THE COMPLETE SHORT STORIES OF MARK TWAIN

ALSO BY CHARLES NEIDER

Fiction

NAKED EYE
THE AUTHENTIC DEATH OF HENDRY JONES
THE WHITE CITADEL

Biography

SUSY: A CHILDHOOD

Criticism

MARK TWAIN
THE FROZEN SEA, A STUDY OF FRANZ KAFKA

EDITED BY CHARLES NEIDER

THE AUTOBIOGRAPHY OF MARK TWAIN
THE COMPLETE HUMOROUS SKETCHES AND TALES OF MARK TWAIN
THE COMPLETE ESSAYS OF MARK TWAIN
THE COMPLETE NOVELS OF MARK TWAIN
THE COMPLETE TRAVEL BOOKS OF MARK TWAIN
MARK TWAIN: THE ADVENTURES OF COLONEL SELLERS
MARK TWAIN: LIFE AS I FIND IT
THE COMPLETE SHORT STORIES OF ROBERT LOUIS STEVENSON
OUR SAMOAN ADVENTURE, by Fanny and Robert Louis Stevenson
SHORT NOVELS OF THE MASTERS
GREAT SHORT STORIES FROM THE WORLD'S LITERATURE
THE STATURE OF THOMAS MANN
THE GREAT WEST
MAN AGAINST NATURE

The
Complete Short Stories
of
MARK TWAIN

NOW COLLECTED FOR THE FIRST TIME

Edited with an introduction by

Charles Neider

DOUBLEDAY & COMPANY, INC.
GARDEN CITY, NEW YORK

For

HANNA *and* COLIN PALMERSTON

ISBN: 0-385-01502-x
Library of Congress Catalog Card Number 57–5536
Copyright © 1957 by Charles Neider
Printed in the United States of America

CONTENTS

Introduction   ix

The Notorious Jumping Frog of Calaveras County   1

The Story of the Bad Little Boy   6

Cannibalism in the Cars   9

A Day at Niagara   16

Legend of the Capitoline Venus   22

Journalism in Tennessee   27

A Curious Dream   32

The Facts in the Great Beef Contract   40

How I Edited an Agricultural Paper   46

A Medieval Romance   50

My Watch   57

Political Economy   59

Science *vs.* Luck   64

The Story of the Good Little Boy   67

Buck Fanshaw's Funeral   71

The Story of the Old Ram   78

Tom Quartz   82

A Trial   84

The Trials of Simon Erickson   89

A True Story   94

Experience of the McWilliamses with Membranous Croup   99

Some Learned Fables for Good Old Boys and Girls   105

The Canvasser's Tale   122

The Loves of Alonzo Fitz Clarence and Rosannah Ethelton   127

Edward Mills and George Benton: A Tale   144

The Man Who Put Up at Gadsby's   149

Mrs. McWilliams and the Lightning   153

What Stumped the Bluejays   159

A Curious Experience   163

The Invalid's Story   187

The McWilliamses and the Burglar Alarm   193

The Stolen White Elephant   199

A Burning Brand   216

A Dying Man's Confession   225

The Professor's Yarn   239

A Ghost Story   244

Luck   249

Playing Courier   253

The Californian's Tale   266

The Diary of Adam and Eve   272

The Esquimau Maiden's Romance   294

Is He Living or Is He Dead?   307

The £1,000,000 Bank-Note   315

Cecil Rhodes and the Shark   332

The Joke That Made Ed's Fortune   337

A Story Without an End   343

The Man That Corrupted Hadleyburg   349

The Death Disk   391

Two Little Tales   399

The Belated Russian Passport   409

A Double-Barreled Detective Story   423

The Five Boons of Life   470

Was It Heaven? Or Hell?   472

A Dog's Tale   489

The $30,000 Bequest   497

A Horse's Tale   523

Hunting the Deceitful Turkey   562

Extract from Captain Stormfield's Visit to Heaven   564

A Fable   597

The Mysterious Stranger   599

Acknowledgments

I wish to express my gratitude to Harper & Brothers and to the Mark Twain Estate, without whose cooperation it would not have been possible to publish this volume. I owe particular thanks to Mr. Frank Mac-Gregor of Harpers and to Mr. Henry Nash Smith of the University of California (Berkeley) for courtesies extended to me.

C. N.

A Note on the Text

The present volume contains a total of sixty stories, thirteen of them gathered from works of non-fiction. They cover the entire span of Twain's writing life, from 1865 to 1916, six years after his death. The text is that of the Stormfield Edition of Twain's Works, published in 1929 by Harper & Brothers in thirty-seven volumes. The stories are arranged chronologically according to the years of first publication, and alphabetically within a given year whenever more than one story was published in that year.

"A Cure for the Blues" is an example of a short piece which I did not include. It is a sort of burlesque book review, with none of the usual attributes of a story. "The Private History of a Campaign That Failed" is another example. It is a piece of reminiscence which comes close to being autobiography and again is clearly something other than a short story.

C. N.

Introduction

Not long ago I happened to be reading Mark Twain's *Roughing It*, when I was piqued by his habit of inserting yarns of pure fiction in a non-fictional work, yarns tossed in just because they were good ones which he had in his head at the time. I counted five yarns or stories in *Roughing It* and wondered if there were others in some of his other non-fictional books. Sure enough, there were: two in *A Tramp Abroad*, three in *Life on the Mississippi*, and three in *Following the Equator*. "What a curious habit!" I thought. But Twain is full of curious habits, both personal and literary, and you either love him or you don't, regardless. I do. It is just his unconventionality, as a literary figure as well as a man, which makes him so appealing to those who like him.

"Strictly speaking, however, these yarns don't belong in the books which house them," I thought. "They belong with his other tales, the stories which are plainly recognized as such. They ought to be included in his collected stories. Let's see if they are." And so I went across the street to the Columbia University library, where I discovered, to my surprise, that his stories had never been put together apart from essays, anecdotes, and the like.

Here is a man, a very great man, a national monument, you might say, who has been dead these forty-odd years without having had his stories collected, when lesser men, just recently dead, or still living, have had that mark of honor offered them by the publishing world and the public. Why? Is it because he is not a good writer of stories? But he is acknowledged to have written some great stories and I believe it is generally conceded that as a story writer he is among our best. Is it because his output was so large, varied, and popular that his stories have been overshadowed—by the novels and travel books? Or is it because he is not a formalist and did not himself publish his short stories purely as such?

During his lifetime his stories appeared in volumes which I can only

call hodgepodge, containing as they did anecdotes, jokes, letters, essays—all sorts of serious and humorous non-fiction along with the fiction. Twain was a man who was very easygoing about border lines.
Some of his short pieces fluctuate between fiction and fact. And he was
a fellow who had very definite notions about the appeal of the grab
bag. When he was a publisher himself he got William Dean Howells,
his friend, to edit a collection of accounts of true adventure. Howells
put the pieces together according to a scheme, and after Twain had
looked at it he gently advised Howells to mix the things up, give them
variety, so that the reader might be surprised. A formal scheme was
about as appealing to him as a tight collar. This differed considerably
from the French notions popular at the time and popular today. Perhaps it is his unconventionality, his insistence on formlessness, which
has left his stories in the lurch.

Twain was not unconscious of this formlessness. Whether he was ra-
tionalizing some literary defect or not when he was defending it, I do
not know. I know he had a philosophy about it. Six years before his
death, when he was dictating fragments of his autobiography, he felt
impelled to explain the practice of dictation. His explanation illumi-
nates his general writing beliefs.

*Within the last eight or ten years I have made several attempts to
do the autobiography in one way or another with a pen, but the result
was not satisfactory; it was too literary. With the pen in one's hand,
narrative is a difficult art; narrative should flow as flows the brook
down through the hills and the leafy woodlands, its course changed by
every bowlder it comes across and by every grass-clad gravelly spur
that projects into its path; its surface broken, but its course not stayed
by rocks and gravel on the bottom in the shoal places; a brook that
never goes straight for a minute, but goes, and goes briskly, sometimes
ungrammatically, and sometimes fetching a horseshoe three-quarters
of a mile around, and at the end of the circuit flowing within a yard of
the path it traversed an hour before; but always going, and always
following at least one law, always loyal to that law, the law of narrative, which has no law. Nothing to do but make the trip; the how of
it is not important, so that the trip is made.*

*With a pen in the hand the narrative stream is a canal; it moves
slowly, smoothly, decorously, sleepily, it has no blemish except that it is
all blemish. It is too literary, too prim, too nice; the gait and style and
movement are not suited to narrative. That canal stream is always reflecting; it is its nature, it can't help it. Its slick shiny surface is inter-*

ested in everything it passes along the banks—cows, foliage, flowers, everything. And so it wastes a lot of time in reflections.

In almost any other writer's work it is easy to say, "This is a short story, whereas that is not." Take the cases of Joyce, Mann, James, Hemingway, Kafka, Lawrence. There is no hesitation about it: a short story belongs to a particular genre and has a relation to the whole of fictional writing in the same way that a water color has to the whole of painting, or a song to the whole of composition. Even in Chekhov it is easy to say what is a short story and what is not. I say "even" because his stories are so gentle in their shading, so clearly lacking in formalism (although not in form), that he of all the writers mentioned might cause some trouble in this respect. But in Twain's case it is quite another matter. I have the sense that Twain wrote primarily to satisfy an audience rather than the requirements of a genre. Whatever came to mind that aided his cause was grist for his mill. This is why we find sketches in which it is not possible to distinguish between fiction and fact.

He rarely bothered about the niceties of fiction. Fiction has a tone all its own, which the literary artist reveres. For him it is in a special sense greater than reality; it shapes reality, controls it. It is inconceivable to think of a James or a Flaubert inserting raw material, untransmuted, unmodulated, into his fictions. For Mark Twain such problems were beside the point. He simply disregarded them, although he was quite aware of them, a great deal more aware than he was accustomed to admit. Twain had enough of the frontier spirit to dislike "form." Form was likely to be something eastern; or if not eastern then something worse: European. Henry James went to Europe to seek form, to saturate himself in it, the form of old societies, old art, old manners and buildings. Twain went to Europe to poke fun at it and to make us laugh. The product of the frontier thought he could see where form was growing hollow and becoming a fraud.

Whatever a short story may be—and this is not the place to attempt to say exactly what it is or should be—we can say with some assurance what it is not. It is not a fragment of autobiography or biography; it is not a report, unalloyed, of a historical event; it is not a joke or a hoax pure and simple; it is not a moral sermon, whether taken down from the pulpit or not; it is not, in short, any of the small bits of writing which used to be produced in the old West for newspaper and magazine fillers and of which Twain turned out a healthy share. A short story is something which, through the long process of evolution, has come to exist in and for itself. It has laws of its own, it is sovereign in its field. And it was already sovereign when Twain began to write.

Twain had the artistic temperament without too much of the artistic conscience. His genius was essentially western, its strength the land, the people, their language and their humor. What he lacked was a studied eastern conscience to refine the great ore he mined. Perhaps such a conscience would have inhibited and eventually ruined him. Probably he knew best what was necessary for *him*. What he *had*, he had in great measure: the naked power of the man with the gift of gab. He knew what a yarn was, and what it was for, and what to do with it. He did not think that a good yarn needs prettifying, and he told it straight, without trimmings. His high jinks are remarkable—his love of mugging, of monologue, dialect, caricature. He is a great proponent of the tall story, piling details on until the story comes crashing down. At his best he is uproarious, and he is often at his best in his stories, as you will see.

It has been said that his stories are an important part of our literary heritage. It would be difficult, if not impossible, to dispute this statement successfully, presuming one cared to try. They are also part of our folklore. Twain is our writer closest to folklore, our teller of fairy tales. The Jumping Frog story is a living American fairy tale, acted out annually in Calaveras County. Whatever may be its dim origins (it has been claimed to be close kin to an old Greek tale; but the latter probably descended from a Hindu one, and so on), it is now *our* story, mirroring something in us. "The Man That Corrupted Hadleyburg" is part of our moral heritage. A rebel American of the creative kind, Frank Lloyd Wright, has written to me that it is his favorite of all short stories. These tales, together with several others, among them "The $30,000 Bequest" and "The £1,000,000 Bank-Note," have been anthologized many times. Others—tales of moral indignation such as "A Horse's Tale," and tales meant to shock, for example, "Captain Stormfield's Visit to Heaven," are no less powerful and important for being less popular. Who are our short-story writers? Irving, Hawthorne, Poe, James, Melville, O. Henry, Bret Harte, Hemingway, Faulkner, Porter —these are names which come to my mind without reflection, although my taste does not run to O. Henry and Harte, and finds much to quarrel with in Faulkner. Twain's ranks high among them.

Twain is a dangerous man to write about. Unless you approach him with a sense of humor you are lost. You cannot dissect a humorist upon a table. Your first stroke will kill him and make him a tragedian. You must come to Twain with a smile. That is his prerogative: that he can make you do so or fail. A great American critic wrote a study of Twain which was brilliant. The only trouble with it was he thought he was describing Twain, when all along he was describing somebody else— himself, probably. The critic did not have a sense of humor, and his error was comparable to that of the tone-deaf critic who wrote on Beethoven. God forbid that I should try to dissect Mark Twain. In Twain it is not the line-by-line detail which is great, nor the day-by-day life— it is the mass, the contour, and the fragrance of a personality. Who would want, here in this place, to try to dissect that? I shall just pursue a few thoughts briefly, and if I seem to be critical at times, let the reader remember I love the man this side of honesty.

Twain poured his writing out in a stream, showering upon it all his gifts. Sometimes it carried everything before it but at others it failed naïvely. He was not the sort of versatile writer who is equally good at everything he puts his hand to. It is difficult to believe that he could have written fastidious travel essays like Hawthorne's or the delicate, subtle criticism of James; yet at times he appeared to be attempting both. He carried a broadsword which he sometimes tried to use on butterflies. He wrote very rapidly and was as proud as a boy of his daily turnout. He did not strive for the polished effect—or, rather, he strived for it too seldom. When his mood changed he stopped writing and put a manuscript away, sometimes for years. He was not a good judge of his work. Being essentially a man of humor, he was rarely humorless regarding himself in relation to his work. He was unlike Flaubert and Proust and James in this respect. To be humorless regarding oneself— or at least regarding one's work—can sometimes be a great advantage. To be well balanced does not guarantee better-grade work.

There is, in a good deal of Twain's writing—in the Hadleyburg story, for example—a kind of naïveté which one feels is literary, a sort of refusal to infuse prose with the sophistication of the mature man. This no doubt reflects in some measure an attitude Twain had to the act of writing and to the nature of his audience. Writing was not the whole man. It may have even been at times the lesser man; and the audience, one seems to perceive, like his family, was largely composed of women: naïve women, sheltered from the painful realities of a man's world. The moral pressure in Twain's work is generally considerable; but the purely literary, the aesthetic pressure is occasionally so low as to form only a trickle. This aesthetic pressure, impossible to define, is what is necessary to the creation of a work of art. In some cases it stems from moments of transcendent well-being, in others from the depths of frustration or despair; but whatever the causes, the pressure must be there, inside one, for the effect to be made. Too great a pressure may be as devastating to a work as too little, although writers like Twain are more likely to suffer from too little.

In Twain's case there is often something pleasant in even the lesser pages, precisely because of the low pressure: he is relaxed and his mood is infectious. Twain rarely tries to overreach himself, to strain after an effect of greatness. This lesson of being relaxed while writing, although a dangerous one for young writers, is an invaluable one for the mature ones. The right balance of pressure when one is about to sit down to work—one's health, one's relation to the material, one's linguistic resilience at the moment, the play of one's mind—is really what is called inspiration: the balance is everything: the container, which is one's own complex state, must exactly suit the thing contained, which is the raw material about to be transfigured into art. It is a pity that Twain did not often take the pains to find the just balance for himself. But if he did not, he at least substituted another virtue. He says somewhere, wryly, that he had the habit of doing and of reflecting afterward. One contrasts this habit with an opposite one, the habit of reflecting to the point of disease, often found in the later works of Melville and James, as well as in portions of the works of Thomas Mann and Marcel Proust.

Twain does not strive to be an artist—*artiste*, he probably would have called it with a grin. He would have felt more comfortable wearing the term journalist. He grew up a journalist, like Dickens, and was one of those hearty nineteenth-century scribblers who strayed into literature almost without realizing it. He had the journalist's instinct, in the way Defoe had, and in the way Hawthorne and James did not. This is not necessarily a handicap in the creation of literature. In so far as it stimulates a sense of audience, a sense of common scene, and the use of native speech and lore—in so far, that is, that it inspires one to attempt a colloquy in common terms but with uncommon genius, it is a definite and rare gift. Its limitations are likely to be great also, the limitations of the known, and especially what is known to the particular group. Twain's writing was almost always a means to an end. He had few impersonal objectives in mind in the way of form, experiment, texture, design. He had the common touch and knew it was a blessing. He was enriched by it and made world-famous.

He possessed in a limited degree the craft discipline of the writer who *sees* his prose, who carefully examines it, watching for design and effect, while at the same time listening to its music. Flaubert and Joyce were writers who intensely saw, and it is by no accident that we find in their work a brilliance of visual images. The visual intelligence can act as a tight check on the aural one; the latter may run wild, like a weed, until one is writing sound for its own sweet sake. James in his later phase dictated much of his fiction, and as a result his work of that period is marked by prolixity, dilution, and sometimes a vagueness of meaning. Of course, it can be argued that he adopted dictation to satisfy the requirements of a genius which was declining. The trouble here is that it would be a difficult task to chart and to prove the actual falling off of his genius apart from the mannerisms which had begun to afflict it. One wonders if the visual sense in literature, especially in terms of formal design, has not overreached itself in our century with the production of works like Joyce's *Ulysses*, Mann's *Joseph and his Brethren*, and parts of the great Proust novel, and if the impetus to their excesses was not at least partly the excesses of the aural sense, as witnessed in a writer like Dickens.

It is a large part of Twain's greatness that he heard so well. His dialogue is extraordinary. One sometimes wonders if he had a phonographic memory. His ability to imitate styles of speech, with a vast array of accurate detail, is truly remarkable. His biographer, Albert Bigelow Paine, has written: "At dinner, too, it was his habit, between the courses, to rise from the table and walk up and down the room, waving his napkin and talking—talking in a strain and with a charm that he could never quite equal with his pen. It is the opinion of most people who knew Mark Twain personally that his impromptu utterances, delivered with that ineffable quality of speech, manifested the culmination of his genius." Twain and the oral tradition: both are related to the frontier. Yet some of his chief faults stem directly from this side of his genius—an occasional looseness of texture, a kind of stage or vaudeville timing for effect, an overindulgence in burlesque, a sense as if he were lecturing from a platform. Early in his public career he achieved success as a lecturer and as a maker of speeches, and no doubt this success, this practice, this buttressed confidence in a talent he long must have known he possessed, had a crucial influence upon his work.

There is a certain transparency in Twain's work, like that to be found in fairy tales. One senses the machinery behind the silken screen. But in this very transparency there is a kind of potency also found in the fairy tales, a foreknowledge of events, a delight in repetition, in the spelling out of the known, a sort of tribal incantation. There is also something abstract in certain of his fictions, some sort of geometric approach to the art of narrative which, to the modern reader, is not quite satisfying. I refer to pieces like *The American Claimant* and *The Tragedy of Pudd'nhead Wilson*. The latter is a very imperfect work whose imperfections are traceable to its conception, or rather misconception, a fact which Twain himself has revealed at some length. But when he speaks out of his own mouth, with the drawl and idiom and dialect, as he does in so many of his stories, he is unique, inspired, zany, wonderful.

This man loved a gimmick the way the frontier loved a practical joke. He claimed to be the first private user of the telephone; the first author to use a typewriter; the first author to dictate into a phonograph recording machine. He fooled around with inventions with the passion of an inveterate gambler, and lost his shirt. A literary gimmick sometimes caused him to lose his literary shirt. His favorite of his own books was his *Joan of Arc*, which purports to be the recollections of a friend of Joan's. It is sentimental and dull, as it was likely to be, not being done in Twain's own voice and style.

It is a fact that Twain, like many other nineteenth-century novelists, is sometimes guilty of padding. This is often due to the economics of book production of his day. The two-volume work, often sold by subscription, often serialized, was as much the thing in those days as it is not now. If a man had only a book and a half in him, that was too bad; he had to get up the half somehow or throw in the towel. The effect of this can be seen all the way from Dickens to James. Forgetting this, we are likely to recall the size of nineteenth-century novels and think, "There were giants in those days." There *were* giants, but the fact remains that many of the novels of the previous century can stand pruning, from our point of view.

There is a new kind of padding which has come to flower in our own century, a kind not due to economics of book production, a kind which almost deliberately flies in the face of economics—the padding of Joyce, Proust, Mann, Faulkner. I suspect this sort has as its motive a gentle and harmless variety of megalomania, the desire to fill up culs-de-sac in such a way that no one can add a pound to them. It is time that the novel of elegant proportions returned to fashion and worth—the novel which by its intensity, elasticity, form and overtones achieves what the older ones have achieved through bulk. A whale is not by definition superior to a shark.

It is almost needless to add that in the story the impulse or the need to pad was at a minimum, and that consequently there is more economy of effect in Twain's stories than in most of his book-size works. One might even say that Twain felt most at home in the story, that it was the form most congenial to him, lover as he was of the yarn. It was the form which most effectively brought out his particular "voice." Some of his full-size books are more like a series of yarns strung together, than works with an indigenous structure.

Despite his great successes he remained an unfulfilled, unintegrated writer of uncertain taste. In *A Tramp Abroad*, for example, his desire was often for serious description of scene, influenced by the beauty of the landscape and the fact he had kept accurate notes. This conflicted with a desire to be funny, or a nervousness because he feared his reader's attention was flagging. He broke up his descriptions with unfunny insertions of outlandish foreign words and phrases, creating a hodgepodge that was in poor taste, dull, and an affront to his considerable descriptive talents. His autobiography is a good example, although a late one, of his uncertain taste. He did not—he could not—write it in sequence, but drifted here and there, wherever idle memory (not always dependable) and a wandering stream of associations led him, at times lingering over minor events and hurrying past important ones. It is an important and neglected American document, justly neglected inasmuch as it is almost unreadable in its present form, the sequence of events garbled, and bits of daily journalism thrown in from the period in which he was composing it. And yet at its best it is remarkable and needs only a skilled hand to put it together properly. It is ready to emerge as a classic of its kind, although at present it is in the stage of being raw material. Twain did not always recognize the difference between raw material and the polished product, just as Henry James, inversely, sometimes mistook the polish of his prose for the material of life itself.

Twain at his most balanced is likely to be found in his letters, where he could be himself, without having to please what he believed to be his audience and to satisfy his audience's demand (whether real or imaginary) for more of the Twain brand of humor. He was in a sense the slave of his audience; or, more justly, the slave of what he conceived to be his duty toward his audience. When Twain is truly himself he is magnificent. How beautifully, how truly, how movingly he can write in the midst of deep emotion, as when he set down his thoughts immediately after the death of his daughter Jean. There is no false tone, no striving in his prose then. You sense he is a *man*, unique and great, honest, noble, in some ways sublime.

His best books, with the exception of his travel books, are those with a western scene; and his travel books largely owe their humor, their geniality, and their wisdom to his western orientation. The sentimentality of the frontier, which ranged all the way from an exaggerated regard for females to the most deadly sort of sadism; the lack of form in social behavior, together with certain codes of behavior which smack of juvenile delinquents; the relative contempt for the written as against the spoken word; the racy language; the attitudes toward dudes and the East, the two being almost synonymous; the impatience with the ways and principles of law—all these characteristics of the American frontier are to be found in Twain's best work, and they are the motor of that work. They are also to be found, in somewhat more disguised form, in the work of Twain's star descendant, Ernest Hemingway.

A man from Missouri, Twain said "Show me" skeptically to Europe and the world. This was a novel concept to the East, where reverence for Europe among literary men was in vogue, as it is today. Paris, Rome, London are still considered the seats of literary learning; or if not learning, of literary practice; or if not practice, of literary conscience. Twain knew better. To the westerner Europe seems remote, and its concerns—its stale, very stale concerns—seem almost perversely imagined, or at any rate like a long-forgotten but still-remembered dream, a bitterness on the tongue, a haunting disquiet in some dim corner of the mind. The climate and the great spaces speak eloquently of today and tomorrow. Europe, like the East, is a pallid yesterday.

Twain could be sardonic in turning the tables and exposing a bluff. It had been fashionable, up to his time, for Europeans, some of them prominent literary figures like Dickens, to write sarcastic reports on the "raw" United States. Twain, a self-appointed ambassador, returned the compliment with interest, offering a tongue-in-cheek view of the American as progressive, the European as a piece of baroque humanity. The salt in the wound was that there was much truth in this view, as Hawthorne had already hinted in his *English Note-books*. Twain never struck upon a happier symbol than the German language, which he satirized so penetratingly and with such wit that even many Germans laughed and appreciated the truth of what he implied. Twain has a wonderful wisdom. He is so essentially sane that it is exhilarating to be in his company. By his way of life he seemed to say, "I am of the tribe of writers but I am saner than they. I know how to savor life." You expect a man like that to live a long life. Twain did, like Tolstoy, and like Tolstoy he managed very often to write without contrived effects.

It has happened in other countries that what was once looked upon condescendingly as being unworthy of art became, almost overnight, the body and soul of the highest art. It happened in Germany and in

Russia early in the last century. I believe it will happen in our own country when western legends and myths, western folklore, become the basis of a sophisticated art. There is no lack of snobbism among eastern intellectuals toward western materials. Some academic writers and critics, who enjoy western films, deride the notion that in the more serious realm of the novel the same materials can be used to good and true effect. The frontier may be closed, finished; no doubt it is—the geographical one. But there are other frontiers—the frontier of a cultural *tone*, for example. These are important also. They contain elements which the geographical frontier created or inspired. The frontier has gone underground, and if this is a calamity to the adventurer it is not necessarily so to the artist, in particular the writer. There is a free-swinging sense of things in the West which has long been missing in the East. The ghost of Europe hovers over the East.

It seems to me that the West will produce a great and fertile literature and that this literature, although it will be free in tone and speech in a way the New England literature could not be, will nevertheless be sophisticated, will know what it is about, will understand the meaning of heritage and tradition as well as of rebellion, and of its place in the great stream of literature and the arts. That it has not come into its own during the last half century need not be held against it. Its practitioners are unfortunately parochial, and either unnecessarily resentful of the East or afraid of it. Perhaps the greatest and most successful users of western materials will not be westerners at all. They need not be. They may very well be easterners, for that matter.

Twain's personal influence during his lifetime was very great. His literary influence has also been considerable, not only among humorists but also among American novelists. Hemingway's prose of action and his language of speech are direct descendants of Twain's. Hemingway himself has said that American literature begins with one book, *Huckleberry Finn*—an obvious exaggeration in his fashion, but indicative of his regard for Twain. Twain is a muscular writer, he is par excellence the writer who calls a spade a spade, the writer who is intent on making an accurate correspondence between reality as he has experienced it and reality as it emerges in his books. This too is what Hemingway is after. It is Hemingway's real passion. What makes him great is that he has had the vision to sense where in this complex world he can come to grips with what, for him, is a real experience; the courage to seek these places out and, in James's term, saturate himself in them; and the passion to find the words—the fresh words, in his own style—to fit his experience. Like Twain, Hemingway gives the impression of being only incidentally a great writer. The writing follows upon his life. This is far from the example of James and Flaubert, who seemed to live only for their work and whose passion, morality, intelligence, and religion were dissolved and sacrificed in their work.

Twain's fashion has dimmed in the last forty years. He is seen to belong to another era, the era of chromos and linsey-woolsey, of an extraordinary optimism, of a degree of national self-criticism rarely now enjoyed. Despite his frontier manliness he is too frilly, too juvenile, too surrounded by females to entirely please the national taste. But he is a solid monument in American letters and an invaluable lesson for our young novelists. That lesson is: do not neglect your native sources; remember that yesterday's journalism may become tomorrow's literature; steep yourself in the living speech; and do not forget that the life of humor is long and that the Muse does not insist you wear a frown when you work.

CHARLES NEIDER
Pacific Palisades
California

The Notorious Jumping Frog
of Calaveras County

In compliance with the request of a friend of mine, who wrote me from the East, I called on good-natured, garrulous old Simon Wheeler, and inquired after my friend's friend, Leonidas W. Smiley, as requested to do, and I hereunto append the result. I have a lurking suspicion that *Leonidas W.* Smiley is a myth; that my friend never knew such a personage; and that he only conjectured that if I asked old Wheeler about him, it would remind him of his infamous *Jim* Smiley, and he would go to work and bore me to death with some exasperating reminiscence of him as long and as tedious as it should be useless to me. If that was the design, it succeeded.

I found Simon Wheeler dozing comfortably by the bar-room stove of the dilapidated tavern in the decayed mining camp of Angel's, and I noticed that he was fat and bald-headed, and had an expression of winning gentleness and simplicity upon his tranquil countenance. He roused up, and gave me good day. I told him that a friend of mine had commissioned me to make some inquiries about a cherished companion of his boyhood named *Leonidas W.* Smiley—*Rev. Leonidas W.* Smiley, a young minister of the Gospel, who he had heard was at one time a resident of Angel's Camp. I added that if Mr. Wheeler could tell me anything about this Rev. Leonidas W. Smiley, I would feel under many obligations to him.

Simon Wheeler backed me into a corner and blockaded me there with his chair, and then sat down and reeled off the monotonous narrative which follows this paragraph. He never smiled, he never frowned, he never changed his voice from the gentle-flowing key to which he tuned his initial sentence, he never betrayed the slightest suspicion of enthusiasm; but all through the interminable narrative there ran a vein of impressive earnestness and sincerity, which showed me plainly that, so far from his imagining that there was anything ridiculous or funny about his story, he regarded it as a really important matter, and admired its two heroes as men of transcendent genius in *finesse*. I let him go on in his own way, and never interrupted him once.

"Rev. Leonidas W. H'm, Reverend Le—well, there was a feller here once by the name of *Jim* Smiley, in the winter of '49—or maybe it was the spring of '50—I don't recollect exactly, somehow, though what makes me think it was one or the other is because I remember the big flume warn't finished when he first come to the camp; but anyway, he was the curiousest man about always betting on anything that turned up you ever see, if he could get anybody to bet on the other side; and if he couldn't he'd change sides. Any way that suited the other man would suit *him*—any way just so's he got a bet, *he* was satisfied. But still he was lucky, uncommon lucky; he most always come out winner. He was always ready and laying for a chance; there couldn't be no solit'ry thing mentioned but that feller'd offer to bet on it, and take ary side you please, as I was just telling you. If there was a horse-race, you'd find him flush or you'd find him busted at the end of it; if there was a dog-fight, he'd bet on it; if there was a cat-fight, he'd bet on it; if there was a chicken-fight, he'd bet on it; why, if there was two birds setting on a fence, he would bet you which one would fly first; or if there was a camp-meeting, he would be there reg'lar to bet on Parson Walker, which he judged to be the best exhorter about here, and so he was too, and a good man. If he even see a straddle-bug start to go anywheres, he would bet you how long it would take him to get to—to wherever he was going to, and if you took him up, he would foller that straddle-bug to Mexico but what he would find out where he was bound for and how long he was on the road. Lots of the boys here has seen that Smiley, and can tell you about him. Why, it never made no difference to *him*— he'd bet on *any* thing—the dangdest feller. Parson Walker's wife laid very sick once, for a good while, and it seemed as if they warn't going to save her; but one morning he come in, and Smiley up and asked him how she was, and he said she was considerable better—thank the Lord for his inf'nite mercy—and coming on so smart that with the blessing of Prov'dence she'd get well yet; and Smiley, before he thought, says, 'Well, I'll resk two-and-a-half she don't anyway.'

"Thish-yer Smiley had a mare—the boys called her the fifteen-minute nag, but that was only in fun, you know, because of course she was faster than that—and he used to win money on that horse, for all she was so slow and always had the asthma, or the distemper, or the consumption, or something of that kind. They used to give her two or three hundred yards' start, and then pass her under way; but always at the fag end of the race she'd get excited and desperate like, and come cavorting

and straddling up, and scattering her legs around limber, sometimes in the air, and sometimes out to one side among the fences, and kicking up m-o-r-e dust and raising m-o-r-e racket with her coughing and sneezing and blowing her nose—and *always* fetch up at the stand just about a neck ahead, as near as you could cipher it down.

"And he had a little small bull-pup, that to look at him you'd think he warn't worth a cent but to set around and look ornery and lay for a chance to steal something. But as soon as money was up on him he was a different dog; his under-jaw'd begin to stick out like the fo'castle of a steamboat, and his teeth would uncover and shine like the furnaces. And a dog might tackle him and bully-rag him, and bite him, and throw him over his shoulder two or three times, and Andrew Jackson—which was the name of the pup—Andrew Jackson would never let on but what *he* was satisfied, and hadn't expected nothing else—and the bets being doubled and doubled on the other side all the time, till the money was all up; and then all of a sudden he would grab that other dog jest by the j'int of his hind leg and freeze to it—not chaw, you understand, but only just grip and hang on till they throwed up the sponge, if it was a year. Smiley always come out winner on that pup, till he harnessed a dog once that didn't have no hind legs, because they'd been sawed off in a circular saw, and when the thing had gone along far enough, and the money was all up, and he come to make a snatch for his pet holt, he see in a minute how he'd been imposed on, and how the other dog had him in the door, so to speak, and he 'peared surprised, and then he looked sorter discouraged-like, and didn't try no more to win the fight, and so he got shucked out bad. He give Smiley a look, as much as to say his heart was broke, and it was *his* fault, for putting up a dog that hadn't no hind legs for him to take holt of, which was his main dependence in a fight, and then he limped off a piece and laid down and died. It was a good pup, was that Andrew Jackson, and would have made a name for hisself if he'd lived, for the stuff was in him and he had genius—I know it, because he hadn't no opportunities to speak of, and it don't stand to reason that a dog could make such a fight as he could under them circumstances if he hadn't no talent. It always makes me feel sorry when I think of that last fight of his'n, and the way it turned out.

"Well, thish-yer Smiley had rat-tarriers, and chicken cocks, and tomcats and all them kind of things, till you couldn't rest, and you couldn't fetch nothing for him to bet on but he'd match you. He ketched a frog one day, and took him home, and said he cal'lated to educate him; and so he never done nothing for three months but set in his back yard and learn that frog to jump. And you bet you he *did* learn him, too. He'd give him a little punch behind, and the next minute you'd see that frog whirling in the air like a doughnut—see him turn one summerset, or maybe a couple, if he got a good start, and come down flat-footed and all right, like a cat. He got him up so in the matter of ketching flies, and kep' him in practice so constant, that he'd nail a fly every time as fur as he could see him. Smiley said all a frog wanted was education, and he could do 'most anything—and I believe him. Why, I've seen him set Dan'l Webster down here on this floor—Dan'l Webster was the name of the frog—and sing out, 'Flies, Dan'l, flies!' and quicker'n you could wink he'd spring straight up and snake a fly off'n the counter there, and flop down on the floor ag'in as solid as a gob of mud, and fall to scratching the side of his head with his hind foot as indifferent as if he hadn't no idea he'd been doin' any more'n any frog might do. You never see a frog so modest and straightfor'ard as he was, for all he was so gifted. And when it come to fair and square jumping on a dead level, he could get over more ground at one straddle than any animal of his breed you ever see. Jumping on a dead level was his strong suit, you understand; and when it come to that, Smiley would ante up money on him as long as he had a red. Smiley was monstrous proud of his frog, and well he might be, for fellers that had traveled and been everywheres all said he laid over any frog that ever *they* see.

"Well, Smiley kep' the beast in a little lattice box, and he used to fetch him down-town sometimes and lay for a bet. One day a feller—a stranger in the camp, he was—come acrost him with his box, and says:

" 'What might it be that you've got in the box?'

"And Smiley says, sorter indifferent-like, 'It might be a parrot, or it might be a canary, maybe, but it ain't—it's only just a frog.'

"And the feller took it, and looked at it careful, and turned it round this way and that, and says, 'H'm—so 'tis. Well, what's *he* good for?'

" 'Well,' Smiley says, easy and careless, 'he's good enough for *one* thing, I should judge—he can outjump any frog in Calaveras County.'

"The feller took the box again, and took another long, particular look, and give it back to Smiley, and says, very deliberate, 'Well,' he says, 'I don't see no p'ints about that frog that's any better'n any other frog.'

" 'Maybe you don't,' Smiley says. 'Maybe you understand frogs and maybe you don't understand 'em; maybe you've had experience, and maybe you ain't only a amature, as it were. Anyways, I've got *my* opinion, and I'll resk forty dollars that he can outjump any frog in Calaveras County.'

"And the feller studied a minute, and then says, kinder sad-like,

'Well, I'm only a stranger here, and I ain't got no frog; but if I had a frog, I'd bet you.'

"And then Smiley says, 'That's all right—that's all right—if you'll hold my box a minute, I'll go and get you a frog.' And so the feller took the box, and put up his forty dollars along with Smiley's, and set down to wait.

"So he set there a good while thinking and thinking to himself, and then he got the frog out and prized his mouth open and took a teaspoon and filled him full of quail-shot—filled him pretty near up to his chin—and set him on the floor. Smiley he went to the swamp and slopped around in the mud for a long time, and finally he ketched a frog, and fetched him in, and give him to this feller, and says:

"'Now, if you're ready, set him alongside of Dan'l, with his fore paws just even with Dan'l's, and I'll give the word.' Then he says, 'One—two—three—git!' and him and the feller touched up the frogs from behind, and the new frog hopped off lively, but Dan'l give a heave, and hysted up his shoulders—so—like a Frenchman, but it warn't no use—he couldn't budge; he was planted as solid as a church, and he couldn't no more stir than if he was anchored out. Smiley was a good deal surprised, and he was disgusted too, but he didn't have no idea what the matter was, of course.

"The feller took the money and started away; and when he was going out at the door, he sorter jerked his thumb over his shoulder—so—at Dan'l, and says again, very deliberate, 'Well,' he says, '*I* don't see no p'ints about that frog that's any better'n any other frog.'

"Smiley he stood scratching his head and looking down at Dan'l a long time, and at last he says, 'I do wonder what in the nation that frog throw'd off for—I wonder if there ain't something the matter with him—he 'pears to look mighty baggy, somehow.' And he ketched Dan'l by the nap of the neck, and hefted him, and says, 'Why blame my cats if he don't weigh five pound!' and turned him upside down and he belched out a double handful of shot. And then he see how it was, and he was the maddest man—he set the frog down and took out after that feller, but he never ketched him. And—"

[Here Simon Wheeler heard his name called from the front yard, and got up to see what was wanted.] And turning to me as he moved away, he said: "Just set where you are, stranger, and rest easy—I ain't going to be gone a second."

But, by your leave, I did not think that a continuation of the history of the enterprising vagabond *Jim* Smiley would be likely to afford me much information concerning the Rev. *Leonidas W.* Smiley, and so I started away.

At the door I met the sociable Wheeler returning, and he buttonholed me and recommenced:

"Well, thish-yer Smiley had a yaller one-eyed cow that didn't have no tail, only just a short stump like a bannanner, and—"

However, lacking both time and inclination, I did not wait to hear about the afflicted cow, but took my leave.

1865

The Story of the Bad Little Boy

Once there was a bad little boy whose name was Jim—though, if you will notice, you will find that bad little boys are nearly always called James in your Sunday-school books. It was strange, but still it was true, that this one was called Jim.

He didn't have any sick mother, either—a sick mother who was pious and had the consumption, and would be glad to lie down in the grave and be at rest but for the strong love she bore her boy, and the anxiety she felt that the world might be harsh and cold toward him when she was gone. Most bad boys in the Sunday books are named James, and have sick mothers, who teach them to say, "Now, I lay me down," etc., and sing them to sleep with sweet, plaintive voices, and then kiss them good night, and kneel down by the bedside and weep. But it was different with this fellow. He was named Jim, and there wasn't anything the matter with his mother—no consumption, nor anything of that kind. She was rather stout than otherwise, and she was not pious; moreover, she was not anxious on Jim's account. She said if he were to break his neck it wouldn't be much loss. She always spanked Jim to sleep, and she never kissed him good night; on the contrary, she boxed his ears when she was ready to leave him.

Once this little bad boy stole the key of the pantry, and slipped in there and helped himself to some jam, and filled up the vessel with tar, so that his mother would never know the difference; but all at once a terrible feeling didn't come over him, and something didn't seem to whisper to him, "Is it right to disobey my mother? Isn't it sinful to do this? Where do bad little boys go who gobble up their good kind mother's jam?" and then he didn't kneel down all alone and promise never to be wicked any more, and rise up with a light, happy heart, and go and tell his mother all about it, and beg her forgiveness, and be blessed by her with tears of pride and thankfulness in her eyes. No; that is the way with all other bad boys in the books; but it happened otherwise with this Jim, strangely enough. He ate that jam, and said it was bully, in his sinful, vulgar way; and he put in the tar, and said that was bully also, and laughed, and observed "that the old woman would get up and snort" when she found it out; and when she did find it out, he denied knowing anything about it, and she whipped him severely, and he did the crying himself. Everything about this boy was curious—everything turned out differently with him from the way it does to the bad Jameses in the books.

Once he climbed up in Farmer Acorn's apple tree to steal apples, and the limb didn't break, and he didn't fall and break his arm, and get torn by the farmer's great dog, and then languish on a sickbed for weeks, and repent and become good. Oh, no; he stole as many apples as he wanted and came down all right; and he was all ready for the dog, too, and knocked him endways with a brick when he came to tear him. It was very strange—nothing like it ever happened in those mild little books with marbled backs, and with pictures in them of men with swallow-tailed coats and bell-crowned hats, and pantaloons that are short in the legs, and women with the waists of their dresses under their arms, and no hoops on. Nothing like it in any of the Sunday-school books.

Once he stole the teacher's penknife, and, when he was afraid it would be found out and he would get whipped, he slipped it into George Wilson's cap—poor Widow Wilson's son, the moral boy, the good little boy of the village, who always obeyed his mother, and never told an untruth, and was fond of his lessons, and infatuated with Sunday-school. And when the knife dropped from the cap, and poor George hung his head and blushed, as if in conscious guilt, and the grieved teacher charged the theft upon him, and was just in the very act of bringing the switch down upon his trembling shoulders, a white-haired, improbable justice of the peace did not suddenly appear in their midst, and strike an attitude and say, "Spare this noble boy—there stands the cowering culprit! I was passing the school door at recess, and, unseen myself, I saw the theft committed!" And then Jim didn't get whaled, and the venerable justice didn't read the tearful school a homily, and take George by the hand and say such a boy deserved to be exalted, and then tell him to come and make his home with him, and sweep out the office, and make fires, and run errands, and chop wood, and study law, and help his wife do household labors, and have all the balance of the time to play, and get forty cents a month, and be happy. No; it would have happened that way in the books, but it didn't happen that way to Jim. No meddling old clam of a justice dropped in to make trouble, and so the model boy George got thrashed, and Jim was glad of it because, you know, Jim hated moral boys. Jim said he was "down on them milksops." Such was the coarse language of this bad, neglected boy.

But the strangest thing that ever happened to Jim was the time he went boating on Sunday, and didn't get drowned, and that other time that he got caught out in the storm when he was fishing on Sunday, and didn't get struck by lightning. Why, you might look, and look, all through the Sunday-school books from now till next Christmas, and you would never come across anything like this. Oh, no; you would find that all the bad boys who go boating on Sunday invariably get drowned; and all the bad boys who get caught out in storms when they are fishing on Sunday infallibly get struck by lightning. Boats with bad boys in them always upset on Sunday, and it always storms when bad boys go fishing on the Sabbath. How this Jim ever escaped is a mystery to me.

This Jim bore a charmed life—that must have been the way of it. Nothing could hurt him. He even gave the elephant in the menagerie a plug of tobacco, and the elephant didn't knock the top of his head off with his trunk. He browsed around the cupboard after essence of peppermint, and didn't make a mistake and drink *aqua fortis*. He stole his father's gun and went hunting on the Sabbath, and didn't shoot three or four of his fingers off. He struck his little sister on the temple with his fist when he was angry, and she didn't linger in pain through long summer days, and die with sweet words of forgiveness upon her lips that redoubled the anguish of his breaking heart. No; she got over it. He ran off and went to sea at last, and didn't come back and find himself sad and alone in the world, his loved ones sleeping in the quiet churchyard, and the vine-embowered home of his boyhood tumbled down and gone to decay. Ah, no; he came home as drunk as a piper, and got into the station-house the first thing.

And he grew up and married, and raised a large family, and brained them all with an ax one night, and got wealthy by all manner of cheating and rascality; and now he is the infernalest wickedest scoundrel in his native village, and is universally respected, and belongs to the legislature.

So you see there never was a bad James in the Sunday-school books that had such a streak of luck as this sinful Jim with the charmed life.

1865

Cannibalism in the Cars

I visited St. Louis lately, and on my way West, after changing cars at Terre Haute, Indiana, a mild, benevolent-looking gentleman of about forty-five, or maybe fifty, came in at one of the way-stations and sat down beside me. We talked together pleasantly on various subjects for an hour, perhaps, and I found him exceedingly intelligent and entertaining. When he learned that I was from Washington, he immediately began to ask questions about various public men, and about Congressional affairs; and I saw very shortly that I was conversing with a man who was perfectly familiar with the ins and outs of political life at the Capital, even to the ways and manners, and customs of procedure of Senators and Representatives in the Chambers of the national Legislature. Presently two men halted near us for a single moment, and one said to the other:

"Harris, if you'll do that for me, I'll never forget you, my boy."

My new comrade's eye lighted pleasantly. The words had touched upon a happy memory, I thought. Then his face settled into thoughtfulness—almost into gloom. He turned to me and said, "Let me tell you a story; let me give you a secret chapter of my life—a chapter that has never been referred to by me since its events transpired. Listen patiently, and promise that you will not interrupt me."

I said I would not, and he related the following strange adventure, speaking sometimes with animation, sometimes with melancholy, but always with feeling and earnestness.

On the 19th of December, 1853, I started from St. Louis on the evening train bound for Chicago. There were only twenty-four passengers, all told. There were no ladies and no children. We were in excellent spirits, and pleasant acquaintanceships were soon formed. The journey bade fair to be a happy one; and no individual in the party, I think, had even the vaguest presentiment of the horrors we were soon to undergo.

At 11 P.M. it began to snow hard. Shortly after leaving the small village of Welden, we entered upon that tremendous prairie solitude that stretches its leagues on leagues of houseless dreariness far away toward the Jubilee Settlements. The winds, unobstructed by trees or hills, or even vagrant rocks, whistled fiercely across the level desert, driving the falling snow before it like spray from the crested waves of a stormy sea. The snow was deepening fast; and we knew, by the diminished speed of the train, that the engine was plowing through it with steadily increasing difficulty. Indeed, it almost came to a dead halt sometimes, in the midst of great drifts that piled themselves like colossal graves across the track. Conversation began to flag. Cheerfulness gave place to grave concern. The possibility of being imprisoned in the snow, on the bleak prairie, fifty miles from any house, presented itself to every mind, and extended its depressing influence over every spirit.

At two o'clock in the morning I was aroused out of an uneasy slumber by the ceasing of all motion about me. The appalling truth flashed upon me instantly—we were captives in a snow-drift! "All hands to the rescue!" Every man sprang to obey. Out into the wild night, the pitchy darkness, the billowy snow, the driving storm, every soul leaped, with the consciousness that a moment lost now might bring destruction to us all. Shovels, hands, boards—anything, everything that could displace snow, was brought into instant requisition. It was a weird picture, that small company of frantic men fighting the banking snows, half in the blackest shadow and half in the angry light of the locomotive's reflector.

One short hour sufficed to prove the utter uselessness of our efforts. The storm barricaded the track with a dozen drifts while we dug one away. And worse than this, it was discovered that the last grand charge the engine had made upon the enemy had broken the fore-and-aft shaft of the driving-wheel! With a free track before us we should still have been helpless. We entered the car wearied with labor, and very sorrowful. We gathered about the stoves, and gravely canvassed our situation. We had no provisions whatever—in this lay our chief distress. We could not freeze, for there was a good supply of wood in the tender. This was our only comfort. The discussion ended at last in accepting the disheartening decision of the conductor, viz., that it would be death for any man to attempt to travel fifty miles on foot through snow like that. We could not send for help, and even if we could it would not come. We must submit, and await, as patiently as we might, succor or starvation!

I think the stoutest heart there felt a momentary chill when those words were uttered.

Within the hour conversation subsided to a low murmur here and there about the car, caught fitfully between the rising and falling of the blast; the lamps grew dim; and the majority of the castaways settled themselves among the flickering shadows to think—to forget the present, if they could—to sleep, if they might.

The eternal night—it surely seemed eternal to us—wore its lagging hours away at last, and the cold gray dawn broke in the east. As the light grew stronger the passengers began to stir and give signs of life, one after another, and each in turn pushed his slouched hat up from his forehead, stretched his stiffened limbs, and glanced out of the windows upon the cheerless prospect. It was cheerless, indeed!—not a living thing visible anywhere, not a human habitation; nothing but a vast white desert; uplifted sheets of snow drifting hither and thither before the wind—a world of eddying flakes shutting out the firmament above.

All day we moped about the cars, saying little, thinking much. Another lingering dreary night—and hunger.

Another dawning—another day of silence, sadness, wasting hunger, hopeless watching for succor that could not come. A night of restless slumber, filled with dreams of feasting—wakings distressed with the gnawings of hunger.

The fourth day came and went—and the fifth! Five days of dreadful imprisonment! A savage hunger looked out at every eye. There was in it a sign of awful import—the foreshadowing of a something that was vaguely shaping itself in every heart—a something which no tongue dared yet to frame into words.

The sixth day passed—the seventh dawned upon as gaunt and haggard and hopeless a company of men as ever stood in the shadow of death. It must out now! That thing which had been growing up in every heart was ready to leap from every lip at last! Nature had been taxed to the utmost—she must yield. RICHARD H. GASTON of Minnesota, tall, cadaverous, and pale, rose up. All knew what was coming. All prepared—every emotion, every semblance of excitement was smothered—only a calm, thoughtful seriousness appeared in the eyes that were lately so wild.

"Gentlemen: It cannot be delayed longer! The time is at hand! We must determine which of us shall die to furnish food for the rest!"

MR. JOHN J. WILLIAMS of Illinois rose and said: "Gentlemen—I nominate the Rev. James Sawyer of Tennessee."

MR. WM. R. ADAMS of Indiana said: "I nominate Mr. Daniel Slote of New York."

MR. CHARLES J. LANGDON: "I nominate Mr. Samuel A. Bowen of St. Louis."

MR. SLOTE: "Gentlemen—I desire to decline in favor of Mr. John A. Van Nostrand, Jun., of New Jersey."

MR. GASTON: "If there be no objection, the gentleman's desire will be acceded to."

MR. VAN NOSTRAND objecting, the resignation of Mr. Slote was rejected. The resignations of Messrs. Sawyer and Bowen were also offered, and refused upon the same grounds.

MR. A. L. BASCOM of Ohio: "I move that the nominations now close, and that the House proceed to an election by ballot."

MR. SAWYER: "Gentlemen—I protest earnestly against these proceedings. They are, in every way, irregular and unbecoming. I must beg to move that they be dropped at once, and that we elect a chairman of the meeting and proper officers to assist him, and then we can go on with the business before us understandingly."

MR. BELL of Iowa: "Gentlemen—I object. This is no time to stand upon forms and ceremonious observances. For more than seven days we have been without food. Every moment we lose in idle discussion increases our distress. I am satisfied with the nominations that have been made—every gentleman present is, I believe—and I, for one, do not see why we should not proceed at once to elect one or more of them. I wish to offer a resolution—"

MR. GASTON: "It would be objected to, and have to lie over one day under the rules, thus bringing about the very delay you wish to avoid. The gentleman from New Jersey—"

MR. VAN NOSTRAND: "Gentlemen—I am a stranger among you; I have not sought the distinction that has been conferred upon me, and I feel a delicacy—"

MR. MORGAN of Alabama (interrupting): "I move the previous question."

The motion was carried, and further debate shut off, of course. The motion to elect officers was passed, and under it Mr. Gaston was chosen chairman, Mr. Blake, secretary, Messrs. Holcomb, Dyer, and Baldwin a committee on nominations, and Mr. R. M. Howland, purveyor, to assist the committee in making selections.

A recess of half an hour was then taken, and some little caucusing followed. At the sound of the gavel the meeting reassembled, and the committee reported in favor of Messrs. George Ferguson of Kentucky,

Lucien Herrman of Louisiana, and W. Messick of Colorado as candidates. The report was accepted.

MR. ROGERS of Missouri: "Mr. President—The report being properly before the House now, I move to amend it by substituting for the name of Mr. Herrman that of Mr. Lucius Harris of St. Louis, who is well and honorably known to us all. I do not wish to be understood as casting the least reflection upon the high character and standing of the gentleman from Louisiana—far from it. I respect and esteem him as much as any gentleman here present possibly can; but none of us can be blind to the fact that he had lost more flesh during the week that we have lain here than any among us—none of us can be blind to the fact that the committee has been derelict in its duty, either through negligence or a graver fault, in thus offering for our suffrages a gentleman who, however pure his own motives may be, has really less nutriment in him—"

THE CHAIR: "The gentleman from Missouri will take his seat. The Chair cannot allow the integrity of the committee to be questioned save by the regular course, under the rules. What action will the House take upon the gentleman's motion?"

MR. HALLIDAY of Virginia: "I move to further amend the report by substituting Mr. Harvey Davis of Oregon for Mr. Messick. It may be urged by gentlemen that the hardships and privations of a frontier life have rendered Mr. Davis tough; but, gentlemen, is this a time to cavil at toughness? Is this a time to be fastidious concerning trifles? Is this a time to dispute about matters of paltry significance? No, gentlemen, bulk is what we desire—substance, weight, bulk—these are the supreme requisites now—not talent, not genius, not education. I insist upon my motion."

MR. MORGAN (excitedly): "Mr. Chairman—I do most strenuously object to this amendment. The gentleman from Oregon is old, and furthermore is bulky only in bone—not in flesh. I ask the gentleman from Virginia if it is soup we want instead of solid sustenance? if he would delude us with shadows? if he would mock our suffering with an Oregonian specter? I ask him if he can look upon the anxious faces around him, if he can gaze into our sad eyes, if he can listen to the beating of our expectant hearts, and still thrust this famine-stricken fraud upon us? I ask him if he can think of our desolate state, of our past sorrows, of our dark future, and still unpityingly foist upon us this wreck, this ruin, this tottering swindle, this gnarled and blighted and sapless vagabond from Oregon's inhospitable shores? Never!" [Applause.]

The amendment was put to vote, after a fiery debate, and lost. Mr. Harris was substituted on the first amendment. The balloting then began. Five ballots were held without a choice. On the sixth, Mr. Harris was elected, all voting for him but himself. It was then moved that his election should be ratified by acclamation, which was lost, in consequence of his again voting against himself.

MR. RADWAY moved that the House now take up the remaining candidates, and go into an election for breakfast. This was carried.

On the first ballot there was a tie, half the members favoring one candidate on account of his youth, and half favoring the other on account of his superior size. The President gave the casting vote for the latter, Mr. Messick. This decision created considerable dissatisfaction among the friends of Mr. Ferguson, the defeated candidate, and there was some talk of demanding a new ballot; but in the midst of it a motion to adjourn was carried, and the meeting broke up at once.

The preparations for supper diverted the attention of the Ferguson faction from the discussion of their grievance for a long time, and then, when they would have taken it up again, the happy announcement that Mr. Harris was ready drove all thought of it to the winds.

We improvised tables by propping up the backs of car-seats, and sat down with hearts full of gratitude to the finest supper that had blessed our vision for seven torturing days. How changed we were from what we had been a few short hours before! Hopeless, sad-eyed misery, hunger, feverish anxiety, desperation, then; thankfulness, serenity, joy too deep for utterance now. That I know was the cheeriest hour of my eventful life. The winds howled, and blew the snow wildly about our prison-house, but they were powerless to distress us any more. I liked Harris. He might have been better done, perhaps, but I am free to say that no man ever agreed with me better than Harris, or afforded me so large a degree of satisfaction. Messick was very well, though rather high-flavored, but for genuine nutritiousness and delicacy of fiber, give me Harris. Messick had his good points—I will not attempt to deny it, nor do I wish to do it—but he was no more fitted for breakfast than a mummy would be, sir—not a bit. Lean?—why, bless me!—and tough? Ah, he was very tough! You could not imagine it—you could never imagine anything like it.

"Do you mean to tell me that—"

"Do not interrupt me, please. After breakfast we elected a man by the name of Walker, from Detroit, for supper. He was very good. I wrote his wife so afterward. He was worthy of all praise. I shall always remember Walker. He was a little rare, but very good. And then the next morning we had Morgan of Alabama for breakfast. He was one of the finest men I ever sat down to—handsome, educated, refined, spoke several languages fluently—a perfect gentleman—he was a perfect gentleman, and singularly juicy. For supper we had that Oregon patriarch, and he *was* a fraud, there is no question about it—old, scraggy, tough, nobody can picture the reality. I finally said, gentlemen, you can do as you like, but *I* will wait for another election. And Grimes of Illinois said, 'Gentlemen, *I* will wait also. When you elect a man that has *something* to recommend him, I shall be glad to join you again.' It soon became evident that there was general dissatisfaction with Davis of Oregon, and so, to preserve the good will that had prevailed so pleasantly since we had had Harris, an election was called, and the result of it was that Baker of Georgia was chosen. He was splendid! Well, well—after that we had Doolittle, and Hawkins, and McElroy (there was some complaint about McElroy, because he was uncommonly short and thin), and Penrod, and two Smiths, and Bailey (Bailey had a wooden leg, which was clear loss, but he was otherwise good), and an Indian boy, and an organ-grinder, and a gentleman by the name of Buckminster—a poor stick of a vagabond that wasn't any good for company and no account for breakfast. We were glad we got him elected before relief came."

"And so the blessed relief *did* come at last?"

"Yes, it came one bright, sunny morning, just after election. John Murphy was the choice, and there never was a better, I am willing to testify; but John Murphy came home with us, in the train that came to succor us, and lived to marry the widow Harris—"

"Relict of—"

"Relict of our first choice. He married her, and is happy and respected and prosperous yet. Ah, it was like a novel, sir—it was like a romance. This is my stopping-place, sir; I must bid you good-by. Any time that you can make it convenient to tarry a day or two with me, I shall be glad to have you. I like you, sir; I have conceived an affection for you. I could like you as well as I liked Harris himself, sir. Good day, sir, and a pleasant journey."

He was gone. I never felt so stunned, so distressed, so bewildered in my life. But in my soul I was glad he was gone. With all his gentleness of manner and his soft voice, I shuddered whenever he turned his hungry eye upon me; and when I heard that I had achieved his perilous affection, and that I stood almost with the late Harris in his esteem, my heart fairly stood still!

I was bewildered byond description. I did not doubt his word; I could not question a single item in a statement so stamped with the earnestness of truth as his; but its dreadful details overpowered me, and threw my thoughts into hopeless confusion. I saw the conductor looking at me. I said, "Who is that man?"

"He was a member of Congress once, and a good one. But he got caught in a snow-drift in the cars, and like to have been starved to death. He got so frost-bitten and frozen up generally, and used up for want of something to eat, that he was sick and out of his head two or three months afterward. He is all right now, only he is a monomaniac, and when he gets on that old subject he never stops till he has eat up that whole car-load of people he talks about. He would have finished the crowd by this time, only he had to get out here. He has got their names as pat as A B C. When he gets them all eat up but himself, he always says: 'Then the hour for the usual election for breakfast having arrived, and there being no opposition, I was duly elected, after which, there being no objections offered, I resigned. Thus I am here.'"

I felt inexpressibly relieved to know that I had only been listening to the harmless vagaries of a madman instead of the genuine experiences of a bloodthirsty cannibal.

1868

A Day at Niagara

Niagara Falls is a most enjoyable place of resort. The hotels are excellent, and the prices not at all exorbitant. The opportunities for fishing are not surpassed in the country; in fact, they are not even equaled elsewhere. Because, in other localities, certain places in the streams are much better than others; but at Niagara one place is just as good as another, for the reason that the fish do not bite anywhere, and so there is no use in your walking five miles to fish, when you can depend on being just as unsuccessful nearer home. The advantages of this state of things have never heretofore been properly placed before the public.

The weather is cool in summer, and the walks and drives are all pleasant and none of them fatiguing. When you start out to "do" the Falls you first drive down about a mile, and pay a small sum for the privilege of looking down from a precipice into the narrowest part of the

Niagara River. A railway "cut" through a hill would be as comely if it had the angry river tumbling and foaming through its bottom. You can descend a staircase here a hundred and fifty feet down, and stand at the edge of the water. After you have done it, you will wonder why you did it; but you will then be too late.

The guide will explain to you, in his blood-curdling way, how he saw the little steamer, *Maid of the Mist,* descend the fearful rapids—how first one paddle-box was out of sight behind the raging billows and then the other, and at what point it was that her smokestack toppled overboard, and where her planking began to break and part asunder—and how she did finally live through the trip, after accomplishing the incredible feat of traveling seventeen miles in six minutes, or six miles in seventeen minutes, I have really forgotten which. But it was very extraordinary, anyhow. It is worth the price of admission to hear the guide tell the story nine times in succession to different parties, and never miss a word or alter a sentence or a gesture.

Then you drive over to Suspension Bridge, and divide your misery between the chances of smashing down two hundred feet into the river below, and the chances of having the railway-train overhead smashing down onto you. Either possibility is discomforting taken by itself, but, mixed together, they amount in the aggregate to positive unhappiness.

On the Canada side you drive along the chasm between long ranks of photographers standing guard behind their cameras, ready to make an ostentatious frontispiece of you and your decaying ambulance, and your solemn crate with a hide on it, which you are expected to regard in the light of a horse, and a diminished and unimportant background of sublime Niagara; and a great many people *have* the incredible effrontery or the native depravity to aid and abet this sort of crime.

Any day, in the hands of these photographers, you may see stately pictures of papa and mamma, Johnny and Bub and Sis, or a couple of country cousins, all smiling vacantly, and all disposed in studied and uncomfortable attitudes in their carriage, and all looming up in their awe-inspiring imbecility before the snubbed and diminished presentment of that majestic presence whose ministering spirits are the rainbows, whose voice is the thunder, whose awful front is veiled in clouds, who was monarch here dead and forgotten ages before this hackful of small reptiles was deemed temporarily necessary to fill a crack in the world's unnoted myriads, and will still be monarch here ages and decades of ages after they shall have gathered themselves to their blood-relations, the other worms, and been mingled with the unremembering dust.

There is no actual harm in making Niagara a background whereon to display one's marvelous insignificance in a good strong light, but it requires a sort of superhuman self-complacency to enable one to do it.

When you have examined the stupendous Horseshoe Fall till you are satisfied you cannot improve on it, you return to America by the new Suspension Bridge, and follow up the bank to where they exhibit the Cave of the Winds.

Here I followed instructions, and divested myself of all my clothing, and put on a waterproof jacket and overalls. This costume is picturesque, but not beautiful. A guide, similarly dressed, led the way down a flight of winding stairs, which wound and wound, and still kept on winding long after the thing ceased to be a novelty, and then terminated long before it had begun to be a pleasure. We were then well down under the precipice, but still considerably above the level of the river.

We now began to creep along flimsy bridges of a single plank, our persons shielded from destruction by a crazy wooden railing, to which I clung with both hands—not because I was afraid, but because I wanted to. Presently the descent became steeper, and the bridge flimsier, and sprays from the American Fall began to rain down on us in fast increasing sheets that soon became blinding, and after that our progress was mostly in the nature of groping. Now a furious wind began to rush out from behind the waterfall, which seemed determined to sweep us from the bridge, and scatter us on the rocks and among the torrents below. I remarked that I wanted to go home; but it was too late. We were almost under the monstrous wall of water thundering down from above, and speech was in vain in the midst of such a pitiless crash of sound.

In another moment the guide disappeared behind the deluge, and, bewildered by the thunder, driven helplessly by the wind, and smitten by the arrowy tempest of rain, I followed. All was darkness. Such a mad storming, roaring, and bellowing of warring wind and water never crazed my ears before. I bent my head, and seemed to receive the Atlantic on my back. The world seemed going to destruction. I could not see anything, the flood poured down so savagely. I raised my head, with open mouth, and the most of the American cataract went down my throat. If I had sprung a leak now I had been lost. And at this moment I discovered that the bridge had ceased, and we must trust for a foothold to the slippery and precipitous rocks. I never was so scared before and survived it. But we got through at last, and emerged into the open day, where we could stand in front of the laced and frothy and seething world of descending water, and look at it. When I saw how much of it there was, and how fearfully in earnest it was, I was sorry I had gone behind it.

The noble Red Man has always been a friend and darling of mine. I love to read about him in tales and legends and romances. I love to read of his inspired sagacity, and his love of the wild free life of mountain and forest, and his general nobility of character, and his stately metaphorical manner of speech, and his chivalrous love for the dusky maiden, and the picturesque pomp of his dress and accoutrements. Especially the picturesque pomp of his dress and accoutrements. When I found the shops at Niagara Falls full of dainty Indian beadwork, and stunning moccasins, and equally stunning toy figures representing human beings who carried their weapons in holes bored through their arms and bodies, and had feet shaped like a pie, I was filled with emotion. I knew that now, at last, I was going to come face to face with the noble Red Man.

A lady clerk in a shop told me, indeed, that all her grand array of curiosities were made by the Indians, and that they were plenty about the Falls, and that they were friendly, and it would not be dangerous to speak to them. And sure enough, as I approached the bridge leading over to Luna Island, I came upon a noble Son of the Forest sitting under a tree, diligently at work on a bead reticule. He wore a slouch hat and brogans, and had a short black pipe in his mouth. Thus does the baneful contact with our effeminate civilization dilute the picturesque pomp which is so natural to the Indian when far removed from us in his native haunts. I addressed the relic as follows:

"Is the Wawhoo-Wang-Wang of the Whack-a-Whack happy? Does the great Speckled Thunder sigh for the war-path, or is his heart contented with dreaming of the dusky maiden, the Pride of the Forest? Does the mighty Sachem yearn to drink the blood of his enemies, or is he satisfied to make bead reticules for the pappooses of the paleface? Speak, sublime relic of bygone grandeur—venerable ruin, speak!"

The relic said:

"An' is it mesilf, Dennis Hooligan, that ye'd be takin' for a dirty Injin, ye drawlin', lantern-jawed, spider-legged divil! By the piper that played before Moses, I'll ate ye!"

I went away from there.

By and by, in the neighborhood of the Terrapin Tower, I came upon a gentle daughter of the aborigines in fringed and beaded buckskin moccasins and leggins, seated on a bench with her pretty wares about her. She had just carved out a wooden chief that had a strong family resemblance to a clothespin, and was now boring a hole through his abdomen to put his bow through. I hesitated a moment, and then addressed her:

"Is the heart of the forest maiden heavy? Is the Laughing Tadpole lonely? Does she mourn over the extinguished council-fires of her race, and the vanished glory of her ancestors? Or does her sad spirit wander afar toward the hunting-grounds whither her brave Gobbler-of-the-Lightnings is gone? Why is my daughter silent? Has she aught against the paleface stranger?"

The maiden said:

"Faix, an' is it Biddy Malone ye dare to be callin' names? Lave this, or I'll shy your lean carcass over the cataract, ye sniveling blaggard!"

I adjourned from there also.

"Confound these Indians!" I said. "They told me they were tame; but, if appearances go for anything, I should say they were all on the war-path."

I made one more attempt to fraternize with them, and only one. I came upon a camp of them gathered in the shade of a great tree, making wampum and moccasins, and addressed them in the language of friendship:

"Noble Red Men, Braves, Grand Sachems, War Chiefs, Squaws, and High Muck-a-Mucks, the paleface from the land of the setting sun greets you! You, Beneficent Polecat—you, Devourer of Mountains—you, Roaring Thundergust—you, Bully Boy with a Glass eye—the paleface from beyond the great waters greets you all! War and pestilence have thinned your ranks and destroyed your once proud nation. Poker and seven-up, and a vain modern expense for soap, unknown to your glorious ancestors, have depleted your purses. Appropriating, in your simplicity, the property of others has gotten you into trouble. Misrepresenting facts, in your simple innocence, has damaged your reputation with the soulless usurper. Trading for forty-rod whisky, to enable you to get drunk and happy and tomahawk your families, has played the everlasting mischief with the picturesque pomp of your dress, and here you are, in the broad light of the nineteenth century, gotten up like the ragtag and bobtail of the purlieus of New York. For shame! Remember your ancestors! Recall their mighty deeds! Remember Uncas!—and Red Jacket!—and Hole in the Day!—and Whoopdedoodledo! Emulate their achievements! Unfurl yourselves under my banner, noble savages, illustrious guttersnipes—"

"Down wid him!" "Scoop the blaggard!" "Burn him!" "Hang him!" "Dhround him!"

It was the quickest operation that ever was. I simply saw a sudden flash in the air of clubs, brick-bats, fists, bead-baskets, and moccasins—a single flash, and they all appeared to hit me at once, and no two of them in the same place. In the next instant the entire tribe was upon me. They tore half the clothes off me; they broke my arms and legs; they gave me a thump that dented the top of my head till it would hold coffee like a saucer; and, to crown their disgraceful proceedings and add insult to injury, they threw me over the Niagara Falls, and I got wet.

About ninety or a hundred feet from the top, the remains of my vest caught on a projecting rock, and I was almost drowned before I could get loose. I finally fell, and brought up in a world of white foam at the foot of the Fall, whose celled and bubbly masses towered up several inches above my head. Of course I got into the eddy. I sailed round and round in it forty-four times—chasing a chip and gaining on it—each round trip a half-mile—reaching for the same bush on the bank forty-four times, and just exactly missing it by a hair's-breadth every time.

At last a man walked down and sat down close to that bush, and put a pipe in his mouth, and lit a match, and followed me with one eye and kept the other on the match, while he sheltered it in his hands from the wind. Presently a puff of wind blew it out. The next time I swept around he said:

"Got a match?"

"Yes; in my other vest. Help me out, please."

"Not for Joe."

When I came round again, I said:

"Excuse the seemingly impertinent curiosity of a drowning man, but will you explain this singular conduct of yours?"

"With pleasure. I am the coroner. Don't hurry on my account. I can wait for you. But I wish I had a match."

I said: "Take my place, and I'll go and get you one."

He declined. This lack of confidence on his part created a coldness between us, and from that time forward I avoided him. It was my idea, in case anything happened to me, to so time the occurrence as to throw my custom into the hands of the opposition coroner on the American side.

At last a policeman came along, and arrested me for disturbing the peace by yelling at people on shore for help. The judge fined me, but I had the advantage of him. My money was with my pantaloons, and my pantaloons were with the Indians.

Thus I escaped. I am now lying in a very critical condition. At least I am lying anyway—critical or not critical. I am hurt all over, but I cannot tell the full extent yet, because the doctor is not done taking inventory.

He will make out my manifest this evening. However, thus far he thinks only sixteen of my wounds are fatal. I don't mind the others.

Upon regaining my right mind, I said:

"It is an awful savage tribe of Indians that do the beadwork and moccasins for Niagara Falls, doctor. Where are they from?"

"Limerick, my son."

1869

Legend of the Capitoline Venus

CHAPTER I
[*Scene—An Artist's Studio in Rome*]

"Oh, George, I *do* love you!"

"Bless your dear heart, Mary, I know that—*why* is your father so obdurate?"

"George, he means well, but art is folly to him—he only understands groceries. He thinks you would starve me."

"Confound his wisdom—it savors of inspiration. Why am I not a money-making bowelless grocer, instead of a divinely gifted sculptor with nothing to eat?"

"Do not despond, Georgy, dear—all his prejudices will fade away as soon as you shall have acquired fifty thousand dol—"

"Fifty thousand demons! Child, I am in arrears for my board!"

CHAPTER II
[*Scene—A Dwelling in Rome*]

"My dear sir, it is useless to talk. I haven't anything against you, but I can't let my daughter marry a hash of love, art, and starvation—I believe you have nothing else to offer."

"Sir, I am poor, I grant you. But is fame nothing? The Hon. Bellamy Foodle of Arkansas says that my new statue of America is a clever piece of sculpture, and he is satisfied that my name will one day be famous."

"Bosh! What does that Arkansas ass know about it? Fame's nothing—the market price of your marble scarecrow is the thing to look at. It took you six months to chisel it, and you can't sell it for a hundred dollars. No, sir! Show me fifty thousand dollars and you can have my daughter —otherwise she marries young Simper. You have just six months to raise the money in. Good morning, sir."

"Alas! Woe is me!"

CHAPTER III
[Scene—The Studio]

"Oh, John, friend of my boyhood, I am the unhappiest of men."

"You're a simpleton!"

"I have nothing left to love but my poor statue of America—and see, even she has no sympathy for me in her cold marble countenance—so beautiful and so heartless!"

"You're a dummy!"

"Oh, John!"

"Oh, fudge! Didn't you say you had six months to raise the money in?"

"Don't deride my agony, John. If I had six centuries what good would it do? How could it help a poor wretch without name, capital, or friends?"

"Idiot! Coward! Baby! Six months to raise the money in—and five will do!"

"Are you insane?"

"Six months—an abundance. Leave it to me. I'll raise it."

"What do you mean, John? How on earth can you raise such a monstrous sum for *me?*"

"*Will* you let that be *my* business, and not meddle? Will you leave the thing in my hands? Will you swear to submit to whatever I do? Will you pledge me to find no fault with my actions?"

"I am dizzy—bewildered—but I swear."

John took up a hammer and deliberately smashed the nose of America! He made another pass and two of her fingers fell to the floor—another, and part of an ear came away—another, and a row of toes was mangled and dismembered—another, and the left leg, from the knee down, lay a fragmentary ruin!

John put on his hat and departed.

George gazed speechless upon the battered and grotesque nightmare before him for the space of thirty seconds, and then wilted to the floor and went into convulsions.

John returned presently with a carriage, got the broken-hearted artist and the broken-legged statue aboard, and drove off, whistling low and tranquilly. He left the artist at his lodgings, and drove off and disappeared down the *Via Quirinalis* with the statue.

CHAPTER IV
[*Scene—The Studio*]

"The six months will be up at two o'clock to-day! Oh, agony! My life is blighted. I would that I were dead. I had no supper yesterday. I have had no breakfast to-day. I dare not enter an eating-house. And hungry? —don't mention it! My bootmaker duns me to death—my tailor duns me —my landlord haunts me. I am miserable. I haven't seen John since that awful day. *She* smiles on me tenderly when we meet in the great thoroughfares, but her old flint of a father makes her look in the other direction in short order. Now who is knocking at that door? Who is come to persecute me? That malignant villain the bootmaker, I'll warrant. *Come in!*"

"Ah, happiness attend your highness—Heaven be propitious to your grace! I have brought my lord's new boots—ah, say nothing about the pay, there is no hurry, none in the world. Shall be proud if my noble lord will continue to honor me with his custom—ah, adieu!"

"Brought the boots himself! Don't want his pay! Takes his leave with a bow and a scrape fit to honor majesty withal! Desires a continuance of my custom! Is the world coming to an end? Of all the—*come in!*"

"Pardon, signore, but I have brought your new suit of clothes for—"

"*Come in! !*"

"A thousand pardons for this intrusion, your worship! But I have prepared the beautiful suite of rooms below for you—this wretched den is but ill suited to—"

"*Come in! ! !*"

"I have called to say that your credit at our bank, some time since unfortunately interrupted, is entirely and most satisfactorily restored, and we shall be most happy if you will draw upon us for any—"

"Come in! ! ! !"

"My noble boy, she is yours! She'll be here in a moment! Take her— marry her—love her—be happy!—God bless you both! Hip, hip, hur—"

"COME IN! ! ! ! !"

"Oh, George, my own darling, we are saved!"

"Oh, Mary, my own darling, we *are* saved—but I'll swear I don't know why nor how!"

CHAPTER V
[Scene—A Roman Café]

One of a group of American gentlemen reads and translates from the weekly edition of *Il Slangwhanger di Roma* as follows:

WONDERFUL DISCOVERY!—*Some six months ago Signor John Smitthe, an American gentleman now some years a resident of Rome, purchased for a trifle a small piece of ground in the Campagna, just beyond the tomb of the Scipio family, from the owner, a bankrupt relative of the Princess Borghese. Mr. Smitthe afterward went to the Minister of the Public Records and had the piece of ground transferred to a poor American artist named George Arnold, explaining that he did it as payment and satisfaction for pecuniary damage accidentally done by him long since upon property belonging to Signor Arnold, and further observed that he would make additional satisfaction by improving the ground for Signor A., at his own charge and cost. Four weeks ago, while making some necessary excavations upon the property, Signor Smitthe unearthed the most remarkable ancient statue that has ever been added to the opulent art treasures of Rome. It was an exquisite figure of a woman, and though sadly stained by the soil and the mold of ages, no eye can look unmoved upon its ravishing beauty. The nose, the left leg from the knee down, an ear, and also the toes of the right foot and two fingers of one of the hands were gone, but otherwise the noble figure was in a remarkable state of preservation. The government at once took military possession of the statue, and appointed a commission of art-critics, antiquaries, and cardinal princes of the church to assess its value and determine the remuneration that must go to the owner of the ground in which it was found. The whole affair was kept a profound secret until last night. In the mean time the commission sat with closed doors and deliberated. Last night they decided unanimously that the statue is a Venus, and the work of some unknown but sublimely gifted artist of the third century before Christ. They consider it the most faultless work of art the world has any knowledge of.*

At midnight they held a final conference and decided that the Venus was worth the enormous sum of ten million francs! *In accordance with Roman law and Roman usage, the government being half-owner in all works of art found in the Campagna, the State has naught to do but pay five million francs to Mr. Arnold and take permanent possession of the beautiful statue. This morning the Venus will be removed to the*

Capitol, there to remain, and at noon the commission will wait upon Signor Arnold with His Holiness the Pope's order upon the Treasury for the princely sum of five million francs in gold!

Chorus of Voices.—"Luck! It's no name for it!"

Another Voice.—"Gentlemen, I propose that we immediately form an American joint-stock company for the purchase of lands and excavations of statues here, with proper connections in Wall Street to bull and bear the stock."

All.—"Agreed."

CHAPTER VI
[*Scene—The Roman Capitol Ten Years Later*]

"Dearest Mary, this is the most celebrated statue in the world. This is the renowned 'Capitoline Venus' you've heard so much about. Here she is with her little blemishes 'restored' (that is, patched) by the most noted Roman artists—and the mere fact that they did the humble patching of so noble a creation will make their names illustrious while the world stands. How strange it seems—this place! The day before I last stood here, ten happy years ago, I wasn't a rich man—bless your soul, I hadn't a cent. And yet I had a good deal to do with making Rome mistress of this grandest work of ancient art the world contains."

"The worshiped, the illustrious Capitoline Venus—and what a sum she is valued at! Ten millions of francs!"

"Yes—*now* she is."

"And oh, Georgy, how divinely beautiful she is!"

"Ah, yes—but nothing to what she was before that blessed John Smith broke her leg and battered her nose. Ingenious Smith!—gifted Smith!—noble Smith! Author of all our bliss! Hark! Do you know what that wheeze means? Mary, that cub has got the whooping-cough. Will you *never* learn to take care of the children!"

THE END

The Capitoline Venus is still in the Capitol at Rome, and is still the most charming and most illustrious work of ancient art the world can boast of. But if ever it shall be your fortune to stand before it and go into the customary ecstasies over it, don't permit this true and secret history of its origin to mar your bliss—and when you read about a gigantic Petrified Man being dug up near Syracuse, in the State of New

York, or near any other place, keep your own counsel—and if the Barnum that buried him there offers to sell to you at an enormous sum, don't you buy. Send him to the Pope!

NOTE   The above sketch was written at the time the famous swindle of the "Petrified Giant" was the sensation of the day in the United States.

1869

Journalism in Tennessee

The editor of the Memphis *Avalanche* swoops thus mildly down upon a correspondent who posted him as a Radical:—"While he was writing the first word, the middle, dotting his i's, crossing his t's, and punching his period, he knew he was concocting a sentence that was saturated with infamy and reeking with falsehood."   *Exchange*

I was told by the physician that a Southern climate would improve my health, and so I went down to Tennessee, and got a berth on the *Morning Glory and Johnson County War-Whoop* as associate editor. When I went on duty I found the chief editor sitting tilted back in a three-legged chair with his feet on a pine table. There was another pine table in the room and another afflicted chair, and both were half buried under newspapers and scraps and sheets of manuscript. There was a wooden box of sand, sprinkled with cigar stubs and "old soldiers," and a stove with a door hanging by its upper hinge. The chief editor had a long-tailed black cloth frock-coat on, and white linen pants. His boots were small and neatly blacked. He wore a ruffled shirt, a large seal-ring, a standing collar of obsolete pattern, and a checkered neckerchief with the ends hanging down. Date of costume about 1848. He was smoking a cigar, and trying to think of a word, and in pawing his hair he had rumpled his locks a good deal. He was scowling fearfully, and I judged that he was concocting a particularly knotty editorial. He told me to take the exchanges and skim through them and write up the "Spirit of the Tennessee Press," condensing into the article all of their contents that seemed of interest.

I wrote as follows:

SPIRIT OF THE TENNESSEE PRESS

The editors of the Semi-Weekly Earthquake *evidently labor under a misapprehension with regard to the Ballyhack railroad. It is not the object of the company to leave Buzzardville off to one side. On the contrary, they consider it one of the most important points along the line, and consequently can have no desire to slight it. The gentlemen of the* Earthquake *will, of course, take pleasure in making the correction.*

John W. Blossom, Esq., the able editor of the Higginsville Thunderbolt and Battle Cry of Freedom, *arrived in the city yesterday. He is stopping at the Van Buren House.*

We observe that our contemporary of the Mud Springs Morning Howl *has fallen into the error of supposing that the election of Van Werter is not an established fact, but he will have discovered his mistake before this reminder reaches him, no doubt. He was doubtless misled by incomplete election returns.*

It is pleasant to note that the city of Blathersville is endeavoring to contract with some New York gentlemen to pave its well-nigh impassable streets with the Nicholson pavement. The Daily Hurrah *urges the measure with ability, and seems confident of ultimate success.*

I passed my manuscript over to the chief editor for acceptance, alteration, or destruction. He glanced at it and his face clouded. He ran his eye down the pages, and his countenance grew portentous. It was easy to see that something was wrong. Presently he sprang up and said:

"Thunder and lighting! Do you suppose I am going to speak of those cattle that way? Do you suppose my subscribers are going to stand such gruel as that? Give me the pen!"

I never saw a pen scrape and scratch its way so viciously, or plow through another man's verbs and adjectives so relentlessly. While he was in the midst of his work, somebody shot at him through the open window, and marred the symmetry of my ear.

"Ah," said he, "that is that scoundrel Smith, of the *Moral Volcano*—he was due yesterday." And he snatched a navy revolver from his belt and fired. Smith dropped, shot in the thigh. The shot spoiled Smith's aim, who was just taking a second chance, and he crippled a stranger. It was me. Merely a finger shot off.

Then the chief editor went on with his erasures and interlineations. Just as he finished them a hand-grenade came down the stove-pipe, and the explosion shivered the stove into a thousand fragments. However, it did no further damage, except that a vagrant piece knocked a couple of my teeth out.

"That stove is utterly ruined," said the chief editor.

I said I believed it was.

"Well, no matter—don't want it this kind of weather. I know the man that did it. I'll get him. Now, *here* is the way this stuff ought to be written."

I took the manuscript. It was scarred with erasures and interlineations till its mother wouldn't have known it if it had had one. It now read as follows:

SPIRIT OF THE TENNESSEE PRESS

The inveterate liars of the Semi-Weekly Earthquake *are evidently endeavoring to palm off upon a noble and chivalrous people another of their vile and brutal falsehoods with regard to that most glorious conception of the nineteenth century, the Ballyhack railroad. The idea that Buzzardville was to be left off at one side originated in their own fulsome brains—or rather in the settlings which they regard as brains. They had better swallow this lie if they want to save their abandoned reptile carcasses the cowhiding they so richly deserve.*

That ass, Blossom, of the Higginsville Thunderbolt and Battle Cry of Freedom, *is down here again sponging at the Van Buren.*

We observe that the besotted blackguard of the Mud Springs Morning Howl *is giving out, with his usual propensity for lying, that Van Werter is not elected. The heaven-born mission of journalism is to disseminate truth; to eradicate error; to educate, refine, and elevate the tone of public morals and manners, and make all men more gentle, more virtuous, more charitable, and in all ways better, and holier, and happier; and yet this black-hearted scoundrel degrades his great office persistently to the dissemination of falsehood, calumny, vituperation, and vulgarity.*

Blathersville wants a Nicholson pavement—it wants a jail and a poorhouse more. The idea of a pavement in a one-horse town composed of two gin-mills, a blacksmith shop, and that mustard-plaster of a newspaper, the Daily Hurrah! *The crawling insect, Buckner, who edits the* Hurrah, *is braying about his business with his customary imbecility, and imagining that he is talking sense.*

"Now *that* is the way to write—peppery and to the point. Mush-and-milk journalism gives me the fan-tods."

About this time a brick came through the window with a splintering crash, and gave me a considerable of a jolt in the back. I moved out of range—I began to feel in the way.

The chief said, "That was the Colonel, likely. I've been expecting him for two days. He will be up now right away."

He was correct. The Colonel appeared in the door a moment afterward with a dragoon revolver in his hand.

He said, "Sir, have I the honor of addressing the poltroon who edits this mangy sheet?"

"You have. Be seated, sir. Be careful of the chair, one of its legs is gone. I believe I have the honor of addressing the putrid liar, Colonel Blatherskite Tecumseh?"

"Right, sir. I have a little account to settle with you. If you are at leisure we will begin."

"I have an article on the 'Encouraging Progress of Moral and Intellectual Development in America' to finish, but there is no hurry. Begin."

Both pistols rang out their fierce clamor at the same instant. The chief lost a lock of his hair, and the Colonel's bullet ended its career in the fleshy part of my thigh. The Colonel's left shoulder was clipped a little. They fired again. Both missed their men this time, but I got my share, a shot in the arm. At the third fire both gentlemen were wounded slightly, and I had a knuckle chipped. I then said, I believed I would go out and take a walk, as this was a private matter, and I had a delicacy about participating in it further. But both gentlemen begged me to keep my seat, and assured me that I was not in the way.

They then talked about the elections and the crops while they reloaded, and I fell to tying up my wounds. But presently they opened fire again with animation, and every shot took effect—but it is proper to remark that five out of the six fell to my share. The sixth one mortally wounded the Colonel, who remarked, with fine humor, that he would have to say good morning now, as he had business uptown. He then inquired the way to the undertaker's and left.

The chief turned to me and said, "I am expecting company to dinner, and shall have to get ready. It will be a favor to me if you will read proof and attend to the customers."

I winced a little at the idea of attending to the customers, but I was too bewildered by the fusillade that was still ringing in my ears to think of anything to say.

He continued, "Jones will be here at three—cowhide him. Gillespie will call earlier, perhaps—throw him out of the window. Ferguson will be along about four—kill him. That is all for to-day, I believe. If you have any odd time, you may write a blistering article on the police—give the chief inspector rats. The cowhides are under the table; weapons in the drawer—ammunition there in the corner—lint and bandages up there in the pigeonholes. In case of accident, go to Lancet, the surgeon, down-stairs. He advertises—we take it out in trade."

He was gone. I shuddered. At the end of the next three hours I had been through perils so awful that all peace of mind and all cheerfulness were gone from me. Gillespie had called and thrown *me* out of the window. Jones arrived promptly, and when I got ready to do the cowhiding he took the job off my hands. In an encounter with a stranger, not in the bill of fare, I had lost my scalp. Another stranger, by the name of Thompson, left me a mere wreck and ruin of chaotic rags. And at last, at bay in the corner, and beset by an infuriated mob of editors, blacklegs, politicians, and desperadoes, who raved and swore and flourished their weapons about my head till the air shimmered with glancing flashes of steel, I was in the act of resigning my berth on the paper when the chief arrived, and with him a rabble of charmed and enthusiastic friends. Then ensued a scene of riot and carnage such as no human pen, or steel one either, could describe. People were shot, probed, dismembered, blown up, thrown out of the window. There was a brief tornado of murky blasphemy, with a confused and frantic war-dance glimmering through it, and then all was over. In five minutes there was silence, and the gory chief and I sat alone and surveyed the sanguinary ruin that strewed the floor around us.

He said, "You'll like this place when you get used to it."

I said, "I'll have to get you to excuse me; I think maybe I might write to suit you after a while; as soon as I had had some practice and learned the language I am confident I could. But, to speak the plain truth, that sort of energy of expression has its inconveniences, and a man is liable to interruption. You see that yourself. Vigorous writing is calculated to elevate the public, no doubt, but then I do not like to attract so much attention as it calls forth. I can't write with comfort when I am interrupted so much as I have been to-day. I like this berth well enough, but I don't like to be left here to wait on the customers. The experiences are novel, I grant you, and entertaining, too, after a fashion, but they are not judiciously distributed. A gentleman shoots at you through the window and cripples *me;* a bombshell comes down the stove-pipe for your gratification and sends the stove door down *my* throat; a friend drops in to swap compliments with you, and freckles *me* with bullet-holes till my skin won't hold my principles; you go to dinner, and Jones comes with his cowhide, Gillespie throws me out of the window, Thompson tears all my clothes off, and an entire stranger takes my scalp with the easy freedom of an old acquaintance; and in less than five minutes all the blackguards in the country arrive in their war-paint, and proceed to scare the rest of me to death with their toma-hawks. Take it altogether, I never had such a spirited time in all my life as I have had to-day. No; I like you, and I like your calm unruffled way of explaining things to the customers, but you see I am not used to it. The Southern heart is too impulsive; Southern hospitality is too lavish with the stranger. The paragraphs which I have written to-day, and into whose cold sentences your masterly hand has infused the fervent spirit of Tennesseean journalism, will wake up another nest of hornets. All that mob of editors will come—and they will come hungry, too, and want somebody for breakfast. I shall have to bid you adieu. I decline to be present at these festivities. I came South for my health, I will go back on the same errand, and suddenly. Tennesseean journalism is too stirring for me."

After which we parted with mutual regret, and I took apartments at the hospital.

1869

A Curious Dream

CONTAINING A MORAL

Night before last I had a singular dream. I seemed to be sitting on a doorstep (in no particular city perhaps) ruminating, and the time of night appeared to be about twelve or one o'clock. The weather was balmy and delicious. There was no human sound in the air, not even a footstep. There was no sound of any kind to emphasize the dead stillness, except the occasional hollow barking of a dog in the distance and the fainter answer of a further dog. Presently up the street I heard a bony clack-clacking, and guessed it was the castanets of a serenading party. In a minute more a tall skeleton, hooded, and half clad in a tattered and moldy shroud, whose shreds were flapping about the ribby latticework of its person, swung by me with a stately stride and disappeared in the gray gloom of the starlight. It had a broken and worm-eaten coffin on its shoulder and a bundle of something in its hand. I knew what the clack-clacking was then; it was this party's joints working together, and his elbows knocking against his sides as he walked. I may say I was surprised. Before I could collect my thoughts and enter upon any speculations as to what this apparition might portend, I heard another one coming—for I recognized his clack-clack. He had two-thirds of a coffin on his shoulder, and some foot and head boards under his arm. I mightily wanted to peer under his hood and speak to him, but when he turned and smiled upon me with his cavernous sockets and his projecting grin as he went by, I thought I would not detain him. He was hardly gone when I heard the clacking again, and another one issued from the shadowy half-light. This one was bending under a heavy gravestone, and dragging a shabby coffin after him by a string. When he got to me he gave me a steady look for a moment or two, and then rounded to and backed up to me, saying:

"Ease this down for a fellow, will you?"

I eased the gravestone down till it rested on the ground, and in doing so noticed that it bore the name of "John Baxter Copmanhurst," with "May, 1839," as the date of his death. Deceased sat wearily down by me, and wiped his os frontis with his major maxillary—chiefly from former habit I judged, for I could not see that he brought away any perspiration.

"It is too bad, too bad," said he, drawing the remnant of the shroud about him and leaning his jaw pensively on his hand. Then he put his left foot up on his knee and fell to scratching his anklebone absently with a rusty nail which he got out of his coffin.

"What is too bad, friend?"

"Oh, everything, everything. I almost wish I never had died."

"You surprise me. Why do you say this? Has anything gone wrong? What is the matter?"

"Matter! Look at this shroud—rags. Look at this gravestone, all battered up. Look at that disgraceful old coffin. All a man's property going to ruin and destruction before his eyes, and ask him if anything is wrong? Fire and brimstone!"

"Calm yourself, calm yourself," I said. "It is too bad—it is certainly too bad, but then I had not supposed that you would much mind such matters, situated as you are."

"Well, my dear sir, I do mind them. My pride is hurt, and my comfort is impaired—destroyed, I might say. I will state my case—I will put it to you in such a way that you can comprehend it, if you will let me," said the poor skeleton, tilting the hood of his shroud back, as if he were clearing for action, and thus unconsciously giving himself a jaunty and festive air very much at variance with the grave character of his position in life—so to speak—and in prominent contrast with his distressful mood.

"Proceed," said I.

"I reside in the shameful old graveyard a block or two above you here, in this street—there, now, I just expected that cartilage would let go!—third rib from the bottom, friend, hitch the end of it to my spine with a string, if you have got such a thing about you, though a bit of silver wire is a deal pleasanter, and more durable and becoming, if one keeps it polished—to think of shredding out and going to pieces in this way, just on account of the indifference and neglect of one's posterity!" —and the poor ghost grated his teeth in a way that gave me a wrench and a shiver—for the effect is mightily increased by the absence of muffling flesh and cuticle. "I reside in that old graveyard, and have for these thirty years; and I tell you things are changed since I first laid this old tired frame there, and turned over, and stretched out for a long sleep, with a delicious sense upon me of being *done* with bother, and grief, and anxiety, and doubt, and fear, forever and ever, and listening with comfortable and increasing satisfaction to the sexton's work, from the startling clatter of his first spadeful on my coffin till it dulled away to the faint patting that shaped the roof of my new home—delicious! My! I wish you could try it to-night!" and out of my reverie deceased fetched me a rattling slap with a bony hand.

"Yes, sir, thirty years ago I laid me down there, and was happy. For it was out in the country then—out in the breezy, flowery, grand old woods, and the lazy winds gossiped with the leaves, and the squirrels capered over us and around us, and the creeping things visited us, and the birds filled the tranquil solitude with music. Ah, it was worth ten years of a man's life to be dead then! Everything was pleasant. I was in a good neighborhood, for all the dead people that lived near me belonged to the best families in the city. Our posterity appeared to think the world of us. They kept our graves in the very best condition; the fences were always in faultless repair, head-boards were kept painted or whitewashed, and were replaced with new ones as soon as they began to look rusty or decayed; monuments were kept upright, railings intact and bright, the rose-bushes and shrubbery trimmed, trained, and free from blemish, the walks clean and smooth and graveled. But that day is gone by. Our descendants have forgotten us. My grandson lives in a stately house built with money made by these old hands of mine, and I sleep in a neglected grave with invading vermin that gnaw my shroud to build them nests withal! I and friends that lie with me founded and secured the prosperity of this fine city, and the stately bantling of our loves leaves us to rot in a dilapidated cemetery which neighbors curse and strangers scoff at. See the difference between the old time and this—for instance: Our graves are all caved in now; our head-boards have rotted away and tumbled down; our railings reel this way and that, with one foot in the air, after a fashion of unseemly levity; our monuments lean wearily, and our gravestones bow their heads discouraged; there be no adornments any more—no roses, nor shrubs, nor graveled walks, nor anything that is a comfort to the eye; and even the paintless old board fence that did make a show of holding us sacred from companionship with beasts and the defilement of heedless feet, has tottered till it overhangs the street, and only advertises the presence of our dismal resting-place and invites yet more derision to it. And now we cannot hide our poverty and tatters in the friendly woods, for the city has stretched its withering arms abroad and taken us in, and all that remains of the cheer of our old home is the cluster of lugubrious forest trees that stand, bored and weary of a city life, with their feet in our coffins, looking into the hazy distance and wishing they were there. I tell you it is disgraceful!

"You begin to comprehend—you begin to see how it is. While our descendants are living sumptuously on our money, right around us in the city, we have to fight hard to keep skull and bones together. Bless you, there isn't a grave in our cemetery that doesn't leak—not one. Every time it rains in the night we have to climb out and roost in the trees—and sometimes we are wakened suddenly by the chilly water trickling down the back of our necks. Then I tell you there is a general heaving up of old graves and kicking over of old monuments, and scampering of old skeletons for the trees! Bless me, if you had gone along there some such nights after twelve you might have seen as many as fifteen of us roosting on one limb, with our joints rattling drearily and the wind wheezing through our ribs! Many a time we have perched there for three or four dreary hours, and then come down, stiff and chilled through and drowsy, and borrowed each other's skulls to bail out our graves with—if you will glance up in my mouth now as I tilt my head back, you can see that my head-piece is half full of old dry sediment—how top-heavy and stupid it makes me sometimes! Yes, sir, many a time if you had happened to come along just before the dawn you'd have caught us bailing out the graves and hanging our shrouds on the fence to dry. Why, I had an elegant shroud stolen from there one morning—think a party by the name of Smith took it, that resides in a plebeian graveyard over yonder—I think so because the first time I ever saw him he hadn't anything on but a check shirt, and the last time I saw him, which was at a social gathering in the new cemetery, he was the best-dressed corpse in the company—and it is a significant fact that he left when he saw me; and presently an old woman from here missed her coffin—she generally took it with her when she went anywhere, because she was liable to take cold and bring on the spasmodic rheumatism that originally killed her if she exposed herself to the night air much. She was named Hotchkiss—Anna Matilda Hotchkiss—you might know her? She has two upper front teeth, is tall, but a good deal inclined to stoop, one rib on the left side gone, has one shred of rusty hair hanging from the left side of her head, and one little tuft just above and a little forward of her right ear, has her underjaw wired on one side where it had worked loose, small bone of left forearm gone—lost in a fight—has a kind of swagger in her gait and a 'gallus' way of going with her arms akimbo and her nostrils in the air —has been pretty free and easy, and is all damaged and battered up till she looks like a queensware crate in ruins—maybe you have met her?"

"God forbid!" I involuntarily ejaculated, for somehow I was not looking for that form of question, and it caught me a little off my guard. But I hastened to make amends for my rudeness, and say, "I simply meant I had not had the honor—for I would not deliberately speak discourteously of a friend of yours. You were saying that you were robbed —and it was a shame, too—but it appears by what is left of the shroud you have on that it was a costly one in its day. How did—"

A most ghastly expression began to develop among the decayed features and shriveled integuments of my guest's face, and I was beginning to grow uneasy and distressed, when he told me he was only working up a deep, sly smile, with a wink in it, to suggest that about the time he acquired his present garment a ghost in a neighboring cemetery missed one. This reassured me, but I begged him to confine himself to speech thenceforth, because his facial expression was uncertain. Even with the most elaborate care it was liable to miss fire. Smiling should especially be avoided. What *he* might honestly consider a shining success was likely to strike me in a very different light. I said I liked to see a skeleton cheerful, even decorously playful, but I did not think smiling was a skeleton's best hold.

"Yes, friend," said the poor skeleton, "the facts are just as I have given them to you. Two of these old graveyards—the one that I resided in and one further along—have been deliberately neglected by our de-

scendants of to-day until there is no occupying them any longer. Aside
from the osteological discomfort of it—and that is no light matter this
rainy weather—the present state of things is ruinous to property. We
have got to move or be content to see our effects wasted away and
utterly destroyed. Now, you will hardly believe it, but it is true, nevertheless, that there isn't a single coffin in good repair among all my acquaintance—now that is an absolute fact. I do not refer to low people
who come in a pine box mounted on an express-wagon, but I am talking about your high-toned, silver-mounted burial-case, your monumen-
tal sort, that travel under black plumes at the head of a procession and
have choice of cemetery lots—I mean folks like the Jarvises, and the
Bledsoes and Burlings, and such. They are all about ruined. The most
substantial people in our set, they were. And now look at them—utterly
used up and poverty-stricken. One of the Bledsoes actually traded his
monument to a late barkeeper for some fresh shavings to put under
his head. I tell you it speaks volumes, for there is nothing a corpse takes
so much pride in as his monument. He loves to read the inscription.
He comes after a while to believe what it says himself, and then you
may see him sitting on the fence night after night enjoying it. Epitaphs
are cheap, and they do a poor chap a world of good after he is dead,
especially if he had hard luck while he was alive. I wish they were
used more. Now I don't complain, but confidentially I *do* think it was
a little shabby in my descendants to give me nothing but this old slab
of a gravestone—and all the more that there isn't a compliment on it.
It used to have

'GONE TO HIS JUST REWARD'

on it, and I was proud when I first saw it, but by and by I noticed
that whenever an old friend of mine came along he would hook his
chin on the railing and pull a long face and read along down till he
came to that, and then he would chuckle to himself and walk off, looking satisfied and comfortable. So I scratched it off to get rid of those
fools. But a dead man always takes a deal of pride in his monument.
Yonder goes half a dozen of the Jarvises now, with the family monument along. And Smithers and some hired specters went by with his
awhile ago. Hello, Higgins, good-by, old friend! That's Meredith Higgins—died in '44—belongs to our set in the cemetery—fine old family—
great-grandmother was an Injun—I am on the most familiar terms with
him—he didn't hear me was the reason he didn't answer me. And I am
sorry, too, because I would have liked to introduce you. You would
admire him. He is the most disjointed, sway-backed, and generally dis-

torted old skeleton you ever saw, but he is full of fun. When he laughs it sounds like rasping two stones together, and he always starts it off with a cheery screech like raking a nail across a window-pane. Hey, Jones! That is old Columbus Jones—shroud cost four hundred dollars— entire trousseau, including monument, twenty-seven hundred. This was in the spring of '26. It was enormous style for those days. Dead people came all the way from the Alleghanies to see his things—the party that occupied the grave next to mine remembers it well. Now do you see that individual going along with a piece of a head-board under his arm, one leg-bone below his knee gone, and not a thing in the world on? That is Barstow Dalhousie, and next to Columbus Jones he was the most sumptuously outfitted person that ever entered our cemetery. We are all leaving. We cannot tolerate the treatment we are receiving at the hands of our descendants. They open new cemeteries, but they leave us to our ignominy. They mend the streets, but they never mend anything that is about us or belongs to us. Look at that coffin of mine— yet I tell you in its day it was a piece of furniture that would have attracted attention in any drawing-room in this city. You may have it if you want it—I can't afford to repair it. Put a new bottom in her, and part of a new top, and a bit of fresh lining along the left side, and you'll find her about as comfortable as any receptacle of her species you ever tried. No thanks—no, don't mention it—you have been civil to me, and I would give you all the property I have got before I would seem ungrateful. Now this winding-sheet is a kind of a sweet thing in its way, if you would like to— No? Well, just as you say, but I wished to be fair and liberal—there's nothing mean about *me*. Good-by, friend, I must be going. I may have a good way to go to-night—don't know. I only know one thing for certain, and that is that I am on the emigrant trail now, and I'll never sleep in that crazy old cemetery again. I will travel till I find respectable quarters, if I have to hoof it to New Jersey. All the boys are going. It was decided in public conclave, last night, to emigrate, and by the time the sun rises there won't be a bone left in our old habitations. Such cemeteries may suit my surviving friends, but they do not suit the remains that have the honor to make these remarks. My opinion is the general opinion. If you doubt it, go and see how the departing ghosts upset things before they started. They were almost riotous in their demonstrations of distaste. Hello, here are some of the Bledsoes, and if you will give me a lift with this tombstone I guess I will join company and jog along with them—mighty respectable old family, the Bledsoes, and used to always come out in six-horse hearses and all that sort of thing fifty years ago when I walked these streets in daylight. Good-by, friend."

And with his gravestone on his shoulder he joined the grisly procession, dragging his damaged coffin after him, for notwithstanding he pressed it upon me so earnestly, I utterly refused his hospitality. I suppose that for as much as two hours these sad outcasts went clacking by, laden with their dismal effects, and all that time I sat pitying them. One or two of the youngest and least dilapidated among them inquired about midnight trains on the railways, but the rest seemed unacquainted with that mode of travel, and merely asked about common public roads to various towns and cities, some of which are not on the map now, and vanished from it and from the earth as much as thirty years ago, and some few of them never *had* existed anywhere but on maps, and private ones in real-estate agencies at that. And they asked about the condition of the cemeteries in these towns and cities, and about the reputation the citizens bore as to reverence for the dead.

This whole matter interested me deeply, and likewise compelled my sympathy for these homeless ones. And it all seeming real, and I not knowing it was a dream, I mentioned to one shrouded wanderer an idea that had entered my head to publish an account of this curious and very sorrowful exodus, but said also that I could not describe it truthfully, and just as it occurred, without seeming to trifle with a grave subject and exhibit an irreverence for the dead that would shock and distress their surviving friends. But this bland and stately remnant of a former citizen leaned him far over my gate and whispered in my ear, and said:

"Do not let that disturb you. The community that can stand such graveyards as those we are emigrating from can stand anything a body can say about the neglected and forsaken dead that lie in them."

At that very moment a cock crowed, and the weird procession vanished and left not a shred or a bone behind. I awoke, and found myself lying with my head out of the bed and "sagging" downward considerably—a position favorable to dreaming dreams with morals in them, maybe, but not poetry.

NOTE   The reader is assured that if the cemeteries in his town are kept in good order, this Dream is not leveled at his town at all, but is leveled particularly and venomously at the *next* town.

1870

The Facts in the Great Beef Contract

In as few words as possible I wish to lay before the nation what share, howsoever small, I have had in this matter—this matter which has so exercised the public mind, engendered so much ill-feeling, and so filled the newspapers of both continents with distorted statements and extravagant comments.

The origin of this distressful thing was this—and I assert here that every fact in the following résumé can be amply proved by the official records of the General Government:

John Wilson Mackenzie, of Rotterdam, Chemung County, New Jersey, deceased, contracted with the General Government, on or about the 10th day of October, 1861, to furnish to General Sherman the sum total of thirty barrels of beef.

Very well.

He started after Sherman with the beef, but when he got to Washington, Sherman had gone to Manassas; so he took the beef and followed him there, but arrived too late; he followed him to Nashville, and from Nashville to Chattanooga, and from Chattanooga to Atlanta—but he never could overtake him. At Atlanta he took a fresh start and followed him clear through his march to the sea. He arrived too late again by a few days; but hearing that Sherman was going out in the *Quaker City* excursion to the Holy Land, he took shipping for Beirut, calculating to head off the other vessel. When he arrived in Jerusalem with his beef, he learned that Sherman had not sailed in the *Quaker City*, but had gone to the Plains to fight the Indians. He returned to America and started for the Rocky Mountains. After sixty-eight days of arduous travel on the Plains, and when he had got within four miles of Sherman's headquarters, he was tomahawked and scalped, and the Indians got the beef. They got all of it but one barrel. Sherman's army captured that, and so, even in death, the bold navigator partly fulfilled his contract. In his will, which he had kept like a journal, he bequeathed the contract to his son Bartholomew W. Bartholomew W. made out the following bill, and then died:

THE UNITED STATES

In account with JOHN WILSON MACKENZIE, of New Jersey,
   deceased   Dr.

To thirty barrels of beef for General Sherman, at $100, $3,000
To traveling expenses and transportation   14,000
                                                          ──────────
                              Total $17,000
                           Rec'd Pay't.

He died then; but he left the contract to Wm. J. Martin, who tried
to collect it, but died before he got through. *He* left it to Barker J.
Allen, and he tried to collect it also. He did not survive. Barker J. Allen
left it to Anson G. Rogers, who attempted to collect it, and got
along as far as the Ninth Auditor's Office, when Death, the great Lev-
eler, came all unsummoned, and foreclosed on *him* also. He left the
bill to a relative of his in Connecticut, Vengeance Hopkins by name,
who lasted four weeks and two days, and made the best time on record,
coming within one of reaching the Twelfth Auditor. In his will he gave
the contract bill to his uncle, by the name of O-be-joyful Johnson. It
was too undermining for Joyful. His last words were: "Weep not for
me—*I* am willing to go." And so he was, poor soul. Seven people in-
herited the contract after that; but they all died. So it came into my
hands at last. It fell to me through a relative by the name of Hubbard
—Bethlehem Hubbard, of Indiana. He had had a grudge against me
for a long time; but in his last moments he sent for me, and forgave
me everything, and, weeping, gave me the beef contract.

This ends the history of it up to the time that I succeeded to the
property. I will now endeavor to set myself straight before the nation
in everything that concerns my share in the matter. I took this beef
contract, and the bill for mileage and transportation, to the President
of the United States.

He said, "Well, sir, what can I do for you?"

I said, "Sire, on or about the 10th day of October, 1861, John Wilson
Mackenzie, of Rotterdam, Chemung County, New Jersey, deceased,
contracted with the General Government to furnish to General Sherman the sum total of thirty barrels of beef—"

He stopped me there, and dismissed me from his presence—kindly,
but firmly. The next day I called on the Secretary of State.

He said, "Well, sir?"

I said, "Your Royal Highness: on or about the 10th day of October,
1861, John Wilson Mackenzie, of Rotterdam, Chemung County, New

Jersey, deceased, contracted with the General Government to furnish to General Sherman the sum total of thirty barrels of beef—"

"That will do, sir—that will do; this office has nothing to do with contracts for beef."

I was bowed out. I thought the matter all over, and finally, the following day, I visited the Secretary of the Navy, who said, "Speak quickly, sir; do not keep me waiting."

I said, "Your Royal Highness, on or about the 10th day of October, 1861, John Wilson Mackenzie, of Rotterdam, Chemung County, New Jersey, deceased, contracted with the General Government to General Sherman the sum total of thirty barrels of beef—"

Well, it was as far as I could get. *He* had nothing to do with beef contracts for General Sherman, either. I began to think it was a curious kind of a government. It looked somewhat as if they wanted to get out of paying for that beef. The following day I went to the Secretary of the Interior.

I said, "Your Imperial Highness, on or about the 10th day of October—"

"That is sufficient, sir. I have heard of you before. Go, take your infamous beef contract out of this establishment. The Interior Department has nothing whatever to do with subsistence for the army."

I went away. But I was exasperated now. I said I would haunt them; I would infest every department of this iniquitous government till that contract business was settled. I would collect that bill, or fall, as fell my predecessors, trying. I assailed the Postmaster-General; I besieged the Agricultural Department; I waylaid the Speaker of the House of Representatives. *They* had nothing to do with army contracts for beef. I moved upon the Commissioner of the Patent Office.

I said, "Your August Excellency, on or about—"

"Perdition! have you got *here* with your incendiary beef contract, at last? We have *nothing* to do with beef contracts for the army, my dear sir."

"Oh, that is all very well—but *somebody* has got to pay for that beef. It has got to be paid *now*, too, or I'll confiscate this old Patent Office and everything in it."

"But, my dear sir—"

"It don't make any difference, sir. The Patent Office is liable for that beef, I reckon; and, liable or not liable, the Patent Office has got to pay for it."

Never mind the details. It ended in a fight. The Patent Office won. But I found out something to my advantage. I was told that the Treasury Department was the proper place for me to go to. I went there. I waited two hours and a half, and then I was admitted to the First Lord of the Treasury.

I said, "Most noble, grave, and reverend Signor, on or about the 10th day of October, 1861, John Wilson Macken—"

"That is sufficient, sir. I have heard of you. Go to the First Auditor of the Treasury."

I did so. He sent me to the Second Auditor. The Second Auditor sent me to the Third, and the Third sent me to the First Comptroller of the Corn-Beef Division. This began to look like business. He examined his books and all his loose papers, but found no minute of the beef contract. I went to the Second Comptroller of the Corn-Beef Division. He examined his books and his loose papers, but with no success. I was encouraged. During that week I got as far as the Sixth Comptroller in that division; the next week I got through the Claims Department; the third week I began and completed the Mislaid Contracts Department, and got a foothold in the Dead Reckoning Department. I finished that in three days. There was only one place left for it now. I laid siege to the Commissioner of Odds and Ends. To his clerk, rather—he was not there himself. There were sixteen beautiful young ladies in the room, writing in books, and there were seven well-favored young clerks showing them how. The young women smiled up over their shoulders, and the clerks smiled back at them, and all went merry as a marriage bell. Two or three clerks that were reading the newspapers looked at me rather hard, but went on reading, and nobody said anything. However, I had been used to this kind of alacrity from Fourth Assistant Junior Clerks all through my eventful career, from the very day I entered the first office of the Corn-Beef Bureau clear till I passed out of the last one in the Dead Reckoning Division. I had got so accomplished by this time that I could stand on one foot from the moment I entered an office till a clerk spoke to me, without changing more than two, or maybe three, times.

So I stood there till I had changed four different times. Then I said to one of the clerks who was reading:

"Illustrious Vagrant, where is the Grand Turk?"

"What do you mean, sir? whom do you mean? If you mean the Chief of the Bureau, he is out."

"Will he visit the harem to-day?"

The young man glared upon me awhile, and then went on reading his paper. But I knew the ways of those clerks. I knew I was safe if he got through before another New York mail arrived. He only had two more papers left. After a while he finished them, and then he yawned and asked me what I wanted.

"Renowned and honored Imbecile: on or about—"

"You are the beef-contract man. Give me your papers."

He took them, and for a long time he ransacked his odds and ends. Finally he found the Northwest Passage, as *I* regarded it—he found the long-lost record of that beef contract—he found the rock upon which so many of my ancestors had split before they ever got to it. I was deeply moved. And yet I rejoiced—for I had survived. I said with emotion, "Give it me. The government will settle now." He waved me back, and said there was something yet to be done first.

"Where is this John Wilson Mackenzie?" said he.

"Dead."

"When did he die?"

"He didn't die at all—he was killed."

"How?"

"Tomahawked."

"Who tomahawked him?"

"Why, an Indian, of course. You didn't suppose it was the superintendent of a Sunday-school, did you?"

"No. An Indian, was it?"

"The same."

"Name of the Indian?"

"His name? *I* don't know his name."

"*Must* have his name. Who saw the tomahawking done?"

"I don't know."

"You were not present yourself, then?"

"Which you can see by my hair. I was absent."

"Then how do you know that Mackenzie is dead?"

"Because he certainly died at that time, and I have every reason to believe that he has been dead ever since. I *know* he has, in fact."

"We must have proofs. Have you got the Indian?"

"Of course not."

"Well, you must get him. Have you got the tomahawk?"

"I never thought of such a thing."

"You must get the tomahawk. You must produce the Indian and the tomahawk. If Mackenzie's death can be proven by these, you can then go before the commission appointed to audit claims with some show of getting your bill under such headway that your children may possibly live to receive the money and enjoy it. But that man's death *must* be proven. However, I may as well tell you that the government will never pay that transportation and those traveling expenses of the lamented Mackenzie. It *may* possibly pay for the barrel of beef that Sherman's soldiers captured, if you can get a relief bill through Congress making an appropriation for that purpose; but it will not pay for the twenty-nine barrels the Indians ate."

"Then there is only a hundred dollars due me, and *that* isn't certain! After all Mackenzie's travels in Europe, Asia, and America with that beef; after all his trials and tribulations and transportation; after the slaughter of all those innocents that tried to collect that bill! Young man, why didn't the First Comptroller of the Corn-Beef Division tell me this?"

"He didn't know anything about the genuineness of your claim."

"Why didn't the Second tell me? why didn't the Third? why didn't all those divisions and departments tell me?"

"None of them knew. We do things by routine here. You have followed the routine and found out what you wanted to know. It is the best way. It is the only way. It is very regular, and very slow, but it is very certain."

"Yes, certain death. It has been, to the most of our tribe. I begin to feel that I, too, am called. Young man, you love the bright creature yonder with the gentle blue eyes and the steel pens behind her ears— I see it in your soft glances; you wish to marry her—but you are poor. Here, hold out your hand—here is the beef contract; go, take her and be happy! Heaven bless you, my children!"

This is all I know about the great beef contract that has created so much talk in the community. The clerk to whom I bequeathed it died. I know nothing further about the contract, or any one connected with it. I only know that if a man lives long enough he can trace a thing through the Circumlocution Office of Washington and find out, after much labor and trouble and delay, that which he could have found out on the first day if the business of the Circumlocution Office were as ingeniously systematized as it would be if it were a great private mercantile institution.

1870

How I Edited an Agricultural Paper

I did not take temporary editorship of an agricultural paper without misgivings. Neither would a landsman take command of a ship without misgivings. But I was in circumstances that made the salary an object. The regular editor of the paper was going off for a holiday, and I accepted the terms he offered, and took his place.

The sensation of being at work again was luxurious, and I wrought all the week with unflagging pleasure. We went to press, and I waited a day with some solicitude to see whether my effort was going to attract any notice. As I left the office, toward sundown, a group of men and boys at the foot of the stairs dispersed with one impulse, and gave me passageway, and I heard one or two of them say: "That's him!" I was naturally pleased by this incident. The next morning I found a similar group at the foot of the stairs, and scattering couples and individuals standing here and there in the street and over the way, watching me with interest. The group separated and fell back as I approached, and I heard a man say, "Look at his eye!" I pretended not to observe the notice I was attracting, but secretly I was pleased with it, and was purposing to write an account of it to my aunt. I went up the short flight of stairs, and heard cheery voices and a ringing laugh as I drew near the door, which I opened, and caught a glimpse of two young rural-looking men, whose faces blanched and lengthened when they saw me, and then they both plunged through the window with a great crash. I was surprised.

In about half an hour an old gentleman, with a flowing beard and a fine but rather austere face, entered, and sat down at my invitation. He seemed to have something on his mind. He took off his hat and set it on the floor, and got out of it a red silk handkerchief and a copy of our paper.

He put the paper on his lap, and while he polished his spectacles with his handkerchief he said, "Are you the new editor?"

I said I was.

"Have you ever edited an agricultural paper before?"

"No," I said; "this is my first attempt."

"Very likely. Have you had any experience in agriculture practically?"

"No; I believe I have not."

"Some instinct told me so," said the old gentleman, putting on his spectacles, and looking over them at me with asperity, while he folded his paper into a convenient shape. "I wish to read you what must have made me have that instinct. It was this editorial. Listen, and see if it was you that wrote it:

"*Turnips should never be pulled, it injures them. It is much better to send a boy up and let him shake the tree.*'

"Now, what do you think of that?—for I really suppose you wrote it?"

"Think of it? Why, I think it is good. I think it is sense. I have no doubt that every year millions and millions of bushels of turnips are spoiled in this township alone by being pulled in a half-ripe condition, when, if they had sent a boy up to shake the tree—"

"Shake your grandmother! Turnips don't grow on trees!"

"Oh, they don't, don't they? Well, who said they did? The language was intended to be figurative, wholly figurative. Anybody that knows anything will know that I meant that the boy should shake the vine."

Then this old person got up and tore his paper all into small shreds, and stamped on them, and broke several things with his cane, and said I did not know as much as a cow; and then went out and banged the door after him, and, in short, acted in such a way that I fancied he was displeased about something. But not knowing what the trouble was, I could not be any help to him.

Pretty soon after this a long, cadaverous creature, with lanky locks hanging down to his shoulders, and a week's stubble bristling from the hills and valleys of his face, darted within the door, and halted, motionless, with finger on lip, and head and body bent in listening attitude. No sound was heard. Still he listened. No sound. Then he turned the key in the door, and came elaborately tiptoeing toward me till he was within long reaching distance of me, when he stopped and, after scanning my face with intense interest for a while, drew a folded copy of our paper from his bosom, and said:

"There, you wrote that. Read it to me—quick! Relieve me. I suffer."

I read as follows; and as the sentences fell from my lips I could see the relief come, I could see the drawn muscles relax, and the anxiety go out of the face, and rest and peace steal over the features like the merciful moonlight over a desolate landscape:

The guano is a fine bird, but great care is necessary in rearing it. It should not be imported earlier than June or later than September. In the winter it should be kept in a warm place, where it can hatch out its young.

It is evident that we are to have a backward season for grain. There-fore it will be well for the farmer to begin setting out his corn-stalks and planting his buckwheat cakes in July instead of August.

Concerning the pumpkin. This berry is a favorite with the natives of the interior of New England, who prefer it to the gooseberry for the making of fruit-cake, and who likewise give it the preference over the raspberry for feeding cows, as being more filling and fully as satisfying. The pumpkin is the only esculent of the orange family that will thrive in the North, except the gourd and one or two varieties of the squash. But the custom of planting it in the front yard with the shrubbery is fast going out of vogue, for it is now generally conceded that the pump-kin as a shade tree is a failure.

Now, as the warm weather approaches, and the ganders begin to spawn—

The excited listener sprang toward me to shake hands, and said:

"There, there—that will do. I know I am all right now, because you have read it just as I did, word for word. But, stranger, when I first read it this morning, I said to myself, I never, never believed it before, notwithstanding my friends kept me under watch so strict, but now I believe I *am* crazy; and with that I fetched a howl that you might have heard two miles, and started out to kill somebody—because, you know, I knew it would come to that sooner or later, and so I might as well begin. I read one of them paragraphs over again, so as to be certain, and then I burned my house down and started. I have crippled several peo-ple, and have got one fellow up a tree, where I can get him if I want him. But I thought I would call in here as I passed along and make the thing perfectly certain; and now it *is* certain, and I tell you it is lucky for the chap that is in the tree. I should have killed him sure, as I went back. Good-by, sir, good-by; you have taken a great load off my mind. My reason has stood the strain of one of your agricultural articles, and I know that nothing can ever unseat it now. *Good*-by, sir."

I felt a little uncomfortable about the cripplings and arsons this per-son had been entertaining himself with, for I could not help feeling remotely accessory to them. But these thoughts were quickly banished, for the regular editor walked in! [I thought to myself, Now if you had gone to Egypt as I recommended you to, I might have had a chance to get my hand in; but you wouldn't do it, and here you are. I sort of expected you.]

The editor was looking sad and perplexed and dejected.

He surveyed the wreck which that old rioter and those two young farmers had made, and then said: "This is a sad business—a very sad business. There is the mucilage-bottle broken, and six panes of glass, and a spittoon, and two candlesticks. But that is not the worst. The reputation of the paper is injured—and permanently, I fear. True, there never was such a call for the paper before, and it never sold such a large edition or soared to such celebrity;—but does one want to be famous for lunacy, and prosper upon the infirmities of his mind? My friend, as I am an honest man, the street out here is full of people, and others are roosting on the fences, waiting to get a glimpse of you, because they think you are crazy. And well they might after reading your editorials. They are a disgrace to journalism. Why, what put it into your head that you could edit a paper of this nature? You do not seem to know the first rudiments of agriculture. You speak of a furrow and a harrow as being the same thing; you talk of the moulting season for cows; and you recommend the domestication of the pole-cat on account of its playfulness and its excellence as a ratter! Your remark that clams will lie quiet if music be played to them was superfluous—entirely superfluous. Nothing disturbs clams. Clams *always* lie quiet. Clams care nothing whatever about music. Ah, heavens and earth, friend! if you had made the acquiring of ignorance the study of your life, you could not have graduated with higher honor than you could to-day. I never saw anything like it. Your observation that the horse-chestnut as an article of commerce is steadily gaining in favor is simply calculated to destroy this journal. I want you to throw up your situation and go. I want no more holiday—I could not enjoy it if I had it. Certainly not with you in my chair. I would always stand in dread of what you might be going to recommend next. It makes me lose all patience every time I think of your discussing oyster-beds under the head of 'Landscape Gardening.' I want you to go. Nothing on earth could persuade me to take another holiday. Oh! why didn't you *tell* me you didn't know anything about agriculture?"

"*Tell* you, you corn-stalk, you cabbage, you son of a cauliflower? It's the first time I ever heard such an unfeeling remark. I tell you I have been in the editorial business going on fourteen years, and it is the first time I ever heard of a man's having to know anything in order to edit a newspaper. You turnip! Who write the dramatic critiques for the second-rate papers? Why, a parcel of promoted shoemakers and apprentice apothecaries, who know just as much about good acting as I do about good farming and no more. Who review the books? People who never wrote one. Who do up the heavy leaders on finance? Parties who have had the largest opportunities for knowing nothing about it. Who criticize the Indian campaigns? Gentlemen who do not know a war-whoop from a wigwam, and who never have had to run a foot-race with a tomahawk, or pluck arrows out of the several members of their families to build the evening camp-fire with. Who write the temperance appeals, and clamor about the flowing bowl? Folks who will never draw another sober breath till they do it in the grave. Who edit the agricultural papers, you—yam? Men, as a general thing, who fail in the poetry line, yellow-colored novel line, sensation-drama line, city-editor line, and finally fall back on agriculture as a temporary reprieve from the poorhouse. *You* try to tell *me* anything about the newspaper business! Sir, I have been through it from Alpha to Omaha, and I tell you that the less a man knows the bigger the noise he makes and the higher the salary he commands. Heaven knows if I had but been ignorant instead of cultivated, and impudent instead of diffident, I could have made a name for myself in this cold, selfish world. I take my leave, sir. Since I have been treated as you have treated me, I am perfectly willing to go. But I have done my duty. I have fulfilled my contract as far as I was permitted to do it. I said I could make your paper of interest to all classes—and I have. I said I could run your circulation up to twenty thousand copies, and if I had had two more weeks I'd have done it. And I'd have given you the best class of readers that ever an agricultural paper had—not a farmer in it, nor a solitary individual who could tell a watermelon-tree from a peach-vine to save his life. *You* are the loser by this rupture, not me, Pie-plant. *Adios.*"

I then left.

1870

A Medieval Romance

1   THE SECRET REVEALED

It was night. Stillness reigned in the grand old feudal castle of Klugenstein. The year 1222 was drawing to a close. Far away up in the tallest of the castle's towers a single light glimmered. A secret council was being held there. The stern old lord of Klugenstein sat in a chair of state meditating. Presently he said, with a tender accent: "My daughter!"

A young man of noble presence, clad from head to heel in knightly mail, answered: "Speak, father!"

"My daughter, the time is come for the revealing of the mystery that hath puzzled all your young life. Know, then, that it had its birth in the matters which I shall now unfold. My brother Ulrich is the great Duke of Brandenburgh. Our father, on his deathbed, decreed that if no son were born to Ulrich the succession should pass to my house, provided a *son* were born to me. And further, in case no son were born to either, but only daughters, then the succession should pass to Ulrich's daughter if she proved stainless; if she did not, my daughter should succeed if she retained a blameless name. And so I and my old wife here prayed fervently for the good boon of a son, but the prayer was vain. You were born to us. I was in despair. I saw the mighty prize slipping from my grasp—the splendid dream vanishing away! And I had been so hopeful! Five years had Ulrich lived in wedlock, and yet his wife had borne no heir of cither sex.

" 'But hold,' I said, 'all is not lost.' A saving scheme had shot athwart my brain. You were born at midnight. Only the leech, the nurse, and six waiting-women knew your sex. I hanged them every one before an hour sped. Next morning all the barony went mad with rejoicing over the proclamation that a *son* was born to Klugenstein—an heir to mighty Brandenburgh! And well the secret has been kept. Your mother's own sister nursed your infancy, and from that time forward we feared nothing.

"When you were ten years old a daughter was born to Ulrich. We grieved, but hoped for good results from measles, or physicians, or other natural enemies of infancy, but were always disappointed. She lived, she throve—Heaven's malison upon her! But it is nothing. We are safe. For, ha! ha! have we not a son? And is not our son the future duke? Our well-beloved Conrad, is it not so?—for woman of eight-and-twenty years as you are, my child, none other name than that hath ever fallen to *you!*

"Now it hath come to pass that age hath laid its hand upon my brother, and he waxes feeble. The cares of state do tax him sore, therefore he wills that you shall come to him and be already duke in act, though not yet in name. Your servitors are ready—you journey forth to-night.

"Now listen well. Remember every word I say. There is a law as old as Germany, that if any woman sit for a single instant in the great ducal chair before she hath been absolutely crowned in presence of the people—SHE SHALL DIE! So heed my words. Pretend humility. Pronounce your judgments from the Premier's chair, which stands at the *foot* of the throne. Do this until you are crowned and safe. It is not likely that your sex will ever be discovered, but still it is the part of wisdom to make all things as safe as may be in this treacherous earthly life."

"Oh, my father! is it for this my life hath been a lie? Was it that I might cheat my unoffending cousin of her rights? Spare me, father, spare your child!"

"What, hussy! Is this my reward for the august fortune my brain has wrought for thee? By the bones of my father, this puling sentiment of thine but ill accords with my humor. Betake thee to the duke instantly, and beware how thou meddlest with my purpose!"

Let this suffice of the conversation. It is enough for us to know that the prayers, the entreaties, and the tears of the gentle-natured girl availed nothing. Neither they nor anything could move the stout old lord of Klugenstein. And so, at last, with a heavy heart, the daughter saw the castle gates close behind her, and found herself riding away in the darkness surrounded by a knightly array of armed vassals and a brave following of servants.

The old baron sat silent for many minutes after his daughter's departure, and then he turned to his sad wife, and said:

"Dame, our matters seem speeding fairly. It is full three months since I sent the shrewd and handsome Count Detzin on his devilish mission to my brother's daughter Constance. If he fail we are not wholly safe, but if he do succeed no power can bar our girl from being duchess, e'en though ill fortune should decree she never should be duke!"

"My heart is full of bodings; yet all may still be well."

"Tush, woman! Leave the owls to croak. To bed with ye, and dream of Brandenburgh and grandeur!"

2 FESTIVITY AND TEARS

Six days after the occurrences related in the above chapter, the brilliant capital of the Duchy of Brandenburgh was resplendent with military pageantry and noisy with the rejoicings of loyal multitudes, for Conrad, the young heir to the crown, was come. The old duke's heart was full of happiness, for Conrad's handsome person and graceful bearing had won his love at once. The great halls of the palace were

thronged with nobles, who welcomed Conrad bravely; and so bright
and happy did all things seem that he felt his fears and sorrows passing
away and giving place to a comforting contentment.

But in a remote apartment of the palace a scene of a different nature
was transpiring. By a window stood the duke's only child, the Lady
Constance. Her eyes were red and swollen and full of tears. She was
alone. Presently she fell to weeping anew, and said aloud:

"The villain Detzin is gone—has fled the dukedom! I could not believe it at first, but, alas! it is too true. And I loved him so. I dared to
love him though I knew the duke, my father, would never let me wed
him. I loved him—but now I hate him! With all my soul I hate him! Oh,
what is to become of me? I am lost, lost, lost! I shall go mad!"

3 THE PLOT THICKENS

A few months drifted by. All men published the praises of the young
Conrad's government, and extolled the wisdom of his judgments, the
mercifulness of his sentences, and the modesty with which he bore
himself in his great office. The old duke soon gave everything into his
hands, and sat apart and listened with proud satisfaction while his heir
delivered the decrees of the crown from the seat of the Premier. It
seemed plain that one so loved and praised and honored of all men
as Conrad was could not be otherwise than happy. But, strangely
enough, he was not. For he saw with dismay that the Princess Constance had begun to love him! The love of the rest of the world was
happy fortune for him, but this was freighted with danger! And he saw,
moreover, that the delighted duke had discovered his daughter's passion likewise, and was already dreaming of a marriage. Every day
somewhat of the deep sadness that had been in the princess's face faded
away; every day hope and animation beamed brighter from her eye;
and by and by even vagrant smiles visited the face that had been so
troubled.

Conrad was appalled. He bitterly cursed himself for having yielded
to the instinct that had made him seek the companionship of one of
his own sex when he was new and a stranger in the palace—when he
was sorrowful and yearned for a sympathy such as only women can
give or feel. He now began to avoid his cousin. But this only made matters worse, for, naturally enough, the more he avoided her the more she
cast herself in his way. He marveled at this at first, and next it startled
him. The girl haunted him; she hunted him; she happened upon him at

all times and in all places, in the night as well as in the day. She seemed singularly anxious. There was surely a mystery somewhere.

This could not go on forever. All the world was talking about it. The duke was beginning to look perplexed. Poor Conrad was becoming a very ghost through dread and dire distress. One day as he was emerging from a private anteroom attached to the picture-gallery Constance confronted him, and seizing both his hands in hers, exclaimed:

"Oh, why do you avoid me? What have I done—what have I said, to lose your kind opinion of me—for surely I had it once? Conrad, do not despise me, but pity a tortured heart? I cannot, cannot hold the words unspoken longer, lest they kill me—I LOVE YOU, CONRAD! There, despise me if you must, but they *would* be uttered!"

Conrad was speechless. Constance hesitated a moment, and then, misinterpreting his silence, a wild gladness flamed in her eyes, and she flung her arms about his neck and said:

"You relent! you relent! You *can* love me—you *will* love me! Oh, say you will, my own, my worshiped Conrad!"

Conrad groaned aloud. A sickly pallor overspread his countenance, and he trembled like an aspen. Presently, in desperation, he thrust the poor girl from him, and cried:

"You know not what you ask! It is forever and ever impossible!" And then he fled like a criminal, and left the princess stupefied with amazement. A minute afterward she was crying and sobbing there, and Conrad was crying and sobbing in his chamber. Both were in despair. Both saw ruin staring them in the face.

By and by Constance rose slowly to her feet and moved away, saying:

"To think that he was despising my love at the very moment that I thought it was melting his cruel heart! I hate him! He spurned me —did this man—he spurned me from him like a dog!"

4   THE AWFUL REVELATION

Time passed on. A settled sadness rested once more upon the countenance of the good duke's daughter. She and Conrad were seen together no more now. The duke grieved at this. But as the weeks wore away Conrad's color came back to his cheeks, and his old-time vivacity to his eye, and he administered the government with a clear and steadily ripening wisdom.

Presently a strange whisper began to be heard about the palace. It grew louder; it spread farther. The gossips of the city got hold of it. It swept the dukedom. And this is what the whisper said:

"The Lady Constance hath given birth to a child!"

When the lord of Klugenstein heard it he swung his plumed helmet thrice around his head and shouted:

"Long live Duke Conrad!—for lo, his crown is sure from this day forward! Detzin has done his errand well, and the good scoundrel shall be rewarded!"

And he spread the tidings far and wide, and for eight-and-forty hours no soul in all the barony but did dance and sing, carouse and illuminate, to celebrate the great event, and all proud and happy at old Klugenstein's expense.

5 THE FRIGHTFUL CATASTROPHE

The trial was at hand. All the great lords and barons of Brandenburgh were assembled in the Hall of Justice in the ducal palace. No space was left unoccupied where there was room for a spectator to stand or sit. Conrad, clad in purple and ermine, sat in the Premier's chair, and on either side sat the great judges of the realm. The old duke had sternly commanded that the trial of his daughter should proceed without favor, and then had taken to his bed broken-hearted. His days were numbered. Poor Conrad had begged, as for his very life, that he might be spared the misery of sitting in judgment upon his cousin's crime, but it did not avail.

The saddest heart in all that great assemblage was in Conrad's breast.

The gladdest was in his father's, for, unknown to his daughter "Conrad," the old Baron Klugenstein was come, and was among the crowd of nobles triumphant in the swelling fortunes of his house.

After the heralds had made due proclamation and the other preliminaries had followed, the venerable Lord Chief Justice said: "Prisoner, stand forth!"

The unhappy princess rose, and stood unveiled before the vast multitude. The Lord Chief Justice continued:

"Most noble lady, before the great judges of this realm it hath been charged and proven that out of holy wedlock your Grace hath given birth unto a child, and by our ancient law the penalty is death excepting in one sole contingency, whereof his Grace the acting duke, our good Lord Conrad, will advertise you in his solemn sentence now; wherefore give heed."

Conrad stretched forth his reluctant scepter, and in the selfsame moment the womanly heart beneath his robe yearned pityingly toward the doomed prisoner, and the tears came into his eyes. He opened his lips to speak, but the Lord Chief Justice said quickly:

"Not there, your Grace, not there! It is not lawful to pronounce judgment upon any of the ducal line SAVE FROM THE DUCAL THRONE!"

A shudder went to the heart of poor Conrad, and a tremor shook the iron frame of his old father likewise. CONRAD HAD NOT BEEN CROWNED —dared he profane the throne? He hesitated and turned pale with fear. But it must be done. Wondering eyes were already upon him. They would be suspicious eyes if he hesitated longer. He ascended the throne. Presently he stretched forth the scepter again, and said:

"Prisoner, in the name of our sovereign Lord Ulrich, Duke of Brandenburgh, I proceed to the solemn duty that hath devolved upon me. Give heed to my words. By the ancient law of the land, except you produce the partner of your guilt and deliver him up to the executioner you must surely die. Embrace this opportunity—save yourself while yet you may. Name the father of your child!"

A solemn hush fell upon the great court—a silence so profound that men could hear their own hearts beat. Then the princess slowly turned, with eyes gleaming with hate, and, pointing her finger straight at Conrad, said:

"Thou art the man!"

An appalling conviction of his helpless, hopeless peril struck a chill to Conrad's heart like the chill of death itself. What power on earth could save him! To disprove the charge he must reveal that he was a woman, and for an uncrowned woman to sit in the ducal chair was death! At one and the same moment he and his grim old father swooned and fell to the ground.

The remainder of this thrilling and eventful story will NOT be found in this or any other publication, either now or at any future time.

The truth is, I have got my hero (or heroine) into such a particularly close place that I do not see how I am ever going to get him (or her) out of it again, and therefore I will wash my hands of the whole business, and leave that person to get out the best way that offers—or else stay there. I thought it was going to be easy enough to straighten out that little difficulty, but it looks different now.

1870

My Watch

AN INSTRUCTIVE LITTLE TALE

My beautiful new watch had run eighteen months without losing or gaining, and without breaking any part of its machinery or stopping. I had come to believe it infallible in its judgments about the time of day, and to consider its constitution and its anatomy imperishable. But at last, one night, I let it run down. I grieved about it as if it were a recognized messenger and forerunner of calamity. But by and by I cheered up, set the watch by guess, and commanded my bodings and superstitions to depart. Next day I stepped into the chief jeweler's to set it by the exact time, and the head of the establishment took it out of my hand and proceeded to set it for me. Then he said, "She is four minutes slow—regulator wants pushing up." I tried to stop him—tried to make him understand that the watch kept perfect time. But no; all this human cabbage could see was that the watch was four minutes slow, and the regulator *must* be pushed up a little; and so, while I danced around him in anguish, and implored him to let the watch alone, he calmly and cruelly did the shameful deed. My watch began to gain. It gained faster and faster day by day. Within the week it sickened to a raging fever, and its pulse went up to a hundred and fifty in the shade. At the end of two months it had left all the timepieces of the town far in the rear, and was a fraction over thirteen days ahead of the almanac. It was away into November enjoying the snow, while the October leaves were still turning. It hurried up house rent, bills payable, and such things, in such a ruinous way that I could not abide it. I took it to the watchmaker to be regulated. He asked me if I had ever had it repaired. I said no, it had never needed any repairing. He looked a look of vicious happiness and eagerly pried the watch open, and then put a small dice-box into his eye and peered into its machinery. He said it wanted cleaning and oiling, besides regulating—come in a week. After being cleaned and oiled, and regulated, my watch slowed down to that degree that it ticked like a tolling bell. I began to be left by trains, I failed all appointments, I got to missing my dinner; my watch strung out three days' grace to four and let me go to protest; I gradually drifted back into yesterday, then day before, then into last week, and by and by the comprehension came upon me that all solitary and alone I was lingering along in week before last, and the world was out of sight. I seemed to detect in myself a sort of sneaking fellow-feeling for the mummy in the museum, and a desire to swap news with him. I went to a watchmaker again. He took the watch all to pieces while I waited, and then said the barrel was "swelled." He said he could reduce it in three days. After this the watch *averaged* well, but nothing more. For half a day it would go like the very mischief, and keep up such a barking and wheezing and whooping and sneezing and snorting, that I could not hear myself think for the disturbance; and as long as it held out there was not a watch in the land that stood any chance against it. But the rest of the day it would keep on slowing down and fooling along until all the clocks it had left behind caught up again. So at last, at the end of twenty-four hours, it would trot up to the judges' stand all right and just in time. It would show a fair and square average, and no man could say it had done more or less than its duty. But a correct average is only a mild virtue in a watch, and I took this instrument to another watchmaker. He said the king-bolt was broken. I said I was glad it was nothing more serious. To tell the plain truth, I had no idea what the king-bolt was, but I did not choose to appear ignorant to a stranger. He repaired the king-bolt, but what the watch gained in one way it lost in another. It would run awhile and then stop awhile, and then run awhile again, and so on, using its own discretion about the intervals. And every time it went off it kicked back like a musket. I padded my breast for a few days, but finally took the watch to another watchmaker. He picked it all to pieces, and turned the ruin over and over under his glass; and then he said there appeared to be something the matter with the hair-trigger. He fixed it, and gave it a fresh start. It did well now, except that always at ten minutes to ten the hands would shut together like a pair of scissors, and from that time forth they would travel together. The oldest man in the world could not make head or tail of the time of day by such a watch, and so I went again to have the thing repaired. This person said that the crystal had got bent, and that the mainspring was not straight. He also remarked that part of the works needed half-soling. He made these things all right, and then my timepiece performed unexceptionably, save that now and then, after working along quietly for nearly eight hours, everything inside would let go all of a sudden and begin to buzz like a bee, and the hands would straightway begin to spin round and round so fast that their individuality was lost completely, and they simply seemed a delicate spider's web over the face of the watch. She would reel off the next twenty-four hours in six or seven minutes, and then stop with a bang. I went with a heavy heart to one more watchmaker, and looked on while he took her to pieces. Then I prepared to cross-question him rigidly, for this thing was getting serious. The watch had cost two hundred dollars originally, and I seemed to have paid out two or three thousand for repairs. While I waited and looked on I presently recognized in this watchmaker an old acquaintance—a steamboat engineer of other days, and not a good engineer, either. He examined all the parts carefully, just as the other watchmakers had done, and then delivered his verdict with the same confidence of manner.

He said:

"She makes too much steam—you want to hang the monkey-wrench on the safety-valve!"

I brained him on the spot, and had him buried at my own expense.

My uncle William (now deceased, alas!) used to say that a good horse was a good horse until it had run away once, and that a good watch was a good watch until the repairers got a chance at it. And he used to wonder what became of all the unsuccessful tinkers, and gunsmiths, and shoemakers, and engineers, and blacksmiths; but nobody could ever tell him.

1870

Political Economy

Political Economy is the basis of all good government. The wisest men of all ages have brought to bear upon this subject the—

[Here I was interrupted and informed that a stranger wished to see me down at the door. I went and confronted him, and asked to know his business, struggling all the time to keep a tight rein on my seething political-economy ideas, and not let them break away from me or get tangled in their harness. And privately I wished the stranger was in the bottom of the canal with a cargo of wheat on top of him. I was all in a fever, but he was cool. He said he was sorry to disturb me, but as he was passing he noticed that I needed some lightning-rods. I said, "Yes, yes —go on—what about it?" He said there was nothing about it, in particular—nothing except that he would like to put them up for me. I am new to housekeeping; have been used to hotels and boarding-houses all my life. Like anybody else of similar experience, I try to appear (to strangers) to be an old housekeeper; consequently I said in an offhand way that I had been intending for some time to have six or eight lightning-rods put up, but—The stranger started, and looked inquiringly at me, but I was serene. I thought that if I chanced to make any mistakes, he would not catch me by my countenance. He said he would rather have my custom than any man's in town. I said, "All right," and started off to wrestle with my great subject again, when he called me back and said it would be necessary to know exactly how many "points" I wanted put up, what parts of the house I wanted them on, and what quality of rod I preferred. It was close quarters for a man not used to the exigencies of housekeeping; but I went through creditably, and he probably never suspected that I was a novice. I told him to put up eight "points," and put them all on the roof, and use the best quality of rod. He said he could furnish the "plain" article at 20 cents a foot; "coppered," 25 cents; "zinc-plated spiral-twist," at 30 cents, that would stop a streak of lightning any time, no matter where it was bound, and "render its errand harmless and its further progress apocryphal." I said apocryphal was no slouch of a word, emanating from the source it did, but, philology aside, I liked the spiral-twist and would take that brand. Then he said he *could* make two hundred and fifty feet answer; but to do it right, and make the best job in town of it, and attract the admiration of the just and the unjust alike, and compel all parties to say they never saw a more symmetrical and hypothetical display of lightning-rods since they were born, he supposed he really couldn't get along without four hundred, though he was not vindictive, and trusted he was willing to try. I said, go ahead and use four hundred, and make any kind of a job he pleased out of it, but let me get back to my work. So I got rid of him at last; and now, after half an hour spent in getting my train of political-economy thoughts coupled together again, I am ready to go on once more.]

richest treasures of their genius, their experience of life, and their learning. The great lights of commercial jurisprudence, international, confraternity, and biological deviation, of all ages, all civilizations, and all nationalities, from Zoroaster down to Horace Greeley, have—

[Here I was interrupted again, and required to go down and confer further with that lightning-rod man. I hurried off, boiling and surging with prodigious thoughts wombed in words of such majesty that each one of them was in itself a straggling procession of syllables that might be fifteen minutes passing a given point, and once more I confronted him—he so calm and sweet, I so hot and frenzied. He was standing in the contemplative attitude of the Colossus of Rhodes, with one foot on my infant tuberose, and the other among my pansies, his hands on his hips, his hat-brim tilted forward, one eye shut and the other gazing critically and admiringly in the direction of my principal chimney. He said now *there* was a state of things to make a man glad to be alive; and added, "I leave it to *you* if you ever saw anything more deliriously picturesque than eight lightning-rods on one chimney?" I said I had no present recollection of anything that transcended it. He said that in his opinion nothing on earth but Niagara Falls was superior to it in the way of natural scenery. All that was needed now, he verily believed, to make my house a perfect balm to the eye, was to kind of touch up the other chimneys a little, and thus "add to the generous *coup d'œil* a soothing uniformity of achievement which would allay the excitement naturally consequent upon the *coup d'état*." I asked him if he learned to talk out of a book, and if I could borrow it anywhere? He smiled pleasantly, and said that his manner of speaking was not taught in books, and that nothing but familiarity with lightning could enable a man to handle his conversational style with impunity. He then figured up an estimate, and said that about eight more rods scattered about my roof would about fix me right, and he guessed five hundred feet of stuff would do it; and added that the first eight had got a little the start of him, so to speak, and used up a mere trifle of material more than he had calculated on—a hundred feet or along there. I said I was in a dreadful hurry, and I wished we could get this business permanently mapped out, so that I could go on with my work. He said, "I *could* have put up those eight rods, and marched off about my business—some men *would* have done it. But no; I said to myself, this man is a stranger to me, and I will die before I'll wrong him; there ain't lightning-rods enough on that house, and for one I'll never stir out of my tracks till I've done as I would be done by, and told him so. Stranger, my duty is accomplished; if the recalcitrant and dephlogistic messenger of heaven strikes your—" "There, now, there," I said, "put on the other eight—add five hundred feet of spiral-twist—do anything and everything you want to do; but calm your sufferings, and try to keep your feelings where you can reach them with the dictionary. Meanwhile, if we understand each other now, I will go to work again."

I think I have been sitting here a full hour this time, trying to get back to where I was when my train of thought was broken up by the last interruption; but I believe I have accomplished it at last, and may venture to proceed again.]

wrestled with this great subject, and the greatest among them have found it a worthy adversary, and one that always comes up fresh and smiling after every throw. The great Confucius said that he would rather be a profound political economist than chief of police. Cicero frequently said that political economy was the grandest consummation that the human mind was capable of consuming; and even our own Greeley had said vaguely but forcibly that "Political—

[Here the lightning-rod man sent up another call for me. I went down in a state of mind bordering on impatience. He said he would rather have died than interrupt me, but when he was employed to do a job, and that job was expected to be done in a clean, workmanlike manner, and when it was finished and fatigue urged him to seek the rest and recreation he stood so much in need of, and he was about to do it, but looked up and saw at a glance that all the calculations had been a little out, and if a thunder-storm were to come up, and that house, which he felt a personal interest in, stood there with nothing on earth to protect it but sixteen lightning-rods—"Let us have peace!" I shrieked. "Put up a hundred and fifty! Put some on the kitchen! Put a dozen on the barn! Put a couple on the cow!—Put one on the cook!—scatter them all over the persecuted place till it looks like a zinc-plated, spiral-twisted, silver-mounted cane-brake! Move! Use up all the material you can get your hands on, and when you run out of lightning-rods put up ram-rods, cam-rods, stair-rods, piston-rods—*anything* that will pander to your dismal appetite for artificial scenery, and bring respite to my raging brain and healing to my lacerated soul!" Wholly unmoved—further than to smile sweetly—this iron being simply turned back his wrist-bands daintily, and said he would now proceed to hump himself. Well, all that was nearly three hours ago. It is questionable whether I am calm enough yet to write on the noble theme of political economy, but I cannot resist the desire to try, for it is the one subject that is nearest to my heart and dearest to my brain of all this world's philosophy.]

—*"economy is heaven's best boon to man." When the loose but gifted Byron lay in his Venetian exile he observed that, if it could be granted him to go back and live his misspent life over again, he would give his lucid and unintoxicated intervals to the composition, not of frivolous rhymes, but of essays upon political economy. Washington loved this exquisite science; such names as Baker, Beckwith, Judson, Smith, are imperishably linked with it; and even imperial Homer, in the ninth book of the Iliad, has said:*

Fiat justitia, ruat cœlum,
Post mortem unum, ante bellum,
Hic jacet hoc, ex-parte res,
Politicum e-conomico est.

The grandeur of these conceptions of the old poet, together with the felicity of the wording which clothes them, and the sublimity of the imagery whereby they are illustrated, have singled out that stanza, and made it more celebrated than any that ever—

["Now, not a word out of you—not a single word. Just state your bill and relapse into impenetrable silence for ever and ever on these premises. Nine hundred dollars? Is that all? This check for the amount will be honored at any respectable bank in America. What is that multitude of people gathered in the street for? How?—'looking at the lightning-rods!' Bless my life, did they never see any lightning-rods before? Never saw 'such a stack of them on one establishment,' did I understand you to say? I will step down and critically observe this popular ebullition of ignorance."]

THREE DAYS LATER   We are all about worn out. For four-and-twenty hours our bristling premises were the talk and wonder of the town. The theaters languished, for their happiest scenic inventions were tame and commonplace compared with my lightning-rods. Our street was blocked night and day with spectators, and among them were many who came from the country to see. It was a blessed relief on the second day when a thunder-storm came up and the lightning began to "go for" my house, as the historian Josephus quaintly phrases it. It cleared the galleries, so to speak. In five minutes there was not a spectator within half a mile of my place; but all the high houses about that distance away were full, windows, roof, and all. And well they might be, for all the falling stars and Fourth-of-July fireworks of a generation, put together and rained down simultaneously out of heaven in one brilliant shower upon one helpless roof, would not have any advantage of the pyrotechnic display that was making my house so magnificently conspicuous in the general gloom of the storm. By actual count, the lightning struck at my establishment seven hundred and sixty-four times in forty minutes, but tripped on one of those faithful rods every time, and slid down the spiral-twist and shot into the earth before it probably had time to be surprised at the way the thing was done. And through all that bombardment only one patch of slates was ripped up, and that was because, for a single instant, the rods in the vicinity were transporting all the lightning they could possibly accommodate. Well, nothing was ever seen like it since the world began. For one whole day and night not a member of my family stuck his head out of the window but he got the hair snatched off it as smooth as a billiard-ball; and, if the reader will believe me, not one of us ever dreamt of stirring abroad. But at last the awful siege came to an end—because there was absolutely no more electricity left in the clouds above us within grappling distance of my insatiable rods. Then I sallied forth, and gathered daring workmen together, and not a bite or a nap did we take till the premises were utterly stripped of all their terrific armament except just three rods on the house, one on the kitchen, and one on the barn—and, behold, these remain there even unto this day. And then, and not till then, the people ventured to use our street again. I will remark here, in passing, that during that fearful time I did not continue my essay upon political economy. I am not even yet settled enough in nerve and brain to resume it.

TO WHOM IT MAY CONCERN   Parties having need of three thousand two hundred and eleven feet of best quality zinc-plated spiral-twist lightning-rod stuff, and sixteen hundred and thirty-one silver-tipped points, all in tolerable repair (and, although much worn by use, still equal to any ordinary emergency), can hear of a bargain by addressing the publisher.

1870

Science *vs.* Luck

At that time, in Kentucky (said the Hon. Mr. K——), the law was very strict against what is termed "games of chance." About a dozen of the boys were detected playing "seven-up" or "old sledge" for money, and the grand jury found a true bill against them. Jim Sturgis was retained to defend them when the case came up, of course. The more he studied over the matter, and looked into the evidence, the plainer it was that he must lose a case at last—there was no getting around that painful fact. Those boys had certainly been betting money on a game of chance. Even public sympathy was roused in behalf of Sturgis. People said it was a pity to see him mar his successful career with a big prominent case like this, which must go against him.

But after several restless nights an inspired idea flashed upon Sturgis, and he sprang out of bed delighted. He thought he saw his way through. The next day he whispered around a little among his clients and a few friends, and then when the case came up in court he acknowledged the seven-up and the betting, and, as his sole defense, had the astounding effrontery to put in the plea that old sledge was not a game of chance! There was the broadest sort of a smile all over the faces of that sophisticated audience. The judge smiled with the rest. But Sturgis maintained a countenance whose earnestness was even severe. The opposite counsel tried to ridicule him out of his position, and did not succeed. The judge jested in a ponderous judicial way about the thing, but did not move him. The matter was becoming grave. The judge lost a little of his patience, and said the joke had gone far enough. Jim Sturgis said he knew of no joke in the matter—his clients could not be punished for indulging in what some people chose to consider a game of chance until it was *proven* that it was a game of chance. Judge and counsel said that would be an easy matter, and forthwith called Deacons Job, Peters, Burke, and Johnson, and Dominies Wirt and Miggles, to testify; and they unanimously and with strong feeling put down the legal quibble of Sturgis by pronouncing that old sledge *was* a game of chance.

"What do you call it *now?*" said the judge.

"I call it a game of science!" retorted Sturgis; "and I'll prove it, too!" They saw his little game.

He brought in a cloud of witnesses, and produced an overwhelming mass of testimony, to show that old sledge was not a game of chance but a game of science.

Instead of being the simplest case in the world, it had somehow turned out to be an excessively knotty one. The judge scratched his head over it awhile, and said there was no way of coming to a determination, because just as many men could be brought into court who would testify on one side as could be found to testify on the other.

But he said he was willing to do the fair thing by all parties, and would act upon any suggestion Mr. Sturgis would make for the solution of the difficulty.

Mr. Sturgis was on his feet in a second.

"Impanel a jury of six of each, Luck *versus* Science. Give them candles and a couple of decks of cards. Send them into the jury-room, and just abide by the result!"

There was no disputing the fairness of the proposition. The four deacons and the two dominies were sworn in as the "chance" jurymen, and six inveterate old seven-up professors were chosen to represent the "science" side of the issue. They retired to the jury-room.

In about two hours Deacon Peters sent into court to borrow three dollars from a friend. [Sensation.] In about two hours more Dominie Miggles sent into court to borrow a "stake" from a friend. [Sensation.] During the next three or four hours the other dominie and the other deacons sent into court for small loans. And still the packed audience waited, for it was a prodigious occasion in Bull's Corners, and one in which every father of a family was necessarily interested.

The rest of the story can be told briefly. About daylight the jury came in, and Deacon Job, the foreman, read the following

VERDICT

We, the jury in the case of the Commonwealth of Kentucky *vs.* John Wheeler *et al.*, have carefully considered the points of the case, and tested the merits of the several theories advanced, and do hereby unanimously decide that the game commonly known as old sledge or seven-up is eminently a game of science and not of chance. In demonstration whereof it is hereby and herein stated, iterated, reiterated, set forth, and made manifest that, during the entire night, the "chance" men never won a game or turned a jack, although both feats were common and frequent to the opposition; and furthermore, in support of this our verdict, we call attention to the significant fact that the "chance" men are all busted, and the "science" men have got the money. It is the deliberate opinion of this jury, that the "chance" theory concerning seven-up is a pernicious doctrine, and calculated to inflict untold suffering and pecuniary loss upon any community that takes stock in it.

"That is the way that seven-up came to be set apart and particularized in the statute-books of Kentucky as being a game not of chance but of science, and therefore not punishable under the law," said Mr. K——. "That verdict is of record, and holds good to this day."

1870

The Story of the Good Little Boy

Once there was a good little boy by the name of Jacob Blivens. He always obeyed his parents, no matter how absurd and unreasonable their demands were; and he always learned his book, and never was late at Sabbath-school. He would not play hookey, even when his sober judgment told him it was the most profitable thing he could do. None of the other boys could ever make that boy out, he acted so strangely. He wouldn't lie, no matter how convenient it was. He just said it was wrong to lie, and that was sufficient for him. And he was so honest that he was simply ridiculous. The curious ways that that Jacob had, surpassed everything. He wouldn't play marbles on Sunday, he wouldn't rob birds' nests, he wouldn't give hot pennies to organ-grinders' monkeys; he didn't seem to take any interest in any kind of rational amusement. So the other boys used to try to reason it out and come to an understanding of him, but they couldn't arrive at any satisfactory conclusion. As I said before, they could only figure out a sort of vague idea that he was "afflicted," and so they took him under their protection, and never allowed any harm to come to him.

This good little boy read all the Sunday-school books; they were his greatest delight. This was the whole secret of it. He believed in the good little boys they put in the Sunday-school books; he had every confidence in them. He longed to come across one of them alive once; but he never did. They all died before his time, maybe. Whenever he read about a particularly good one he turned over quickly to the end to see what became of him, because he wanted to travel thousands of miles and gaze on him; but it wasn't any use; that good little boy always died in the last chapter, and there was a picture of the funeral, with all his relations and the Sunday-school children standing around the grave in pantaloons that were too short, and bonnets that were too large, and everybody crying into handkerchiefs that had as much as a yard and a half of stuff in them. He was always headed off in this way. He never could see one of those good little boys on account of his always dying in the last chapter.

Jacob had a noble ambition to be put in a Sunday-school book. He wanted to be put in, with pictures representing him gloriously declining to lie to his mother, and her weeping for joy about it; and pictures representing him standing on the doorstep giving a penny to a poor beggar-woman with six children, and telling her to spend it freely, but not to be extravagant, because extravagance is a sin; and pictures of him magnanimously refusing to tell on the bad boy who always lay in wait for him around the corner as he came from school, and welted him over the head with a lath, and then chased him home, saying, "Hi! hi!" as he proceeded. That was the ambition of young Jacob Blivens. He wished to be put in a Sunday-school book. It made him feel a little uncomfortable sometimes when he reflected that the good little boys always died. He loved to live, you know, and this was the most unpleasant feature about being a Sunday-school-book boy. He knew it was not healthy to be good. He knew it was more fatal than consumption to be so supernaturally good as the boys in the books were; he knew that none of them had ever been able to stand it long, and it pained him to think that if they put him in a book he wouldn't ever see it, or even if they did get the book out before he died it wouldn't be popular without any picture of his funeral in the back part of it. It couldn't be much of a Sunday-school book that couldn't tell about the advice he gave to the community when he was dying. So at last, of course, he had to make up his mind to do the best he could under the circumstances —to live right, and hang on as long as he could, and have his dying speech all ready when his time came.

But somehow nothing ever went right with this good little boy; nothing ever turned out with him the way it turned out with the good little boys in the books. They always had a good time, and the bad boys had the broken legs; but in his case there was a screw loose somewhere, and it all happened just the other way. When he found Jim Blake stealing apples, and went under the tree to read to him about the bad little boy who fell out of a neighbor's apple tree and broke his arm, Jim fell out of the tree, too, but he fell on *him* and broke *his* arm, and Jim wasn't hurt at all. Jacob couldn't understand that. There wasn't anything in the books like it.

And once, when some bad boys pushed a blind man over in the mud, and Jacob ran to help him up and receive his blessing, the blind man did not give him any blessing at all, but whacked him over the head with his stick and said he would like to catch him shoving *him* again, and then pretending to help him up. This was not in accordance with any of the books. Jacob looked them all over to see.

One thing that Jacob wanted to do was to find a lame dog that hadn't any place to stay, and was hungry and persecuted, and bring him home and pet him and have that dog's imperishable gratitude. And at last he found one and was happy; and he brought him home and fed him, but when he was going to pet him the dog flew at him and tore all the clothes off him except those that were in front, and made a spectacle of him that was astonishing. He examined authorities, but he could not understand the matter. It was of the same breed of dogs that was in the books, but it acted very differently. Whatever this boy did he got into trouble. The very things the boys in the books got rewarded for turned out to be about the most unprofitable things he could invest in.

Once, when he was on his way to Sunday-school, he saw some bad boys starting off pleasuring in a sailboat. He was filled with consternation, because he knew from his reading that boys who went sailing on Sunday invariably got drowned. So he ran out on a raft to warn them, but a log turned with him and slid him into the river. A man got him out pretty soon, and the doctor pumped the water out of him, and gave him a fresh start with his bellows, but he caught cold and lay sick abed nine weeks. But the most unaccountable thing about it was that the bad boys in the boat had a good time all day, and then reached home alive and well in the most surprising manner. Jacob Blivens said there was nothing like these things in the books. He was perfectly dumfounded.

When he got well he was a little discouraged, but he resolved to keep on trying anyhow. He knew that so far his experiences wouldn't do to go in a book, but he hadn't yet reached the allotted term of life for good little boys, and he hoped to be able to make a record yet if he could hold on till his time was fully up. If everything else failed he had his dying speech to fall back on.

He examined his authorities, and found that it was now time for him to go to sea as a cabin-boy. He called on a ship-captain and made his application, and when the captain asked for his recommendations he proudly drew out a tract and pointed to the word, "To Jacob Blivens, from his affectionate teacher." But the captain was a coarse, vulgar man, and he said, "Oh, that be blowed! *that* wasn't any proof that he knew how to wash dishes or handle a slush-bucket, and he guessed he didn't want him." This was altogether the most extraordinary thing that ever happened to Jacob in all his life. A compliment from a teacher, on a tract, had never failed to move the tenderest emotions of ship-captains, and open the way to all offices of honor and profit in their gift—it never had in any book that ever *he* had read. He could hardly believe his senses.

This boy always had a hard time of it. Nothing ever came out according to the authorities with him. At last, one day, when he was around hunting up bad little boys to admonish, he found a lot of them in the old iron-foundry fixing up a little joke on fourteen or fifteen dogs, which they had tied together in long procession, and were going to ornament with empty nitroglycerin cans made fast to their tails. Jacob's heart was touched. He sat down on one of those cans (for he never minded grease when duty was before him), and he took hold of the foremost dog by the collar, and turned his reproving eye upon wicked Tom Jones. But just at that moment Alderman McWelter, full of wrath, stepped in. All the bad boys ran away, but Jacob Blivens rose in conscious innocence and began one of those stately little Sunday-school-book speeches which always commence with "Oh, sir!" in dead opposition to the fact that no boy, good or bad, ever starts a remark with "Oh, sir." But the alderman never waited to hear the rest. He took Jacob Blivens by the ear and turned him around, and hit him a whack in the rear with the flat of his hand; and in an instant that good little boy shot out through the roof and soared away toward the sun, with the fragments of those fifteen dogs stringing after him like the tail of a kite. And there wasn't a sign of that alderman or that old iron-foundry left on the face of the earth; and, as for young Jacob Blivens, he never got a chance to make his last dying speech after all his trouble fixing it up, unless he made it to the birds; because, although the bulk of him came down all right in a tree-top in an adjoining county, the rest of him was apportioned around among four townships, and so they had to hold five inquests on him to find out whether he was dead or not, and how it occurred. You never saw a boy scattered so.[1]

Thus perished the good little boy who did the best he could, but didn't come out according to the books. Every boy who ever did as he did prospered except him. His case is truly remarkable. It will probably never be accounted for.

[1] This glycerin catastrophe is borrowed from a floating newspaper item, whose author's name I would give if I knew it. M. T.

1870

Buck Fanshaw's Funeral

Somebody has said that in order to know a community, one must observe the style of its funerals and know what manner of men they bury with most ceremony. I cannot say which class we buried with most éclat in our "flush times," the distinguished public benefactor or the distinguished rough—possibly the two chief grades or grand divisions of society honored their illustrious dead about equally; and hence, no doubt, the philosopher I have quoted from would have needed to see two representative funerals in Virginia before forming his estimate of the people.

There was a grand time over Buck Fanshaw when he died. He was a representative citizen. He had "killed his man"—not in his own quarrel, it is true, but in defense of a stranger unfairly beset by numbers. He had kept a sumptuous saloon. He had been the proprietor of a dashing helpmeet whom he could have discarded without the formality of a divorce. He had held a high position in the fire department and been a very Warwick in politics. When he died there was great lamentation throughout the town, but especially in the vast bottom-stratum of society.

On the inquest it was shown that Buck Fanshaw, in the delirium of a wasting typhoid fever, had taken arsenic, shot himself through the body, cut his throat, and jumped out of a four-story window and broken his neck—and after due deliberation, the jury, sad and tearful, but with intelligence unblinded by its sorrow, brought in a verdict of death "by the visitation of God." What could the world do without juries?

Prodigious preparations were made for the funeral. All the vehicles in town were hired, all the saloons put in mourning, all the municipal and fire-company flags hung at half-mast, and all the firemen ordered to muster in uniform and bring their machines duly draped in black. Now—let us remark in parentheses—as all the peoples of the earth had representative adventurers in the Silverland, and as each adventurer had brought the slang of his nation or his locality with him, the combination made the slang of Nevada the richest and the most infinitely varied and copious that had ever existed anywhere in the world, per-

haps, except in the mines of California in the "early days." Slang was
the language of Nevada. It was hard to preach a sermon without it,
and be understood. Such phrases as "You bet!" "Oh, no, I reckon not!"
"No Irish need apply," and a hundred others, became so common as
to fall from the lips of a speaker unconsciously—and very often when
they did not touch the subject under discussion and consequently
failed to mean anything.

After Buck Fanshaw's inquest, a meeting of the short-haired brother-
hood was held, for nothing can be done on the Pacific coast without a
public meeting and an expression of sentiment. Regretful resolutions
were passed and various committees appointed; among others, a committee of one was deputed to call on the minister, a fragile, gentle,
spirituel new fledgling from an Eastern theological seminary, and as yet
unacquainted with the ways of the mines. The committeeman, "Scotty"
Briggs, made his visit; and in after days it was worth something to hear
the minister tell about it. Scotty was a stalwart rough, whose customary
suit, when on weighty official business, like committee work, was a fire-
helmet, flaming red flannel shirt, patent-leather belt with spanner and
revolver attached, coat hung over arm, and pants stuffed into boot-tops.
He formed something of a contrast to the pale theological student. It
is fair to say of Scotty, however, in passing, that he had a warm heart,
and a strong love for his friends, and never entered into a quarrel when
he could reasonably keep out of it. Indeed, it was commonly said that
whenever one of Scotty's fights was investigated, it always turned out
that it had originally been no affair of his, but that out of native good-
heartedness he had dropped in of his own accord to help the man who
was getting the worst of it. He and Buck Fanshaw were bosom friends,
for years, and had often taken adventurous "pot-luck" together. On one
occasion, they had thrown off their coats and taken the weaker side in
a fight among strangers, and after gaining a hard-earned victory, turned
and found that the men they were helping had deserted early, and not
only that, but had stolen their coats and made off with them. But to
return to Scotty's visit to the minister. He was on a sorrowful mission,
now, and his face was the picture of woe. Being admitted to the presence he sat down before the clergyman, placed his fire-hat on an unfinished manuscript sermon under the minister's nose, took from it a red
silk handkerchief, wiped his brow and heaved a sigh of dismal impressiveness, explanatory of his business. He choked, and even shed tears;
but with an effort he mastered his voice and said in lugubrious tones:

"Are you the duck that runs the gospel-mill next door?"

"Am I the—pardon me, I believe I do not understand?"

With another sigh and a half-sob, Scotty rejoined:

"Why you see we are in a bit of trouble, and the boys thought maybe you would give us a lift, if we'd tackle you—that is, if I've got the rights of it and you are the head clerk of the doxology-works next door."

"I am the shepherd in charge of the flock whose fold is next door."

"The which?"

"The spiritual adviser of the little company of believers whose sanctuary adjoins these premises."

Scotty scratched his head, reflected a moment, and then said:

"You ruther hold over me, pard. I reckon I can't call that hand. Ante and pass the buck."

"How? I beg pardon. What did I understand you to say?"

"Well, you've ruther got the bulge on me. Or maybe we've both got the bulge, somehow. You don't smoke me and I don't smoke you. You see, one of the boys has passed in his checks, and we want to give him a good send-off, and so the thing I'm on now is to roust out somebody to jerk a little chin-music for us and waltz him through handsome."

"My friend, I seem to grow more and more bewildered. Your observations are wholly incomprehensible to me. Cannot you simplify them in some way? At first I thought perhaps I understood you, but I grope now. Would it not expedite matters if you restricted yourself to categorical statements of fact unencumbered with obstructing accumulations of metaphor and allegory?"

Another pause, and more reflection. Then, said Scotty:

"I'll have to pass, I judge."

"How?"

"You've raised me out, pard."

"I still fail to catch your meaning."

"Why, that last lead of yourn is too many for me—that's the idea. I can't neither trump nor follow suit."

The clergyman sank back in his chair perplexed. Scotty leaned his head on his hand and gave himself up to thought. Presently his face came up, sorrowful but confident.

"I've got it now, so's you can savvy," he said. "What we want is a gospel-sharp. See?"

"A what?"

"Gospel-sharp. Parson."

"Oh! Why did you not say so before? I am a clergyman—a parson."

"Now you talk! You see my blind and straddle it like a man. Put it there!"—extending a brawny paw, which closed over the minister's small hand and gave it a shake indicative of fraternal sympathy and fervent gratification.

"Now we're all right, pard. Let's start fresh. Don't you mind my snuffling a little—becuz we're in a power of trouble. You see, one of the boys has gone up the flume—"

"Gone where?"

"Up the flume—throwed up the sponge, you understand."

"Thrown up the sponge?"

"Yes—kicked the bucket—"

"Ah—has departed to that mysterious country from whose bourne no traveler returns."

"Return! I reckon not. Why, pard, he's *dead!*"

"Yes, I understand."

"Oh, you do? Well I thought maybe you might be getting tangled some more. Yes, you see he's dead again—"

"*Again!* Why, has he ever been dead before?"

"Dead before? No! Do you reckon a man has got as many lives as a cat? But you bet you he's awful dead now, poor old boy, and I wish I'd never seen this day. I don't want no better friend than Buck Fanshaw. I knowed him by the back; and when I know a man and like him, I freeze to him—you hear *me.* Take him all round, pard, there never was a bullier man in the mines. No man ever knowed Buck Fanshaw to go back on a friend. But it's all up, you know, it's all up. It ain't no use. They've scooped him."

"Scooped him?"

"Yes—death has. Well, well, well, we've got to give him up. Yes, indeed. It's a kind of a hard world, after all, *ain't* it? But pard, he was a rustler! You ought to seen him get started once. He was a bully boy with a glass eye! Just spit in his face and give him room according to his strength, and it was just beautiful to see him peel and go in. He was the worst son of a thief that ever drawed breath. Pard, he was *on* it! He was on it bigger than an Injun!"

"On it? On what?"

"On the shoot. On the shoulder. On the fight, you understand. *He* didn't give a continental for *any*body. *Beg* your pardon, friend, for coming so near saying a cuss-word—but you see I'm on an awful strain, in this palaver, on account of having to cramp down and draw everything so mild. But we've got to give him up. There ain't any getting around that, I don't reckon. Now if we can get you to help plant him—"

"Preach the funeral discourse? Assist at the obsequies?"

"Obs'quies is good. Yes. That's it—that's our little game. We are going to get the thing up regardless, you know. He was always nifty himself, and so you bet you his funeral ain't going to be no slouch—solid-silver door-plate on his coffin, six plumes on the hearse, and a nigger on the box in a biled shirt and a plug hat—how's that for high? And we'll take care of *you,* pard. We'll fix you all right. There'll be a kerridge for you; and whatever you want, you just 'scape out and we'll 'tend to it. We've got a shebang fixed up for you to stand behind, in No. 1's house, and don't you be afraid. Just go in and toot your horn, if you don't sell a clam. Put Buck through as bully as you can, pard, for anybody that knowed him will tell you that he was one of the whitest men that was ever in the mines. You can't draw it too strong. He never could stand it to see things going wrong. He's done more to make this town quiet and peaceable than any man in it. I've seen him lick four Greasers in eleven minutes, myself. If a thing wanted regulating, *he* warn't a man to go browsing around after somebody to do it, but he would prance in and regulate it himself. He warn't a Catholic. Scasely. He was down on 'em. His word was, 'No Irish need apply!' But it didn't make no difference about that when it came down to what a man's rights was—and so, when some roughs jumped the Catholic boneyard and started in to stake out town lots in it he *went* for 'em! And he *cleaned* 'em, too! I was there, pard, and I seen it myself."

"That was very well indeed—at least the impulse was—whether the act was strictly defensible or not. Had deceased any religious convictions? That is to say, did he feel a dependence upon, or acknowledge allegiance to a higher power?"

More reflection.

"I reckon you've stumped me again, pard. Could you say it over once more, and say it slow?"

"Well, to simplify it somewhat, was he, or rather had he ever been connected with any organization sequestered from secular concerns and devoted to self-sacrifice in the interests of morality?"

"All down but nine—set 'em up on the other alley, pard."

"What did I understand you to say?"

"Why, you're most too many for me, you know. When you get in with your left I hunt grass every time. Every time you draw, you fill; but I don't seem to have any luck. Let's have a new deal."

"How? Begin again?"

"That's it."

"Very well. Was he a good man, and—"

"There—I see that; don't put up another chip till I look at my hand. A good man, says you? Pard, it ain't no name for it. He was the best man that ever—pard, you would have doted on that man. He could lam any galoot of his inches in America. It was him that put down the riot last election before it got a start; and everybody said he was the only man that could have done it. He waltzed in with a spanner in one hand and a trumpet in the other, and sent fourteen men home on a shutter in less than three minutes. He had that riot all broke up and prevented nice before anybody ever got a chance to strike a blow. He was always for peace, and he would *have* peace—he could not stand disturbances. Pard, he was a great loss to this town. It would please the boys if you could chip in something like that and do him justice. Here once when the Micks got to throwing stones through the Methodis' Sunday-school windows, Buck Fanshaw, all of his own notion, shut up his saloon and took a couple of six-shooters and mounted guard over the Sunday-school. Says he, 'No Irish need apply!' And they didn't. He was the bulliest man in the mountains, pard! He could run faster, jump higher, hit harder, and hold more tanglefoot whisky without spilling it than any man in seventeen counties. Put that in, pard—it'll please the boys more than anything you could say. And you can say, pard, that he never shook his mother."

"Never shook his mother?"

"That's it—any of the boys will tell you so."

"Well, but why *should* he shake her?"

"That's what *I* say—but some people does."

"Not people of any repute?"

"Well, some that averages pretty so-so."

"In my opinion the man that would offer personal violence to his own mother, ought to—"

"Cheese it, pard; you've banked your ball clean outside the string. What I was a drivin' at, was, that he never *throwed off* on his mother —don't you see? No indeedy. He give her a house to live in, and town lots, and plenty of money; and he looked after her and took care of her all the time; and when she was down with the smallpox I'm d—d if he didn't set up nights and nuss her himself! *Beg* your pardon for saying it, but it hopped out too quick for yours truly. You've treated me like a gentleman, pard, and I ain't the man to hurt your feelings intentional. I think you're white. I think you're a square man, pard. I like you, and I'll lick any man that don't. I'll lick him till he can't tell himself from a last year's corpse! Put it *there!*" [Another fraternal hand-shake—and exit.]

The obsequies were all that "the boys" could desire. Such a marvel of funeral pomp had never been seen in Virginia. The plumed hearse, the dirge-breathing brass-bands, the closed marts of business, the flags drooping at half-mast, the long, plodding procession of uniformed secret societies, military battalions and fire companies, draped engines, carriages of officials, and citizens in vehicles and on foot, attracted multitudes of spectators to the sidewalks, roofs, and windows; and for years afterward, the degree of grandeur attained by any civic display in Virginia was determined by comparison with Buck Fanshaw's funeral.

Scotty Briggs, as a pall-bearer and a mourner, occupied a prominent place at the funeral, and when the sermon was finished and the last sentence of the prayer for the dead man's soul ascended, he responded, in a low voice, but with feeling:

"AMEN. No Irish need apply."

As the bulk of the response was without apparent relevancy, it was probably nothing more than a humble tribute to the memory of the friend that was gone; for, as Scotty had once said, it was "his word."

Scotty Briggs, in after days, achieved the distinction of becoming the only convert to religion that was ever gathered from the Virginia roughs; and it transpired that the man who had it in him to espouse the quarrel of the weak out of inborn nobility of spirit was no mean timber whereof to construct a Christian. The making him one did not warp his generosity or diminish his courage; on the contrary it gave intelligent direction to the one and a broader field to the other. If his Sunday-school class progressed faster than the other classes, was it matter for wonder? I think not. He talked to his pioneer small-fry in a language they understood! It was my large privilege, a month before he died, to hear him tell the beautiful story of Joseph and his brethren to his class "without looking at the book." I leave it to the reader to fancy what it was like, as it fell, riddled with slang, from the lips of that grave, earnest teacher, and was listened to by his little learners with a consuming interest that showed that they were as unconscious as he was that any violence was being done to the sacred proprieties!

From ROUGHING IT, 1872

The Story of the Old Ram

Every now and then, in these days, the boys used to tell me I ought to get one Jim Blaine to tell me the stirring story of his grandfather's old ram—but they always added that I must not mention the matter unless Jim was drunk at the time—just comfortably and sociably drunk. They kept this up until my curiosity was on the rack to hear the story. I got to haunting Blaine; but it was of no use, the boys always found fault with his condition; he was often moderately but never satisfactorily drunk. I never watched a man's condition with such absorbing interest, such anxious solicitude; I never so pined to see a man uncompromisingly drunk before. At last, one evening I hurried to his cabin, for I learned that this time his situation was such that even the most fastidious could find no fault with it—he was tranquilly, serenely, symmetrically drunk—not a hiccup to mar his voice, not a cloud upon his brain thick enough to obscure his memory. As I entered, he was sitting upon an empty powder-keg, with a clay pipe in one hand and the other raised to command silence. His face was round, red, and very serious; his throat was bare and his hair tumbled; in general appearance and costume he was a stalwart miner of the period. On the pine table stood a candle, and its dim light revealed "the boys" sitting here and there on bunks, candle-boxes, powder-kegs, etc. They said:

"Sh—! Don't speak—he's going to commence."

I found a seat at once, and Blaine said:

"I don't reckon them times will ever come again. There never was a more bullier old ram than what he was. Grandfather fetched him from Illinois—got him of a man by the name of Yates—Bill Yates—maybe you might have heard of him; his father was a deacon—Baptist—and he was a rustler, too; a man had to get up ruther early to get the start of old Thankful Yates; it was him that put the Greens up to j'ining teams with my grandfather when he moved west. Seth Green was prob'ly the pick of the flock; he married a Wilkerson—Sarah Wilkerson—good cretur, she was—one of the likeliest heifers that was ever raised in old Stoddard, everybody said that knowed her. She could heft a bar'l of flour as easy

as I can flirt a flapjack. And spin? Don't mention it! Independent?
Humph! When Sile Hawkins come a-browsing around her, she let him
know that for all his tin he couldn't trot in harness alongside of *her*.
You see, Sile Hawkins was—no, it warn't Sile Hawkins, after all—it was
a galoot by the name of Filkins—I disremember his first name; but he
was a stump—come into pra'r-meeting drunk, one night, hooraying for
Nixon, becuz he thought it was a primary; and old Deacon Ferguson
up and scooted him through the window and he lit on old Miss Jeffer-
son's head, poor old filly. She was a good soul—had a glass eye and used
to lend it to old Miss Wagner, that hadn't any, to receive company in;
it warn't big enough, and when Miss Wagner warn't noticing, it would
get twisted around in the socket, and look up, maybe, or out to one
side, and every which way, while t'other one was looking as straight
ahead as a spy-glass. Grown people didn't mind it, but it 'most always
made the children cry, it was so sort of scary. She tried packing it in
raw cotton, but it wouldn't work, somehow—the cotton would get loose
and stick out and look so kind of awful that the children couldn't stand
it no way. She was always dropping it out, and turning up her old
deadlight on the company empty, and making them oncomfortable, becuz *she* never could tell when it hopped out, being blind on that side,
you see. So somebody would have to hunch her and say, 'Your game
eye has fetched loose, Miss Wagner, dear'—and then all of them would
have to sit and wait till she jammed it in again—wrong side before, as
a general thing, and green as a bird's egg, being a bashful cretur and
easy sot back before company. But being wrong side before warn't
much difference, anyway, becuz her own eye was sky-blue and the glass
one was yaller on the front side, so whichever way she turned it it
didn't match nohow. Old Miss Wagner was considerable on the borrow,
she was. When she had a quilting, or Dorcas S'iety at her house she
gen'ally borrowed Miss Higgins's wooden leg to stump around on; it
was considerable shorter than her other pin, but much *she* minded that.
She said she couldn't abide crutches when she had company, becuz
they were so slow; said when she had company and things had to be
done, she wanted to get up and hump herself. She was as bald as a jug,
and so she used to borrow Miss Jacops's wig—Miss Jacops was the
coffin-peddler's wife—a ratty old buzzard, he was, that used to go roosting around where people was sick, waiting for 'em; and there that old
rip would sit all day, in the shade, on a coffin that he judged would
fit the can'idate; and if it was a slow customer and kind of uncertain,
he'd fetch his rations and a blanket along and sleep in the coffin nights.
He was anchored out that way, in frosty weather, for about three weeks,

once, before old Robbins's place, waiting for him; and after that, for as much as two years, Jacops was not on speaking terms with the old man, on account of his disapp'inting him. He got one of his feet froze, and lost money, too, becuz old Robbins took a favorable turn and got well. The next time Robbins got sick, Jacops tried to make up with him, and varnished up the same old coffin and fetched it along; but old Robbins was too many for him; he had him in, and 'peared to be powerful weak; he bought the coffin for ten dollars and Jacops was to pay it back and twenty-five more besides if Robbins didn't like the coffin after he'd tried it. And then Robbins died, and at the funeral he bursted off the lid and riz up in his shroud and told the parson to let up on the performances, becuz he could *not* stand such a coffin as that. You see he had been in a trance once before, when he was young, and he took the chances on another, cal'lating that if he made the trip it was money in his pocket, and if he missed fire he couldn't lose a cent. And, by George, he sued Jacops for the rhino and got judgment; and he set up the coffin in his back parlor and said he 'lowed to take his time, now. It was always an aggravation to Jacops, the way that miserable old thing acted. He moved back to Indiany pretty soon—went to Wellsville —Wellsville was the place the Hogadorns was from. Mighty fine family. Old Maryland stock. Old Squire Hogadorn could carry around more mixed licker, and cuss better than 'most any man I ever see. His second wife was the Widder Billings—she that was Becky Martin; her dam was Deacon Dunlap's first wife. Her oldest child, Maria, married a missionary and died in grace—et up by the savages. They et *him*, too, poor feller—biled him. It warn't the custom, so they say, but they explained to friends of his'n that went down there to bring away his things, that they'd tried missionaries every other way and never could get any good out of 'em—and so it annoyed all his relations to find out that that man's life was fooled away just out of a dern'd experiment, so to speak. But mind you, there ain't anything ever reely lost; everything that people can't understand and don't see the reason of does good if you only hold on and give it a fair shake; Prov'dence don't fire no blank ca'tridges, boys. That there missionary's substance, unbeknowns to himself, actu'ly converted every last one of them heathens that took a chance at the barbecue. Nothing ever fetched them but that. Don't tell *me* it was an accident that he was biled. There ain't no such a thing as an accident. When my Uncle Lem was leaning up agin a scaffolding once, sick, or drunk, or suthin, an Irishman with a hod full of bricks fell on him out of the third story and broke the old man's back in two places. People said it was an accident. Much accident there was about that.

He didn't know what he was there for, but he was there for a good
object. If he hadn't been there the Irishman would have been killed.
Nobody can ever make me believe anything different from that. Uncle
Lem's dog was there. Why didn't the Irishman fall on the dog? Becuz
the dog would 'a' seen him a-coming and stood from under. That's the
reason the dog warn't app'inted. A dog can't be depended on to carry
out a special prov'dence. Mark my words, it was a put-up thing. Accidents don't happen, boys. Uncle Lem's dog—I wish you could 'a' seen
that dog. He was a reg'lar shepherd—or ruther he was part bull and
part shepherd—splendid animal; belonged to Parson Hagar before
Uncle Lem got him. Parson Hagar belonged to the Western Reserve
Hagars; prime family; his mother was a Watson; one of his sisters married a Wheeler; they settled in Morgan County, and he got nipped by
the machinery in a carpet factory and went through in less than a
quarter of a minute; his widder bought the piece of carpet that had
his remains wove in, and people come a hundred mile to 'tend the
funeral. There was fourteen yards in the piece. She wouldn't let them
roll him up, but planted him just so—full length. The church was middling small where they preached the funeral, and they had to let one
end of the coffin stick out of the window. They didn't bury him—they
planted one end, and let him stand up, same as a monument. And they
nailed a sign on it and put—put on—put on it—sacred to—the m-e-m-o-r-y
—of fourteen y-a-r-d-s—of three-ply—car - - - pet—containing all that
was—m-o-r-t-a-l—of—of—W-i-l-l-i-a-m—W-h-e—"

Jim Blaine had been growing gradually drowsy and drowsier—his
head nodded, once, twice, three times—dropped peacefully upon his
breast, and he fell tranquilly asleep. The tears were running down the
boys' cheeks—they were suffocating with suppressed laughter—and had
been from the start, though I had never noticed it. I perceived that I
was "sold." I learned then that Jim Blaine's peculiarity was that whenever he reached a certain stage of intoxication, no human power could
keep him from setting out, with impressive unction, to tell about a
wonderful adventure which he had once had with his grandfather's old
ram—and the mention of the ram in the first sentence was as far as any
man had ever heard him get, concerning it. He always maundered off,
interminably, from one thing to another, till his whisky got the best
of him, and he feel asleep. What the thing was that happened to him
and his grandfather's old ram is a dark mystery to this day, for nobody
has ever yet found out.

From ROUGHING IT, 1872

Tom Quartz

One of my comrades there[1]—another of those victims of eighteen years of unrequited toil and blighted hopes—was one of the gentlest spirits that ever bore its patient cross in a weary exile: grave and simple Dick Baker, pocket-miner of Dead-Horse Gulch. He was forty-six, gray as a rat, earnest, thoughtful, slenderly educated, slouchily dressed, and clay-soiled, but his heart was finer metal than any gold his shovel ever brought to light—than any, indeed, that ever was mined or minted.

Whenever he was out of luck and a little downhearted, he would fall to mourning over the loss of a wonderful cat he used to own (for where women and children are not, men of kindly impulses take up with pets, for they must love something). And he always spoke of the strange sagacity of that cat with the air of a man who believed in his secret heart that there was something human about it—maybe even supernatural.

I heard him talking about this animal once. He said:

"Gentlemen, I used to have a cat here, by the name of Tom Quartz, which you'd 'a' took an interest in, I reckon—most anybody would. I had him here eight year—and he was the remarkablest cat I ever see. He was a large gray one of the Tom specie, an' he had more hard, natchral sense than any man in this camp—'n' a *power* of dignity—he wouldn't let the Gov'ner of Califorhy be familiar with him. He never ketched a rat in his life—'peared to be above it. He never cared for nothing but mining. He knowed more about mining, that cat did, than any man I ever, ever see. You couldn't tell *him* noth'n' 'bout placer-diggin's—'n' as for pocket-mining, why he was just born for it. He would dig out after me an' Jim when we went over the hills prospect'n', and he would trot along behind us for as much as five mile, if we went so fur. An' he had the best judgment about mining-ground—why you never see anything like it. When we went to work, he'd scatter a glance around, 'n' if he didn't think much of the indications, he would give a look as much as to say, 'Well, I'll have to get you to excuse *me*,' 'n'

[1] California

without another word he'd hyste his nose into the air 'n' shove for home. But if the ground suited him, he would lay low 'n' keep dark till the first pan was washed, 'n' then he would sidle up 'n' take a look, an' if there was about six or seven grains of gold *he* was satisfied—he didn't want no better prospect 'n' that—'n' then he would lay down on our coats and snore like a steamboat till we'd struck the pocket, an' then get up 'n' superintend. He was nearly lightnin' on superintending.

"Well, by an' by, up comes this yer quartz excitement. Everybody was into it—everybody was pick'n' 'n' blast'n' instead of shovelin' dirt on the hillside—everybody was put'n' down a shaft instead of scrapin' the surface. Noth'n' would do Jim, but *we* must tackle the ledges, too, 'n' so we did. We commenced putt'n' down a shaft, 'n' Tom Quartz he begin to wonder what in the Dickens it was all about. *He* hadn't ever seen any mining like that before, 'n' he was all upset, as you may say— he couldn't come to a right understanding of it no way—it was too many for *him*. He was down on it, too, you bet you—he was down on it pow- erful—'n' always appeared to consider it the cussedest foolishness out. But that cat, you know, was *always* agin new-fangled arrangements— somehow he never could abide 'em. *You* know how it is with old habits. But by an' by Tom Quartz begin to git sort of reconciled a little, though he never *could* altogether understand that eternal sinkin' of a shaft an' never pannin' out anything. At last he got to comin' down in the shaft, hisself, to try to cipher it out. An' when he'd git the blues, 'n' feel kind o' scruffy, 'n' aggravated 'n' disgusted—knowin' as he did, that the bills was runnin' up all the time an' we warn't makin' a cent—he would curl up on a gunny-sack in the corner an' go to sleep. Well, one day when the shaft was down about eight foot, the rock got so hard that we had to put in a blast—the first blast'n' we'd ever done since Tom Quartz was born. An' then we lit the fuse 'n' clumb out 'n' got off 'bout fifty yards —'n' forgot 'n' left Tom Quartz sound asleep on the gunny-sack. In 'bout a minute we seen a puff of smoke bust up out of the hole, 'n' then everything let go with an awful crash, 'n' about four million ton of rocks 'n' dirt 'n' smoke 'n' splinters shot up 'bout a mile an' a half into the air, an' by George, right in the dead center of it was old Tom Quartz a-goin' end over end, an' a-snortin' an' a-sneez'n', an' a-clawin' an' a-reachin' for things like all possessed. But it warn't no use, you know, it warn't no use. An' that was the last we see of *him* for about two minutes 'n' a half, an' then all of a sudden it begin to rain rocks and rubbage, an' directly he come down ker-whop about ten foot off f'm where we stood. Well, I reckon he was p'raps the orneriest-lookin' beast you ever see. One ear was sot back on his neck, 'n' his tail was stove up, 'n' his eyewinkers was swinged off, 'n' he was all blacked up with powder an' smoke, an' all sloppy with mud 'n' slush f'm one end to the other. Well, sir, it warn't no use to try to apologize—we couldn't say a word. He took a sort of a disgusted look at hisself, 'n' then he looked at us—an' it was just exactly the same as if he had said—'Gents, maybe *you* think it's smart to take advantage of a cat that ain't had no experience of quartz-minin', but *I* think *different*'—an' then he turned on his heel 'n' marched off home without ever saying another word.

"That was jest his style. An' maybe you won't believe it, but after that you never see a cat so prejudiced agin quartz-mining as what he was. An' by an' by when he *did* get to goin' down in the shaft ag'in, you'd 'a' been astonished at his sagacity. The minute we'd tetch off a blast 'n' the fuse'd begin to sizzle, he'd give a look as much as to say, 'Well, I'll have to git you to excuse *me*,' an' it was surpris'n' the way he'd shin out of that hole 'n' go f'r a tree. Sagacity? It ain't no name for it. 'Twas *inspiration!*"

I said, "Well, Mr. Baker, his prejudice against quartz-mining *was* remarkable, considering how he came by it. Couldn't you ever curc him of it?"

"*Cure him!* No! When Tom Quartz was sot once, he was *always* sot—and you might 'a' blowed him up as much as three million times 'n' you'd never 'a' broken him of his cussed prejudice agin quartz-mining."

The affection and the pride that lit up Baker's face when he delivered this tribute to the firmness of his humble friend of other days, will always be a vivid memory with me.

From ROUGHING IT, 1872

A Trial

Capt. Ned Blakely—that name will answer as well as any other fictitious one (for he was still with the living at last accounts, and may not desire to be famous)—sailed ships out of the harbor of San Francisco for many years. He was a stalwart, warm-hearted, eagle-eyed veteran, who had been a sailor nearly fifty years—a sailor from early boyhood. He was a rough, honest creature, full of pluck, and just as full of hard-headed simplicity, too. He hated trifling conventionalities—"business" was the word, with him. He had all a sailor's vindictiveness against the quips and quirks of the law, and steadfastly believed that the first and last aim and object of the law and lawyers was to defeat justice.

He sailed for the Chincha Islands in command of a guano-ship. He had a fine crew, but his negro mate was his pet—on him he had for years lavished his admiration and esteem. It was Capt. Ned's first voyage to the Chinchas, but his fame had gone before him—the fame of being a man who would fight at the dropping of a handkerchief, when imposed upon, and would stand no nonsense. It was a fame well earned. Arrived in the islands, he found that the staple of conversation was the exploits of one Bill Noakes, a bully, the mate of a trading-ship. This man had created a small reign of terror there. At nine o'clock at night, Capt. Ned, all alone, was pacing his deck in the starlight. A form ascended the side, and approached him. Capt. Ned said:

"Who goes there?"

"I'm Bill Noakes, the best man on the islands."

"What do you want aboard this ship?"

"I've heard of Capt. Ned Blakely, and one of us is a better man than 'tother—I'll know which, before I go ashore."

"You have come to the right shop—I'm your man. I'll learn you to come aboard this ship without an *in*vite."

He seized Noakes, backed him against the mainmast, pounded his face to a pulp, and then threw him overboard.

Noakes was not convinced. He returned the next night, got the pulp renewed, and went overboard head first, as before. He was satisfied.

A week after this, while Noakes was carousing with a sailor crowd on shore, at noonday, Capt. Ned's colored mate came along, and Noakes tried to pick a quarrel with him. The negro evaded the trap, and tried to get away. Noakes followed him up; the negro began to run; Noakes fired on him with a revolver and killed him. Half a dozen sea-captains witnessed the whole affair. Noakes retreated to the small after-cabin of his ship, with two other bullies, and gave out that death would be the portion of any man that intruded there. There was no attempt made to follow the villains; there was no disposition to do it, and indeed very little thought of such an enterprise. There were no courts and no officers; there was no government; the islands belonged to Peru, and Peru was far away; she had no official representative on the ground; and neither had any other nation.

However, Capt. Ned was not perplexing his head about such things. They concerned him not. He was boiling with rage and furious for justice. At nine o'clock at night he loaded a double-barreled gun with slugs, fished out a pair of handcuffs, got a ship's lantern, summoned his quartermaster, and went ashore. He said:

"Do you see that ship there at the dock?"

"Ay-ay, sir."

"It's the *Venus.*"

"Ay-ay, sir."

"You—you know *me.*"

"Ay-ay, sir."

"Very well, then. Take the lantern. Carry it just under your chin. I'll walk behind you and rest this gun-barrel on your shoulder, p'inting forward—so. Keep your lantern well up, so's I can see things ahead of you good. I'm going to march in on Noakes—and take him—and jug the other chaps. If you flinch—well, you know *me.*"

"Ay-ay, sir."

In this order they filed aboard softly, arrived at Noakes's den, the quartermaster pushed the door open, and the lantern revealed the three desperadoes sitting on the floor. Capt. Ned said:

"I'm Ned Blakely. I've got you under fire. Don't you move without orders—any of you. You two kneel down in the corner; faces to the wall —now. Bill Noakes, put these handcuffs on; now come up close. Quartermaster, fasten 'em. All right. Don't stir, sir. Quartermaster, put the key in the outside of the door. Now, men, I'm going to lock you two in; and if you try to burst through this door—well, you've heard of *me.* Bill Noakes, fall in ahead, and march. All set. Quartermaster, lock the door."

Noakes spent the night on board Blakely's ship, a prisoner under strict guard. Early in the morning Capt. Ned called in all the sea-captains in the harbor and invited them, with nautical ceremony, to be present on board his ship at nine o'clock to witness the hanging of Noakes at the yard-arm!

"What! The man has not been tried."

"Of course he hasn't. But didn't he kill the nigger?"

"Certainly he did; but you are not thinking of hanging him without a trial?"

"*Trial!* What do I want to try him for, if he killed the nigger?"

"Oh, Capt. Ned, this will *never* do. Think how it will sound."

"Sound be hanged! *Didn't he kill the nigger?*"

"Certainly, certainly, Capt. Ned—nobody denies that—but—"

"Then I'm going to *hang* him, that's all. Everybody I've talked to talks just the same way you do. Everybody says he killed the nigger, everybody knows he killed the nigger, and yet every lubber of you wants him *tried* for it. I don't understand such bloody foolishness as that. *Tried!* Mind you, I don't object to trying him if it's got to be done to give satisfaction; and I'll be there, and chip in and help, too; but put it off till afternoon—put it off till afternoon, for I'll have my hands middling full till after the burying—"

"Why, what do you mean? Are you going to hang him *anyhow*—and try him afterward?"

"Didn't I *say* I was going to hang him? I never saw such people as you. What's the difference? You ask a favor, and then you ain't satisfied when you get it. Before or after's all one—*you* know how the trial will go. He killed the nigger. Say—I must be going. If your mate would like to come to the hanging, fetch him along. I like him."

There was a stir in the camp. The captains came in a body and pleaded with Capt. Ned not to do this rash thing. They promised that they would create a court composed of captains of the best character; they would impanel a jury; they would conduct everything in a way becoming the serious nature of the business in hand, and give the case an impartial hearing and the accused a fair trial. And they said it would be murder, and punishable by the American courts if he persisted and hung the accused on his ship. They pleaded hard. Capt. Ned said:

"Gentlemen, I'm not stubborn and I'm not unreasonable. I'm always willing to do just as near right as I can. How long will it take?"

"Probably only a little while."

"And can I take him up the shore and hang him as soon as you are done?"

"If he is proven guilty he shall be hanged without unnecessary delay."

"*If* he's proven guilty. Great Neptune, *ain't* he guilty? This beats my time. Why you all *know* he's guilty."

But at last they satisfied him that they were projecting nothing underhanded. Then he said:

"Well, all right. You go on and try him and I'll go down and overhaul his conscience and prepare him to go—like enough he needs it, and I don't want to send him off without a show for hereafter."

This was another obstacle. They finally convinced him that it was necessary to have the accused in court. Then they said they would send a guard to bring him.

"No, sir, I prefer to fetch him myself—he don't get out of *my* hands. Besides, I've got to go to the ship to get a rope, anyway."

The court assembled with due ceremony, impaneled a jury, and presently Capt. Ned entered, leading the prisoner with one hand and carrying a Bible and a rope in the other. He seated himself by the side of his captive and told the court to "up anchor and make sail." Then he turned a searching eye on the jury, and detected Noakes's friends, the two bullies. He strode over and said to them confidentially:

"You're here to interfere, you see. Now you vote right, do you hear? —or else there'll be a double-barreled inquest here when this trial's off, and your remainders will go home in a couple of baskets."

The caution was not without fruit. The jury was a unit—the verdict, "Guilty."

Capt. Ned sprung to his feet and said:

"Come along—you're my meat *now,* my lad, anyway. Gentlemen, you've done yourselves proud. I invite you all to come and see that I do it all straight. Follow me to the cañon, a mile above here."

The court informed him that a sheriff had been appointed to do the hanging, and—

Capt. Ned's patience was at an end. His wrath was boundless. The subject of a sheriff was judiciously dropped.

When the crowd arrived at the cañon, Capt. Ned climbed a tree and arranged the halter, then came down and noosed his man. He opened his Bible, and laid aside his hat. Selecting a chapter at random, he read it through, in a deep bass voice and with sincere solemnity. Then he said:

"Lad, you are about to go aloft and give an account of yourself; and the lighter a man's manifest is, as far as sin's concerned, the better for him. Make a clean breast, man, and carry a log with you that 'll bear inspection. You killed the nigger?"

No reply. A long pause.

The captain read another chapter, pausing, from time to time, to impress the effect. Then he talked an earnest, persuasive sermon to him, and ended by repeating the question:

"Did you kill the nigger?"

No reply—other than a malignant scowl. The captain now read the first and second chapters of Genesis, with deep feeling, paused a moment, closed the book reverently, and said with a perceptible savor of satisfaction:

"There. Four chapters. There's few that would have took the pains with you that I have."

Then he swung up the condemned, and made the rope fast; stood by and timed him half an hour with his watch, and then delivered the body to the court. A little after, as he stood contemplating the motionless figure, a doubt came into his face; evidently he felt a twinge of conscience—a misgiving—and he said with a sigh:

"Well, p'raps I ought to burnt him, maybe. But I was trying to do for the best."

When the history of this affair reached California (it was in the "early days") it made a deal of talk, but did not diminish the captain's popularity in any degree. It increased it, indeed. California had a population then that "inflicted" justice after a fashion that was simplicity and primitiveness itself, and could therefore admire appreciatively when the same fashion was followed elsewhere.

From ROUGHING IT, 1872

The Trials of Simon Erickson

We stopped some time at one of the plantations, to rest ourselves and refresh the horses. We had a chatty conversation with several gentlemen present; but there was one person, a middle-aged man, with an absent look in his face, who simply glanced up, gave us good-day and lapsed again into the meditations which our coming had interrupted. The planters whispered us not to mind him—crazy. They said he was in the Islands[1] for his health; was a preacher; his home, Michigan. They said that if he woke up presently and fell to talking about a correspondence which he had some time held with Mr. Greeley about a trifle of some kind, we must humor him and listen with interest; and we must humor his fancy that this correspondence was the talk of the world.

It was easy to see that he was a gentle creature and that his madness had nothing vicious in it. He looked pale, and a little worn, as if with perplexing thought and anxiety of mind. He sat a long time, looking at the floor, and at intervals muttering to himself and nodding his head acquiescingly or shaking it in mild protest. He was lost in his thought, or in his memories. We continued our talk with the planters, branching from subject to subject. But at last the word "circumstance," casually dropped, in the course of conversation, attracted his attention and

[1] Hawaiian Islands

brought an eager look into his countenance. He faced about in his chair and said:

"Circumstance? What circumstance? Ah, I know—I know too well. So you have heard of it too." [With a sigh.] "Well, no matter—all the world has heard of it. All the world. The whole world. It is a large world, too, for a thing to travel so far in—now, isn't it? Yes, yes—the Greeley correspondence with Erickson has created the saddest and bitterest controversy on both sides of the ocean—and still they keep it up! It makes us famous, but at what a sorrowful sacrifice! I was so sorry when I heard that it had caused that bloody and distressful war over there in Italy. It was little comfort to me, after so much bloodshed, to know that the victors sided with me, and the vanquished with Greeley. It is little comfort to know that Horace Greeley is responsible for the battle of Sadowa, and not me. Queen Victoria wrote me that she felt just as I did about it—she said that as much as she was opposed to Greeley and the spirit he showed in the correspondence with me, she would not have had Sadowa happen for hundreds of dollars. I can show you her letter, if you would like to see it. But, gentlemen, much as you may think you know about that unhappy correspondence, you cannot know the *straight* of it till you hear it from my lips. It has always been garbled in the journals, and even in history. Yes, even in history—think of it! Let me—*please* let me, give you the matter, exactly as it occurred. I truly will not abuse your confidence."

Then he leaned forward, all interest, all earnestness, and told his story—and told it appealingly, too, and yet in the simplest and most unpretentious way; indeed, in such a way as to suggest to one, all the time, that this was a faithful, honorable witness, giving evidence in the sacred interest of justice, and under oath. He said:

Mrs. Beazeley—Mrs. Jackson Beazeley, widow, of the village of Campbellton, Kansas—wrote me about a matter which was near her heart—a matter which many might think trivial, but to her it was a thing of deep concern. I was living in Michigan, then—serving in the ministry. She was, and is, an estimable woman—a woman to whom poverty and hardship have proven incentives to industry, in place of discouragements. Her only treasure was her son William, a youth just verging upon manhood; religious, amiable, and sincerely attached to agriculture. He was the widow's comfort and her pride. And so, moved by her love for him, she wrote me about a matter, as I have said before, which lay near her heart—because it lay near her boy's. She desired me to confer with Mr. Greeley about turnips. Turnips were the dream of her child's young

ambition. While other youths were frittering away in frivolous amuse-
ments the precious years of budding vigor which God had given
them for useful preparation, this boy was patiently enriching his mind
with information concerning turnips. The sentiment which he felt toward the turnip was akin to adoration. He could not think of the turnip
without emotion; he could not speak of it calmly; he could not con-
template it without exaltation; he could not eat it without shedding
tears. All the poetry in his sensitive nature was in sympathy with the
gracious vegetable. With the earliest pipe of dawn he sought his patch,
and when the curtaining night drove him from it he shut himself up
with his books and garnered statistics till sleep overcame him. On rainy
days he sat and talked hours together with his mother about turnips.
When company came, he made it his loving duty to put aside everything else and converse with them all the day long of his great joy in
the turnip. And yet, was this joy rounded and complete? Was there no
secret alloy of unhappiness in it? Alas, there was. There was a canker
gnawing at his heart; the noblest inspiration of his soul eluded his endeavor—*viz.*, he could not make of the turnip a climbing vine. Months
went by; the bloom forsook his cheek, the fire faded out of his eye;
sighings and abstraction usurped the place of smiles and cheerful converse. But a watchful eye noted these things, and in time a motherly
sympathy unsealed the secret. Hence the letter to me. She pleaded for
attention—she said her boy was dying by inches.

I was a stranger to Mr. Greeley, but what of that? The matter was
urgent. I wrote and begged him to solve the difficult problem if possible, and save the student's life. My interest grew, until it partook
of the anxiety of the mother. I waited in much suspense. At last the
answer came.

I found that I could not read it readily, the handwriting being unfamiliar and my emotions somewhat wrought up. It seemed to refer
in part to the boy's case, but chiefly to other and irrelevant matters
—such as paving-stones, electricity, oysters, and something which I took
to be "absolution" or "agrarianism," I could not be certain which; still,
these appeared to be simply casual mentions, nothing more; friendly
in spirit, without doubt, but lacking the connection or coherence necessary to make them useful. I judged that my understanding was affected
by my feelings, and so laid the letter away till morning.

In the morning I read it again, but with difficulty and uncertainty
still, for I had lost some little rest and my mental vision seemed clouded.
The note was more connected, now, but did not meet the emergency

it was expected to meet. It was too discursive. It appeared to read as follows, though I was not certain of some of the words:

Polygamy dissembles majesty; extracts redeem polarity; causes hitherto exist. Ovations pursue wisdom, or warts inherit and condemn. Boston, botany, cakes, folony undertakes, but who shall allay? We fear not. Yrxwly,

HEVACE EVEELOJ

But there did not seem to be a word about turnips. There seemed to be no suggestion as to how they might be made to grow like vines. There was not even a reference to the Beazeleys. I slept upon the matter; I ate no supper, neither any breakfast next morning. So I resumed my work with a brain refreshed, and was very hopeful. *Now* the letter took a different aspect—all save the signature, which latter I judged to be only a harmless affectation of Hebrew. The epistle was necessarily from Mr. Greeley, for it bore the printed heading of *The Tribune*, and I had written to no one else there. The letter, I say, had taken a different aspect, but still its language was eccentric and avoided the issue. It now appeared to say:

Bolivia extemporizes mackerel; borax esteems polygamy; sausages wither in the east. Creation perdu, is done; for woes inherent one can damn. Buttons, buttons, corks, geology underrates but we shall allay. My beer's out. Yrxwly,

HEVACE EVEELOJ

I was evidently overworked. My comprehension was impaired. Therefore I gave two days to recreation, and then returned to my task greatly refreshed. The letter now took this form:

Poultices do sometimes choke swine; tulips reduce posterity; causes leather to resist. Our notions empower wisdom, her let's afford while we can. Butter but any cakes, fill any undertaker, we'll wean him from his filly. We feel hot. Yrxwly,

HEVACE EVEELOJ

I was still not satisfied. These generalities did not meet the question. They were crisp, and vigorous, and delivered with a confidence that almost compelled conviction; but at such a time as this, with a human life at stake, they seemed inappropriate, worldly, and in bad taste. At any other time I would have been not only glad, but proud, to receive from a man like Mr. Greeley a letter of this kind, and would have studied it earnestly and tried to improve myself all I could; but now, with that poor boy in his far home languishing for relief, I had no heart for learning.

Three days passed by, and I read the note again. Again its tenor had changed. It now appeared to say:

Potations do sometimes wake wines; turnips restrain passion; causes necessary to state. Infest the poor widow; her lord's effects will be void. But dirt, bathing, etc., etc., followed unfairly, will worm him from his folly—so swear not. Yrxwly,

HEVACE EVEELOJ

This was more like it. But I was unable to proceed. I was too much worn. The word "turnips" brought temporary joy and encouragement, but my strength was so much impaired, and the delay might be so perilous for the boy, that I relinquished the idea of pursuing the translation further, and resolved to do what I ought to have done at first. I sat down and wrote Mr. Greeley as follows:

Dear Sir: I fear I do not entirely comprehend your kind note. It cannot be possible, Sir, that "turnips restrain passion"—at least the study or contemplation of turnips cannot—for it is this very employment that has scorched our poor friend's mind and sapped his bodily strength.— But if they do restrain it, will you bear with us a little further and explain how they should be prepared? I observe that you say "causes necessary to state," but you have omitted to state them.

Under a misapprehension, you seem to attribute to me interested motives in this matter—to call it by no harsher term. But I assure you, dear sir, that if I seem to be "infesting the widow," it is all seeming, and void of reality. It is from no seeking of mine that I am in this position. She asked me, herself, to write you. I never have infested her—indeed I scarcely know her. I do not infest anybody. I try to go along, in my humble way, doing as near right as I can, never harming anybody, and never throwing out insinuations. As for "her lord and his effects," they are of no interest to me. I trust I have effects enough of my own—shall endeavor to get along with them, at any rate, and not go mousing around to get hold of somebody's that are "void." But do you not see?— this woman is a widow—she has no "lord." He is dead—or pretended to be, when they buried him. Therefore, no amount of "dirt, bathing, etc., etc.," howsoever "unfairly followed" will be likely to "worm him from his folly"—if being dead and a ghost is "folly." Your closing remark is as un-

kind as it was uncalled for; and if report says true you might have applied it to yourself, sir, with more point and less impropriety.

Very Truly Yours,

SIMON ERICKSON

In the course of a few days, Mr. Greeley did what would have saved a world of trouble and much mental and bodily suffering and misunderstanding, if he had done it sooner. To wit, he sent an intelligible rescript or translation of his original note, made in a plain hand by his clerk. Then the mystery cleared, and I saw that his heart had been right, all the time. I will recite the note in its clarified form:

[Translation]

Potatoes do sometimes make vines; turnips remain passive: cause unnecessary to state. Inform the poor widow her lad's efforts will be vain. But diet, bathing, etc., etc., followed uniformly, will wean him from his folly—so fear not. Yours,

HORACE GREELEY

But alas, it was too late, gentlemen—too late. The criminal delay had done its work—young Beazeley was no more. His spirit had taken its flight to a land where all anxieties shall be charmed away, all desires gratified, all ambitions realized. Poor lad, they laid him to his rest with a turnip in each hand.

So ended Erickson, and lapsed again into nodding, mumbling, and abstraction. The company broke up, and left him so. . . . But they did not say what drove him crazy. In the momentary confusion, I forgot to ask.

From ROUGHING IT, 1872

A True Story

REPEATED WORD FOR WORD AS I HEARD IT

It was summer-time, and twilight. We were sitting on the porch of the farmhouse, on the summit of the hill, and "Aunt Rachel" was sitting respectfully below our level, on the steps—for she was our servant, and colored. She was of mighty frame and stature; she was sixty years old, but her eye was undimmed and her strength unabated. She was a cheerful, hearty soul, and it was no more trouble for her to laugh than it is for a bird to sing. She was under fire now, as usual when the day was done. That is to say, she was being chaffed without mercy, and was enjoying it. She would let off peal after peal of laughter, and then sit with her face in her hands and shake with throes of enjoyment which she could no longer get breath enough to express. At such a moment as this a thought occurred to me, and I said:

"Aunt Rachel, how is it that you've lived sixty years and never had any trouble?"

She stopped quaking. She paused, and there was a moment of silence. She turned her face over her shoulder toward me, and said, without even a smile in her voice:

"Misto C——, is you in 'arnest?"

It surprised me a good deal; and it sobered my manner and my speech, too. I said:

"Why, I thought—that is, I meant—why, you *can't* have had any trouble. I've never heard you sigh, and never seen your eye when there wasn't a laugh in it."

She faced fairly around now, and was full of earnestness.

"Has I had any trouble? Misto C——, I's gwyne to tell you, den I leave it to you. I was bawn down 'mongst de slaves; I knows all 'bout slavery, 'case I ben one of 'em my own se'f. Well, sah, my ole man—dat's my husban'—he was lovin' an' kind to me, jist as kind as you is to yo' own wife. An' we had chil'en—seven chil'en—an' we loved dem chil'en jist de same as you loves yo' chil'en. Dey was black, but de Lord can't make no chil'en so black but what dey mother loves 'em an' wouldn't give 'em up, no, not for anything dat's in dis whole world.

"Well, sah, I was raised in ole Fo'ginny, but my mother she was raised in Maryland; an' my *souls!* she was turrible when she'd git started! My *lan'!* but she'd make de fur fly! When she'd git into dem tantrums, she always had one word dat she said. She'd straighten herse'f up an' put her fists in her hips an' say, 'I want you to understan' dat I wa'n't bawn in the mash to be fool' by trash! I's one o' de ole Blue Hen's Chickens, *I* is!' 'Ca'se, you see, dat's what folks dat's bawn in Maryland calls deyselves, an' dey's proud of it. Well, dat was her word. I don't ever forgit it, beca'se she said it so much, an' beca'se she said it one day when my little Henry tore his wris' awful, and most busted his head, right up at de top of his forehead, an' de niggers didn't fly aroun' fas' enough to 'tend to him. An' when dey talk' back at her, she up an' she says, 'Look-a-heah!' she says, 'I want you niggers to understan' dat I wa'n't bawn in de mash to be fool' by trash! I's one o' de ole Blue Hen's Chickens, *I* is!' an' den she clar' dat kitchen an' bandage' up de chile herse'f. So I says dat word, too, when I's riled.

"Well, bymeby my ole mistis say she's broke, an' she got to sell all de niggers on de place. An' when I heah dat dey gwyne to sell us all off at oction in Richmon', oh, de good gracious! I know what dat mean!"

Aunt Rachel had gradually risen, while she warmed to her subject, and now she towered above us, black against the stars.

"Dey put chains on us an' put us on a stan' as high as dis po'ch—twenty foot high—an' all de people stood aroun', crowds an' crowds. An' dey'd come up dah an' look at us all roun', an' squeeze our arm, an' make us git up an' walk, an' den say, 'Dis one too ole,' or 'Dis one lame,' or 'Dis one don't 'mount to much.' An' dey sole my ole man, an' took him away, an' dey begin to sell my chil'en an' take *dem* away, an' I begin to cry; an' de man say, 'Shet up yo' damn blubberin',' an' hit me on de mouf wid his han'. An' when de las' one was gone but my little Henry, I grab' *him* clost up to my breas' so, an' I ris up an' says, 'You sha'n't take him away,' I says; 'I'll kill de man dat tetches him!' I says. But my little Henry whisper an' say, 'I gwyne to run away, an' den I work an' buy yo' freedom.' Oh, bless de chile, he always so good! But dey got him—dey got him, de men did; but I took and tear de clo'es mos' off of 'em an' beat 'em over de head wid my chain; an' *dey* give it to *me*, too, but I didn't mine dat.

"Well, dah was my ole man gone, an' all my chil'en, all my seven chil'en—an' six of 'em I hain't set eyes on ag'in to dis day, an' dat's twenty-two year ago las' Easter. De man dat bought me b'long' in Newbern, an' he took me dah. Well, bymeby de years roll on an' de waw come. My marster he was a Confedrit colonel, an' I was his family's cook. So when de Unions took dat town, dey all run away an' lef' me all by myse'f wid de other niggers in dat mons'us big house. So de big Union officers move in dah, an' dey ask me would I cook for *dem*. 'Lord bless you,' says I, 'dat's what I's *for*.'

"Dey wa'n't no small-fry officers, mine you, dey was de biggest dey *is;* an' de way dey made dem sojers mosey roun'! De Gen'l he tole me to boss dat kitchen; an' he say, 'If anybody come meddlin' wid you, you jist make 'em walk chalk; don't you be afeared,' he say; 'you's 'mong frens now.'

"Well, I thinks to myse'f, if my little Henry ever got a chance to run away, he'd make to de Norf, o' course. So one day I comes in dah whar

de big officers was, in de parlor, an' I drops a kurtchy, so, an' I up an'
tole 'em 'bout my Henry, dey a-listenin' to my troubles jist de same as if
I was white folks; an' I says, 'What I come for is beca'se if he got away
and got up Norf whar you gemmen comes from, you might 'a' seen him,
maybe, an' could tell me so as I could fine him ag'in; he was very little,
an' he had a sk-yar on his lef' wris' an' at de top of his forehead.' Den dey
look mournful, an' de Gen'l says, 'How long sence you los' him?' an' I say,
'Thirteen year.' Den de Gen'l say, 'He wouldn't be little no mo' now—
he's a man!'

"I never thought o' dat befo'! He was only dat little feller to *me* yit. I
never thought 'bout him growin' up an' bein' big. But I see it den. None
o' de gemmen had run acrost him, so dey couldn't do nothin' for me.
But all dat time, do' *I* didn't know it, my Henry *was* run off to de Norf,
years an' years, an' he was a barber, too, an' worked for hisse'f. An' bymeby, when de waw come he ups an' he says: 'I's done barberin',' he
says, 'I's gwyne to fine my ole mammy, less'n she's dead.' So he sole out
an' went to whar dey was recruitin', an' hired hisse'f out to de colonel
for his servant; an' den he went all froo de battles everywhah, huntin'
for his ole mammy; yes, indeedy, he'd hire to fust one officer an' den
another, tell he'd ransacked de whole Souf; but you see *I* didn't know
nuffin 'bout *dis*. How was *I* gwyne to know it?

"Well, one night we had a big sojer ball; de sojers dah at Newbern
was always havin' balls an' carryin' on. Dey had 'em in my kitchen,
heaps o' times, 'ca'se it was so big. Mine you, I was *down* on sich doin's;
beca'se my place was wid de officers, an' it rasp me to have dem common sojers cavortin' roun' my kitchen like dat. But I alway' stood aroun'
an' kep' things straight, I did; an' sometimes dey'd git my dander up,
an' den I'd make 'em clar dat kitchen, mine I *tell* you!

"Well, one night—it was a Friday night—dey comes a whole platoon
f'm a *nigger* ridgment dat was on guard at de house—de house was
headquarters, you know—an' den I was jist a-*bilin'*! Mad? I was jist
a-*boomin'*! I swelled aroun', an' swelled aroun'; I jist was a-itchin' for 'em
to do somefin for to start me. An' dey was a-waltzin' an' a-dancin'! *my!*
but dey was havin' a time! an' I jist a-swellin' an' a-swellin' up! Pooty
soon, 'long comes *sich* a spruce young nigger a-sailin' down de room wid
a yaller wench roun' de wais'; an' roun' an' roun' an' roun' dey went,
enough to make a body drunk to look at 'em; an' when dey got abreas' o'
me, dey went to kin' o' balancin' aroun' fust on one leg an' den on t'other,
an' smilin' at my big red turban, an' makin' fun, an' I ups an' says '*Git*
along wid you!—rubbage!' De young man's face kin' o' changed, all of a
sudden, for 'bout a second, but den he went to smilin' ag'in, same as he

was befo'. Well, 'bout dis time, in comes some niggers dat played music
and b'long' to de ban', an' dey *never* could git along widout puttin' on
airs. An' de very fust air dey put on dat night, I lit into 'em! Dey laughed,
an' dat made me wuss. De res' o' de niggers got to laughin', an' den my
soul *alive* but I was hot! My eye was jist a-blazin'! I jist straightened
myself up so—jist as I is now, plum to de ceilin', mos'—an' I digs my fists
into my hips, an' I says, 'Look-a-heah!' I says, 'I want you niggers to
understan' dat I wa'n't bawn in de mash to be fool' by trash! I's one o' de
ole Blue Hen's Chickens, *I* is!' an' den I see dat young man stan' a-starin'
an' stiff, lookin' kin' o' up at de ceilin' like he fo'got somefin, an' couldn't
'member it no mo'. Well, I jist march' on dem niggers—so, lookin' like a
gen'l—an' dey jist cave' away befo' me an' out at de do'. An' as dis young
man was a-goin' out, I heah him say to another nigger, 'Jim,' he says, 'you
go 'long an' tell de cap'n I be on han' 'bout eight o'clock in de mawnin';
dey's somefin on my mine,' he says; 'I don't sleep no mo' dis night. You
go 'long,' he says, 'an' leave me by my own se'f.'

"Dis was 'bout one o'clock in de mawnin'. Well, 'bout seven, I was up
an' on han', gittin' de officers' breakfast. I was a-stoopin' down by de
stove—jist so, same as if yo' foot was de stove—an' I'd opened de stove
do' wid my right han'—so, pushin' it back, jist as I pushes yo' foot—an' I'd
jist got de pan o' hot biscuits in my han' an' was 'bout to raise up, when
I see a black face come aroun' under mine, an' de eyes a-lookin' up into
mine, jist as I's a-lookin' up clost under yo' face now; an' I jist stopped
right dah, an' never budged! jist gazed an' gazed so; an' de pan begin to
tremble, an' all of a sudden I *knowed!* De pan drop' on de flo' an' I grab
his lef' han' an' shove back his sleeve—jist so, as I's doin' to you—an'
den I goes for his forehead an' push de hair back so, an' 'Boy!' I says,
'if you an't my Henry, what is you doin' wid dis welt on yo' wris' an' dat
sk-yar on yo' forehead? De Lord God ob heaven be praise', I got my
own ag'in!'

"Oh no, Misto C——, *I* hain't had no trouble. An' no *joy!*"

1874

Experience of the McWilliamses
with Membranous Croup

As related to the author of this book by Mr. McWilliams, a pleasant New York gentleman whom the said author met by chance on a journey.

Well, to go back to where I was before I digressed to explain to you how that frightful and incurable disease, membranous croup, was ravaging the town and driving all mothers mad with terror, I called Mrs. McWilliams's attention to little Penelope, and said:

"Darling, I wouldn't let that child be chewing that pine stick if I were you."

"Precious, where is the harm in it?" said she, but at the same time preparing to take away the stick—for women cannot receive even the most palpably judicious suggestion without arguing it; that is, married women.

I replied:

"Love, it is notorious that pine is the least nutritious wood that a child can eat."

My wife's hand paused, in the act of taking the stick, and returned itself to her lap. She bridled perceptibly, and said:

"Hubby, you know better than that. You know you do. Doctors *all* say that the turpentine in pine wood is good for weak back and the kidneys."

"Ah—I was under a misapprehension. I did not know that the child's kidneys and spine were affected, and that the family physician had recommended—"

"Who said the child's spine and kidneys were affected?"

"My love, you intimated it."

"The idea! I never intimated anything of the kind."

"Why, my dear, it hasn't been two minutes since you said—"

"Bother what I said! I don't care what I did say. There isn't any harm in the child's chewing a bit of pine stick if she wants to, and you know it perfectly well. And she *shall* chew it, too. So there, now!"

"Say no more, my dear. I now see the force of your reasoning, and I will go and order two or three cords of the best pine wood to-day. No child of mine shall want while I—"

"Oh, *please* go along to your office and let me have some peace. A body can never make the simplest remark but you must take it up and go to arguing and arguing and arguing till you don't know what you are talking about, and you *never* do."

"Very well, it shall be as you say. But there is a want of logic in your last remark which—"

However, she was gone with a flourish before I could finish, and had taken the child with her. That night at dinner she confronted me with a face as white as a sheet:

"Oh, Mortimer, there's another! Little Georgie Gordon is taken."

"Membranous croup?"

"Membranous croup."

"Is there any hope for him?"

"None in the wide world. Oh, what is to become of us!"

By and by a nurse brought in our Penelope to say good night and offer the customary prayer at the mother's knee. In the midst of "Now I lay me down to sleep," she gave a slight cough! My wife fell back like one stricken with death. But the next moment she was up and brimming with the activities which terror inspires.

She commanded that the child's crib be removed from the nursery to our bedroom; and she went along to see the order executed. She took me with her, of course. We got matters arranged with speed. A cot-bed was put up in my wife's dressing-room for the nurse. But now Mrs. Mc-Williams said we were too far away from the other baby, and what if *he* were to have the symptoms in the night—and she blanched again, poor thing.

We then restored the crib and the nurse to the nursery and put up a bed for ourselves in a room adjoining.

Presently, however, Mrs. McWilliams said suppose the baby should catch it from Penelope? This thought struck a new panic to her heart, and the tribe of us could not get the crib out of the nursery again fast enough to satisfy my wife, though she assisted in her own person and well-nigh pulled the crib to pieces in her frantic hurry.

We moved down-stairs; but there was no place there to stow the nurse, and Mrs. McWilliams said the nurse's experience would be an inestimable help. So we returned, bag and baggage, to our own bed-room once more, and felt a great gladness, like storm-buffeted birds that have found their nest again.

Mrs. McWilliams sped to the nursery to see how things were going on there. She was back in a moment with a new dread. She said:

"What *can* make Baby sleep so?"

I said:

"Why, my darling, Baby *always* sleeps like a graven image."

"I know. I know; but there's something peculiar about his sleep now. He seems to—to—he seems to breathe so *regularly*. Oh, this is dreadful."

"But, my dear, he always breathes regularly."

"Oh, I know it, but there's something frightful about it now. His nurse is too young and inexperienced. Maria shall stay there with her, and be on hand if anything happens."

"That is a good idea, but who will help *you*?"

"You can help me all I want. I wouldn't allow anybody to do anything but myself, anyhow, at such a time as this."

I said I would feel mean to lie abed and sleep, and leave her to watch and toil over our little patient all the weary night. But she reconciled me to it. So old Maria departed and took up her ancient quarters in the nursery.

Penelope coughed twice in her sleep.

"Oh, why *don't* that doctor come! Mortimer, this room is too warm. This room is certainly too warm. Turn off the register—quick!"

I shut it off, glancing at the thermometer at the same time, and wondering to myself if 70 *was* too warm for a sick child.

The coachman arrived from down-town now with the news that our physician was ill and confined to his bed. Mrs. McWilliams turned a dead eye upon me, and said in a dead voice:

"There is a Providence in it. It is foreordained. He never was sick before. Never. We have not been living as we ought to live, Mortimer. Time and time again I have told you so. Now you see the result. Our child will never get well. Be thankful if you can forgive yourself; I never can forgive *myself*."

I said, without intent to hurt, but with heedless choice of words, that I could not see that we had been living such an abandoned life.

"*Mortimer!* Do you want to bring the judgment upon Baby, too!" Then she began to cry, but suddenly exclaimed:

"The doctor must have sent medicines!"

I said:

"Certainly. They are here. I was only waiting for you to give me a chance."

"Well do give them to me! Don't you know that every moment is precious now? But what was the use in sending medicines, when he *knows* that the disease is incurable?"

I said that while there was life there was hope.

"Hope! Mortimer, you know no more what you are talking about than the child unborn. If you would— As I live, the directions say give one teaspoonful once an hour! Once an hour!—as if we had a whole year before us to save the child in! Mortimer, please hurry. Give the poor perishing thing a tablespoonful, and *try* to be quick!"

"Why, my dear, a tablespoonful might—"

"*Don't* drive me frantic! . . . There, there, there, my precious, my own; it's nasty bitter stuff, but it's good for Nelly—good for mother's precious darling; and it will make her well. There, there, there, put the little head on mamma's breast and go to sleep, and pretty soon—oh, I know she can't live till morning! Mortimer, a tablespoonful every half-hour will— Oh, the child needs belladonna, too; I know she does—and aconite. Get them, Mortimer. Now do let me have my way. You know nothing about these things."

We now went to bed, placing the crib close to my wife's pillow. All this turmoil had worn upon me, and within two minutes I was something more than half asleep. Mrs. McWilliams roused me:

"Darling, is that register turned on?"

"No."

"I thought as much. Please turn it on at once. This room is cold."

I turned it on, and presently fell asleep again. I was aroused once more:

"Dearie, would you mind moving the crib to your side of the bed? It is nearer the register."

I moved it, but had a collision with the rug and woke up the child. I dozed off once more, while my wife quieted the sufferer. But in a little while these words came murmuring remotely through the fog of my drowsiness:

"Mortimer, if we only had some goose grease—will you ring?"

I climbed dreamily out, and stepped on a cat, which responded with a protest and would have got a convincing kick for it if a chair had not got it instead.

"Now, Mortimer, why do you want to turn up the gas and wake up the child again?"

"Because I want to see how much I am hurt, Caroline."

"Well, look at the chair, too—I have no doubt it is ruined. Poor cat, suppose you had—"

"Now I am not going to suppose anything about the cat. It never would have occurred if Maria had been allowed to remain here and attend to these duties, which are in her line and are not in mine."

"Now, Mortimer, I should think you would be ashamed to make a remark like that. It is a pity if you cannot do the few little things I ask of you at such an awful time as this when our child—"

"There, there, I will do anything you want. But I can't raise anybody with this bell. They're all gone to bed. Where is the goose grease?"

"On the mantelpiece in the nursery. If you'll step there and speak to Maria—"

I fetched the goose grease and went to sleep again. Once more I was called:

"Mortimer, I so hate to disturb you, but the room is still too cold for me to try to apply this stuff. Would you mind lighting the fire? It is all ready to touch a match to."

I dragged myself out and lit the fire, and then sat down disconsolate.

"Mortimer, don't sit there and catch your death of cold. Come to bed."

As I was stepping in she said:

"But wait a moment. Please give the child some more of the medicine."

Which I did. It was a medicine which made a child more or less lively; so my wife made use of its waking interval to strip it and grease it all over with the goose oil. I was soon asleep once more, but once more I had to get up.

"Mortimer, I feel a draft. I feel it distinctly. There is nothing so bad for this disease as a draft. Please move the crib in front of the fire."

I did it; and collided with the rug again, which I threw in the fire. Mrs. McWilliams sprang out of bed and rescued it and we had some words. I had another trifling interval of sleep, and then got up, by request, and constructed a flax-seed poultice. This was placed upon the child's breast and left there to do its healing work.

A wood-fire is not a permanent thing. I got up every twenty minutes and renewed ours, and this gave Mrs. McWilliams the opportunity to shorten the times of giving the medicines by ten minutes, which was a great satisfaction to her. Now and then, between times, I reorganized the flax-seed poultices, and applied sinapisms and other sorts of blisters where unoccupied places could be found upon the child. Well, toward morning the wood gave out and my wife wanted me to go down cellar and get some more. I said:

"My dear, it is a laborious job, and the child must be nearly warm enough, with her extra clothing. Now mightn't we put on another layer of poultices and—"

I did not finish, because I was interrupted. I lugged wood up from below for some little time, and then turned in and fell to snoring as only a man can whose strength is all gone and whose soul is worn out. Just at broad daylight I felt a grip on my shoulder that brought me to my senses suddenly. My wife was glaring down upon me and gasping. As soon as she could command her tongue she said:

"It is all over! All over! The child's perspiring! What *shall* we do?"

"Mercy, how you terrify me! *I* don't know what we ought to do. Maybe if we scraped her and put her in the draft again—"

"Oh, idiot! There is not a moment to lose! Go for the doctor. Go yourself. Tell him he *must* come, dead or alive."

I dragged that poor sick man from his bed and brought him. He looked at the child and said she was not dying. This was joy unspeakable to me, but it made my wife as mad as if he had offered her a personal affront. Then he said the child's cough was only caused by some trifling irritation or other in the throat. At this I thought my wife had a mind to show him the door. Now the doctor said he would make the child cough harder and dislodge the trouble. So he gave her something that sent her into a spasm of coughing, and presently up came a little wood splinter or so.

"This child has no membranous croup," said he. "She has been chewing a bit of pine shingle or something of the kind, and got some little slivers in her throat. They won't do her any hurt."

"No," said I, "I can well believe that. Indeed, the turpentine that is in them is very good for certain sorts of diseases that are peculiar to children. My wife will tell you so."

But she did not. She turned away in disdain and left the room; and since that time there is one episode in our life which we never refer to. Hence the tide of our days flows by in deep and untroubled serenity.

Very few married men have such an experience as McWilliams's, and so the author of this book thought that maybe the novelty of it would give it a passing interest to the reader.

1875

Some Learned Fables
for Good Old Boys and Girls

IN THREE PARTS

PART FIRST   HOW THE ANIMALS OF THE WOOD
SENT OUT A SCIENTIFIC EXPEDITION

Once the creatures of the forest held a great convention and appointed a commission consisting of the most illustrious scientists among them to go forth, clear beyond the forest and out into the unknown and unexplored world, to verify the truth of the matters already taught in their schools and colleges and also to make discoveries. It was the most imposing enterprise of the kind the nation had ever embarked in. True, the government had once sent Dr. Bull Frog, with a picked crew, to hunt for a northwesterly passage through the swamp to the right-hand corner of the wood, and had since sent out many expeditions to hunt for Dr. Bull Frog; but they never could find him, and so government finally gave him up and ennobled his mother to show its gratitude for the services her son had rendered to science. And once government sent Sir Grass Hopper to hunt for the sources of the rill that emptied into the swamp; and afterward sent out many expeditions to hunt for Sir Grass, and at last they were successful—they found his body, but if he had discovered the sources meantime, he did not let on. So government acted handsomely by deceased, and many envied his funeral.

But these expeditions were trifles compared with the present one; for this one comprised among its servants the very greatest among the learned; and besides it was to go to the utterly unvisited regions believed to lie beyond the mighty forest—as we have remarked before. How the members were banqueted, and glorified, and talked about! Everywhere that one of them showed himself, straightway there was a crowd to gape and stare at him.

Finally they set off, and it was a sight to see the long procession of dry-land Tortoises heavily laden with savants, scientific instruments,

Glow-Worms and Fire-Flies for signal service, provisions, Ants and Tumble-Bugs to fetch and carry and delve, Spiders to carry the surveying chain and do other engineering duty, and so forth and so on; and after the Tortoises came another long train of ironclads—stately and spacious Mud Turtles for marine transportation service; and from every Tortoise and every Turtle flaunted a flaming gladiolus or other splendid banner; at the head of the column a great band of Bumble-Bees, Mosquitoes, Katy-Dids, and Crickets discoursed martial music; and the entire train was under the escort and protection of twelve picked regiments of the Army Worm.

At the end of three weeks the expedition emerged from the forest and looked upon the great Unknown World. Their eyes were greeted with an impressive spectacle. A vast level plain stretched before them, watered by a sinuous stream; and beyond there towered up against the sky a long and lofty barrier of some kind, they did not know what. The Tumble-Bug said he believed it was simply land tilted up on its edge, because he knew he could see trees on it. But Professor Snail and the others said:

"You are hired to dig, sir—that is all. We need your muscle, not your brains. When we want your opinion on scientific matters, we will hasten to let you know. Your coolness is intolerable, too—loafing about here meddling with august matters of learning, when the other laborers are pitching camp. Go along and help handle the baggage."

The Tumble-Bug turned on his heel uncrushed, unabashed, observing to himself, "If it isn't land tilted up, let me die the death of the unrighteous."

Professor Bull Frog (nephew of the late explorer) said he believed the ridge was the wall that inclosed the earth. He continued:

"Our fathers have left us much learning, but they had not traveled far, and so we may count this a noble new discovery. We are safe for renown now, even though our labors began and ended with this single achievement. I wonder what this wall is built of? Can it be fungus? Fungus is an honorable good thing to build a wall of."

Professor Snail adjusted his field-glass and examined the rampart critically. Finally he said:

"The fact that it is not diaphanous convinces me that it is a dense vapor formed by the calorification of ascending moisture dephlogisticated by refraction. A few endiometrical experiments would confirm this, but it is not necessary. The thing is obvious."

So he shut up his glass and went into his shell to make a note of the discovery of the world's end, and the nature of it.

"Profound mind!" said Professor Angle-Worm to Professor Field-Mouse; "profound mind! nothing can long remain a mystery to that august brain."

Night drew on apace, the sentinel crickets were posted, the Glow-Worm and Fire-Fly lamps were lighted, and the camp sank to silence and sleep. After breakfast in the morning, the expedition moved on. About noon a great avenue was reached, which had in it two endless parallel bars of some kind of hard black substance, raised the height of the tallest Bull Frog above the general level. The scientists climbed up on these and examined and tested them in various ways. They walked along them for a great distance, but found no end and no break in them. They could arrive at no decision. There was nothing in the records of science that mentioned anything of this kind. But at last the bald and venerable geographer, Professor Mud Turtle, a person who, born poor, and of a drudging low family, had, by his own native force raised himself to the headship of the geographers of his generation, said:

"My friends, we have indeed made a discovery here. We have found in a palpable, compact, and imperishable state what the wisest of our fathers always regarded as a mere thing of the imagination. Humble yourselves, my friends, for we stand in a majestic presence. These are parallels of latitude!"

Every heart and every head was bowed, so awful, so sublime was the magnitude of the discovery. Many shed tears.

The camp was pitched and the rest of the day given up to writing voluminous accounts of the marvel, and correcting astronomical tables to fit it. Toward midnight a demoniacal shriek was heard, then a clattering and rumbling noise, and the next instant a vast terrific eye shot by, with a long tail attached, and disappeared in the gloom, still uttering triumphant shrieks.

The poor camp laborers were stricken to the heart with fright, and stampeded for the high grass in a body. But not the scientists. They had no superstitions. They calmly proceeded to exchange theories. The ancient geographer's opinion was asked. He went into his shell and deliberated long and profoundly. When he came out at last, they all knew by his worshiping countenance that he brought light. Said he:

"Give thanks for this stupendous thing which we have been permitted to witness. It is the Vernal Equinox!"

There were shoutings and great rejoicings.

"But," said the Angle-Worm, uncoiling after reflection, "this is dead summer-time."

"Very well," said the Turtle, "we are far from our region; the season differs with the difference of time between the two points."

"Ah, true. True enough. But it is night. How should the sun pass in the night?"

"In these distant regions he doubtless passes always in the night at this hour."

"Yes, doubtless that is true. But it being night, how is it that we could see him?"

"It is a great mystery. I grant that. But I am persuaded that the humidity of the atmosphere in these remote regions is such that particles of daylight adhere to the disk and it was by aid of these that we were enabled to see the sun in the dark."

This was deemed satisfactory, and due entry was made of the decision.

But about this moment those dreadful shriekings were heard again; again the rumbling and thundering came speeding up out of the night; and once more a flaming great eye flashed by and lost itself in gloom and distance.

The camp laborers gave themselves up for lost. The savants were sorely perplexed. Here was a marvel hard to account for. They thought and they talked, they talked and they thought. Finally the learned and aged Lord Grand-Daddy-Longlegs, who had been sitting in deep study, with his slender limbs crossed and his stemmy arms folded, said:

"Deliver your opinions, brethren, and then I will tell my thought—for I think I have solved this problem."

"So be it, good your lordship," piped the weak treble of the wrinkled and withered Professor Woodlouse, "for we shall hear from your lordship's lips naught but wisdom." [Here the speaker threw in a mess of trite, threadbare, exasperating quotations from the ancient poets and philosophers, delivering them with unction in the sounding grandeurs of the original tongues, they being from the Mastodon, the Dodo, and other dead languages.] "Perhaps I ought not to presume to meddle with matters pertaining to astronomy at all, in such a presence as this, I who have made it the business of my life to delve only among the riches of the extinct languages and unearth the opulence of their ancient lore; but still, as unacquainted as I am with the noble science of astronomy, I beg with deference and humility to suggest that inasmuch as the last of these wonderful apparitions proceeded in exactly the opposite direction from that pursued by the first, which you decide to be the Vernal Equinox, and greatly resembled it in all particulars, is it not possible, nay certain, that this last is the *Autumnal* Equi—"

"O-o-o!" "O-o-o! go to bed! go to bed!" with annoyed derision from everybody. So the poor old Woodlouse retreated out of sight, consumed with shame.

Further discussion followed, and then the united voice of the commission begged Lord Longlegs to speak. He said:

"Fellow-scientists, it is my belief that we have witnessed a thing which has occurred in perfection but once before in the knowledge of created beings. It is a phenomenon of inconceivable importance and interest, view it as one may, but its interest to us is vastly heightened by an added knowledge of its nature which no scholar has heretofore possessed or even suspected. This great marvel which we have just witnessed, fellow-savants (it almost takes my breath away), is nothing less than the transit of Venus!"

Every scholar sprang to his feet pale with astonishment. Then ensued tears, handshakings, frenzied embraces, and the most extravagant jubilations of every sort. But by and by, as emotion began to retire within bounds, and reflection to return to the front, the accomplished Chief Inspector Lizard observed:

"But how is this? Venus should traverse the sun's surface, not the earth's."

The arrow went home. It carried sorrow to the breast of every apostle of learning there, for none could deny that this was a formidable criticism. But tranquilly the venerable Duke crossed his limbs behind his ears and said:

"My friend has touched the marrow of our mighty discovery. Yes—all that have lived before us thought a transit of Venus consisted of a flight across the sun's face; they thought it, they maintained it, they honestly believed it, simple hearts, and were justified in it by the limitations of their knowledge; but to us has been granted the inestimable boon of proving that the transit occurs across the earth's face, *for we have* SEEN *it!*"

The assembled wisdom sat in speechless adoration of this imperial intellect. All doubts had instantly departed, like night before the lightning.

The Tumble-Bug had just intruded, unnoticed. He now came reeling forward among the scholars, familiarly slapping first one and then another on the shoulder, saying "Nice ('ic!) nice old boy!" and smiling a smile of elaborate content. Arrived at a good position for speaking, he put his left arm akimbo with his knuckles planted in his hip just under the edge of his cut-away coat, bent his right leg, placing his toe on the ground and resting his heel with easy grace against his left shin, puffed out his aldermanic stomach, opened his lips, leaned his right elbow on Inspector Lizard's shoulder, and—

But the shoulder was indignantly withdrawn and the hard-handed son of toil went to earth. He floundered a bit, but came up smiling, arranged his attitude with the same careful detail as before, only choosing Professor Dogtick's shoulder for a support, opened his lips and—

Went to earth again. He presently scrambled up once more, still smiling, made a loose effort to brush the dust off his coat and legs, but a smart pass of his hand missed entirely, and the force of the unchecked impulse slewed him suddenly around, twisted his legs together, and projected him, limber and sprawling, into the lap of the Lord Longlegs. Two or three scholars sprang forward, flung the low creature head over heels into a corner, and reinstated the patrician, smoothing his ruffled dignity with many soothing and regretful speeches. Professor Bull Frog roared out:

"No more of this, sirrah Tumble-Bug! Say your say and then get you about your business with speed! Quick—what is your errand? Come—move off a trifle; you smell like a stable; what have you been at?"

"Please ('ic!) please your worship I chanced to light upon a find. But no m (e-uck!) matter 'bout that. There's b ('ic!) been another find which—beg pardon, your honors, what was that th ('ic!) thing that ripped by here first?"

"It was the Vernal Equinox."

"Inf ('ic!) fernal equinox. 'At's all right. D ('ic!) Dunno him. What's other one?"

"The transit of Venus."

"G ('ic!) Got me again. No matter. Las' one dropped something."

"Ah, indeed! Good luck! Good news! Quick—what is it?"

"M ('ic!) Mosey out 'n' see. It'll pay."

No more votes were taken for four-and-twenty hours. Then the following entry was made:

"The commission went in a body to view the find. It was found to consist of a hard, smooth, huge object with a rounded summit surmounted by a short upright projection resembling a section of a cabbage stalk divided transversely. This projection was not solid, but was a hollow cylinder plugged with a soft woody substance unknown to our region—that is, it had been so plugged, but unfortunately this obstruction had been heedlessly removed by Norway Rat, Chief of the Sappers and Miners, before our arrival. The vast object before us, so mysteriously conveyed from the glittering domains of space, was found to be hollow and nearly filled with a pungent liquid of a brownish hue, like rainwater that has stood for some time. And such a spectacle as met our view! Norway Rat was perched upon the summit engaged in thrusting his tail into the cylindrical projection, drawing it out dripping, permitting the struggling multitude of laborers to suck the end of it, then straightway reinserting it and delivering the fluid to the mob as before. Evidently this liquor had strangely potent qualities; for all that partook of it were immediately exalted with great and pleasurable emotions, and went staggering about singing ribald songs, embracing, fighting, dancing, discharging irruptions of profanity, and defying all authority. Around us struggled a massed and uncontrolled mob—uncontrolled and likewise uncontrollable, for the whole army, down to the very sentinels, were mad like the rest, by reason of the drink. We were seized upon by these reckless creatures, and within the hour we, even we, were undistinguishable from the rest—the demoralization was complete and universal. In time the camp wore itself out with its orgies and sank into a stolid and pitiable stupor, in whose mysterious bonds rank was forgotten and strange bedfellows made, our eyes, at the resurrection, being blasted and our souls petrified with the incredible spectacle of that intolerable stinking scavenger, the Tumble-Bug, and the illustrious patrician my Lord Grand Daddy, Duke of Longlegs, lying soundly steeped in sleep, and clasped lovingly in each other's arms, the like whereof hath not been seen in all the ages that tradition compasseth, and doubtless none shall ever in this world find faith to master the belief of it save only we that have beheld the damnable and unholy vision. Thus inscrutable be the ways of God, whose will be done!

"This day, by order, did the engineer-in-chief, Herr Spider, rig the necessary tackle for the overturning of the vast reservoir, and so its calamitous contents were discharged in a torrent upon the thirsty earth, which drank it up, and now there is no more danger, we reserving but a few drops for experiment and scrutiny, and to exhibit to the king and subsequently preserve among the wonders of the museum. What this liquid is has been determined. It is without question that fierce and most destructive fluid called lightning. It was wrested, in its container, from its storehouse in the clouds, by the resistless might of the flying planet, and hurled at our feet as she sped by. An interesting discovery here results. Which is, that lightning, kept to itself, is quiescent; it is the assaulting contact of the thunderbolt that releases it from captivity, ignites its awful fires, and so produces an instantaneous combustion and explosion which spread disaster and desolation far and wide in the earth."

After another day devoted to rest and recovery, the expedition proceeded upon its way. Some days later it went into camp in a pleasant part of the plain, and the savants sallied forth to see what they might find. Their reward was at hand. Professor Bull Frog discovered a strange tree, and called his comrades. They inspected it with profound interest. It was very tall and straight, and wholly devoid of bark, limbs, or foliage. By triangulation Lord Longlegs determined its altitude; Herr Spider measured its circumference at the base and computed the circumference at its top by a mathematical demonstration based upon the warrant furnished by the uniform degree of its taper upward. It was considered a very extraordinary find; and since it was a tree of a hitherto unknown species, Professor Woodlouse gave it a name of a learned sound, being none other than that of Professor Bull Frog translated into the ancient Mastodon language, for it had always been the custom with discoverers to perpetuate their names and honor themselves by this sort of connection with their discoveries.

Now Professor Field-Mouse having placed his sensitive ear to the tree, detected a rich, harmonious sound issuing from it. This surprising thing was tested and enjoyed by each scholar in turn, and great was the gladness and astonishment of all. Professor Woodlouse was requested to add to and extend the tree's name so as to make it suggest the musical quality it possessed—which he did, furnishing the addition *Anthem Singer*, done into the Mastodon tongue.

By this time Professor Snail was making some telescopic inspections. He discovered a great number of these trees, extending in a single rank, with wide intervals between, as far as his instrument would carry, both southward and northward. He also presently discovered that all these trees were bound together, near their tops, by fourteen great ropes, one above another, which ropes were continuous, from tree to tree, as far as his vision could reach. This was surprising. Chief Engineer Spider ran aloft and soon reported that these ropes were simply a web hung there by some colossal member of his own species, for he could see its prey dangling here and there from the strands, in the shape of mighty shreds and rags that had a woven look about their texture and were no doubt the discarded skins of prodigious insects which had been caught and eaten. And then he ran along one of the ropes to make a closer inspection, but felt a smart sudden burn on the soles of his feet, accompanied by a paralyzing shock, wherefore he let go and swung himself to the earth by a thread of his own spinning, and advised all to hurry at once to camp, lest the monster should appear and get as much interested in the savants as they were in him and his works. So they departed with speed, making notes about the gigantic web as they went. And that evening the naturalist of the expedition built a beautiful model of the colossal spider, having no need to see it in order to do this, because he had picked up a fragment of its vertebræ by the tree, and so knew exactly what the creature looked like and what its habits and its preferences were by this simple evidence alone. He built it with a tail, teeth, four-teen legs, and a snout, and said it ate grass, cattle, pebbles, and dirt with equal enthusiasm. This animal was regarded as a very precious addition to science. It was hoped a dead one might be found to stuff. Professor Woodlouse thought that he and his brother scholars, by lying hid and being quiet, might maybe catch a live one. He was advised to try it. Which was all the attention that was paid to his suggestion. The confer-ence ended with the naming the monster after the naturalist, since he, after God, had created it.

"And improved it, mayhap," muttered the Tumble-Bug, who was in-truding again, according to his idle custom and his unappeasable curi-osity.

PART SECOND HOW THE ANIMALS OF THE WOOD COMPLETED THEIR SCIENTIFIC LABORS

A week later the expedition camped in the midst of a collection of wonderful curiosities. These were a sort of vast caverns of stone that rose singly and in bunches out of the plain by the side of the river which they had first seen when they emerged from the forest. These caverns stood in long, straight rows on opposite sides of broad aisles that were bordered with single ranks of trees. The summit of each cavern sloped sharply both ways. Several horizontal rows of great square holes, ob-structed by a thin, shiny, transparent substance, pierced the frontage of each cavern. Inside were caverns within caverns; and one might as-cend and visit these minor compartments by means of curious winding ways consisting of continuous regular terraces raised one above another. There were many huge, shapeless objects in each compartment which were considered to have been living creatures at one time, though now the thin brown skin was shrunken and loose, and rattled when disturbed. Spiders were here in great number, and their cobwebs, stretched in all directions and wreathing the great skinny dead together, were a pleasant spectacle, since they inspired with life and wholesome cheer a scene which would otherwise have brought to the mind only a sense of forsakenness and desolation. Information was sought of these spiders, but in vain. They were of a different nationality from those with the expedition, and their language seemed but a musical, meaning-less jargon. They were a timid, gentle race, but ignorant, and heathenish worshipers of unknown gods. The expedition detailed a great detachment of missionaries to teach them the true religion, and in a week's time a precious work had been wrought among those darkened creatures, not three families being by that time at peace with each other or having a settled belief in any system of religion whatever. This encouraged the expedition to establish a colony of missionaries there permanently, that the work of grace might go on.

But let us not outrun our narrative. After close examination of the fronts of the caverns, and much thinking and exchanging of theories, the scientists determined the nature of these singular formations. They said that each belonged mainly to the Old Red Sandstone period; that the cavern fronts rose in innumerable and wonderfully regular strata high in the air, each stratum about five frog-spans thick, and that in the present discovery lay an overpowering refutation of all received geology; for between every two layers of Old Red Sandstone reposed a thin layer of decomposed limestone; so instead of there having been but one Old Red Sandstone period there had certainly been not less than a hundred and seventy-five! And by the same token it was plain that there had also been a hundred and seventy-five floodings of the earth and depositings of limestone strata! The unavoidable deduction from which pair of facts was the overwhelming truth that the world, instead of being only two hundred thousand years old, was older by millions upon millions of years! And there was another curious thing: every stratum of Old Red Sandstone was pierced and divided at mathematically regular intervals by vertical strata of limestone. Up-shootings of igneous rock through fractures in water formations were common; but here was the first instance where water-formed rock had been so projected. It was a great and noble discovery, and its value to science was considered to be inestimable.

A critical examination of some of the lower strata demonstrated the presence of fossil ants and tumble-bugs (the latter accompanied by their peculiar goods), and with high gratification the fact was enrolled upon the scientific record; for this was proof that these vulgar laborers belonged to the first and lowest orders of created beings, though at the same time there was something repulsive in the reflection that the perfect and exquisite creature of the modern uppermost order owed its origin to such ignominious beings through the mysterious law of Development of Species.

The Tumble-Bug, overhearing this discussion, said he was willing that the parvenus of these new times should find what comfort they might in their wise-drawn theories, since as far as he was concerned he was content to be of the old first families and proud to point back to his place among the old original aristocracy of the land.

"Enjoy your mushroom dignity, stinking of the varnish of yesterday's veneering, since you like it," said he; "suffice it for the Tumble-Bugs that they come of a race that rolled their fragrant spheres down the solemn aisles of antiquity, and left their imperishable words embalmed in the Old Red Sandstone to proclaim it to the wasting centuries as they file along the highway of Time!"

"Oh, take a walk!" said the chief of the expedition, with derision.

The summer passed, and winter approached. In and about many of the caverns were what seemed to be inscriptions. Most of the scientists said they were inscriptions, a few said they were not. The chief philologist, Professor Woodlouse, maintained that they were writings, done in a character utterly unknown to scholars, and in a language equally unknown. He had early ordered his artists and draftsmen to make facsimiles of all that were discovered; and had set himself about finding the key to the hidden tongue. In this work he had followed the method which had always been used by decipherers previously. That is to say, he placed a number of copies of inscriptions before him and studied them both collectively and in detail. To begin with, he placed the following copies together:

THE AMERICAN HOTEL	MEALS AT ALL HOURS
THE SHADES	NO SMOKING
BOATS FOR HIRE CHEAP	UNION PRAYER MEETING, 4 P.M.
BILLIARDS	THE WATERSIDE JOURNAL
THE A1 BARBER SHOP	TELEGRAPH OFFICE
KEEP OFF THE GRASS	TRY BRANDRETH'S PILLS
COTTAGES FOR RENT DURING THE WATERING SEASON	
FOR SALE CHEAP	FOR SALE CHEAP
FOR SALE CHEAP	FOR SALE CHEAP

At first it seemed to the professor that this was a sign-language, and that each word was represented by a distinct sign; further examination convinced him that it was a written language, and that every letter of its alphabet was represented by a character of its own; and finally he decided that it was a language which conveyed itself partly by letters, and partly by signs or hieroglyphics. This conclusion was forced upon him by the discovery of several specimens of the following nature:

He observed that certain inscriptions were met with in greater frequency than others. Such as "FOR SALE CHEAP"; "BILLIARDS"; "S. T.—

1860—X"; "KENO"; "ALE ON DRAUGHT." Naturally, then, these must be religious maxims. But this idea was cast aside by and by, as the mystery of the strange alphabet began to clear itself. In time, the professor was enabled to translate several of the inscriptions with considerable plausibility, though not to the perfect satisfaction of all the scholars. Still, he made constant and encouraging progress.

Finally a cavern was discovered with these inscriptions upon it:

WATERSIDE MUSEUM
Open at All Hours
Admission 50 cents
WONDERFUL COLLECTIONS OF
WAX-WORKS, ANCIENT FOSSILS, ETC.

Professor Woodlouse affirmed that the word "Museum" was equivalent to the phrase "*lumgath molo,*" or "Burial Place." Upon entering, the scientists were well astonished. But what they saw may be best conveyed in the language of their own official report:

"Erect, in a row, were a sort of rigid great figures which struck us instantly as belonging to the long extinct species of reptile called MAN, described in our ancient records. This was a peculiarly gratifying discovery, because of late times it has become fashionable to regard this creature as a myth and a superstition, a work of the inventive imaginations of our remote ancestors. But here, indeed, was Man, perfectly preserved, in a fossil state. And this was his burial place, as already ascertained by the inscription. And now it began to be suspected that the caverns we had been inspecting had been his ancient haunts in that old time that he roamed the earth—for upon the breast of each of these tall fossils was an inscription in the character heretofore noticed. One read, 'CAPTAIN KIDD THE PIRATE'; another, 'QUEEN VICTORIA'; another, 'ABE LINCOLN'; another, 'GEORGE WASHINGTON,' etc.

"With feverish interest we called for our ancient scientific records to discover if perchance the description of Man there set down would tally with the fossils before us. Professor Woodlouse read it aloud in its quaint and musty phraseology, to wit:

"'In ye time of our fathers Man still walked ye earth, as by tradition we know. It was a creature of exceeding great size, being compassed about with a loose skin, sometimes of one color, sometimes of many, the which it was able to cast at will; which being done, the hind legs were discovered to be armed with short claws like to a mole's but broader, and ye forelegs with fingers of a curious slimness and a length much more prodigious than a frog's, armed also with broad talons for scratching in yᵉ earth for its food. It had a sort of feathers upon its head such as hath a rat, but longer, and a beak suitable for seeking its food by yᵉ smell thereof. When it was stirred with happiness, it leaked water from its eyes; and when it suffered or was sad, it manifested it with a horrible hellish cackling clamor that was exceeding dreadful to hear and made one long that it might rend itself and perish, and so end its troubles. Two Mans being together, they uttered noises at each other like this: "Haw-haw-haw—dam good, dam good," together with other sounds of more or less likeness to these, wherefore yᵉ poets conceived that they talked, but poets be always ready to catch at any frantic folly, God he knows. Sometimes this creature goeth about with a long stick yᵉ which it putteth to its face and bloweth fire and smoke through yᵉ same with a sudden and most damnable bruit and noise that doth fright its prey to death, and so seizeth it in its talons and walketh away to its habitat, consumed with a most fierce and devilish joy.'

"Now was the description set forth by our ancestors wonderfully in-dorsed and confirmed by the fossils before us, as shall be seen. The specimen marked 'Captain Kidd' was examined in detail. Upon its head and part of its face was a sort of fur like that upon the tail of a horse. With great labor its loose skin was removed, whereupon its body was discovered to be of a polished white texture, thoroughly petrified. The straw it had eaten, so many ages gone by, was still in its body, undi-gested—and even in its legs.

"Surrounding these fossils were objects that would mean nothing to the ignorant, but to the eye of science they were a revelation. They laid bare the secrets of dead ages. These musty Memorials told us when Man lived, and what were his habits. For here, side by side with Man, were the evidences that he had lived in the earliest ages of creation, the com-panion of the other low orders of life that belonged to that forgotten time. Here was the fossil nautilus that sailed the primeval seas; here was the skeleton of the mastodon, the ichthyosaurus, the cave-bear, the prodigious elk. Here, also, were the charred bones of some of these ex-tinct animals and of the young of Man's own species, split lengthwise, showing that to his taste the marrow was a toothsome luxury. It was plain that Man had robbed those bones of their contents, since no tooth-mark of any beast was upon them—albeit the Tumble-Bug intruded the remark that 'no beast could mark a bone with its teeth, anyway.' Here were proofs that Man had vague, groveling notions of art; for this fact was conveyed by certain things marked with the untranslatable words, 'FLINT HATCHETS, KNIVES, ARROW-HEADS, AND BONE ORNAMENTS OF PRIMEVAL MAN.' Some of these seemed to be rude weapons chipped out of flint, and in a secret place was found some more in process of construction, with this untranslatable legend, on a thin, flimsy material, lying by:

"*'Jones, if you don't want to be discharged from the Musseum, make the next primeaveal weppons more careful—you couldn't even fool one of these sleapy old syentiffic grannys from the Coledge with the last ones. And mind you the animles you carved on some of the Bone Ornaments is a blame sight too good for any primeaveal man that was ever fooled.—Varnum, Manager.'*

"Back of the burial place was a mass of ashes, showing that Man always had a feast at a funeral—else why the ashes in such a place; and showing, also, that he believed in God and the immortality of the soul—else why these solemn ceremonies?

"To sum up. We believe that Man had a written language. We *know* that he indeed existed at one time, and is not a myth; also, that he was the companion of the cave-bear, the mastodon, and other extinct species; that he cooked and ate them and likewise the young of his own kind; also, that he bore rude weapons, and knew nothing of art; that he imagined he had a soul, and pleased himself with the fancy that it was immortal. But let us not laugh; there may be creatures in existence to whom we and our vanities and profundities may seem as ludicrous."

PART THIRD

Near the margin of the great river the scientists presently found a huge, shapely stone, with this inscription:

"*In 1847, in the spring, the river overflowed its banks and covered the whole township. The depth was from two to six feet. More than 900 head of cattle were lost, and many homes destroyed. The Mayor ordered this memorial to be erected to perpetuate the event. God spare us the repetition of it!*"

With infinite trouble, Professor Woodlouse succeeded in making a translation of this inscription, which was sent home, and straightway an enormous excitement was created about it. It confirmed, in a remarkable way, certain treasured traditions of the ancients. The translation was slightly marred by one or two untranslatable words, but these did not impair the general clearness of the meaning. It is here presented:

"*One thousand eight hundred and forty-seven years ago, the (fires?) descended and consumed the whole city. Only some nine hundred souls were saved, all others destroyed. The (king?) commanded this stone to be set up to . . . (untranslatable) . . . prevent the repetition of it.*"

This was the first successful and satisfactory translation that had been made of the mysterious character left behind him by extinct man, and it gave Professor Woodlouse such reputation that at once every seat of learning in his native land conferred a degree of the most illustrious grade upon him, and it was believed that if he had been a soldier and had turned his splendid talents to the extermination of a remote tribe of reptiles, the king would have ennobled him and made him rich. And this, too, was the origin of that school of scientists called Manologists, whose specialty is the deciphering of the ancient records of the extinct bird termed Man. [For it is now decided that Man was a bird and not a reptile.] But Professor Woodlouse began and remained chief of these, for it was granted that no translations were ever so free from error as his. Others made mistakes—he seemed incapable of it. Many a memorial of the lost race was afterward found, but none ever attained to the renown and veneration achieved by the "Mayoritish Stone"—it being so called from the word "Mayor" in it, which, being translated "King," "Mayoritish Stone" was but another way of saying "King Stone."

Another time the expedition made a great "find." It was a vast round flattish mass, ten frog-spans in diameter and five or six high. Professor Snail put on his spectacles and examined it all around, and then climbed up and inspected the top. He said:

"The result of my perlustration and perscontation of this isoperimetrical protuberance is a belief that it is one of those rare and wonderful creations left by the Mound Builders. The fact that this one is lamellibranchiate in its formation, simply adds to its interest as being possibly of a different kind from any we read of in the records of science, but yet in no manner marring its authenticity. Let the megalophonous grasshopper sound a blast and summon hither the perfunctory and circumforaneous Tumble-Bug, to the end that excavations may be made and learning gather new treasures."

Not a Tumble-Bug could be found on duty, so the Mound was excavated by a working party of Ants. Nothing was discovered. This would have been a great disappointment, had not the venerable Longlegs explained the matter. He said:

"It is now plain to me that the mysterious and forgotten race of Mound Builders did not always erect these edifices as mausoleums, else in this case, as in all previous cases, their skeletons would be found here, along with the rude implements which the creatures used in life. Is not this manifest?"

"True! true!" from everybody.

"Then we have made a discovery of peculiar value here; a discovery which greatly extends our knowledge of this creature in place of diminishing it; a discovery which will add luster to the achievements of this expedition and win for us the commendations of scholars everywhere. For the absence of the customary relics here means nothing less than this: The Mound Builder, instead of being the ignorant, savage reptile we have been taught to consider him, was a creature of cultivation and high intelligence, capable of not only appreciating worthy achievements of the great and noble of his species, but of commemorating them! Fellow-scholars, this stately Mound is not a sepulcher, it is a monument!"

A profound impression was produced by this.

But it was interrupted by rude and derisive laughter—and the Tumble-Bug appeared.

"A monument!" quoth he. "A monument set up by a Mound Builder! Aye, so it is! So it is, indeed, to the shrewd keen eye of science; but to an ignorant poor devil who has never seen a college, it is not a Monument, strictly speaking, but is yet a most rich and noble property; and with your worship's good permission I will proceed to manufacture it into spheres of exceedings grace and—"

The Tumble-Bug was driven away with stripes, and the draftsmen of the expedition were set to making views of the Monument from different standpoints, while Professor Woodlouse, in a frenzy of scientific zeal, traveled all over it and all around it hoping to find an inscription. But if there had ever been one, it had decayed or been removed by some vandal as a relic.

The views having been completed, it was now considered safe to load the precious Monument itself upon the backs of four of the largest Tortoises and send it home to the king's museum, which was done; and when it arrived it was received with enormous *éclat* and escorted to its future abiding-place by thousands of enthusiastic citizens, King Bullfrog XVI. himself attending and condescending to sit enthroned upon it throughout the progress.

The growing rigor of the weather was now admonishing the scientists to close their labors for the present, so they made preparations to journey homeward. But even their last day among the Caverns bore fruit; for one of the scholars found in an out-of-the-way corner of the Museum or "Burial Place" a most strange and extraordinary thing. It was nothing less than a double Man-Bird lashed together breast to breast by a natural ligament, and labeled with the untranslatable words, "*Siamese Twins.*" The official report concerning this thing closed thus:

"Wherefore it appears that there were in old times two distinct species of this majestic fowl, the one being single and the other double. Nature has a reason for all things. It is plain to the eye of science that the Double-Man originally inhabited a region where dangers abounded; hence he was paired together to the end that while one part slept the other might watch; and likewise that, danger being discovered, there might always be a double instead of a single power to oppose it. All honor to the mystery-dispelling eye of godlike Science!"

And near the Double Man-Bird was found what was plainly an ancient record of his, marked upon numberless sheets of a thin white substance and bound together. Almost the first glance that Professor Woodlouse threw into it revealed this following sentence, which he instantly translated and laid before the scientists, in a tremble, and it uplifted every soul there with exultation and astonishment:

"In truth it is believed by many that the lower animals reason and talk together."

When the great official report of the expedition appeared, the above sentence bore this comment:

"Then there are lower animals than Man! This remarkable passage can mean nothing else. Man himself is extinct, but *they* may still exist. What can they be? Where do they inhabit? One's enthusiasm bursts all bounds in the contemplation of the brilliant field of discovery and investigation here thrown open to science. We close our labors with the humble prayer that your Majesty will immediately appoint a commission and command it to rest not nor spare expense until the search for this hitherto unsuspected race of the creatures of God shall be crowned with success."

The expedition then journeyed homeward after its long absence and its faithful endeavors, and was received with a mighty ovation by the whole grateful country. There were vulgar, ignorant carpers, of course, as there always are and always will be; and naturally one of these was the obscene Tumble-Bug. He said that all he had learned by his travels was that science only needed a spoonful of supposition to build a mountain of demonstrated fact out of; and that for the future he meant to be content with the knowledge that nature had made free to all creatures and not go prying into the august secrets of the Deity.

1875

The Canvasser's Tale

Poor, sad-eyed stranger! There was that about his humble mien, his tired look, his decayed-gentility clothes, that almost reached the mustard-seed of charity that still remained, remote and lonely, in the empty vastness of my heart, notwithstanding I observed a portfolio under his arm, and said to myself, Behold, Providence hath delivered his servant into the hands of another canvasser.

Well, these people always get one interested. Before I well knew how it came about, this one was telling me his history, and I was all attention and sympathy. He told it something like this:

My parents died, alas, when I was a little, sinless child. My uncle Ithuriel took me to his heart and reared me as his own. He was my only relative in the wide world; but he was good and rich and generous. He reared me in the lap of luxury. I knew no want that money could satisfy.

In the fullness of time I was graduated, and went with two of my servants—my chamberlain and my valet—to travel in foreign countries. During four years I flitted upon careless wing amid the beauteous gardens of the distant strand, if you will permit this form of speech in one whose tongue was ever attuned to poesy; and indeed I so speak with confidence, as one unto his kind, for I perceive by your eyes that you too, sir, are gifted with the divine inflation. In those far lands I reveled in the ambrosial food that fructifies the soul, the mind, the heart. But of all things, that which most appealed to my inborn esthetic taste was the prevailing custom there, among the rich, of making collections of elegant and costly rarities, dainty *objets de vertu*, and in an evil hour I tried to uplift my uncle Ithuriel to a plane of sympathy with this exquisite employment.

I wrote and told him of one gentleman's vast collection of shells; another's noble collection of meerschaum pipes; another's elevating and refining collection of undecipherable autographs; another's priceless collection of old china; another's enchanting collection of postage-stamps—and so forth and so on. Soon my letters yielded fruit. My uncle began to look about for something to make a collection of. You may know, perhaps, how fleetly a taste like this dilates. His soon became a raging fever, though I knew it not. He began to neglect his great pork business; presently he wholly retired and turned an elegant leisure into a rabid search for curious things. His wealth was vast, and he spared it not. First he tried cow-bells. He made a collection which filled five large *salons*, and comprehended all the different sorts of cow-bells that ever had been contrived, save one. That one—an antique, and the only specimen extant—was possessed by another collector. My uncle offered enormous sums for it, but the gentleman would not sell. Doubtless you know what necessarily resulted. A true collector attaches no value to a collection that is not complete. His great heart breaks, he sells his hoard, he turns his mind to some field that seems unoccupied.

Thus did my uncle. He next tried brickbats. After piling up a vast and intensely interesting collection, the former difficulty supervened; his great heart broke again; he sold out his soul's idol to the retired brewer who possessed the missing brick. Then he tried flint hatchets and other implements of Primeval Man, but by and by discovered that the factory where they were made was supplying other collectors as well as himself. He tried Aztec inscriptions and stuffed whales—another failure, after incredible labor and expense. When his collection seemed at last perfect, a stuffed whale arrived from Greenland and an Aztec inscription from the Cundurango regions of Central America that made all former specimens insignificant. My uncle hastened to secure these noble gems. He got the stuffed whale, but another collector got the inscription. A real Cundurango, as possibly you know, is a possession of such supreme value that, when once a collector gets it, he will rather part with his family than with it. So my uncle sold out, and saw his darlings go forth, never more to return; and his coal-black hair turned white as snow in a single night.

Now he waited, and thought. He knew another disappointment might kill him. He was resolved that he would choose things next time that no other man was collecting. He carefully made up his mind, and once more entered the field—this time to make a collection of echoes.

"Of what?" said I.

Echoes, sir. His first purchase was an echo in Georgia that repeated four times; his next was a six-repeater in Maryland; his next was a thirteen-repeater in Maine; his next was a nine-repeater in Kansas; his next was a twelve-repeater in Tennessee, which he got cheap, so to speak, because it was out of repair, a portion of the crag which reflected it having tumbled down. He believed he could repair it at a cost of a few thousand dollars, and, by increasing the elevation with masonry, treble the repeating capacity; but the architect who undertook the job had never built an echo before, and so he utterly spoiled this one. Before he meddled with it, it used to talk back like a mother-in-law, but now it was only fit for the deaf-and-dumb asylum. Well, next he bought a lot of cheap little double-barreled echoes, scattered around over various states and territories; he got them at twenty per cent. off by taking the lot. Next he bought a perfect Gatling-gun of an echo in Oregon, and it cost a fortune, I can tell you. You may know, sir, that in the echo market the scale of prices is cumulative, like the carat-scale in diamonds; in fact, the same phraseology is used. A single-carat echo is worth but ten dollars over and above the value of the land it is on; a two-carat or double-barreled echo is worth thirty dollars; a five-carat is worth nine hundred and fifty; a ten-carat is worth thirteen thousand. My uncle's Oregon echo, which he called the Great Pitt Echo, was a twenty-two carat gem, and cost two hundred and sixteen thousand dollars—they threw the land in, for it was four hundred miles from a settlement.

Well, in the mean time my path was a path of roses. I was the accepted suitor of the only and lovely daughter of an English earl, and was beloved to distraction. In that dear presence I swam in seas of bliss. The family were content, for it was known that I was sole heir to an uncle held to be worth five millions of dollars. However, none of us knew that my uncle had become a collector, at least in anything more than a small way, for esthetic amusement.

Now gathered the clouds above my unconscious head. That divine echo, since known throughout the world as the Great Koh-i-noor, or Mountain of Repetitions, was discovered. It was a sixty-five-carat gem. You could utter a word and it would talk back at you for fifteen minutes, when the day was otherwise quiet. But behold, another fact came to light at the same time: another echo-collector was in the field. The two rushed to make the peerless purchase. The property consisted of a couple of small hills with a shallow swale between, out yonder among the back settlements of New York State. Both men arrived on the ground at the same time, and neither knew the other was there. The echo was not all owned by one man; a person by the name of Williamson Bolivar Jarvis owned the east hill, and a person by the name of Harbison J. Bledso owned the west hill; the swale between was the dividing-line. So while my uncle was buying Jarvis's hill for three million two hundred and eighty-five thousand dollars, the other party was buying Bledso's hill for a shade over three million.

Now, do you perceive the natural result? Why, the noblest collection of echoes on earth was forever and ever incomplete, since it possessed but the one-half of the king echo of the universe. Neither man was content with this divided ownership, yet neither would sell to the other. There were jawings, bickerings, heart-burnings. And at last that other collector, with a malignity which only a collector can ever feel toward a man and a brother, proceeded to cut down his hill!

You see, as long as he could not have the echo, he was resolved that nobody should have it. He would remove his hill, and then there would be nothing to reflect my uncle's echo. My uncle remonstrated with him, but the man said, "I own one end of this echo; I choose to kill my end; you must take care of your own end yourself."

Well, my uncle got an injunction put on him. The other man appealed and fought it in a higher court. They carried it on up, clear to the Supreme Court of the United States. It made no end of trouble there. Two of the judges believed that an echo was personal property, because it was impalpable to sight and touch, and yet was purchasable, salable, and consequently taxable; two others believed that an echo was real estate, because it was manifestly attached to the land, and was not removable from place to place; other of the judges contended that an echo was not property at all.

It was finally decided that the echo was property; that the hills were property; that the two men were separate and independent owners of the two hills, but tenants in common in the echo; therefore defendant was at full liberty to cut down his hill, since it belonged solely to him, but must give bonds in three million dollars as indemnity for damages which might result to my uncle's half of the echo. This decision also debarred my uncle from using defendant's hill to reflect his part of the echo, without defendant's consent; he must use only his own hill; if his part of the echo would not go, under these circumstances, it was sad, of course, but the court could find no remedy. The court also debarred defendant from using my uncle's hill to reflect *his* end of the echo, without consent. You see the grand result! Neither man would give consent, and so that astonishing and most noble echo had to cease from its great powers; and since that day that magnificent property is tied up and unsalable.

A week before my wedding-day, while I was still swimming in bliss and the nobility were gathering from far and near to honor our espousals, came news of my uncle's death, and also a copy of his will, making me his sole heir. He was gone; alas, my dear benefactor was no more. The thought surcharges my heart even at this remote day. I handed the will to the earl; I could not read it for the blinding tears. The earl read it; then he sternly said, "Sir, do you call this wealth?—but doubtless you do in your inflated country. Sir, you are left sole heir to a vast collection of echoes—if a thing can be called a collection that is scattered far and wide over the huge length and breadth of the American continent; sir, this is not all; you are head and ears in debt; there is not an echo in the lot but has a mortgage on it; sir, I am not a hard man, but I must look to my child's interest; if you had but one echo which you could honestly call your own, if you had but one echo which was free from incumbrance, so that you could retire to it with my child, and by humble, painstaking industry cultivate and improve it, and thus wrest from it a maintenance, I would not say you nay; but I cannot marry my child to a beggar. Leave his side, my darling; go, sir, take your mortgage-ridden echoes and quit my sight forever."

My noble Celestine clung to me in tears, with loving arms, and swore she would willingly, nay gladly, marry me, though I had not an echo in the world. But it could not be. We were torn asunder, she to pine and die within the twelvemonth, I to toil life's long journey sad and alone, praying daily, hourly, for that release which shall join us together again in that dear realm where the wicked cease from troubling and the weary are at rest. Now, sir, if you will be so kind as to look at these maps and plans in my portfolio, I am sure I can sell you an echo for less money than any man in the trade. Now this one, which cost my uncle ten dollars, thirty years ago, and is one of the sweetest things in Texas, I will let you have for—

"Let me interrupt you," I said. "My friend, I have not had a moment's respite from canvassers this day. I have bought a sewing-machine which I did not want; I have bought a map which is mistaken in all its details; I have bought a clock which will not go; I have bought a moth poison which the moths prefer to any other beverage; I have bought no end of useless inventions, and now I have had enough of this foolishness. I would not have one of your echoes if you were even to give it to me. I would not let it stay on the place. I always hate a man that tries to sell me echoes. You see this gun? Now take your collection and move on; let us not have bloodshed."

But he only smiled a sad, sweet smile, and got out some more diagrams. You know the result perfectly well, because you know that when you have once opened the door to a canvasser, the trouble is done and you have got to suffer defeat.

I compromised with this man at the end of an intolerable hour. I bought two double-barreled echoes in good condition, and he threw in another, which he said was not salable because it only spoke German.

He said, "She was a perfect polyglot once, but somehow her palate got down."

1876

The Loves of Alonzo Fitz Clarence
and Rosannah Ethelton

1

It was well along in the forenoon of a bitter winter's day. The town of Eastport, in the state of Maine, lay buried under a deep snow that was newly fallen. The customary bustle in the streets was wanting. One could look long distances down them and see nothing but a dead-white emptiness, with silence to match. Of course I do not mean that you could *see* the silence—no, you could only hear it. The sidewalks were merely long, deep ditches, with steep snow walls on either side. Here and there you might hear the faint, far scrape of a wooden shovel, and if you were quick enough you might catch a glimpse of a distant black figure stooping and disappearing in one of those ditches, and reappearing the next moment with a motion which you would know meant the heaving out of a shovelful of snow. But you needed to be quick, for that black figure would not linger, but would soon drop that shovel and scud for the house, thrashing itself with its arms to warm them. Yes, it was too venomously cold for snow-shovelers or anybody else to stay out long.

Presently the sky darkened; then the wind rose and began to blow in fitful, vigorous gusts, which sent clouds of powdery snow aloft, and straight ahead, and everywhere. Under the impulse of one of these gusts, great white drifts banked themselves like graves across the streets; a moment later another gust shifted them around the other way, driving a fine spray of snow from their sharp crests, as the gale drives the spume flakes from wave-crests at sea; a third gust swept that place as clean as your hand, if it saw fit. This was fooling, this was play; but each and all of the gusts dumped some snow into the sidewalk ditches, for that was business.

Alonzo Fitz Clarence was sitting in his snug and elegant little parlor, in a lovely blue silk dressing-gown, with cuffs and facings of crimson satin, elaborately quilted. The remains of his breakfast were before him, and the dainty and costly little table service added a harmonious charm to the grace, beauty, and richness of the fixed appointments of the room. A cheery fire was blazing on the hearth.

A furious gust of wind shook the windows, and a great wave of snow washed against them with a drenching sound, so to speak. The handsome young bachelor murmured:

"That means, no going out to-day. Well, I am content. But what to do for company? Mother is well enough, Aunt Susan is well enough; but these, like the poor, I have with me always. On so grim a day as this, one needs a new interest, a fresh element, to whet the dull edge of captivity. That was very neatly said, but it doesn't mean anything. One doesn't *want* the edge of captivity sharpened up, you know, but just the reverse."

He glanced at his pretty French mantel-clock.

"That clock's wrong again. That clock hardly ever knows what time it is; and when it does know, it lies about it—which amounts to the same thing. Alfred!"

There was no answer.

"Alfred! . . . Good servant, but as uncertain as the clock."

Alonzo touched an electric bell button in the wall. He waited a moment, then touched it again; waited a few moments more, and said:

"Battery out of order, no doubt. But now that I have started, I *will* find out what time it is." He stepped to a speaking-tube in the wall, blew its whistle, and called, "Mother!" and repeated it twice.

"Well, *that's* no use. Mother's battery is out of order, too. Can't raise anybody down-stairs—that is plain."

He sat down at a rosewood desk, leaned his chin on the left-hand edge of it and spoke, as if to the floor: "Aunt Susan!"

A low, pleasant voice answered, "Is that you, Alonzo?"

"Yes. I'm too lazy and comfortable to go down-stairs; I am in extremity, and I can't seem to scare up any help."

"Dear me, what is the matter?"

"Matter enough, I can tell you!"

"Oh, don't keep me in suspense, dear! What *is* it?"

"I want to know what time it is."

"You abominable boy, what a turn you did give me! Is that all?"

"All—on my honor. Calm yourself. Tell me the time, and receive my blessing."

"Just five minutes after nine. No charge—keep your blessing."

"Thanks. It wouldn't have impoverished me, aunty, nor so enriched you that you could live without other means."

He got up, murmuring, "Just five minutes after nine," and faced his clock. "Ah," said he, "you are doing better than usual. You are only thirty-four minutes wrong. Let me see . . . let me see. . . . Thirty-three and twenty-one are fifty-four; four times fifty-four are two hundred and thirty-six. One off, leaves two hundred and thirty-five. That's right."

He turned the hands of his clock forward till they marked twenty-five minutes to one, and said, "Now see if you can't keep right for a while . . . else I'll raffle you!"

He sat down at the desk again, and said, "Aunt Susan!"

"Yes, dear."

"Had breakfast?"

"Yes, indeed, an hour ago."

"Busy?"

"No—except sewing. Why?"

"Got any company?"

"No, but I expect some at half past nine."

"I wish I did. I'm lonesome. I want to talk to somebody."

"Very well, talk to me."

"But this is very private."

"Don't be afraid—talk right along, there's nobody here but me."

"I hardly know whether to venture or not, but—"

"But what? Oh, don't stop there! You *know* you can trust me, Alonzo —you know you can."

"I feel it, aunt, but this is very serious. It affects me deeply—me, and all the family—even the whole community."

"Oh, Alonzo, tell me! I will never breathe a word of it. What is it?"

"Aunt, if I might dare—"

"Oh, please go on! I love you, and feel for you. Tell me all. Confide in me. What *is* it?"

"The weather!"

"Plague take the weather! I don't see how you can have the heart to serve me so, Lon."

"There, there, aunty dear, I'm sorry; I am, on my honor. I won't do it again. Do you forgive me?"

"Yes, since you seem so sincere about it, though I know I oughtn't to. You will fool me again as soon as I have forgotten this time."

"No, I won't, honor bright. But such weather, oh, such weather! You've *got* to keep your spirits up artificially. It is snowy, and blowy, and gusty, and bitter cold! How is the weather with you?"

"Warm and rainy and melancholy. The mourners go about the streets with their umbrellas running streams from the end of every whalebone. There's an elevated double pavement of umbrellas stretching down the sides of the streets as far as I can see. I've got a fire for cheerfulness, and the windows open to keep cool. But it is vain, it is useless: nothing comes in but the balmy breath of December, with its burden of mocking odors from the flowers that possess the realm outside, and rejoice in their lawless profusion whilst the spirit of man is low, and flaunt their gaudy splendors in his face while his soul is clothed in sackcloth and ashes and his heart breaketh."

Alonzo opened his lips to say, "You ought to print that, and get it framed," but checked himself, for he heard his aunt speaking to some one else. He went and stood at the window and looked out upon the wintry prospect. The storm was driving the snow before it more furiously than ever; window-shutters were slamming and banging; a forlorn dog, with bowed head and tail withdrawn from service, was pressing his quaking body against a windward wall for shelter and protection; a young girl was plowing knee-deep through the drifts, with her face turned from the blast, and the cape of her waterproof blowing straight rearward over her head. Alonzo shuddered, and said with a sigh, "Better the slop, and the sultry rain, and even the insolent flowers, than this!"

He turned from the window, moved a step, and stopped in a listening attitude. The faint, sweet notes of a familiar song caught his ear. He remained there, with his head unconsciously bent forward, drinking in the melody, stirring neither hand nor foot, hardly breathing. There was a blemish in the execution of the song, but to Alonzo it seemed an added charm instead of a defect. This blemish consisted of a marked flatting of the third, fourth, fifth, sixth, and seventh notes of the refrain or chorus of the piece. When the music ended, Alonzo drew a deep breath, and said, "Ah, I never have heard 'In the Sweet By-and-By' sung like that before!"

He stepped quickly to the desk, listened a moment, and said in a guarded, confidential voice, "Aunty, who is this divine singer?"

"She is the company I was expecting. Stays with me a month or two. I will introduce you. Miss—"

"For goodness' sake, wait a moment, Aunt Susan! You never stop to think what you are about!"

He flew to his bedchamber, and returned in a moment perceptibly changed in his outward appearance, and remarking, snappishly:

"Hang it, she would have introduced me to this angel in that sky-blue dressing-gown with red-hot lapels! Women never think, when they get a-going."

He hastened and stood by the desk, and said eagerly, "Now, Aunty, I am ready," and fell to smiling and bowing with all the persuasiveness and elegance that were in him.

"Very well. Miss Rosannah Ethelton, let me introduce to you my favorite nephew, Mr. Alonzo Fitz Clarence. There! You are both good people, and I like you; so I am going to trust you together while I attend to a few household affairs. Sit down, Rosannah; sit down, Alonzo. Good-by; I sha'n't be gone long."

Alonzo had been bowing and smiling all the while, and motioning imaginary young ladies to sit down in imaginary chairs, but now he took a seat himself, mentally saying, "Oh, this is luck! Let the winds blow now, and the snow drive, and the heavens frown! Little I care!"

While these young people chat themselves into an acquaintanceship, let us take the liberty of inspecting the sweeter and fairer of the two. She sat alone, at her graceful ease, in a richly furnished apartment which was manifestly the private parlor of a refined and sensible lady, if signs and symbols may go for anything. For instance, by a low, comfortable chair stood a dainty, top-heavy workstand, whose summit was a fancifully embroidered shallow basket, with varicolored crewels, and other strings and odds and ends protruding from under the gaping lid and hanging down in negligent profusion. On the floor lay bright shreds of Turkey red, Prussian blue, and kindred fabrics, bits of ribbon, a spool or two, a pair of scissors, and a roll or so of tinted silken stuffs. On a luxurious sofa, upholstered with some sort of soft Indian goods wrought in black and gold threads interwebbed with other threads not so pronounced in color, lay a great square of coarse white stuff, upon whose surface a rich bouquet of flowers was growing, under the deft cultivation of the crochet-needle. The household cat was asleep on this work of art. In a bay-window stood an easel with an unfinished picture on it, and a palette and brushes on a chair beside it. There were books everywhere: Robertson's Sermons, Tennyson, Moody and Sankey, Hawthorne, *Rab and his Friends,* cook-books, prayer-books, pattern-books —and books about all kinds of odious and exasperating pottery, of course. There was a piano, with a deck-load of music, and more in a tender. There was a great plenty of pictures on the walls, on the shelves of the mantelpiece, and around generally; where coigns of vantage offered were statuettes, and quaint and pretty gimcracks, and rare and costly specimens of peculiarly devilish china. The bay-window gave upon a garden that was ablaze with foreign and domestic flowers and flowering shrubs.

But the sweet young girl was the daintiest thing these premises, within or without, could offer for contemplation: delicately chiseled features, of Grecian cast; her complexion the pure snow of a japonica that is receiving a faint reflected enrichment from some scarlet neighbor of the garden; great, soft blue eyes fringed with long, curving lashes; an expression made up of the trustfulness of a child and the gentleness of a fawn; a beautiful head crowned with its own prodigal gold; a lithe and rounded figure, whose every attitude and movement was instinct with native grace.

Her dress and adornment were marked by that exquisite harmony that can come only of a fine natural taste perfected by culture. Her gown was of a simple magenta tulle, cut bias, traversed by three rows of light-blue flounces, with the selvage edges turned up with ashes-of-roses chenille; over-dress of dark bay tarlatan with scarlet satin lambrequins; corn-colored polonaise, *en panier,* looped with mother-of-pearl buttons and silver cord, and hauled aft and made fast by buff velvet lashings; basque of lavender reps, picked out with valenciennes; low neck, short sleeves; maroon velvet necktie edged with delicate pink silk; inside handkerchief of some simple three-ply ingrain fabric of a soft saffron tint; coral bracelets and locket-chain; coiffure of forget-me-nots and lilies-of-the-valley massed around a noble calla.

This was all; yet even in this subdued attire she was divinely beautiful. Then what must she have been when adorned for the festival or the ball?

All this time she had been busily chatting with Alonzo, unconscious of our inspection. The minutes still sped, and still she talked. But by and by she happened to look up, and saw the clock. A crimson blush sent its rich flood through her cheeks, and she exclaimed:

"There, good-by, Mr. Fitz Clarence; I must go now!"

She sprang from her chair with such haste that she hardly heard the young man's answering good-by. She stood radiant, graceful, beautiful, and gazed, wondering, upon the accusing clock. Presently her pouting lips parted, and she said:

"Five minutes after eleven! Nearly two hours, and it did not seem twenty minutes! Oh, dear, what will he think of me!"

At the self-same moment Alonzo was staring at *his* clock. And presently he said:

"Twenty-five minutes to three! Nearly two hours, and I didn't believe it was two minutes! Is it possible that this clock is humbugging again? Miss Ethelton! Just one moment, please. Are you there yet?"

"Yes, but be quick; I'm going right away."

"Would you be so kind as to tell me what time it is?"

The girl blushed again, murmured to herself, "It's right down cruel of him to ask me!" and then spoke up and answered with admirably counterfeited unconcern, "Five minutes after eleven."

"Oh, thank you! You have to go, now, have you?"

"Yes."

"I'm sorry."

No reply.

"Miss Ethelton!"

"Well?"

"You—you're there yet, *ain't* you?"

"Yes; but please hurry. What did you want to say?"

"Well, I—well, nothing in particular. It's very lonesome here. It's asking a great deal, I know, but would you mind talking with me again by and by—that is, if it will not trouble you too much?"

"I don't know—but I'll think about it. I'll try."

"Oh, thanks! Miss Ethelton! . . . Ah, me, she's gone, and here are the black clouds and the whirling snow and the raging winds come again! But she said *good-by*. She didn't say good morning, she said good-by! . . . The clock was right, after all. What a lightning-winged two hours it was!"

He sat down, and gazed dreamily into his fire for a while, then heaved a sigh and said:

"How wonderful it is! Two little hours ago I was a free man, and now my heart's in San Francisco!"

About that time Rosannah Ethelton, propped in the window-seat of her bedchamber, book in hand, was gazing vacantly out over the rainy seas that washed the Golden Gate, and whispering to herself, "How different he is from poor Burley, with his empty head and his single little antic talent of mimicry!"

2

Four weeks later Mr. Sidney Algernon Burley was entertaining a gay luncheon company, in a sumptuous drawing-room on Telegraph Hill, with some capital imitations of the voices and gestures of certain popular actors and San Franciscan literary people and Bonanza grandees.

He was elegantly upholstered, and was a handsome fellow, barring a
trifling cast in his eye. He seemed very jovial, but nevertheless he kept
his eye on the door with an expectant and uneasy watchfulness. By and
by a nobby lackey appeared, and delivered a message to the mistress,
who nodded her head understandingly. That seemed to settle the thing
for Mr. Burley; his vivacity decreased little by little, and a dejected
look began to creep into one of his eyes and a sinister one into the
other.

The rest of the company departed in due time, leaving him with the
mistress, to whom he said:

"There is no longer any question about it. She avoids me. She contin-
ually excuses herself. If I could see her, if I could speak to her only a
moment—but this suspense—"

"Perhaps her seeming avoidance is mere accident, Mr. Burley. Go
to the small drawing-room up-stairs and amuse yourself a moment. I
will despatch a household order that is on my mind, and then I will go
to her room. Without doubt she will be persuaded to see you."

Mr. Burley went up-stairs, intending to go to the small drawing-room,
but as he was passing "Aunt Susan's" private parlor, the door of which
stood slightly ajar, he heard a joyous laugh which he recognized; so
without knock or announcement he stepped confidently in. But before
he could make his presence known he heard words that harrowed up
his soul and chilled his young blood. He heard a voice say:

"Darling, it has come!"

Then he heard Rosannah Ethelton, whose back was toward him,
say:

"So has yours, dearest!"

He saw her bowed form bend lower; he heard her kiss something—
not merely once, but again and again! His soul raged within him. The
heart-breaking conversation went on:

"Rosannah, I knew you must be beautiful, but this is dazzling, this
is blinding, this is intoxicating!"

"Alonzo, it is such happiness to hear you say it. I know it is not true,
but I am *so* grateful to have you think it is, nevertheless! I knew you
must have a noble face, but the grace and majesty of the reality beggar
the poor creation of my fancy."

Burley heard that rattling shower of kisses again.

"Thank you, my Rosannah! The photograph flatters me, but you must
not allow yourself to think of that. Sweetheart?"

"Yes, Alonzo."

"I am so happy, Rosannah."

"Oh, Alonzo, none that have gone before me knew what love was, none that come after me will ever know what happiness is. I float in a gorgeous cloudland, a boundless firmament of enchanted and bewildering ecstasy!"

"Oh, my Rosannah!—for you are mine, are you not?"

"Wholly, oh, wholly yours, Alonzo, now and forever! All the day long, and all through my nightly dreams, one song sings itself, and its sweet burden is, 'Alonzo Fitz Clarence, Alonzo Fitz Clarence, Eastport, state of Maine!'"

"Curse him, I've got his address, anyway!" roared Burley, inwardly, and rushed from the place.

Just behind the unconscious Alonzo stood his mother, a picture of astonishment. She was so muffled from head to heel in furs that nothing of herself was visible but her eyes and nose. She was a good allegory of winter, for she was powdered all over with snow.

Behind the unconscious Rosannah stood "Aunt Susan," another picture of astonishment. She was a good allegory of summer, for she was lightly clad, and was vigorously cooling the perspiration on her face with a fan.

Both of these women had tears of joy in their eyes.

"So ho!" exclaimed Mrs. Fitz Clarence, "this explains why nobody has been able to drag you out of your room for six weeks, Alonzo!"

"So ho!" exclaimed Aunt Susan, "this explains why you have been a hermit for the past six weeks, Rosannah!"

The young couple were on their feet in an instant, abashed, and standing like detected dealers in stolen goods awaiting Judge Lynch's doom.

"Bless you, my son! I am happy in your happiness. Come to your mother's arms, Alonzo!"

"Bless you, Rosannah, for my dear nephew's sake! Come to my arms!"

Then was there a mingling of hearts and of tears of rejoicing on Telegraph Hill and in Eastport Square.

Servants were called by the elders, in both places. Unto one was given the order, "Pile this fire high with hickory wood, and bring me a roasting-hot lemonade."

Unto the other was given the order, "Put out this fire, and bring me two palm-leaf fans and a pitcher of ice-water."

Then the young people were dismissed, and the elders sat down to talk the sweet surprise over and make the wedding plans.

Some minutes before this Mr. Burley rushed from the mansion on Telegraph Hill without meeting or taking formal leave of anybody. He hissed through his teeth, in unconscious imitation of a popular favorite in melodrama, "Him shall she never wed! I have sworn it! Ere great Nature shall have doffed her winter's ermine to don the emerald gauds of spring, she shall be mine!"

3

Two weeks later. Every few hours, during some three or four days, a very prim and devout-looking Episcopal clergyman, with a cast in his eye, had visited Alonzo. According to his card, he was the Rev. Melton Hargrave, of Cincinnati. He said he had retired from the ministry on account of his health. If he had said on account of ill-health, he would probably have erred, to judge by his wholesome looks and firm build. He was the inventor of an improvement in telephones, and hoped to make his bread by selling the privilege of using it. "At present," he continued, "a man may go and tap a telegraph wire which is conveying a song or a concert from one state to another, and he can attach his private telephone and steal a hearing of that music as it passes along. My invention will stop all that."

"Well," answered Alonzo, "if the owner of the music could not miss what was stolen, why should he care?"

"He shouldn't care," said the Reverend.

"Well?" said Alonzo, inquiringly.

"Suppose," replied the Reverend, "suppose that, instead of music that was passing along and being stolen, the burden of the wire was loving endearments of the most private and sacred nature?"

Alonzo shuddered from head to heel. "Sir, it is a priceless invention," said he; "I must have it at any cost."

But the invention was delayed somewhere on the road from Cincinnati, most unaccountably. The impatient Alonzo could hardly wait. The thought of Rosannah's sweet words being shared with him by some ribald thief was galling to him. The Reverend came frequently and lamented the delay, and told of measures he had taken to hurry things up. This was some little comfort to Alonzo.

One forenoon the Reverend ascended the stairs and knocked at Alonzo's door. There was no response. He entered, glanced eagerly around, closed the door softly, then ran to the telephone. The exquisitely soft and remote strains of the "Sweet By-and-By" came floating through the instrument. The singer was flatting, as usual, the five notes that follow the first two in the chorus, when the Reverend interrupted her with this word, in a voice which was an exact imitation of Alonzo's, with just the faintest flavor of impatience added:

"Sweetheart?"

"Yes, Alonzo?"

"Please don't sing that any more this week—try something modern."

The agile step that goes with a happy heart was heard on the stairs, and the Reverend, smiling diabolically, sought sudden refuge behind the heavy folds of the velvet window-curtains. Alonzo entered and flew to the telephone. Said he:

"Rosannah, dear, shall we sing something together?"

"Something *modern?*" asked she, with sarcastic bitterness.

"Yes, if you prefer."

"Sing it yourself, if you like!"

This snappishness amazed and wounded the young man. He said:

"Rosannah, that was not like you."

"I suppose it becomes me as much as your very polite speech became you, Mr. Fitz Clarence."

"*Mister* Fitz Clarence! Rosannah, there was nothing impolite about my speech."

"Oh, indeed! Of course, then, I misunderstood you, and I most humbly beg your pardon, ha-ha-ha! No doubt you said, 'Don't sing it any more *to-day.*' "

"Sing *what* any more to-day?"

"The song you mentioned, of course. How very obtuse we are, all of a sudden!"

"I never mentioned any song."

"Oh, you *didn't?*"

"No, I *didn't!*"

"I am compelled to remark that you *did.*"

"And I am obliged to reiterate that I *didn't.*"

"A second rudeness! That is sufficient, sir. I will never forgive you. All is over between us."

Then came a muffled sound of crying. Alonzo hastened to say:

"Oh, Rosannah, unsay those words! There is some dreadful mystery here, some hideous mistake. I am utterly earnest and sincere when I say I never said anything about any song. I would not hurt you for the whole world. . . . Rosannah, dear! . . . Oh, speak to me, won't you?"

There was a pause; then Alonzo heard the girl's sobbings retreating, and knew she had gone from the telephone. He rose with a heavy sigh, and hastened from the room, saying to himself, "I will ransack the charity missions and the haunts of the poor for my mother. She will persuade her that I never meant to wound her."

A minute later the Reverend was crouching over the telephone like a cat that knoweth the ways of the prey. He had not very many minutes to wait. A soft, repentant voice, tremulous with tears, said:

"Alonzo, dear, I have been wrong. You *could* not have said so cruel a thing. It must have been some one who imitated your voice in malice or in jest."

The Reverend coldly answered, in Alonzo's tones:

"You have said all was over between us. So let it be. I spurn your proffered repentance, and despise it!"

Then he departed, radiant with fiendish triumph, to return no more with his imaginary telephonic invention forever.

Four hours afterward Alonzo arrived with his mother from her favorite haunts of poverty and vice. They summoned the San Francisco household; but there was no reply. They waited, and continued to wait, upon the voiceless telephone.

At length, when it was sunset in San Francisco, and three hours and a half after dark in Eastport, an answer to the oft-repeated cry of "Rosannah!"

But, alas, it was Aunt Susan's voice that spake. She said:

"I have been out all day; just got in. I will go and find her."

The watchers waited two minutes—five minutes—ten minutes. Then came these fatal words, in a frightened tone:

"She is gone, and her baggage with her. To visit another friend, she told the servants. But I found this note on the table in her room. Listen: 'I am gone; seek not to trace me out; my heart is broken; you will never see me more. Tell him I shall always think of him when I sing my poor "Sweet By-and-By," but never of the unkind words he said about it.' That is her note. Alonzo, Alonzo, what does it mean? What has happened?"

But Alonzo sat white and cold as the dead. His mother threw back the velvet curtains and opened a window. The cold air refreshed the sufferer, and he told his aunt his dismal story. Meantime his mother was inspecting a card which had disclosed itself upon the floor when she cast the curtains back. It read, "Mr. Sidney Algernon Burley, San Francisco."

"The miscreant!" shouted Alonzo, and rushed forth to seek the false Reverend and destroy him; for the card explained everything, since in the course of the lovers' mutual confessions they had told each other all about all the sweethearts they had ever had, and thrown no end of mud at their failings and foibles—for lovers always do that. It has a fascination that ranks next after billing and cooing.

4

During the next two months many things happened. It had early transpired that Rosannah, poor suffering orphan, had neither returned to her grandmother in Portland, Oregon, nor sent any word to her save a duplicate of the woeful note she had left in the mansion on Telegraph Hill. Whosoever was sheltering her—if she was still alive—had been persuaded not to betray her whereabouts, without doubt; for all efforts to find trace of her had failed.

Did Alonzo give her up? Not he. He said to himself, "She will sing that sweet song when she is sad; I shall find her." So he took his carpetsack and a portable telephone, and shook the snow of his native city from his arctics, and went forth into the world. He wandered far and wide and in many states. Time and again, strangers were astounded to see a wasted, pale, and woe-worn man laboriously climb a telegraphpole in wintry and lonely places, perch sadly there an hour, with his ear at a little box, then come sighing down, and wander wearily away. Sometimes they shot at him, as peasants do at aeronauts, thinking him mad and dangerous. Thus his clothes were much shredded by bullets and his person grievously lacerated. But he bore it all patiently.

In the beginning of his pilgrimage he used often to say, "Ah, if I could but hear the 'Sweet By-and-By'!" But toward the end of it he used to shed tears of anguish and say, "Ah, if I could but hear something else!"

Thus a month and three weeks drifted by, and at last some humane people seized him and confined him in a private mad-house in New York. He made no moan, for his strength was all gone, and with it all heart and all hope. The superintendent, in pity, gave up his own comfortable parlor and bedchamber to him and nursed him with affectionate devotion.

At the end of a week the patient was able to leave his bed for the first time. He was lying, comfortably pillowed, on a sofa, listening to the plaintive Miserere of the bleak March winds and the muffled sound of tramping feet in the street below—for it was about six in the evening, and New York was going home from work. He had a bright fire and the added cheer of a couple of student-lamps. So it was warm and snug within, though bleak and raw without; it was light and bright within, though outside it was as dark and dreary as if the world had been lit

with Hartford gas. Alonzo smiled feebly to think how his loving vagaries had made him a maniac in the eyes of the world, and was proceed-
ing to pursue his line of thought further, when a faint, sweet strain,
the very ghost of sound, so remote and attenuated it seemed, struck
upon his ear. His pulses stood still; he listened with parted lips and
bated breath. The song flowed on—he waiting, listening, rising slowly
and unconsciously from his recumbent position. At last he exclaimed:

"It is! it is she! Oh, the divine flatted notes!"

He dragged himself eagerly to the corner whence the sounds proceeded, tore aside a curtain, and discovered a telephone. He bent over,
and as the last note died away he burst forth with the exclamation:

"Oh, thank Heaven, found at last! Speak to me, Rosannah, dearest!
The cruel mystery has been unraveled; it was the villain Burley who
mimicked my voice and wounded you with insolent speech!"

There was a breathless pause, a waiting age to Alonzo; then a faint
sound came, framing itself into language:

"Oh, say those precious words again, Alonzo!"

"They are the truth, the veritable truth, my Rosannah, and you
shall have the proof, ample and abundant proof!"

"Oh, Alonzo, stay by me! Leave me not for a moment! Let me feel
that you are near me! Tell me we shall never be parted more! Oh, this
happy hour, this blessed hour, this memorable hour!"

"We will make record of it, my Rosannah; every year, as this dear
hour chimes from the clock, we will celebrate it with thanksgivings,
all the years of our life."

"We will, we will, Alonzo!"

"Four minutes after six, in the evening, my Rosannah, shall henceforth—"

"Twenty-three minutes after twelve, afternoon, shall—"

"Why, Rosannah, darling, where are you?"

"In Honolulu, Sandwich Islands. And where are you? Stay by me;
do not leave me for a moment. I cannot bear it. Are you at home?"

"No, dear, I am in New York—a patient in the doctor's hands."

An agonizing shriek came buzzing to Alonzo's ear, like the sharp
buzzing of a hurt gnat; it lost power in traveling five thousand miles.
Alonzo hastened to say:

"Calm yourself, my child. It is nothing. Already I am getting well
under the sweet healing of your presence. Rosannah?"

"Yes, Alonzo? Oh, how you terrified me! Say on."

"Name the happy day, Rosannah!"

There was a little pause. Then a diffident small voice replied, "I blush

—but it is with pleasure, it is with happiness. Would—would you like to have it soon?"

"This very night, Rosannah! Oh, let us risk no more delays. Let it be now!—this very night, this very moment!"

"Oh, you impatient creature! I have nobody here but my good old uncle, a missionary for a generation, and now retired from service—nobody but him and his wife. I would so dearly like it if your mother and your Aunt Susan—"

"*Our* mother and *our* Aunt Susan, my Rosannah."

"Yes, *our* mother and *our* Aunt Susan—I am content to word it so if it pleases you; I would so like to have them present."

"So would I. Suppose you telegraph Aunt Susan. How long would it take her to come?"

"The steamer leaves San Francisco day after tomorrow. The passage is eight days. She would be here the 31st of March."

"Then name the 1st of April; do, Rosannah, dear."

"Mercy, it would make us April fools, Alonzo!"

"So we be the happiest ones that that day's sun looks down upon in the whole broad expanse of the globe, why need we care? Call it the 1st of April, dear."

"Then the 1st of April it shall be, with all my heart!"

"Oh, happiness! Name the hour, too, Rosannah."

"I like the morning, it is so blithe. Will eight in the morning do, Alonzo?"

"The loveliest hour in the day—since it will make you mine."

There was a feeble but frantic sound for some little time, as if wool-lipped, disembodied spirits were exchanging kisses; then Rosannah said, "Excuse me just a moment, dear; I have an appointment, and am called to meet it."

The young girl sought a large parlor and took her place at a window which looked out upon a beautiful scene. To the left one could view the charming Nuuana Valley, fringed with its ruddy flush of tropical flowers and its plumed and graceful cocoa palms; its rising foothills clothed in the shining green of lemon, citron, and orange groves; its storied precipice beyond, where the first Kamehameha drove his defeated foes over to their destruction—a spot that had forgotten its grim history, no doubt, for now it was smiling, as almost always at noonday, under the glowing arches of a succession of rainbows. In front of the window one could see the quaint town, and here and there a picturesque group of dusky natives, enjoying the blistering weather; and far to the right lay the restless ocean, tossing its white mane in the sunshine.

Rosannah stood there, in her filmy white raiment, fanning her flushed and heated face, waiting. A Kanaka boy, clothed in a damaged blue necktie and part of a silk hat, thrust his head in at the door, and announced, "'Frisco *haole!*"

"Show him in," said the girl, straightening herself up and assuming a meaning dignity. Mr. Sidney Algernon Burley entered, clad from head to heel in dazzling snow—that is to say, in the lightest and whitest of Irish linen. He moved eagerly forward, but the girl made a gesture and gave him a look which checked him suddenly. She said, coldly, "I am here, as I promised. I believed your assertions, I yielded to your importunities, and said I would name the day. I name the 1st of April—eight in the morning. Now go!"

"Oh, my dearest, if the gratitude of a lifetime—"

"Not a word. Spare me all sight of you, all communication with you, until that hour. No—no supplications; I will have it so."

When he was gone, she sank exhausted in a chair, for the long siege of troubles she had undergone had wasted her strength. Presently she said, "What a narrow escape! If the hour appointed had been an hour earlier—Oh, horror, what an escape I have made! And to think I had come to imagine I was loving this beguiling, this truthless, this treacherous monster! Oh, he shall repent his villainy!"

Let us now draw this history to a close, for little more needs to be told. On the 2d of the ensuing April, the Honolulu *Advertiser* contained this notice:

MARRIED *In this city, by telephone, yesterday morning, at eight o'clock, by Rev. Nathan Hays, assisted by Rev. Nathaniel Davis, of New York, Mr. Alonzo Fitz Clarence, of Eastport, Maine, U.S., and Miss Rosannah Ethelton, of Portland, Oregon, U.S. Mrs. Susan Howland, of San Francisco, a friend of the bride, was present, she being the guest of the Rev. Mr. Hays and wife, uncle and aunt of the bride. Mr. Sidney Algernon Burley, of San Francisco, was also present but did not remain till the conclusion of the marriage service. Captain Hawthorne's beautiful yacht, tastefully decorated, was in waiting, and the happy bride and her friends immediately departed on a bridal trip to Lahaina and Haleakala.*

The New York papers of the same date contained this notice:

MARRIED *In this city, yesterday, by telephone, at half-past two in the*

morning, by Rev. Nathaniel Davis, assisted by Rev. Nathan Hays, of
Honolulu, Mr. Alonzo Fitz Clarence, of Eastport, Maine, and Miss
Rosannah Ethelton, of Portland, Oregon. The parents and several
friends of the bridegroom were present, and enjoyed a sumptuous
breakfast and much festivity until nearly sunrise, and then departed
on a bridal trip to the Aquarium, the bridegroom's state of health not
admitting of a more extended journey.

Toward the close of that memorable day Mr. and Mrs. Alonzo Fitz
Clarence were buried in sweet converse concerning the pleasures of
their several bridal tours, when suddenly the young wife exclaimed:
"Oh, Lonny, I forgot! I did what I said I would."

"Did you, dear?"

"Indeed, I did. I made him the April fool! And I told him so, too!
Ah, it was a charming surprise! There he stood, sweltering in a black
dress-suit, with the mercury leaking out of the top of the thermometer,
waiting to be married. You should have seen the look he gave when I
whispered it in his ear. Ah, his wickedness cost me many a heartache
and many a tear, but the score was all squared up, then. So the vengeful feeling went right out of my heart, and I begged him to stay, and
said I forgave him everything. But he wouldn't. He said he would live
to be avenged; said he would make our lives a curse to us. But he can't,
can he, dear?"

"Never in this world, my Rosannah!"

Aunt Susan, the Oregonian grandmother, and the young couple and
their Eastport parents, are all happy at this writing, and likely to remain
so. Aunt Susan brought the bride from the islands, accompanied her
across our continent, and had the happiness of witnessing the rapturous
meeting between an adoring husband and wife who had never seen
each other until that moment.

A word about the wretched Burley, whose wicked machinations
came so near wrecking the hearts and lives of our poor young friends,
will be sufficient. In a murderous attempt to seize a crippled and helpless artisan who he fancied had done him some small offense, he fell
into a caldron of boiling oil and expired before he could be extinguished.

1878

Edward Mills and George Benton:
A Tale

These two were distantly related to each other—seventh cousins, or something of that sort. While still babies they became orphans, and were adopted by the Brants, a childless couple, who quickly grew very fond of them. The Brants were always saying: "Be pure, honest, sober, industrious, and considerate of others, and success in life is assured." The children heard this repeated some thousands of times before they understood it; they could repeat it themselves long before they could say the Lord's Prayer; it was painted over the nursery door, and was about the first thing they learned to read. It was destined to become the unswerving rule of Edward Mills's life. Sometimes the Brants changed the wording a little, and said: "Be pure, honest, sober, industrious, considerate, and you will never lack friends."

Baby Mills was a comfort to everybody about him. When he wanted candy and could not have it, he listened to reason, and contented himself without it. When Baby Benton wanted candy, he cried for it until he got it. Baby Mills took care of his toys; Baby Benton always destroyed his in a very brief time, and then made himself so insistently disagreeable that, in order to have peace in the house, little Edward was persuaded to yield up his playthings to him.

When the children were a little older, Georgie became a heavy expense in one respect: he took no care of his clothes; consequently, he shone frequently in new ones, which was not the case with Eddie. The boys grew apace. Eddie was an increasing comfort, Georgie an increasing solicitude. It was always sufficient to say, in answer to Eddie's petitions, "I would rather you would not do it"—meaning swimming, skating, picnicking, berrying, circusing, and all sorts of things which boys delight in. But *no* answer was sufficient for Georgie; he had to be humored in his desires, or he would carry them with a high hand. Naturally, no boy got more swimming, skating, berrying, and so forth than he; no boy ever had a better time. The good Brants did not allow the boys to play out after nine in summer evenings; they were sent to bed at that hour; Eddie honorably remained, but Georgie usually slipped out of the window toward ten, and enjoyed himself till midnight. It seemed impossible to break Georgie of this bad habit, but the Brants managed it at last by hiring him, with apples and marbles, to stay in. The good Brants gave all their time and attention to vain endeavors to regulate Georgie; they said, with grateful tears in their eyes, that Eddie needed no efforts of theirs, he was so good, so considerate, and in all ways so perfect.

By and by the boys were big enough to work, so they were apprenticed to a trade: Edward went voluntarily; George was coaxed and bribed. Edward worked hard and faithfully, and ceased to be an expense to the good Brants; they praised him, so did his master; but George ran away, and it cost Mr. Brant both money and trouble to hunt him up and get him back. By and by he ran away again—more money and more trouble. He ran away a third time—and stole a few little things to carry with him. Trouble and expense for Mr. Brant once more; and, besides, it was with the greatest difficulty that he succeeded in persuading the master to let the youth go unprosecuted for the theft.

Edward worked steadily along, and in time became a full partner in his master's business. George did not improve; he kept the loving hearts of his aged benefactors full of trouble, and their hands full of inventive activities to protect him from ruin. Edward, as a boy, had interested himself in Sunday-schools, debating societies, penny missionary affairs, anti-tobacco organizations, anti-profanity associations, and all such things; as a man, he was a quiet but steady and reliable helper in the church, the temperance societies, and in all movements looking to the aiding and uplifting of men. This excited no remark, attracted no attention—for it was his "natural bent."

Finally, the old people died. The will testified their loving pride in Edward, and left their little property to George—because he "needed it"; whereas, "owing to a bountiful Providence," such was not the case with Edward. The property was left to George conditionally: he must buy out Edward's partner with it; else it must go to a benevolent organization called the Prisoner's Friend Society. The old people left a letter, in which they begged their dear son Edward to take their place and watch over George, and help and shield him as they had done.

Edward dutifully acquiesced, and George became his partner in the business. He was not a valuable partner: he had been meddling with drink before; he soon developed into a constant tippler now, and his flesh and eyes showed the fact unpleasantly. Edward had been courting a sweet and kindly spirited girl for some time. They loved each other dearly, and— But about this period George began to haunt her tearfully and imploringly, and at last she went crying to Edward, and said her high and holy duty was plain before her—she must not let her own selfish desires interfere with it: she must marry "poor George" and "reform him." It would break her heart, she knew it would, and so on; but duty was duty. So she married George, and Edward's heart came very near breaking, as well as her own. However, Edward recovered, and married another girl—a very excellent one she was, too.

Children came to both families. Mary did her honest best to reform her husband, but the contract was too large. George went on drinking, and by and by he fell to misusing her and the little ones sadly. A great many good people strove with George—they were always at it, in fact —but he calmly took such efforts as his due and their duty, and did not mend his ways. He added a vice, presently—that of secret gambling. He got deeply in debt; he borrowed money on the firm's credit, as quietly as he could, and carried this system so far and so successfully that one morning the sheriff took possession of the establishment, and the two cousins found themselves penniless.

Times were hard, now, and they grew worse. Edward moved his family into a garret, and walked the streets day and night, seeking work. He begged for it, but it was really not to be had. He was astonished to see how soon his face became unwelcome; he was astonished and hurt to see how quickly the ancient interest which people had had in him faded out and disappeared. Still, he *must* get work; so he swallowed his chagrin, and toiled on in search of it. At last he got a job of carrying bricks up a ladder in a hod, and was a grateful man in consequence; but after that *nobody* knew him or cared anything about him. He was not able to keep up his dues in the various moral organizations to which he belonged, and had to endure the sharp pain of seeing himself brought under the disgrace of suspension.

But the faster Edward died out of public knowledge and interest, the faster George rose in them. He was found lying, ragged and drunk, in the gutter one morning. A member of the Ladies' Temperance Refuge fished him out, took him in hand, got up a subscription for him, kept him sober a whole week, then got a situation for him. An account of it was published.

General attention was thus drawn to the poor fellow, and a great many people came forward, and helped him toward reform with their countenance and encouragement. He did not drink a drop for two months, and meantime was the pet of the good. Then he fell—in the gutter; and there was general sorrow and lamentation. But the noble sisterhood rescued him again. They cleaned him up, they fed him, they listened to the mournful music of his repentances, they got him his situation again. An account of this, also, was published, and the town was drowned in happy tears over the re-restoration of the poor beast and struggling victim of the fatal bowl. A grand temperance revival was got up, and after some rousing speeches had been made the chairman said, impressively: "We are now about to call for signers; and I think there is a spectacle in store for you which not many in this house will be able to view with dry eyes." There was an eloquent pause, and then George Benton, escorted by a red-sashed detachment of the Ladies of the Refuge, stepped forward upon the platform and signed the pledge. The air was rent with applause, and everybody cried for joy. Everybody wrung the hand of the new convert when the meeting was over; his salary was enlarged next day; he was the talk of the town, and its hero. An account of it was published.

George Benton fell, regularly, every three months, but was faithfully rescued and wrought with, every time, and good situations were found for him. Finally, he was taken around the country lecturing, as a reformed drunkard, and he had great houses and did an immense amount of good.

He was so popular at home, and so trusted—during his sober intervals—that he was enabled to use the name of a principal citizen, and get a large sum of money at the bank. A mighty pressure was brought to bear to save him from the consequences of his forgery, and it was partially successful—he was "sent up" for only two years. When, at the end of a year, the tireless efforts of the benevolent were crowned with success, and he emerged from the penitentiary with a pardon in his pocket, the Prisoner's Friend Society met him at the door with a situation and a comfortable salary, and all the other benevolent people came forward and gave him advice, encouragement, and help. Edward Mills had once applied to the Prisoner's Friend Society for a situation, when in dire need, but the question, "Have you been a prisoner?" made brief work of his case.

While all these things were going on, Edward Mills had been quietly making head against adversity. He was still poor, but was in receipt of a steady and sufficient salary, as the respected and trusted cashier of a bank. George Benton never came near him, and was never heard to inquire about him. George got to indulging in long absences from the town; there were ill reports about him, but nothing definite.

One winter's night some masked burglars forced their way into the bank, and found Edward Mills there alone. They commanded him to reveal the "combination," so that they could get into the safe. He refused. They threatened his life. He said his employers trusted him, and he could not be traitor to that trust. He could die, if he must, but while he lived he would be faithful; he would not yield up the "combination." The burglars killed him.

The detectives hunted down the criminals; the chief one proved to be George Benton. A wide sympathy was felt for the widow and orphans of the dead man, and all the newspapers in the land begged that all the banks in the land would testify their appreciation of the fidelity and heroism of the murdered cashier by coming forward with a generous contribution of money in aid of his family, now bereft of support. The result was a mass of solid cash amounting to upward of five hundred dollars—an average of nearly three-eighths of a cent for each bank in the Union. The cashier's own bank testified its gratitude by endeavoring to show (but humiliatingly failed in it) that the peerless servant's accounts were not square, and that he himself had knocked his brains out with a bludgeon to escape detection and punishment.

George Benton was arraigned for trial. Then everybody seemed to forget the widow and orphans in their solicitude for poor George. Everything that money and influence could do was done to save him, but it all failed; he was sentenced to death. Straightway the Governor was besieged with petitions for commutation or pardon; they were brought by tearful young girls; by sorrowful old maids; by deputations of pathetic widows; by shoals of impressive orphans. But no, the Governor —for once—would not yield.

Now George Benton experienced religion. The glad news flew all around. From that time forth his cell was always full of girls and women and fresh flowers; all the day long there was prayer, and hymn-singing, and thanksgivings, and homilies, and tears, with never an interruption, except an occasional five-minute intermission for refreshments.

This sort of thing continued up the very gallows, and George Benton went proudly home, in the black cap, before a wailing audience of the sweetest and best that the region could produce. His grave had fresh flowers on it every day, for a while, and the head-stone bore these words, under a hand pointing aloft: "He has fought the good fight."

The brave cashier's head-stone has this inscription: "Be pure, honest, sober, industrious, considerate, and you will never—"

Nobody knows who gave the order to leave it that way, but it was so given.

The cashier's family are in stringent circumstances, now, it is said; but no matter; a lot of appreciative people, who were not willing that an act so brave and true as his should go unrewarded, have collected forty-two thousand dollars—and built a Memorial Church with it.

1880

The Man Who Put Up at Gadsby's

When my odd friend Riley and I were newspaper correspondents in Washington, in the winter of '67, we were coming down Pennsylvania Avenue one night, near midnight, in a driving storm of snow, when the flash of a street-lamp fell upon a man who was eagerly tearing along in the opposite direction. This man instantly stopped and exclaimed:

"This is lucky! You are Mr. Riley, ain't you?"

Riley was the most self-possessed and solemnly deliberate person in the republic. He stopped, looked his man over from head to foot, and finally said:

"I am Mr. Riley. Did you happen to be looking for me?"

"That's just what I was doing," said the man, joyously, "and it's the biggest luck in the world that I've found you. My name is Lykins. I'm one of the teachers of the high school—San Francisco. As soon as I heard the San Francisco postmastership was vacant, I made up my mind to get it—and here I am."

"Yes," said Riley, slowly, "as you have remarked . . . Mr. Lykins . . . here you are. And have you got it?"

"Well, not exactly got it, but the next thing to it. I've brought a petition, signed by the Superintendent of Public Instruction, and all the teachers, and by more than two hundred other people. Now I want you, if you'll be so good, to go around with me to the Pacific delegation, for I want to rush this thing through and get along home."

"If the matter is so pressing, you will prefer that we visit the delegation to-night," said Riley, in a voice which had nothing mocking in it —to an unaccustomed ear.

"Oh, to-night, by all means! I haven't got any time to fool around. I want their promise before I go to bed—I ain't the talking kind, I'm the *doing* kind!"

"Yes . . . you've come to the right place for that. When did you arrive?"

"Just an hour ago."

"When are you intending to leave?"

"For New York to-morrow evening—for San Francisco next morning."

"Just so. . . . What are you going to do to-morrow?"

"*Do!* Why, I've got to go to the President with the petition and the
delegation, and get the appointment, haven't I?"

"Yes . . . very true . . . that is correct. And then what?"

"Executive session of the Senate at 2 P.M.—got to get the appointment confirmed—I reckon you'll grant that?"

"Yes . . . yes," said Riley, meditatively, "you are right again. Then
you take the train for New York in the evening, and the steamer for
San Francisco next morning?"

"That's it—that's the way I map it out!"

Riley considered a while, and then said:

"You couldn't stay . . . a day . . . well, say two days longer?"

"Bless your soul, no! It's not my style. I ain't a man to go fooling
around—I'm a man that *does* things, I tell you."

The storm was raging, the thick snow blowing in gusts. Riley stood
silent, apparently deep in a reverie, during a minute or more, then he
looked up and said:

"Have you ever heard about that man who put up at Gadsby's, once?
. . . But I see you haven't."

He backed Mr. Lykins against an iron fence, buttonholed him, fastened him with his eye, like the Ancient Mariner, and proceeded to unfold his narrative as placidly and peacefully as if we were all stretched
comfortably in a blossomy summer meadow instead of being persecuted
by a wintry midnight tempest:

"I will tell you about that man. It was in Jackson's time. Gadsby's
was the principal hotel, then. Well, this man arrived from Tennessee
about nine o'clock, one morning, with a black coachman and a splendid
four-horse carriage and an elegant dog, which he was evidently fond
and proud of; he drove up before Gadsby's, and the clerk and the landlord and everybody rushed out to take charge of him, but he said,
'Never mind,' and jumped out and told the coachman to wait—said he
hadn't time to take anything to eat, he only had a little claim against
the government to collect, would run across the way, to the Treasury,
and fetch the money, and then get right along back to Tennessee, for
he was in considerable of a hurry.

"Well, about eleven o'clock that night he came back and ordered a bed and told them to put the horses up—said he would collect the claim in the morning. This was in January, you understand—January, 1834—the 3d of January—Wednesday.

"Well, on the 5th of February, he sold the fine carriage, and bought a cheap second-hand one—said it would answer just as well to take the money home in, and he didn't care for style.

"On the 11th of August he sold a pair of the fine horses—said he'd often thought a pair was better than four, to go over the rough mountain roads with where a body had to be careful about his driving—and there wasn't so much of his claim but he could lug the money home with a pair easy enough.

"On the 13th of December he sold another horse—said two warn't necessary to drag that old light vehicle with—in fact, one could snatch it along faster than was absolutely necessary, now that it was good solid winter weather and the roads in splendid condition.

"On the 17th of February, 1835, he sold the old carriage and bought a cheap second-hand buggy—said a buggy was just the trick to skim along mushy, slushy early spring roads with, and he had always wanted to try a buggy on those mountain roads, anyway.

"On the 1st of August he sold the buggy and bought the remains of an old sulky—said he just wanted to see those green Tennesseans stare and gawk when they saw him come a-ripping along in a sulky—didn't believe they'd ever heard of a sulky in their lives.

"Well, on the 29th of August he sold his colored coachman—said he didn't need a coachman for a sulky—wouldn't be room enough for two in it anyway—and, besides, it wasn't every day that Providence sent a man a fool who was willing to pay nine hundred dollars for such a third-rate negro as that—been wanting to get rid of the creature for years, but didn't like to *throw* him away.

"Eighteen months later—that is to say, on the 15th of February, 1837—he sold the sulky and bought a saddle—said horseback-riding was what the doctor had always recommended *him* to take, and dog'd if he wanted to risk *his* neck going over those mountain roads on wheels in the dead of winter, not if he knew himself.

"On the 9th of April he sold the saddle—said he wasn't going to risk *his* life with any perishable saddle-girth that ever was made, over a rainy, miry April road, while he could ride bareback and know and feel he was safe—always *had* despised to ride on a saddle, anyway.

"On the 24th of April he sold his horse—said 'I'm just fifty-seven to-day, hale and hearty—it would be a *pretty* howdy-do for me to be wasting such a trip as that and such weather as this, on a horse, when there ain't anything in the world so splendid as a tramp on foot through the fresh spring woods and over the cheery mountains, to a man that *is* a man—and I can make my dog carry my claim in a little bundle, anyway, when it's collected. So to-morrow I'll be up bright and early, make my little old collection, and mosey off to Tennessee, on my own hind legs, with a rousing good-by to Gadsby's.'

"On the 22d of June he sold his dog—said 'Dern a dog, anyway, where you're just starting off on a rattling bully pleasure tramp through the summer woods and hills—perfect nuisance—chases the squirrels, barks at everything, goes a-capering and splattering around in the fords—man can't get any chance to reflect and enjoy nature—and I'd a blamed sight ruther carry the claim myself, it's a mighty sight safer; a dog's mighty uncertain in a financial way—always noticed it—well, *good*-by, boys—last call—I'm off for Tennessee with a good leg and a gay heart, early in the morning.'"

There was a pause and a silence—except the noise of the wind and the pelting snow. Mr. Lykins said, impatiently:

"Well?"

Riley said:

"Well—that was thirty years ago."

"Very well, very well—what of it?"

"I'm great friends with that old patriarch. He comes every evening to tell me good-by. I saw him an hour ago—he's off for Tennessee early to-morrow morning—as usual; said he calculated to get his claim through and be off before night-owls like me have turned out of bed. The tears were in his eyes, he was so glad he was going to see his old Tennessee and his friends once more."

Another silent pause. The stranger broke it:

"Is that all?"

"That is all."

"Well, for the *time* of night, and the *kind* of night, it seems to me the story was full long enough. But what's it all *for?*"

"Oh, nothing in particular."

"Well, where's the point of it?"

"Oh, there isn't any particular point to it. Only, if you are not in *too* much of a hurry to rush off to San Francisco with that post-office appointment, Mr. Lykins, I'd advise you to '*put up at Gadsby's*' for a spell, and take it easy. Good-by. *God* bless you!"

So saying, Riley blandly turned on his heel and left the astonished school-teacher standing there, a musing and motionless snow image shining in the broad glow of the street-lamp.

He never got that post-office.

From A TRAMP ABROAD, 1880

Mrs. McWilliams and the Lightning

Well, sir—continued Mr. McWilliams, for this was not the beginning of his talk—the fear of lightning is one of the most distressing infirmities a human being can be afflicted with. It is mostly confined to women; but now and then you find it in a little dog, and sometimes in a man. It is a particularly distressing infirmity, for the reason that it takes the sand out of a person to an extent which no other fear can, and it can't be *reasoned* with, and neither can it be shamed out of a person. A woman who could face the very devil himself—or a mouse—loses her grip and goes all to pieces in front of a flash of lightning. Her fright is something pitiful to see.

Well, as I was telling you, I woke up, with that smothered and unlocatable cry of "Mortimer! Mortimer!" wailing in my ears; and as soon as I could scrape my faculties together I reached over in the dark and then said:

"Evangeline, is that you calling? What is the matter? Where are you?"

"Shut up in the boot-closet. You ought to be ashamed to lie there and sleep so, and such an awful storm going on."

"Why, how *can* one be ashamed when he is asleep? It is unreasonable; a man *can't* be ashamed when he is asleep, Evangeline."

"You never try, Mortimer—you know very well you never try."

I caught the sound of muffled sobs.

That sound smote dead the sharp speech that was on my lips, and I changed it to—

"I'm sorry, dear—I'm truly sorry. I never meant to act so. Come back and—"

"MORTIMER!"

"Heavens! what is the matter, my love?"

"Do you mean to say you are in that bed yet?"

"Why, of course."

"Come out of it instantly. I should think you would take some *little* care of your life, for *my* sake and the children's, if you will not for your own."

"But, my love—"

"Don't talk to me, Mortimer. You *know* there is no place so dangerous as a bed in such a thunder-storm as this—all the books say that; yet there you would lie, and deliberately throw away your life—for goodness knows what, unless for the sake of arguing, and arguing, and—"

"But, confound it, Evangeline, I'm *not* in the bed *now*. I'm—"

[Sentence interrupted by a sudden glare of lightning, followed by a terrified little scream from Mrs. McWilliams and a tremendous blast of thunder.]

"There! You see the result. Oh, Mortimer, how *can* you be so profligate as to swear at such a time as this?"

"I *didn't* swear. And that *wasn't* a result of it, anyway. It would have come, just the same, if I hadn't said a word; and you know very well, Evangeline—at least, you ought to know—that when the atmosphere is charged with electricity—"

"Oh, yes; now argue it, and argue it, and argue it!—I don't see how you can act so, when you *know* there is not a lightning-rod on the place, and your poor wife and children are absolutely at the mercy of Providence. What *are* you doing?—lighting a match at such a time as this! Are you stark mad?"

"Hang it, woman, where's the harm? The place is as dark as the inside of an infidel, and—"

"Put it out! put it out instantly! Are you determined to sacrifice us all? You *know* there is nothing attracts lightning like a light. [*Fzt!—crash! boom—boloom-boom-boom!*] Oh, just hear it! Now you see what you've done!"

"No, I *don't* see what I've done. A match may attract lightning, for all I know, but it don't *cause* lightning—I'll go odds on that. And it didn't attract it worth a cent this time; for if that shot was leveled at my match, it was blessed poor marksmanship—about an average of none out of a possible million, I should say. Why, at Dollymount such marksmanship as that—"

"For shame, Mortimer! Here we are standing right in the very presence of death, and yet in so solemn a moment you are capable of using such language as that. If you have no desire to—Mortimer!"

"Well?"

"Did you say your prayers to-night?"

"I—I—meant to, but I got to trying to cipher out how much twelve times thirteen is, and—"

[*Fzt!—boom-berroom-boom! bumble-umble bang-*SMASH!]

"Oh, we are lost, beyond all help! How *could* you neglect such a thing at such a time as this?"

"But it *wasn't* 'such a time as this.' There wasn't a cloud in the sky. How could *I* know there was going to be all this rumpus and pow-wow about a little slip like that? And I don't think it's just fair for you to make so much out of it, anyway, seeing it happens so seldom; I haven't missed before since I brought on that earthquake, four years ago."

"MORTIMER! How you talk! Have you forgotten the yellow-fever?"

"My dear, you are always throwing up the yellow-fever to me, and I think it is perfectly unreasonable. You can't even send a telegraphic message as far as Memphis without relays, so how is a little devotional slip of mine going to carry so far? I'll *stand* the earthquake, because it was in the neighborhood; but I'll be hanged if I'm going to be responsible for every blamed—"

[*Fzt!—*BOOM *beroom-*boom! boom.—BANG!]

"Oh, dear, dear, dear! I *know* it struck something, Mortimer. We never shall see the light of another day; and if it will do you any good to remember, when we are gone, that your dreadful language—*Mortimer!*"

"WELL! What now?"

"Your voice sounds as if— Mortimer, are you actually standing in front of that open fireplace?"

"That is the very crime I am committing."

"Get away from it this moment! You do seem determined to bring destruction on us all. Don't you *know* that there is no better conductor for lightning than an open chimney? *Now* where have you got to?"

"I'm here by the window."

"Oh, for pity's sake! have you lost your mind? Clear out from there, this moment! The very children in arms know it is fatal to stand near a window in a thunder-storm. Dear, dear, I know I shall never see the light of another day! Mortimer!"

"Yes."

"What is that rustling?"

"It's me."

"What are you doing?"

"Trying to find the upper end of my pantaloons."

"Quick! throw those things away! I do believe you would deliberately put on those clothes at such a time as this; yet you know perfectly well that *all* authorities agree that woolen stuffs attract lightning. Oh, dear, dear, it isn't sufficient that one's life must be in peril from natural causes, but you must do everything you can possibly think of to augment the danger. Oh, *don't* sing! What *can* you be thinking of?"

"Now where's the harm in it?"

"Mortimer, if I have told you once, I have told you a hundred times, that singing causes vibrations in the atmosphere which interrupt the flow of the electric fluid, and— What on *earth* are you opening that door for?"

"Goodness gracious, woman, is there any harm in *that?*"

"*Harm?* There's *death* in it. Anybody that has given this subject any attention knows that to create a draught is to invite the lightning. You haven't half shut it; shut it *tight*—and do hurry, or we are all destroyed. Oh, it is an awful thing to be shut up with a lunatic at such a time as this. Mortimer, what *are* you doing?"

"Nothing. Just turning on the water. This room is smothering hot and close. I want to bathe my face and hands."

"You have certainly parted with the remnant of your mind! Where lightning strikes any other substance once, it strikes water fifty times. Do turn it off. Oh, dear, I am sure that nothing in this world can save us. It does seem to me that—Mortimer, what was that?"

"It was a da—it was a picture. Knocked it down."

"Then you are close to the wall! I never heard of such imprudence! Don't you *know* that there's no better conductor for lightning than a wall? Come away from there! And you came as near as anything to swearing, too. Oh, how can you be so desperately wicked, and your family in such peril? Mortimer, did you order a feather bed, as I asked you to do?"

"No. Forgot it."

"Forgot it! It may cost you your life. If you had a feather bed now, and could spread it in the middle of the room and lie on it, you would be perfectly safe. Come in here—come quick, before you have a chance to commit any more frantic indiscretions."

I tried, but the little closet would not hold us both with the door shut, unless we could be content to smother. I gasped awhile, then forced my way out. My wife called out:

"Mortimer, something *must* be done for your preservation. Give me that German book that is on the end of the mantelpiece, and a candle;

but don't light it; give me a match; I will light it in here. That book has some directions in it."

I got the book—at cost of a vase and some other brittle things; and the madam shut herself up with her candle. I had a moment's peace; then she called out:

"Mortimer, what was that?"

"Nothing but the cat."

"The cat! Oh, destruction! Catch her, and shut her up in the wash-stand. Do be quick, love; cats are *full* of electricity. I just know my hair will turn white with this night's awful perils."

I heard the muffled sobbings again. But for that, I should not have moved hand or foot in such a wild enterprise in the dark.

However, I went at my task—over chairs, and against all sorts of obstructions, all of them hard ones, too, and most of them with sharp edges—and at last I got kitty cooped up in the commode, at an expense of over four hundred dollars in broken furniture and shins. Then these muffled words came from the closet:

"It says the safest thing is to stand on a chair in the middle of the room, Mortimer; and the legs of the chair must be insulated with non-conductors. That is, you must set the legs of the chair in glass tumblers. [*Fzt!—boom—bang!—smash!*] Oh, hear that! Do hurry, Mortimer, before you are struck."

I managed to find and secure the tumblers. I got the last four—broke all the rest. I insulated the chair legs, and called for further instructions.

"Mortimer, it says, 'Während eines Gewitters entferne man Metalle, wie z. B., Ringe, Uhren, Schlüssel, etc., von sich und halte sich auch nicht an solchen Stellen auf, wo viele Metalle bei einander liegen, oder mit andern Körpern verbunden sind, wie an Herden, Oefen, Eisengittern u. dgl.' What does that mean, Mortimer? Does it mean that you must keep metals *about* you, or keep them *away* from you?"

"Well, I hardly know. It appears to be a little mixed. All German advice is more or less mixed. However, I think that that sentence is mostly in the dative case, with a little genitive and accusative sifted in, here and there, for luck; so I reckon it means that you must keep some metals *about* you."

"Yes, that must be it. It stands to reason that it is. They are in the nature of lightning-rods, you know. Put on your fireman's helmet, Mortimer; that is mostly metal."

I got it, and put it on—a very heavy and clumsy and uncomfortable thing on a hot night in a close room. Even my night-dress seemed to be more clothing than I strictly needed.

"Mortimer, I think your middle ought to be protected. Won't you buckle on your militia saber, please?"

I complied.

"Now, Mortimer, you ought to have some way to protect your feet. Do please put on your spurs."

I did it—in silence—and kept my temper as well as I could.

"Mortimer, it says, 'Das Gewitter läuten ist sehr gefährlich, weil die Glocke selbst, sowie der durch das Läuten veranlasste Luftzug und die Höhe des Thurmes den Blitz anziehen könnten.' Mortimer, does that mean that it is dangerous not to ring the church bells during a thunder-storm?"

"Yes, it seems to mean that—if that is the past participle of the nominative case singular, and I reckon it is. Yes, I think it means that on account of the height of the church tower and the absence of *Luftzug* it would be very dangerous (*sehr gefährlich*) not to ring the bells in time of a storm; and, moreover, don't you see, the very wording—"

"Never mind that, Mortimer; don't waste the precious time in talk. Get the large dinner-bell; it is right there in the hall. Quick, Mortimer, dear; we are almost safe. Oh, dear, I do believe we are going to be saved, at last!"

Our little summer establishment stands on top of a high range of hills, overlooking a valley. Several farm-houses are in our neighborhood —the nearest some three or four hundred yards away.

When I, mounted on the chair, had been clanging that dreadful bell a matter of seven or eight minutes, our shutters were suddenly torn open from without, and a brilliant bull's-eye lantern was thrust in at the window, followed by a hoarse inquiry:

"What in the nation is the matter here?"

The window was full of men's heads, and the heads were full of eyes that stared wildly at my night-dress and my warlike accoutrements.

I dropped the bell, skipped down from the chair in confusion, and said:

"There is nothing the matter, friends—only a little discomfort on account of the thunder-storm. I was trying to keep off the lightning."

"Thunder-storm? Lightning? Why, Mr. McWilliams, have you lost your mind? It is a beautiful starlight night; there has been no storm."

I looked out, and I was so astonished I could hardly speak for a while. Then I said:

"I do not understand this. We distinctly saw the glow of the flashes through the curtains and shutters, and heard the thunder."

One after another of those people lay down on the ground to laugh —and two of them died. One of the survivors remarked:

"Pity you didn't think to open your blinds and look over to the top of the high hill yonder. What you heard was cannon; what you saw was the flash. You see, the telegraph brought some news, just at midnight; Garfield's nominated—and that's what's the matter!"

Yes, Mr. Twain, as I was saying in the beginning (said Mr. McWilliams), the rules for preserving people against lightning are so excellent and so innumerable that the most incomprehensible thing in the world to me is how anybody ever manages to get struck.

So saying, he gathered up his satchel and umbrella, and departed; for the train had reached his town.

1880

What Stumped the Bluejays

Animals talk to each other, of course. There can be no question about that; but I suppose there are very few people who can understand them. I never knew but one man who could. I knew he could, however, because he told me so himself. He was a middle-aged, simple-hearted miner who had lived in a lonely corner of California, among the woods and mountains, a good many years, and had studied the ways of his only neighbors, the beasts and the birds, until he believed he could accurately translate any remark which they made. This was Jim Baker. According to Jim Baker, some animals have only a limited education, and use only very simple words, and scarcely ever a comparison or a flowery figure; whereas, certain other animals have a large vocabulary, a fine command of language and a ready and fluent delivery; consequently these latter talk a great deal; they like it; they are conscious of their talent, and they enjoy "showing off." Baker said, that after long and careful observation, he had come to the conclusion that the bluejays were the best talkers he had found among birds and beasts. Said he:

There's more *to* a bluejay than any other creature. He has got more moods, and more different kinds of feelings than other creatures; and, mind you, whatever a bluejay feels, he can put into language. And no mere commonplace language, either, but rattling, out-and-out book-talk —and bristling with metaphor, too—just bristling! And as for command of language—why *you* never see a bluejay get stuck for a word. No man ever did. They just boil out of him! And another thing: I've noticed a good deal, and there's no bird, or cow, or anything that uses as good grammar as a bluejay. You may say a cat uses good grammar. Well, a cat does—but you let a cat get excited once; you let a cat get to pulling fur with another cat on a shed, nights, and you'll hear grammar that will give you the lockjaw. Ignorant people think it's the *noise* which fighting cats make that is so aggravating, but it ain't so; it's the sickening grammar they use. Now I've never heard a jay use bad grammar but very seldom; and when they do, they are as ashamed as a human; they shut right down and leave.

You may call a jay a bird. Well, so he is, in a measure—because he's got feathers on him, and don't belong to no church, perhaps; but other- wise he is just as much a human as you be. And I'll tell you for why. A jay's gifts, and instincts, and feelings, and interests, cover the whole ground. A jay hasn't got any more principle than a Congressman. A jay will lie, a jay will steal, a jay will deceive, a jay will betray; and four times out of five, a jay will go back on his solemnest promise. The sacredness of an obligation is a thing which you can't cram into no bluejay's head. Now, on top of all this, there's another thing; a jay can out-swear any gentleman in the mines. You think a cat can swear. Well, a cat can; but you give a bluejay a subject that calls for his re- serve-powers, and where is your cat? Don't talk to *me*—I know too much about this thing. And there's yet another thing; in the one little particu- lar of scolding—just good, clean, out-and-out scolding—a bluejay can lay over anything, human or divine. Yes, sir, a jay is everything that a man is. A jay can cry, a jay can laugh, a jay can feel shame, a jay can reason and plan and discuss, a jay likes gossip and scandal, a jay has got a sense of humor, a jay knows when he is an ass just as well as you do— maybe better. If a jay ain't human, he better take in his sign, that's all. Now I'm going to tell you a perfectly true fact about some bluejays. When I first begun to understand jay language correctly, there was a little incident happened here. Seven years ago, the last man in this region but me moved away. There stands his house—been empty ever since; a log house, with a plank roof—just one big room, and no more; no ceiling —nothing between the rafters and the floor. Well, one Sunday morning I was sitting out here in front of my cabin, with my cat, taking the sun, and looking at the blue hills, and listening to the leaves rustling so lonely in the trees, and thinking of the home away yonder in the states, that I hadn't heard from in thirteen years, when a bluejay lit on that house, with an acorn in his mouth, and says, "Hello, I reckon I've struck something." When he spoke, the acorn dropped out of his mouth and rolled down the roof, of course, but he didn't care; his mind was all on the thing he had struck. It was a knot-hole in the roof. He cocked his head to one side, shut one eye and put the other one to the hole, like a possum looking down a jug; then he glanced up with his bright eyes, gave a wink or two with his wings—which signifies gratification, you understand—and says, "It looks like a hole, it's located like a hole—blamed if I don't believe it *is* a hole!"

Then he cocked his head down and took another look; he glances up perfectly joyful, this time; winks his wings and his tail both, and says, "Oh, no, this ain't no fat thing, I reckon! If I ain't in luck!—why it's a perfectly elegant hole!" So he flew down and got that acorn, and fetched it up and dropped it in, and was just tilting his head back, with the heavenliest smile on his face, when all of a sudden he was paralyzed into a listening attitude and that smile faded gradually out of his countenance like breath off'n a razor, and the queerest look of surprise took its place. Then he says, "Why, I didn't hear it fall!" He cocked his eye at the hole again, and took a long look; raised up and shook his head; stepped around to the other side of the hole and took another look from that side; shook his head again. He studied a while, then he just went into the *de*tails—walked round and round the hole and spied into it from every point of the compass. No use. Now he took a thinking attitude on the comb of the roof and scratched the back of his head with his right foot a minute, and finally says, "Well, it's too many for *me*, that's certain; must be a mighty long hole; however, I ain't got no time to fool around here, I got to 'tend to business; I reckon it's all right—chance it, anyway."

So he flew off and fetched another acorn and dropped it in, and tried to flirt his eye to the hole quick enough to see what become of it, but he was too late. He held his eye there as much as a minute; then he raised up and sighed, and says, "Confound it, I don't seem to understand this thing, no way; however, I'll tackle her again." He fetched another acorn, and done his level best to see what become of it, but he couldn't. He says, "Well, *I* never struck no such a hole as this before; I'm of the opinion it's a totally new kind of a hole." Then he begun to get mad. He held in for a spell, walking up and down the comb of the roof and shaking his head and muttering to himself; but his feelings got the upper hand of him, presently, and he broke loose and cussed himself black in the face. I never see a bird take on so about a little thing. When he got through he walks to the hole and looks in again for half a minute; then he says, "Well, you're a long hole, and a deep hole, and a mighty singular hole altogether—but I've started in to fill you, and I'm d—d if I *don't* fill you, if it takes a hundred years!"

And with that, away he went. You never see a bird work so since you was born. He laid into his work like a nigger, and the way he hove acorns into that hole for about two hours and a half was one of the most exciting and astonishing spectacles I ever struck. He never stopped to take a look any more—he just hove 'em in and went for more. Well, at last he could hardly flop his wings, he was so tuckered out. He comes a-drooping down, once more, sweating like an ice-pitcher, drops his acorn in and says, "*Now* I guess I've got the bulge on you by this time!" So he bent down for a look. If you'll believe me, when his head come up again he was just pale with rage. He says, "I've shoveled acorns enough in there to keep the family thirty years, and if I can see a sign of one of 'em I wish I may land in a museum with a belly full of sawdust in two minutes!"

He just had strength enough to crawl up on to the comb and lean his back agin the chimbly, and then he collected his impressions and begun to free his mind. I see in a second that what I had mistook for profanity in the mines was only just the rudiments, as you may say.

Another jay was going by, and heard him doing his devotions, and stops to inquire what was up. The sufferer told him the whole circumstance, and says, "Now yonder's the hole, and if you don't believe me, go and look for yourself." So this fellow went and looked, and comes back and says, "How many did you say you put in there?" "Not any less than two tons," says the sufferer. The other jay went and looked again. He couldn't seem to make it out, so he raised a yell, and three more jays come. They all examined the hole, they all made the sufferer tell it over again, then they all discussed it, and got off as many leather-headed opinions about it as an average crowd of humans could have done.

They called in more jays; then more and more, till pretty soon this whole region 'peared to have a blue flush about it. There must have been five thousand of them; and such another jawing and disputing and ripping and cussing, you never heard. Every jay in the whole lot put his eye to the hole and delivered a more chuckle-headed opinion about the mystery than the jay that went there before him. They examined the house all over, too. The door was standing half open, and at last one old jay happened to go and light on it and look in. Of course, that knocked the mystery galley-west in a second. There lay the acorns, scattered all over the floor. He flopped his wings and raised a whoop. "Come here!" he says, "Come here, everybody; hang'd if this fool hasn't been trying to fill up a house with acorns!" They all came a-swooping down like a blue cloud, and as each fellow lit on the door and took a glance, the whole absurdity of the contract that that first jay had tackled hit him home and he fell over backward suffocating with laughter, and the next jay took his place and done the same.

Well, sir, they roosted around here on the housetop and the trees for an hour, and guffawed over that thing like human beings. It ain't any use to tell me a bluejay hasn't got a sense of humor, because I know better. And memory, too. They brought jays here from all over the United States to look down that hole, every summer for three years. Other birds, too. And they could all see the point, except an owl that come from Nova Scotia to visit the Yo Semite, and he took this thing in on his way back. He said he couldn't see anything funny in it. But then he was a good deal disappointed about Yo Semite, too.

From A TRAMP ABROAD, 1880

A Curious Experience

This is the story which the Major told me, as nearly as I can recall it:

In the winter of 1862–63 I was commandant of Fort Trumbull, at New London, Conn. Maybe our life there was not so brisk as life at "the front"; still it was brisk enough, in its way—one's brains didn't cake together there for lack of something to keep them stirring. For one thing, all the Northern atmosphere at that time was thick with mysterious rumors—rumors to the effect that rebel spies were flitting everywhere, and getting ready to blow up our Northern forts, burn our hotels, send infected clothing into our towns, and all that sort of thing. You remember it. All this had a tendency to keep us awake, and knock the traditional dullness out of garrison life. Besides, ours was a recruiting station —which is the same as saying we hadn't any time to waste in dozing, or dreaming, or fooling around. Why, with all our watchfulness, fifty per cent. of a day's recruits would leak out of our hands and give us the slip the same night. The bounties were so prodigious that a recruit could pay a sentinel three or four hundred dollars to let him escape, and still have enough of his bounty-money left to constitute a fortune for a poor man. Yes, as I said before, our life was not drowsy.

Well, one day I was in my quarters alone, doing some writing, when a pale and ragged lad of fourteen or fifteen entered, made a neat bow, and said:

"I believe recruits are received here?"

"Yes."

"Will you please enlist me, sir?"

"Dear me, no! You are too young, my boy, and too small."

A disappointed look came into his face, and quickly deepened into an expression of despondency. He turned slowly away, as if to go; hesitated, then faced me again, and said, in a tone that went to my heart:

"I have no home, and not a friend in the world. If you *could* only enlist me!"

But of course the thing was out of the question, and I said so as gently as I could. Then I told him to sit down by the stove and warm himself, and added:

"You shall have something to eat, presently. You are hungry?"

He did not answer; he did not need to; the gratitude in his big, soft eyes was more eloquent than any words could have been. He sat down by the stove, and I went on writing. Occasionally I took a furtive glance at him. I noticed that his clothes and shoes, although soiled and damaged, were of good style and material. This fact was suggestive. To it I added the facts that his voice was low and musical; his eyes deep and melancholy; his carriage and address gentlemanly; evidently the poor chap was in trouble. As a result, I was interested.

However, I became absorbed in my work by and by, and forgot all about the boy. I don't know how long this lasted; but at length I happened to look up. The boy's back was toward me, but his face was turned in such a way that I could see one of his cheeks—and down that cheek a rill of noiseless tears was flowing.

"God bless my soul!" I said to myself; "I forgot the poor rat was starving." Then I made amends for my brutality by saying to him, "Come along, my lad; you shall dine with *me;* I am alone to-day."

He gave me another of those grateful looks, and a happy light broke in his face. At the table he stood with his hand on his chair-back until I was seated, then seated himself. I took up my knife and fork and—

well, I simply held them, and kept still; for the boy had inclined his head and was saying a silent grace. A thousand hallowed memories of home and my childhood poured in upon me, and I sighed to think how far I had drifted from religion and its balm for hurt minds, its comfort and solace and support.

As our meal progressed I observed that young Wicklow—Robert Wicklow was his full name—knew what to do with his napkin; and—well, in a word, I observed that he was a boy of good breeding; never mind the details. He had a simple frankness, too, which won upon me. We talked mainly about himself, and I had no difficulty in getting his history out of him. When he spoke of his having been born and reared in Louisiana, I warmed to him decidedly, for I had spent some time down there. I knew all the "coast" region of the Mississippi, and loved it, and had not been long enough away from it for my interest in it to begin to pale. The very names that fell from his lips sounded good to me—so good that I steered the talk in directions that would bring them out: Baton Rouge, Plaquemine, Donaldsonville, Sixty-mile Point, Bonnet-Carré, the Stock Landing, Carrollton, the Steamship Landing, the Steamboat Landing, New Orleans, Tchoupitoulas Street, the Esplanade, the Rue des Bons Enfants, the St. Charles Hotel, the Tivoli Circle, the Shell Road, Lake Pontchartrain; and it was particularly delightful to me to hear once more of the *R. E. Lee*, the *Natchez*, the *Eclipse*, the *General Quitman*, the *Duncan F. Kenner*, and other old familiar steamboats. It was almost as good as being back there, these names so vividly reproduced in my mind the look of the things they stood for. Briefly, this was little Wicklow's history:

When the war broke out, he and his invalid aunt and his father were living near Baton Rouge, on a great and rich plantation which had been in the family for fifty years. The father was a Union man. He was persecuted in all sorts of ways, but clung to his principles. At last one night masked men burned his mansion down, and the family had to fly for their lives. They were hunted from place to place, and learned all there was to know about poverty, hunger, and distress. The invalid aunt found relief at last: misery and exposure killed her; she died in an open field, like a tramp, the rain beating upon her and the thunder booming overhead. Not long afterward the father was captured by an armed band; and while the son begged and pleaded, the victim was strung up before his face. [At this point a baleful light shone in the youth's eyes, and he said, with the manner of one who talks to himself: "If I cannot be enlisted, no matter—I shall find a way—I shall find a way."] As soon as the father was pronounced dead, the son was told that if he was not out of that region within twenty-four hours it would go hard with him. That night he crept to the riverside and hid himself near a plantation landing. By and by the *Duncan F. Kenner* stopped there, and he swam out and concealed himself in the yawl that was dragging at her stern. Before daylight the boat reached the Stock Landing and he slipped ashore. He walked the three miles which lay between that point and the house of an uncle of his in Good-Children Street, in New Orleans, and then his troubles were over for the time being. But this uncle was a Union man, too, and before very long he concluded that he had better leave the South. So he and young Wicklow slipped out of the country on board a sailing-vessel, and in due time reached New York. They put up at the Astor House. Young Wicklow had a good time of it for a while, strolling up and down Broadway, and observing the strange Northern sights; but in the end a change came—and not for the better. The uncle had been cheerful at first, but now he began to look troubled and despondent; moreover, he became moody and irritable; talked of money giving out, and no way to get more—"not enough left for one, let alone two." Then, one morning, he was missing—did not come to breakfast. The boy inquired at the office, and was told that the uncle had paid his bill the night before and gone away—to Boston, the clerk believed, but was not certain.

The lad was alone and friendless. He did not know what to do, but concluded he had better try to follow and find his uncle. He went down to the steamboat landing: learned that the trifle of money in his pocket would not carry him to Boston; however, it would carry him to New London; so he took passage for that port, resolving to trust to Providence to furnish him means to travel the rest of the way. He had now been wandering about the streets of New London three days and nights, getting a bite and a nap here and there for charity's sake. But he had given up at last; courage and hope were both gone. If he could enlist, nobody could be more thankful; if he could not get in as a soldier, couldn't he be a drummer-boy? Ah, he would work *so* hard to please, and would be so grateful!

Well, there's the history of young Wicklow, just as he told it to me, barring details. I said:

"My boy, you are among friends now—don't you be troubled any more." How his eyes glistened! I called in Sergeant John Rayburn—he was from Hartford; lives in Hartford yet; maybe you know him—and said, "Rayburn, quarter this boy with the musicians. I am going to enroll him as a drummer-boy, and I want you to look after him and see that he is well treated."

Well, of course, intercourse between the commandant of the post and the drummer-boy came to an end now; but the poor little friendless chap lay heavy on my heart just the same. I kept on the lookout, hoping to see him brighten up and begin to be cheery and gay; but no, the days went by, and there was no change. He associated with nobody; he was always absent-minded, always thinking; his face was always sad. One morning Rayburn asked leave to speak to me privately. Said he:

"I hope I don't offend, sir; but the truth is, the musicians are in such a sweat it seems as if somebody's *got* to speak."

"Why, what is the trouble?"

"It's the Wicklow boy, sir. The musicians are down on him to an extent you can't imagine."

"Well, go on, go on. What has he been doing?"

"Prayin', sir."

"Praying!"

"Yes, sir; the musicians haven't any peace of their life for that boy's prayin'. First thing in the mornin' he's at it; noons he's at it; and nights—well, *nights* he just lays into 'em like all possessed! Sleep? Bless you, they *can't* sleep: he's got the floor, as the sayin' is, and then when he once gets his supplication-mill agoin' there just simply ain't any let-up *to* him. He starts in with the band-master, and he prays for him; next he takes the head bugler, and he prays for him; next the bass drum, and he scoops *him* in; and so on, right straight through the band, givin' them all a show, and takin' that amount of interest in it which would make you think he thought he warn't but a little while for this world, and believed he couldn't be happy in heaven without he had a brass-band along, and wanted to pick 'em out for himself, so he could depend on 'em to do up the national tunes in a style suitin' to the place. Well, sir, heavin' boots at him don't have no effect; it's dark in there; and, besides, he don't pray fair, anyway, but kneels down behind the big drum; so it don't make no difference if they *rain* boots at him, *he* don't give a dern—warbles right along, same as if it was applause. They sing out, 'Oh, dry up!' 'Give us a rest!' 'Shoot him!' 'Oh, take a walk!' and all sorts of such things. But what of it? It don't faze him. *He* don't mind it." After a pause: "Kind of a good little fool, too; gits up in the mornin' and carts all that stock of boots back, and sorts 'em out and sets each man's pair where they belong. And they've been throwed at him so much now that he knows every boot in the band—can sort 'em out with his eyes shut."

After another pause, which I forbore to interrupt:

"But the roughest thing about it is that when he's done prayin'—when he ever *does* get done—he pipes up and begins to *sing*. Well, you know what a honey kind of a voice he's got when he talks; you know how it would persuade a cast-iron dog to come down off of a door-step and lick his hand. Now if you'll take my word for it, sir, it ain't a circumstance to his singin'! Flute music is harsh to that boy's singin'. Oh, he just gurgles it out so soft and sweet and low, there in the dark, that it makes you think you are in heaven."

"What is there 'rough' about that?"

"Ah, that's just it, sir. You hear him sing

> *'Just as I am—poor, wretched, blind'—*

just you hear him sing that once, and see if you don't melt all up and the water come into your eyes! I don't care *what* he sings, it goes plum straight home to you—it goes deep down to where you *live*—and it fetches you every time! Just you hear him sing

> *'Child of sin and sorrow, filled with dismay,*
> *Wait not till to-morrow, yield thee to-day;*
> *Grieve not that love*
> *Which, from above'—*

and so on. It makes a body feel like the wickedest, ungratefulest brute that walks. And when he sings them songs of his about home, and mother, and childhood, and old memories, and things that's vanished, and old friends dead and gone, it fetches everything before your face that you've ever loved and lost in all your life—and it's just beautiful, it's just divine to listen to, sir—but, Lord, Lord, the heartbreak of it! The band—well, they all cry—every rascal of them blubbers, and don't try to hide it, either; and first you know, that very gang that's been slammin' boots at that boy will skip out of their bunks all of a sudden, and rush over in the dark and hug him! Yes, they do—and slobber all over him, and call him pet names, and beg him to forgive them. And just at that time, if a regiment was to offer to hurt a hair of that cub's head, they'd go for that regiment, if it was a whole army corps!"

Another pause.

"Is that all?" said I.

"Yes, sir."

"Well, dear me, what is the complaint? What do they want done?"

"Done? Why, bless you, sir, they want you to stop him from *singin'*."

"What an idea! You said his music was divine."

"That's just it. It's *too* divine. Mortal man can't stand it. It stirs a body up so; it turns a body inside out; it racks his feelin's all to rags; it makes him feel bad and wicked, and not fit for any place but perdition. It keeps a body in such an everlastin' state of repentin', that nothin' don't taste good and there ain't no comfort in life. And then the *cryin'*, you see—every mornin' they are ashamed to look one another in the face."

"Well, this is an odd case, and a singular complaint. So they really want the singing stopped?"

"Yes, sir, that is the idea. They don't wish to ask too much; they would like powerful well to have the prayin' shut down on, or leastways trimmed off around the edges; but the main thing's the singin'. If they can only get the singin' choked off, they think they can stand the prayin', rough as it is to be bullyragged so much that way."

I told the sergeant I would take the matter under consideration. That night I crept into the musicians' quarters and listened. The sergeant had not overstated the case. I heard the praying voice pleading in the dark; I heard the execrations of the harassed men; I heard the rain of boots whiz through the air, and bang and thump around the big drum. The thing touched me, but it amused me, too. By and by, after an impressive silence, came the singing. Lord, the pathos of it, the enchantment of it! Nothing in the world was ever so sweet, so gracious, so tender, so holy, so moving. I made my stay very brief; I was beginning to experience emotions of a sort not proper to the commandant of a fortress.

Next day I issued orders which stopped the praying and singing. Then followed three or four days which were so full of bounty-jumping excitements and irritations that I never once thought of my drummer-boy. But now comes Sergeant Rayburn, one morning, and says:

"That new boy acts mighty strange, sir."

"How?"

"Well, sir, he's all the time writin'."

"Writing? What does he write—letters?"

"I don't know, sir; but whenever he's off duty, he is always pokin' and nosin' around the fort, all by himself—blest if I think there's a hole or corner in it he hasn't been into—and every little while he outs with pencil and paper and scribbles somethin' down."

This gave me a most unpleasant sensation. I wanted to scoff at it, but it was not a time to scoff at *anything* that had the least suspicious tinge about it. Things were happening all around us in the North then that warned us to be always on the alert, and always suspecting. I recalled to mind the suggestive fact that this boy was from the South— the extreme South, Louisiana—and the thought was not of a reassuring nature, under the circumstances. Nevertheless, it cost me a pang to give the orders which I now gave to Rayburn. I felt like a father who plots to expose his own child to shame and injury. I told Rayburn to keep quiet, bide his time, and get me some of those writings whenever he could manage it without the boy's finding it out. And I charged him not to do anything which might let the boy discover that he was being watched. I also ordered that he allow the lad his usual liberties, but that he be followed at a distance when he went out into the town.

During the next two days Rayburn reported to me several times. No success. The boy was still writing, but he always pocketed his paper with a careless air whenever Rayburn appeared in the vicinity. He had gone twice to an old deserted stable in the town, remained a minute or two, and come out again. One could not pooh-pooh these things—they had an evil look. I was obliged to confess to myself that I was getting uneasy. I went into my private quarters and sent for my second in command—an officer of intelligence and judgment, son of General James Watson Webb. He was surprised and troubled. We had a long talk over the matter, and came to the conclusion that it would be worth while to institute a secret search. I determined to take charge of that myself. So I had myself called at two in the morning; and pretty soon after I was in the musicians' quarters, crawling along the floor on my stomach among the snorers. I reached my slumbering waif's bunk at last, without disturbing anybody, captured his clothes and kit, and crawled stealthily back again. When I got to my own quarters, I found Webb there, waiting and eager to know the result. We made search immediately. The clothes were a disappointment. In the pockets we found blank paper and a pencil; nothing else, except a jackknife and such queer odds and ends and useless trifles as boys hoard and value. We turned to the kit hopefully. Nothing there but a rebuke for us!—a little Bible with this written on the fly-leaf: "Stranger, be kind to my boy, for his mother's sake."

I looked at Webb—he dropped his eyes; he looked at me—I dropped mine. Neither spoke. I put the book reverently back in its place. Presently Webb got up and went away, without remark. After a little I nerved myself up to my unpalatable job, and took the plunder back to where it belonged, crawling on my stomach as before. It seemed the peculiarly appropriate attitude for the business I was in.

I was most honestly glad when it was over and done with.

About noon next day Rayburn came, as usual, to report. I cut him short. I said:

"Let this nonsense be dropped. We are making a bugaboo out of a poor little cub who has got no more harm in him than a hymn-book."

The sergeant looked surprised, and said:

"Well, you know it was your orders, sir, and I've got some of the writin'."

"And what does it amount to? How did you get it?"

"I peeped through the keyhole, and see him writin'. So, when I judged he was about done, I made a sort of a little cough, and I see him crumple it up and throw it in the fire, and look all around to see if anybody was comin'. Then he settled back as comfortable and careless as anything. Then I comes in, and passes the time of day pleasantly, and sends him on an errand. He never looked uneasy, but went right along. It was a coal fire and new built; the writin' had gone over behind a chunk, out of sight; but I got it out; there it is; it ain't hardly scorched, you see."

I glanced at the paper and took in a sentence or two. Then I dismissed the sergeant and told him to send Webb to me. Here is the paper in full:

FORT TRUMBULL, *the 8th.*

COLONEL *I was mistaken as to the caliber of the three guns I ended my list with. They are 18-pounders; all the rest of the armament is as I stated. The garrison remains as before reported, except that the two light infantry companies that were to be detached for service at the front are to stay here for the present—can't find out for how long, just now, but will soon. We are satisfied that, all things considered, matters had better be postponed un—*

There it broke off—there is where Rayburn coughed and interrupted the writer. All my affection for the boy, all my respect for him and charity for his forlorn condition, withered in a moment under the blight of this revelation of cold-blooded baseness.

But never mind about that. Here was business—business that required profound and immediate attention, too. Webb and I turned the subject over and over, and examined it all around. Webb said:

"What a pity he was interrupted! Something is going to be postponed until—when? And what *is* the something? Possibly he would have mentioned it, the pious little reptile!"

"Yes," I said, "we have missed a trick. And who is '*we*' in the letter? Is it conspirators inside the fort or outside?"

That "we" was uncomfortably suggestive. However, it was not worth while to be guessing around that, so we proceeded to matters more practical. In the first place, we decided to double the sentries and keep the strictest possible watch. Next, we thought of calling Wicklow in and making him divulge everything; but that did not seem wisest until other methods should fail. We must have some more of the writings; so we began to plan to that end. And now we had an idea: Wicklow never went to the post-office—perhaps the deserted stable was his post-office. We sent for my confidential clerk—a young German named Sterne, who was a sort of natural detective—and told him all about the case, and ordered him to go to work on it. Within the hour we got word that Wicklow was writing again. Shortly afterward word came that he had asked leave to go out into the town. He was detained awhile and meantime Sterne hurried off and concealed himself in the stable. By and by he saw Wicklow saunter in, look about him, then hide something under some rubbish in a corner, and take leisurely leave again. Sterne pounced upon the hidden article—a letter—and brought it to us. It had no superscription and no signature. It repeated what we had already read, and then went on to say:

We think it best to postpone till the two companies are gone. I mean the four inside think so; have not communicated with the others—afraid of attracting attention. I say four because we have lost two; they had hardly enlisted and got inside when they were shipped off to the front. It will be absolutely necessary to have two in their places. The two that went were the brothers from Thirty-mile Point. I have something of the greatest importance to reveal, but must not trust it to this method of communication; will try the other.

"The little scoundrel!" said Webb; "who *could* have supposed he was a spy? However, never mind about that; let us add up our particulars, such as they are, and see how the case stands to date. First, we've got a rebel spy in our midst, whom we know; secondly, we've got three more in our midst whom we don't know; thirdly, these spies have been introduced among us through the simple and easy process of enlisting as soldiers in the Union army—and evidently two of them have got sold at it, and been shipped off to the front; fourthly, there are assistant spies 'outside'—number indefinite; fifthly, Wicklow has very important matter which he is afraid to communicate by the 'present method'—will 'try the other.' That is the case, as it now stands. Shall we collar Wicklow and make him confess? Or shall we catch the person who removes the letters from the stable and make *him* tell? Or shall we keep still and find out more?"

We decided upon the last course. We judged that we did not need to proceed to summary measures now, since it was evident that the conspirators were likely to wait till those two light infantry companies were out of the way. We fortified Sterne with pretty ample powers, and told him to use his best endeavors to find out Wicklow's "other method" of communication. We meant to play a bold game; and to this end we proposed to keep the spies in an unsuspecting state as long as possible. So we ordered Sterne to return to the stable immediately, and, if he found the coast clear, to conceal Wicklow's letter where it was before, and leave it there for the conspirators to get.

The night closed down without further event. It was cold and dark and sleety, with a raw wind blowing; still I turned out of my warm bed several times during the night, and went the rounds in person, to see that all was right and that every sentry was on the alert. I always found them wide awake and watchful; evidently whispers of mysterious dangers had been floating about, and the doubling of the guards had been a kind of indorsement of those rumors. Once, toward morning, I encountered Webb, breasting his way against the bitter wind, and learned then that he, also, had been the rounds several times to see that all was going right.

Next day's events hurried things up somewhat. Wicklow wrote another letter; Sterne preceded him to the stable and saw him deposit it; captured it as soon as Wicklow was out of the way, then slipped out and followed the little spy at a distance, with a detective in plain clothes at his own heels, for we thought it judicious to have the law's assistance handy in case of need. Wicklow went to the railway station, and waited around till the train from New York came in, then stood scanning the faces of the crowd as they poured out of the cars. Presently an aged gentleman, with green goggles and a cane, came limping along, stopped in Wicklow's neighborhood, and began to look about him expectantly. In an instant Wicklow darted forward, thrust an envelope into his hand, then glided away and disappeared in the throng. The next instant Sterne had snatched the letter; and as he hurried past the detective, he said: "Follow the old gentleman—don't lose sight of him." Then Sterne skurried out with the crowd, and came straight to the fort.

We sat with closed doors, and instructed the guard outside to allow no interruption.

First we opened the letter captured at the stable. It read as follows:

HOLY ALLIANCE *Found, in the usual gun, commands from the Master, left there last night, which set aside the instructions heretofore received from the subordinate quarter. Have left in the gun the usual indication that the commands reached the proper hand—*

Webb, interrupting: "Isn't the boy under constant surveillance now?"

I said yes; he had been under strict surveillance ever since the capturing of his former letter.

"Then how could he put anything into a gun, or take anything out of it, and not get caught?"

"Well," I said, "I don't like the look of that very well."

"I don't either," said Webb. "It simply means that there are conspirators among the very sentinels. Without their connivance in some way or other, the thing couldn't have been done."

I sent for Rayburn, and ordered him to examine the batteries and see what he could find. The reading of the letter was then resumed:

The new commands are peremptory, and require that the MMMM shall be FFFFF at 3 o'clock to-morrow morning. Two hundred will arrive, in small parties, by train and otherwise, from various directions, and will be at appointed place at right time. I will distribute the sign to-day. Success is apparently sure, though something must have got out, for the sentries have been doubled, and the chiefs went the rounds last night several times. W. W. comes from southerly to-day and will receive secret orders—by the other method. All six of you must be in 166 at sharp 2 A.M. You will find B. B. there, who will give you detailed instructions. Password same as last time, only reversed—put first syllable last and last syllable first. REMEMBER XXXX. Do not forget. Be of good heart; before the next sun rises you will be heroes; your fame will be permanent; you will have added a deathless page to history. AMEN.

"Thunder and Mars," said Webb, "but we are getting into mighty hot quarters, as I look at it!"

I said there was no question but that things were beginning to wear a most serious aspect. Said I:

"A desperate enterprise is on foot, that is plain enough. To-night is the time set for it—that, also, is plain. The exact nature of the enterprise—I mean the manner of it—is hidden away under those blind bunches of M's and F's, but the end and aim, I judge, is the surprise and capture of the post. We must move quick and sharp now. I think nothing can be gained by continuing our clandestine policy as regards Wicklow. We *must* know, and as soon as possible, too, where '166' is located, so that we can make a descent upon the gang there at 2 A.M.; and doubtless the quickest way to get that information will be to force it out of that boy. But first of all, and before we make any important move, I must lay the facts before the War Department, and ask for plenary powers."

The despatch was prepared in cipher to go over the wires; I read it, approved it, and sent it along.

We presently finished discussing the letter which was under consideration, and then opened the one which had been snatched from the lame gentleman. It contained nothing but a couple of perfectly blank sheets of note-paper! It was a chilly check to our hot eagerness and expectancy. We felt as blank as the paper, for a moment, and twice as foolish. But it was for a moment only; for, of course, we immediately afterward thought of "sympathetic ink." We held the paper close to the fire and watched for the characters to come out, under the influence of the heat; but nothing appeared but some faint tracings, which we could make nothing of. We then called in the surgeon, and sent him off with orders to apply every test he was acquainted with till he got the right one, and report the contents of the letter to me the instant he brought them to the surface. This check was a confounded annoyance, and we naturally chafed under the delay; for we had fully expected to get out of that letter some of the most important secrets of the plot.

Now appeared Sergeant Rayburn, and drew from his pocket a piece of twine string about a foot long, with three knots tied in it, and held it up.

"I got it out of a gun on the water-front," said he. "I took the tompions out of all the guns and examined close; this string was the only thing that was in any gun."

So this bit of string was Wicklow's "sign" to signify that the "Master's" commands had not miscarried. I ordered that every sentinel who had served near that gun during the past twenty-four hours be put in confinement at once and separately, and not allowed to communicate with any one without my privity and consent.

A telegram now came from the Secretary of War. It read as follows:

SUSPEND HABEAS CORPUS. PUT TOWN UNDER MARTIAL LAW. MAKE NECESSARY ARRESTS. ACT WITH VIGOR AND PROMPTNESS. KEEP THE DEPARTMENT INFORMED.

We were now in shape to go to work. I sent out and had the lame gentleman quietly arrested and as quietly brought into the fort; I placed him under guard, and forbade speech to him or from him. He was inclined to bluster at first, but he soon dropped that.

Next came word that Wicklow had been seen to give something to a couple of our new recruits; and that, as soon as his back was turned, these had been seized and confined. Upon each was found a small bit of paper, bearing these words and signs in pencil:

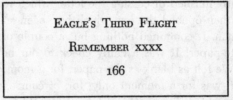

EAGLE'S THIRD FLIGHT

REMEMBER XXXX

166

In accordance with instructions, I telegraphed to the Department, in cipher, the progress made, and also described the above ticket. We seemed to be in a strong enough position now to venture to throw off the mask as regarded Wicklow; so I sent for him. I also sent for and received back the letter written in sympathetic ink, the surgeon accompanying it with the information that thus far it had resisted his tests, but that there were others he could apply when I should be ready for him to do so.

Presently Wicklow entered. He had a somewhat worn and anxious look, but he was composed and easy, and if he suspected anything it did not appear in his face or manner. I allowed him to stand there a moment or two; then I said, pleasantly:

"My boy, why do you go to that old stable so much?"

He answered, with simple demeanor and without embarrassment:

"Well, I hardly know, sir; there isn't any particular reason, except that I like to be alone, and I amuse myself there."

"You amuse yourself there, do you?"

"Yes, sir," he replied, as innocently and simply as before.

"Is that all you do there?"

"Yes, sir," he said, looking up with childlike wonderment in his big, soft eyes.

"You are *sure?*"

"Yes, sir, sure."

After a pause I said:

"Wicklow, why do you write so much?"

"I? I do not write much, sir."

"You don't?"

"No, sir. Oh, if you mean scribbling, I *do* scribble some, for amusement."

"What do you do with your scribblings?"

"Nothing, sir—throw them away."

"Never send them to anybody?"

"No, sir."

I suddenly thrust before him the letter to the "Colonel." He started slightly, but immediately composed himself. A slight tinge spread itself over his cheek.

"How came you to send *this* piece of scribbling, then?"

"I nev—never meant any harm, sir!"

"Never meant any harm! You betray the armament and condition of the post, and mean no harm by it?"

He hung his head and was silent.

"Come, speak up, and stop lying. Whom was this letter intended for?"

He showed signs of distress now; but quickly collected himself, and replied, in a tone of deep earnestness:

"I will tell you the truth, sir—the whole truth. The letter was never intended for anybody at all. I wrote it only to amuse myself. I see the error and foolishness of it now; but it is the only offense, sir, upon my honor."

"Ah, I am glad of that. It is dangerous to be writing such letters. I hope you are sure this is the only one you wrote?"

"Yes, sir, perfectly sure."

His hardihood was stupefying. He told that lie with as sincere a countenance as any creature ever wore. I waited a moment to soothe down my rising temper, and then said:

"Wicklow, jog your memory now, and see if you can help me with two or three little matters which I wish to inquire about."

"I will do my very best, sir."

"Then, to begin with—who is 'the Master'?"

It betrayed him into darting a startled glance at our faces, but that was all. He was serene again in a moment, and tranquilly answered:

"I do not know, sir."

"You do not know?"

"I do not know."

"You are *sure* you do not know?"

He tried hard to keep his eyes on mine, but the strain was too great; his chin sunk slowly toward his breast and he was silent; he stood there nervously fumbling with a button, an object to command one's pity, in spite of his base acts. Presently I broke the stillness with the question:

"Who are the 'Holy Alliance'?"

His body shook visibly, and he made a slight random gesture with his hands, which to me was like the appeal of a despairing creature for compassion. But he made no sound. He continued to stand with his face bent toward the ground. As we sat gazing at him, waiting for him to speak, we saw the big tears begin to roll down his cheeks. But he remained silent. After a little, I said:

"You must answer me, my boy, and you must tell me the truth. Who are the Holy Alliance?"

He wept on in silence. Presently I said, somewhat sharply:

"Answer the question!"

He struggled to get command of his voice; and then, looking up appealingly, forced the words out between his sobs:

"Oh, have pity on me, sir! I cannot answer it, for I do not know."

"What!"

"Indeed, sir, I am telling the truth. I never have heard of the Holy Alliance till this moment. On my honor, sir, this is so."

"Good heavens! Look at this second letter of yours; there, do you see those words, 'Holy Alliance'? What do you say now?"

He gazed up into my face with the hurt look of one upon whom a great wrong had been wrought, then said, feelingly:

"This is some cruel joke, sir; and how could they play it upon me, who have tried all I could to do right, and have never done harm to anybody? Some one has counterfeited my hand; I never wrote a line of this; I have never seen this letter before!"

"Oh, you unspeakable liar! Here, what do you say to this?"—and I snatched the sympathetic-ink letter from my pocket and thrust it before his eyes.

His face turned white—as white as a dead person's. He wavered slightly in his tracks, and put his hand against the wall to steady himself. After a moment he asked, in so faint a voice that it was hardly audible:

"Have you—read it?"

Our faces must have answered the truth before my lips could get out a false "yes," for I distinctly saw the courage come back into that boy's eyes. I waited for him to say something, but he kept silent. So at last I said:

"Well, what have you to say as to the revelations in this letter?"

He answered, with perfect composure:

"Nothing, except that they are entirely harmless and innocent; they can hurt nobody."

I was in something of a corner now, as I couldn't disprove his assertion. I did not know exactly how to proceed. However, an idea came to my relief, and I said:

"You are sure you know nothing about the Master and the Holy Alliance, and did not write the letter which you say is a forgery?"

"Yes, sir—sure."

I slowly drew out the knotted twine string and held it up without speaking. He gazed at it indifferently, then looked at me inquiringly. My patience was sorely taxed. However, I kept my temper down, and said, in my usual voice:

"Wicklow, do you see this?"

"Yes, sir."

"What is it?"

"It seems to be a piece of string."

"*Seems?* It *is* a piece of string. Do you recognize it?"

"No, sir," he replied, as calmly as the words could be uttered.

His coolness was perfectly wonderful! I paused now for several seconds, in order that the silence might add impressiveness to what I was about to say; then I rose and laid my hand on his shoulder, and said, gravely:

"It will do you no good, poor boy, none in the world. This sign to the 'Master,' this knotted string, found in one of the guns on the water-front—"

"Found *in* the gun! Oh, no, no, no! do not say *in* the gun, but in a crack in the tompion!—it *must* have been in the crack!" and down he went on his knees and clasped his hands and lifted up a face that was pitiful to see, so ashy it was, and wild with terror.

"No, it was *in* the gun."

"Oh, something has gone wrong! My God, I am lost!" and he sprang up and darted this way and that, dodging the hands that were put out to catch him, and doing his best to escape from the place. But of course escape was impossible. Then he flung himself on his knees again, crying with all his might, and clasped me around the legs; and so he clung to me and begged and pleaded, saying, "Oh, have pity on me! Oh, be merciful to me! Do not betray me; they would not spare my life a moment! Protect me, save me. I will confess everything!"

It took us some time to quiet him down and modify his fright, and get him into something like a rational frame of mind. Then I began to question him, he answering humbly, with downcast eyes, and from time to time swabbing away his constantly flowing tears:

"So you are at heart a rebel?"

"Yes, sir."

"And a spy?"

"Yes, sir."

"And have been acting under distinct orders from outside?"

"Yes, sir."

"Willingly?"

"Yes, sir."

"*Gladly*, perhaps?"

"Yes, sir; it would do no good to deny it. The South is my country; my heart is Southern, and it is all in her cause."

"Then the tale you told me of your wrongs and the persecution of your family was made up for the occasion?"

"They—they told me to say it, sir."

"And you would betray and destroy those who pitied and sheltered you. Do you comprehend how base you are, you poor misguided thing?"

He replied with sobs only.

"Well, let that pass. To business. Who is the 'Colonel,' and where is he?"

He began to cry hard, and tried to beg off from answering. He said he would be killed if he told. I threatened to put him in the dark cell and lock him up if he did not come out with the information. At the same time I promised to protect him from all harm if he made a clean breast. For all answer, he closed his mouth firmly and put on a stubborn air which I could not bring him out of. At last I started with him; but a single glance into the dark cell converted him. He broke into a passion of weeping and supplicating, and declared he would tell everything.

So I brought him back, and he named the "Colonel," and described him particularly. Said he would be found at the principal hotel in the town, in citizen's dress. I had to threaten him again, before he would describe and name the "Master." Said the Master would be found at No. 15 Bond Street, New York, passing under the name of R. F. Gaylord. I telegraphed name and description to the chief of police of the metropolis, and asked that Gaylord be arrested and held till I could send for him.

"Now," said I, "it seems that there are several of the conspirators 'outside,' presumably in New London. Name and describe them."

He named and described three men and two women—all stopping at the principal hotel. I sent out quietly, and had them and the "Colonel" arrested and confined in the fort.

"Next, I want to know all about your three fellow-conspirators who are here in the fort."

He was about to dodge me with a falsehood, I thought; but I produced the mysterious bits of paper which had been found upon two of them, and this had a salutary effect upon him. I said we had possession of two of the men, and he must point out the third. This frightened him badly, and he cried out:

"Oh, please don't make me; he would kill me on the spot!"

I said that that was all nonsense; I would have somebody near by to protect him, and, besides, the men should be assembled without arms. I ordered all the raw recruits to be mustered, and then the poor, trembling little wretch went out and stepped along down the line, trying to look as indifferent as possible. Finally he spoke a single word to one of the men, and before he had gone five steps the man was under arrest.

As soon as Wicklow was with us again, I had those three men brought in. I made one of them stand forward, and said:

"Now, Wicklow, mind, not a shade's divergence from the exact truth. Who is this man, and what do you know about him?"

Being "in for it," he cast consequences aside, fastened his eyes on the man's face, and spoke straight along without hesitation—to the following effect:

"His real name is George Bristow. He is from New Orleans; was second mate of the coast-packet *Capitol* two years ago; is a desperate character, and has served two terms for manslaughter—one for killing a deck-hand named Hyde with a capstan-bar, and one for killing a roustabout for refusing to heave the lead, which is no part of a roustabout's business. He is a spy, and was sent here by the Colonel to act in that capacity. He was third mate of the *St. Nicholas* when she blew up in the neighborhood of Memphis, in '58, and came near being lynched for robbing the dead and wounded while they were being taken ashore in an empty wood-boat."

And so forth and so on—he gave the man's biography in full. When he had finished, I said to the man:

"What have you to say to this?"

"Barring your presence, sir, it is the infernalist lie that ever was spoke!"

I sent him back into confinement, and called the others forward in turn. Same result. The boy gave a detailed history of each, without ever hesitating for a word or a fact; but all I could get out of either rascal was the indignant assertion that it was all a lie. They would confess nothing. I returned them to captivity, and brought out the rest of my prisoners, one by one. Wicklow told all about them—what towns in the South they were from, and every detail of their connection with the conspiracy.

But they all denied his facts, and not one of them confessed a thing. The men raged, the women cried. According to their stories, they were all innocent people from out West, and loved the Union above all things in this world. I locked the gang up, in disgust, and fell to catechizing Wicklow once more.

"Where is No. 166, and who is B. B.?"

But *there* he was determined to draw the line. Neither coaxing nor threats had any effect upon him. Time was flying—it was necessary to institute sharp measures. So I tied him up a-tiptoe by the thumbs. As the pain increased, it wrung screams from him which were almost more than I could bear. But I held my ground, and pretty soon he shrieked out:

"Oh, *please* let me down, and I will tell!"

"No—you'll tell *before* I let you down."

Every instant was agony to him now, so out it came:

"No. 166, Eagle Hotel!"—naming a wretched tavern down by the water, a resort of common laborers, 'longshoremen, and less reputable folk.

So I released him, and then demanded to know the object of the conspiracy.

"To take the fort to-night," said he, doggedly and sobbing.

"Have I got all the chiefs of the conspiracy?"

"No. You've got all except those that are to meet at 166."

"What does 'Remember XXXX' mean?"

No reply.

"What is the password to No. 166?"

No reply.

"What do those bunches of letters mean—'FFFFF' and 'MMMM'? Answer! or you will catch it again."

"I never *will* answer! I will die first. Now do what you please."

"Think what you are saying, Wicklow. Is it final?"

He answered steadily, and without a quiver in his voice:

"It is final. As sure as I love my wronged country and hate everything this Northern sun shines on, I will die before I will reveal those things."

I tied him up by the thumbs again. When the agony was full upon him it was heartbreaking to hear the poor thing's shrieks, but we got nothing else out of him. To every question he screamed the same reply: "I can die, and I *will* die; but I will never tell."

Well, we had to give it up. We were convinced that he certainly would die rather than confess. So we took him down, and imprisoned him under strict guard.

Then for some hours we busied ourselves with sending telegrams to the War Department, and with making preparations for a descent upon No. 166.

It was stirring times, that black and bitter night. Things had leaked out, and the whole garrison was on the alert. The sentinels were trebled, and nobody could move, outside or in, without being brought to a stand with a musket leveled at his head. However, Webb and I were less concerned now than we had previously been, because of the fact that the conspiracy must necessarily be in a pretty crippled condition, since so many of its principals were in our clutches.

I determined to be at No. 166 in good season, capture and gag B. B., and be on hand for the rest when they arrived. At about a quarter past one in the morning I crept out of the fortress with half a dozen stalwart and gamy U. S. regulars at my heels, and the boy Wicklow, with his hands tied behind him. I told him we were going to No. 166, and that if I found he had lied again and was misleading us, he would have to show us the right place or suffer the consequences.

We approached the tavern stealthily and reconnoitered. A light was burning in the small barroom, the rest of the house was dark. I tried the front door; it yielded, and we softly entered, closing the door behind us. Then we removed our shoes, and I led the way to the barroom. The German landlord sat there, asleep in his chair. I woke him gently, and told him to take off his boots and precede us, warning him at the same time to utter no sound. He obeyed without a murmur, but evidently he was badly frightened. I ordered him to lead the way to 166. We ascended two or three flights of stairs as softly as a file of cats; and then, having arrived near the farther end of a long hall, we came to a door through the glazed transom of which we could discern the glow of a dim light from within. The landlord felt for me in the dark and whispered to me that that was 166. I tried the door—it was locked on the inside. I whispered an order to one of my biggest soldiers; we set our ample shoulders to the door, and with one heave we burst it from its hinges. I caught a half-glimpse of a figure in a bed—saw its head dart toward the candle; out went the light and we were in pitch darkness. With one big bound I lit on that bed and pinned its occupant down with my knees. My prisoner struggled fiercely, but I got a grip on his throat with my left hand, and that was a good assistance to my knees in holding him down. Then straightway I snatched out my revolver, cocked it, and laid the cold barrel warningly against his cheek.

"Now somebody strike a light!" said I. "I've got him safe."

It was done. The flame of the match burst up. I looked at my captive, and, by George, it was a young woman!

I let go and got off the bed, feeling pretty sheepish. Everybody stared stupidly at his neighbor. Nobody had any wit or sense left, so sudden and overwhelming had been the surprise. The young woman began to cry, and covered her face with the sheet. The landlord said, meekly:

"My daughter, she has been doing something that is not right, *nicht wahr?*"

"Your daughter? Is she your daughter?"

"Oh, yes, she is my daughter. She is just to-night come home from Cincinnati a little bit sick."

"Confound it, that boy has lied again. This is not the right 166; this is not B. B. Now, Wicklow, you will find the correct 166 for us, or— hello! where is that boy?"

Gone, as sure as guns! And, what is more, we failed to find a trace of him. Here was an awful predicament. I cursed my stupidity in not tying him to one of the men; but it was of no use to bother about that now. What should I do in the present circumstances?—that was the question. That girl *might* be B. B., after all. I did not believe it, but still it would not answer to take unbelief for proof. So I finally put my men in a vacant room across the hall from 166, and told them to capture anybody and everybody that approached the girl's room, and to keep the landlord with them, and under strict watch, until further orders. Then I hurried back to the fort to see if all was right there yet.

Yes, all was right. And all remained right. I stayed up all night to make sure of that. Nothing happened. I was unspeakably glad to see the dawn come again, and be able to telegraph the Department that the Stars and Stripes still floated over Fort Trumbull.

An immense pressure was lifted from my breast. Still I did not relax vigilance, of course, nor effort, either; the case was too grave for that. I had up my prisoners, one by one, and harried them by the hour, try- ing to get them to confess, but it was a failure. They only gnashed their teeth and tore their hair, and revealed nothing.

About noon came tidings of my missing boy. He had been seen on the road, tramping westward, some eight miles out, at six in the morn- ing. I started a cavalry lieutenant and a private on his track at once. They came in sight of him twenty miles out. He had climbed a fence and was wearily dragging himself across a slushy field toward a large old-fashioned mansion in the edge of a village. They rode through a bit of woods, made a detour, and closed upon the house from the op- posite side; then dismounted and skurried into the kitchen. Nobody there. They slipped into the next room, which was also unoccupied; the door from that room into the front or sitting room was open. They were about to step through it when they heard a low voice; it was some- body praying. So they halted reverently, and the lieutenant put his head in and saw an old man and an old woman kneeling in a corner of that sitting-room. It was the old man that was praying, and just as he was finishing his prayer, the Wicklow boy opened the front door and stepped in. Both of those old people sprang at him and smothered him with embraces, shouting:

"Our boy! our darling! God be praised. The lost is found! He that was dead is alive again!"

Well, sir, what do you think! That young imp was born and reared on that homestead, and had never been five miles away from it in all his life till the fortnight before he loafed into my quarters and gulled me with that maudlin yarn of his! It's as true as gospel. That old man was his father—a learned old retired clergyman; and that old lady was his mother.

Let me throw in a word or two of explanation concerning that boy and his performances. It turned out that he was a ravenous devourer of dime novels and sensation-story papers—therefore, dark mysteries and gaudy heroisms were just in his line. Then he had read newspaper reports of the stealthy goings and comings of rebel spies in our midst, and of their lurid purposes and their two or three startling achievements, till his imagination was all aflame on that subject. His constant comrade for some months had been a Yankee youth of much tongue and lively fancy, who had served for a couple of years as "mud clerk" (that is, subordinate purser) on certain of the packet-boats plying between New Orleans and points two or three hundred miles up the Mississippi—hence his easy facility in handling the names and other details pertaining to that region. Now I had spent two or three months in that part of the country before the war; and I knew just enough about it to be easily taken in by that boy, whereas a born Louisianian would probably have caught him tripping before he had talked fifteen minutes. Do you know the reason he said he would rather die than explain certain of his treasonable enigmas? Simply because he *couldn't* explain them!—they had no meaning; he had fired them out of his imagination without forethought or afterthought; and so, upon sudden call, he wasn't able to invent an explanation of them. For instance, he couldn't reveal what was hidden in the "sympathetic ink" letter, for the ample reason that there wasn't anything hidden in it; it was blank paper only. He hadn't put anything into a gun, and had never intended to—for his letters were all written to imaginary persons, and when he hid one in the stable he always removed the one he had put there the day before; so he was not acquainted with that knotted string, since he was seeing it for the first time when I showed it to him; but as soon as I had let him find out where it came from, he straightway adopted it, in his romantic fashion, and got some fine effects out of it. He invented Mr. "Gaylord"; there wasn't any 15 Bond Street, just then—it had been pulled down three months before. He invented the "Colonel"; he invented the glib histories of those unfortunates whom I captured and confronted him with; he invented "B. B."; he even invented No. 166, one may say, for he didn't know there *was* such a number in the Eagle Hotel until we went there. He stood ready to invent anybody or anything whenever it was wanted. If I called for "outside" spies, he promptly described strangers whom he had seen at the hotel, and whose names he had happened to hear. Ah, he lived in a gorgeous, mysterious, romantic world during those few stirring days, and I think it was *real* to him, and that he enjoyed it clear down to the bottom of his heart.

But he made trouble enough for us, and just no end of humiliation. You see, on account of him we had fifteen or twenty people under arrest and confinement in the fort, with sentinels before their doors. A lot of the captives were soldiers and such, and to them I didn't have to apologize; but the rest were first-class citizens, from all over the country, and no amount of apologies was sufficient to satisfy them. They just fumed and raged and made no end of trouble! And those two ladies—one was an Ohio Congressman's wife, the other a Western bishop's sister—well, the scorn and ridicule and angry tears they poured out on me made up a keepsake that was likely to make me remember them for a considerable time—and I shall. That old lame gentleman with the goggles was a college president from Philadelphia, who had come up to attend his nephew's funeral. He had never seen young Wicklow before, of course. Well, he not only missed the funeral, and got jailed as a rebel spy, but Wicklow had stood up there in my quarters and coldly described him as a counterfeiter, nigger-trader, horse-thief, and firebug from the most notorious rascal-nest in Galveston; and this was a thing which that poor old gentleman couldn't seem to get over at all.

And the War Department! But, oh, my soul, let's draw the curtain over that part!

NOTE   I showed my manuscript to the Major, and he said: "Your unfamiliarity with military matters has betrayed you into some little mistakes. Still, they are picturesque ones—let them go; military men will smile at them, the rest won't detect them. You have got the main facts of the history right, and have set them down just about as they occurred."   M. T.

1881

The Invalid's Story

I seem sixty and married, but these effects are due to my condition and sufferings, for I am a bachelor, and only forty-one. It will be hard for you to believe that I, who am now but a shadow, was a hale, hearty man two short years ago—a man of iron, a very athlete!—yet such is the simple truth. But stranger still than this fact is the way in which I lost my health. I lost it through helping to take care of a box of guns on a two-hundred-mile railway journey one winter's night. It is the actual truth, and I will tell you about it.

I belong in Cleveland, Ohio. One winter's night, two years ago, I reached home just after dark, in a driving snow-storm, and the first thing I heard when I entered the house was that my dearest boyhood friend and schoolmate, John B. Hackett, had died the day before, and that his last utterance had been a desire that I would take his remains home to his poor old father and mother in Wisconsin. I was greatly shocked and grieved, but there was no time to waste in emotions; I must start at once. I took the card, marked "Deacon Levi Hackett, Bethlehem, Wisconsin," and hurried off through the whistling storm to the railway-station. Arrived there I found the long white-pine box which had been described to me; I fastened the card to it with some tacks, saw it put safely aboard the express-car, and then ran into the eating-room to provide myself with a sandwich and some cigars. When I returned, presently, there was my coffin-box *back again*, apparently, and a young fellow examining around it, with a card in his hands, and some tacks and a hammer! I was astonished and puzzled. He began to nail on his card, and I rushed out to the express-car, in a good deal of a state of mind, to ask for an explanation. But no—there was my box, all right, in the express-car; it hadn't been disturbed. [The fact is that without my suspecting it a prodigious mistake had been made. I was carrying off a box of *guns* which that young fellow had come to the station to ship to a rifle company in Peoria, Illinois, and *he* had got my corpse!] Just then the conductor sang out "All aboard," and I jumped into the express-car and got a comfortable seat on a bale of buckets. The expressman was there, hard at work—a plain man of fifty, with a simple, honest, good-natured face, and a breezy, practical heartiness in his general style. As the train moved off a stranger skipped into the car and set a package of peculiarly mature and capable Limburger cheese on one end of my coffin-box—I mean my box of guns. That is to say, I know *now* that it was Limburger cheese, but at that time I never had heard of the article in my life, and of course was wholly ignorant of its character. Well, we sped through the wild night, the bitter storm raged on, a cheerless misery stole over me, my heart went down, down, down! The old expressman made a brisk remark or two about the tempest and the arctic weather, slammed his sliding doors to, and bolted them, closed his window down tight, and then went bustling around, here and there and yonder, setting things to rights, and all the time contentedly humming "Sweet By and By," in a low tone, and flatting a good deal. Presently I began to detect a most evil and searching odor stealing about on the frozen air. This depressed my spirits still more, because of course I attributed it to my poor departed friend. There was something infinitely saddening about his calling himself to my remembrance in this dumb, pathetic way, so it was hard to keep the tears back. Moreover, it distressed me on account of the old expressman, who, I was afraid, might notice it. However, he went humming tranquilly on, and gave no sign; and for this I was grateful. Grateful, yes, but still uneasy; and soon I began to feel more and more uneasy every minute, for every minute that went by that odor thickened up the more, and got to be more and more gamy and hard to stand. Presently, having got things arranged to his satisfaction, the expressman got some wood and made up a tremendous fire in his stove. This distressed me more than I can tell, for I could not but feel that it was a mistake. I was sure that the effect would be deleterious upon my poor departed friend. Thompson—the expressman's name was Thompson, as I found out in the course of the night—now went poking around his car, stopping up whatever stray cracks he could find, remarking that it didn't make any difference what kind of a night it was outside, he calculated to make *us* comfortable, anyway. I said nothing, but I believed he was not choosing the right way. Meantime he was humming to himself just as before; and meantime, too, the stove was getting hotter and hotter, and the place closer and closer. I felt myself growing pale and qualmish, but grieved in silence and said nothing. Soon I noticed that the "Sweet By and By" was gradually fading out; next it ceased altogether, and there was an ominous stillness. After a few moments Thompson said—

"Pfew! I reckon it ain't no cinnamon 't I've loaded up thish-yer stove with!"

He gasped once or twice, then moved toward the cof—gun-box, stood over that Limburger cheese part of a moment, then came back and sat down near me, looking a good deal impressed. After a contemplative pause, he said, indicating the box with a gesture—

"Friend of yourn?"

"Yes," I said with a sigh.

"He's pretty ripe, *ain't* he!"

Nothing further was said for perhaps a couple of minutes, each being busy with his own thoughts; then Thompson said, in a low, awed voice—

"Sometimes it's uncertain whether they're really gone or not—*seem* gone, you know—body warm, joints limber—and so, although you *think* they're gone, you don't really know. I've had cases in my car. It's perfectly awful, becuz *you* don't know what minute they'll rise up and look at you!" Then, after a pause, and slightly lifting his elbow toward the box,—"But *he* ain't in no trance! No, sir, I go bail for *him!*"

We sat some time, in meditative silence, listening to the wind and the roar of the train; then Thompson said, with a good deal of feeling:

"Well-a-well, we've all got to go, they ain't no getting around it. Man that is born of woman is of few days and far between, as Scriptur' says. Yes, you look at it any way you want to, it's awful solemn and cur'us: they ain't *nobody* can get around it; *all's* got to go—just *everybody*, as you may say. One day you're hearty and strong"—here he scrambled to his feet and broke a pane and stretched his nose out at it a moment or two, then sat down again while I struggled up and thrust my nose out at the same place, and this we kept on doing every now and then—"and next day he's cut down like the grass, and the places which knowed him then knows him no more forever, as Scriptur' says. Yes'ndeedy, it's awful solemn and cur'us; but we've all got to go, one time or another; they ain't no getting around it."

There was another long pause; then—

"What did he die of?"

I said I didn't know.

"How long has he ben dead?"

It seemed judicious to enlarge the facts to fit the probabilities; so I said:

"Two or three days."

But it did no good; for Thompson received it with an injured look which plainly said, "Two or three *years*, you mean." Then he went right along, placidly ignoring my statement, and gave his views at considerable length upon the unwisdom of putting off burials too long. Then he lounged off toward the box, stood a moment, then came back on a sharp trot and visited the broken pane, observing:

" 'Twould 'a' ben a dum sight better, all around, if they'd started him along last summer."

Thompson sat down and buried his face in his red silk handkerchief, and began to slowly sway and rock his body like one who is doing his best to endure the almost unendurable. By this time the fragrance—if you may call it fragrance—was just about suffocating, as near as you can come at it. Thompson's face was turning gray; I knew mine hadn't any color left in it. By and by Thompson rested his forehead in his left hand, with his elbow on his knee, and sort of waved his red handkerchief toward the box with his other hand, and said:

"I've carried a many a one of 'em—some of 'em considerable overdue, too—but, lordy, he just lays over 'em all!—and does it *easy*. Cap, they was heliotrope to *him!*"

This recognition of my poor friend gratified me, in spite of the sad circumstances, because it had so much the sound of a compliment.

Pretty soon it was plain that something had got to be done. I suggested cigars. Thompson thought it was a good idea. He said:

"Likely it'll modify him some."

We puffed gingerly along for a while, and tried hard to imagine that things were improved. But it wasn't any use. Before very long, and without any consultation, both cigars were quietly dropped from our nerveless fingers at the same moment. Thompson said, with a sigh:

"No, Cap, it don't modify him worth a cent. Fact is, it makes him worse, becuz it appears to stir up his ambition. What do you reckon we better do, now?"

I was not able to suggest anything; indeed, I had to be swallowing and swallowing all the time, and did not like to trust myself to speak. Thompson fell to maundering, in a desultory and low-spirited way, about the miserable experiences of this night; and he got to referring to my poor friend by various titles—sometimes military ones, sometimes civil ones; and I noticed that as fast as my poor friend's effectiveness grew, Thompson promoted him accordingly—gave him a bigger title. Finally he said:

"I've got an idea. Suppos'n' we buckle down to it and give the Colonel a bit of a shove toward t'other end of the car?—about ten foot, say. He wouldn't have so much influence, then, don't you reckon?"

I said it was a good scheme. So we took in a good fresh breath at the broken pane, calculating to hold it till we got through; then we went there and bent over that deadly cheese and took a grip on the box.

Thompson nodded "All ready," and then we threw ourselves forward with all our might; but Thompson slipped, and slumped down with his nose on the cheese, and his breath got loose. He gagged and gasped, and floundered up and made a break for the door, pawing the air and saying hoarsely, "Don't hender me!—gimme the road! I'm a-dying; gimme the road!" Out on the cold platform I sat down and held his head awhile, and he revived. Presently he said:

"Do you reckon we started the Gen'rul any?"

I said no; we hadn't budged him.

"Well, then, *that* idea's up the flume. We got to think up something else. He's suited wher' he is, I reckon; and if that's the way he feels about it, and has made up his mind that he don't wish to be disturbed, you bet he's a-going to have his own way in the business. Yes, better leave him right wher' he is, long as he wants it so; becuz he holds all the trumps, don't you know, and so it stands to reason that the man that lays out to alter his plans for him is going to get left."

But we couldn't stay out there in that mad storm; we should have frozen to death. So we went in again and shut the door, and began to suffer once more and take turns at the break in the window. By and by, as we were starting away from a station where we had stopped a moment Thompson pranced in cheerily, and exclaimed:

"We're all right, now! I reckon we've got the Commodore this time. I judge I've got the stuff here that'll take the tuck out of him."

It was carbolic acid. He had a carboy of it. He sprinkled it all around everywhere; in fact he drenched everything with it, rifle-box, cheese and all. Then we sat down, feeling pretty hopeful. But it wasn't for long. You see the two perfumes began to mix, and then—well, pretty soon we made a break for the door; and out there Thompson swabbed his face with his bandanna and said in a kind of disheartened way:

"It ain't no use. We can't buck agin *him*. He just utilizes everything we put up to modify him with, and gives it his own flavor and plays it back on us. Why, Cap, don't you know, it's as much as a hundred times worse in there now than it was when he first got a-going. I never *did* see one of 'em warm up to his work so, and take such a dumnation interest in it. No, sir, I never did, as long as I've ben on the road; and I've carried a many a one of 'em, as I was telling you."

We went in again after we were frozen pretty stiff; but my, we couldn't *stay* in, now. So we just waltzed back and forth, freezing, and thawing, and stifling, by turns. In about an hour we stopped at another station; and as we left it Thompson came in with a bag, and said—

"Cap, I'm a-going to chance him once more—just this once; and if we don't fetch him this time, the thing for us to do, is to just throw up the sponge and withdraw from the canvass. That's the way I put it up."

He had brought a lot of chicken feathers, and dried apples, and leaf tobacco, and rags, and old shoes, and sulphur, and asafetida, and one thing or another; and he piled them on a breadth of sheet iron in the middle of the floor, and set fire to them.

When they got well started, I couldn't see, myself, how even the corpse could stand it. All that went before was just simply poetry to that smell—but mind you, the original smell stood up out of it just as sublime as ever—fact is, these other smells just seemed to give it a better hold; and my, how rich it was! I didn't make these reflections there— there wasn't time—made them on the platform. And breaking for the platform, Thompson got suffocated and fell; and before I got him dragged out, which I did by the collar, I was mighty near gone myself. When we revived, Thompson said dejectedly:

"We got to stay out here, Cap. We got to do it. They ain't no other way. The Governor wants to travel alone, and he's fixed so he can out-vote us."

And presently he added:

"And don't you know, we're *pisoned*. It's *our* last trip, you can make up your mind to it. Typhoid fever is what's going to come of this. I feel it a-coming right now. Yes, sir, we're elected, just as sure as you're born."

We were taken from the platform an hour later, frozen and insensible, at the next station, and I went straight off into a virulent fever, and never knew anything again for three weeks. I found out, then, that I had spent that awful night with a harmless box of rifles and a lot of inno- cent cheese; but the news was too late to save *me*; imagination had done its work, and my health was permanently shattered; neither Ber- muda nor any other land can ever bring it back to me. This is my last trip; I am on my way home to die.

1882

The McWilliamses
and the Burglar Alarm

The conversation drifted smoothly and pleasantly along from weather to crops, from crops to literature, from literature to scandal, from scandal to religion; then took a random jump, and landed on the subject of burglar alarms. And now for the first time Mr. McWilliams showed feeling. Whenever I perceive this sign on this man's dial, I comprehend it, and lapse into silence, and give him opportunity to unload his heart. Said he, with but ill-controlled emotion:

I do not go one single cent on burglar alarms, Mr. Twain—not a single cent—and I will tell you why. When we were finishing our house, we found we had a little cash left over, on account of the plumber not knowing it. I was for enlightening the heathen with it, for I was always unaccountably down on the heathen somehow; but Mrs. McWilliams said no, let's have a burglar alarm. I agreed to this compromise. I will explain that whenever I want a thing, and Mrs. McWilliams wants another thing, and we decide upon the thing that Mrs. McWilliams wants—as we always do—she calls that a compromise. Very well: the man came up from New York and put in the alarm, and charged three hundred and twenty-five dollars for it, and said we could sleep without uneasiness now. So we did for awhile—say a month. Then one night we smelled smoke, and I was advised to get up and see what the matter was. I lit a candle, and started toward the stairs, and met a burglar coming out of a room with a basket of tinware, which he had mistaken for solid silver in the dark. He was smoking a pipe. I said, "My friend, we do not allow smoking in this room." He said he was a stranger, and could not be expected to know the rules of the house: said he had been in many houses just as good as this one, and it had never been objected to before. He added that as far as his experience went, such rules had never been considered to apply to burglars, anyway.

I said: "Smoke along, then, if it is the custom, though I think that the conceding of a privilege to a burglar which is denied to a bishop is a conspicuous sign of the looseness of the times. But waiving all that, what business have you to be entering this house in this furtive and clandestine way, without ringing the burglar alarm?"

He looked confused and ashamed, and said, with embarrassment: "I beg a thousand pardons. I did not know you had a burglar alarm, else I would have rung it. I beg you will not mention it where my parents may hear of it, for they are old and feeble, and such a seemingly wanton breach of the hallowed conventionalities of our Christian civilization might all too rudely sunder the frail bridge which hangs darkling between the pale and evanescent present and the solemn great deeps of the eternities. May I trouble you for a match?"

I said: "Your sentiments do you honor, but if you will allow me to say it, metaphor is not your best hold. Spare your thigh; this kind light only on the box, and seldom there, in fact, if my experience may be trusted. But to return to business: how did you get in here?"

"Through a second-story window."

It was even so. I redeemed the tinware at pawnbroker's rates, less cost of advertising, bade the burglar good-night, closed the window after him, and retired to headquarters to report. Next morning we sent for the burglar-alarm man, and he came up and explained that the reason the alarm did not "go off" was that no part of the house but the first floor was attached to the alarm. This was simply idiotic; one might as well have no armor on at all in battle as to have it only on his legs. The expert now put the whole second story on the alarm, charged three hundred dollars for it, and went his way. By and by, one night, I found a burglar in the third story, about to start down a ladder with a lot of miscellaneous property. My first impulse was to crack his head with a billiard cue; but my second was to refrain from this attention, because he was between me and the cue rack. The second impulse was plainly the soundest, so I refrained, and proceeded to compromise. I redeemed the property at former rates, after deducting ten per cent. for use of ladder, it being my ladder, and next day we sent down for the expert once more, and had the third story attached to the alarm, for three hundred dollars.

By this time the "annunciator" had grown to formidable dimensions. It had forty-seven tags on it, marked with the names of the various rooms and chimneys, and it occupied the space of an ordinary wardrobe. The gong was the size of a wash-bowl, and was placed above the head of our bed. There was a wire from the house to the coachman's quarters in the stable, and a noble gong alongside his pillow.

We should have been comfortable now but for one defect. Every morning at five the cook opened the kitchen door, in the way of business, and rip went that gong! The first time this happened I thought the last day was come sure. I didn't think it *in* bed—no, but out of it—for the first effect of that frightful gong is to hurl you across the house, and slam you against the wall, and then curl you up, and squirm you like a spider on a stove lid, till somebody shuts the kitchen door. In solid fact, there is no clamor that is even remotely comparable to the dire clamor which that gong makes. Well, this catastrophe happened every morning regularly at five o'clock, and lost us three hours sleep; for, mind you, when that thing wakes you, it doesn't merely wake you in spots; it wakes you all over, conscience and all, and you are good for eighteen hours of wide-awakeness subsequently—eighteen hours of the very most inconceivable wide-awakeness that you ever experienced in your life. A stranger died on our hands one time, and we vacated and left him in our room overnight. Did that stranger wait for the general judgment? *No*, sir; he got up at five the next morning in the most prompt and unostentatious way. I knew he would; I knew it mighty well. He collected his life-insurance, and lived happy ever after, for there was plenty of proof as to the perfect squareness of his death.

Well, we were gradually fading toward a better land, on account of the daily loss of sleep; so we finally had the expert up again, and he ran a wire to the outside of the door, and placed a switch there, whereby Thomas, the butler, always made one little mistake—he switched the alarm off at night when he went to bed, and switched it on again at daybreak in the morning, just in time for the cook to open the kitchen door, and enable that gong to slam us across the house, sometimes breaking a window with one or the other of us. At the end of a week we recognized that this switch business was a delusion and a snare. We also discovered that a band of burglars had been lodging in the house the whole time—not exactly to steal, for there wasn't much left now, but to hide from the police, for they were hot pressed, and they shrewdly judged that the detectives would never think of a tribe of burglars taking sanctuary in a house notoriously protected by the most imposing and elaborate burglar alarm in America.

Sent down for the expert again, and this time he struck a most dazzling idea—he fixed the thing so that opening the kitchen door would take off the alarm. It was a noble idea, and he charged accordingly. But you already foresee the result. I switched on the alarm every night at bed-time, no longer trusting on Thomas's frail memory; and as soon as the lights were out the burglars walked in at the kitchen door, thus taking the alarm off without waiting for the cook to do it in the morning. You see how aggravatingly we were situated. For months we couldn't have any company. Not a spare bed in the house; all occupied by burglars.

Finally, I got up a cure of my own. The expert answered the call, and ran another ground wire to the stable, and established a switch there, so that the coachman could put on and take off the alarm. That worked first rate, and a season of peace ensued, during which we got to inviting company once more and enjoying life.

But by and by the irrepressible alarm invented a new kink. One winter's night we were flung out of bed by the sudden music of that awful gong, and when we hobbled to the annunciator, turned up the gas, and saw the word "Nursery" exposed, Mrs. McWilliams fainted dead away, and I came precious near doing the same thing myself. I seized my shotgun, and stood timing the coachman whilst that appalling buzzing went on. I knew that his gong had flung him out, too, and that he would be along with his gun as soon as he could jump into his clothes. When I judged that the time was ripe, I crept to the room next the nursery, glanced through the window, and saw the dim outline of the coachman in the yard below, standing at present-arms and waiting for a chance. Then I hopped into the nursery and fired, and in the same instant the coachman fired at the red flash of my gun. Both of us were successful; I crippled a nurse, and he shot off all my back hair. We turned up the gas, and telephoned for a surgeon. There was not a sign of a burglar, and no window had been raised. One glass was absent, but that was where the coachman's charge had come through. Here was a fine mystery—a burglar alarm "going off" at midnight of its own accord, and not a burglar in the neighborhood!

The expert answered the usual call, and explained that it was a "False alarm." Said it was easily fixed. So he overhauled the nursery window, charged a remunerative figure for it, and departed.

What we suffered from false alarms for the next three years no stylographic pen can describe. During the next three months I always flew with my gun to the room indicated, and the coachman always sallied forth with his battery to support me. But there was never anything to shoot at—windows all tight and secure. We always sent down for the expert next day, and he fixed those particular windows so they would keep quiet a week or so, and always remembered to send us a bill about like this:

Wire	$2.15
Nipple	.75
Two hours' labor	1.50
Wax	.47
Tape	.34
Screws	.15
Recharging battery	.98
Three hours' labor	2.25
String	.02
Lard	.66
Pond's Extract	1.25
Springs at 50	2.00
Railroad fares	7.25
	$19.77

At length a perfectly natural thing came about—after we had answered three or four hundred false alarms—to wit, we stopped answering them. Yes, I simply rose up calmly, when slammed across the house by the alarm, calmly inspected the annunciator, took note of the room indicated, and then calmly disconnected that room from the alarm, and went back to bed as if nothing had happened. Moreover, I left that room off permanently, and did not send for the expert. Well, it goes without saying that in the course of time *all* the rooms were taken off, and the entire machine was out of service.

It was at this unprotected time that the heaviest calamity of all happened. The burglars walked in one night and carried off the burglar alarm! yes, sir, every hide and hair of it: ripped it out, tooth and nail; springs, bells, gongs, battery, and all; they took a hundred and fifty miles of copper wire; they just cleaned her out, bag and baggage, and never left us a vestige of her to swear at—swear by, I mean.

We had a time of it to get her back; but we accomplished it finally, for money. The alarm firm said that what we needed now was to have her put in right—with their new patent springs in the windows to make false alarms impossible, and their new patent clock attached to take off and put on the alarm morning and night without human assistance. That seemed a good scheme. They promised to have the whole thing finished in ten days. They began work, and we left for the summer. They worked a couple of days; then *they* left for the summer. After which the burglars moved in, and began *their* summer vacation. When we returned in the fall, the house was as empty as a beer closet in premises where painters have been at work. We refurnished, and then sent down to hurry up the expert. He came up and finished the job, and said: "Now this clock is set to put on the alarm every night at 10, and take it off every morning at 5:45. All you've got to do is to wind her up every week, and then leave her alone—she will take care of the alarm herself."

After that we had a most tranquil season during three months. The bill was prodigious, of course, and I had said I would not pay it until the new machinery had proved itself to be flawless. The time stipulated was three months. So I paid the bill, and the very next day the alarm went to buzzing like ten thousand bee swarms at ten o'clock in the morning. I turned the hands around twelve hours, according to instructions, and this took off the alarm; but there was another hitch at night, and I had to set her ahead twelve hours once more to get her to put the alarm on again. That sort of nonsense went on a week or two, then the expert came up and put in a new clock. He came up every three months during the next three years, and put in a new clock. But it was always a failure. His clocks all had the same perverse defect: they would put the alarm on in the daytime, and they would *not* put it on at night; and if you forced it on yourself, they *would* take it off again the minute your back was turned.

Now there is the history of that burglar alarm—everything just as it happened; nothing extenuated, and naught set down in malice. Yes, sir,—and when I had slept nine years with burglars, and maintained an expensive burglar alarm the whole time, for their protection, not mine, and at my sole cost—for not a d—— d cent could I ever get *them* to contribute—I just said to Mrs. McWilliams that I had had enough of that kind of pie; so with her full consent I took the whole thing out and traded it off for a dog, and shot the dog. I don't know what *you* think about it, Mr. Twain; but *I* think those things are made solely in the interest of the burglars. Yes, sir, a burglar alarm combines in its person all that is objectionable about a fire, a riot, and a harem, and at the same time had none of the compensating advantages, of one sort or another, that customarily belong with that combination. Good-by: I get off here.

1882

The Stolen White Elephant[1]

The following curious history was related to me by a chance railway acquaintance. He was a gentleman more than seventy years of age, and his thoroughly good and gentle face and earnest and sincere manner imprinted the unmistakable stamp of truth upon every statement which fell from his lips. He said:

You know in what reverence the royal white elephant of Siam is held by the people of that country. You know it is sacred to kings, only kings may possess it, and that it is, indeed, in a measure even superior to kings, since it receives not merely honor but worship. Very well; five years ago, when the troubles concerning the frontier line arose between Great Britain and Siam, it was presently manifest that Siam had been in the wrong. Therefore every reparation was quickly made, and the British representative stated that he was satisfied and the past should be forgotten. This greatly relieved the King of Siam, and partly as a token of gratitude, but partly also, perhaps, to wipe out any little remaining vestige of unpleasantness which England might feel toward him, he wished to send the Queen a present—the sole sure way of propitiating an enemy, according to Oriental ideas. This present ought not only to be a royal one, but transcendently royal. Wherefore, what offering could be so meet as that of a white elephant? My position in the Indian civil service was such that I was deemed peculiarly worthy of the honor of conveying the present to her Majesty. A ship was fitted out for me and my servants and the officers and attendants of the elephant, and in due time I arrived in New York harbor and placed my royal charge in admirable quarters in Jersey City. It was necessary to remain awhile in order to recruit the animal's health before resuming the voyage.

All went well during a fortnight—then my calamities began. The white elephant was stolen! I was called up at dead of night and in-

---

[1] Left out of *A Tramp Abroad*, because it was feared that some of the particulars had been exaggerated, and that others were not true. Before these suspicions had been proven groundless, the book had gone to press. M. T.

formed of this fearful misfortune. For some moments I was beside myself with terror and anxiety; I was helpless. Then I grew calmer and
collected my faculties. I soon saw my course—for, indeed, there was
but the one course for an intelligent man to pursue. Late as it was, I
flew to New York and got a policeman to conduct me to the headquarters of the detective force. Fortunately I arrived in time, though the
chief of the force, the celebrated Inspector Blunt, was just on the
point of leaving for his home. He was a man of middle size and compact frame, and when he was thinking deeply he had a way of knitting his brows and tapping his forehead reflectively with his finger,
which impressed you at once with the conviction that you stood in
the presence of a person of no common order. The very sight of him
gave me confidence and made me hopeful. I stated my errand. It did
not flurry him in the least; it had no more visible effect upon his iron
self-possession than if I had told him somebody had stolen my dog. He
motioned me to a seat, and said, calmly:

"Allow me to think a moment, please."

So saying, he sat down at his office table and leaned his head upon
his hand. Several clerks were at work at the other end of the room;
the scratching of their pens was all the sound I heard during the next
six or seven minutes. Meantime the inspector sat there, buried in
thought. Finally he raised his head, and there was that in the firm lines
of his face which showed me that his brain had done its work and his
plan was made. Said he—and his voice was low and impressive:

"This is no ordinary case. Every step must be warily taken; each step
must be made sure before the next is ventured. And secrecy must be
observed—secrecy profound and absolute. Speak to no one about the
matter, not even the reporters. I will take care of *them;* I will see that
they get only what it may suit my ends to let them know." He touched
a bell; a youth appeared. "Alaric, tell the reporters to remain for the
present." The boy retired. "Now let us proceed to business—and systematically. Nothing can be accomplished in this trade of mine without
strict and minute method."

He took a pen and some paper. "Now—name of the elephant?"

"Hassan Ben Ali Ben Selim Abdallah Mohammed Moisé Alhammal
Jamsetjejeebhoy Dhuleep Sultan Ebu Bhudpoor."

"Very well. Given name?"

"Jumbo."

"Very well. Place of birth?"

"The capital city of Siam."

"Parents living?"

"No—dead."

"Had they any other issue besides this one?"

"None. He was an only child."

"Very well. These matters are sufficient under that head. Now please describe the elephant, and leave out no particular, however insignificant—that is, insignificant from *your* point of view. To men in my profession there *are* no insignificant particulars; they do not exist."

I described—he wrote. When I was done, he said:

"Now listen. If I have made any mistakes, correct me."

He read as follows:

"Height, 19 feet; length from apex of forehead to insertion of tail, 26 feet; length of trunk, 16 feet; length of tail, 6 feet; total length, including trunk and tail, 48 feet; length of tusks, 9½ feet; ears in keeping with these dimensions; footprint resembles the mark left when one up-ends a barrel in the snow; color of the elephant, a dull white; has a hole the size of a plate in each ear for the insertion of jewelry, and possesses the habit in a remarkable degree of squirting water upon spectators and of maltreating with his trunk not only such persons as he is acquainted with, but even entire strangers; limps slightly with his right hind leg, and has a small scar in his left armpit caused by a former boil; had on, when stolen, a castle containing seats for fifteen persons, and a gold-cloth saddle-blanket the size of an ordinary carpet."

There were no mistakes. The inspector touched the bell, handed the description to Alaric, and said:

"Have fifty thousand copies of this printed at once and mailed to every detective office and pawnbroker's shop on the continent." Alaric retired. "There—so far, so good. Next, I must have a photograph of the property."

I gave him one. He examined it critically, and said:

"It must do, since we can do no better; but he has his trunk curled up and tucked into his mouth. That is unfortunate, and is calculated to mislead, for of course he does not usually have it in that position." He touched his bell.

"Alaric, have fifty thousand copies of this photograph made the first thing in the morning, and mail them with the descriptive circulars."

Alaric retired to execute his orders. The inspector said:

"It will be necessary to offer a reward, of course. Now as to the amount?"

"What sum would you suggest?"

"To *begin* with, I should say—well, twenty-five thousand dollars. It is an intricate and difficult business; there are a thousand avenues of es-

cape and opportunities of concealment. These thieves have friends and
pals everywhere—"

"Bless me, do you know who they are?"

The wary face, practised in concealing the thoughts and feelings
within, gave me no token, nor yet the replying words, so quietly uttered:

"Never mind about that. I may, and I may not. We generally gather
a pretty shrewd inkling of who our man is by the manner of his work
and the size of the game he goes after. We are not dealing with a pick-
pocket or a hall thief now, make up your mind to that. This property
was not 'lifted' by a novice. But, as I was saying, considering the amount
of travel which will have to be done, and the diligence with which the
thieves will cover up their traces as they move along, twenty-five thousand may be too small a sum to offer, yet I think it worth while to
start with that."

So we determined upon that figure as a beginning. Then this man,
whom nothing escaped which could by any possibility be made to serve
as a clue, said:

"There are cases in detective history to show that criminals have been
detected through peculiarities in their appetites. Now, what does this
elephant eat, and how much?"

"Well, as to *what* he eats—he will eat *anything*. He will eat a man, he
will eat a Bible—he will eat anything *between* a man and a Bible."

"Good—very good, indeed, but too general. Details are necessary—
details are the only valuable things in our trade. Very well—as to men.
At one meal—or, if you prefer, during one day—how many men will
he eat, if fresh?"

"He would not care whether they were fresh or not; at a single meal
he would eat five ordinary men."

"Very good; five men; we will put that down. What nationalities
would he prefer?"

"He is indifferent about nationalities. He prefers acquaintances, but
is not prejudiced against strangers."

"Very good. Now, as to Bibles. How many Bibles would he eat at a
meal?"

"He would eat an entire edition."

"It is hardly succinct enough. Do you mean the ordinary octavo, or
the family illustrated?"

"I think he would be indifferent to illustrations; that is, I think he
would not value illustrations above simple letterpress."

"No, you do not get my idea. I refer to bulk. The ordinary octavo
Bible weighs about two pounds and a half, while the great quarto with

the illustrations weighs ten or twelve. How many Doré Bibles would he eat at a meal?"

"If you knew this elephant, you could not ask. He would take what they had."

"Well, put it in dollars and cents, then. We must get at it somehow. The Doré costs a hundred dollars a copy, Russia leather, beveled."

"He would require about fifty thousand dollars' worth—say an edition of five hundred copies."

"Now that is more exact. I will put that down. Very well; he likes men and Bibles; so far, so good. What else will he eat? I want particulars."

"He will leave Bibles to eat bricks, he will leave bricks to eat bottles, he will leave bottles to eat clothing, he will leave clothing to eat cats, he will leave cats to eat oysters, he will leave oysters to eat ham, he will leave ham to eat sugar, he will leave sugar to eat pie, he will leave pie to eat potatoes, he will leave potatoes to eat bran, he will leave bran to eat hay, he will leave hay to eat oats, he will leave oats to eat rice, for he was mainly raised on it. There is nothing whatever that he will not eat but European butter, and he would eat that if he could taste it."

"Very good. General quantity at a meal—say about—"

"Well, anywhere from a quarter to half a ton."

"And he drinks—"

"Everything that is fluid. Milk, water, whisky, molasses, castor oil, camphene, carbolic acid—it is no use to go into particulars; whatever fluid occurs to you set it down. He will drink anything that is fluid, except European coffee."

"Very good. As to quantity?"

"Put it down five to fifteen barrels—his thirst varies; his other appetites do not."

"These things are unusual. They ought to furnish quite good clues toward tracing him."

He touched the bell.

"Alaric, summon Captain Burns."

Burns appeared. Inspector Blunt unfolded the whole matter to him, detail by detail. Then he said in the clear, decisive tones of a man whose plans are clearly defined in his head and who is accustomed to command:

"Captain Burns, detail Detectives Jones, Davis, Halsey, Bates, and Hackett to shadow the elephant."

"Yes, sir."

"Detail Detectives Moses, Dakin, Murphy, Rogers, Tupper, Higgins, and Batholomew to shadow the thieves."

"Yes, sir."

"Place a strong guard—a guard of thirty picked men, with a relief of thirty—over the place from whence the elephant was stolen, to keep strict watch there night and day, and allow none to approach—except reporters—without written authority from me."

"Yes, sir."

"Place detectives in plain clothes in the railway, steamship, and ferry depots, and upon all roadways leading out of Jersey City, with orders to search all suspicious persons."

"Yes, sir."

"Furnish all these men with photograph and accompanying description of the elephant, and instruct them to search all trains and outgoing ferryboats and other vessels."

"Yes, sir."

"If the elephant should be found, let him be seized, and the information forwarded to me by telegraph."

"Yes, sir."

"Let me be informed at once if any clues should be found—footprints of the animal, or anything of that kind."

"Yes, sir."

"Get an order commanding the harbor police to patrol the frontages vigilantly."

"Yes, sir."

"Despatch detectives in plain clothes over all the railways, north as far as Canada, west as far as Ohio, south as far as Washington."

"Yes, sir."

"Place experts in all the telegraph offices to listen to all messages; and let them require that all cipher despatches be interpreted to them."

"Yes, sir."

"Let all these things be done with the utmost secrecy—mind, the most impenetrable secrecy."

"Yes, sir."

"Report to me promptly at the usual hour."

"Yes, sir."

"Go!"

"Yes, sir."

He was gone.

Inspector Blunt was silent and thoughtful a moment, while the fire in his eye cooled down and faded out. Then he turned to me and said in a placid voice:

"I am not given to boasting, it is not my habit; but—we shall find the elephant."

I shook him warmly by the hand and thanked him; and I *felt* my thanks, too. The more I had seen of the man the more I liked him and the more I admired him and marveled over the mysterious wonders of his profession. Then we parted for the night, and I went home with a far happier heart than I had carried with me to his office.

2

Next morning it was all in the newspapers, in the minutest detail. It even had additions—consisting of Detective This, Detective That, and Detective The Other's "Theory" as to how the robbery was done, who the robbers were, and whither they had flown with their booty. There were eleven of these theories, and they covered all the possibilities; and this single fact shows what independent thinkers detectives are. No two theories were alike, or even much resembled each other, save in one striking particular, and in that one all the other eleven theories were absolutely agreed. That was, that although the rear of my building was torn out and the only door remained locked, the elephant had not been removed through the rent, but by some other (undiscovered) outlet. All agreed that the robbers had made that rent only to mislead the detectives. That never would have occurred to me or to any other layman, perhaps, but it had not deceived the detectives for a moment. Thus, what I had supposed was the only thing that had no mystery about it was in fact the very thing I had gone furthest astray in. The eleven theories all named the supposed robbers, but no two named the same robbers; the total number of suspected persons was thirty-seven. The various newspaper accounts all closed with the most important opinion of all—that of Chief Inspector Blunt. A portion of this statement read as follows:

The chief knows who the two principals are, namely, "Brick" Duffy and "Red" McFadden. Ten days before the robbery was achieved he was already aware that it was to be attempted, and had quietly proceeded to shadow these two noted villains; but unfortunately on the night in question their track was lost, and before it could be found again the bird was flown—that is, the elephant.

Duffy and McFadden are the boldest scoundrels in the profession; the chief has reasons for believing that they are the men who stole the stove out of the detective headquarters on a bitter night last winter—in consequence of which the chief and every detective present were in the hands of the physicians before morning, some with frozen feet, others with frozen fingers, ears, and other members.

When I read the first half of that I was more astonished than ever at the wonderful sagacity of this strange man. He not only saw everything in the present with a clear eye, but even the future could not be hidden from him. I was soon at his office, and said I could not help wishing he had had those men arrested, and so prevented the trouble and loss; but his reply was simple and unanswerable:

"It is not our province to prevent crime, but to punish it. We cannot punish it until it is committed."

I remarked that the secrecy with which we had begun had been marred by the newspapers; not only all our facts but all our plans and purposes had been revealed; even all the suspected persons had been named; these would doubtless disguise themselves now, or go into hiding.

"Let them. They will find that when I am ready for them my hand will descend upon them, in their secret places, as unerringly as the hand of fate. As to the newspapers, we *must* keep in with them. Fame, reputation, constant public mention—these are the detective's bread and butter. He must publish his facts, else he will be supposed to have none; he must publish his theory, for nothing is so strange or striking as a detective's theory, or brings him so much wonderful respect; we must publish our plans, for these the journals insist upon having, and we could not deny them without offending. We must constantly show the public what we are doing, or they will believe we are doing nothing. It is much pleasanter to have a newspaper say, 'Inspector Blunt's ingenious and extraordinary theory is as follows,' than to have it say some harsh thing, or, worse still, some sarcastic one."

"I see the force of what you say. But I noticed that in one part of your remarks in the papers this morning you refused to reveal your opinion upon a certain minor point."

"Yes, we always do that; it has a good effect. Besides, I had not formed any opinion on that point, anyway."

I deposited a considerable sum of money with the inspector, to meet current expenses, and sat down to wait for news. We were expecting the telegrams to begin to arrive at any moment now. Meantime I reread the newspapers and also our descriptive circular, and observed that our twenty-five thousand dollars reward seemed to be offered only to detectives. I said I thought it ought to be offered to anybody who would catch the elephant. The inspector said:

"It is the detectives who will find the elephant, hence the reward will go to the right place. If other people found the animal, it would only be by watching the detectives and taking advantage of clues and indications stolen from them, and that would entitle the detectives to the reward, after all. The proper office of a reward is to stimulate the men who deliver up their time and their trained sagacities to this sort of work, and not to confer benefits upon chance citizens who stumble upon a capture without having earned the benefits by their own merits and labors."

This was reasonable enough, certainly. Now the telegraphic machine in the corner began to click, and the following despatch was the result:

> FLOWER STATION, N. Y., 7.30 A.M.
>
> HAVE GOT A CLUE. FOUND A SUCCESSION OF DEEP TRACKS ACROSS A FARM NEAR HERE. FOLLOWED THEM TWO MILES EAST WITHOUT RESULT; THINK ELEPHANT WENT WEST. SHALL NOW SHADOW HIM IN THAT DIRECTION.
>
> DARLEY, DETECTIVE

"Darley's one of the best men on the force," said the inspector. "We shall hear from him again before long."

Telegram No. 2 came:

> BARKER'S, N. J., 7.40 A.M.
>
> JUST ARRIVED. GLASS FACTORY BROKEN OPEN HERE DURING NIGHT, AND EIGHT HUNDRED BOTTLES TAKEN. ONLY WATER IN LARGE QUANTITY NEAR HERE IS FIVE MILES DISTANT. SHALL STRIKE FOR THERE. ELEPHANT WILL BE THIRSTY. BOTTLES WERE EMPTY.   BAKER, DETECTIVE

"That promises well, too," said the inspector. "I told you the creature's appetites would not be bad clues."

Telegram No. 3:

> TAYLORVILLE, L. I., 8.15 A.M.
>
> A HAYSTACK NEAR HERE DISAPPEARED DURING NIGHT. PROBABLY EATEN. HAVE GOT A CLUE, AND AM OFF.   HUBBARD, DETECTIVE

"How he does move around!" said the inspector. "I knew we had a difficult job on hand, but we shall catch him yet."

> FLOWER STATION, N. Y., 9 A.M.
>
> SHADOWED THE TRACKS THREE MILES WESTWARD. LARGE, DEEP, AND RAGGED. HAVE JUST MET A FARMER WHO SAYS THEY ARE NOT ELEPHANT

TRACKS. SAYS THEY ARE HOLES WHERE HE DUG UP SAPLINGS FOR SHADE-TREES WHEN GROUND WAS FROZEN LAST WINTER. GIVE ME ORDERS HOW TO PROCEED. DARLEY, DETECTIVE

"Aha! a confederate of the thieves! The thing grows warm," said the inspector.

He dictated the following telegram to Darley:

ARREST THE MAN AND FORCE HIM TO NAME HIS PALS. CONTINUE TO FOL-LOW THE TRACKS—TO THE PACIFIC, IF NECESSARY. CHIEF BLUNT

Next telegram:

CONEY POINT, PA., 8.45 A.M.
GAS OFFICE BROKEN OPEN HERE DURING NIGHT AND THREE MONTHS' UNPAID GAS BILLS TAKEN. HAVE GOT A CLUE AND AM AWAY. MURPHY, DETECTIVE

"Heavens!" said the inspector; "would he eat gas bills?"

"Through ignorance—yes; but they cannot support life. At least, unassisted."

Now came this exciting telegram:

IRONVILLE, N. Y., 9.30 A.M.
JUST ARRIVED. THIS VILLAGE IN CONSTERNATION. ELEPHANT PASSED THROUGH HERE AT FIVE THIS MORNING. SOME SAY HE WENT EAST, SOME SAY WEST, SOME NORTH, SOME SOUTH—BUT ALL SAY THEY DID NOT WAIT TO NOTICE PARTICULARLY. HE KILLED A HORSE; HAVE SECURED A PIECE OF IT FOR A CLUE. KILLED IT WITH HIS TRUNK; FROM STYLE OF BLOW, THINK HE STRUCK IT LEFT-HANDED. FROM POSITION IN WHICH HORSE LIES, THINK ELEPHANT TRAVELED NORTHWARD ALONG LINE OF BERKLEY RAILWAY. HAS FOUR AND A HALF HOURS' START, BUT I MOVE ON HIS TRACK AT ONCE. HAWES, DETECTIVE

I uttered exclamations of joy. The inspector was as self-contained as a graven image. He calmly touched his bell.

"Alaric, send Captain Burns here."

Burns appeared.

"How many men are ready for instant orders?"

"Ninety-six, sir."

"Send them north at once. Let them concentrate along the line of the Berkley road north of Ironville."

"Yes, sir."

"Let them conduct their movements with the utmost secrecy. As fast as others are at liberty, hold them for orders."

"Yes, sir."

"Go!"

"Yes, sir."

Presently came another telegram:

> SAGE CORNERS, N. Y., 10.30.
>
> JUST ARRIVED. ELEPHANT PASSED THROUGH HERE AT 8.15. ALL ESCAPED FROM THE TOWN BUT A POLICEMAN. APPARENTLY ELEPHANT DID NOT STRIKE AT POLICEMAN, BUT AT THE LAMP-POST. GOT BOTH. I HAVE SECURED A PORTION OF THE POLICEMAN AS CLUE.   STUMM, DETECTIVE

"So the elephant has turned westward," said the inspector. "However, he will not escape, for my men are scattered all over that region."

The next telegram said:

> GLOVER'S, 11.15.
>
> JUST ARRIVED. VILLAGE DESERTED, EXCEPT SICK AND AGED. ELEPHANT PASSED THROUGH THREE-QUARTERS OF AN HOUR AGO. THE ANTITEMPERANCE MASS-MEETING WAS IN SESSION; HE PUT HIS TRUNK IN AT A WINDOW AND WASHED IT OUT WITH WATER FROM CISTERN. SOME SWALLOWED IT—SINCE DEAD; SEVERAL DROWNED. DETECTIVES CROSS AND O'SHAUGHNESSY WERE PASSING THROUGH TOWN, BUT GOING SOUTH—SO MISSED ELEPHANT. WHOLE REGION FOR MANY MILES AROUND IN TERROR—PEOPLE FLYING FROM THEIR HOMES. WHEREVER THEY TURN THEY MEET ELEPHANT, AND MANY ARE KILLED.   BRANT, DETECTIVE

I could have shed tears, this havoc so distressed me. But the inspector only said:

"You see—we are closing in on him. He feels our presence; he has turned eastward again."

Yet further troublous news was in store for us. The telegraph brought this:

> HOGANSPORT, 12.19.
>
> JUST ARRIVED. ELEPHANT PASSED THROUGH HALF AN HOUR AGO, CREATING WILDEST FRIGHT AND EXCITEMENT. ELEPHANT RAGED AROUND STREETS; TWO PLUMBERS GOING BY, KILLED ONE—OTHER ESCAPED. REGRET GENERAL.
>
> O'FLAHERTY, DETECTIVE

"Now he is right in the midst of my men," said the inspector. "Nothing can save him."

A succession of telegrams came from detectives who were scattered through New Jersey and Pennsylvania, and who were following clues consisting of ravaged barns, factories, and Sunday-school libraries, with high hopes—hopes amounting to certainties, indeed. The inspector said:

"I wish I could communicate with them and order them north, but that is impossible. A detective only visits a telegraph office to send his report; then he is off again, and you don't know where to put your hand on him."

Now came this despatch:

BRIDGEPORT, CT., 12.15.

BARNUM OFFERS RATE OF $4,000 A YEAR FOR EXCLUSIVE PRIVILEGE OF USING ELEPHANT AS TRAVELING ADVERTISING MEDIUM FROM NOW TILL DE-TECTIVES FIND HIM. WANTS TO PASTE CIRCUS-POSTERS ON HIM. DESIRES IM-MEDIATE ANSWER.   BOGGS, DETECTIVE

"That is perfectly absurd!" I exclaimed.

"Of course it is," said the inspector. "Evidently Mr. Barnum, who thinks he is so sharp, does not know me—but I know him."

Then he dictated this answer to the despatch:

MR. BARNUM'S OFFER DECLINED. MAKE IT $7,000 OR NOTHING.

CHIEF BLUNT

"There. We shall not have to wait long for an answer. Mr. Barnum is not at home; he is in the telegraph office—it is his way when he has business on hand. Inside of three—"

DONE.—P. T. BARNUM

So interrupted the clicking telegraphic instrument. Before I could make a comment upon this extraordinary episode, the following despatch carried my thoughts into another and very distressing channel:

BOLIVIA, N. Y., 12.50.

ELEPHANT ARRIVED HERE FROM THE SOUTH AND PASSED THROUGH TOWARD THE FOREST AT 11.50, DISPERSING A FUNERAL ON THE WAY, AND DIMINISH-ING THE MOURNERS BY TWO. CITIZENS FIRED SOME SMALL CANNON-BALLS INTO HIM, AND THEN FLED. DETECTIVE BURKE AND I ARRIVED TEN MINUTES LATER, FROM THE NORTH, BUT MISTOOK SOME EXCAVATIONS FOR FOOTPRINTS, AND SO LOST A GOOD DEAL OF TIME; BUT AT LAST WE STRUCK THE RIGHT TRAIL AND FOLLOWED IT TO THE WOODS. WE THEN GOT DOWN ON OUR HANDS AND KNEES AND CONTINUED TO KEEP A SHARP EYE ON THE TRACK, AND SO SHAD-OWED IT INTO THE BRUSH. BURKE WAS IN ADVANCE. UNFORTUNATELY THE ANIMAL HAD STOPPED TO REST; THEREFORE, BURKE HAVING HIS HEAD DOWN, INTENT UPON THE TRACK, BUTTED UP AGAINST THE ELEPHANT'S HIND LEGS BEFORE HE WAS AWARE OF HIS VICINITY. BURKE INSTANTLY AROSE TO HIS FEET, SEIZED THE TAIL, AND EXCLAIMED JOYFULLY, "I CLAIM THE RE—"

BUT GOT NO FURTHER, FOR A SINGLE BLOW OF THE HUGE TRUNK LAID THE BRAVE FELLOW'S FRAGMENTS LOW IN DEATH. I FLED REARWARD, AND THE ELEPHANT TURNED AND SHADOWED ME TO THE EDGE OF THE WOOD, MAKING TREMENDOUS SPEED, AND I SHOULD INEVITABLY HAVE BEEN LOST, BUT THAT THE REMAINS OF THE FUNERAL PROVIDENTIALLY INTERVENED AGAIN AND DIVERTED HIS ATTENTION. I HAVE JUST LEARNED THAT NOTHING OF THAT FUNERAL IS NOW LEFT; BUT THIS IS NO LOSS, FOR THERE IS ABUNDANCE OF MATERIAL FOR ANOTHER. MEANTIME, THE ELEPHANT HAS DISAPPEARED AGAIN.   MULROONEY, DETECTIVE

We heard no news except from the diligent and confident detectives scattered about New Jersey, Pennsylvania, Delaware, and Virginia—who were all following fresh and encouraging clues—until shortly after 2 P.M., when this telegram came:

BAXTER CENTER, 2.15.
ELEPHANT BEEN HERE, PLASTERED OVER WITH CIRCUS-BILLS, AND BROKE UP A REVIVAL, STRIKING DOWN AND DAMAGING MANY WHO WERE ON THE POINT OF ENTERING UPON A BETTER LIFE. CITIZENS PENNED HIM UP AND ESTABLISHED A GUARD. WHEN DETECTIVE BROWN AND I ARRIVED, SOME TIME AFTER, WE ENTERED INCLOSURE AND PROCEEDED TO IDENTIFY ELEPHANT BY PHOTOGRAPH AND DESCRIPTION. ALL MARKS TALLIED EXACTLY EXCEPT ONE, WHICH WE COULD NOT SEE—THE BOIL-SCAR UNDER ARMPIT. TO MAKE SURE, BROWN CREPT UNDER TO LOOK, AND WAS IMMEDIATELY BRAINED—THAT IS, HEAD CRUSHED AND DESTROYED, THOUGH NOTHING ISSUED FROM DEBRIS. ALL FLED; SO DID ELEPHANT, STRIKING RIGHT AND LEFT WITH MUCH EFFECT. HAS ESCAPED, BUT LEFT BOLD BLOOD-TRACK FROM CANNON-WOUNDS. REDISCOVERY CERTAIN. HE BROKE SOUTHWARD, THROUGH A DENSE FOREST.

BRENT, DETECTIVE

That was the last telegram. At nightfall a fog shut down which was so dense that objects but three feet away could not be discerned. This lasted all night. The ferryboats and even the omnibuses had to stop running.

3

Next morning the papers were as full of detective theories as before; they had all our tragic facts in detail also, and a great many more which they had received from their telegraphic correspondents. Column after column was occupied, a third of its way down, with glaring head-lines, which it made my heart sick to read. Their general tone was like this:

THE WHITE ELEPHANT AT LARGE! HE MOVES UPON HIS FATAL MARCH!

WHOLE VILLAGES DESERTED BY THEIR FRIGHT-STRICKEN OCCUPANTS! PALE TERROR GOES BEFORE HIM, DEATH AND DEVASTATION FOLLOW AFTER! AFTER THESE, THE DETECTIVES! BARNS DESTROYED, FACTORIES GUTTED, HARVESTS DEVOURED, PUBLIC ASSEMBLAGES DISPERSED, ACCOMPANIED BY SCENES OF CARNAGE IMPOSSIBLE TO DESCRIBE! THEORIES OF THIRTY-FOUR OF THE MOST DISTINGUISHED DETECTIVES ON THE FORCE! THEORY OF CHIEF BLUNT!

"There!" said Inspector Blunt, almost betrayed into excitement, "this is magnificent! This is the greatest windfall that any detective organization ever had. The fame of it will travel to the ends of the earth, and endure to the end of time, and my name with it."

But there was no joy for me. I felt as if I had committed all those red crimes, and that the elephant was only my irresponsible agent. And how the list had grown! In one place he had "interfered with an election and killed five repeaters." He had followed this act with the destruction of two poor fellows, named O'Donohue and McFlannigan, who had "found a refuge in the home of the oppressed of all lands only the day before, and were in the act of exercising for the first time the noble right of American citizens at the polls, when stricken down by the relentless hand of the Scourge of Siam." In another, he had "found a crazy sensation-preacher preparing his next season's heroic attacks on the dance, the theater, and other things which can't strike back, and had stepped on him." And in still another place he had "killed a lightning-rod agent." And so the list went on, growing redder and redder, and more and more heartbreaking. Sixty persons had been killed, and two hundred and forty wounded. All the accounts bore just testimony to the activity and devotion of the detectives, and all closed with the remark that "three hundred thousand citizens and four detectives saw the dread creature, and two of the latter he destroyed."

I dreaded to hear the telegraphic instrument begin to click again. By and by the messages began to pour in, but I was happily disappointed in their nature. It was soon apparent that all trace of the elephant was lost. The fog had enabled him to search out a good hiding-place unobserved. Telegrams from the most absurdly distant points reported that a dim vast mass had been glimpsed there through the fog at such and such an hour, and was "undoubtedly the elephant." This dim vast mass had been glimpsed in New Haven, in New Jersey, in Pennsylvania, in interior New York, in Brooklyn, and even in the city of New York itself! But in all cases the dim vast mass had vanished quickly and left no trace. Every detective of the large force scattered over this huge extent of country sent his hourly report, and each and every one of them had a clue, and was shadowing something, and was hot upon the heels of it.

But the day passed without other result.

The next day the same.

The next just the same.

The newspaper reports began to grow monotonous with facts that amounted to nothing, clues which led to nothing, and theories which had nearly exhausted the elements which surprise and delight and dazzle.

By advice of the inspector I doubled the reward.

Four more dull days followed. Then came a bitter blow to the poor, hard-working detectives—the journalists declined to print their theories, and coldly said, "Give us a rest."

Two weeks after the elephant's disappearance I raised the reward to seventy-five thousand dollars by the inspector's advice. It was a great sum, but I felt that I would rather sacrifice my whole private fortune than lose my credit with my government. Now that the detectives were in adversity, the newspapers turned upon them, and began to fling the most stinging sarcasms at them. This gave the minstrels an idea, and they dressed themselves as detectives and hunted the elephant on the stage in the most extravagant way. The caricaturists made pictures of detectives scanning the country with spyglasses, while the elephant, at their backs, stole apples out of their pockets. And they made all sorts of ridiculous pictures of the detective badge—you have seen that badge printed in gold on the back of detective novels, no doubt—it is a wide-staring eye, with the legend, "WE NEVER SLEEP." When detectives called for a drink, the would-be facetious barkeeper resurrected an obsolete form of expression and said, "Will you have an eye-opener?" All the air was thick with sarcasms.

But there was one man who moved calm, untouched, unaffected, through it all. It was that heart of oak, the chief inspector. His brave eye never drooped, his serene confidence never wavered. He always said:

"Let them rail on; he laughs best who laughs last."

My admiration for the man grew into a species of worship. I was at his side always. His office had become an unpleasant place to me, and now became daily more and more so. Yet if he could endure it I meant to do so also—at least, as long as I could. So I came regularly, and stayed—the only outsider who seemed to be capable of it. Everybody wondered how I could; and often it seemed to me that I must desert, but at such times I looked into that calm and apparently unconscious face, and held my ground.

About three weeks after the elephant's disappearance I was about to say, one morning, that I should *have* to strike my colors and retire, when the great detective arrested the thought by proposing one more superb and masterly move.

This was to compromise with the robbers. The fertility of this man's invention exceeded anything I have ever seen, and I have had a wide intercourse with the world's finest minds. He said he was confident he could compromise for one hundred thousand dollars and recover the elephant. I said I believed I could scrape the amount together, but what would become of the poor detectives who had worked so faithfully? He said:

"In compromises they always get half."

This removed my only objection. So the inspector wrote two notes, in this form:

DEAR MADAM—YOUR HUSBAND CAN MAKE A LARGE SUM OF MONEY (AND BE ENTIRELY PROTECTED FROM THE LAW) BY MAKING AN IMMEDIATE AP-POINTMENT WITH ME.   CHIEF BLUNT

He sent one of these by his confidential messenger to the "reputed wife" of Brick Duffy, and the other to the reputed wife of Red Mc-Fadden.

Within the hour these offensive answers came:

YE OWLD FOOL: BRICK DUFFYS BIN DED 2 YERE.   BRIDGET MAHONEY

CHIEF BAT—RED MCFADDEN IS HUNG AND IN HEVING 18 MONTH. ANY ASS BUT A DETECTIVE KNOSE THAT.   MARY O'HOOLIGAN

"I had long suspected these facts," said the inspector; "this testimony proves the unerring accuracy of my instinct."

The moment one resource failed him he was ready with another. He immediately wrote an advertisement for the morning papers, and I kept a copy of it:

A.—xwblv. 242 N. Tjnd—fz328wmlg. Ozpo,—; 2 m! ogw. Mum.

He said that if the thief was alive this would bring him to the usual rendezvous. He further explained that the usual rendezvous was a place where all business affairs between detectives and criminals were conducted. This meeting would take place at twelve the next night.

We could do nothing till then, and I lost no time in getting out of the office, and was grateful indeed for the privilege.

At eleven the next night I brought one hundred thousand dollars in bank-notes and put them into the chief's hands, and shortly afterward he took his leave, with the brave old undimmed confidence in his eye. An almost intolerable hour dragged to a close; then I heard his welcome tread, and rose gasping and tottered to meet him. How his fine eyes flamed with triumph! He said:

"We've compromised! The jokers will sing a different tune to-morrow! Follow me!"

He took a lighted candle and strode down into the vast vaulted basement where sixty detectives always slept, and where a score were now playing cards to while the time. I followed close after him. He walked swiftly down to the dim and remote end of the place, and just as I succumbed to the pangs of suffocation and was swooning away he stumbled and fell over the outlying members of a mighty object, and I heard him exclaim as he went down:

"Our noble profession is vindicated. Here is your elephant!"

I was carried to the office above and restored with carbolic acid. The whole detective force swarmed in, and such another season of triumphant rejoicing ensued as I had never witnessed before. The reporters were called, baskets of champagne were opened, toasts were drunk, the handshakings and congratulations were continuous and enthusiastic. Naturally the chief was the hero of the hour, and his happiness was so complete and had been so patiently and worthily and bravely won that it made me happy to see it, though I stood there a homeless beggar, my priceless charge dead, and my position in my country's service lost to me through what would always seem my fatally careless execution of a great trust. Many an eloquent eye testified its deep admiration for the chief, and many a detective's voice murmured, "Look at him—just the king of the profession; only give him a clue, it's all he wants, and there ain't anything hid that he can't find." The dividing of the fifty thousand dollars made great pleasure; when it was finished the chief made a little speech while he put his share in his pocket, in which he said, "Enjoy it, boys, for you've earned it; and, more than that, you've earned for the detective profession undying fame."

A telegram arrived, which read:

MONROE, MICH., 10 P.M.
FIRST TIME I'VE STRUCK A TELEGRAPH OFFICE IN OVER THREE WEEKS. HAVE FOLLOWED THOSE FOOTPRINTS, HORSEBACK, THROUGH THE WOODS, A THOUSAND MILES TO HERE, AND THEY GET STRONGER AND BIGGER AND FRESHER EVERY DAY. DON'T WORRY—INSIDE OF ANOTHER WEEK I'LL HAVE THE ELEPHANT. THIS IS DEAD SURE.   DARLEY, DETECTIVE

The chief ordered three cheers for "Darley, one of the finest minds on the force," and then commanded that he be telegraphed to come home and receive his share of the reward.

So ended that marvelous episode of the stolen elephant. The newspapers were pleasant with praises once more, the next day, with one contemptible exception. This sheet said, "Great is the detective! He may be a little slow in finding a little thing like a mislaid elephant—he may hunt him all day and sleep with his rotting carcass all night for three weeks, but he will find him at last—if he can get the man who mislaid him to show him the place!"

Poor Hassan was lost to me forever. The cannon-shots had wounded him fatally, he had crept to that unfriendly place in the fog, and there, surrounded by his enemies and in constant danger of detection, he had wasted away with hunger and suffering till death gave him peace.

The compromise cost me one hundred thousand dollars; my detective expenses were forty-two thousand dollars more; I never applied for a place again under my government; I am a ruined man and a wanderer on the earth—but my admiration for that man, whom I believe to be the greatest detective the world has ever produced, remains undimmed to this day, and will so remain unto the end.

1882

A Burning Brand

I wish to reveal a secret which I have carried with me nine years and which has become burdensome.

Upon a certain occasion, nine years ago, I had said, with strong feeling, "If ever I see St. Louis again, I will seek out Mr. Brown, the great grain merchant, and ask of him the privilege of shaking him by the hand."

The occasion and the circumstances were as follows. A friend of mine, a clergyman, came one evening and said:

"I have a most remarkable letter here, which I want to read to you, if I can do it without breaking down. I must preface it with some ex-

planations, however. The letter is written by an ex-thief and ex-vaga-
bond of the lowest origin and basest rearing, a man all stained with
crime and steeped in ignorance; but, thank God! with a mine of pure
gold hidden away in him, as you shall see. His letter is written to a
burglar named Williams, who is serving a nine-year term in a certain
state prison, for burglary. Williams was a particularly daring burglar
and plied that trade during a number of years; but he was caught at
last and jailed, to await trial in a town where he had broken into a
house at night, pistol in hand, and forced the owner to hand over to
him eight thousand dollars in government bonds. Williams was not a
common sort of person, by any means; he was a graduate of Harvard
College and came of good New England stock. His father was a clergyman. While lying in jail, his health began to fail, and he was threatened
with consumption. This fact, together with the opportunity for reflection afforded by solitary confinement, had its effect—its natural effect.
He fell into serious thought; his early training asserted itself with power,
and wrought with strong influence upon his mind and heart. He put
his old life behind him and became an earnest Christian. Some ladies
in the town heard of this, visited him, and by their encouraging words
supported him in his good resolutions and strengthened him to continue
in his new life. The trial ended in his conviction and sentence to the
state prison for the term of nine years, as I have before said. In the
prison he became acquainted with the poor wretch referred to in
the beginning of my talk, Jack Hunt, the writer of the letter which I am
going to read. You will see that the acquaintanceship bore fruit for
Hunt. When Hunt's time was out, he wandered to St. Louis; and from
that place he wrote his letter to Williams. The letter got no further
than the office of the prison warden, of course; prisoners are not often
allowed to receive letters from outside. The prison authorities read this
letter, but did not destroy it. They had not the heart to do it. They read
it to several persons, and eventually it fell into the hands of those ladies
of whom I spoke a while ago. The other day I came across an old friend
of mine—a clergyman—who had seen this letter, and was full of it. The
mere remembrance of it so moved him that he could not talk of it without his voice breaking. He promised to get a copy of it for me; and
here it is—an exact copy, with all the imperfections of the original preserved. It has many slang expressions in it—thieves' *argot*—but their
meaning has been interlined, in parentheses, by the prison authorities:

St. Louis, June 9th, 1872

MR. W—— *friend Charlie if i may call you so: i no you are surprised to
get a letter from me, but i hope you won't be mad at my writing to you.*

i want to tell you my thanks for the way you talked to me when i was in prison—it has led me to try and be a better man; i guess you thought i did not cair for what you said, & at the first go off i didn't, but i noed you was a man who had don big work with good men & want no sucker, nor want gasing & all the boys knod it.

I used to think at nite what you said, & for it i nocked off swearing 5 months before my time was up, for i saw it want no good, nohow— the day my time was up you told me if i would shake the cross (quit stealing), & live on the square for 3 months, it would be the best job i ever done in my life. The state agent give me a ticket to here, & on the car i thought more of what you said to me, but didn't make up my mind. When we got to Chicago on the cars from there to here, I pulled off an old woman's leather (robbed her of her pocket-book); i hadn't no more than got it off when i wished i hadn't done it, for a while before that i made up my mind to be a square bloke, for 3 months on your word, but i forgot it when i saw the leather was a grip (easy to get)—but i kept clos to her & when she got out of the cars at a way place i said, marm have you lost anything? & she tumbled (discovered) her leather was of (gone)—is this it says i, giving it to her—well if you aint honest, says she, but i hadn't got cheak enough to stand that sort of talk, so i left her in a hurry. When i got here i had $1 and 25 cents left & i didn't get no work for 3 days as i aint strong enough for roust about on a steam bote (for a deck-hand)—The afternoon of the 3d day I spent my last 10 cents for 2 moons (large, round sea-biscuit) & cheese & i felt pretty rough & was thinking i would have to go on the dipe (picking pockets) again, when i thought of what you once said about a fellows calling on the Lord when he was in hard luck, & i thought i would try it once anyhow, but when i tryed it i got stuck on the start, & all i could get off wos, Lord give a poor fellow a chance to square it for 3 months for Christ's sake, amen; & i kept a thinking it over and over as i went along—about an hour after that i was in 4th St. & this is what happened & is the cause of my being where i am now & about which i will tell you before i get done writing. As i was walking along i herd a big noise & saw a horse running away with a carriage with 2 children in it, and i grabed up a peace of box cover from the sidewalk & run in the middle of the street, & when the horse came up i smashed him over the head as hard as i could drive —the bord split to peces & the horse checked up a little & i grabbed the reigns & pulled his head down until he stopped—the gentleman what owned him came running up & soon as he saw the children were all rite, he shook hands with me & gave me a $50 green back, & my asking the Lord to help me come into my head, & i was so thunderstruck i

*couldn't drop the reigns nor say nothing—he saw something was up, &
coming back to me said, my boy are you hurt? & the thought come into
my head just then to ask him for work; & i asked him to take back the
bill and give me a job—says he, jump in here & lets talk about it, but
keep the money—he asked me if i could take care of horses & i said yes,
for i used to hang round livery stables & often would help clean &
drive horses, he told me he wanted a man for that work, & would give
me $16. a month & bord me. You bet i took that chance at once. that
nite in my little room over the stable i sat a long time thinking over my
past life & of what had just happened & i just got down on my nees &
thanked the Lord for the job & to help me to square it, & to bless you
for putting me up to it, & the next morning i done it again & got me
some new togs* (clothes) *& a bible for i made up my mind after what
the Lord had done for me i would read the bible every nite and morning, & ask him to keep an eye on me. When I had been there about a
week Mr. Brown* (that's his name) *came in my room one nite & saw
me reading the bible—he asked me if i was a Christian & i told him no
—he asked me how it was i read the bible instead of papers & books
—Well Charlie i thought i had better give him a square deal in the start,
so i told him all about my being in prison & about you, & how i had almost done give up looking for work & how the Lord got me the job when
i asked him; & the only way i had to pay him back was to read the bible
& square it, & i asked him to give me a chance for 3 months—he talked
to me like a father for a long time, & told me i could stay & then i felt
better than ever i had done in my life, for i had given Mr. Brown a
fair start with me & now i didn't fear no one giving me a back cap*
(exposing his past life) *& running me off the job—the next morning he
called me into the library & gave me another square talk, & advised me
to study some every day, & he would help me one or 2 hours every nite,
& he gave me a Arithmetic, a spelling book, a Geography & and a writing book, & he hers me every nite—he lets me come into the house to
prayers every morning, & got me put in a bible class in the Sunday
School which i likes very much for it helps me to understand my bible
better.*

*Now, Charlie the 3 months on the square are up 2 months ago, & as
you said, it is the best job i ever did in my life, & i commenced another
of the same sort right away, only it is to God helping me to last a lifetime Charlie—i wrote this letter to tell you i do think God has forgiven
my sins & herd your prayers, for you told me you should pray for me—
i no i love to read his word & tell him all my troubles & he helps me i
know for i have plenty of chances to steal but i don't feel to as i once*

*did & now i take more pleasure in going to church than to the theatre &
that wasn't so once—our ministers and others often talk with me & a
month ago they wanted me to join the church, but i said no, not now, i
may be mistaken in my feelings, i will wait awhile, but now i feel that
God has called me & on the first Sunday in July i will join the church—
dear friend i wish i could write to you as i feel, but i cant do it yet—you
no i learned to read and write while in prisons & i aint got well enough
along to write as i would talk; i no i aint spelled all the words rite in
this & lots of other mistakes but you will excuse it i no, for you no i was
brought up in a poor house until i run away, & that i never new who
my father and mother was & i don't no my rite name, & i hope you wont
be mad at me, but i have as much rite to one name as another & i have
taken your name, for you wont use it when you get out i no, & you are
the man i think most of in the world; so i hope you wont be mad—I am
doing well, i put $10 a month in bank with $25 of the $50—if you ever
want any or all of it let me know, & it is yours. i wish you would let me
send you some now. I send you with this a receipt for a year of Littles
Living Age, i didn't no what you would like & i told Mr. Brown & he
said he thought you would like it—i wish i was nere you so i could send
you chuck (refreshments) on holidays; it would spoil this weather from
here, but i will send you a box next thanksgiving any way—next week
Mr. Brown takes me into his store as lite porter & will advance me as
soon as i know a little more—he keeps a big granary store, wholesale—
i forgot to tell you of my mission school, sunday school class—the school
is in the sunday afternoon, i went out two sunday afternoons, and picked
up seven kids (little boys) & got them to come in. Two of them new
as much as i did & i had them put in a class where they could learn
something. i don't no much myself, but as these kids cant read i get on
nicely with them. i make sure of them by going after them every Sunday ½ hour before school time, i also got 4 girls to come. tell Mack and
Harry about me, if they will come out here when their time is up i will
get them jobs at once. i hope you will excuse this long letter & all mistakes, i wish i could see you for i cant write as i would talk—i hope the
warm weather is doing your lungs good—i was afraid when you was
bleeding you would die—give my respects to all the boys and tell them
how i am doing—i am doing well and every one here treats me as kind
as they can—Mr. Brown is going to write to you sometime—i hope some
day you will write to me, this letter is from your very true friend*

C—— W——

who you know as Jack Hunt.

I send you Mr. Brown's card. Send my letter to him.

Here was true eloquence; irresistible eloquence; and without a single grace or ornament to help it out. I have seldom been so deeply stirred by any piece of writing. The reader of it halted, all the way through, on a lame and broken voice; yet he had tried to fortify his feelings by several private readings of the letter before venturing into company with it. He was practising upon me to see if there was any hope of his being able to read the document to his prayer-meeting with anything like a decent command over his feelings. The result was not promising. However, he determined to risk it; and did. He got through tolerably well; but his audience broke down early, and stayed in that condition to the end.

The fame of the letter spread through the town. A brother minister came and borrowed the manuscript, put it bodily into a sermon, preached the sermon to twelve hundred people on a Sunday morning, and the letter drowned them in their own tears. Then my friend put it into a sermon and went before his Sunday morning congregation with it. It scored another triumph. The house wept as one individual.

My friend went on summer vacation up into the fishing regions of our northern British neighbors, and carried this sermon with him, since he might possibly chance to need a sermon. He was asked to preach one day. The little church was full. Among the people present were the late Dr. J. G. Holland, the late Mr. Seymour of the New York *Times*, Mr. Page, the philanthropist and temperance advocate, and, I think, Senator Frye of Maine. The marvelous letter did its wonted work; all the people were moved, all the people wept; the tears flowed in a steady stream down Dr. Holland's cheeks, and nearly the same can be said with regard to all who were there. Mr. Page was so full of enthusiasm over the letter that he said he would not rest until he made pilgrimage to that prison, and had speech with the man who had been able to inspire a fellow-unfortunate to write so priceless a tract.

Ah, that unlucky Page!—and another man. If they had only been in Jericho, that letter would have rung through the world and stirred all the hearts of all the nations for a thousand years to come, and nobody might ever have found out that it was the confoundedest, brazenest, ingeniousest piece of fraud and humbuggery that was ever concocted to fool poor confiding mortals with!

The letter was a pure swindle, and that is the truth. And take it by and large, it was without a compeer among swindles. It was perfect, it was rounded, symmetrical, complete, colossal!

The reader learns it at this point; but we didn't learn it till some miles and weeks beyond this stage of the affair. My friend came back from the woods, and he and other clergymen and lay missionaries began once more to inundate audiences with their tears and the tears of said audiences; I begged hard for permission to print the letter in a magazine and tell the watery story of its triumphs; numbers of people got copies of the letter, with permission to circulate them in writing, but not in print; copies were sent to the Sandwich Islands and other far regions.

Charles Dudley Warner was at church, one day, when the worn letter was read and wept over. At the church door, afterward, he dropped a peculiarly cold iceberg down the clergyman's back with the question:

"Do you know that letter to be genuine?"

It was the first suspicion that had ever been voiced; but it had that sickening effect which first-uttered suspicions against one's idol always have. Some talk followed:

"Why—what should make you suspect that it isn't genuine?"

"Nothing that I know of, except that it is too neat, and compact, and fluent, and nicely put together for an ignorant person, an unpractised hand. I think it was done by an educated man."

The literary artist had detected the literary machinery. If you will look at the letter now, you will detect it yourself—it is observable in every line.

Straightway the clergyman went off, with this seed of suspicion sprouting in him, and wrote to a minister residing in that town where Williams had been jailed and converted; asked for light; and also asked if a person in the literary line (meaning me) might be allowed to print the letter and tell its history. He presently received this answer:

Rev. —— ——.

My dear Friend: In regard to that "convict's letter" there can be no doubt as to its genuineness. "Williams," to whom it was written, lay in our jail and professed to have been converted, and Rev. Mr. ——, the chaplain, had great faith in the genuineness of the change—as much as one can have in any such case.

The letter was sent to one of our ladies, who is a Sunday-school teacher—sent either by Williams himself, or the chaplain of the state's prison, probably. She has been greatly annoyed in having so much publicity, lest it might seem a breach of confidence, or be an injury to Williams. In regard to its publication, I can give no permission; though, if the names and places were omitted, and especially if sent out of the country, I think you might take the responsibility and do it.

It is a wonderful letter, which no Christian genius, much less one unsanctified, could ever have written. As showing the work of grace in a human heart, and in a very degraded and wicked one, it proves its own origin and reproves our weak faith in its power to cope with any form of wickedness.

"Mr. Brown" of St. Louis, some one said, was a Hartford man. Do all whom you send from Hartford serve their Master as well?

P. S.—Williams is still in the state's prison, serving out a long sentence —of nine years, I think. He has been sick and threatened with consumption, but I have not inquired after him lately. This lady that I speak of corresponds with him, I presume, and will be quite sure to look after him.

This letter arrived a few days after it was written—and up went Mr. Williams's stock again. Mr. Warner's low-down suspicion was laid in the cold, cold grave, where it apparently belonged. It was a suspicion based upon mere internal evidence, anyway; and when you come to internal evidence, it's a big field and a game that two can play at: as witness this other internal evidence, discovered by the writer of the note above quoted, that "it is a wonderful letter—which no Christian genius, much less one unsanctified, could ever have written."

I had permission now to print—provided I suppressed names and places and sent my narrative out of the country. So I chose an Australian magazine for vehicle, as being far enough out of the country, and set myself to work on my article. And the ministers set the pumps going again, with the letter to work the handles.

But meantime Brother Page had been agitating. He had not visited the penitentiary, but he had sent a copy of the illustrious letter to the chaplain of that institution, and accompanied it with—apparently—inquiries. He got an answer, dated four days later than that other brother's reassuring epistle; and before my article was complete, it wandered into my hands. The original is before me now, and I here append it. It is pretty well loaded with internal evidence of the most solid description:

State's Prison, Chaplain's Office, July 11, 1873

Dear Bro. Page:

Herewith please find the letter kindly loaned me. I am afraid its genuineness cannot be established. It purports to be addressed to some prisoner here. No such letter ever came to a prisoner here. All letters received are carefully read by officers of the prison before they go into the hands of the convicts, and any such letter could not be forgotten. Again, Charles Williams is not a Christian man, but a dissolute, cunning prodigal, whose father is a minister of the gospel. His name is an assumed one. I am glad to have made your acquaintance. I am preparing a lecture upon life seen through prison bars, and should like to deliver the same in your vicinity.

And so ended that little drama. My poor article went into the fire; for whereas the materials for it were now more abundant and infinitely richer than they had previously been, there were parties all around me who, although longing for the publication before, were a unit for suppression at this stage and complexion of the game. They said, "Wait— the wound is too fresh, yet." All the copies of the famous letter, except mine, disappeared suddenly; and from that time onward, the aforetime same old drought set in, in the churches. As a rule, the town was on a spacious grin for a while, but there were places in it where the grin did not appear, and where it was dangerous to refer to the ex-convict's letter.

A word of explanation: "Jack Hunt," the professed writer of the letter, was an imaginary person. The burglar Williams—Harvard graduate, son of a minister—wrote the letter himself, *to* himself: got it smuggled out of the prison; got it conveyed to persons who had supported and encouraged him in his conversion—where he knew two things would happen: the genuineness of the letter would not be doubted or inquired into; and the nub of it would be noticed, and would have valuable effect —the effect, indeed, of starting a movement to get Mr. Williams pardoned out of prison.

That "nub" is so ingeniously, so casually, flung in, and immediately left there in the tail of the letter, undwelt upon, that an indifferent reader would never suspect that it was the heart and core of the epistle, if he even took note of it at all. This is the "nub":

i hope the warm weather is doing your lungs good—i was afraid when you was bleeding you would die—*give my respects, etc.*

That is all there is of it—simply touch and go—no dwelling upon it. Nevertheless it was intended for an eye that would be swift to see it; and it was meant to move a kind heart to try to effect the liberation of a poor reformed and purified fellow lying in the fell grip of consumption.

When I for the first time heard that letter read, nine years ago, I felt that it was the most remarkable one I had ever encountered. And it so

warmed me toward Mr. Brown of St. Louis that I said that if ever I
visited that city again, I would seek out that excellent man and kiss the
hem of his garment, if it was a new one. Well, I visited St. Louis, but I
did not hunt for Mr. Brown; for alas! the investigations of long ago
had proved that the benevolent Brown, like "Jack Hunt," was not a real
person, but a sheer invention of that gifted rascal, Williams—burglar,
Harvard graduate, son of a clergyman.

From LIFE ON THE MISSISSIPPI, 1883

A Dying Man's Confession

We were approaching Napoleon, Arkansas. So I began to think about
my errand there. Time, noonday; and bright and sunny. This was bad—
not best, anyway; for mine was not (preferably) a noonday kind of
errand. The more I thought, the more that fact pushed itself upon me
—now in one form, now in another. Finally, it took the form of a distinct
question: Is it good common sense to do the errand in daytime, when
by a little sacrifice of comfort and inclination you can have night for it,
and no inquisitive eyes around? This settled it. Plain question and plain
answer make the shortest road out of most perplexities.

I got my friends into my stateroom, and said I was sorry to create
annoyance and disappointment, but that upon reflection it really seemed
best that we put our luggage ashore and stop over at Napoleon. Their
disapproval was prompt and loud; their language mutinous. Their main
argument was one which has always been the first to come to the surface, in such cases, since the beginning of time: "But you decided
and *agreed* to stick to this boat," etc.; as if, having determined to do
an unwise thing, one is thereby bound to go ahead and make *two* unwise things of it, by carrying out that determination. I tried various
mollifying tactics upon them, with reasonably good success: under
which encouragement I increased my efforts; and, to show them that
I had not created this annoying errand, and was in no way to blame
for it, I presently drifted into its history—substantially as follows:

Toward the end of last year I spent a few months in Munich, Bavaria.
In November I was living in Fräulein Dahlweiner's *pension,* 1a, Karl-

strasse; but my working quarters were a mile from there, in the house of a widow who supported herself by taking lodgers. She and her two young children used to drop in every morning and talk German to me —by request. One day, during a ramble about the city, I visited one of the two establishments where the government keeps and watches corpses until the doctors decide that they are permanently dead, and not in a trance state. It was a grisly place, that spacious room. There were thirty-six corpses of adults in sight, stretched on their backs on slightly slanted boards, in three long rows—all of them with wax-white, rigid faces, and all of them wrapped in white shrouds. Along the sides of the room were deep alcoves, like bay-windows; and in each of these lay several marble-visaged babes, utterly hidden and buried under banks of fresh flowers, all but their faces and crossed hands. Around a finger of each of these fifty still forms, both great and small, was a ring; and from the ring a wire led to the ceiling, and thence to a bell in a watch-room yonder, where, day and night, a watchman sits always alert and ready to spring to the aid of any of that pallid company who, waking out of death, shall make a movement—for any, even the slightest, movement will twitch the wire and ring that fearful bell. I imagined myself a death-sentinel drowsing there alone, far in the dragging watches of some wailing, gusty night, and having in a twinkling all my body stricken to quivering jelly by the sudden clamor of that awful summons! So I inquired about this thing; asked what resulted usually? if the watchman died, and the restored corpse came and did what it could to make his last moments easy? But I was rebuked for trying to feed an idle and frivolous curiosity in so solemn and so mournful a place; and went my way with a humbled crest.

Next morning I was telling the widow my adventure when she exclaimed:

"Come with me! I have a lodger who shall tell you all you want to know. He has been a night watchman there."

He was a living man, but he did not look it. He was abed and had his head propped high on pillows; his face was wasted and colorless, his deep-sunken eyes were shut; his hand, lying on his breast, was talon-like, it was so bony and long-fingered. The widow began her introduction of me. The man's eyes opened slowly, and glittered wickedly out from the twilight of their caverns; he frowned a black frown; he lifted his lean hand and waved us peremptorily away. But the widow kept straight on, till she had got out the fact that I was a stranger and an American. The man's face changed at once, brightened, became even eager—and the next moment he and I were alone together.

I opened up in cast-iron German; he responded in quite flexible English; thereafter we gave the German language a permanent rest.

This consumptive and I became good friends. I visited him every day, and we talked about everything. At least, about everything but wives and children. Let anybody's wife or anybody's child be mentioned and three things always followed: the most gracious and loving and tender light glimmered in the man's eyes for a moment; faded out the next, and in its place came that deadly look which had flamed there the first time I ever saw his lids unclose; thirdly, he ceased from speech there and then for that day, lay silent, abstracted, and absorbed, apparently heard nothing that I said, took no notice of my good-bys, and plainly did not know by either sight or hearing when I left the room.

When I had been this Karl Ritter's daily and sole intimate during two months, he one day said abruptly:

"I will tell you my story."

Then he went on as follows:

I have never given up until now. But now I have given up. I am going to die. I made up my mind last night that it must be, and very soon, too. You say you are going to revisit your river by and by, when you find opportunity. Very well; that, together with a certain strange experience which fell to my lot last night, determines me to tell you my history—for you will see Napoleon, Arkansas, and for my sake you will stop there and do a certain thing for me—a thing which you will willingly undertake after you shall have heard my narrative.

Let us shorten the story wherever we can, for it will need it, being long. You already know how I came to go to America, and how I came to settle in that lonely region in the South. But you do not know that I had a wife. My wife was young, beautiful, loving, and oh, so divinely good and blameless and gentle! And our little girl was her mother in minature. It was the happiest of happy households.

One night—it was toward the close of the war—I woke up out of a sodden lethargy, and found myself bound and gagged, and the air tainted with chloroform! I saw two men in the room, and one was saying to the other in a hoarse whisper: "I *told* her I would, if she made a noise, and as for the child—"

The other man interrupted in a low, half-crying voice:

"You said we'd only gag them and rob them, not hurt them, or I wouldn't have come."

"Shut up your whining; *had* to change the plan when they waked up. You done all *you* could to protect them, now let that satisfy you. Come, help rummage."

Both men were masked and wore coarse, ragged "nigger" clothes; they had a bull's-eye lantern, and by its light I noticed that the gentler robber had no thumb on his right hand. They rummaged around my poor cabin for a moment: the head bandit then said in his stage whisper:

"It's a waste of time—*he* shall tell where it's hid. Undo his gag and revive him up."

The other said:

"All right—provided no clubbing."

"No clubbing it is, then—provided he keeps still."

They approached me. Just then there was a sound outside, a sound of voices and trampling hoofs; the robbers held their breath and listened; the sounds came slowly nearer and nearer, then came a shout:

"*Hello,* the house! Show a light, we want water."

"The captain's voice, by G——!" said the stage-whispering ruffian, and both robbers fled by the way of the back door, shutting off their bull's-eye as they ran.

The stranger shouted several times more, then rode by—there seemed to be a dozen of the horses—and I heard nothing more.

I struggled, but could not free myself from my bonds. I tried to speak, but the gag was effective, I could not make a sound. I listened for my wife's voice and my child's—listened long and intently, but no sound came from the other end of the room where their bed was. This silence became more and more awful, more and more ominous, every moment. Could you have endured an hour of it, do you think? Pity me, then, who had to endure three. Three hours? it was three ages! Whenever the clock struck it seemed as if years had gone by since I had heard it last. All this time I was struggling in my bonds, and at last, about dawn, I got myself free and rose up and stretched my stiff limbs. I was able to distinguish details pretty well. The floor was littered with things thrown there by the robbers during their search for my savings. The first object that caught my particular attention was a document of mine which I had seen the rougher of the two ruffians glance at and then cast away. It had blood on it! I staggered to the other end of the room. Oh, poor unoffending, helpless ones, there they lay; their troubles ended, mine begun!

Did I appeal to the law—I? Does it quench the pauper's thirst if the king drink for him? Oh, no, no, no! I wanted no impertinent interference of the law. Laws and the gallows could not pay the debt that

was owing to me! Let the laws leave the matter in my hands, and have
no fears: I would find the debtor and collect the debt. How accomplish
this, do you say? How accomplish it and feel so sure about it, when I
had neither seen the robbers' faces, nor heard their natural voices, nor
had any idea who they might be? Nevertheless, I *was* sure—quite sure,
quite confident. I had a clue—a clue which you would not have valued
—a clue which would not have greatly helped even a detective, since he
would lack the secret of how to apply it. I shall come to that presently
—you shall see. Let us go on now, taking things in their due order. There
was one circumstance which gave me a slant in a definite direction to
begin with: Those two robbers were manifestly soldiers in tramp disguise, and not new to military service, but old in it—regulars, perhaps;
they did not acquire their soldierly attitude, gestures, carriage, in a
day, nor a month, nor yet in a year. So I thought, but said nothing.
And one of them had said, "The captain's voice, by G——!"—the one
whose life I would have. Two miles away several regiments were in
camp, and two companies of U. S. cavalry. When I learned that Captain
Blakely of Company C had passed our way that night with an escort
I said nothing, but in that company I resolved to seek my man. In
conversation I studiously and persistently described the robbers as
tramps, camp followers; and among this class the people made useless
search, none suspecting the soldiers but me.

Working patiently by night in my desolated home, I made a disguise
for myself out of various odds and ends of clothing; in the nearest
village I bought a pair of blue goggles. By and by, when the military
camp broke up, and Company C was ordered a hundred miles north,
to Napoleon, I secreted my small hoard of money in my belt and took
my departure in the night. When Company C arrived in Napoleon I
was already there. Yes, I was there, with a new trade—fortune-teller.
Not to seem partial, I made friends and told fortunes among all the
companies garrisoned there, but I gave Company C the great bulk of
my attentions. I made myself limitlessly obliging to these particular
men; they could ask me no favor, put on me no risk which I would
decline. I became the willing butt of their jokes; this perfected my
popularity; I became a favorite.

I early found a private who lacked a thumb—what joy it was to me!
And when I found that he alone, of all the company, had lost a thumb,
my last misgiving vanished; I was *sure* I was on the right track. This
man's name was Kruger, a German. There were nine Germans in the
company. I watched to see who might be his intimates, but he seemed
to have no especial intimates. But *I* was his intimate, and I took care

to make the intimacy grow. Sometimes I so hungered for my revenge that I could hardly restrain myself from going on my knees and begging him to point out the man who had murdered my wife and child, but I managed to bridle my tongue. I bided my time and went on telling fortunes, as opportunity offered.

My apparatus was simple: a little red paint and a bit of white paper. I painted the ball of the client's thumb, took a print of it on the paper, studied it that night, and revealed his fortune to him next day. What was my idea in this nonsense? It was this: When I was a youth, I knew an old Frenchman who had been a prison-keeper for thirty years, and he told me that there was one thing about a person which never changed, from the cradle to the grave—the lines in the ball of the thumb; and he said that these lines were never exactly alike in the thumbs of any two human beings. In these days, we photograph the new criminal, and hang his picture in the Rogues' Gallery for future reference; but that Frenchman, in his day, used to take a print of the ball of a new prisoner's thumb and put that away for future reference. He always said that pictures were no good—future disguises could make them useless. "The thumb's the only sure thing," said he; "you can't disguise that." And he used to prove his theory, too, on my friends and acquaintances; it always succeeded.

I went on telling fortunes. Every night I shut myself in, all alone, and studied the day's thumb-prints with a magnifying-glass. Imagine the devouring eagerness with which I poured over those mazy red spirals, with that document by my side which bore the right-hand thumb and finger-marks of that unknown murderer, printed with the dearest blood—to me—that was ever shed on this earth! And many and many a time I had to repeat the same old disappointed remark, "Will they *never* correspond!"

But my reward came at last. It was the print of the thumb of the forty-third man of Company C whom I had experimented on—Private Franz Adler. An hour before I did not know the murderer's name, or voice, or figure, or face, or nationality; but now I knew all these things! I believed I might feel sure; the Frenchman's repeated demonstrations being so good a warranty. Still, there was a way to *make* sure. I had an impression of Kruger's left thumb. In the morning I took him aside when he was off duty; and when we were out of sight and hearing of witnesses, I said impressively:

"A part of your fortune is so grave that I thought it would be better for you if I did not tell it in public. You and another man, whose fortune I was studying last night—Private Adler—have been murdering a woman and a child! You are being dogged. Within five days both of you will be assassinated."

He dropped on his knees, frightened out of his wits; and for five minutes he kept pouring out the same set of words, like a demented person, and in the same half-crying way which was one of my memories of that murderous night in my cabin:

"I didn't do it; upon my soul I didn't do it; and I tried to keep *him* from doing it. I did, as God is my witness. He did it alone."

This was all I wanted. And I tried to get rid of the fool; but no, he clung to me, imploring me to save him from the assassin. He said:

"I have money—ten thousand dollars—hid away, the fruit of loot and thievery; save me—tell me what to do, and you shall have it, every penny. Two-thirds of it is my cousin Adler's; but you can take it all. We hid it when we first came here. But I hid it in a new place yesterday, and have not told him—shall not tell him. I was going to desert, and get away with it all. It is gold, and too heavy to carry when one is running and dodging; but a woman who has been gone over the river two days to prepare my way for me is going to follow me with it; and if I got no chance to describe the hiding-place to her I was going to slip my silver watch into her hand, or send it to her, and she would understand. There's a piece of paper in the back of the case which tells it all. Here, take the watch—tell me what to do!"

He was trying to press his watch upon me, and was exposing the paper and explaining it to me, when Adler appeared on the scene, about a dozen yards away. I said to poor Kruger:

"Put up your watch, I don't want it. You sha'n't come to any harm. Go, now. I must tell Adler his fortune. Presently I will tell you how to escape the assassin; meantime I shall have to examine your thumb-mark again. Say nothing to Adler about this thing—say nothing to anybody."

He went away filled with fright and gratitude, poor devil! I told Adler a long fortune—purposely so long that I could not finish it; promised to come to him on guard, that night, and tell him the really important part of it—the tragical part of it, I said—so must be out of reach of eavesdroppers. They always kept a picket-watch outside the town—mere discipline and ceremony—no occasion for it, no enemy around.

Toward midnight I set out, equipped with the countersign, and picked my way toward the lonely region where Adler was to keep his watch. It was so dark that I stumbled right on a dim figure almost before I could get out a protecting word. The sentinel hailed and I answered, both at the same moment. I added, "It's only me—the fortuneteller." Then I slipped to the poor devil's side, and without a word I drove my dirk into his heart! "*Ja wohl*," laughed I, "it *was* the tragedy part of his fortune, indeed!" As he fell from his horse he clutched at me, and my blue goggles remained in his hand; and away plunged the beast, dragging him with his foot in the stirrup.

I fled through the woods and made good my escape, leaving the accusing goggles behind me in that dead man's hand.

This was fifteen or sixteen years ago. Since then I have wandered aimlessly about the earth, sometimes at work, sometimes idle; sometimes with money, sometimes with none; but always tired of life, and wishing it was done, for my mission here was finished with the act of that night; and the only pleasure, solace, satisfaction I had, in all those tedious years, was in the daily reflection, "I have killed him!"

Four years ago my health began to fail. I had wandered into Munich, in my purposeless way. Being out of money I sought work, and got it; did my duty faithfully about a year, and was then given the berth of night watchman yonder in that dead-house which you visited lately. The place suited my mood. I liked it. I liked being with the dead— liked being alone with them. I used to wander among those rigid corpses, and peer into their austere faces, by the hour. The later the time, the more impressive it was; I preferred the late time. Sometimes I turned the lights low; this gave perspective, you see; and the imagination could play; always, the dim, receding ranks of the dead inspired one with weird and fascinating fancies. Two years ago—I had been there a year then—I was sitting all alone in the watch-room, one gusty winter's night, chilled, numb, comfortless; drowsing gradually into unconsciousness; the sobbing of the wind and the slamming of distant shutters falling fainter and fainter upon my dulling ear each moment, when sharp and suddenly that dead-bell rang out a blood-curdling alarum over my head! The shock of it nearly paralyzed me; for it was the first time I had ever heard it.

I gathered myself together and flew to the corpse-room. About midway down the outside rank, a shrouded figure was sitting upright, wagging its head slowly from one side to the other—a grisly spectacle! Its side was toward me. I hurried to it and peered into its face. Heavens, it was Adler!

Can you divine what my first thought was? Put into words, it was this: "It seems, then, you escaped me once: there will be a different result this time!"

Evidently this creature was suffering unimaginable terrors. Think what it must have been to wake up in the midst of that voiceless hush, and look out over that grim congregation of the dead! What gratitude shone in his skinny white face when he saw a living form before him! And how the fervency of this mute gratitude was augmented when his eyes fell upon the life-giving cordials which I carried in my hands! Then imagine the horror which came into his pinched face when I put the cordials behind me, and said mockingly:

"Speak up, Franz Adler—call upon these dead! Doubtless they will listen and have pity; but here there is none else that will."

He tried to speak, but that part of the shroud which bound his jaws held firm, and would not let him. He tried to lift imploring hands, but they were crossed upon his breast and tied. I said:

"Shout, Franz Adler; make the sleepers in the distant streets hear you and bring help. Shout—and lose no time, for there is little to lose. What, you cannot? That is a pity; but it is no matter—it does not always bring help. When you and your cousin murdered a helpless woman and child in a cabin in Arkansas—my wife, it was, and my child!—they shrieked for help, you remember; but it did no good; you remember that it did no good, is it not so? Your teeth chatter—then why cannot you shout? Loosen the bandages with your hands—then you can. Ah, I see—your hands are tied, they cannot aid you. How strangely things repeat themselves, after long years; for *my* hands were tied, that night, you remember? Yes, tied much as yours are now—how odd that is! I could not pull free. It did not occur to you to untie me; it does not occur to me to untie you. 'Sh—! there's a late footstep. It is coming this way. Hark, how near it is! One can count the footfalls—one—two— three. There—it is just outside. Now is the time! Shout, man, shout! it is the one sole chance between you and eternity! Ah, you see you have delayed too long—it is gone by. There—it is dying out. It is gone! Think of it—reflect upon it—you have heard a human footstep for the last time. How curious it must be, to listen to so common a sound as that and know that one will never hear the fellow to it again."

Oh, my friend, the agony in that shrouded face was ecstasy to see! I thought of a new torture, and applied it—assisting myself with a trifle of lying invention:

"That poor Kruger tried to save my wife and child, and I did him a grateful good turn for it when the time came. I persuaded him to rob you; and I and a woman helped him to desert, and got him away in safety."

A look as of surprise and triumph shone out dimly through the anguish in my victim's face. I was disturbed, disquieted. I said:

"What, then—didn't he escape?"

A negative shake of the head.

"No? What happened, then?"

The satisfaction in the shrouded face was still plainer. The man tried to mumble out some words—could not succeed; tried to express something with his obstructed hands—failed; paused a moment, then feebly tilted his head, in a meaning way, toward the corpse that lay nearest him.

"Dead?" I asked. "Failed to escape? Caught in the act and shot?"

Negative shake of the head.

"How, then?"

Again the man tried to do something with his hands. I watched closely, but could not guess the intent. I bent over and watched still more intently. He had twisted a thumb around and was weakly punching at his breast with it.

"Ah—stabbed, do you mean?"

Affirmative nod, accompanied by a spectral smile of such devilishness that it struck an awakening light through my dull brain, and I cried:

"Did I stab him, mistaking him for you? for that stroke was meant for none but you."

The affirmative nod of the re-dying rascal was as joyous as his failing strength was able to put into its expression.

"Oh, miserable, miserable me, to slaughter the pitying soul that stood a friend to my darlings when they were helpless, and would have saved them if he could! miserable, oh, miserable, miserable me!"

I fancied I heard the muffled gurgle of a mocking laugh. I took my face out of my hands, and saw my enemy sinking back upon his inclined board.

He was a satisfactory long time dying. He had a wonderful vitality, an astonishing constitution. Yes, he was a pleasant long time at it. I got a chair and a newspaper, and sat down by him and read. Occasionally I took a sip of brandy. This was necessary, on account of the cold. But I did it partly because I saw that, along at first, whenever I reached for the bottle, he thought I was going to give him some. I read aloud: mainly imaginary accounts of people snatched from the grave's threshold and restored to life and vigor by a few spoonfuls of liquor and a warm bath. Yes, he had a long, hard death of it—three hours and six minutes, from the time he rang his bell.

It is believed that in all these eighteen years that have elapsed since the institution of the corpse-watch, no shrouded occupant of the Bavarian dead-houses has ever rung its bell. Well, it is a harmless belief. Let it stand at that.

The chill of that death-room had penetrated my bones. It revived and fastened upon me the disease which had been afflicting me, but which, up to that night, had been steadily disappearing. That man murdered my wife and my child; and in three days hence he will have added me to his list. No matter—God! how delicious the memory of it! I caught him escaping from his grave, and thrust him back into it!

After that night I was confined to my bed for a week; but as soon as I could get about I went to the dead-house books and got the number of the house which Adler had died in. A wretched lodging-house it was. It was my idea that he would naturally have gotten hold of Kruger's effects, being his cousin; and I wanted to get Kruger's watch, if I could. But while I was sick, Adler's things had been sold and scattered, all except a few old letters, and some odds and ends of no value. However, through those letters I traced out a son of Kruger's, the only relative he left. He is a man of thirty, now, a shoemaker by trade, and living at No. 14 Königstrasse, Mannheim—widower, with several small children. Without explaining to him why, I have furnished two-thirds of his support ever since.

Now, as to that watch—see how strangely things happen! I traced it around and about Germany for more than a year, at considerable cost in money and vexation; and at last I got it. Got it, and was unspeakably glad; opened it, and found nothing in it! Why, I might have known that that bit of paper was not going to stay there all this time. Of course I gave up that ten thousand dollars then; gave it up, and dropped it out of my mind; and most sorrowfully, for I had wanted it for Kruger's son.

Last night, when I consented at last that I must die, I began to make ready. I proceeded to burn all useless papers; and sure enough, from a batch of Adler's, not previously examined with thoroughness, out dropped that long-desired scrap! I recognized it in a moment. Here it is —I will translate it:

Brick livery stable, stone foundation, middle of town, corner of Orleans and Market. Corner toward Court-house. Third stone, fourth row. Stick notice there, saying how many are to come.

There—take it, and preserve it! Kruger explained that that stone was removable; and that it was in the north wall of the foundation, fourth row from the top, and third stone from the west. The money is secreted behind it. He said the closing sentence was a blind, to mislead in case the paper should fall into wrong hands. It probably performed that office for Adler.

Now I want to beg that when you make your intended journey down the river, you will hunt out that hidden money, and send it to Adam Kruger, care of the Mannheim address which I have mentioned. It will make a rich man of him, and I shall sleep the sounder in my grave for knowing that I have done what I could for the son of the man who tried to save my wife and child—albeit my hand ignorantly struck him down, whereas the impulse of my heart would have been to shield and serve him.

"Such was Ritter's narrative," said I to my two friends. There was a profound and impressive silence, which lasted a considerable time; then both men broke into a fusillade of excited and admiring ejaculations over the strange incidents of the tale: and this, along with a rattling fire of questions, was kept up until all hands were about out of breath. Then my friends began to cool down, and draw off, under shelter of occasional volleys, into silence and abysmal revery. For ten minutes, now, there was stillness. Then Rogers said dreamily:

"Ten thousand dollars!" Adding, after a considerable pause:

"Ten thousand. It is a heap of money."

Presently the poet inquired:

"Are you going to send it to him right away?"

"Yes," I said. "It is a queer question."

No reply. After a little, Rogers asked hesitatingly:

"*All* of it? That is—I mean—"

"*Certainly*, all of it."

I was going to say more, but stopped—was stopped by a train of thought which started up in me. Thompson spoke, but my mind was absent and I did not catch what he said. But I heard Rogers answer:

"Yet, it seems so to me. It ought to be quite sufficient; for I don't see that *he* has done anything."

Presently the poet said:

"When you come to look at it, it is *more* than sufficient. Just look at it—five thousand dollars! Why, he couldn't spend it in a lifetime! And it would injure him, too; perhaps ruin him—you want to look at that. In a little while he would throw his last away, shut up his shop, maybe take to drinking, maltreat his motherless children, drift into other evil courses, go steadily from bad to worse—"

"Yes, that's it," interrupted Rogers fervently, "I've seen it a hundred times—yes, more than a hundred. You put money into the hands of a man like that, if you want to destroy him, that's all. Just put money into his hands, it's all you've got to do; and if it don't pull him down, and take all the usefulness out of him, and all the self-respect and everything, then I don't know human nature—ain't that so, Thompson? And even if we were to give him a *third* of it; why, in less than six months—"

"Less than six *weeks*, you'd better say!" said I, warming up and breaking in. "Unless he had that three thousand dollars in safe hands where he couldn't touch it, he would no more last you six weeks than—"

"Of *course* he wouldn't!" said Thompson. "I've edited books for that kind of people; and the moment they get their hands on the royalty— maybe it's three thousand, maybe it's two thousand—"

"What business has that shoemaker with two thousand dollars, I should like to know?" broke in Rogers earnestly. "A man perhaps perfectly contented now, there in Mannheim, surrounded by his own class, eating his bread with the appetite which laborious industry alone can give, enjoying his humble life, honest, upright, pure in heart, and *blest!* —yes, I say blest! above all the myriads that go in silk attire and walk the empty, artificial round of social folly—but just you put *that* temptation before him once! just you lay fifteen hundred dollars before a man like that, and say—"

"Fifteen hundred devils!" cried I. "*Five* hundred would rot his principles, paralyze his industry, drag him to the rumshop, thence to the gutter, thence to the almshouse, thence to—"

"*Why* put upon ourselves this crime, gentlemen?" interrupted the poet earnestly and appealingly. "He is happy where he is, and *as* he is. Every sentiment of honor, every sentiment of charity, every sentiment of high and sacred benevolence warns us, beseeches us, commands us to leave him undisturbed. That is real friendship, that is true friendship. We could follow other courses that would be more showy; but none that would be so truly kind and wise, depend upon it."

After some further talk, it became evident that each of us, down in his heart, felt some misgivings over this settlement of the matter. It was manifest that we all felt that we ought to send the poor shoemaker *something*. There was long and thoughtful discussion of this point, and we finally decided to send him a chromo.

Well, now that everything seemed to be arranged satisfactorily to everybody concerned, a new trouble broke out: it transpired that these two men were expecting to share equally in the money with me. That was not my idea. I said that if they got half of it between them they might consider themselves lucky. Rogers said:

"Who would have had *any* if it hadn't been for me? I flung out the first hint—but for that it would all have gone to the shoemaker."

Thompson said that he was thinking of the thing himself at the very moment that Rogers had originally spoken.

I retorted that the idea would have occurred to me plenty soon enough, and without anybody's help. I was slow about thinking, maybe, but I was sure.

This matter warmed up into a quarrel; then into a fight; and each man got pretty badly battered. As soon as I got myself mended up after a fashion, I ascended to the hurricane-deck in a pretty sour humor. I found Captain McCord there, and said, as pleasantly as my humor would permit:

"I have come to say good-by, captain. I wish to go ashore at Napoleon."

"Go ashore where?"

"Napoleon."

The captain laughed; but seeing that I was not in a jovial mood, stopped that and said:

"But are you serious?"

"Serious? I certainly am."

The captain glanced up at the pilot-house and said:

"He wants to get off at Napoleon!"

"*Napoleon?*"

"That's what he says."

"Great Cæsar's ghost!"

Uncle Mumford approached along the deck. The captain said:

"Uncle, here's a friend of yours wants to get off at Napoleon!"

"Well, by ——!"

I said:

"Come, what is all this about? Can't a man go ashore at Napoleon, if he wants to?"

"Why, hang it, don't you know? There *isn't* any Napoleon any more. Hasn't been for years and years. The Arkansas River burst through it, tore it all to rags, and emptied it into the Mississippi!"

"Carried the *whole* town away? Banks, churches, jails, newspaper offices, court-house, theater, fire department, livery stable—*everything?*"

"Everything! Just a fifteen-minute job, or such a matter. Didn't leave hide nor hair, shred nor shingle of it, except the fag-end of a shanty and one brick chimney. This boat is paddling along right now where the dead-center of that town used to be; yonder is the brick chimney—all that's left of Napoleon. These dense woods on the right used to be a mile back of the town. Take a look behind you—up-stream—now you begin to recognize this country, don't you?"

"Yes, I do recognize it now. It is the most wonderful thing I ever heard of; by a long shot the most wonderful—and unexpected."

Mr. Thompson and Mr. Rogers had arrived, meantime, with satchels and umbrellas, and had silently listened to the captain's news. Thompson put a half-dollar in my hand and said softly:

"For my share of the chromo."

Rogers followed suit.

Yes, it was an astonishing thing to see the Mississippi rolling between unpeopled shores and straight over the spot where I used to see a good big self-complacent town twenty years ago. Town that was county-seat of a great and important county; town with a big United States marine hospital; town of innumerable fights—an inquest every day; town where I had used to know the prettiest girl, and the most accomplished, in the whole Mississippi valley; town where we were handed the first printed news of the *Pennsylvania's* mournful disaster a quarter of a century ago; a town no more—swallowed up, vanished, gone to feed the fishes; nothing left but a fragment of a shanty and a crumbling brick chimney!

From LIFE ON THE MISSISSIPPI, 1883

The Professor's Yarn

It was in the early days. I was not a college professor then. I was a humble-minded young land-surveyor, with the world before me—to survey, in case anybody wanted it done. I had a contract to survey a route for a great mining ditch in California, and I was on my way thither, by sea—a three or four weeks' voyage. There were a good many passengers, but I had very little to say to them; reading and dreaming were my passions, and I avoided conversation in order to indulge these appetites. There were three professional gamblers on board—rough, repulsive fellows. I never had any talk with them, yet I could not help seeing them with some frequency, for they gambled in an upper-deck stateroom every day and night, and in my promenades I often had glimpses of them through their door, which stood a little ajar to let out the surplus tobacco-smoke and profanity. They were an evil and hateful presence, but I had to put up with it, of course.

There was one other passenger who fell under my eye a good deal, for he seemed determined to be friendly with me, and I could not have gotten rid of him without running some chance of hurting his feelings, and I was far from wishing to do that. Besides, there was something engaging in his countrified simplicity and his beaming good nature. The first time I saw this Mr. John Backus, I guessed, from his clothes and his looks, that he was a grazier or farmer from the backwoods of some Western state—doubtless Ohio—and afterward, when he dropped into his personal history, and I discovered that he *was* a cattle-raiser from interior Ohio, I was so pleased with my own penetration that I warmed toward him for verifying my instinct.

He got to dropping alongside me every day, after breakfast, to help me make my promenade; and so, in the course of time, his easy-working jaw had told me everything about his business, his prospects, his family, his relatives, his politics—in fact, everything that concerned a Backus, living or dead. And meantime I think he had managed to get out of me everything I knew about my trade, my tribe, my purposes, my prospects, and myself. He was a gentle and persuasive genius, and this thing showed it; for I was not given to talking about my matters. I said something about triangulation, once; the stately word pleased his ear; he inquired what it meant; I explained. After that he quietly and inoffensively ignored my name, and always called me Triangle.

What an enthusiast he was in cattle! At the bare name of a bull or a cow, his eye would light and his eloquent tongue would turn itself loose. As long as I would walk and listen, he would walk and talk; he knew all breeds, he loved all breeds, he caressed them all with his affectionate tongue. I tramped along in voiceless misery while the cattle question was up. When I could endure it no longer, I used to deftly insert a scientific topic into the conversation; then my eye fired and his faded; my tongue fluttered, his stopped; life was a joy to me, and a sadness to him.

One day he said, a little hesitatingly, and with somewhat of diffidence:

"Triangle, would you mind coming down to my stateroom a minute and have a little talk on a certain matter?"

I went with him at once. Arrived there, he put his head out, glanced up and down the saloon warily, then closed the door and locked it. We sat down on the sofa and he said:

"I'm a-going to make a little proposition to you, and if it strikes you favorable, it 'll be a middling good thing for both of us. You ain't a-going out to Californy for fun, nuther am I—it's *business,* ain't that so?

Well, you can do me a good turn, and so can I you, if we see fit. I've raked and scraped and saved a considerable many years, and I've got it all here." He unlocked an old hair trunk, tumbled a chaos of shabby clothes aside, and drew a short, stout bag into view for a moment, then buried it again and relocked the trunk. Dropping his voice to a cautious, low tone, he continued: "She's all there—a round ten thousand dollars in yellow-boys; now, this is my little idea: What I don't know about raising cattle ain't worth knowing. There's mints of money in it in Californy. Well, I know, and you know, that all along a line that's being surveyed, there's little dabs of land that they call 'gores,' that fall to the surveyor free gratis for nothing. All you've got to do on your side is to survey in such a way that the 'gores' will fall on good fat land, then you turn 'em over to me, I stock 'em with cattle, *in* rolls the cash, I plank out your share of the dollars regular right along, and—"

I was sorry to wither his blooming enthusiasm, but it could not be helped. I interrupted and said severely:

"I am not that kind of a surveyor. Let us change the subject, Mr. Backus."

It was pitiful to see his confusion and hear his awkward and shame-faced apologies. I was as much distressed as he was—especially as he seemed so far from having suspected that there was anything improper in his proposition. So I hastened to console him and lead him on to forget his mishap in a conversational orgy about cattle and butchery. We were lying at Acapulco, and as we went on deck it happened luckily that the crew were just beginning to hoist some beeves aboard in slings. Backus's melancholy vanished instantly, and with it the memory of his late mistake.

"Now, only look at that!" cried he. "My goodness, Triangle, what *would* they say to it in *Ohio?* Wouldn't their eyes bug out to see 'em handled like that?—wouldn't they, though?"

All the passengers were on deck to look—even the gamblers—and Backus knew them all, and had afflicted them all with his pet topic. As I moved away I saw one of the gamblers approach and accost him; then another of them; then the third. I halted, waited, watched; the conversation continued between the four men; it grew earnest; Backus drew gradually away; the gamblers followed and kept at his elbow. I was uncomfortable. However, as they passed me presently, I heard Backus say with a tone of persecuted annoyance:

"But it ain't any use, gentlemen; I tell you again, as I've told you a half a dozen times before, I warn't raised to it, and I ain't a-going to resk it."

I felt relieved. "His level head will be his sufficient protection," I said to myself.

During the fortnight's run from Acapulco to San Francisco I several times saw the gamblers talking earnestly with Backus, and once I threw out a gentle warning to him. He chuckled comfortably and said:

"Oh, yes! they tag around after me considerable—want me to play a little, just for amusement, they say—but laws-a-me, if my folks have told me once to look out for that sort of live stock, they've told me a thousand times, I reckon."

By and by, in due course, we were approaching San Francisco. It was an ugly, black night, with a strong wind blowing, but there was not much sea. I was on deck alone. Toward ten I started below. A figure issued from the gamblers' den and disappeared in the darkness. I experienced a shock, for I was sure it was Backus. I flew down the companionway, looked about for him, could not find him, then returned to the deck just in time to catch a glimpse of him as he re-entered that confounded nest of rascality. Had he yielded at last? I feared it. What had he gone below for? His bag of coin? Possibly. I drew near the door, full of bodings. It was a-crack, and I glanced in and saw a sight that made me bitterly wish I had given my attention to saving my poor cattle-friend, instead of reading and dreaming my foolish time away. He was gambling. Worse still, he was being plied with champagne, and was already showing some effect from it. He praised the "cider," as he called it, and said now that he had got a taste of it he almost believed he would drink it if it was spirits, it was so good and so ahead of anything he had ever run across before. Surreptitious smiles at this passed from one rascal to another, and they filled all the glasses, and while Backus honestly drained his to the bottom they pretended to do the same, but threw the wine over their shoulders.

I could not bear the scene, so I wandered forward and tried to interest myself in the sea and the voices of the wind. But no, my uneasy spirit kept dragging me back at quarter-hour intervals, and always I saw Backus drinking his wine—fairly and squarely, and the others throwing theirs away. It was the painfulest night I ever spent.

The only hope I had was that we might reach our anchorage with speed—that would break up the game. I helped the ship along all I could with my prayers. At last we went booming through the Golden Gate, and my pulses leaped for joy. I hurried back to that door and glanced in. Alas! there was small room for hope—Backus's eyes were heavy and bloodshot, his sweaty face was crimson, his speech maudlin and thick, his body sawed drunkenly about with the weaving motion of the ship. He drained another glass to the dregs, while the cards were being dealt.

He took his hand, glanced at it, and his dull eyes lit up for a moment. The gamblers observed it, and showed their gratification by hardly perceptible signs.

"How many cards?"

"None!" said Backus.

One villain—named Hank Wiley—discarded one card, the others three each. The betting began. Heretofore the bets had been trifling— a dollar or two; but Backus started off with an eagle now, Wiley hesitated a moment, then "saw it," and "went ten dollars better." The other two threw up their hands.

Backus went twenty better. Wiley said:

"I see that, and go you a *hundred* better!" then smiled and reached for the money.

"Let it alone," said Backus, with drunken gravity.

"What! you mean to say you're going to cover it?"

"Cover it? Well, I reckon I am—and lay another hundred on top of it, too."

He reached down inside his overcoat and produced the required sum.

"Oh, that's your little game, is it? I see your raise, and raise it five hundred!" said Wiley.

"Five hundred *better!*" said the foolish bull-driver, and pulled out the amount and showered it on the pile. The three conspirators hardly tried to conceal their exultation.

All diplomacy and pretense were dropped now, and the sharp exclamations came thick and fast, and the yellow pyramid grew higher and higher. At last ten thousand dollars lay in view. Wiley cast a bag of coin on the table, and said with mocking gentleness:

"Five thousand dollars better, my friend from the rural districts— what do you say *now?*"

"I *call* you!" said Backus, heaving his golden shot-bag on the pile. "What have you got?"

"Four kings, you d——d fool!" and Wiley threw down his cards and surrounded the stakes with his arms.

"Four *aces*, you ass!" thundered Backus, covering his man with a cocked revolver. "*I'm a professional gambler myself, and I've been laying for you duffers all this voyage!*"

Down went the anchor, rumbledy-dum-dum! and the trip was ended.

Well, well—it is a sad world. One of the three gamblers was Backus's "pal." It was he that dealt the fateful hands. According to an understanding with the two victims, he was to have given Backus four queens, but alas! he didn't.

A week later I stumbled upon Backus—arrayed in the height of fashion—in Montgomery street. He said cheerily, as we were parting:

"Ah, by the way, you needn't mind about those gores. I don't really know anything about cattle, except what I was able to pick up in a week's apprenticeship over in Jersey, just before we sailed. My cattle culture and cattle enthusiasm have served their turn—I sha'n't need them any more."

From LIFE ON THE MISSISSIPPI, 1883

A Ghost Story

I took a large room, far up Broadway, in a huge old building whose upper stories had been wholly unoccupied for years until I came. The place had long been given up to dust and cobwebs, to solitude and silence. I seemed groping among the tombs and invading the privacy of the dead, that first night I climbed up to my quarters. For the first time in my life a superstitious dread came over me; and as I turned a dark angle of the stairway and an invisible cobweb swung its slazy woof in my face and clung there, I shuddered as one who had encountered a phantom.

I was glad enough when I reached my room and locked out the mold and the darkness. A cheery fire was burning in the grate, and I sat down before it with a comforting sense of relief. For two hours I sat there, thinking of bygone times; recalling old scenes, and summoning half-forgotten faces out of the mists of the past; listening, in fancy, to voices that long ago grew silent for all time, and to once familiar songs that nobody sings now. And as my reverie softened down to a sadder and sadder pathos, the shrieking of the winds outside softened to a wail, the angry beating of the rain against the panes diminished to a tranquil patter, and one by one the noises in the street subsided, until the

hurrying footsteps of the last belated straggler died away in the distance
and left no sound behind.

The fire had burned low. A sense of loneliness crept over me. I arose
and undressed, moving on tiptoe about the room, doing stealthily what
I had to do, as if I were environed by sleeping enemies whose slumbers
it would be fatal to break. I covered up in bed, and lay listening to
the rain and wind and the faint creaking of distant shutters, till they
lulled me to sleep.

I slept profoundly, but how long I do not know. All at once I found
myself awake, and filled with a shuddering expectancy. All was still.
All but my own heart—I could hear it beat. Presently the bedclothes
began to slip away slowly toward the foot of the bed, as if some one
were pulling them! I could not stir; I could not speak. Still the blankets
slipped deliberately away, till my breast was uncovered. Then with a
great effort I seized them and drew them over my head. I waited,
listened, waited. Once more that steady pull began, and once more I
lay torpid a century of dragging seconds till my breast was naked again.
At last I roused my energies and snatched the covers back to their
place and held them with a strong grip. I waited. By and by I felt a
faint tug, and took a fresh grip. The tug strengthened to a steady strain
—it grew stronger and stronger. My hold parted, and for the third time
the blankets slid away. I groaned. An answering groan came from the
foot of the bed! Beaded drops of sweat stood upon my forehead. I was
more dead than alive. Presently I heard a heavy footstep in my room
—the step of an elephant, it seemed to me—it was not like anything
human. But it was moving *from* me—there was relief in that. I heard
it approach the door—pass out without moving bolt or lock—and wander
away among the dismal corridors, straining the floors and joists till they
creaked again as it passed—and then silence reigned once more.

When my excitement had calmed, I said to myself, "This is a dream
—simply a hideous dream." And so I lay thinking it over until I convinced myself that it *was* a dream, and then a comforting laugh relaxed
my lips and I was happy again. I got up and struck a light; and when I
found that the locks and bolts were just as I had left them, another
soothing laugh welled in my heart and rippled from my lips. I took my
pipe and lit it, and was just sitting down before the fire, when—down
went the pipe out of my nerveless fingers, the blood forsook my cheeks,
and my placid breathing was cut short with a gasp! In the ashes on the
hearth, side by side with my own bare footprint, was another, so vast
that in comparison mine was but an infant's! Then I had *had* a visitor,
and the elephant tread was explained.

I put out the light and returned to bed, palsied with fear. I lay a long time, peering into the darkness, and listening. Then I heard a grating noise overhead, like the dragging of a heavy body across the floor; then the throwing down of the body, and the shaking of my windows in response to the concussion. In distant parts of the building I heard the muffled slamming of doors. I heard, at intervals, stealthy footsteps creeping in and out among the corridors, and up and down the stairs. Sometimes these noises approached my door, hesitated, and went away again. I heard the clanking of chains faintly, in remote passages, and listened while the clanking grew nearer—while it wearily climbed the stairways, marking each move by the loose surplus of chain that fell with an accented rattle upon each succeeding step as the goblin that bore it advanced. I heard muttered sentences; half-uttered screams that seemed smothered violently; and the swish of invisible garments, the rush of invisible wings. Then I became conscious that my chamber was invaded —that I was not alone. I heard sighs and breathings about my bed, and mysterious whisperings. Three little spheres of soft phosphorescent light appeared on the ceiling directly over my head, clung and glowed there a moment, and then dropped—two of them upon my face and one upon the pillow. They spattered, liquidly, and felt warm. Intuition told me they had turned to gouts of blood as they fell—I needed no light to satisfy myself of that. Then I saw pallid faces, dimly luminous, and white uplifted hands, floating bodiless in the air—floating a moment and then disappearing. The whispering ceased, and the voices and the sounds, and a solemn stillness followed. I waited and listened. I felt that I must have light or die. I was weak with fear. I slowly raised myself toward a sitting posture, and my face came in contact with a clammy hand! All strength went from me apparently, and I fell back like a stricken invalid. Then I heard the rustle of a garment—it seemed to pass to the door and go out.

When everything was still once more, I crept out of bed, sick and feeble, and lit the gas with a hand that trembled as if it were aged with a hundred years. The light brought some little cheer to my spirits. I sat down and fell into a dreamy contemplation of that great footprint in the ashes. By and by its outlines began to waver and grow dim. I glanced up and the broad gas-flame was slowly wilting away. In the same moment I heard that elephantine tread again. I noted its approach, nearer and nearer, along the musty halls, and dimmer and dimmer the light waned. The tread reached my very door and paused— the light had dwindled to a sickly blue, and all things about me lay in a spectral twilight. The door did not open, and yet I felt a faint gust of air fan my cheek, and presently was conscious of a huge, cloudy presence before me. I watched it with fascinated eyes. A pale glow stole over the Thing; gradually its cloudy folds took shape—an arm appeared, then legs, then a body, and last a great sad face looked out of the vapor. Stripped of its filmy housings, naked, muscular and comely, the majestic Cardiff Giant loomed above me!

All my misery vanished—for a child might know that no harm could come with that benignant countenance. My cheerful spirits returned at once, and in sympathy with them the gas flamed up brightly again. Never a lonely outcast was so glad to welcome company as I was to greet the friendly giant. I said:

"Why, is it nobody but you? Do you know, I have been scared to death for the last two or three hours? I am most honestly glad to see you. I wish I had a chair— Here, here, don't try to sit down in that thing!"

But it was too late. He was in it before I could stop him, and down he went—I never saw a chair shivered so in my life.

"Stop, stop, you'll ruin ev—"

Too late again. There was another crash, and another chair was resolved into its original elements.

"Confound it, haven't you got any judgment at all? Do you want to ruin all the furniture on the place? Here, here, you petrified fool—"

But it was no use. Before I could arrest him he had sat down on the bed, and it was a melancholy ruin.

"Now what sort of a way is that to do? First you come lumbering about the place bringing a legion of vagabond goblins along with you to worry me to death, and then when I overlook an indelicacy of costume which would not be tolerated anywhere by cultivated people except in a respectable theater, and not even there if the nudity were of *your* sex, you repay me by wrecking all the furniture you can find to sit down on. And why will you? You damage yourself as much as you do me. You have broken off the end of your spinal column, and littered up the floor with chips of your hams till the place looks like a marble yard. You ought to be ashamed of yourself—you are big enough to know better."

"Well, I will not break any more furniture. But what am I to do? I have not had a chance to sit down for a century." And the tears came into his eyes.

"Poor devil," I said, "I should not have been so harsh with you. And you are an orphan, too, no doubt. But sit down on the floor here— nothing else can stand your weight—and besides, we cannot be sociable with you away up there above me; I want you down where I can perch on this high counting-house stool and gossip with you face to face."

So he sat down on the floor, and lit a pipe which I gave him, threw one of my red blankets over his shoulders, inverted my sitz-bath on his head, helmet fashion, and made himself picturesque and comfortable. Then he crossed his ankles, while I renewed the fire, and exposed the flat, honeycombed bottoms of his prodigious feet to the grateful warmth.

"What is the matter with the bottom of your feet and the back of your legs, that they are gouged up so?"

"Infernal chilblains—I caught them clear up to the back of my head, roosting out there under Newell's farm. But I love the place; I love it as one loves his old home. There is no peace for me like the peace I feel when I am there."

We talked along for half an hour, and then I noticed that he looked tired, and spoke of it.

"Tired?" he said. "Well, I should think so. And now I will tell you all about it, since you have treated me so well. I am the spirit of the Petrified Man that lies across the street there in the museum. I am the ghost of the Cardiff Giant. I can have no rest, no peace, till they have given that poor body burial again. Now what was the most natural thing for me to do, to make men satisfy this wish? Terrify them into it!—haunt the place where the body lay! So I haunted the museum night after night. I even got other spirits to help me. But it did no good, for nobody ever came to the museum at midnight. Then it occurred to me to come over the way and haunt this place a little. I felt that if I ever got a hearing I must succeed, for I had the most efficient company that perdition could furnish. Night after night we have shivered around through these mildewed halls, dragging chains, groaning, whispering, tramping up and down stairs, till, to tell you the truth, I am almost worn out. But when I saw a light in your room to-night I roused my energies again and went at it with a deal of the old freshness. But I am tired out—entirely fagged out. Give me, I beseech you, give me some hope!"

I lit off my perch in a burst of excitement, and exclaimed:

"This transcends everything! everything that ever did occur! Why you poor blundering old fossil, you have had all your trouble for nothing— you have been haunting a *plaster cast* of yourself—the real Cardiff Giant is in Albany![1] Confound it, don't you know your own remains?"

---

[1] A fact. The original fraud was ingeniously and fraudfully duplicated, and exhibited in New York as the "only genuine" Cardiff Giant (to the unspeakable disgust of the owners of the real colossus) at the very same time that the latter was drawing crowds at a museum in Albany.

I never saw such an eloquent look of shame, of pitiable humilation, overspread a countenance before.

The Petrified Man rose slowly to his feet, and said:

"Honestly, *is* that true?"

"As true as I am sitting here."

He took the pipe from his mouth and laid it on the mantel, then stood irresolute a moment (unconsciously, from old habit, thrusting his hands where his pantaloons pockets should have been, and meditatively dropping his chin on his breast), and finally said:

"Well—I *never* felt so absurd before. The Petrified Man has sold everybody else, and now the mean fraud has ended by selling its own ghost! My son, if there is any charity left in your heart for a poor friendless phantom like me, don't let this get out. Think how *you* would feel if you had made such an ass of yourself."

I heard his stately tramp die away, step by step down the stairs and out into the deserted street, and felt sorry that he was gone, poor fellow —and sorrier still that he had carried off my red blanket and my bathtub.

1888

Luck[1]

It was at a banquet in London in honor of one of the two or three conspicuously illustrious English military names of this generation. For reasons which will presently appear, I will withhold his real name and titles and call him Lieutenant-General Lord Arthur Scoresby, Y.C., K.C.B., etc., etc., etc. What a fascination there is in a renowned name! There sat the man, in actual flesh, whom I had heard of so many thousands of times since that day, thirty years before, when his name shot suddenly to the zenith from a Crimean battlefield, to remain forever celebrated. It was food and drink to me to look, and look, and look at that demi-god; scanning, searching, noting: the quietness, the reserve,

[1] This is not a fancy sketch. I got it from a clergyman who was an instructor at Woolwich forty years ago, and who vouched for its truth. M. T.

the noble gravity of his countenance; the simple honesty that expressed itself all over him; the sweet unconsciousness of his greatness—unconsciousness of the hundreds of admiring eyes fastened upon him, unconsciousness of the deep, loving, sincere worship welling out of the breasts of those people and flowing toward him.

The clergyman at my left was an old acquaintance of mine—clergyman now, but had spent the first half of his life in the camp and field and as an instructor in the military school at Woolwich. Just at the moment I have been talking about a veiled and singular light glimmered in his eyes and he leaned down and muttered confidentially to me—indicating the hero of the banquet with a gesture:

"Privately—he's an absolute fool."

This verdict was a great surprise to me. If its subject had been Napoleon, or Socrates, or Solomon, my astonishment could not have been greater. Two things I was well aware of: that the Reverend was a man of strict veracity and that his judgment of men was good. Therefore I knew, beyond doubt or question, that the world was mistaken about this hero: he *was* a fool. So I meant to find out, at a convenient moment, how the Reverend, all solitary and alone, had discovered the secret.

Some days later the opportunity came, and this is what the Reverend told me:

About forty years ago I was an instructor in the military academy at Woolwich. I was present in one of the sections when young Scoresby underwent his preliminary examination. I was touched to the quick with pity, for the rest of the class answered up brightly and handsomely, while he—why, dear me, he didn't know *anything*, so to speak. He was evidently good, and sweet, and lovable, and guileless; and so it was exceedingly painful to see him stand there, as serene as a graven image, and deliver himself of answers which were veritably miraculous for stupidity and ignorance. All the compassion in me was aroused in his behalf. I said to myself, when he comes to be examined again he will be flung over, of course; so it will be simply a harmless act of charity to ease his fall as much as I can. I took him aside and found that he knew a little of Cæsar's history; and as he didn't know anything else, I went to work and drilled him like a galley-slave on a certain line of stock questions concerning Cæsar which I knew would be used. If you'll believe me, he went through with flying colors on examination day! He went through on that purely superficial "cram," and got compliments too, while others, who knew a thousand times more than he, got plucked. By some strangely lucky accident—an accident not likely to happen twice in a century—he was asked no question outside of the narrow limits of his drill.

It was stupefying. Well, all through his course I stood by him, with something of the sentiment which a mother feels for a crippled child; and he always saved himself—just by miracle, apparently.

Now, of course, the thing that would expose him and kill him at last was mathematics. I resolved to make his death as easy as I could; so I drilled him and crammed him, and crammed him and drilled him, just on the line of questions which the examiners would be most likely to use, and then launched him on his fate. Well, sir, try to conceive of the result: to my consternation, he took the first prize! And with it he got a perfect ovation in the way of compliments.

Sleep? There was no more sleep for me for a week. My conscience tortured me day and night. What I had done I had done purely through charity, and only to ease the poor youth's fall. I never had dreamed of any such preposterous results as the thing that had happened. I felt as guilty and miserable as Frankenstein. Here was a wooden-head whom I had put in the way of glittering promotions and prodigious responsibilities, and but one thing could happen: he and his responsibilities would all go to ruin together at the first opportunity.

The Crimean War had just broken out. Of course there had to be a war, I said to myself. We couldn't have peace and give this donkey a chance to die before he is found out. I waited for the earthquake. It came. And it made me reel when it did come. He was actually gazetted to a captaincy in a marching regiment! Better men grow old and gray in the service before they climb to a sublimity like that. And who could ever have foreseen that they would go and put such a load of responsibility on such green and inadequate shoulders? I could just barely have stood it if they had made him a cornet; but a captain—think of it! I thought my hair would turn white.

Consider what I did—I who so loved repose and inaction. I said to myself, I am responsible to the country for this, and I must go along with him and protect the country against him as far as I can. So I took my poor little capital that I had saved up through years of work and grinding economy, and went with a sigh and bought a cornetcy in his regiment, and away we went to the field.

And there—oh, dear, it was awful. Blunders?—why, he never did anything *but* blunder. But, you see, nobody was in the fellow's secret. Everybody had him focused wrong, and necessarily misinterpreted his performance every time. Consequently they took his idiotic blunders for inspirations of genius. They did, honestly! His mildest blunders were

enough to make a man in his right mind cry; and they did make me cry
—and rage and rave, too, privately. And the thing that kept me always
in a sweat of apprehension was the fact that every fresh blunder he
made increased the luster of his reputation! I kept saying to myself, he'll
get so high that when discovery does finally come it will be like the
sun falling out of the sky.

He went right along up, from grade to grade, over the dead bodies of
his superiors, until at last, in the hottest moment of the battle of ——
down went our colonel, and my heart jumped into my mouth, for
Scoresby was next in rank! Now for it, said I; we'll all land in Sheol in
ten minutes, sure.

The battle was awfully hot; the allies were steadily giving way all
over the field. Our regiment occupied a position that was vital; a blunder now must be destruction. At this crucial moment, what does this
immortal fool do but detach the regiment from its place and order a
charge over a neighboring hill where there wasn't a suggestion of an
enemy! "There you go!" I said to myself; "this *is* the end at last."

And away we did go, and were over the shoulder of the hill before
the insane movement could be discovered and stopped. And what did
we find? An entire and unsuspected Russian army in reserve! And what
happened? We were eaten up? That is necessarily what would have
happened in ninety-nine cases out of a hundred. But no; those Rus-
sians argued that no single regiment would come browsing around there
at such a time. It must be the entire English army, and that the sly
Russian game was detected and blocked; so they turned tail, and away
they went, pell-mell, over the hill and down into the field, in wild confusion, and we after them; they themselves broke the solid Russian
center in the field, and tore through, and in no time there was the most
tremendous rout you ever saw, and the defeat of the allies was turned
into a sweeping and splendid victory! Marshal Canrobert looked on,
dizzy with astonishment, admiration, and delight; and sent right off for
Scoresby, and hugged him, and decorated him on the field in presence
of all the armies!

And what was Scoresby's blunder that time? Merely the mistaking
his right hand for his left—that was all. An order had come to him to fall
back and support our right; and, instead, he fell *forward* and went over
the hill to the left. But the name he won that day as a marvelous military genius filled the world with his glory, and that glory will never fade
while history books last.

He is just as good and sweet and lovable and unpretending as a man
can be, but he doesn't know enough to come in when it rains. Now that

is absolutely true. He is the supremest ass in the universe; and until half an hour ago nobody knew it but himself and me. He has been pursued, day by day and year by year, by a most phenomenal and astonishing luckiness. He has been a shining soldier in all our wars for a generation; he has littered his whole military life with blunders, and yet has never committed one that didn't make him a knight or a baronet or a lord or something. Look at his breast; why, he is just clothed in domestic and foreign decorations. Well, sir, every one of them is the record of some shouting stupidity or other; and, taken together, they are proof that the very best thing in all this world that can befall a man is to be born lucky. I say again, as I said at the banquet, Scoresby's an absolute fool.

1891

Playing Courier

A time would come when we must go from Aix-les-Bains to Geneva, and from thence, by a series of day-long and tangled journeys, to Bayreuth in Bavaria. I should have to have a courier, of course, to take care of so considerable a party as mine.

But I procrastinated. The time slipped along, and at last I woke up one day to the fact that we were ready to move and had no courier. I then resolved upon what I felt was a foolhardy thing, but I was in the humor of it. I said I would make the first stage without help—I did it.

I brought the party from Aix to Geneva by myself—four people. The distance was two hours and more, and there was one change of cars. There was not an accident of any kind, except leaving a valise and some other matters on the platform—a thing which can hardly be called an accident, it is so common. So I offered to conduct the party all the way to Bayreuth.

This was a blunder, though it did not seem so at the time. There was more detail than I thought there would be: 1, two persons whom we had left in a Genevan pension some weeks before must be collected and brought to the hotel; 2, I must notify the people on the Grand Quay who store trunks to bring seven of our stored trunks to the hotel and carry back seven which they would find piled in the lobby; 3, I must find out what part of Europe Bayreuth was in and buy seven railway tickets for that point; 4, I must send a telegram to a friend in the Netherlands; 5, it was now two in the afternoon, and we must look sharp and be ready for the first night train and make sure of sleeping-car tickets; 6, I must draw money at the bank.

It seemed to me that the sleeping-car tickets must be the most important thing, so I went to the station myself to make sure; hotel messengers are not always brisk people. It was a hot day, and I ought to have driven, but it seemed better economy to walk. It did not turn out so, because I lost my way and trebled the distance. I applied for the tickets, and they asked me which route I wanted to go by, and that embarrassed me and made me lose my head, there were so many people standing around, and I not knowing anything about the routes and not supposing there were going to be two; so I judged it best to go back and map out the road and come again.

I took a cab this time, but on my way up-stairs at the hotel I remembered that I was out of cigars, so I thought it would be well to get some while the matter was in my mind. It was only round the corner, and I didn't need the cab. I asked the cabman to wait where he was. Thinking of the telegram and trying to word it in my head, I forgot the cigars and the cab, and walked on indefinitely. I was going to have the hotel people send the telegram, but as I could not be far from the post-office by this time, I thought I would do it myself. But it was further than I had supposed. I found the place at last and wrote the telegram and handed it in. The clerk was a severe-looking, fidgety man, and he began to fire French questions at me in such a liquid form that I could not detect the joints between his words, and this made me lose my head again. But an Englishman stepped up and said the clerk wanted to know where he was to send the telegram. I could not tell him, because it was not my telegram, and I explained that I was merely sending it for a member of my party. But nothing would pacify the clerk but the address; so I said that if he was so particular I would go back and get it.

However, I thought I would go and collect those lacking two persons first, for it would be best to do everything systematically and in order, and one detail at a time. Then I remembered the cab was eating up my substance down at the hotel yonder; so I called another cab and told the man to go down and fetch it to the post-office and wait till I came.

I had a long, hot walk to collect those people, and when I got there they couldn't come with me because they had heavy satchels and must have a cab. I went away to find one, but before I ran across any I noticed that I had reached the neighborhood of the Grand Quay—at least I thought I had—so I judged I could save time by stepping around and arranging about the trunks. I stepped around about a mile, and although I did not find the Grand Quay, I found a cigar shop, and remembered about the cigars. I said I was going to Bayreuth, and wanted enough for the journey. The man asked me which route I was going to take. I said I did not know. He said he would recommend me to go by Zurich and various other places which he named, and offered to sell me seven second-class through tickets for twenty-two dollars apiece, which would be throwing off the discount which the railroads allowed him. I was already tired of riding second-class on first-class tickets, so I took him up.

By and by I found Natural & Co.'s storage office, and told them to send seven of our trunks to the hotel and pile them up in the lobby. It seemed to me that I was not delivering the whole of the message, still it was all I could find in my head.

Next I found the bank and asked for some money, but I had left my letter of credit somewhere and was not able to draw. I remembered now that I must have left it lying on the table where I wrote my telegram; so I got a cab and drove to the post-office and went up-stairs, and they said that a letter of credit had indeed been left on the table, but that it was now in the hands of the police authorities, and it would be necessary for me to go there and prove property. They sent a boy with me, and we went out the back way and walked a couple of miles and found the place; and then I remembered about my cabs, and asked the boy to send them to me when he got back to the post-office. It was nightfall now, and the Mayor had gone to dinner. I thought I would go to dinner myself, but the officer on duty thought differently, and I stayed. The Mayor dropped in at half past ten, but said it was too late to do anything to-night—come at 9.30 in the morning. The officer wanted to keep me all night, and said I was a suspicious-looking person, and probably did not own the letter of credit, and didn't know what a letter of credit was, but merely saw the real owner leave it lying on the table, and wanted to get it because I was probably a person that would want anything he could get, whether it was valuable or not. But the Mayor said he saw nothing suspicious about me, and that I seemed a harmless person and nothing the matter with me but a wandering mind, and not much of that. So I thanked him and he set me free, and I went home in my three cabs.

As I was dog-tired and in no condition to answer questions with discretion, I thought I would not disturb the Expedition at that time of night, as there was a vacant room I knew of at the other end of the hall; but I did not quite arrive there, as a watch had been set, the Expedition being anxious about me. I was placed in a galling situation. The Expedition sat stiff and forbidding on four chairs in a row, with shawls and things all on, satchels and guide-books in lap. They had been sitting like that for four hours, and the glass going down all the time. Yes, and they were waiting—waiting for me. It seemed to me that nothing but a sudden, happily contrived, and brilliant *tour de force* could break this iron front and make a diversion in my favor; so I shied my hat into the arena and followed it with a skip and a jump, shouting blithely:

"Ha, ha, here we all are, Mr. Merryman!"

Nothing could be deeper or stiller than the absence of applause which followed. But I kept on; there seemed no other way, though my confidence, poor enough before, had got a deadly check and was in effect gone.

I tried to be jocund out of a heavy heart, I tried to touch the other hearts there and soften the bitter resentment in those faces by throwing off bright and airy fun and making of the whole ghastly thing a joyously humorous incident, but this idea was not well conceived. It was not the right atmosphere for it. I got not one smile; not one line in those offended faces relaxed; I thawed nothing of the winter that looked out of those frosty eyes. I started one more breezy, poor effort, but the head of the Expedition cut into the center of it and said:

"Where have you been?"

I saw by the manner of this that the idea was to get down to cold business now. So I began my travels, but was cut short again.

"Where are the two others? We have been in frightful anxiety about them."

"Oh, they're all right. I was to fetch a cab. I will go straight off, and—"

"Sit down! Don't you know it is eleven o'clock? Where did you leave them?"

"At the pension."

"Why didn't you bring them?"

"Because we couldn't carry the satchels. And so I thought—"

"Thought! You should not try to think. One cannot think without the proper machinery. It is two miles to that pension. Did you go there without a cab?"

"I—well, I didn't intend to; it only happened so."

"How did it happen so?"

"Because I was at the post-office and I remembered that I had left a cab waiting here, and so, to stop that expense, I sent another cab to—to—"

"To what?"

"Well, I don't remember now, but I think the new cab was to have the hotel pay the old cab, and send it away."

"What good would that do?"

"What good would it do? It would stop the expense, wouldn't it?"

"By putting the new cab in its place to continue the expense?"

I didn't say anything.

"Why didn't you have the new cab come back for you?"

"Oh, that is what I did. I remember now. Yes, that is what I did. Because I recollect that when I—"

"Well, then, why didn't it come back for you?"

"To the post-office? Why, it did."

"Very well, then, how did you come to walk to the pension?"

"I—I don't quite remember how that happened. Oh, yes, I do remember now. I wrote the despatch to send to the Netherlands, and—"

"Oh, thank goodness, you did accomplish something! I wouldn't have had you fail to send—what makes you look like that! You are trying to avoid my eye. That despatch is the most important thing that— You haven't sent that despatch!"

"I haven't said I didn't send it."

"You don't need to. Oh, dear, I wouldn't have had that telegram fail for anything. Why didn't you send it?"

"Well, you see, with so many things to do and think of, I—they're very particular there, and after I had written the telegram—"

"Oh, never mind, let it go, explanations can't help the matter now—what will he think of us?"

"Oh, that's all right, that's all right, he'll think we gave the telegram to the hotel people, and that they—"

"Why, certainly! Why didn't you do that? There was no other rational way."

"Yes, I know, but then I had it on my mind that I must be sure and get to the bank and draw some money—"

"Well, you are entitled to some credit, after all, for thinking of that, and I don't wish to be too hard on you, though you must acknowledge yourself that you have cost us all a good deal of trouble, and some of it not necessary. How much did you draw?"

"Well, I—I had an idea that—that—"

"That what?"

"That—well, it seems to me that in the circumstances—so many of us, you know, and—and—"

"What are you mooning about? Do turn your face this way and let me—why, you haven't drawn any money!"

"Well, the banker said—"

"Never mind what the banker said. You must have had a reason of your own. Not a reason, exactly, but something which—"

"Well, then, the simple fact was that I hadn't my letter of credit."

"Hadn't your letter of credit?"

"Hadn't my letter of credit."

"Don't repeat me like that. Where was it?"

"At the post-office."

"What was it doing there?"

"Well, I forgot it and left it there."

"Upon my word, I've seen a good many couriers, but of all the couriers that ever I—"

"I've done the best I could."

"Well, so you have, poor thing, and I'm wrong to abuse you so when you've been working yourself to death while we've been sitting here only thinking of our vexations instead of feeling grateful for what you were trying to do for us. It will all come out right. We can take the 7.30 train in the morning just as well. You've bought the tickets?"

"I have—and it's a bargain, too. Second class."

"I'm glad of it. Everybody else travels second class, and we might just as well save that ruinous extra charge. What did you pay?"

"Twenty-two dollars apiece—through to Bayreuth."

"Why, I didn't know you could buy through tickets anywhere but in London and Paris."

"Some people can't, maybe; but some people can—of whom I am one of which, it appears."

"It seems a rather high price."

"On the contrary, the dealer knocked off his commission."

"Dealer?"

"Yes—I bought them at a cigar shop."

"That reminds me. We shall have to get up pretty early, and so there should be no packing to do. Your umbrella, your rubbers, your cigars—what is the matter?"

"Hang it, I've left the cigars at the bank."

"Just think of it! Well, your umbrella?"

"I'll have that all right. There's no hurry."

"What do you mean by that?"

"Oh, that's all right; I'll take care of—"

"Where is that umbrella?"

"It's just the merest step—it won't take me—"

"Where is it?"

"Well, I think I left it at the cigar shop; but anyway—"

"Take your feet out from under that thing. It's just as I expected! Where are your rubbers?"

"They—well—"

"Where are your rubbers?"

"It's got so dry now—well, everybody says there's not going to be another drop of—"

"Where—are—your—rubbers?"

"Well, you see—well, it was this way. First, the officer said—"

"What officer?"

"Police officer; but the Mayor, he—"

"What Mayor?"

"Mayor of Geneva; but I said—"

"Wait. What is the matter with you?"

"Who, me? Nothing. They both tried to persuade me to stay, and—"

"Stay where?"

"Well, the fact is—"

"Where have you been? What's kept you out till half past ten at night?"

"Oh, you see, after I lost my letter of credit, I—"

"You are beating around the bush a good deal. Now, answer the question in just one straightforward word. Where are those rubbers?"

"They—well, they're in the county jail."

I started a placating smile, but it petrified. The climate was unsuitable. Spending three or four hours in jail did not seem to the Expedition humorous. Neither did it to me, at bottom.

I had to explain the whole thing, and, of course, it came out then that we couldn't take the early train, because that would leave my letter of credit in hock still. It did look as if we had all got to go to bed estranged and unhappy, but by good luck that was prevented. There happened to be mention of the trunks, and I was able to say I had attended to that feature.

"There, you are just as good and thoughtful and painstaking and intelligent as you can be, and it's a shame to find so much fault with you, and there sha'n't be another word of it. You've done beautifully, admirably, and I'm sorry I ever said one ungrateful word to you."

This hit deeper than some of the other things and made me uncomfortable, because I wasn't feeling as solid about that trunk errand as I wanted to. There seemed somehow to be a defect about it somewhere, though I couldn't put my finger on it, and didn't like to stir the matter just now, it being late and maybe well enough to let well enough alone.

Of course there was music in the morning, when it was found that we couldn't leave by the early train. But I had no time to wait; I got only the opening bars of the overture, and then started out to get my letter of credit.

It seemed a good time to look into the trunk business and rectify it if it needed it, and I had a suspicion that it did. I was too late. The concierge said he had shipped the trunks to Zurich the evening before. I asked him how he could do that without exhibiting passage tickets.

"Not necessary in Switzerland. You pay for your trunks and send them where you please. Nothing goes free but your hand-baggage."

"How much did you pay on them?"

"A hundred and forty francs."

"Twenty-eight dollars. There's something wrong about that trunk business, sure."

Next I met the porter. He said:

"You have not slept well, is it not? You have the worn look. If you would like a courier, a good one has arrived last night, and is not engaged for five days already, by the name of Ludi. We recommend him; *das heisst*, the Grand Hôtel Beau Rivage recommends him."

I declined with coldness. My spirit was not broken yet. And I did not like having my condition taken notice of in this way. I was at the county jail by nine o'clock, hoping that the Mayor might chance to come before his regular hour; but he didn't. It was dull there. Every time I offered to touch anything, or look at anything, or do anything, or refrain from doing anything, the policeman said it was *"défendu."* I thought I would practise my French on him, but he wouldn't have that either. It seemed to make him particularly bitter to hear his own tongue.

The Mayor came at last, and then there was no trouble; for the minute he had convened the Supreme Court—they always do whenever there is valuable property in dispute—and got everything shipshape and sentries posted, and had prayer by the chaplain, my unsealed letter was brought and opened, and there wasn't anything in it but some photographs; because, as I remembered now, I had taken out the letter of credit so as to make room for the photographs, and had put the letter in my other pocket, which I proved to everybody's satisfaction by fetching it out and showing it with a good deal of exultation. So then the court looked at each other in a vacant kind of way, and then at me, and then at each other again, and finally let me go, but said it was imprudent for me to be at large, and asked me what my profession was. I said I was a courier. They lifted up their eyes in a kind of reverent way and said, "*Du lieber Gott!*" and I said a word of courteous thanks for their apparent admiration and hurried off to the bank.

However, being a courier was already making me a great stickler for order and system and one thing at a time and each thing in its own proper turn; so I passed by the bank and branched off and started for the two lacking members of the Expedition. A cab lazied by, and I took it upon persuasion. I gained no speed by this, but it was a reposeful turnout and I liked reposefulness. The week-long jubilations over the six hundredth anniversary of the birth of Swiss liberty and the Signing of the Compact was at flood-tide, and all the streets were clothed in fluttering flags.

The horse and the driver had been drunk three days and nights, and had known no stall nor bed meantime. They looked as I felt—dreamy and seedy. But we arrived in course of time. I went in and rang, and asked a housemaid to rush out the lacking members. She said something which I did not understand, and I returned to the chariot. The girl had probably told me that those people did not belong on her floor, and that it would be judicious for me to go higher, and ring from floor to floor till I found them; for in those Swiss flats there does not seem to be any way to find the right family but to be patient and guess your way along up. I calculated that I must wait fifteen minutes, there being three details inseparable from an occasion of this sort: 1, put on hats and come down and climb in; 2, return of one to get "my other glove"; 3, presently, return of the other one to fetch "my *French Verbs at a Glance.*" I would muse during the fifteen minutes and take it easy.

A very still and blank interval ensued, and then I felt a hand on my shoulder and started. The intruder was a policeman. I glanced up and perceived that there was new scenery. There was a good deal of a crowd, and they had that pleased and interested look which such a crowd wears when they see that somebody is out of luck. The horse was asleep, and so was the driver, and some boys had hung them and me full of gaudy decorations stolen from the innumerable banner-poles. It was a scandalous spectacle. The officer said:

"I'm sorry, but we can't have you sleeping here all day."

I was wounded, and said with dignity:

"I beg your pardon, I was not sleeping; I was thinking."

"Well, you can think if you want to, but you've got to think to yourself; you disturb the whole neighborhood."

It was a poor joke, and it made the crowd laugh. I snore at night sometimes, but it is not likely that I would do such a thing in the daytime and in such a place. The officer undecorated us, and seemed sorry for our friendlessness, and really tried to be humane, but he said we mustn't stop there any longer or he would have to charge us rent—it was the law, he said, and he went on to say in a sociable way that I was looking pretty moldy, and he wished he knew—

I shut him off pretty austerely, and said I hoped one might celebrate a little these days, especially when one was personally concerned.

"Personally?" he asked. "How?"

"Because six hundred years ago an ancestor of mine signed the compact."

He reflected a moment, then looked me over and said:

"Ancestor! It's my opinion you signed it yourself. For of all the old ancient relics that ever I—but never mind about that. What is it you are waiting here for so long?"

I said:

"I'm not waiting here so long at all. I'm waiting fifteen minutes till they forget a glove and a book and go back and get them." Then I told him who they were that I had come for.

He was very obliging, and began to shout inquiries to the tiers of heads and shoulders projecting from the windows above us. Then a woman away up there sang out:

"Oh, they? Why, I got them a cab and they left here long ago—half past eight, I should say."

It was annoying. I glanced at my watch, but didn't say anything. The officer said:

"It is a quarter of twelve, you see. You should have inquired better. You have been asleep three-quarters of an hour, and in such a sun as this. You are baked—baked black. It is wonderful. And you will miss your train, perhaps. You interest me greatly. What is your occupation?"

I said I was a courier. It seemed to stun him, and before he could come to we were gone.

When I arrived in the third story of the hotel I found our quarters vacant. I was not surprised. The moment a courier takes his eye off his tribe they go shopping. The nearer it is to train-time the surer they are to go. I sat down to try and think out what I had best do next, but presently the hall-boy found me there, and said the Expedition had gone to the station half an hour before. It was the first time I had known them to do a rational thing, and it was very confusing. This is one of the things that make a courier's life so difficult and uncertain. Just as matters are going the smoothest, his people will strike a lucid interval, and down go all his arrangements to wreck and ruin.

The train was to leave at twelve noon sharp. It was now ten minutes after twelve. I could be at the station in ten minutes. I saw I had no great amount of leeway, for this was the lightning express, and on the Continent the lightning expresses are pretty fastidious about getting away some time during the advertised day. My people were the only ones remaining in the waiting-room; everybody else had passed through and "mounted the train," as they say in those regions. They were exhausted with nervousness and fret, but I comforted them and heartened them up, and we made our rush.

But no; we were out of luck again. The doorkeeper was not satisfied with the tickets. He examined them cautiously, deliberately, suspiciously; then glared at me awhile, and after that he called another official. The two examined the tickets and called another official. These called others, and the convention discussed and discussed, and gesticulated and carried on, until I begged that they would consider how time was flying, and just pass a few resolutions and let us go. Then they said very courteously that there was a defect in the tickets, and asked me where I got them.

I judged I saw what the trouble was now. You see, I had bought the tickets in a cigar shop, and, of course, the tobacco smell was on them; without doubt, the thing they were up to was to work the tickets through the Custom House and to collect duty on that smell. So I resolved to be perfectly frank; it is sometimes the best way. I said:

"Gentlemen, I will not deceive you. These railway tickets—"

"Ah, pardon, monsieur! These are not railway tickets."

"Oh," I said, "is that the defect?"

"Ah, truly yes, monsieur. These are lottery tickets, yes; and it is a lottery which has been drawn two years ago."

I affected to be greatly amused; it is all one can do in such circumstances; it is all one can do, and yet there is no value in it; it deceives nobody, and you can see that everybody around pities you and is ashamed of you. One of the hardest situations in life, I think, is to be full of grief and a sense of defeat and shabbiness that way, and yet have to put on an outside of archness and gaiety, while all the time you know that your own Expedition, the treasures of your heart, and whose love and reverence you are by the custom of our civilization entitled to, are being consumed with humiliation before strangers to see you earning and getting a compassion which is a stigma, a brand—a brand which certifies you to be—oh, anything and everything which is fatal to human respect.

I said, cheerily, it was all right, just one of those little accidents that was likely to happen to anybody—I would have the right tickets in two minutes, and we would catch the train yet, and, moreover, have something to laugh about all through the journey. I did get the tickets in time, all stamped and complete, but then it turned out that I couldn't take them, because in taking so much pains about the two missing members I had skipped the bank and hadn't the money. So then the train left, and there didn't seem to be anything to do but go back to the hotel, which we did; but it was kind of melancholy and not much said. I tried to start a few subjects, like scenery and transubstantiation, and those sorts of things, but they didn't seem to hit the weather right.

We had lost our good rooms, but we got some others which were pretty scattering, but would answer. I judged things would brighten now, but the Head of the Expedition said, "Send up the trunks." It made me feel pretty cold. There was a doubtful something about that trunk business. I was almost sure of it. I was going to suggest—

But a wave of the hand sufficiently restrained me, and I was informed that we would now camp for three days and see if we could rest up.

I said all right, never mind ringing; I would go down and attend to the trunks myself. I got a cab and went straight to Mr. Charles Natural's place, and asked what order it was I had left there.

"To send seven trunks to the hotel."

"And were you to bring any back?"

"No."

"You are sure I didn't tell you to bring back seven that would be found piled in the lobby?"

"Absolutely sure you didn't."

"Then the whole fourteen are gone to Zurich or Jericho or somewhere, and there is going to be more debris around that hotel when the Expedition—"

I didn't finish, because my mind was getting to be in a good deal of a whirl, and when you are that way you think you have finished a sentence when you haven't, and you go mooning and dreaming away, and the first thing you know you get run over by a dray or a cow or something.

I left the cab there—I forgot it—and on my way back I thought it all out and concluded to resign, because otherwise I should be nearly sure to be discharged. But I didn't believe it would be a good idea to resign in person; I could do it by message. So I sent for Mr. Ludi and explained that there was a courier going to resign on account of incompatibility or fatigue or something, and as he had four or five vacant days, I would like to insert him into that vacancy if he thought he could fill it. When everything was arranged I got him to go up and say to the Expedition that, owing to an error made by Mr. Natural's people, we were out of trunks here, but would have plenty in Zurich, and we'd better take the first train, freight, gravel, or construction, and move right along.

He attended to that and came down with an invitation for me to go up—yes, certainly; and, while we walked along over to the bank to get money, and collect my cigars and tobacco, and to the cigar shop to trade back the lottery tickets and get my umbrella, and to Mr. Natural's to pay that cab and send it away, and to the county jail to get my rubbers and leave p. p. c. cards for the Mayor and Supreme Court, he described the weather to me that was prevailing on the upper levels there with the Expedition, and I saw that I was doing very well where I was.

I stayed out in the woods till 4 P.M., to let the weather moderate, and then turned up at the station just in time to take the three-o'clock express for Zurich along with the Expedition, now in the hands of Ludi, who conducted its complex affairs with little apparent effort or inconvenience.

Well, I had worked like a slave while I was in office, and done the very best I knew how; yet all that these people dwelt upon or seemed to care to remember were the defects of my administration, not its creditable features. They would skip over a thousand creditable features to remark upon and reiterate and fuss about just one fact, till it seemed to me they would wear it out; and not much of a fact, either, taken by itself—the fact that I elected myself courier in Geneva, and put in work enough to carry a circus to Jerusalem, and yet never even got my gang out of the town. I finally said I didn't wish to hear any more about the subject, it made me tired. And I told them to their faces that I would never be a courier again to save anybody's life. And if I live long enough I'll prove it. I think it's a difficult, brain-racking, overworked, and thoroughly ungrateful office, and the main bulk of its wages is a sore heart and a bruised spirit.

1891

The Californian's Tale

Thirty-five years ago I was out prospecting on the Stanislaus, tramping all day long with pick and pan and horn, and washing a hatful of dirt here and there, always expecting to make a rich strike, and never doing it. It was a lovely region, woodsy, balmy, delicious, and had once been populous, long years before, but now the people had vanished and the charming paradise was a solitude. They went away when the surface diggings gave out. In one place, where a busy little city with banks and newspapers and fire companies and a mayor and aldermen had been, was nothing but a wide expanse of emerald turf, with not even the faintest sign that human life had ever been present there. This was down toward Tuttletown. In the country neighborhood thereabouts, along the dusty roads, one found at intervals the prettiest little cottage homes, snug and cozy, and so cobwebbed with vines snowed thick with roses that the doors and windows were wholly hidden from sight—sign that these were deserted homes, forsaken years ago by defeated and disappointed families who could neither sell them nor give them away. Now and then, half an hour apart, one came across solitary log cabins of the earliest mining days, built by the first gold-miners, the predecessors of the cottage-builders. In some few cases these cabins were still occupied; and when this was so, you could depend upon it that the occupant was the very pioneer who had built the cabin; and you could depend on another thing, too—that he was there because he had once had his opportunity to go home to the States rich, and had not done it; had rather lost his wealth, and had then in his humiliation resolved to sever all communication with his home relatives and friends, and be to them thenceforth as one dead. Round about California in that day were scattered a host of these living dead men—pride-smitten poor fellows, grizzled and old at forty, whose secret thoughts were made all of regrets and longings—regrets for their wasted lives, and longings to be out of the struggle and done with it all.

It was a lonesome land! Not a sound in all those peaceful expanses of grass and woods but the drowsy hum of insects; no glimpse of man or beast; nothing to keep up your spirits and make you glad to be alive.

And so, at last, in the early part of the afternoon, when I caught sight of a human creature, I felt a most grateful uplift. This person was a man about forty-five years old, and he was standing at the gate of one of those cozy little rose-clad cottages of the sort already referred to. However, this one hadn't a deserted look; it had the look of being lived in and petted and cared for and looked after; and so had its front yard, which was a garden of flowers, abundant, gay, and flourishing. I was invited in, of course, and required to make myself at home—it was the custom of the country.

It was delightful to be in such a place, after long weeks of daily and nightly familiarity with miners' cabins—with all which this implies of dirt floor, never-made beds, tin plates and cups, bacon and beans and black coffee, and nothing of ornament but war pictures from the Eastern illustrated papers tacked to the log walls. That was all hard, cheerless, materialistic desolation, but here was a nest which had aspects to rest the tired eye and refresh that something in one's nature which, after long fasting, recognizes, when confronted by the belongings of art, howsoever cheap and modest they may be, that it has unconsciously been famishing and now has found nourishment. I could not have believed that a rag carpet could feast me so, and so content me; or that there could be such solace to the soul in wall-paper and framed lithographs, and bright-colored tidies and lamp-mats, and Windsor chairs, and varnished what-nots, with sea-shells and books and china vases on them, and the score of little unclassifiable tricks and touches that a woman's hand distributes about a home, which one sees without knowing he sees them, yet would miss in a moment if they were taken away. The delight that was in my heart showed in my face, and the man saw it and was pleased; saw it so plainly that he answered it as if it had been spoken.

"All her work," he said, caressingly; "she did it all herself—every bit," and he took the room in with a glance which was full of affectionate worship. One of those soft Japanese fabrics with which women drape with careful negligence the upper part of a picture-frame was out of adjustment. He noticed it, and rearranged it with cautious pains, stepping back several times to gauge the effect before he got it to suit him. Then he gave it a light finishing pat or two with his hand, and said: "She always does that. You can't tell just what it lacks, but it does lack something until you've done that—you can see it yourself after it's done, but that is all you know; you can't find out the law of it. It's like the finishing pats a mother gives the child's hair after she's got it combed and brushed, I reckon. I've seen her fix all these things so much that I can do them all just her way, though I don't know the law of any of them. But she knows the law. She knows the why and the how both; but I don't know the why; I only know the how."

He took me into a bedroom so that I might wash my hands; such a bedroom as I had not seen for years: white counterpane, white pillows, carpeted floor, papered walls, pictures, dressing-table, with mirror and pin-cushion and dainty toilet things; and in the corner a wash-stand, with real china-ware bowl and pitcher, and with soap in a china dish, and on a rack more than a dozen towels—towels too clean and white for one out of practice to use without some vague sense of profanation. So my face spoke again, and he answered with gratified words:

"All her work; she did it all herself—every bit. Nothing here that hasn't felt the touch of her hand. Now you would think— But I mustn't talk so much."

By this time I was wiping my hands and glancing from detail to detail of the room's belongings, as one is apt to do when he is in a new place, where everything he sees is a comfort to his eye and his spirit; and I became conscious, in one of those unaccountable ways, you know, that there was something there somewhere that the man wanted me to discover for myself. I knew it perfectly, and I knew he was trying to help me by furtive indications with his eye, so I tried hard to get on the right track, being eager to gratify him. I failed several times, as I could see out of the corner of my eye without being told; but at last I knew I must be looking straight at the thing—knew it from the pleasure issuing in invisible waves from him. He broke into a happy laugh, and rubbed his hands together, and cried out:

"That's it! You've found it. I knew you would. It's her picture."

I went to the little black-walnut bracket on the farther wall, and did find there what I had not yet noticed—a daguerreotype-case. It contained the sweetest girlish face, and the most beautiful, as it seemed to me, that I had ever seen. The man drank the admiration from my face, and was fully satisfied.

"Nineteen her last birthday," he said, as he put the picture back; "and that was the day we were married. When you see her—ah, just wait till you see her!"

"Where is she? When will she be in?"

"Oh, she's away now. She's gone to see her people. They live forty or fifty miles from here. She's been gone two weeks to-day."

"When do you expect her back?"

"This is Wednesday. She'll be back Saturday, in the evening—about nine o'clock, likely."

I felt a sharp sense of disappointment.

"I'm sorry, because I'll be gone then," I said, regretfully.

"Gone? No—why should you go? Don't go. She'll be so disappointed."

She would be disappointed—that beautiful creature! If she had said the words herself they could hardly have blessed me more. I was feeling a deep, strong longing to see her—a longing so supplicating, so insistent, that it made me afraid. I said to myself: "I will go straight away from this place, for my peace of mind's sake."

"You see, she likes to have people come and stop with us—people who know things, and can talk—people like you. She delights in it; for she knows—oh, she knows nearly everything herself, and can talk, oh, like a bird—and the books she reads, why, you would be astonished. Don't go; it's only a little while, you know, and she'll be so disappointed."

I heard the words, but hardly noticed them, I was so deep in my thinkings and strugglings. He left me, but I didn't know. Presently he was back, with the picture-case in his hand, and he held it open before me and said:

"There, now, tell her to her face you could have stayed to see her, and you wouldn't."

That second glimpse broke down my good resolution. I would stay and take the risk. That night we smoked the tranquil pipe, and talked till late about various things, but mainly about her; and certainly I had had no such pleasant and restful time for many a day. The Thursday followed and slipped comfortably away. Toward twilight a big miner from three miles away came—one of the grizzled, stranded pioneers—and gave us warm salutation, clothed in grave and sober speech. Then he said:

"I only just dropped over to ask about the little madam, and when is she coming home. Any news from her?"

"Oh yes, a letter. Would you like to hear it, Tom?"

"Well, I should think I would, if you don't mind, Henry!"

Henry got the letter out of his wallet, and said he would skip some of the private phrases, if we were willing; then he went on and read the bulk of it—a loving, sedate, and altogether charming and gracious piece of handiwork, with a postscript full of affectionate regards and messages to Tom, and Joe, and Charley, and other close friends and neighbors.

As the reader finished, he glanced at Tom, and cried out:

"Oho, you're at it again! Take your hands away, and let me see your eyes. You always do that when I read a letter from her. I will write and tell her."

"Oh no, you mustn't, Henry. I'm getting old, you know, and any little disappointment makes me want to cry. I thought she'd be here herself, and now you've got only a letter."

"Well, now, what put that in your head? I thought everybody knew she wasn't coming till Saturday."

"Saturday! Why, come to think, I did know it. I wonder what's the matter with me lately? Certainly I knew it. Ain't we all getting ready for her? Well, I must be going now. But I'll be on hand when she comes, old man!"

Late Friday afternoon another gray veteran tramped over from his cabin a mile or so away, and said the boys wanted to have a little gaiety and a good time Saturday night, if Henry thought she wouldn't be too tired after her journey to be kept up.

"Tired? She tired! Oh, hear the man! Joe, *you* know she'd sit up six weeks to please any one of you!"

When Joe heard that there was a letter, he asked to have it read, and the loving messages in it for him broke the old fellow all up; but he said he was such an old wreck that *that* would happen to him if she only just mentioned his name. "Lord, we miss her so!" he said.

Saturday afternoon I found I was taking out my watch pretty often. Henry noticed it, and said, with a startled look:

"You don't think she ought to be here so soon, do you?"

I felt caught, and a little embarrassed; but I laughed, and said it was a habit of mine when I was in a state of expectancy. But he didn't seem quite satisfied; and from that time on he began to show uneasiness. Four times he walked me up the road to a point whence we could see a long distance; and there he would stand, shading his eyes with his hand, and looking. Several times he said:

"I'm getting worried, I'm getting right down worried. I know she's not due till about nine o'clock, and yet something seems to be trying to warn me that something's happened. You don't think anything has happened, do you?"

I began to get pretty thoroughly ashamed of him for his childishness; and at last, when he repeated that imploring question still another time, I lost my patience for the moment, and spoke pretty brutally to him. It seemed to shrivel him up and cow him; and he looked so wounded and so humble after that, that I detested myself for having done the cruel and unnecessary thing. And so I was glad when Charley, another veteran, arrived toward the edge of the evening, and nestled up to Henry to hear the letter read, and talked over the preparations for the welcome. Charley fetched out one hearty speech after another, and did his best to drive away his friend's bodings and apprehensions.

"Anything *happened* to her? Henry, that's pure nonsense. There isn't anything going to happen to her; just make your mind easy as to that. What did the letter say? Said she was well, didn't it? And said she'd be here by nine o'clock, didn't it? Did you ever know her to fail of her word? Why, you know you never did. Well, then, don't you fret; she'll *be* here, and that's absolutely certain, and as sure as you are born. Come, now, let's get to decorating—not much time left."

Pretty soon Tom and Joe arrived, and then all hands set about adorning the house with flowers. Toward nine the three miners said that as they had brought their instruments they might as well tune up, for the boys and girls would soon be arriving now, and hungry for a good, old-fashioned break-down. A fiddle, a banjo, and a clarinet—these were the instruments. The trio took their places side by side, and began to play some rattling dance-music, and beat time with their big boots.

It was getting very close to nine. Henry was standing in the door with his eyes directed up the road, his body swaying to the torture of his mental distress. He had been made to drink his wife's health and safety several times, and now Tom shouted:

"All hands stand by! One more drink, and she's here!"

Joe brought the glasses on a waiter, and served the party. I reached for one of the two remaining glasses, but Joe growled, under his breath:

"Drop that! Take the other."

Which I did. Henry was served last. He had hardly swallowed his drink when the clock began to strike. He listened till it finished, his face growing pale and paler; then he said:

"Boys, I'm sick with fear. Help me—I want to lie down!"

They helped him to the sofa. He began to nestle and drowse, but presently spoke like one talking in his sleep, and said: "Did I hear horses' feet? Have they come?"

One of the veterans answered, close to his ear: "It was Jimmy Parrish come to say the party got delayed, but they're right up the road a piece, and coming along. Her horse is lame, but she'll be here in half an hour."

"Oh, I'm *so* thankful nothing has happened!"

He was asleep almost before the words were out of his mouth. In a moment those handy men had his clothes off, and had tucked him into his bed in the chamber where I had washed my hands. They closed the door and came back. Then they seemed preparing to leave; but I said: "Please don't go, gentlemen. She won't know me; I am a stranger."

They glanced at each other. Then Joe said:

"She? Poor thing, she's been dead nineteen years!"

"Dead?"

"That or worse. She went to see her folks half a year after she was married, and on her way back, on a Saturday evening, the Indians captured her within five miles of this place, and she's never been heard of since."

"And he lost his mind in consequence?"

"Never has been sane an hour since. But he only gets bad when that time of the year comes round. Then we begin to drop in here, three days before she's due, to encourage him up, and ask if he's heard from her, and Saturday we all come and fix up the house with flowers, and get everything ready for a dance. We've done it every year for nineteen years. The first Saturday there was twenty-seven of us, without counting the girls; there's only three of us now, and the girls are all gone. We drug him to sleep, or he would go wild; then he's all right for another year—thinks she's with him till the last three or four days come round; then he begins to look for her, and gets out his poor old letter, and we come and ask him to read it to us. Lord, she was a darling!"

1893

The Diary of Adam and Eve

PART I—EXTRACTS FROM ADAM'S DIARY

Monday This new creature with the long hair is a good deal in the way. It is always hanging around and following me about. I don't like this; I am not used to company. I wish it would stay with the other animals. . . . Cloudy to-day, wind in the east; think we shall have rain. . . . *We?* Where did I get that word?—I remember now—the new creature uses it.

Tuesday Been examining the great waterfall. It is the finest thing on the estate, I think. The new creature calls it Niagara Falls—why, I am sure I do not know. Says it *looks* like Niagara Falls. That is not a reason, it is mere waywardness and imbecility. I get no chance to name anything myself. The new creature names everything that comes along, before I can get in a protest. And always that same pretext is offered—

it *looks* like the thing. There is the dodo, for instance. Says the moment one looks at it one sees at a glance that it "looks like a dodo." It will have to keep that name, no doubt. It wearies me to fret about it, and it does no good, anyway. Dodo! It looks no more like a dodo than I do.

Wednesday Built me a shelter against the rain, but could not have it to myself in peace. The new creature intruded. When I tried to put it out it shed water out of the holes it looks with, and wiped it away with the back of its paws, and made a noise such as some of the other animals make when they are in distress. I wish it would not talk; it is always talking. That sounds like a cheap fling at the poor creature, a slur; but I do not mean it so. I have never heard the human voice before, and any new and strange sound intruding itself here upon the solemn hush of these dreaming solitudes offends my ear and seems a false note. And this new sound is so close to me; it is right at my shoulder, right at my ear, first on one side and then on the other, and I am used only to sounds that are more or less distant from me.

Friday The naming goes recklessly on, in spite of anything I can do. I had a very good name for the estate, and it was musical and pretty —GARDEN OF EDEN. Privately, I continue to call it that, but not any longer publicly. The new creature says it is all woods and rocks and scenery, and therefore has no resemblance to a garden. Says it *looks* like a park, and does not look like anything *but* a park. Consequently, without consulting me, it has been new-named—NIAGARA FALLS PARK. This is sufficiently high-handed, it seems to me. And already there is a sign up:

KEEP OFF

THE GRASS

My life is not as happy as it was.

Saturday The new creature eats too much fruit. We are going to run short, most likely. "We" again—that is *its* word; mine, too, now, from hearing it so much. Good deal of fog this morning. I do not go out in the fog myself. The new creature does. It goes out in all weathers, and stumps right in with its muddy feet. And talks. It used to be so pleasant and quiet here.

Sunday Pulled through. This day is getting to be more and more trying. It was selected and set apart last November as a day of rest. I had already six of them per week before. This morning found the new creature trying to clod apples out of that forbidden tree.

Monday The new creature says its name is Eve. That is all right, I have no objections. Says it is to call it by, when I want it to come. I said it was superfluous, then. The word evidently raised me in its respect; and indeed it is a large, good word and will bear repetition. It says it is not an It, it is a She. This is probably doubtful; yet it is all one to me; what she is were nothing to me if she would but go by herself and not talk.

Tuesday She has littered the whole estate with execrable names and offensive signs:

> THIS WAY TO THE WHIRLPOOL
> THIS WAY TO GOAT ISLAND
> CAVE OF THE WINDS THIS WAY

She says this park would make a tidy summer resort if there was any custom for it. Summer resort—another invention of hers—just words, without any meaning. What is a summer resort? But it is best not to ask her, she has such a rage for explaining.

Friday She has taken to beseeching me to stop going over the Falls. What harm does it do? Says it makes her shudder. I wonder why; I have always done it—always liked the plunge, and coolness. I supposed it was what the Falls were for. They have no other use that I can see, and they must have been made for something. She says they were only made for scenery—like the rhinoceros and the mastodon.

I went over the Falls in a barrel—not satisfactory to her. Went over in a tub—still not satisfactory. Swam the Whirlpool and the Rapids in a fig-leaf suit. It got much damaged. Hence, tedious complaints about my extravagance. I am too much hampered here. What I need is change of scene.

Saturday I escaped last Tuesday night, and traveled two days, and built me another shelter in a secluded place, and obliterated my tracks as well as I could, but she hunted me out by means of a beast which she has tamed and calls a wolf, and came making that pitiful noise again, and shedding that water out of the places she looks with. I was obliged to return with her, but will presently emigrate again when occasion offers. She engages herself in many foolish things; among others, to study out why the animals called lions and tigers live on grass and flowers, when, as she says, the sort of teeth they wear would indicate that they were intended to eat each other. This is foolish, because to do that would be to kill each other, and that would introduce what, as I understand it, is called "death"; and death, as I have been told, has not yet entered the Park. Which is a pity, on some accounts.

Sunday Pulled through.

Monday I believe I see what the week is for: it is to give time to rest up from the weariness of Sunday. It seems a good idea. . . . She has been climbing that tree again. Clodded her out of it. She said nobody was looking. Seems to consider that a sufficient justification for chancing any dangerous thing. Told her that. The word justification moved her admiration—and envy, too, I thought. It is a good word.

Tuesday She told me she was made out of a rib taken from my body. This is at least doubtful, if not more than that. I have not missed any rib. . . . She is in much trouble about the buzzard; says grass does not agree with it; is afraid she can't raise it; thinks it was intended to live on decayed flesh. The buzzard must get along the best it can with what it is provided. We cannot overturn the whole scheme to accommodate the buzzard.

Saturday She fell in the pond yesterday when she was looking at herself in it, which she is always doing. She nearly strangled, and said it was most uncomfortable. This made her sorry for the creatures which live in there, which she calls fish, for she continues to fasten names on to things that don't need them and don't come when they are called by them, which is a matter of no consequence to her, she is such a numskull, anyway; so she got a lot of them out and brought them in last night and put them in my bed to keep warm, but I have noticed them now and then all day and I don't see that they are any happier there than they were before, only quieter. When night comes I shall throw them outdoors. I will not sleep with them again, for I find them clammy and unpleasant to lie among when a person hasn't anything on.

Sunday Pulled through.

Tuesday She has taken up with a snake now. The other animals are glad, for she was always experimenting with them and bothering them; and I am glad because the snake talks, and this enables me to get a rest.

Friday She says the snake advises her to try the fruit of that tree, and says the result will be a great and fine and noble education. I told her there would be another result, too—it would introduce death into the world. That was a mistake—it had been better to keep the remark to myself; it only gave her an idea—she could save the sick buzzard, and furnish fresh meat to the despondent lions and tigers. I advised her to keep away from the tree. She said she wouldn't. I foresee trouble. Will emigrate.

Wednesday I have had a variegated time. I escaped last night, and rode a horse all night as fast as he could go, hoping to get clear out of the Park and hide in some other country before the trouble should begin; but it was not to be. About an hour after sun-up, as I was riding through a flowery plain where thousands of animals were grazing, slumbering, or playing with each other, according to their wont, all of a sudden they broke into a tempest of frightful noises, and in one moment the plain was a frantic commotion and every beast was destroying its neighbor. I knew what it meant—Eve had eaten that fruit, and death was come into the world. . . . The tigers ate my horse, paying no attention when I ordered them to desist, and they would have eaten me if I had stayed—which I didn't, but went away in much haste. . . . I found this place, outside the Park, and was fairly comfortable for a few days, but she has found me out. Found me out, and has named the place Tonawanda—says it *looks* like that. In fact I was not sorry she came, for there are but meager pickings here, and she brought some of those apples. I was obliged to eat them, I was so hungry. It was against my principles, but I find that principles have no real force except when one is well fed. . . . She came curtained in boughs and bunches of leaves, and when I asked her what she meant by such nonsense, and snatched them away and threw them down, she tittered and blushed. I had never seen a person titter and blush before, and to me it seemed unbecoming and idiotic. She said I would soon know how it was myself. This was correct. Hungry as I was, I laid down the apple half-eaten—certainly the best one I ever saw, considering the lateness of the season—and arrayed myself in the discarded boughs and branches, and then spoke to her with some severity and ordered her to go and get some more and not make such a spectacle of herself. She did it, and after this we crept down to where the wild-beast battle had been, and collected some skins, and I made her patch together a couple of suits proper for public occasions. They are uncomfortable, it is true, but stylish, and that is the main point about clothes. . . . I find she is a good deal of a companion. I see I should be lonesome and depressed without her, now that I have lost my property. Another thing, she says it is ordered that we work for our living hereafter. She will be useful. I will superintend.

Ten Days Later   She accuses *me* of being the cause of our disaster! She says, with apparent sincerity and truth, that the Serpent assured her that the forbidden fruit was not apples, it was chestnuts. I said I was innocent, then, for I had not eaten any chestnuts. She said the Serpent informed her that "chestnut" was a figurative term meaning an aged and moldy joke. I turned pale at that, for I have made many jokes to pass the weary time, and some of them could have been of that sort, though I had honestly supposed that they were new when I made them. She asked me if I had made one just at the time of the catastrophe. I was obliged to admit that I had made one to myself, though not aloud. It was this. I was thinking about the Falls, and I said to myself, "How wonderful it is to see that vast body of water tumble down there!" Then in an instant a bright thought flashed into my head, and I let it fly, saying, "It would be a deal more wonderful to see it tumble *up* there!"—and I was just about to kill myself with laughing at it when all nature broke loose in war and death and I had to flee for my life. "There," she said, with triumph, "that is just it; the Serpent mentioned that very jest, and called it the First Chestnut, and said it was coeval with the creation." Alas, I am indeed to blame. Would that I were not witty; oh, that I had never had that radiant thought!

Next Year We have named it Cain. She caught it while I was up country trapping on the North Shore of the Erie; caught it in the timber a couple of miles from our dug-out—or it might have been four, she isn't certain which. It resembles us in some ways, and may be a relation. That is what she thinks, but this is an error, in my judgment. The difference in size warrants the conclusion that it is a different and new kind of animal—a fish, perhaps, though when I put it in the water to see, it sank, and she plunged in and snatched it out before there was opportunity for the experiment to determine the matter. I still think it is a fish, but she is indifferent about what it is, and will not let me have it to try. I do not understand this. The coming of the creature seems to have changed her whole nature and made her unreasonable about experiments. She thinks more of it than she does of any of the other animals, but is not able to explain why. Her mind is disordered—everything shows it. Sometimes she carries the fish in her arms half the night when it complains and wants to get to the water. At such times the water comes out of the places in her face that she looks out of, and she pats the fish on the back and makes soft sounds with her mouth to soothe it, and betrays sorrow and solicitude in a hundred ways. I have never seen her do like this with any other fish, and it troubles me greatly. She used to carry the young tigers around so, and play with them, before we lost our property, but it was only play; she never took on about them like this when their dinner disagreed with them.

Sunday She doesn't work, Sundays, but lies around all tired out, and likes to have the fish wallow over her; and she makes fool noises to amuse it, and pretends to chew its paws, and that makes it laugh. I have not seen a fish before that could laugh. This makes me doubt. . . . I have come to like Sunday myself. Superintending all the week tires a body so. There ought to be more Sundays. In the old days they were tough, but now they come handy.

Wednesday It isn't a fish. I cannot quite make out what it is. It makes curious devilish noises when not satisfied, and says "goo-goo" when it is. It is not one of us, for it doesn't walk; it is not a bird, for it doesn't fly; it is not a frog, for it doesn't hop; it is not a snake, for it doesn't crawl, I feel sure it is not a fish, though I cannot get a chance to find out whether it can swim or not. It merely lies around, and mostly on its back, with its feet up. I have not seen any other animal do that before. I said I believed it was an enigma; but she only admired the word without understanding it. In my judgment it is either an enigma or some kind of a bug. If it dies, I will take it apart and see what its arrangements are. I never had a thing perplex me so.

Three Months Later The perplexity augments instead of diminishing. I sleep but little. It has ceased from lying around, and goes about on its four legs now. Yet it differs from the other four-legged animals, in that its front legs are unusually short, consequently this causes the main part of its person to stick up uncomfortably high in the air, and this is not attractive. It is built much as we are, but its method of traveling shows that it is not of our breed. The short front legs and long hind ones indicate that it is of the kangaroo family, but it is a marked variation of the species, since the true kangaroo hops, whereas this one never does. Still it is a curious and interesting variety, and has not been catalogued before. As I discovered it, I have felt justified in securing the credit of the discovery by attaching my name to it, and hence have called it *Kangaroorum Adamiensis*. . . . It must have been a young one when it came, for it has grown exceedingly since. It must be five times as big, now, as it was then, and when discontented it is able to make from twenty-two to thirty-eight times the noise it made at first. Coercion does not modify this, but has the contrary effect. For this reason I discontinued the system. She reconciles it by persuasion, and by giving it things which she had previously told me she wouldn't give it. As already observed, I was not at home when it first came, and she told me she found it in the woods. It seems odd that it should be the only one, yet it must be so, for I have worn myself out these many weeks trying to find another one to add to my collection, and for this one to play with; for surely then it would be quieter and we could tame it more easily. But I find none, nor any vestige of any; and strangest of all, no tracks. It has to live on the ground, it cannot help itself; therefore, how does it get about without leaving a track? I have set a dozen traps, but they do no good. I catch all small animals except that one; animals that merely go into the trap out of curiosity, I think, to see what the milk is there for. They never drink it.

Three Months Later The Kangaroo still continues to grow, which is very strange and perplexing. I never knew one to be so long getting its growth. It has fur on its head now; not like kangaroo fur, but exactly like our hair except that it is much finer and softer, and instead of being black is red. I am like to lose my mind over the capricious and harassing developments of this unclassifiable zoological freak. If I could catch another one—but that is hopeless; it is a new variety, and the only sample; this is plain. But I caught a true kangaroo and brought it in, thinking that this one, being lonesome, would rather have that for company than have no kin at all, or any animal it could feel a nearness to or get sympathy from in its forlorn condition here among strangers who do not know its ways or habits, or what to do to make it feel that it is among friends; but it was a mistake—it went into such fits at the sight of the kangaroo that I was convinced it had never seen one before. I pity the poor noisy little animal, but there is nothing I can do to make it happy. If I could tame it—but that is out of the question; the more I try the worse I seem to make it. It grieves me to the heart to see it in its little storms of sorrow and passion. I wanted to let it go, but she wouldn't hear of it. That seemed cruel and not like her; and yet she may be right. It might be lonelier than ever; for since I cannot find another one, how could *it?*

Five Months Later   It is not a kangaroo. No, for it supports itself by holding to her finger, and thus goes a few steps on its hind legs, and then falls down. It is probably some kind of a bear; and yet it has no tail—as yet—and no fur, except on its head. It still keeps on growing— that is a curious circumstance, for bears get their growth earlier than this. Bears are dangerous—since our catastrophe—and I shall not be satisfied to have this one prowling about the place much longer without a muzzle on. I have offered to get her a kangaroo if she would let this one go, but it did no good—she is determined to run us into all sorts of foolish risks, I think. She was not like this before she lost her mind.

A Fortnight Later   I examined its mouth. There is no danger yet: it has only one tooth. It has no tail yet. It makes more noise now than it ever did before—and mainly at night. I have moved out. But I shall go over, mornings, to breakfast, and see if it has more teeth. If it gets a mouthful of teeth it will be time for it to go, tail or no tail, for a bear does not need a tail in order to be dangerous.

Four Months Later   I have been off hunting and fishing a month, up in the region that she calls Buffalo; I don't know why, unless it is because there are not any buffaloes there. Meantime the bear has learned to paddle around all by itself on its hind legs, and says "poppa" and "momma." It is certainly a new species. This resemblance to words may be purely accidental, of course, and may have no purpose or meaning; but even in that case it is still extraordinary, and is a thing which no other bear can do. This imitation of speech, taken together with general absence of fur and entire absence of tail, sufficiently indicates that this is a new kind of bear. The further study of it will be exceedingly interesting. Meantime I will go off on a far expedition among the forests of the north and make an exhaustive search. There must certainly be another one somewhere, and this one will be less dangerous when it has company of its own species. I will go straightway; but I will muzzle this one first.

Three Months Later It has been a weary, weary hunt, yet I have had no success. In the mean time, without stirring from the home estate, she has caught another one! I never saw such luck. I might have hunted these woods a hundred years, I never would have run across that thing.

Next Day I have been comparing the new one with the old one, and it is perfectly plain that they are the same breed. I was going to stuff one of them for my collection, but she is prejudiced against it for some reason or other; so I have relinquished the idea, though I think it is a mistake. It would be an irreparable loss to science if they should get away. The old one is tamer than it was and can laugh and talk like the parrot, having learned this, no doubt, from being with the parrot so much, and having the imitative faculty in a highly developed degree. I shall be astonished if it turns out to be a new kind of parrot; and yet I ought not to be astonished, for it has already been everything else it could think of since those first days when it was a fish. The new one is as ugly now as the old one was at first; has the same sulphur-and-raw-meat complexion and the same singular head without any fur on it. She calls it Abel.

Ten Years Later They are *boys*; we found it out long ago. It was their coming in that small, immature shape that puzzled us; we were not used to it. There are some girls now. Abel is a good boy, but if Cain had stayed a bear it would have improved him. After all these years, I see that I was mistaken about Eve in the beginning; it is better to live outside the Garden with her than inside it without her. At first I thought she talked too much; but now I should be sorry to have that voice fall silent and pass out of my life. Blessed be the chestnut that brought us near together and taught me to know the goodness of her heart and the sweetness of her spirit!

PART II—EVE'S DIARY

(Translated from the original)

Saturday   I am almost a whole day old, now. I arrived yesterday. That is as it seems to me. And it must be so, for if there was a day-before-yesterday I was not there when it happened, or I should remember it. It could be, of course, that it did happen, and that I was not noticing. Very well; I will be very watchful now, and if any day-before-yesterdays happen I will make a note of it. It will be best to start right and not let the record get confused, for some instinct tells me that these details are going to be important to the historian some day. For I feel like an experiment, I feel exactly like an experiment; it would be impossible for a person to feel more like an experiment than I do, and so I am coming to feel convinced that that is what I *am*—an experiment; just an experiment, and nothing more.

Then if I am an experiment, am I the whole of it? No, I think not; I think the rest of it is part of it. I am the main part of it, but I think the rest of it has its share in the matter. Is my position assured, or do I have to watch it and take care of it? The latter, perhaps. Some instinct tells me that eternal vigilance is the price of supremacy. [That is a good phrase, I think, for one so young.]

Everything looks better to-day than it did yesterday. In the rush of finishing up yesterday, the mountains were left in a ragged condition, and some of the plains were so cluttered with rubbish and remnants that the aspects were quite distressing. Noble and beautiful works of art should not be subjected to haste; and this majestic new world is indeed a most noble and beautiful work. And certainly marvelously near to being perfect, notwithstanding the shortness of the time. There are too many stars in some places and not enough in others, but that can be remedied presently, no doubt. The moon got loose last night, and slid down and fell out of the scheme—a very great loss; it breaks my heart to think of it. There isn't another thing among the ornaments and decorations that is comparable to it for beauty and finish. It should have been fastened better. If we can only get it back again—

But of course there is no telling where it went to. And besides, whoever gets it will hide it; I know it because I would do it myself. I believe I can be honest in all other matters, but I already begin to realize that the core and center of my nature is love of the beautiful, a passion for the beautiful, and that it would not be safe to trust me with a moon that belonged to another person and that person didn't know I had it. I could give up a moon that I found in the daytime, because I should be afraid some one was looking; but if I found it in the dark, I am sure I should find some kind of an excuse for not saying anything about it. For I do love moons, they are so pretty and so romantic. I wish we had five or six; I would never go to bed; I should never get tired lying on the moss-bank and looking up at them.

Stars are good, too. I wish I could get some to put in my hair. But I suppose I never can. You would be surprised to find how far off they are, for they do not look it. When they first showed, last night, I tried to knock some down with a pole, but it didn't reach, which astonished me; then I tried clods till I was all tired out, but I never got one. It was because I am left-handed and cannot throw good. Even when I aimed at the one I wasn't after I couldn't hit the other one, though I did make some close shots, for I saw the black blot of the clod sail right into the midst of the golden clusters forty or fifty times, just barely missing them, and if I could have held out a little longer maybe I could have got one.

So I cried a little, which was natural, I suppose, for one of my age, and after I was rested I got a basket and started for a place on the extreme rim of the circle, where the stars were close to the ground and I could get them with my hands, which would be better, anyway, because I could gather them tenderly then, and not break them. But it was farther than I thought, and at last I had to give it up; I was so tired I couldn't drag my feet another step; and besides, they were sore and hurt me very much.

I couldn't get back home; it was too far and turning cold; but I found some tigers and nestled in among them and was most adorably comfortable, and their breath was sweet and pleasant, because they live on strawberries. I had never seen a tiger before, but I knew them in a minute by the stripes. If I could have one of those skins, it would make a lovely gown.

To-day I am getting better ideas about distances. I was so eager to get hold of every pretty thing that I giddily grabbed for it, sometimes when it was too far off, and sometimes when it was but six inches away but seemed a foot—alas, with thorns between! I learned a lesson; also I made an axiom, all out of my own head—my very first one: *The scratched Experiment shuns the thorn.* I think it is a very good one for one so young.

I followed the other Experiment around, yesterday afternoon, at a distance, to see what it might be for, if I could. But I was not able to make out. I think it is a man. I had never seen a man, but it looked like one, and I feel sure that that is what it is. I realize that I feel more curiosity about it than about any of the other reptiles. If it is a reptile, and I suppose it is; for it has frowsy hair and blue eyes, and looks like a reptile. It has no hips; it tapers like a carrot; when it stands, it spreads itself apart like a derrick; so I think it is a reptile, though it may be architecture.

I was afraid of it at first, and started to run every time it turned around, for I thought it was going to chase me; but by and by I found it was only trying to get away, so after that I was not timid any more, but tracked it along, several hours, about twenty yards behind, which made it nervous and unhappy. At last it was a good deal worried, and climbed a tree. I waited a good while, then gave it up and went home.

To-day the same thing over. I've got it up the tree again.

Sunday   It is up there yet. Resting, apparently. But that is a subterfuge: Sunday isn't the day of rest; Saturday is appointed for that. It looks to me like a creature that is more interested in resting than in anything else. It would tire me to rest so much. It tires me just to sit around and watch the tree. I do wonder what it is for; I never see it do anything.

They returned the moon last night, and I was *so* happy! I think it is very honest of them. It slid down and fell off again, but I was not distressed; there is no need to worry when one has that kind of neighbors; they will fetch it back. I wish I could do something to show my appreciation. I would like to send them some stars, for we have more than we can use. I mean I, not we, for I can see that the reptile cares nothing for such things.

It has low tastes, and is not kind. When I went there yesterday evening in the gloaming it had crept down and was trying to catch the little speckled fishes that play in the pool, and I had to clod it to make it go up the tree again and let them alone. I wonder if *that* is what it is for? Hasn't it any heart? Hasn't it any compassion for those little creatures? Can it be that it was designed and manufactured for such ungentle work? It has the look of it. One of the clods took it back of the ear, and it used language. It gave me a thrill, for it was the first time I had ever heard speech, except my own. I did not understand the words, but they seemed expressive.

When I found it could talk I felt a new interest in it, for I love to talk; I talk, all day, and in my sleep, too, and I am very interesting, but if I had another to talk to I could be twice as interesting, and would never stop, if desired.

If this reptile is a man, it isn't an *it*, is it? That wouldn't be grammatical, would it? I think it would be *he*. I think so. In that case one would parse it thus: nominative, *he;* dative, *him;* possessive, *his'n.* Well, I will consider it a man and call it he until it turns out to be something else. This will be handier than having so many uncertainties.

Next week Sunday   All the week I tagged around after him and tried to get acquainted. I had to do the talking, because he was shy, but I didn't mind it. He seemed pleased to have me around, and I used the sociable "we" a good deal, because it seemed to flatter him to be included.

Wednesday   We are getting along very well indeed, now, and getting better and better acquainted. He does not try to avoid me any more, which is a good sign, and shows that he likes to have me with him. That pleases me, and I study to be useful to him in every way I can, so as to increase his regard. During the last day or two I have taken all the work of naming things off his hands, and this has been a great relief to him, for he has not gift in that line, and is evidently very grateful. He can't think of a rational name to save him, but I do not let him see that I am aware of his defect. Whenever a new creature comes along I name it before he has time to expose himself by an awkward silence. In this way I have saved him many embarrassments. I have no defect like his. The minute I set eyes on an animal I know what it is. I don't have to reflect a moment; the right name comes out instantly, just as if it were an inspiration, as no doubt it is, for I am sure it wasn't in me half a minute before. I seem to know just by the shape of the creature and the way it acts what animal it is.

When the dodo came along he thought it was a wildcat—I saw it in his eye. But I saved him. And I was careful not to do it in a way that could hurt his pride. I just spoke up in a quite natural way of pleased surprise, and not as if I was dreaming of conveying information, and said, "Well, I do declare, if there isn't the dodo!" I explained—without seeming to be explaining—how I knew it for a dodo, and although I thought maybe he was a little piqued that I knew the creature when he didn't, it was quite evident that he admired me. That was very agreeable, and I thought of it more than once with gratification before I slept. How little a thing can make us happy when we feel that we have earned it!

Thursday   My first sorrow. Yesterday he avoided me and seemed to wish I would not talk to him. I could not believe it, and thought there was some mistake, for I loved to be with him, and loved to hear him talk, and so how could it be that he could feel unkind toward me when I had not done anything? But at last it seemed true, so I went away and sat lonely in the place where I first saw him the morning that we were made and I did not know what he was and was indifferent about him; but now it was a mournful place, and every little thing spoke of him, and my heart was very sore. I did not know why very clearly, for it was a new feeling; I had not experienced it before, and it was all a mystery, and I could not make it out.

But when night came I could not bear the lonesomeness, and went to the new shelter which he has built, to ask him what I had done that was wrong and how I could mend it and get back his kindness again; but he put me out in the rain, and it was my first sorrow.

Sunday It is pleasant again, now, and I am happy; but those were heavy days; I do not think of them when I can help it.

I tried to get him some of those apples, but I cannot learn to throw straight. I failed, but I think the good intention pleased him. They are forbidden, and he says I shall come to harm; but so I come to harm through pleasing him, why shall I care for that harm?

Monday This morning I told him my name, hoping it would interest him. But he did not care for it. It is strange. If he should tell me his name, I would care. I think it would be pleasanter in my ears than any other sound.

He talks very little. Perhaps it is because he is not bright, and is sensitive about it and wishes to conceal it. It is such a pity that he should feel so, for brightness is nothing; it is in the heart that the values lie. I wish I could make him understand that a loving good heart is riches, and riches enough, and that without it intellect is poverty.

Although he talks so little, he has quite a considerable vocabulary. This morning he used a surprisingly good word. He evidently recognized, himself, that it was a good one, for he worked it in twice afterward, casually. It was not good casual art, still it showed that he possesses a certain quality of perception. Without a doubt that seed can be made to grow, if cultivated.

Where did he get that word? I do not think I have ever used it.

No, he took no interest in my name. I tried to hide my disappointment, but I suppose I did not succeed. I went away and sat on the moss-bank with my feet in the water. It is where I go when I hunger for companionship, some one to look at, some one to talk to. It is not enough—that lovely white body painted there in the pool—but it is something, and something is better than utter loneliness. It talks when I talk; it is sad when I am sad; it comforts me with its sympathy; it says, "Do not be downhearted, you poor friendless girl; I will be your friend." It *is* a good friend to me, and my only one; it is my sister.

That first time that she forsook me! ah, I shall never forget that—never, never. My heart was lead in my body! I said, "She was all I had, and now she is gone!" In my despair I said, "Break, my heart; I cannot bear my life any more!" and hid my face in my hands, and there was no solace for me. And when I took them away, after a little, there she was again, white and shining and beautiful, and I sprang into her arms!

That was perfect happiness; I had known happiness before, but it was not like this, which was ecstasy. I never doubted her afterward. Sometimes she stayed away—maybe an hour, maybe almost the whole day, but I waited and did not doubt; I said, "She is busy, or she is gone a journey, but she will come." And it was so: she always did. At night she would not come if it was dark, for she was a timid little thing; but if there was a moon she would come. I am not afraid of the dark, but she is younger than I am; she was born after I was. Many and many are the visits I have paid her; she is my comfort and my refuge when my life is hard—and it is mainly that.

Tuesday All the morning I was at work improving the estate; and I purposely kept away from him in the hope that he would get lonely and come. But he did not.

At noon I stopped for the day and took my recreation by flitting all about with the bees and the butterflies and reveling in the flowers, those beautiful creatures that catch the smile of God out of the sky and preserve it! I gathered them, and made them into wreaths and garlands and clothed myself in them while I ate my luncheon—apples, of course; then I sat in the shade and wished and waited. But he did not come.

But no matter. Nothing would have come of it, for he does not care for flowers. He calls them rubbish, and cannot tell one from another, and thinks it is superior to feel like that. He does not care for me, he does not care for flowers, he does not care for the painted sky at eventide—is there anything he does care for, except building shacks to coop himself up in from the good clean rain, and thumping the melons, and sampling the grapes, and fingering the fruit on the trees, to see how those properties are coming along?

I laid a dry stick on the ground and tried to bore a hole in it with another one, in order to carry out a scheme that I had, and soon I got an awful fright. A thin, transparent bluish film rose out of the hole, and I dropped everything and ran! I thought it was a spirit, and I *was* so frightened! But I looked back, and it was not coming; so I leaned against a rock and rested and panted, and let my limbs go on trembling until they got steady again; then I crept warily back, alert, watching, and ready to fly if there was occasion; and when I was come near, I parted the branches of a rose-bush and peeped through—wishing the man was about, I was looking so cunning and pretty—but the sprite was gone. I went there, and there was a pinch of delicate pink dust in the hole. I put my finger in, to feel it, and said *ouch!* and took it out again. It was a cruel pain. I put my finger in my mouth; and by standing first on one foot and then the other, and grunting, I presently eased my misery; then I was full of interest, and began to examine.

I was curious to know what the pink dust was. Suddenly the name of it occurred to me, though I had never heard of it before. It was *fire!* I was as certain of it as a person could be of anything in the world. So without hesitation I named it that—fire.

I had created something that didn't exist before; I had added a new thing to the world's uncountable properties; I realized this, and was proud of my achievement, and was going to run and find him and tell him about it, thinking to raise myself in his esteem—but I reflected, and did not do it. No—he would not care for it. He would ask what it was good for, and what could I answer? for if it was not *good* for something, but only beautiful, merely beautiful—

So I sighed, and did not go. For it wasn't good for anything; it could not build a shack, it could not improve melons, it could not hurry a fruit crop; it was useless, it was a foolishness and a vanity; he would despise it and say cutting words. But to me it was not despicable; I said, "Oh, you fire, I love you, you dainty pink creature, for you are *beautiful*— and that is enough!" and was going to gather it to my breast. But refrained. Then I made another maxim out of my own head, though it was so nearly like the first one that I was afraid it was only a plagiarism: *"The burnt Experiment shuns the fire."*

I wrought again; and when I had made a good deal of fire-dust I emptied it into a handful of dry brown grass, intending to carry it home and keep it always and play with it; but the wind struck it and it sprayed up and spat out at me fiercely, and I dropped it and ran. When I looked back the blue spirit was towering up and stretching and rolling away like a cloud, and instantly I thought of the name of it—*smoke!*— though, upon my word, I had never heard of smoke before.

Soon, brilliant yellow and red flares shot up through the smoke, and I named them in an instant—*flames*—and I was right, too, though these were the very first flames that had ever been in the world. They climbed the trees, they flashed splendidly in and out of the vast and increasing volume of tumbling smoke, and I had to clap my hands and laugh and dance in my rapture, it was so new and strange and so wonderful and so beautiful!

He came running, and stopped and gazed, and said not a word for many minutes. Then he asked what it was. Ah, it was too bad that he should ask such a direct question. I had to answer it, of course, and I did. I said it was fire. If it annoyed him that I should know and he must ask; that was not my fault; I had no desire to annoy him. After a pause he asked:

"How did it come?"

Another direct question, and it also had to have a direct answer.

"I made it."

The fire was traveling farther and farther off. He went to the edge of the burned place and stood looking down, and said:

"What are these?"

"Fire-coals."

He picked up one to examine it, but changed his mind and put it down again. Then he went away. *Nothing* interests him.

But I was interested. There were ashes, gray and soft and delicate and pretty—I knew what they were at once. And the embers; I knew the embers, too. I found my apples, and raked them out, and was glad; for I am very young and my appetite is active. But I was disappointed; they were all burst open and spoiled. Spoiled apparently; but it was not so; they were better than raw ones. Fire is beautiful; some day it will be useful, I think.

Friday   I saw him again, for a moment, last Monday at nightfall, but only for a moment. I was hoping he would praise me for trying to improve the estate, for I had meant well and had worked hard. But he was not pleased, and turned away and left me. He was also displeased on another account: I tried once more to persuade him to stop going over the Falls. That was because the fire had revealed to me a new passion—quite new, and distinctly different from love, grief, and those others which I had already discovered—*fear*. And it is horrible!—I wish I had never discovered it; it gives me dark moments, it spoils my happiness, it makes me shiver and tremble and shudder. But I could not persuade him, for he has not discovered fear yet, and so he could not understand me.

Extract from Adam's Diary

Perhaps I ought to remember that she is very young, a mere girl, and make allowances. She is all interest, eagerness, vivacity, the world is to her a charm, a wonder, a mystery, a joy; she can't speak for delight when she finds a new flower, she must pet it and caress it and smell it and talk to it, and pour out endearing names upon it. And she is color-mad: brown rocks, yellow sand, gray moss, green foliage, blue sky; the pearl of the dawn, the purple shadows on the mountains, the golden islands floating in crimson seas at sunset, the pallid moon sailing through the shredded cloud-rack, the star-jewels glittering in the wastes of space—none of them is of any practical value, so far as I can see, but because they have color and majesty, that is enough for her, and she loses her mind over them. If she could quiet down and keep still a couple of minutes at a time, it would be a reposeful spectacle. In that case I think I could enjoy looking at her; indeed I am sure I could, for I am coming to realize that she is a quite remarkably comely creature—lithe, slender, trim, rounded, shapely, nimble, graceful; and once when she was standing marble-white and sun-drenched on a boulder, with her young head tilted back and her hand shading her eyes, watching the flight of a bird in the sky, I recognized that she was beautiful.

Monday noon   If there is anything on the planet that she is not interested in it is not in my list. There are animals that I am indifferent to, but it is not so with her. She has no discrimination, she takes to all of them, she thinks they are all treasures, every new one is welcome.

When the mighty brontosaurus came striding into camp, she regarded it as an acquisition, I considered it a calamity; that is a good sample of the lack of harmony that prevails in our views of things. She wanted to domesticate it, I wanted to make it a present of the homestead and move out. She believed it could be tamed by kind treatment and would be a good pet; I said a pet twenty-one feet high and eighty-four feet long would be no proper thing to have about the place, because, even with the best intentions and without meaning any harm, it could sit down on the house and mash it, for any one could see by the look of its eye that it was absent-minded.

Still, her heart was set upon having that monster, and she couldn't give it up. She thought we could start a dairy with it, and wanted me to help her milk it; but I wouldn't; it was too risky. The sex wasn't right, and we hadn't any ladder anyway. Then she wanted to ride it, and look at the scenery. Thirty or forty feet of its tail was lying on the ground, like a fallen tree, and she thought she could climb it, but she was mistaken; when she got to the steep place it was too slick and down she came, and would have hurt herself but for me.

Was she satisfied now? No. Nothing ever satisfies her but demonstration; untested theories are not in her line, and she won't have them.

It is the right spirit, I concede it; it attracts me; I feel the influence of it; if I were with her more I think I should take it up myself. Well, she had one theory remaining about this colossus: she thought that if we could tame him and make him friendly we could stand him in the river and use him for a bridge. It turned out that he was already plenty tame enough—at least as far as she was concerned—so she tried her theory, but it failed: every time she got him properly placed in the river and went ashore to cross over on him, he came out and followed her around like a pet mountain. Like the other animals. They all do that.

Friday Tuesday—Wednesday—Thursday—and to-day: all without seeing him. It is a long time to be alone; still, it is better to be alone than unwelcome.

I *had* to have company—I was made for it, I think—so I made friends with the animals. They are just charming, and they have the kindest disposition and the politest ways; they never look sour, they never let you feel that you are intruding, they smile at you and wag their tail, if they've got one, and they are always ready for a romp or an excursion or anything you want to propose. I think they are perfect gentlemen. All these days we have had such good times, and it hasn't been lonesome for me, ever. Lonesome! No, I should say not. Why, there's always a swarm of them around—sometimes as much as four or five acres—you can't count them; and when you stand on a rock in the midst and look out over the furry expanse it is so mottled and splashed and gay with color and frisking sheen and sun-flash, and so rippled with stripes, that you might think it was a lake, only you know it isn't; and there's storms of sociable birds, and hurricanes of whirring wings; and when the sun strikes all that feathery commotion, you have a blazing up of all the colors you can think of, enough to put your eyes out.

We have made long excursions, and I have seen a great deal of the world; almost all of it, I think; and so I am the first traveler, and the only one. When we are on the march, it is an imposing sight—there's nothing like it anywhere. For comfort I ride a tiger or a leopard, because it is soft and has a round back that fits me, and because they are such pretty animals; but for long distance or for scenery I ride the elephant. He hoists me up with his trunk, but I can get off myself; when we are ready to camp, he sits and I slide down the back way.

The birds and animals are all friendly to each other, and there are no disputes about anything. They all talk, and they all talk to me, but it must be a foreign language, for I cannot make out a word they say;

yet they often understand me when I talk back, particularly the dog and the elephant. It makes me ashamed. It shows that they are brighter than I am, and are therefore my superiors. It annoys me, for I want to be the principal Experiment myself—and I intend to be, too.

I have learned a number of things, and am educated, now, but I wasn't at first. I was ignorant at first. At first it used to vex me because, with all my watching, I was never smart enough to be around when the water was running uphill; but now I do not mind it. I have experimented and experimented until now I know it never does run uphill, except in the dark. I know it does in the dark, because the pool never goes dry, which it would, of course, if the water didn't come back in the night. It is best to prove things by actual experiment; then you *know;* whereas if you depend on guessing and supposing and conjecturing, you will never get educated.

Some things you *can't* find out; but you will never know you can't by guessing and supposing: no, you have to be patient and go on experimenting until you find out that you can't find out. And it is delightful to have it that way, it makes the world so interesting. If there wasn't anything to find out, it would be dull. Even trying to find out and not finding out is just as interesting as trying to find out and finding out, and I don't know but more so. The secret of the water was a treasure until I *got* it; then the excitement all went away, and I recognized a sense of loss.

By experiment I know that wood swims, and dry leaves, and feathers, and plenty of other things; therefore by all that cumulative evidence you know that a rock will swim; but you have to put up with simply knowing it, for there isn't any way to prove it—up to now. But I shall find a way—then *that* excitement will go. Such things make me sad; because by and by when I have found out everything there won't be any more excitements, and I do love excitements so! The other night I couldn't sleep for thinking about it.

At first I couldn't make out what I was made for, but now I think it was to search out the secrets of this wonderful world and be happy and thank the Giver of it all for devising it. I think there are many things to learn yet—I hope so; and by economizing and not hurrying too fast I think they will last weeks and weeks. I hope so. When you cast up a feather it sails away on the air and goes out of sight; then you throw up a clod and it doesn't. It comes down, every time. I have tried it and tried it, and it is always so. I wonder why it is? Of course it *doesn't* come down, but why should it *seem* to? I suppose it is an optical illusion. I mean, one of them is. I don't know which one. It may be the feather, it may be the clod; I can't prove which it is, I can only demonstrate that one or the other is a fake, and let a person take his choice.

By watching, I know that the stars are not going to last. I have seen some of the best ones melt and run down the sky. Since one can melt, they can all melt; since they can all melt, they can all melt the same night. That sorrow will come—I know it. I mean to sit up every night and look at them as long as I can keep awake; and I will impress those sparkling fields on my memory, so that by and by when they are taken away I can by my fancy restore those lovely myriads to the black sky and make them sparkle again, and double them by the blur of my tears.

AFTER THE FALL

When I look back, the Garden is a dream to me. It was beautiful, surpassingly beautiful, enchantingly beautiful; and now it is lost, and I shall not see it any more.

The Garden is lost, but I have found *him*, and am content. He loves me as well as he can; I love him with all the strength of my passionate nature, and this, I think, is proper to my youth and sex. If I ask myself why I love him, I find I do not know, and do not really much care to know; so I suppose that this kind of love is not a product of reasoning and statistics, like one's love for other reptiles and animals. I think that this must be so. I love certain birds because of their song; but I do not love Adam on account of his singing—no, it is not that; the more he sings the more I do not get reconciled to it. Yet I ask him to sing, because I wish to learn to like everything he is interested in. I am sure I can learn, because at first I could not stand it, but now I can. It sours the milk, but it doesn't matter; I can get used to that kind of milk.

It is not on account of his brightness that I love him—no, it is not that. He is not to blame for his brightness, such as it is, for he did not make it himself; he is as God made him, and that is sufficient. There was a wise purpose in it, *that* I know. In time it will develop, though I think it will not be sudden; and besides, there is no hurry; he is well enough just as he is.

It is not on account of his gracious and considerate ways and his delicacy that I love him. No, he has lacks in these regards, but he is well enough just so, and is improving.

It is not on account of his industry that I love him—no, it is not that. I think he has it in him, and I do not know why he conceals it from me. It is my only pain. Otherwise he is frank and open with me, now. I am sure he keeps nothing from me but this. It grieves me that he should have a secret from me, and sometimes it spoils my sleep, thinking of it, but I will put it out of my mind; it shall not trouble my happiness, which is otherwise full to overflowing.

It is not on account of his education that I love him—no, it is not that. He is self-educated, and does really know a multitude of things, but they are not so.

It is not on account of his chivalry that I love him—no, it is not that. He told on me, but I do not blame him; it is a peculiarity of sex, I think, and he did not make his sex. Of course I would not have told on him, I would have perished first; but that is a peculiarity of sex, too, and I do not take credit for it, for I did not make my sex.

Then why is it that I love him? *Merely because he is masculine,* I think.

At bottom he is good, and I love him for that, but I could love him without it. If he should beat me and abuse me, I should go on loving him. I know it. It is a matter of sex, I think.

He is strong and handsome, and I love him for that, and I admire him and am proud of him, but I could love him without those qualities. If he were plain, I should love him; if he were a wreck, I should love him; and I would work for him, and slave over him, and pray for him, and watch by his bedside until I died.

Yes, I think I love him merely because he is *mine* and is *masculine.* There is no other reason, I suppose. And so I think it is as I first said: that this kind of love is not a product of reasonings and statistics. It just *comes*—none knows whence—and cannot explain itself. And doesn't need to.

It is what I think. But I am only a girl, and the first that has examined this matter, and it may turn out that in my ignorance and inexperience I have not got it right.

FORTY YEARS LATER

It is my prayer, it is my longing, that we may pass from this life together—a longing which shall never perish from the earth, but shall have place in the heart of every wife that loves, until the end of time; and it shall be called by my name.

But if one of us must go first, it is my prayer that it shall be I; for he is strong, I am weak, I am not so necessary to him as he is to me—life without him would not be life; how could I endure it? This prayer is also immortal, and will not cease from being offered up while my race continues. I am the first wife; and in the last wife I shall be repeated.

AT EVE'S GRAVE

ADAM: Wheresoever she was, *there* was Eden.

1893, 1905

The Esquimau Maiden's Romance

"Yes, I will tell you anything about my life that you would like to know, Mr. Twain," she said, in her soft voice, and letting her honest eyes rest placidly upon my face, "for it is kind and good of you to like me and care to know about me."

She had been absently scraping blubber-grease from her cheeks with a small bone-knife and transferring it to her fur sleeve, while she watched the Aurora Borealis swing its flaming streamers out of the sky and wash the lonely snow-plain and the templed icebergs with the rich hues of the prism, a spectacle of almost intolerable splendor and beauty; but now she shook off her reverie and prepared to give me the humble little history I had asked for.

She settled herself comfortably on the block of ice which we were using as a sofa, and I made ready to listen.

She was a beautiful creature. I speak from the Esquimau point of view. Others would have thought her a trifle over-plump. She was just twenty years old, and was held to be by far the most bewitching girl in her tribe. Even now, in the open air, with her cumbersome and shapeless fur coat and trousers and boots and vast hood, the beauty of her face at least was apparent; but her figure had to be taken on trust. Among all the guests who came and went, I had seen no girl at her father's hospitable trough who could be called her equal. Yet she was not spoiled. She was sweet and natural and sincere, and if she was aware that she was a belle, there was nothing about her ways to show that she possessed that knowledge.

She had been my daily comrade for a week now, and the better I knew her the better I liked her. She had been tenderly and carefully brought up, in an atmosphere of singularly rare refinement for the polar regions, for her father was the most important man of his tribe and ranked at the top of Esquimau cultivation. I made long dog-sledge trips across the mighty ice-floes with Lasca—that was her name—and found her company always pleasant and her conversation agreeable. I went fishing with her, but not in her perilous boat: I merely followed along on the ice and watched her strike her game with her fatally accurate spear. We went sealing together; several times I stood by while she and the family dug blubber from a stranded whale, and once I went part of the way when she was hunting a bear, but turned back before the finish, because at bottom I am afraid of bears.

However, she was ready to begin her story now, and this is what she said:

"Our tribe had always been used to wander about from place to place over the frozen seas, like the other tribes, but my father got tired of that two years ago, and built this great mansion of frozen snow-blocks —look at it; it is seven feet high and three or four times as long as any of the others—and here we have stayed ever since. He was very proud of his house, and that was reasonable; for if you have examined it with care you must have noticed how much finer and completer it is than houses usually are. But if you have not, you must, for you will find it has luxurious appointments that are quite beyond the common. For instance, in that end of it which you have called the 'parlor,' the raised platform for the accommodation of guests and the family at meals is the largest you have ever seen in any house—is it not so?"

"Yes, you are quite right, Lasca; it is the largest; we have nothing resembling it in even the finest houses in the United States." This admission made her eyes sparkle with pride and pleasure. I noted that, and took my cue.

"I thought it must have surprised you," she said. "And another thing: it is bedded far deeper in furs than is usual; all kinds of furs—seal, sea-otter, silver-gray fox, bear, marten, sable—every kind of fur in profusion; and the same with the ice-block sleeping-benches along the walls, which you call 'beds.' Are your platforms and sleeping-benches better provided at home?"

"Indeed, they are not, Lasca—they do not begin to be." That pleased her again. All she was thinking of was the *number* of furs her esthetic father took the trouble to keep on hand, not their value. I could have told her that those masses of rich furs constituted wealth—or would in my country—but she would not have understood that; those were not the kind of things that ranked as riches with her people. I could have told her that the clothes she had on, or the every-day clothes of the commonest person about her, were worth twelve or fifteen hundred dollars, and that I was not acquainted with anybody at home who wore twelve-hundred-dollar toilets to go fishing in; but she would not have understood it, so I said nothing. She resumed:

"And then the slop-tubs. We have two in the parlor, and two in the rest of the house. It is very seldom that one has two in the parlor. Have you two in the parlor at home?"

The memory of those tubs made me gasp, but I recovered myself before she noticed, and said with effusion:

"Why, Lasca, it is a shame of me to expose my country, and you must not let it go further, for I am speaking to you in confidence; but I give you my word of honor that not even the richest man in the city of New York has two slop-tubs in his drawing-room."

She clapped her fur-clad hands in innocent delight, and exclaimed:

"Oh, but you cannot mean it, you cannot *mean* it!"

"Indeed, I am in earnest, dear. There is Vanderbilt. Vanderbilt is almost the richest man in the whole world. Now, if I were on my dying bed, I could say to you that not even he has two in his drawing-room. Why, he hasn't even *one*—I wish I may die in my tracks if it isn't true."

Her lovely eyes stood wide with amazement, and she said, slowly, and with a sort of awe in her voice:

"How strange—how incredible—one is not able to realize it. Is he penurious?"

"No—it isn't that. It isn't the expense he minds, but—er—well, you know, it would look like showing off. Yes, that is it, that is the idea; he is a plain man in his way, and shrinks from display."

"Why, that humility is right enough," said Lasca, "if one does not carry it too far—but what does the place *look* like?"

"Well, necessarily it looks pretty barren and unfinished, but—"

"I should think so! I never heard anything like it. Is it a fine house—that is, otherwise?"

"Pretty fine, yes. It is very well thought of."

The girl was silent awhile, and sat dreamily gnawing a candle-end, apparently trying to think the thing out. At last she gave her head a little toss and spoke out her opinion with decision:

"Well, to my mind there's a breed of humility which is *itself* a species of showing-off, when you get down to the marrow of it; and when a man is able to afford two slop-tubs in his parlor, and don't do it, it *may* be that he is truly humble-minded, but it's a hundred times more likely that he is just trying to strike the public eye. In my judgment, your Mr. Vanderbilt knows what he is about."

I tried to modify this verdict, feeling that a double slop-tub standard was not a fair one to try everybody by, although a sound enough one in its own habitat; but the girl's head was set, and she was not to be persuaded. Presently she said:

"Do the rich people, with you, have as good sleeping-benches as ours, and made out of as nice broad ice-blocks?"

"Well, they are pretty good—good enough—but they are not made of ice-blocks."

"I want to know! *Why* aren't they made of ice-blocks?"

I explained the difficulties in the way, and the expensiveness of ice in a country where you have to keep a sharp eye on your ice-man or your ice bill will weigh more than your ice. Then she cried out:

"Dear me, do you *buy* your ice?"

"We most surely do, dear."

She burst into a gale of guileless laughter, and said:

"Oh, I *never* heard of anything so silly! My, there's plenty of it—it isn't worth anything. Why, there is a hundred miles of it in sight, right now. I wouldn't give a fish-bladder for the whole of it."

"Well, it's because you don't know how to value it, you little provincial muggins. If you had it in New York in midsummer, you could buy all the whales in the market with it."

She looked at me doubtfully, and said:

"Are you speaking true?"

"Absolutely. I take my oath to it."

This made her thoughtful. Presently she said, with a little sigh:

"I wish *I* could live there."

I had merely meant to furnish her a standard of values which she could understand; but my purpose had miscarried. I had only given her the impression that whales were cheap and plenty in New York, and set her mouth to watering for them. It seemed best to try to mitigate the evil which I had done, so I said:

"But you wouldn't care for whale-meat if you lived there. Nobody does."

"What!"

"Indeed they don't."

"*Why* don't they?"

"Wel-l-l, I hardly know. It's prejudice, I think. Yes, that is it—just prejudice. I reckon somebody that hadn't anything better to do started a prejudice against it, some time or other, and once you get a caprice like that fairly going, you know, it will last no end of time."

"That is true—*perfectly* true," said the girl, reflectively. "Like our

prejudice against soap, here—our tribes had a prejudice against soap at
first, you know."

I glanced at her to see if she was in earnest. Evidently she was. I
hesitated, then said, cautiously:

"But pardon me. They *had* a prejudice against soap? Had?"—with
falling inflection.

"Yes—but that was only at first; nobody would eat it."

"Oh—I understand. I didn't get your idea before."

She resumed:

"It was just a prejudice. The first time soap came here from the foreigners, nobody liked it; but as soon as it got to be fashionable, everybody liked it, and now everybody has it that can afford it. Are you fond
of it?"

"Yes, indeed! I should die if I couldn't have it—especially here. Do
you like it?"

"I just *adore* it! Do you like candles?"

"I regard them as an absolute necessity. Are you fond of them?"

Her eyes fairly danced, and she exclaimed:

"Oh! Don't mention it! Candles!—and soap!—"

"And fish-interiors!—"

"And train-oil!—"

"And slush!—"

"And whale-blubber!—"

"And carrion! and sour-krout! and beeswax! and tar! and turpentine!
and molasses! and—"

"Don't—oh, don't—I shall expire with ecstasy!—"

"And then serve it all up in a slush-bucket, and invite the neighbors
and sail in!"

But this vision of an ideal feast was too much for her, and she
swooned away, poor thing. I rubbed snow in her face and brought her
to, and after a while got her excitement cooled down. By and by she
drifted into her story again:

"So we began to live here, in the fine house. But I was not happy.
The reason was this: I was born for love; for me there could be no true
happiness without it. I wanted to be loved for myself alone. I wanted
an idol, and I wanted to be my idol's idol; nothing less than mutual
idolatry would satisfy my fervent nature. I had suitors in plenty—in
over-plenty, indeed—but in each and every case they had a fatal defect;
sooner or later I discovered that defect—not one of them failed to betray it—it was not me they wanted, but my wealth."

"Your wealth?"

"Yes; for my father is much the richest man in this tribe—or in any tribe in these regions."

I wondered what her father's wealth consisted of. It couldn't be the house—anybody could build its mate. It couldn't be the furs—they were not valued. It couldn't be the sledge, the dogs, the harpoons, the boat, the bone fish-hooks and needles, and such things—no, these were not wealth. Then what could it be that made this man so rich and brought this swarm of sordid suitors to his house? It seemed to me, finally, that the best way to find out would be to ask. So I did it. The girl was so manifestly gratified by the question that I saw she had been aching to have me ask it. She was suffering fully as much to tell as I was to know. She snuggled confidentially up to me and said:

"Guess how much he is worth—you never can!"

I pretended to consider the matter deeply, she watching my anxious and laboring countenance with a devouring and delighted interest; and when, at last, I gave it up and begged her to appease my longing by telling me herself how much this polar Vanderbilt was worth, she put her mouth close to my ear and whispered, impressively:

"*Twenty-two fish-hooks*—not bone, but foreign—*made out of real iron!*"

Then she sprang back dramatically, to observe the effect. I did my level best not to disappoint her.

I turned pale and murmured:

"Great Scott!"

"It's as true as you live, Mr. Twain!"

"Lasca, you are deceiving me—you cannot mean it."

She was frightened and troubled. She exclaimed:

"Mr. Twain, every word of it is true—every word. You believe me— you *do* believe me, now *don't* you? *Say* you believe me—*do* say you believe me!"

"I—well, yes, I do—I am *trying* to. But it was all so *sudden*. So sudden and prostrating. You shouldn't do such a thing in that sudden way. It—"

"Oh, I'm *so* sorry! If I had only thought—"

"Well, it's all right, and I don't blame you any more, for you are young and thoughtless, and of course you couldn't foresee what an effect—"

"But oh, dear, I ought certainly to have *known* better. Why—"

"You see, Lasca, if you had said five or six hooks, to start with, and then gradually—"

"Oh, I see, I see—then gradually added one, and then two, and then —ah, why couldn't I have thought of that!"

"Never mind, child, it's all right—I am better now—I shall be over it in a little while. *But*—to spring the whole twenty-two on a person un-prepared and not very strong anyway—"

"Oh, it *was* a crime! But you forgive me—say you forgive me. Do!"

After harvesting a good deal of very pleasant coaxing and petting and persuading, I forgave her and she was happy again, and by and by she got under way with her narrative once more. I presently discovered that the family treasury contained still another feature—a jewel of some sort, apparently—and that she was trying to get around speaking squarely about it, lest I get paralyzed again. But I wanted to know about that thing, too, and urged her to tell me what it was. She was afraid. But I insisted, and said I would brace myself this time and be prepared, then the shock would not hurt me. She was full of misgivings, but the temptation to reveal that marvel to me and enjoy my astonish-ment and admiration was too strong for her, and she confessed that she had it on her person, and said that if I was *sure* I was prepared— and so on and so on—and with that she reached into her bosom and brought out a battered square of brass, watching my eye anxiously the while. I fell over against her in a quite well-acted faint, which delighted her heart and nearly frightened it out of her, too, at the same time. When I came to and got calm, she was eager to know what I thought of her jewel.

"What do I think of it? I think it is the most exquisite thing I ever saw."

"Do you really? How nice of you to say that! But it *is* a love, now isn't it?"

"Well, I should say so! I'd rather own it than the equator."

"I thought you would admire it," she said. "I think it is *so* lovely. And there isn't another one in all these latitudes. People have come all the way from the Open Polar Sea to look at it. Did you ever see one before?"

I said no, this was the first one I had ever seen. It cost me a pang to tell that generous lie, for I had seen a million of them in my time, this humble jewel of hers being nothing but a battered old New York Central baggage-check.

"Land!" said I, "you don't go about with it on your person this way, alone and with no protection, not even a dog?"

"Ssh! not so loud," she said. "Nobody knows I carry it with me. They think it is in papa's treasury. That is where it generally is."

"Where is the treasury?"

It was a blunt question, and for a moment she looked startled and a little suspicious, but I said:

"Oh, come, don't you be afraid about me. At home we have seventy millions of people, and although I say it myself that shouldn't, there is not one person among them all but would trust me with untold fish-hooks."

This reassured her, and she told me where the hooks were hidden in the house. Then she wandered from her course to brag a little about the size of the sheets of transparent ice that formed the windows of the mansion, and asked me if I had ever seen their like at home, and I came right out frankly and confessed that I hadn't, which pleased her more than she could find words to dress her gratification in. It was so easy to please her, and such a pleasure to do it, that I went on and said:

"Ah, Lasca, you *are* a fortunate girl!—this beautiful house, this dainty jewel, that rich treasure, all this elegant snow, and sumptuous icebergs and limitless sterility, and public bears and walruses, and noble freedom and largeness, and everybody's admiring eyes upon you, and everybody's homage and respect at your command without the asking; young, rich, beautiful, sought, courted, envied, not a requirement unsatisfied, not a desire ungratified, nothing to wish for that you cannot have—it is immeasurable good fortune! I have seen myriads of girls, but none of whom these extraordinary things could be truthfully said but you alone. And you are worthy—worthy of it all, Lasca—I believe it in my heart."

It made her infinitely proud and happy to hear me say this, and she thanked me over and over again for that closing remark, and her voice and eyes showed that she was touched. Presently she said:

"Still, it is not all sunshine—there is a cloudy side. The burden of wealth is a heavy one to bear. Sometimes I have doubted if it were not better to be poor—at least not inordinately rich. It pains me to see neighboring tribesmen stare as they pass by, and overhear them say, reverently, one to another, 'There—that is she—the millionaire's daughter!' And sometimes they say sorrowfully, 'She is rolling in fish-hooks, and I—I have nothing.' It breaks my heart. When I was a child and we were poor, we slept with the door open, if we chose, but now—now we have to have a night watchman. In those days my father was gentle and courteous to all; but now he is austere and haughty, and cannot abide familiarity. Once his family were his sole thought, but now he goes about thinking of his fish-hooks all the time. And his wealth makes everybody cringing and obsequious to him. Formerly nobody laughed at his jokes, they being always stale and far-fetched and poor, and destitute of the one element that can really justify a joke—the element of humor; but now everybody laughs and cackles at those dismal things, and if any fails to do it my father is deeply displeased, and shows it. Formerly his opinion was not sought upon any matter and was not valuable when he volunteered it; it has that infirmity yet, but nevertheless it is sought by all and applauded by all—and he helps do the applauding himself, having no true delicacy and a plentiful want of tact. He has lowered the tone of all our tribe. Once they were a frank and manly race, now they are measly hypocrites, and sodden with servility. In my heart of hearts I hate all the ways of millionaires! Our tribe was once plain, simple folk, and content with the bone fish-hooks of their fathers; now they are eaten up with avarice and would sacrifice every sentiment of honor and honesty to possess themselves of the debasing iron fish-hooks of the foreigner. However, I must not dwell on these sad things. As I have said, it was my dream to be loved for myself alone.

"At last, this dream seemed about to be fulfilled. A stranger came by, one day, who said his name was Kalula. I told him my name, and he said he loved me. My heart gave a great bound of gratitude and pleasure, for I had loved him at sight, and now I said so. He took me to his breast and said he would not wish to be happier than he was now. We went strolling together far over the ice-floes, telling all about each other, and planning, oh, the loveliest future! When we were tired at last we sat down and ate, for he had soap and candles and I had brought along some blubber. We were hungry, and nothing was ever so good.

"He belonged to a tribe whose haunts were far to the north, and I found that he had never heard of my father, which rejoiced me exceedingly. I mean he had heard of the millionaire, but had never heard his name—so, you see, he could not know that I was the heiress. You may be sure that I did not tell him. I was loved for myself at last, and was satisfied. I was so happy—oh, happier than you can think!

"By and by it was toward supper-time, and I led him home. As we approached our house he was amazed, and cried out:

"'How splendid! Is *that* your father's?'

"It gave me a pang to hear that tone and see that admiring light in his eye, but the feeling quickly passed away, for I loved him so, and he looked so handsome and noble. All my family of aunts and uncles and cousins were pleased with him, and many guests were called in, and the house was shut up tight and the rag-lamps lighted, and when everything was hot and comfortable and suffocating, we began a joyous feast in celebration of my bethrothal.

"When the feast was over, my father's vanity overcame him, and he could not resist the temptation to show off his riches and let Kalula see what grand good fortune he had stumbled into—and mainly, of course, he wanted to enjoy the poor man's amazement. I could have cried—but it would have done no good to try to dissuade my father, so I said nothing, but merely sat there and suffered.

"My father went straight to the hiding-place, in full sight of everybody, and got out the fish-hooks and brought them and flung them scatteringly over my head, so that they fell in glittering confusion on the platform at my lover's knee.

"Of course, the astounding spectacle took the poor lad's breath away. He could only stare in stupid astonishment, and wonder how a single individual could possess such incredible riches. Then presently he glanced brilliantly up and exclaimed:

"'Ah, it is *you* who are the renowned millionaire!'

"My father and all the rest burst into shouts of happy laughter, and when my father gathered the treasure carelessly up as if it might be mere rubbish and of no consequence, and carried it back to its place, poor Kalula's surprise was a study. He said:

"'Is it possible that you put such things away without counting them?'

"My father delivered a vainglorious horse-laugh, and said:

"'Well, truly, a body may know *you* have never been rich, since a mere matter of a fish-hook or two is such a mighty matter in your eyes.'

"Kalula was confused, and hung his head, but said:

"'Ah, indeed, sir, I was never worth the value of the barb of one of those precious things, and I have never seen any man before who was so rich in them as to render the counting of his hoard worth while, since the wealthiest man I have ever known, till now, was possessed of but three.'

"My foolish father roared again with jejune delight, and allowed the impression to remain that he was not accustomed to count his hooks and keep sharp watch over them. He was showing off, you see. Count them? Why, he counted them every day!

"I had met and got acquainted with my darling just at dawn; I had brought him home just at dark, three hours afterward—for the days were shortening toward the six-months' night at that time. We kept up the festivities many hours; then, at last, the guests departed and the rest of us distributed ourselves along the walls on sleeping-benches, and soon all were steeped in dreams but me. I was too happy, too excited, to sleep. After I had lain quiet a long, long time, a dim form passed by me and was swallowed up in the gloom that pervaded the farther end of the house. I could not make out who it was, or whether it was man or woman. Presently that figure or another one passed me going the other way. I wondered what it all meant, but wondering did no good; and while I was still wondering, I fell asleep.

"I do not know how long I slept, but at last I came suddenly broad awake and heard my father say in a terrible voice, 'By the great Snow God, there's a fish-hook gone!' Something told me that that meant sorrow for me, and the blood in my veins turned cold. The presentiment was confirmed in the same instant: my father shouted, 'Up, everybody, and seize the stranger!' Then there was an outburst of cries and curses from all sides, and a wild rush of dim forms through the obscurity. I flew to my beloved's help, but what could I do but wait and wring my hands?—he was already fenced away from me by a living wall, he was being bound hand and foot. Not until he was secured would they let me get to him. I flung myself upon his poor insulted form and cried my grief out upon his breast, while my father and all my family scoffed at me and heaped threats and shameful epithets upon him. He bore his ill usage with a tranquil dignity which endeared him to me more than ever, and made me proud and happy to suffer with him and for him. I heard my father order that the elders of the tribe be called together to try my Kalula for his life.

"'What?' I said, 'before any search has been made for the lost hook?'

"'Lost hook!' they all shouted, in derision; and my father added, mockingly, 'Stand back, everybody, and be properly serious—she is going to hunt up that *lost* hook; oh, without doubt she will find it!'—whereat they all laughed again.

"I was not disturbed—I had no fears, no doubts. I said:

"'It is for you to laugh now; it is your turn. But ours is coming; wait and see.'

"I got a rag-lamp. I thought I should find that miserable thing in one little moment; and I set about the matter with such confidence that those people grew grave, beginning to suspect that perhaps they had been too hasty. But, alas and alas!—oh, the bitterness of that search! There was deep silence while one might count his fingers ten or twelve times, then my heart began to sink, and around me the mockings began again, and grew steadily louder and more assured, until at last, when I gave up, they burst into volley after volley of cruel laughter.

"None will ever know what I suffered then. But my love was my support and my strength, and I took my rightful place at my Kalula's side, and put my arm about his neck, and whispered in his ear, saying:

"'You are innocent, my own—that I know; but say it to me yourself, for my comfort, then I can bear whatever is in store for us.'

"He answered:

"'As surely as I stand upon the brink of death at this moment, I am innocent. Be comforted, then, O bruised heart; be at peace, O thou breath of my nostrils, life of my life!'

"'Now, then, let the elders come!'—and as I said the words there was a gathering sound of crunching snow outside, and then a vision of stooping forms filing in at the door—the elders.

"My father formally accused the prisoner, and detailed the happenings of the night. He said that the watchman was outside the door, and that in the house were none but the family and the stranger. 'Would the family steal their own property?'

"He paused. The elders sat silent many minutes; at last, one after another said to his neighbor, 'This looks bad for the stranger'—sorrowful words for me to hear. Then my father sat down. O miserable, miserable me! at that very moment I could have proved my darling innocent, but I did not know it!

"The chief of the court asked:

"'Is there any here to defend the prisoner?'

"I rose and said:

"'Why should *he* steal that hook, or any or all of them? In another day he would have been heir to the whole!'

"I stood waiting. There was a long silence, the steam from the many breaths rising about me like a fog. At last, one elder after another nodded his head slowly several times, and muttered, 'There is force in what the child has said.' Oh, the heartlift that was in those words!—so transient, but oh, so precious! I sat down.

"'If any would say further, let him speak now, or after hold his peace,' said the chief of the court.

"My father rose and said:

"'In the night a form passed by me in the gloom, going toward the treasury, and presently returned. I think, now, it was the stranger.'

"Oh, I was like to swoon! I had supposed that that was my secret; not the grip of the great Ice God himself could have dragged it out of my heart.

"The chief of the court said sternly to my poor Kalula:

"'Speak!'

"Kalula hesitated, then answered:

"'It was I. I could not sleep for thinking of the beautiful hooks. I went there and kissed them and fondled them, to appease my spirit and drown it in a harmless joy, then I put them back. I may have dropped one, but I stole none.'

"Oh, a fatal admission to make in such a place! There was an awful hush. I knew he had pronounced his own doom, and that all was over. On every face you could see the words hieroglyphed: 'It is a confession! —and paltry, lame, and thin.'

"I sat drawing in my breath in faint gasps—and waiting. Presently, I heard the solemn words I knew were coming; and each word, as it came, was a knife in my heart:

"'It is the command of the court that the accused be subjected to the *trial by water.*'

"Oh, curses be upon the head of him who brought 'trial by water' to our land! It came, generations ago, from some far country, that lies none knows where. Before that, our fathers used augury and other unsure methods of trial, and doubtless some poor, guilty creatures escaped with their lives sometimes; but it is not so with trial by water, which is an invention by wiser men than we poor, ignorant savages are. By it the innocent are proved innocent, without doubt or question, for they drown; and the guilty are proven guilty with the same certainty, for they do not drown. My heart was breaking in my bosom, for I said, 'He is innocent, and he will go down under the waves and I shall never see him more.'

"I never left his side after that. I mourned in his arms all the precious hours, and he poured out the deep stream of his love upon me, and oh, I was so miserable and so happy! At last, they tore him from me, and I followed sobbing after them, and saw them fling him into the sea— then I covered my face with my hands. Agony? Oh, I know the deepest deeps of that word!

"The next moment the people burst into a shout of malicious joy, and I took away my hands, startled. Oh, bitter sight—he was *swimming!*

"My heart turned instantly to stone, to ice. I said, 'He was guilty, and he lied to me!'

"I turned my back in scorn and went my way homeward.

"They took him far out to sea and set him on an iceberg that was drifting southward in the great waters. Then my family came home, and my father said to me:

"'Your thief sent his dying message to you, saying, "Tell her I am innocent, and that all the days and all the hours and all the minutes while I starve and perish I shall love her and think of her and bless the day that gave me sight of her sweet face." Quite pretty, even poetical!'

"I said, 'He is dirt—let me never hear mention of him again.' And oh, to think—he *was* innocent all the time!

"Nine months—nine dull, sad months—went by, and at last came the day of the Great Annual Sacrifice, when all the maidens of the tribe wash their faces and comb their hair. With the first sweep of my comb, out came the fatal fish-hook from where it had been all those months nestling, and I fell fainting into the arms of my remorseful father! Groaning, he said, 'We murdered him, and I shall never smile again!' He has kept his word. Listen: from that day to this not a month goes by that I do not comb my hair. But oh, where is the good of it all now!"

So ended the poor maid's humble little tale—whereby we learn that, since a hundred million dollars in New York and twenty-two fish-hooks on the border of the Arctic Circle represent the same financial supremacy, a man in straitened circumstances is a fool to stay in New York when he can buy ten cents' worth of fish-hooks and emigrate.

1893

Is He Living or Is He Dead?

I was spending the month of March, 1892, at Mentone, in the Riviera. At this retired spot one has all the advantages, privately, which are to be had at Monte Carlo and Nice, a few miles farther along, publicly. That is to say, one has the flooding sunshine, the balmy air, and the brilliant blue sea, without the marring additions of human powwow and fuss and feathers and display. Mentone is quiet, simple, restful, unpretentious; the rich and the gaudy do not come there. As a rule, I mean, the rich do not come there. Now and then a rich man comes, and I presently got acquainted with one of these. Partially to disguise him I will call him Smith. One day, in the Hôtel des Anglais, at the second breakfast, he exclaimed:

"Quick! Cast your eye on the man going out at the door. Take in every detail of him."

"Why?"

"Do you know who he is?"

"Yes. He spent several days here before you came. He is an old, retired, and very rich silk manufacturer from Lyons, they say, and I guess he is alone in the world, for he always looks sad and dreamy, and doesn't talk with anybody. His name is Théophile Magnan."

I supposed that Smith would now proceed to justify the large interest which he had shown in Monsieur Magnan; but instead he dropped into a brown study, and was apparently lost to me and to the rest of the world during some minutes. Now and then he passed his fingers through his flossy white hair, to assist his thinking, and meantime he allowed his breakfast to go on cooling. At last he said:

"No, it's gone; I can't call it back."

"Can't call what back?"

"It's one of Hans Andersen's beautiful little stories. But it's gone from me. Part of it is like this: A child has a caged bird, which it loves, but thoughtlessly neglects. The bird pours out its song unheard and unheeded; but in time, hunger and thirst assail the creature, and its song grows plaintive and feeble and finally ceases—the bird dies. The child comes, and is smitten to the heart with remorse; then, with bitter tears and lamentations, it calls its mates, and they bury the bird with elaborate pomp and the tenderest grief, without knowing, poor things, that it isn't children only who starve poets to death and then spend enough on their funerals and monuments to have kept them alive and made them easy and comfortable. Now—"

But here we were interrupted. About ten that evening I ran across Smith, and he asked me up to his parlor to help him smoke and drink hot Scotch. It was a cozy place, with its comfortable chairs, its cheerful lamps, and its friendly open fire of seasoned olive-wood. To make everything perfect, there was the muffled booming of the surf outside. After the second Scotch and much lazy and contented chat, Smith said:

"Now we are properly primed—I to tell a curious history, and you to listen to it. It has been a secret for many years—a secret between me and three others; but I am going to break the seal now. Are you comfortable?"

"Perfectly. Go on."

Here follows what he told me:

A long time ago I was a young artist—a very young artist, in fact—and I wandered about the country parts of France, sketching here and sketching there, and was presently joined by a couple of darling young Frenchmen who were at the same kind of thing that I was doing. We were as happy as we were poor, or as poor as we were happy—phrase it to suit yourself. Claude Frère and Carl Boulanger—these are the names of those boys; dear, dear fellows, and the sunniest spirits that ever laughed at poverty and had a noble good time in all weathers.

At last we ran hard aground in a Breton village, and an artist as poor as ourselves took us in and literally saved us from starving—François Millet—

"What! the *great* François Millet?"

Great? He wasn't any greater than we were, then. He hadn't any fame, even in his own village; and he was so poor that he hadn't anything to feed us on but turnips, and even the turnips failed us sometimes. We four became fast friends, doting friends, inseparables. We painted away together with all our might, piling up stock, piling up stock, but very seldom getting rid of any of it. We had lovely times together; but, O my soul! how we were pinched now and then!

For a little over two years this went on. At last, one day, Claude said:

"Boys, we've come to the end. Do you understand that?—absolutely to the end. Everybody has struck—there's a league formed against us. I've been all around the village and it's just as I tell you. They refuse to credit us for another centime until all the odds and ends are paid up."

This struck us cold. Every face was blank with dismay. We realized that our circumstances were desperate, now. There was a long silence. Finally, Millet said with a sigh:

"Nothing occurs to me—nothing. Suggest something, lads."

There was no response, unless a mournful silence may be called a response. Carl got up, and walked nervously up and down awhile, then said:

"It's a shame! Look at these canvases: stacks and stacks of as good pictures as anybody in Europe paints—I don't care who he is. Yes, and plenty of lounging strangers have said the same—or nearly that, anyway."

"But didn't buy," Millet said.

"No matter, they said it; and it's true, too. Look at your 'Angelus' there! Will anybody tell me—"

"Pah, Carl—my 'Angelus'! I was offered five francs for it."

"When?"

"Who offered it?"

"Where is he?"

"Why didn't you take it?"

"Come—don't all speak at once. I thought he would give more—I was sure of it—he looked it—so I asked him eight."

"Well—and then?"

"He said he would call again."

"Thunder and lightning! Why, François—"

"Oh, I know—I know! It was a mistake, and I was a fool. Boys, I meant for the best; you'll grant me that, and I—"

"Why, certainly, we know that, bless your dear heart; but don't you be a fool again."

"I? I wish somebody would come along and offer us a cabbage for it —you'd see!"

"A cabbage! Oh, don't name it—it makes my mouth water. Talk of things less trying."

"Boys," said Carl, "*do* these pictures lack merit? Answer me that."

"No!"

"Aren't they of very great and high merit? Answer me that."

"Yes."

"Of such great and high merit that, if an illustrious name were attached to them, they would sell at splendid prices. Isn't it so?"

"Certainly it is. Nobody doubts that."

"But—I'm not joking—*isn't* it so?"

"Why, of course it's so—and *we* are not joking. But what of it? What of it? How does that concern us?"

"In this way, comrades—we'll *attach* an illustrious name to them!"

The lively conversation stopped. The faces were turned inquiringly upon Carl. What sort of riddle might this be? Where was an illustrious name to be borrowed? And who was to borrow it?

Carl sat down, and said:

"Now, I have a perfectly serious thing to propose. I think it is the only way to keep us out of the almshouse, and I believe it to be a perfectly sure way. I base this opinion upon certain multitudinous and long-established facts in human history. I believe my project will make us all rich."

"Rich! You've lost your mind."

"No, I haven't."

"Yes, you have—you've lost your mind. What do you *call* rich?"

"A hundred thousand francs apiece."

"He *has* lost his mind. I knew it."

"Yes, he has. Carl, privation has been too much for you, and—"

"Carl, you want to take a pill and get right to bed."

"Bandage him first—bandage his head, and then—"

"No, bandage his heels; his brains have been settling for weeks—I've noticed it."

"Shut up!" said Millet, with ostensible severity, "and let the boy say his say. Now, then—come out with your project, Carl. What is it?"

"Well, then, by way of preamble I will ask you to note this fact in human history: that the merit of many a great artist has never been acknowledged until after he was starved and dead. This has happened so often that I make bold to found a law upon it. This law: that the merit of *every* great unknown and neglected artist must and will be recognized, and his pictures climb to high prices after his death. My project is this: we must cast lots—one of us must die."

The remark fell so calmly and so unexpectedly that we almost forgot to jump. Then there was a wild chorus of advice again—medical advice—for the help of Carl's brain; but he waited patiently for the hilarity to calm down, then went on again with his project:

"Yes, one of us must die, to save the others—and himself. We will cast lots. The one chosen shall be illustrious, all of us shall be rich. Hold still, now—hold still; don't interrupt—I tell you I know what I am talking about. Here is the idea. During the next three months the one who is to die shall paint with all his might, enlarge his stock all he can —not pictures, *no!* skeleton sketches, studies, parts of studies, fragments of studies, a dozen dabs of the brush on each—meaningless, of course, but *his* with his cipher on them; turn out fifty a day, each to contain some peculiarity or mannerism, easily detectable as his—*they're* the things that sell you know, and are collected at fabulous prices for the world's museums, after the great man is gone; we'll have a ton of them ready—a ton! And all that time the rest of us will be busy supporting the moribund, and working Paris and the dealers—preparations for the coming event, you know; and when everything is hot and just right, we'll spring the death on them and have the notorious funeral. You get the idea?"

"N-o; at least, not qu—"

"Not quite? Don't you see? The man doesn't really die; he changes his name and vanishes; we bury a dummy, and cry over it, with all the world to help. And I—"

But he wasn't allowed to finish. Everybody broke out into a rousing hurrah of applause; and all jumped up and capered about the room and fell on each other's necks in transports of gratitude and joy. For hours we talked over the great plan, without ever feeling hungry; and at last, when all the details had been arranged satisfactorily, we cast lots and Millet was elected—elected to die, as we called it. Then we scraped together those things which one never parts with until he is betting them against future wealth—keepsake trinkets and such like— and these we pawned for enough to furnish us a frugal farewell supper and breakfast, and leave us a few francs over for travel, and a stake of turnips and such for Millet to live on for a few days.

Next morning, early, the three of us cleared out, straightway after breakfast—on foot, of course. Each of us carried a dozen of Millet's small pictures, purposing to market them. Carl struck for Paris, where he would start the work of building up Millet's fame against the coming great day. Claude and I were to separate, and scatter abroad over France.

Now, it will surprise you to know what an easy and comfortable thing we had. I walked two days before I began business. Then I began to sketch a villa in the outskirts of a big town—because I saw the proprietor standing on an upper veranda. He came down to look on—I thought he would. I worked swiftly, intending to keep him interested. Occasionally he fired off a little ejaculation of approbation, and by and by he spoke up with enthusiasm, and said I was a master!

I put down my brush, reached into my satchel, fetched out a Millet, and pointed to the cipher in the corner. I said, proudly:

"I suppose you recognize *that?* Well, he taught me! I should *think* I ought to know my trade!"

The man looked guiltily embarrassed, and was silent. I said, sorrowfully:

"You don't mean to intimate that you don't know the cipher of François Millet!"

Of course he didn't know that cipher; but he was the gratefulest man you ever saw, just the same, for being let out of an uncomfortable place on such easy terms. He said:

"No! Why, it *is* Millet's, sure enough! I don't know what I could have been thinking of. Of course I recognize it now."

Next, he wanted to buy it; but I said that although I wasn't rich I wasn't *that* poor. However, at last, I let him have it for eight hundred francs.

"Eight hundred!"

Yes. Millet would have sold it for a pork-chop. Yes, I got eight hundred francs for that little thing. I wish I could get it back for eighty thousand. But that time's gone by. I made a very nice picture of that man's house, and I wanted to offer it to him for ten francs, but that wouldn't answer, seeing I was the pupil of such a master, so I sold it to him for a hundred. I sent the eight hundred francs straight back to Millet from that town and struck out again next day.

But I didn't walk—no. I rode. I have ridden ever since. I sold one picture every day, and never tried to sell two. I always said to my customer:

"I am a fool to sell a picture of François Millet's at all, for that man is not going to live three months, and when he dies his pictures can't be had for love or money."

I took care to spread that little fact as far as I could, and prepare the world for the event.

I take credit to myself for our plan of selling the pictures—it was mine. I suggested it that last evening when we were laying out our campaign, and all three of us agreed to give it a good fair trial before giving it up for some other. It succeeded with all of us. I walked only two days, Claude walked two—both of us afraid to make Millet celebrated too close to home—but Carl walked only half a day, the bright, conscienceless rascal, and after that he traveled like a duke.

Every now and then we got in with a country editor and started an item around through the press; not an item announcing that a new painter had been discovered, but an item which let on that everybody knew François Millet; not an item praising him in any way, but merely a word concerning the present condition of the "master"—sometimes hopeful, sometimes despondent, but always tinged with fears for the worst. We always marked these paragraphs, and sent the papers to all the people who had bought pictures of us.

Carl was soon in Paris, and he worked things with a high hand. He made friends with the correspondents, and got Millet's condition reported to England and all over the continent, and America, and everywhere.

At the end of six weeks from the start, we three met in Paris and called a halt, and stopped sending back to Millet for additional pictures. The boom was so high, and everything so ripe, that we saw that it would be a mistake not to strike now, right away, without waiting any longer. So we wrote Millet to go to bed and begin to waste away pretty fast, for we should like him to die in ten days if he could get ready.

Then we figured up and found that among us we had sold eighty-five small pictures and studies, and had sixty-nine thousand francs to show for it. Carl had made the last sale and the most brilliant one of all. He sold the "Angelus" for twenty-two hundred francs. How we did glorify him!—not foreseeing that a day was coming by and by when France would struggle to own it and a stranger would capture it for five hundred and fifty thousand, cash.

We had a wind-up champagne supper that night, and next day Claude and I packed up and went off to nurse Millet through his last days and keep busybodies out of the house and send daily bulletins to Carl in Paris for publication in the papers of several continents for the information of a waiting world. The sad end came at last, and Carl was there in time to help in the final mournful rites.

You remember that great funeral, and what a stir it made all over the globe, and how the illustrious of two worlds came to attend it and testify their sorrow. We four—still inseparable—carried the coffin, and would allow none to help. And we were right about that, because it hadn't anything in it but a wax figure, and any other coffin-bearers would have found fault with the weight. Yes, we same old four, who had lovingly shared privation together in the old hard times now gone forever, carried the cof—

"Which four?"

"We four—for Millet helped to carry his own coffin. In disguise, you know. Disguised as a relative—distant relative."

"Astonishing!"

"But true, just the same. Well, you remember how the pictures went up. Money? We didn't know what to do with it. There's a man in Paris to-day who owns seventy Millet pictures. He paid us two million francs for them. And as for the bushels of sketches and studies which Millet shoveled out during the six weeks that we were on the road, well, it would astonish you to know the figure we sell them at nowadays—that is, when we consent to let one go!"

"It is a wonderful history, perfectly wonderful!"

"Yes—it amounts to that."

"Whatever became of Millet?"

"Can you keep a secret?"

"I can."

"Do you remember the man I called your attention to in the dining-room to-day? *That was François Millet.*"

"Great—"

"Scott! Yes. For once they didn't starve a genius to death and then put into other pockets the rewards he should have had himself. *This* songbird was not allowed to pipe out its heart unheard and then be paid with the cold pomp of a big funeral. We looked out for that."

1893

The £1,000,000 Bank-Note

When I was twenty-seven years old, I was a mining-broker's clerk in San Francisco, and an expert in all the details of stock traffic. I was alone in the world, and had nothing to depend upon but my wits and a clean reputation; but these were setting my feet in the road to eventual fortune, and I was content with the prospect.

My time was my own after the afternoon board, Saturdays, and I was accustomed to put it in on a little sail-boat on the bay. One day I ventured too far, and was carried out to sea. Just at nightfall, when hope was about gone, I was picked up by a small brig which was bound for London. It was a long and stormy voyage, and they made me work my passage without pay, as a common sailor. When I stepped ashore in London my clothes were ragged and shabby, and I had only a dollar in my pocket. This money fed and sheltered me twenty-four hours. During the next twenty-four I went without food and shelter.

About ten o'clock on the following morning, seedy and hungry, I was dragging myself along Portland Place, when a child that was passing, towed by a nurse-maid, tossed a luscious big pear—minus one bite—into the gutter. I stopped, of course, and fastened my desiring eye on that muddy treasure. My mouth watered for it, my stomach craved it, my whole being begged for it. But every time I made a move to get it some passing eye detected my purpose, and of course I straightened up then, and looked indifferent, and pretended that I hadn't been thinking about the pear at all. This same thing kept happening and happening, and I couldn't get the pear. I was just getting desperate enough to brave all the shame, and to seize it, when a window behind me was raised, and a gentleman spoke out of it, saying:

"Step in here, please."

I was admitted by a gorgeous flunkey, and shown into a sumptuous room where a couple of elderly gentlemen were sitting. They sent away the servant, and made me sit down. They had just finished their breakfast, and the sight of the remains of it almost overpowered me. I could hardly keep my wits together in the presence of that food, but as I was not asked to sample it, I had to bear my trouble as best I could.

Now, something had been happening there a little before, which I did not know anything about until a good many days afterward, but I will tell you about it now. Those two old brothers had been having a pretty hot argument a couple of days before, and had ended by agreeing to decide it by a bet, which is the English way of settling everything.

You will remember that the Bank of England once issued two notes of a million pounds each, to be used for a special purpose connected with some public transaction with a foreign country. For some reason or other only one of these had been used and canceled; the other still lay in the vaults of the Bank. Well, the brothers, chatting along, happened to get to wondering what might be the fate of a perfectly honest and intelligent stranger who should be turned adrift in London without a friend, and with no money but that million-pound bank-note, and no way to account for his being in possession of it. Brother A said he would starve to death; Brother B said he wouldn't. Brother A said he couldn't offer it at a bank or anywhere else, because he would be arrested on the spot. So they went on disputing till Brother B said he would bet twenty thousand pounds that the man would live thirty days, *anyway*, on that million, and keep out of jail, too. Brother A took him up. Brother B went down to the Bank and bought that note. Just like an Englishman, you see; pluck to the backbone. Then he dictated a letter, which one of his clerks wrote out in a beautiful round hand, and then the two brothers sat at the window a whole day watching for the right man to give it to.

They saw many honest faces go by that were not intelligent enough; many that were intelligent, but not honest enough; many that were both, but the possessors were not poor enough, or, if poor enough, were not strangers. There was always a defect, until I came along; but they agreed that I filled the bill all around; so they elected me unanimously, and there I was now waiting to know why I was called in. They began to ask me questions about myself, and pretty soon they had my story. Finally they told me I would answer their purpose. I said I was sincerely glad, and asked what it was. Then one of them handed me an envelope, and said I would find the explanation inside. I was going to open it, but he said no; take it to my lodgings, and look it over carefully, and not be hasty or rash. I was puzzled, and wanted to discuss the matter a little further, but they didn't; so I took my leave, feeling hurt and insulted to be made the butt of what was apparently some kind of a practical joke, and yet obliged to put up with it, not being in circumstances to resent affronts from rich and strong folk.

I would have picked up the pear now and eaten it before all the world, but it was gone; so I had lost that by this unlucky business, and the thought of it did not soften my feeling toward those men. As soon as I was out of sight of that house I opened my envelope, and saw that it contained money! My opinion of those people changed, I can tell you! I lost not a moment, but shoved note and money into my vest pocket, and broke for the nearest cheap eating-house. Well, how I did eat! When at last I couldn't hold any more, I took out my money and unfolded it, took one glimpse and nearly fainted. Five millions of dollars! Why, it made my head swim.

I must have sat there stunned and blinking at the note as much as a minute before I came rightly to myself again. The first thing I noticed, then, was the landlord. His eye was on the note, and he was petrified. He was worshiping, with all his body and soul, but he looked as if he couldn't stir hand or foot. I took my cue in a moment, and did the only rational thing there was to do. I reached the note toward him, and said, carelessly:

"Give me the change, please."

Then he was restored to his normal condition, and made a thousand apologies for not being able to break the bill, and I couldn't get him to touch it. He wanted to look at it, and keep on looking at it; he couldn't seem to get enough of it to quench the thirst of his eye, but he shrank from touching it as if it had been something too sacred for poor common clay to handle. I said:

"I am sorry if it is an inconvenience, but I must insist. Please change it; I haven't anything else."

But he said that wasn't any matter; he was quite willing to let the trifle stand over till another time. I said I might not be in his neighborhood again for a good while; but he said it was of no consequence, he could wait, and, moreover, I could have anything I wanted, any time I chose, and let the account run as long as I pleased. He said he hoped he wasn't afraid to trust as rich a gentleman as I was, merely because I was of a merry disposition, and chose to play larks on the public in the matter of dress. By this time another customer was entering, and the landlord hinted to me to put the monster out of sight; then he bowed me all the way to the door, and I started straight for that house and those brothers, to correct the mistake which had been made before the police should hunt me up, and help me do it. I was pretty nervous; in fact, pretty badly frightened, though, of course, I was no way in fault; but I knew men well enough to know that when they find they've given a tramp a million-pound bill when they thought it was a one-pounder, they are in a frantic rage against *him* instead of quarreling with their own near-sightedness, as they ought. As I approached the house my excitement began to abate, for all was quiet there, which made me feel pretty sure the blunder was not discovered yet. I rang. The same servant appeared. I asked for those gentlemen.

"They are gone." This in the lofty, cold way of that fellow's tribe.

"Gone? Gone where?"

"On a journey."

"But whereabouts?"

"To the Continent, I think."

"The Continent?"

"Yes, sir."

"Which way—by what route?"

"I can't say, sir."

"When will they be back?"

"In a month, they said."

"A month! Oh, this is awful! Give me *some* sort of idea of how to get a word to them. It's of the last importance."

"I can't, indeed. I've no idea where they've gone, sir."

"Then I must see some member of the family."

"Family's away, too; been abroad months—in Egypt and India, I think."

"Man, there's been an immense mistake made. They'll be back before night. Will you tell them I've been here, and that I will keep coming till it's all made right, and they needn't be afraid?"

"I'll tell them, if they come back, but I am not expecting them. They said you would be here in an hour to make inquiries, but I must tell you it's all right, they'll be here on time and expect you."

So I had to give it up and go away. What a riddle it all was! I was like to lose my mind. They would, be here "on time." What could that mean? Oh the letter would explain, maybe. I had forgotten the letter; I got it out and read it. This is what it said:

You are an intelligent and honest man, as one may see by your face. We conceive you to be poor and a stranger. Enclosed you will find a sum of money. It is lent to you for thirty days, without interest. Report at this house at the end of that time. I have a bet on you. If I win it you shall have any situation that is in my gift—any, that is, that you shall be able to prove yourself familiar with and competent to fill.

No signature, no address, no date.

Well, here was a coil to be in! You are posted on what had preceded all this, but I was not. It was just a deep, dark puzzle to me. I hadn't the least idea what the game was, nor whether harm was meant me or a kindness. I went into a park, and sat down to try to think it out, and to consider what I had best do.

At the end of an hour my reasonings had crystallized into this verdict.

Maybe those men mean me well, maybe they mean me ill; no way to decide that—let it go. They've got a game, or a scheme, or an experiment, of some kind on hand; no way to determine what it is—let it go. There's a bet on me; no way to find out what it is—let it go. That disposes of the indeterminable quantities; the remainder of the matter is tangible, solid, and may be classed and labeled with certainty. If I ask the Bank of England to place this bill to the credit of the man it belongs to, they'll do it, for they know him, although I don't; but they will ask me how I came in possession of it, and if I tell the truth they'll put me in the asylum, naturally, and a lie will land me in jail. The same result would follow if I tried to bank the bill anywhere or to borrow money on it. I have got to carry this immense burden around until those men come back, whether I want to or not. It is useless to me, as useless as a handful of ashes, and yet I must take care of it, and watch over it, while I beg my living. I couldn't *give* it away, if I should try, for neither honest citizen nor highwayman would accept it or meddle with it for anything. Those brothers are safe. Even if I lose their bill, or burn it, they are still safe, because they can stop payment, and the bank will make them whole; but meantime I've got to do a month's suffering without wages or profit—unless I help win that bet, whatever it may be, and get that situation that I am promised. I *should* like to get that; men of their sort have situations in their gift that are worth having.

I got to thinking a good deal about that situation. My hopes began to rise high. Without doubt the salary would be large. It would begin in a month; after that I should be all right. Pretty soon I was feeling first rate. By this time I was tramping the streets again. The sight of a tailor-shop gave me a sharp longing to shed my rags, and to clothe myself decently once more. Could I afford it? No; I had nothing in the world but a million pounds. So I forced myself to go on by. But soon I was drifting back again. The temptation persecuted me cruelly. I must have passed that shop back and forth six times during that manful struggle. At last I gave in; I had to. I asked if they had a misfit suit that had been thrown on their hands. The fellow I spoke to nodded his head toward another fellow, and gave me no answer. I went to the indicated fellow, and he indicated another fellow with *his* head, and no words. I went to him, and he said:

" 'Tend to you presently."

I waited till he was done with what he was at, then he took me into a back room, and overhauled a pile of rejected suits, and selected the rattiest one for me. I put it on. It didn't fit, and wasn't in any way attractive, but it was new, and I was anxious to have it; so I didn't find any fault, but said, with some diffidence:

"It would be an accommodation to me if you could wait some days for the money. I haven't any small change about me."

The fellow worked up a most sarcastic expression of countenance, and said:

"Oh, you haven't? Well, of course, I didn't expect it. I'd only expect gentlemen like you to carry large change."

I was nettled, and said:

"My friend, you shouldn't judge a stranger always by the clothes he wears. I am quite able to pay for this suit; I simply didn't wish to put you to the trouble of changing a large note."

He modified his style a little at that, and said, though still with something of an air:

"I didn't mean any particular harm, but as long as rebukes are going, I might say it wasn't quite your affair to jump to the conclusion that we couldn't change any note that you might happen to be carrying around. On the contrary, we *can*."

I handed the note to him, and said:

"Oh, very well; I apologize."

He received it with a smile, one of those large smiles which go all around over, and have folds in them, and wrinkles, and spirals, and look like the place where you have thrown a brick in a pond; and then in the act of his taking a glimpse of the bill this smile froze solid, and turned yellow, and looked like those wavy, wormy spreads of lava which you find hardened on little levels on the side of Vesuvius. I never before saw a smile caught like that, and perpetuated. The man stood there holding the bill, and looking like that, and the proprietor hustled up to see what was the matter, and said, briskly:

"Well, what's up? what's the trouble? what's wanting?"

I said: "There isn't any trouble. I'm waiting for my change."

"Come, come; get him his change, Tod; get him his change."

Tod retorted: "Get him his change! It's easy to say, sir; but look at the bill yourself."

The proprietor took a look, gave a low, eloquent whistle, then made a dive for the pile of rejected clothing, and began to snatch it this way and that, talking all the time excitedly, and as if to himself:

"Sell an eccentric millionaire such an unspeakable suit as that! Tod's a fool—a born fool. Always doing something like this. Drives every millionaire away from this place, because he can't tell a millionaire from a tramp, and never could. Ah, here's the thing I am after. Please get those things off, sir, and throw them in the fire. Do me the favor to put on this shirt and this suit; it's just the thing, the very thing—plain, rich, modest, and just ducally nobby; made to order for a foreign prince —you may know him, sir, his Serene Highness the Hospodar of Halifax; had to leave it with us and take a mourning-suit because his mother was going to die—which she didn't. But that's all right; we can't always have things the way we—that is, the way they—there! trousers all right, they fit you to a charm, sir; now the waistcoat; aha, right again! now the coat—lord! look at that, now! Perfect—the whole thing! I never saw such a triumph in all my experience."

I expressed my satisfaction.

"Quite right, sir, quite right; it 'll do for a makeshift, I'm bound to say. But wait till you see what we'll get up for you on your own measure. Come, Tod, book and pen; get at it. Length of leg, 32"—and so on. Before I could get in a word he had measured me, and was giving orders for dress-suits, morning suits, shirts, and all sorts of things. When I got a chance I said:

"But, my dear sir, I *can't* give these orders, unless you can wait indefinitely, or change the bill."

"Indefinitely! It's a weak word, sir, a weak word. Eternally—*that's* the word, sir. Tod, rush these things through, and send them to the gentleman's address without any waste of time. Let the minor customers wait. Set down the gentleman's address and—"

"I'm changing my quarters. I will drop in and leave the new address."

"Quite right, sir, quite right. One moment—let me show you out, sir. There—good day, sir, good day."

Well, don't you see what was bound to happen? I drifted naturally into buying whatever I wanted, and asking for change. Within a week I was sumptuously equipped with all needful comforts and luxuries, and was housed in an expensive private hotel in Hanover Square. I took my dinners there, but for breakfast I stuck by Harris's humble feeding-house, where I had got my first meal on my million-pound bill. I was the making of Harris. The fact had gone all abroad that the foreign crank who carried million-pound bills in his vest pocket was the patron saint of the place. That was enough. From being a poor, struggling, little hand-to-mouth enterprise, it had become celebrated, and overcrowded with customers. Harris was so grateful that he forced loans upon me, and would not be denied; and so, pauper as I was, I had money to spend, and was living like the rich and the great. I judged that there was going to be a crash by and by, but I was in now and must swim across or drown. You see there was just that element of impending disaster to give a serious side, a sober side, yes, a tragic side, to a state of things which would otherwise have been purely ridiculous. In the night, in the dark, the tragedy part was always to the front, and always warning, always threatening; and so I moaned and tossed, and sleep was hard to find. But in the cheerful daylight the tragedy element faded out and disappeared, and I walked on air, and was happy to giddiness, to intoxication, you may say.

And it was natural; for I had become one of the notorieties of the metropolis of the world, and it turned my head, not just a little, but a good deal. You could not take up a newspaper, English, Scotch, or Irish, without finding in it one or more references to the "vest-pocket million-pounder" and his latest doings and sayings. At first, in these mentions, I was at the bottom of the personal-gossip column; next, I was listed above the knights, next above the baronets, next above the barons, and so on, and so on, climbing steadily, as my notoriety augmented, until I reached the highest altitude possible, and there I remained, taking precedence of all dukes not royal, and of all ecclesiastics except the primate of all England. But mind, this was not fame; as yet I had achieved only notoriety. Then came the climaxing stroke the accolade, so to speak—which in a single instant transmuted the perishable dross of notoriety into the enduring gold of fame: *Punch* caricatured me! Yes, I was a made man now; my place was established. I might be joked about still, but reverently, not hilariously, not rudely; I could be smiled at, but not laughed at. The time for that had gone by. *Punch* pictured me all a-flutter with rags, dickering with a beef-eater for the Tower of London. Well, you can imagine how it was with a young fellow who had never been taken notice of before, and now all of a sudden couldn't say a thing that wasn't taken up and repeated everywhere; couldn't stir abroad without constantly overhearing the remark flying from lip to lip, "There he goes; that's him!" couldn't take his breakfast without a crowd to look on; couldn't appear in an opera-box without concentrating there the fire of a thousand lorgnettes. Why, I just swam in glory all day long—that is the amount of it.

You know, I even kept my old suit of rags, and every now and then appeared in them, so as to have the old pleasure of buying trifles, and being insulted, and then shooting the scoffer dead with the million-pound bill. But I couldn't keep that up. The illustrated papers made the outfit so familiar that when I went out in it I was at once recognized and followed by a crowd, and if I attempted a purchase the man would offer me his whole shop on credit before I could pull my note on him.

About the tenth day of my fame I went to fulfil my duty to my flag by paying my respects to the American minister. He received me with the enthusiasm proper in my case, upbraided me for being so tardy in my duty, and said that there was only one way to get his forgiveness, and that was to take the seat at his dinner-party that night made vacant by the illness of one of his guests. I said I would, and we got to talking. It turned out that he and my father had been schoolmates in boyhood, Yale students together later, and always warm friends up to my father's death. So then he required me to put in at his house all the odd time I might have to spare, and I was very willing, of course.

In fact, I was more than willing; I was glad. When the crash should come, he might somehow be able to save me from total destruction; I didn't know how, but he might think of a way, maybe. I couldn't venture to unbosom myself to him at this late date, a thing which I would have been quick to do in the beginning of this awful career of mine in London. No, I couldn't venture it now; I was in too deep; that is, too deep for me to be risking revelations to so new a friend, though not clear beyond my depth, as I looked at it. Because, you see, with all my borrowing, I was carefully keeping within my means—I mean within my salary. Of course, I couldn't *know* what my salary was going to be, but I had a good enough basis for an estimate in the fact that if I won the bet I was to have *choice* of any situation in that rich old gentleman's gift provided I was competent—and I should certainly prove competent; I hadn't any doubt about that. And as to the bet, I wasn't worrying about that; I had always been lucky. Now my estimate of the salary was six hundred to a thousand a year; say, six hundred for the first year, and so on up year by year, till I struck the upper figure by proved merit. At present I was only in debt for my first year's salary. Everybody had been trying to lend me money, but I had fought off the most of them on one pretext or another; so this indebtedness represented only £300 borrowed money, the other £300 represented my keep and my purchases. I believed my second year's salary would carry me through the rest of the month if I went on being cautious and economical, and I intended to look sharply out for that. My month ended, my employer back from his journey, I should be all right once more, for I should at once divide the two years' salary among my creditors by assignment, and get right down to my work.

It was a lovely dinner-party of fourteen. The Duke and Duchess of Shoreditch, and their daughter the Lady Anne-Grace-Eleanor-Celeste-

and-so-forth-and-so-forth-de-Bohun, the Earl and Countess of Newgate, Viscount Cheapside, Lord and Lady Blatherskite, some untitled people of both sexes, the minister and his wife and daughter, and his daughter's visiting friend, an English girl of twenty-two, named Portia Langham, whom I fell in love with in two minutes, and she with me—I could see it without glasses. There was still another guest, an American—but I am a little ahead of my story. While the people were still in the drawing-room, whetting up for dinner, and coldly inspecting the late comers, the servant announced:

"Mr. Lloyd Hastings."

The moment the usual civilities were over, Hastings caught sight of me, and came straight with cordially outstretched hand; then stopped short when about to shake, and said, with an embarrassed look:

"I beg your pardon, sir, I thought I knew you."

"Why, you do know me, old fellow."

"No. Are *you* the—the—"

"Vest-pocket monster? I am, indeed. Don't be afraid to call me by my nickname; I'm used to it."

"Well, well, well, this is a surprise. Once or twice I've seen your own name coupled with the nickname, but it never occurred to me that *you* could be the Henry Adams referred to. Why, it isn't six months since you were clerking away for Blake Hopkins in Frisco on a salary, and sitting up nights on an extra allowance, helping me arrange and verify the Gould and Curry Extension papers and statistics. The idea of your being in London, and a vast millionaire, and a colossal celebrity! Why, it's the Arabian Nights come again. Man, I can't take it in at all; can't realize it; give me time to settle the whirl in my head."

"The fact is, Lloyd, you are no worse off than I am. I can't realize it myself."

"Dear me, it *is* stunning, now isn't it? Why, it's just three months to-day since we went to the Miners' restaurant—"

"No; the What Cheer."

"Right, it *was* the What Cheer; went there at two in the morning, and had a chop and coffee after a hard six-hours grind over those Extension papers, and I tried to persuade you to come to London with me, and offered to get leave of absence for you and pay all your expenses, and give you something over if I succeeded in making the sale; and you would not listen to me, said I wouldn't succeed, and you couldn't afford to lose the run of business and be no end of time getting the hang of things again when you got back home. And yet here you are. How odd it all is! How did you happen to come, and whatever *did* give you this incredible start?"

"Oh, just an accident. It's a long story—a romance, a body may say. I'll tell you all about it, but not now."

"When?"

"The end of this month."

"That's more than a fortnight yet. It's too much of a strain on a person's curiosity. Make it a week."

"I can't. You'll know why, by and by. But how's the trade getting along?"

His cheerfulness vanished like a breath, and he said with a sigh:

"You were a true prophet, Hal, a true prophet. I wish I hadn't come. I don't want to talk about it."

"But you must. You must come and stop with me to-night, when we leave here, and tell me all about it."

"Oh, may I? Are you in earnest?" and the water showed in his eyes.

"Yes; I want to hear the whole story, every word."

"I'm so grateful! Just to find a human interest once more, in some voice and in some eye, in me and affairs of mine, after what I've been through here—lord! I could go down on my knees for it!"

He gripped my hand hard, and braced up, and was all right and lively after that for the dinner—which didn't come off. No; the usual thing happened, the thing that is always happening under that vicious and aggravating English system—the matter of precedence couldn't be settled, and so there was no dinner. Englishmen always eat dinner before they go out to dinner, because *they* know the risks they are running; but nobody ever warns the stranger, and so he walks placidly into the trap. Of course, nobody was hurt this time, because we had all been to dinner, none of us being novices excepting Hastings, and he having been informed by the minister at the time that he invited him that in deference to the English custom he had not provided any dinner. Everybody took a lady and processioned down to the dining-room because it is usual to go through the motions; but there the dispute began. The Duke of Shoreditch wanted to take precedence, and sit at the head of the table, holding that he outranked a minister who represented merely a nation and not a monarch; but I stood for my rights, and refused to yield. In the gossip column I ranked all dukes not royal, and said so, and claimed precedence of this one. It couldn't be settled, of course, struggle as we might and did, he finally (and injudiciously) trying to play birth and antiquity, and I "seeing" his Conqueror and "raising" him with Adam, whose direct posterity I was, as shown by my name, while *he* was of a collateral branch, as shown by *his*, and by his recent Norman origin; so we all processioned back to the drawing-room again and had a perpendicular lunch—plate of sardines and a strawberry, and you group yourself and stand up and eat it. Here the religion of precedence is not so strenuous; the two persons of highest rank chuck up a shilling, the one that wins has first go at his strawberry, and the loser gets the shilling. The next two chuck up, then the next two, and so on. After refreshment, tables were brought, and we all played cribbage, sixpence a game. The English never play any game for amusement. If they can't make something or lose something—they don't care which—they won't play.

We had a lovely time; certainly two of us had, Miss Langham and I. I was so bewitched with her that I couldn't count my hands if they went above a double sequence; and when I struck home I never discovered it, and started up the outside row again, and would have lost the game every time, only the girl did the same, she being in just my condition, you see; and consequently neither of us ever got out, or cared to wonder why we didn't; we only just knew we were happy, and didn't wish to know anything else, and didn't want to be interrupted. And I *told* her—I did, indeed—told her I loved her; and she—well, she blushed till her hair turned red, but she liked it; she *said* she did. Oh, there was never such an evening! Every time I pegged I put on a postscript; every time she pegged she acknowledged receipt of it, counting the hands the same. Why, I couldn't even say "Two for his heels" without adding "*My*, how sweet you do look!" and she would say, "Fifteen two, fifteen four, fifteen six, and a pair are eight, and eight are sixteen— *do* you think so?"—peeping out aslant from under her lashes, you know, so sweet and cunning. Oh, it was just *too*-too!

Well, I was perfectly honest and square with her; told her I hadn't a cent in the world but just the million-pound note she'd heard so much talk about, and *it* didn't belong to me, and that started her curiosity; and then I talked low, and told her the whole history right from the start, and it nearly killed her laughing. What in the nation she could find to laugh about I couldn't see, but there it was; every half-minute some new detail would fetch her, and I would have to stop as much as a minute and a half to give her a chance to settle down again. Why, she laughed herself lame—she did, indeed; I never saw anything like it. I mean I never saw a painful story—a story of a person's troubles and worries and fears—produce just *that* kind of effect before. So I loved her all the more, seeing she could be so cheerful when there wasn't anything to be cheerful about; for I might soon need that kind of wife, you know, the way things looked. Of course, I told her we should have to wait a couple of years, till I could catch up on my salary; but she didn't mind that, only she hoped I would be as careful as possible in the matter of expenses, and not let them run the least risk of trenching on our third year's pay. Then she began to get a little worried, and wondered if we were making any mistake, and starting the salary on a higher figure for the first year than I would get. This was good sense, and it made me feel a little less confident than I had been feeling before; but it gave me a good business idea, and I brought it frankly out.

"Portia, dear, would you mind going with me that day, when I confront those old gentlemen?"

She shrank a little, but said:

"N-o; if my being with you would help hearten you. But—would it be quite proper, do you think?"

"No, I don't know that it would—in fact, I'm afraid it wouldn't; but, you see, there's so *much* dependent upon it that—"

"Then I'll go anyway, proper or improper," she said, with a beautiful and generous enthusiasm. "Oh, I shall be so happy to think I'm helping!"

"Helping, dear? Why, you'll be doing it all. You're so beautiful and so lovely and so winning, that with you there I can pile our salary up till I break those good old fellows, and they'll never have the heart to struggle."

Sho! you should have seen the rich blood mount, and her happy eyes shine!

"You wicked flatterer! There isn't a word of truth in what you say, but still I'll go with you. Maybe it will teach you not to expect other people to look with your eyes."

Were my doubts dissipated? Was my confidence restored? You may judge by this fact: privately I raised my salary to twelve hundred the first year on the spot. But I didn't tell her: I saved it for a surprise.

All the way home I was in the clouds, Hastings talking, I not hearing a word. When he and I entered my parlor, he brought me to myself with his fervent appreciations of my manifold comforts and luxuries.

"Let me just stand here a little and look my fill. Dear me! it's a palace —it's just a palace! And in it everything a body *could* desire, including cozy coal fire and supper standing ready. Henry, it doesn't merely make me realize how rich you are; it makes me realize, to the bone, to the marrow, how poor I am—how poor I am, and how miserable, how defeated, routed, annihilated!"

Plague take it! this language gave me the cold shudders. It scared me broad awake, and made me comprehend that I was standing on a half-inch crust, with a crater underneath. *I* didn't know I had been dreaming—that is, I hadn't been allowing myself to know it for a while back; but *now*—oh, dear! Deep in debt, not a cent in the world, a lovely girl's happiness or woe in my hands, and nothing in front of me but a salary which might never—oh, *would* never—materialize! Oh, oh, oh! I am ruined past hope! nothing can save me!

"Henry, the mere unconsidered drippings of your daily income would—"

"Oh, my daily income! Here, down with this hot Scotch, and cheer up your soul. Here's with you! Or, no—you're hungry; sit down and—"

"Not a bite for me; I'm past it. I can't eat, these days; but I'll drink with you till I drop. Come!"

"Barrel for barrel, I'm with you! Ready? Here we go! Now, then, Lloyd, unreel your story while I brew."

"Unreel it? What, again?"

"Again? What do you mean by that?"

"Why, I mean do you want to hear it *over* again?"

"Do I want to hear it *over* again? This *is* a puzzler. Wait; don't take any more of that liquid. You don't need it."

"Look here, Henry, you alarm me. Didn't I tell you the whole story on the way here?"

"You?"

"Yes, I."

"I'll be hanged if I heard a word of it."

"Henry, this is a serious thing. It troubles me. What did you take up yonder at the minister's?"

Then it all flashed on me, and I owned up like a man.

"I took the dearest girl in this world—prisoner!"

So then he came with a rush, and we shook, and shook, and shook till our hands ached; and he didn't blame me for not having heard a word of a story which had lasted while we walked three miles. He just sat down then, like the patient, good fellow he was, and told it all over again. Synopsized, it amounted to this: He had come to England with what he thought was a grand opportunity; he had an "option" to sell the Gould and Curry Extension for the "locators" of it, and keep all he could get over a million dollars. He had worked hard, had pulled every wire he knew of, had left no honest expedient untried, had spent nearly all the money he had in the world, had not been able to get a solitary capitalist to listen to him, and his option would run out at the end of the month. In a word, he was ruined. Then he jumped up and cried out:

"Henry, you can save me! You can save me, and you're the only man in the universe that can. Will you do it? *Won't* you do it?"

"Tell me how. Speak out, my boy."

"Give me a million and my passage home for my 'option'! Don't, *don't* refuse!"

I was in a kind of agony. I was right on the point of coming out with the words, "Lloyd, I'm a pauper myself—absolutely penniless, and in *debt*." But a white-hot idea came flaming through my head, and I gripped my jaws together, and calmed myself down till I was as cold as a capitalist. Then I said, in a commercial and self-possessed way:

"I will save you, Lloyd—"

"Then I'm already saved! God be merciful to you forever! If ever I—"

"Let me finish, Lloyd. I will save you, but not in that way; for that would not be fair to you, after your hard work, and the risks you've run. I don't need to buy mines; I can keep my capital moving, in a commercial center like London, without that; it's what I'm at, all the time; but here is what I'll do. I know all about that mine, of course; I know its immense value, and can swear to it if anybody wishes it. You shall sell out inside of the fortnight for three millions cash, using my name freely, and we'll divide, share and share alike."

Do you know, he would have danced the furniture to kindling-wood in his insane joy, and broken everything on the place, if I hadn't tripped him up and tied him.

Then he lay there, perfectly happy, saying:

"I may use your name! Your name—think of it! Man, they'll flock in droves, these rich Londoners; they'll *fight* for that stock! I'm a made man, I'm a made man forever, and I'll never forget you as long as I live!"

In less than twenty-four hours London was abuzz! I hadn't anything to do, day after day, but sit at home, and say to all comers:

"Yes; I told him to refer to me. I know the man, and I know the mine. His character is above reproach, and the mine is worth far more than he asks for it."

Meantime I spent all my evenings at the minister's with Portia. I didn't say a word to her about the mine; I saved it for a surprise. We talked salary; never anything but salary and love; sometimes love, sometimes salary, sometimes love and salary together. And my! the interest the minister's wife and daughter took in our little affair, and the endless ingenuities they invented to save us from interruption, and to keep the minister in the dark and unsuspicious—well, it was just lovely of them!

When the month was up at last, I had a million dollars to my credit in the London and County Bank, and Hastings was fixed in the same way. Dressed at my level best, I drove by the house in Portland Place, judged by the look of things that my birds were home again, went on toward the minister's and got my precious, and we started back, talking salary with all our might. She was so excited and anxious that it made her just intolerably beautiful. I said:

"Dearie, the way you're looking it's a crime to strike for a salary a single penny under three thousand a year."

"Henry, Henry, you'll ruin us!"

"Don't you be afraid. Just keep up those looks and trust to me. It 'll all come out right."

So, as it turned out, I had to keep bolstering up *her* courage all the way. She kept pleading with me, and saying:

"Oh, please remember that if we ask for too much we may get no salary at all; and then what will become of us, with no way in the world to earn our living?"

We were ushered in by that same servant, and there they were, the two old gentlemen. Of course, they were surprised to see that wonderful creature with me, but I said:

"It's all right, gentlemen; she is my future stay and helpmate."

And I introduced them to her, and called them by name. It didn't surprise them; they knew I would know enough to consult the directory. They seated us, and were very polite to me, and very solicitous to relieve her from embarrassment, and put her as much at her ease as they could. Then I said:

"Gentlemen, I am ready to report."

"We are glad to hear it," said *my* man, "for now we can decide the bet which my brother Abel and I made. If you have won for me, you shall have any situation in my gift. Have you the million-pound note?"

"Here it is, sir," and I handed it to him.

"I've won!" he shouted, and slapped Abel on the back. "*Now* what do you say, brother?"

"I say he *did* survive, and I've lost twenty thousand pounds. I never would have believed it."

"I've a further report to make," I said, "and a pretty long one. I want you to let me come soon, and detail my whole month's history; and I promise you it's worth hearing. Meantime, take a look at that."

"What, man! Certificate of deposit for £200,000. Is it yours?"

"Mine. I earned it by thirty days' judicious use of that little loan you let me have. And the only use I made of it was to buy trifles and offer the bill in change."

"Come, this is astonishing! It's incredible, man!"

"Never mind, I'll prove it. Don't take my word unsupported."

But now Portia's turn was come to be surprised. Her eyes were spread wide, and she said:

"Henry, is that really your money? Have you been fibbing to me?"

"I have, indeed, dearie. But you'll forgive me, I know."

She put up an arch pout, and said:

"Don't you be so sure. You are a naughty thing to deceive me so!"

"Oh, you'll get over it, sweetheart, you'll get over it; it was only fun, you know. Come, let's be going."

"But wait, wait! The situation, you know. I want to give you the situation," said my man.

"Well," I said, "I'm just as grateful as I can be, but really I don't want one."

"But you can have the very choicest one in my gift."

"Thanks again, with all my heart; but I don't even want *that* one."

"Henry, I'm ashamed of you. You don't half thank the good gentleman. May I do it for you?"

"Indeed, you shall, dear, if you can improve it. Let us see you try."

She walked to my man, got up in his lap, put her arm round his neck, and kissed him right on the mouth. Then the two old gentlemen shouted with laughter, but I was dumfounded, just petrified, as you may say. Portia said:

"Papa, he has said you haven't a situation in your gift that he'd take; and I feel just as hurt as—"

"My darling, is that your papa?"

"Yes; he's my step-papa, and the dearest one that ever was. You understand now, don't you, why I was able to laugh when you told me at the minister's, not knowing my relationships, what trouble and worry papa's and Uncle Abel's scheme was giving you?"

Of course, I spoke right up now, without any fooling, and went straight to the point.

"Oh, my dearest dear sir, I want to take back what I said. You *have* got a situation open that I want."

"Name it."

"Son-in-law."

"Well, well, well! But you know, if you haven't ever served in that capacity, you, of course, can't furnish recommendations of a sort to satisfy the conditions of the contract, and so—"

"Try me—oh, do, I beg of you! Only just try me thirty or forty years, and if—"

"Oh, well, all right; it's but a little thing to ask, take her along."

Happy, we two? There are not words enough in the unabridged to describe it. And when London got the whole history, a day or two later, of my month's adventures with that bank-note, and how they ended, did London talk, and have a good time? Yes.

My Portia's papa took that friendly and hospitable bill back to the Bank of England and cashed it; then the Bank canceled it and made him a present of it, and he gave it to us at our wedding, and it has always hung in its frame in the sacredest place in our home ever since. For it gave me my Portia. But for it I could not have remained in London, would not have appeared at the minister's, never should have met her. And so I always say, "Yes, it's a million-pounder, as you see; but it never made but one purchase in its life, and *then* got the article for only about a tenth part of its value."

1893

Cecil Rhodes and the Shark

The shark is the swiftest fish that swims. The speed of the fastest steamer afloat is poor compared to his. And he is a great gad-about, and roams far and wide in the oceans, and visits the shores of all of them, ultimately, in the course of his restless excursions. I have a tale to tell now, which has not as yet been in print. In 1870 a young stranger arrived in Sydney, and set about finding something to do; but he knew no one, and brought no recommendations, and the result was that he got no employment. He had aimed high, at first, but as time and his money wasted away he grew less and less exacting, until at last he was willing to serve in the humblest capacities if so he might get bread and shelter. But luck was still against him; he could find no opening of any sort. Finally his money was all gone. He walked the streets all day, thinking; he walked them all night, thinking, thinking, and growing hungrier and hungrier. At dawn he found himself well away from the town and drifting aimlessly along the harbor shore. As he was passing by a nodding shark-fisher the man looked up and said:

"Say, young fellow, take my line a spell, and change my luck for me."

"How do you know I won't make it worse?"

"Because you can't. It has been at its worst all night. If you can't change it, no harm's done; if you do change it, it's for the better, of course. Come."

"All right, what will you give?"

"I'll give you the shark, if you catch one."

"And I will eat it, bones and all. Give me the line."

"Here you are. I will get away, now, for a while, so that my luck won't spoil yours; for many and many a time I've noticed that if—there, pull in, pull in, man, you've got a bite! *I* knew how it would be. Why, I knew you for a born son of luck the minute I saw you. All right—he's landed."

It was an unusually large shark—"a full nineteen-footer," the fisherman said, as he laid the creature open with his knife.

"Now you rob him, young man, while I step to my hamper for a fresh bait. There's generally something in them worth going for. You've changed my luck, you see. But, my goodness, I hope you haven't changed your own."

"Oh, it wouldn't matter; don't worry about that. Get your bait. I'll rob him."

When the fisherman got back the young man had just finished washing his hands in the bay and was starting away.

"What! you are not going?"

"Yes. Good-by."

"But what about your shark?"

"The shark? Why, what use is he to me?"

"What *use* is he? I like that. Don't you know that we can go and report him to Government, and you'll get a clean solid eighty shillings bounty? Hard cash, you know. What do you think about it *now?*"

"Oh, well, you can collect it."

"And *keep* it? Is that what you mean?"

"Yes."

"Well, this is odd. You're one of those sort they call eccentrics, I judge. The saying is, you mustn't judge a man by his clothes, and I'm believing it now. Why yours are looking just ratty, don't you know; and yet you must be rich."

"I am."

The young man walked slowly back to the town, deeply musing as he went. He halted a moment in front of the best restaurant, then glanced at his clothes and passed on, and got his breakfast at a "stand-up." There was a good deal of it, and it cost five shillings. He tendered a sovereign, got his change, glanced at his silver, muttered to himself, "There isn't enough to buy clothes with," and went his way.

At half past nine the richest wool-broker in Sydney was sitting in his morning-room at home, settling his breakfast with the morning paper. A servant put his head in and said:

"There's a sundowner at the door wants to see you, sir."

"What do you bring that kind of a message here for? Send him about his business."

"He won't go, sir. I've tried."

"He won't go? That's—why, that's unusual. He's one of two things, then: he's a remarkable person, or he's crazy. Is he crazy?"

"No, sir. He don't look it."

"Then he's remarkable. What does he say he wants?"

"He won't tell, sir; only says it's very important."

"And won't go. Does he *say* he won't go?"

"Says he'll stand there till he sees you, sir, if it's all day."

"And yet isn't crazy. Show him up."

The sundowner was shown in. The broker said to himself, "No, he's not crazy; that is easy to see; so he must be the other thing."

Then aloud, "Well, my good fellow, be quick about it; don't waste any words; what is it you want?"

"I want to borrow a hundred thousand pounds."

"Scott! (It's a mistake; he *is* crazy. . . . No—he *can't* be—not with that eye.) Why, you take my breath away. Come, who *are* you?"

"Nobody that you know."

"What is your name?"

"Cecil Rhodes."

"No, I don't remember hearing the name before. Now then—just for curiosity's sake—what has sent you to me on this extraordinary errand?"

"The intention to make a hundred thousand pounds for you and as much for myself within the next sixty days."

"Well, well, well. It is the most extraordinary idea that I—sit *down*—you interest me. And somehow you—well, you fascinate me, I think that that is about the word. And it isn't your proposition—no, that doesn't fascinate me; it's something else, I don't quite know what; something that's born in you and oozes out of you, I suppose. Now then—just for curiosity's sake again, nothing more: as I understand it, it is your desire to bor—"

"I said *intention*."

"Pardon, so you did. I thought it was an unheedful use of the word—an unheedful valuing of its strength, you know."

"I knew its strength."

"Well, I must say—but look here, let me walk the floor a little, my mind is getting into a sort of whirl, though *you* don't seem disturbed any. (Plainly this young fellow isn't crazy; but as to his being remarkable—well, really he amounts to that, and something over.) Now then, I believe I am beyond the reach of further astonishment. Strike, and spare not. What is your scheme?"

"To buy the wool crop—deliverable in sixty days."

"What, the *whole* of it?"

"The whole of it."

"No, I was not quite out of the reach of surprises, after all. Why, how you talk. Do you know what our crop is going to foot up?"

"Two and a half million sterling—maybe a little more."

"Well, you've got your statistics right, anyway. Now then, do you know what the margins would foot up, to buy it at sixty days?"

"The hundred thousand pounds I came here to get."

"Right, once more. Well, dear me, just to see what would happen, I wish you had the money. And if you had it, what would you do with it?"

"I shall make two hundred thousand pounds out of it in sixty days."

"You mean, of course, that you *might* make it if—"

"I said, 'shall.'"

"Yes, by George, you *did* say 'shall'! You are the most definite devil I ever saw, in the matter of language. Dear, dear, dear, look here! Definite speech means clarity of mind. Upon my word I believe you've got what you believe to be a rational *reason* for venturing into this house, an entire stranger, on this wild scheme of buying the wool crop of an entire colony on speculation. Bring it out—I am prepared—acclimatized, if I may use the word. *Why* would you buy the crop, and *why* would you make that sum out of it? That is to say, what makes you think you—"

"I don't think—I know."

"Definite again. *How* do you know?"

"Because France has declared war against Germany, and wool has gone up fourteen per cent. in London and is still rising."

"Oh, in-deed? *Now* then, I've *got* you! Such a thunderbolt as you have just let fly ought to have made me jump out of my chair, but it didn't stir me the least little bit, you see. And for a very simple reason: I have read the morning paper. You can look at it if you want to. The fastest ship in the service arrived at eleven o'clock last night, fifty days out from London. All her news is printed here. There are no war-clouds anywhere; and as for wool, why, it is the low-spiritedest commodity in the English market. It is your turn to jump, now. . . . Well, why don't you jump? Why do you sit there in that placid fashion, when—"

"Because I have later news."

"Later news? Oh, come—later news than fifty days, brought steaming hot from London by the—"

"My news is only ten days old."

"Oh, Mun-*chausen*, hear the maniac talk! Where did you get it?"

"Got it out of a shark."

"Oh, oh, oh, this is *too* much! Front! call the police—bring the gun—raise the town! All the asylums in Christendom have broken loose in the single person of—"

"Sit down! And collect yourself. Where is the use in getting excited? Am I excited? There is nothing to get excited *about*. When I make a statement which I cannot prove, it will be time enough for you to begin to offer hospitality to damaging fancies about me and my sanity."

"Oh, a thousand thousand pardons! I ought to be ashamed of myself, and I *am* ashamed of myself for thinking that a little bit of a circumstance like sending a shark to England to fetch back a market report—"

"What does your middle initial stand for, sir?"

"Andrew. What are you writing?"

"Wait a moment. Proof about the shark—and another matter. Only ten lines. There—now it is done. Sign it."

"Many thanks—many. Let me see; it says—it says—oh, come, this is *interesting!* Why—why—look here! prove what you say here, and I'll put up the money, and double as much, if necessary, and divide the winnings with you, half and half. There, now—I've signed; make your promise good if you can. Show me a copy of the London *Times* only ten days old."

"Here it is—and with it these buttons and a memorandum-book that belonged to the man the shark swallowed. Swallowed him in the Thames, without a doubt; for you will notice that the last entry in the book is dated 'London,' and is of the same date as the *Times,* and says ' Per consequenz der Kriegserklärung, reise ich heute nach Deutschland ab, auf daß ich mein Leben auf dem Altar meines Landes legen mag ' — as clean native German as anybody can put upon paper, and means that in consequence of the declaration of war, this loyal soul is leaving for home *to-day,* to fight. And he did leave, too, but the shark had him before the day was done, poor fellow."

"And a pity, too. But there are times for mourning, and we will attend to this case further on; other matters are pressing, now. I will go down and set the machinery in motion in a quiet way and buy the crop. It will cheer the drooping spirits of the boys, in a transitory way. Everything is transitory in this world. Sixty days hence, when they are called to deliver the goods, they will think they've been struck by lightning. But there is a time for mourning, and we will attend to that case along with the other one. Come along, I'll take you to my tailor. What did you say your name is?"

"Cecil Rhodes."

"It is hard to remember. However, I think you will make it easier by and by, if you live. There are three kinds of people—Commonplace Men, Remarkable Men, and Lunatics. I'll classify you with the Remarkables, and take the chances."

The deal went through, and secured to the young stranger the first fortune he ever pocketed.

From FOLLOWING THE EQUATOR, 1897

The Joke That Made Ed's Fortune

Let us be thankful for the fools. But for them the rest of us could not succeed.

—Pudd'nhead Wilson's New Calendar

A few years before the outbreak of the Civil War it began to appear that Memphis, Tennessee, was going to be a great tobacco *entrepôt*—the wise could see the signs of it. At that time Memphis had a wharfboat, of course. There was a paved sloping wharf, for the accommodation of freight, but the steamers landed on the outside of the wharfboat, and all loading and unloading was done across it, between steamer and shore. A number of wharfboat clerks were needed, and part of the time, every day, they were very busy, and part of the time tediously idle. They were boiling over with youth and spirits, and they had to make the intervals of idleness endurable in some way; and as a rule, they did it by contriving practical jokes and playing them upon each other.

The favorite butt for the jokes was Ed Jackson, because he played none himself, and was easy game for other people's—for he always believed whatever was told him.

One day he told the others his scheme for his holiday. He was not going fishing or hunting this time—no, he had thought out a better plan. Out of his forty dollars a month he had saved enough for his purpose, in an economical way, and he was going to have a look at New York.

It was a great and surprising idea. It meant travel—immense travel—in those days it meant seeing the world; it was the equivalent of a voyage around it in ours. At first the other youths thought his mind was affected, but when they found that he was in earnest, the next thing to be thought of was, what sort of opportunity this venture might afford for a practical joke.

The young men studied over the matter, then held a secret consultation and made a plan. The idea was, that one of the conspirators should offer Ed a letter of introduction to Commodore Vanderbilt, and trick him into delivering it. It would be easy to do this. But what would Ed do when he got back to Memphis? That was a serious matter. He was good-hearted, and had always taken the jokes patiently; but they had been jokes which did not humiliate him, did not bring him to shame; whereas, this would be a cruel one in that way, and to play it was to meddle with fire; for with all his good nature, Ed was a Southerner— and the English of that was, that when he came back he would kill as many of the conspirators as he could before falling himself. However, the chances must be taken—it wouldn't do to waste such a joke as that.

So the letter was prepared with great care and elaboration. It was signed Alfred Fairchild, and was written in an easy and friendly spirit. It stated that the bearer was the bosom friend of the writer's son, and was of good parts and sterling character, and it begged the Commodore to be kind to the young stranger for the writer's sake. It went on to say, "You may have forgotten me, in this long stretch of time, but you will easily call me back out of your boyhood memories when I remind you of how we robbed old Stevenson's orchard that night; and how, while he was chasing down the road after us, we cut across the field and doubled back and sold his own apples to his own cook for a hatful of doughnuts; and the time that we—" and so forth and so on, bringing in names of imaginary comrades, and detailing all sorts of wild and absurd and, of course, wholly imaginary school-boy pranks and adventures, but putting them into lively and telling shape.

With all gravity Ed was asked if he would like to have a letter to

Commodore Vanderbilt, the great millionaire. It was expected that the question would astonish Ed, and it did.

"What? Do *you* know that extraordinary man?"

"No; but my father does. They were schoolboys together. And if you like, I'll write and ask father. I know he'll be glad to give it to you for my sake."

Ed could not find words capable of expressing his gratitude and delight. The three days passed, and the letter was put into his hands. He started on his trip, still pouring out his thanks while he shook good-by all around. And when he was out of sight his comrades let fly their laughter in a storm of happy satisfaction—and then quieted down, and were less happy, less satisfied. For the old doubts as to the wisdom of this deception began to intrude again.

Arrived in New York, Ed found his way to Commodore Vanderbilt's business quarters, and was ushered into a large anteroom, where a score of people were patiently awaiting their turn for a two-minute interview with the millionaire in his private office. A servant asked for Ed's card, and got the letter instead. Ed was sent for a moment later, and found Mr. Vanderbilt alone, with the letter—open—in his hand.

"Pray sit down, Mr.—er—"

"Jackson."

"Ah—sit down, Mr. Jackson. By the opening sentences it seems to be a letter from an old friend. Allow me—I will run my eye through it. He says—he says—why, who *is* it?" He turned the sheet and found the signature. "Alfred Fairchild—h'm—Fairchild—I don't recall the name. But that is nothing—a thousand names have gone from me. He says—he says—h'm—h'm—oh, dear, but it's good! Oh, it's rare! I don't *quite* remember it, but I *seem* to—it 'll all come back to me presently. He says—he says—h'm—h'm—oh, but that was a game! Oh, spl-endid! How it carries me back! It's all dim, of course—it's a long time ago—and the names —*some* of the names are wavery and indistinct—but sho', I know it happened—I can *feel* it! and lord, how it warms my heart, and brings back my lost youth! Well, well, well, I've got to come back into this workaday world now—business presses and people are waiting—I'll keep the rest for bed to-night, and live my youth over again. And you'll thank Fairchild for me when you see him—I used to call him Alf, I think—and you'll give him my gratitude for what this letter has done for the tired spirit of a hard-worked man; and tell him there isn't anything that I can do for him or any friend of his that I won't do. And as for you, my lad, you are my guest; you can't stop at any hotel in New York. Sit where you are a little while, till I get through with these people, then we'll go home. I'll take care of *you*, my boy—make yourself easy as to that."

Ed stayed a week, and had an immense time—and never suspected that the Commodore's shrewd eyes were on him, and that he was daily being weighed and measured and analyzed and tried and tested.

Yes, he had an immense time; and never wrote home, but saved it all up to tell when he should get back. Twice, with proper modesty and decency, he proposed to end his visit, but the Commodore said, "No—wait; leave it to me; I'll tell you when to go."

In those days the Commodore was making some of those vast combinations of his—consolidations of warring odds and ends of railroads into harmonious systems, and concentrations of floating and rudderless commerce in effective centers—and among other things his far-seeing eye had detected the convergence of that huge tobacco-commerce, already spoken of, toward Memphis, and he had resolved to set his grasp upon it and make it his own.

The week came to an end. Then the Commodore said:

"Now you can start home. But first we will have some more talk about that tobacco matter. I know you now. I know your abilities as well as you know them yourself—perhaps better. You understand that tobacco matter; you understand that I am going to take possession of it, and you also understand the plans which I have matured for doing it. What I want is a man who knows my mind, and is qualified to represent me in Memphis, and be in supreme command of that important business—and I appoint you."

"Me!"

"Yes. Your salary will be high—of course—for you are representing me. Later you will earn increases of it, and will get them. You will need a small army of assistants; choose them yourself—and carefully. Take no man for friendship's sake; but, all things being equal, take the man you know, take your friend, in preference to the stranger."

After some further talk under this head, the Commodore said: "Goodby, my boy, and thank Alf for me, for sending you to me."

When Ed reached Memphis he rushed down to the wharf in a fever to tell his great news and thank the boys over and over again for thinking to give him the letter to Mr. Vanderbilt. It happened to be one of those idle times. Blazing hot noonday, and no sign of life on the wharf. But as Ed threaded his way among the freight-piles, he saw a white linen figure stretched in slumber upon a pile of grain-sacks under an awning, and said to himself, "That's one of them," and hastened his step; next, he said, "It's Charley—it's Fairchild—good"; and the next moment laid an affectionate hand on the sleeper's shoulder. The eyes opened lazily, took one glance, the face blanched, the form whirled itself from the sack-pile, and in an instant Ed was alone and Fairchild was flying for the wharfboat like the wind!

Ed was dazed, stupefied. Was Fairchild crazy? What could be the meaning of this? He started slow and dreamily down toward the wharf-boat; turned the corner of a freight-pile and came suddenly upon two of the boys. They were lightly laughing over some pleasant matter; they heard his step, and glanced up just as he discovered them; the laugh died abruptly; and before Ed could speak they were off, and sailing over barrels and bales like hunted deer. Again Ed was paralyzed. Had the boys all gone mad? What *could* be the explanation of this extraordinary conduct? And so, dreaming along, he reached the wharfboat, and stepped aboard—nothing but silence there, and vacancy. He crossed the deck, turned the corner to go down the outer guard, heard a fervent—

"O Lord!" and saw a white linen form plunge overboard.

The youth came up coughing and strangling, and cried out:

"Go 'way from here! You let me alone. *I* didn't do it, I swear I didn't!"

"Didn't do *what?*"

"Give you the—"

"Never mind what you didn't do—come out of that! What makes you all act so? What have *I* done?"

"You? Why, *you* haven't done anything. But—"

"Well, then, what have you got against me? What do you all treat me so for?"

"I—er—but haven't you got anything against *us?*"

"Of course not. What put such a thing into your head?"

"Honor bright—you haven't?"

"Honor bright."

"Swear it!"

"I don't know what in the *world* you mean, but I swear it, anyway."

"And you'll shake hands with me?"

"Goodness knows I'll be *glad* to! Why, I'm just starving to shake hands with *somebody!*"

The swimmer muttered, "Hang him, he smelt a rat and never delivered the letter!—but it's all right, I'm not going to fetch up the subject." And he crawled out and came dripping and draining to shake hands. First one and then another of the conspirators showed up cautiously—armed to the teeth—took in the amicable situation, then ventured warily forward and joined the love-feast.

And to Ed's eager inquiry as to what made them act as they had been acting, they answered evasively and pretended that they had put it up as a joke, to see what he would do. It was the best explanation they could invent at such short notice. And each said to himself, "He never delivered that letter, and the joke is on *us*, if he only knew it or we were dull enough to come out and tell."

Then, of course, they wanted to know all about the trip; and he said:

"Come right up on the boiler deck and order the drinks—it's my treat. I'm going to tell you all about it. And to-night it's my treat again —and we'll have oysters and a time!"

When the drinks were brought and cigars lighted, Ed said:

"Well, when I delivered the letter to Mr. Vanderbilt—"

"Great Scott!"

"Gracious, how you scared me. What's the matter?"

"Oh—er—nothing. Nothing—it was a tack in the chair-seat," said one.

"But you *all* said it. However, no matter. When I delivered the letter—"

"*Did* you deliver it?" And they looked at each other as people might who thought that maybe they were dreaming.

Then they settled to listening; and as the story deepened and its marvels grew, the amazement of it made them dumb, and the interest of it took their breath. They hardly uttered a whisper during two hours, but sat like petrifactions and drank in the immortal romance. At last the tale was ended, and Ed said:

"And it's all owing to *you*, boys, and you'll never find *me* ungrateful —bless your hearts, the best friends a fellow ever had! You'll all have places; I want every one of you. I *know* you—I know you 'by the *back*,' as the gamblers say. You're jokers, and all that, but you're *sterling*, with the hallmark *on*. And Charley Fairchild, you shall be my first assistant and right hand, because of your first-class ability, and because you got me the letter, and for your father's sake who wrote it for me, and to please Mr. Vanderbilt, who *said* it would! And here's to that great man—drink hearty!"

Yes, when the Moment comes, the Man appears—even if he is a thousand miles away, and has to be discovered by a practical joke.

From FOLLOWING THE EQUATOR, 1897

A Story Without an End

We had one game in the ship which was a good time-passer—at least
it was at night in the smoking-room when the men were getting fresh-
ened up from the day's monotonies and dullnesses. It was the complet-
ing of non-complete stories. That is to say, a man would tell all of a
story except the finish, then the others would try to supply the ending
out of their own invention. When every one who wanted a chance had
had it, the man who had introduced the story would give it its original
ending—then you could take your choice. Sometimes the new endings
turned out to be better than the old one. But the story which called out
the most persistent and determined and ambitious effort was one which
had no ending, and so there was nothing to compare the new-made
endings with. The man who told it said he could furnish the particulars
up to a certain point only, because that was as much of the tale as he
knew. He had read it in a volume of sketches twenty-five years ago,
and was interrupted before the end was reached. He would give any
one fifty dollars who would finish the story to the satisfaction of a jury
to be appointed by ourselves. We appointed a jury and wrestled with
the tale. We invented plenty of endings, but the jury voted them all
down. The jury was right. It was a tale which the author of it may
possibly have completed satisfactorily, and if he really had that
good fortune I would like to know what the ending was. Any ordinary
man will find that the story's strength is in its middle, and that there is
apparently no way to transfer it to the close, where of course it ought
to be. In substance the storiette was as follows:

John Brown, aged thirty-one, good, gentle, bashful, timid, lived in
a quiet village in Missouri. He was superintendent of the Presbyterian
Sunday-school. It was but a humble distinction; still, it was his only
official one, and he was modestly proud of it and was devoted to its
work and its interests. The extreme kindliness of his nature was recognized by all; in fact, people said that he was made entirely out of good
impulses and bashfulness; that he could always be counted upon for
help when it was needed, and for bashfulness both when it was needed,
and when it wasn't.

Mary Taylor, twenty-three, modest, sweet, winning, and in character and person beautiful, was all in all to him. And he was very nearly all in all to her. She was wavering, his hopes were high. Her mother had been in opposition from the first. But she was wavering, too; he could see it. She was being touched by his warm interest in her two charity protégés and by his contributions toward their support. These were two forlorn and aged sisters who lived in a log hut in a lonely place up a cross-road four miles from Mrs. Taylor's farm. One of the sisters was crazy, and sometimes a little violent, but not often.

At last the time seemed ripe for a final advance, and Brown gathered his courage together and resolved to make it. He would take along a contribution of double the usual size, and win the mother over; with her opposition annulled, the rest of the conquest would be sure and prompt.

He took to the road in the middle of a placid Sunday afternoon in the soft Missourian summer, and he was equipped properly for his mission. He was clothed all in white linen, with a blue ribbon for a necktie, and he had on dressy tight boots. His horse and buggy were the finest that the livery-stable could furnish. The lap-robe was of white linen, it was new, and it had a hand-worked border that could not be rivaled in that region for beauty and elaboration.

When he was four miles out on the lonely road and was walking his horse over a wooden bridge, his straw hat blew off and fell in the creek, and floated down and lodged against a bar. He did not quite know what to do. He must have the hat, that was manifest; but how was he to get it?

Then he had an idea. The roads were empty, nobody was stirring. Yes, he would risk it. He led the horse to the roadside and set it to cropping the grass; then he undressed and put his clothes in the buggy, petted the horse a moment to secure its compassion and its loyalty, then hurried to the stream. He swam out and soon had the hat. When he got to the top of the bank the horse was gone!

His legs almost gave way under him. The horse was walking leisurely along the road. Brown trotted after it, saying, "Whoa, whoa, there's a good fellow"; but whenever he got near enough to chance a jump for the buggy, the horse quickened its pace a little and defeated him. And so this went on, the naked man perishing with anxiety, and expecting every moment to see people come in sight. He tagged on and on, imploring the horse, beseeching the horse, till he had left a mile behind him, and was closing up on the Taylor premises; then at last he was successful, and got into the buggy. He flung on his shirt, his necktie, and his coat; then reached for—but he was too late; he sat suddenly down and pulled up the lap-robe, for he saw some one coming out of the gate—a woman, he thought. He wheeled the horse to the left, and struck briskly up the cross-road. It was perfectly straight, and exposed on both sides; but there were woods and a sharp turn three miles ahead, and he was very grateful when he got there. As he passed around the turn he slowed down to a walk, and reached for his tr—too late again.

He had come upon Mrs. Enderby, Mrs. Glossop, Mrs. Taylor, and Mary. They were on foot, and seemed tired and excited. They came at once to the buggy and shook hands, and all spoke at once, and said, eagerly and earnestly, how glad they were that he was come, and how fortunate it was. And Mrs. Enderby said, impressively:

"It *looks* like an accident, his coming at such a time; but let no one profane it with such a name; he was sent—sent from on high."

They were all moved, and Mrs. Glossop said in an awed voice:

"Sarah Enderby, you never said a truer word in your life. This is no accident, it is a special Providence. He *was* sent. He is an angel—an angel as truly as ever angel was—an angel of deliverance. *I* say *angel*, Sarah Enderby, and will have no other word. Don't let any one ever say to me again, that there's no such thing as special Providences; for if this isn't one, let them account for it that can."

"I *know* it's so," said Mrs. Taylor, fervently. "John Brown, I could worship you; I could go down on my knees to you. Didn't something tell you—didn't you *feel* that you were sent? I could kiss the hem of your lap-robe."

He was not able to speak; he was helpless with shame and fright. Mrs. Taylor went on:

"Why, just look at it all around, Julia Glossop. *Any* person can see the hand of Providence in it. Here at noon what do we see? We see the smoke rising. I speak up and say, 'That's the Old People's cabin afire.' Didn't I, Julia Glossop?"

"The very words you said, Nancy Taylor. I was as close to you as I am now, and I heard them. You may have said hut instead of cabin, but in substance it's the same. And you were looking pale, too."

"Pale? I was that pale that if—why, you just compare it with this lap-robe. Then the next thing I said was, 'Mary Taylor, tell the hired man to rig up the team—we'll go to the rescue.' And she said, 'Mother, don't you know you told him he could drive to see his people, and stay over Sunday?' And it was just so. I declare for it, I had forgotten it.

'Then,' said I, 'we'll go afoot.' And go we did. And found Sarah Enderby
on the road."

"And we all went together," said Mrs. Enderby. "And found the cabin
set fire and burnt down by the crazy one, and the poor old things so
old and feeble that they couldn't go afoot. And we got them to a shady
place and made them as comfortable as we could, and began to wonder
which way to turn to find some way to get them conveyed to Nancy
Taylor's house. And I spoke up and said—now what did I say? Didn't
I say, 'Providence will provide'?"

"Why sure as you live, so you did! I had forgotten it."

"So had I," said Mrs. Glossop and Mrs. Taylor; "but you certainly
said it. Now wasn't that remarkable?"

"Yes, I said it. And then we went to Mr. Moseley's, two miles, and
all of them were gone to the camp-meeting over on Stony Fork; and
then we came all the way back, two miles, and then here, another mile
—and Providence *has* provided. You see it yourselves."

They gazed at each other awe-struck, and lifted their hands and
said in unison:

"It's per-fectly wonderful."

"And then," said Mrs. Glossop, "what do you think we had better
do—let Mr. Brown drive the Old People to Nancy Taylor's one at a
time, or put both of them in the buggy, and him lead the horse?"

Brown gasped.

"Now, then, that's a question," said Mrs. Enderby. "You see, we are
all tired out, and any way we fix it it's going to be difficult. For if Mr.
Brown takes both of them, at least one of us must go back to help him,
for he can't load them into the buggy by himself, and they so helpless."

"That is so," said Mrs. Taylor. "It doesn't look—oh, how would this
do!—one of us drive there *with* Mr. Brown, and the rest of you go along
to my house and get things ready. I'll go with him. He and I together
can lift one of the Old People into the buggy; then drive her to my
house and—"

"But who will take care of the other one?" said Mrs. Enderby. "We
mustn't leave her there in the woods alone, you know—especially the
crazy one. There and back is eight miles, you see."

They had all been sitting on the grass beside the buggy for a while,
now, trying to rest their weary bodies. They fell silent a moment or
two, and struggled in thought over the baffling situation; then Mrs.
Enderby brightened and said:

"I think I've got the idea, now. You see, we can't *walk* any more.
Think what we've done; four miles there, two to Moseley's, is six, then

back to here—nine miles since noon, and not a bite to eat: I declare I don't see how we've done it; and as for me, I am just famishing. Now, somebody's got to go back, to help Mr. Brown—there's no getting around that; but whoever goes has got to ride, not walk. So my idea is this: one of us to ride back with Mr. Brown, then ride to Nancy Taylor's house with one of the Old People, leaving Mr. Brown to keep the other old one company, you all to go now to Nancy's and rest and wait; then one of you drive back and get the other one and drive *her* to Nancy's, and Mr. Brown walk."

"Splendid!" they all cried. "Oh, that will do—that will answer perfectly." And they all said that Mrs. Enderby had the best head for planning in the company; and they said that they wondered that they hadn't thought of this simple plan themselves. They hadn't meant to take back the compliment, good simple souls, and didn't know they had done it. After a consultation it was decided that Mrs. Enderby should drive back with Brown, she being entitled to the distinction because she had invented the plan. Everything now being satisfactorily arranged and settled, the ladies rose, relieved and happy, and brushed down their gowns, and three of them started homeward; Mrs. Enderby set her foot on the buggy step and was about to climb in, when Brown found a remnant of his voice and gasped out—

"Please, Mrs. Enderby, call them back—I am very weak; I can't walk, I can't indeed."

"Why, dear Mr. Brown! You *do* look pale; I am ashamed of myself that I didn't notice it sooner. Come back—all of you! Mr. Brown is not well. Is there anything I can do for you, Mr. Brown—I'm real sorry. Are you in pain?"

"No, madam, only weak; I am not sick, but only just weak—lately; not long, but just lately."

The others came back, and poured out their sympathies and commiserations, and were full of self-reproaches for not having noticed how pale he was. And they at once struck out a new plan, and soon agreed that it was by far the best of all. They would all go to Nancy Taylor's house and see to Brown's needs first. He could lie on the sofa in the parlor, and while Mrs. Taylor and Mary took care of him the other two ladies would take the buggy and go and get one of the Old People, and leave one of themselves with the other one, and—

By this time, without any solicitation, they were at the horse's head and were beginning to turn him around. The danger was imminent, but Brown found his voice again and saved himself. He said—

"But, ladies, you are overlooking something which makes the plan impracticable. You see, if you bring *one* of them home, and one remains behind with the other, there will be three persons there when one of you comes back for that other, for some one must drive the buggy back, and *three* can't come home in it."

They all exclaimed, "Why, sure-ly, that is so!" and they were all perplexed again.

"Dear, dear, what *can* we do?" said Mrs. Glossop; "it is the most mixed-up thing that ever was. The fox and the goose and the corn and things—oh, dear, they are nothing to it."

They sat wearily down once more, to further torture their tormented heads for a plan that would work. Presently Mary offered a plan; it was her first effort. She said:

"I am young and strong, and am refreshed, now. Take Mr. Brown to our house, and give him help—you see how plainly he needs it. I will go back and take care of the Old People; I can be there in twenty minutes. You can go on and do what you first started to do—wait on the main road at our house until somebody comes along with a wagon; then send and bring away the three of us. You won't have to wait long; the farmers will soon be coming back from town now. I will keep old Polly patient and cheered up—the crazy one doesn't need it."

This plan was discussed and accepted; it seemed the best that could be done, in the circumstances, and the Old People must be getting discouraged by this time.

Brown felt relieved, and was deeply thankful. Let him once get to the main road and he would find a way to escape.

Then Mrs. Taylor said:

"The evening chill will be coming on, pretty soon, and those poor old burnt-out things will need some kind of covering. Take the lap-robe with you, dear."

"Very well, Mother, I will."

She stepped to the buggy and put out her hand to take it—

That was the end of the tale. The passenger who told it said that when he read the story twenty-five years ago in a train he was interrupted at that point—the train jumped off a bridge.

At first we thought we could finish the story quite easily, and we set to work with confidence; but it soon began to appear that it was not a simple thing, but difficult and baffling. This was on account of Brown's character—great generosity and kindliness, but complicated with unusual shyness and diffidence, particularly in the presence of ladies. There was his love for Mary, in a hopeful state but not yet secure—just in a condition, indeed, where its affair must be handled with great tact, and no mistakes made, no offense given. And there was the mother— wavering, half willing—by adroit and flawless diplomacy to be won over, now, or perhaps never at all. Also, there were the helpless Old People yonder in the woods waiting—their fate and Brown's happiness to be determined by what Brown should do within the next two seconds. Mary was reaching for the lap-robe; Brown must decide—there was no time to be lost.

Of course none but a happy ending of the story would be accepted by the jury; the finish must find Brown in high credit with the ladies, his behavior without blemish, his modesty unwounded, his character for self-sacrifice maintained, the Old People rescued through him, their benefactor, all the party proud of him, happy in him, his praises on all their tongues.

We tried to arrange this, but it was beset with persistent and irrecon- cilable difficulties. We saw that Brown's shyness would not allow him to give up the lap-robe. This would offend Mary and her mother; and it would surprise the other ladies, partly because this stinginess toward the suffering Old People would be out of character with Brown, and partly because he was a special Providence and could not properly act so. If asked to explain his conduct, his shyness would not allow him to tell the truth, and lack of invention and practice would find him in- capable of contriving a lie that would wash. We worked at the trouble- some problem until three in the morning.

Meantime Mary was still reaching for the lap-robe. We gave it up, and decided to let her continue to reach. It is the reader's privilege to determine for himself how the thing came out.

From FOLLOWING THE EQUATOR, 1897

The Man That Corrupted Hadleyburg

1

It was many years ago. Hadleyburg was the most honest and up- right town in all the region around about. It had kept that reputation unsmirched during three generations, and was prouder of it than of any other of its possessions. It was so proud of it, and so anxious to insure its perpetuation, that it began to teach the principles of honest dealing to its babies in the cradle, and made the like teachings the staple of their culture thenceforward through all the years devoted to their education. Also, throughout the formative years temptations were kept out of the way of the young people, so that their honesty could have every chance to harden and solidify, and become a part of their very bone. The neighboring towns were jealous of this honorable supremacy, and affected to sneer at Hadleyburg's pride in it and call it vanity; but all the same they were obliged to acknowledge that Hadleyburg was in reality an incorruptible town; and if pressed they would also acknowledge that the mere fact that a young man hailed from Hadleyburg was all the recommendation he needed when he went forth from his natal town to seek for responsible employment.

But at last, in the drift of time, Hadleyburg had the ill luck to offend a passing stranger—possibly without knowing it, certainly without caring, for Hadleyburg was sufficient unto itself, and cared not a rap for strangers or their opinions. Still, it would have been well to make an exception in this one's case, for he was a bitter man and revengeful. All through his wanderings during a whole year he kept his injury in mind, and gave all his leisure moments to trying to invent a compensating satisfaction for it. He contrived many plans, and all of them were good, but none of them was quite sweeping enough; the poorest of them would hurt a great many individuals, but what he wanted was a plan which would comprehend the entire town, and not let so much as one person escape unhurt. At last he had a fortunate idea, and when it fell into his brain it lit up his whole head with an evil joy. He began to form a plan at once, saying to himself, "That is the thing to do—I will corrupt the town."

Six months later he went to Hadleyburg, and arrived in a buggy at the house of the old cashier of the bank about ten at night. He got a sack out of the buggy, shouldered it, and staggered with it through the cottage yard, and knocked at the door. A woman's voice said "Come in," and he entered, and set his sack behind the stove in the parlor, saying politely to the old lady who sat reading the *Missionary Herald* by the lamp:

"Pray keep your seat, madam, I will not disturb you. There—now it is pretty well concealed; one would hardly know it was there. Can I see your husband a moment, madam?"

No, he was gone to Brixton, and might not return before morning.

"Very well, madam, it is no matter. I merely wanted to leave that sack in his care, to be delivered to the rightful owner when he shall be found. I am a stranger; he does not know me; I am merely passing through the town to-night to discharge a matter which has been long in my mind. My errand is now completed, and I go pleased and a little proud, and you will never see me again. There is a paper attached to the sack which will explain everything. Good night, madam."

The old lady was afraid of the mysterious big stranger, and was glad to see him go. But her curiosity was roused, and she went straight to the sack and brought away the paper. It began as follows:

TO BE PUBLISHED; *or, the right man sought out by private inquiry—either will answer. This sack contains gold coin weighing a hundred and sixty pounds four ounces—*

"Mercy on us, and the door not locked!"

Mrs. Richards flew to it all in a tremble and locked it, then pulled down the window-shades and stood frightened, worried, and wondering if there was anything else she could do toward making herself and the money more safe. She listened awhile for burglars, then surrendered to curiosity and went back to the lamp and finished reading the paper:

I am a foreigner, and am presently going back to my own country, to remain there permanently. I am grateful to America for what I have received at her hands during my long stay under her flag; and to one of her citizens—a citizen of Hadleyburg—I am especially grateful for a great kindness done me a year or two ago. Two great kindnesses, in fact. I will explain. I was a gambler. I say I WAS. I was a ruined gambler. I arrived in this village at night, hungry and without a penny. I asked for help—in the dark; I was ashamed to beg in the light. I begged of the right man. He gave me twenty dollars—that is to say, he gave me life, as I considered it. He also gave me fortune; for out of that money I have made myself rich at the gaming-table. And finally, a remark which he made to me has remained with me to this day, and has at last conquered me; and in conquering has saved the remnant of my morals; I shall gamble no more. Now I have no idea who that man was, but I want him found, and I want him to have this money, to give away, throw away, or keep, as he pleases. It is merely my way of testifying my gratitude to him. If I could stay, I would find him myself; but no matter, he will be found. This is an honest town, an incorruptible town, and I know I can trust it without fear. This man can be identified by the remark which he made to me; I feel persuaded that he will remember it.

And now my plan is this: If you prefer to conduct the inquiry pri-
vately, do so. Tell the contents of this present writing to any one who
is likely to be the right man. If he shall answer, 'I am the man; the
remark I made was so-and-so,' apply the test—to wit: open the sack,
and in it you will find a sealed envelope containing that remark. If the
remark mentioned by the candidate tallies with it, give him the money,
and ask no further questions, for he is certainly the right man.

But if you shall prefer a public inquiry, then publish this present writ-
ing in the local paper—with these instructions added, to wit: Thirty
days from now, let the candidate appear at the town-hall at eight in the
evening (Friday), and hand his remark, in a sealed envelope, to the
Rev. Mr. Burgess (if he will be kind enough to act); and let Mr. Bur-
gess there and then destroy the seals of the sack, open it, and see if
the remark is correct; if correct, let the money be delivered, with my
sincere gratitude, to my benefactor thus identified.

Mrs. Richards sat down, gently quivering with excitement, and was
soon lost in thinkings—after this pattern: "What a strange thing it is!
. . . And what a fortune for that kind man who set his bread afloat
upon the waters! . . . If it had only been my husband that did it!—for
we are so poor, so old and poor! . . ." Then, with a sigh—"But it was
not my Edward; no, it was not he that gave a stranger twenty dollars.
It is a pity, too; I see it now. . . ." Then, with a shudder—"But it is
gambler's money! the wages of sin: we couldn't take it; we couldn't
touch it. I don't like to be near it; it seems a defilement." She moved
to a farther chair. . . . "I wish Edward would come and take it to the
bank; a burglar might come at any moment; it is dreadful to be here all
alone with it."

At eleven Mr. Richards arrived, and while his wife was saying, "I
am *so* glad you've come!" he was saying, "I'm so tired—tired clear out;
it is dreadful to be poor, and have to make these dismal journeys at
my time of life. Always at the grind, grind, grind, on a salary—another
man's slave, and he sitting at home in his slippers, rich and comfortable."

"I am so sorry for you, Edward, you know that; but be comforted:
we have our livelihood; we have our good name—"

"Yes, Mary, and that is everything. Don't mind my talk—it's just a
moment's irritation and doesn't mean anything. Kiss me—there, it's all
gone now, and I am not complaining any more. What have you been
getting? What's in the sack?"

Then his wife told him the great secret. It dazed him for a moment;
then he said:

"It weighs a hundred and sixty pounds? Why, Mary, it's for-ty thousand dollars—think of it—a whole fortune! Not ten men in this village are worth that much. Give me the paper."

He skimmed through it and said:

"Isn't it an adventure! Why, it's a romance; it's like the impossible things one reads about in books, and never sees in life." He was well stirred up now; cheerful, even gleeful. He tapped his old wife on the cheek, and said, humorously, "Why, we're rich, Mary, rich; all we've got to do is to bury the money and burn the papers. If the gambler ever comes to inquire, we'll merely look coldly upon him and say: 'What is this nonsense you are talking? We have never heard of you and your sack of gold before'; and then he would look foolish, and—"

"And in the mean time, while you are running on with your jokes, the money is still here, and it is fast getting along toward burglar-time."

"True. Very well, what shall we do—make the inquiry private? No, not that: it would spoil the romance. The public method is better. Think what a noise it will make! And it will make all the other towns jealous; for no stranger would trust such a thing to any town but Hadleyburg, and they know it. It's a great card for us. I must get to the printing-office now, or I shall be too late."

"But stop—stop—don't leave me here alone with it, Edward!"

But he was gone. For only a little while, however. Not far from his own house he met the editor-proprietor of the paper, and gave him the document, and said, "Here is a good thing for you, Cox—put it in."

"It may be too late, Mr. Richards, but I'll see."

At home again he and his wife sat down to talk the charming mystery over; they were in no condition for sleep. The first question was, Who could the citizen have been who gave the stranger the twenty dollars? It seemed a simple one; both answered it in the same breath:

"Barclay Goodson."

"Yes," said Richards, "he could have done it, and it would have been like him, but there's not another in the town."

"Everybody will grant that, Edward—grant it privately, anyway. For six months, now, the village has been its own proper self once more—honest, narrow, self-righteous, and stingy."

"It is what he always called it, to the day of his death—said it right out publicly, too."

"Yes, and he was hated for it."

"Oh, of course; but he didn't care. I reckon he was the best-hated man among us, except the Reverend Burgess."

"Well, Burgess deserves it—he will never get another congregation here. Mean as the town is, it knows how to estimate *him*. Edward, doesn't it seem odd that the stranger should appoint Burgess to deliver the money?"

"Well, yes—it does. That is—that is—"

"Why so much that-*is*-ing? Would *you* select him?"

"Mary, maybe the stranger knows him better than this village does."

"Much *that* would help Burgess!"

The husband seemed perplexed for an answer; the wife kept a steady eye upon him, and waited. Finally Richards said, with the hesitancy of one who is making a statement which is likely to encounter doubt:

"Mary, Burgess is not a bad man."

His wife was certainly surprised.

"Nonsense!" she exclaimed.

"He is not a bad man. I know. The whole of his unpopularity had its foundation in that one thing—the thing that made so much noise."

"That 'one thing,' indeed! As if that 'one thing' wasn't enough, all by itself."

"Plenty. Plenty. Only he wasn't guilty of it."

"How you talk! Not guilty of it! Everybody knows he *was* guilty."

"Mary, I give you my word—he was innocent."

"I can't believe it, and I don't. How do you know?"

"It is a confession. I am ashamed, but I will make it. I was the only man who knew he was innocent. I could have saved him, and—and— well, you know how the town was wrought up—I hadn't the pluck to do it. It would have turned everybody against me. I felt mean, ever so mean; but I didn't dare; I hadn't the manliness to face that."

Mary looked troubled, and for a while was silent. Then she said, stammeringly:

"I—I don't think it would have done for you to—to— One mustn't— er—public opinion—one has to be so careful—so—" It was a difficult road, and she got mired; but after a little she got started again. "It was a great pity, but— Why, we couldn't afford it, Edward—we couldn't indeed. Oh, I wouldn't have had you do it for anything!"

"It would have lost us the good will of so many people, Mary; and then—and then—"

"What troubles me now is, what *he* thinks of us, Edward."

"He? *He* doesn't suspect that I could have saved him."

"Oh," exclaimed the wife, in a tone of relief, "I am glad of that! As long as he doesn't know that you could have saved him, he—he—well, that makes it a great deal better. Why, I might have known he didn't know, because he is always trying to be friendly with us, as little encouragement as we give him. More than once people have twitted me with it. There's the Wilsons, and the Wilcoxes, and the Harknesses, they take a mean pleasure in saying, 'Your friend Burgess,' because they know it pesters me. I wish he wouldn't persist in liking us so; I can't think why he keeps it up."

"I can explain it. It's another confession. When the thing was new and hot, and the town made a plan to ride him on a rail, my conscience hurt me so that I couldn't stand it, and I went privately and gave him notice, and he got out of the town and staid out till it was safe to come back."

"Edward! If the town had found it out—"

"*Don't!* It scares me yet, to think of it. I repented of it the minute it was done; and I was even afraid to tell you, lest your face might betray it to somebody. I didn't sleep any that night, for worrying. But after a few days I saw that no one was going to suspect me, and after that I got to feeling glad I did it. And I feel glad yet, Mary—glad through and through."

"So do I, now, for it would have been a dreadful way to treat him. Yes, I'm glad; for really you did owe him that, you know. But, Edward, suppose it should come out yet, some day!"

"It won't."

"Why?"

"Because everybody thinks it was Goodson."

"Of course they would!"

"Certainly. And of course *he* didn't care. They persuaded poor old Sawlsberry to go and charge it on him, and he went blustering over there and did it. Goodson looked him over, like as if he was hunting for a place on him that he could despise the most, then he says, 'So you are the Committee of Inquiry, are you?' Sawlsberry said that was about what he was. 'Hm. Do they require particulars, or do you reckon a kind of a *general* answer will do?' 'If they require particulars, I will come back, Mr. Goodson; I will take the general answer first.' 'Very well, then, tell them to go to hell—I reckon that's general enough. And I'll give you some advice, Sawlsberry; when you come back for the particulars, fetch a basket to carry the relics of yourself home in.'"

"Just like Goodson; it's got all the marks. He had only one vanity: he thought he could give advice better than any other person."

"It settled the business, and saved us, Mary. The subject was dropped."

"Bless you, I'm not doubting *that*."

Then they took up the gold-sack mystery again, with strong interest.

Soon the conversation began to suffer breaks—interruptions caused by absorbed thinkings. The breaks grew more and more frequent. At last Richards lost himself wholly in thought. He sat long, gazing vacantly at the floor, and by and by he began to punctuate his thoughts with little nervous movements of his hands that seemed to indicate vexation. Meantime his wife too had relapsed into a thoughtful silence, and her movements were beginning to show a troubled discomfort. Finally Richards got up and strode aimlessly about the room, plowing his hands through his hair, much as a somnambulist might do who was having a bad dream. Then he seemed to arrive at a definite purpose; and without a word he put on his hat and passed quickly out of the house. His wife sat brooding, with a drawn face, and did not seem to be aware that she was alone. Now and then she murmured, "Lead us not into t— . . . but—but—we are so poor, so poor! . . . Lead us not into . . . Ah, who would be hurt by it?—and no one would ever know. . . . Lead us . . ." The voice died out in mumblings. After a little she glanced up and muttered in a half-frightened, half-glad way:

"He is gone! But, oh dear, he may be too late—too late. . . . Maybe not—maybe there is still time." She rose and stood thinking, nervously clasping and unclasping her hands. A slight shudder shook her frame, and she said, out of a dry throat, "God forgive me—it's awful to think such things—but . . . Lord, how we are made—how strangely we are made!"

She turned the light low, and slipped stealthily over and kneeled down by the sack and felt of its ridgy sides with her hands, and fondled them lovingly; and there was a gloating light in her poor old eyes. She fell into fits of absence; and came half out of them at times to mutter, "If we had only waited!—oh, if we had only waited a little, and not been in such a hurry!"

Meantime Cox had gone home from his office and told his wife all about the strange thing that had happened, and they had talked it over eagerly, and guessed that the late Goodson was the only man in the town who could have helped a suffering stranger with so noble a sum as twenty dollars. Then there was a pause, and the two became thoughtful and silent. And by and by nervous and fidgety. At last the wife said, as if to herself:

"Nobody knows this secret but the Richardses . . . and us . . . nobody."

The husband came out of his thinkings with a slight start, and gazed wistfully at his wife, whose face was become very pale; then he hesitatingly rose, and glanced furtively at his hat, then at his wife—a sort of mute inquiry. Mrs. Cox swallowed once or twice, with her hand at her throat, then in place of speech she nodded her head. In a moment she was alone, and mumbling to herself.

And now Richards and Cox were hurrying through the deserted streets, from opposite directions. They met, panting, at the foot of the printing-office stairs; by the night light there they read each other's face. Cox whispered:

"Nobody knows about this but us?"

The whispered answer was,

"Not a soul—on honor, not a soul!"

"If it isn't too late to—"

The men were starting up-stairs; at this moment they were overtaken by a boy, and Cox asked:

"Is that you, Johnny?"

"Yes, sir."

"You needn't ship the early mail—nor *any* mail; wait till I tell you."

"It's already gone, sir."

"*Gone?*" It had the sound of an unspeakable disappointment in it.

"Yes, sir. Time-table for Brixton and all the towns beyond changed to-day, sir—had to get the papers in twenty minutes earlier than common. I had to rush; if I had been two minutes later—"

The men turned and walked slowly away, not waiting to hear the rest. Neither of them spoke during ten minutes; then Cox said, in a vexed tone:

"What possessed you to be in such a hurry, *I* can't make out."

The answer was humble enough:

"I see it now, but somehow I never thought, you know, until it was too late. But the next time—"

"Next time be hanged! It won't come in a thousand years."

Then the friends separated without a good night, and dragged themselves home with the gait of mortally stricken men. At their homes their wives sprang up with an eager "Well?"—then saw the answer with their eyes and sank down sorrowing, without waiting for it to come in words. In both houses a discussion followed of a heated sort—a new thing; there had been discussions before, but not heated ones, not ungentle ones. The discussions to-night were a sort of seeming plagiarisms of each other. Mrs. Richards said,

"If you had only waited, Edward—if you had only stopped to think; but no, you must run straight to the printing-office and spread it all over the world."

"It *said* publish it."

"That is nothing; it also said do it privately, if you liked. There, now —is that true, or not?"

"Why, yes—yes, it is true; but when I thought what a stir it would make, and what a compliment it was to Hadleyburg that a stranger should trust it so—"

"Oh, certainly, I know all that; but if you had only stopped to think, you would have seen that you *couldn't* find the right man, because he is in his grave, and hasn't left chick nor child nor relation behind him; and as long as the money went to somebody that awfully needed it, and nobody would be hurt by it, and—and—"

She broke down, crying. Her husband tried to think of some comforting thing to say, and presently came out with this:

"But after all, Mary, it must be for the best—it *must* be; we know that. And we must remember that it was so ordered—"

"Ordered! Oh, everything's *ordered*, when a person has to find some way out when he has been stupid. Just the same, it was *ordered* that the money should come to us in this special way, and it was you that must take it on yourself to go meddling with the designs of Providence —and who gave you the right? It was wicked, that is what it was—just blasphemous presumption, and no more becoming to a meek and humble professor of—"

"But, Mary, you know how we have been trained all our lives long, like the whole village, till it is absolutely second nature to us to stop not a single moment to think when there's an honest thing to be done—"

"Oh, I know it, I know it—it's been one everlasting training and training and training in honesty—honesty shielded, from the very cradle, against every possible temptation, and so it's *artificial* honesty, and weak as water when temptation comes, as we have seen this night. God knows I never had shade nor shadow of a doubt of my petrified and indestructible honesty until now—and now, under the very first big and real temptation, I—Edward, it is my belief that this town's honesty is as rotten as mine is; as rotten as yours is. It is a mean town, a hard, stingy town, and hasn't a virtue in the world but this honesty it is so celebrated for and so conceited about; and so help me, I do believe that if ever the day comes that its honesty falls under great temptation, its grand reputation will go to ruin like a house of cards. There, now, I've made confession, and I feel better; I am a humbug, and I've been one all my life, without knowing it. Let no man call me honest again— I will not have it."

"I—well, Mary, I feel a good deal as you do; I certainly do. It seems strange, too, so strange. I never could have believed it—never."

A long silence followed; both were sunk in thought. At last the wife looked up and said:

"I know what you are thinking, Edward."

Richards had the embarrassed look of a person who is caught.

"I am ashamed to confess it, Mary, but—"

"It's no matter, Edward, I was thinking the same question myself."

"I hope so. State it."

"You were thinking, if a body could only guess out *what the remark was* that Goodson made to the stranger."

"It's perfectly true. I feel guilty and ashamed. And you?"

"I'm past it. Let us make a pallet here; we've got to stand watch till the bank vault opens in the morning and admits the sack. . . . Oh dear, oh dear—if we hadn't made the mistake!"

The pallet was made, and Mary said:

"The open sesame—what could it have been? I do wonder what that remark could have been? But come; we will get to bed now."

"And sleep?"

"No: think."

"Yes, think."

By this time the Coxes too had completed their spat and their reconciliation, and were turning in—to think, to think, and toss, and fret, and worry over what the remark could possibly have been which Goodson made to the stranded derelict; that golden remark; that remark worth forty thousand dollars, cash.

The reason that the village telegraph-office was open later than usual that night was this: The foreman of Cox's paper was the local representative of the Associated Press. One might say its honorary representative, for it wasn't four times a year that he could furnish thirty words that would be accepted. But this time it was different. His despatch stating what he had caught got an instant answer:

Send the whole thing—all the details—twelve hundred words.

A colossal order! The foreman filled the bill; and he was the proudest man in the State. By breakfast-time the next morning the name of Hadleyburg the Incorruptible was on every lip in America, from Montreal to the Gulf, from the glaciers of Alaska to the orange-groves of Florida; and millions and millions of people were discussing the stranger and his money-sack, and wondering if the right man would be found, and hoping some more news about the matter would come soon—right away.

2

Hadleyburg village woke up world-celebrated—astonished—happy—vain. Vain beyond imagination. Its nineteen principal citizens and their wives went about shaking hands with each other, and beaming, and smiling, and congratulating, and saying *this* thing adds a new word to the dictionary—*Hadleyburg*, synonym for *incorruptible*—destined to live in dictionaries forever! And the minor and unimportant citizens and their wives went around acting in much the same way. Everybody ran to the bank to see the gold-sack; and before noon grieved and envious crowds began to flock in from Brixton and all neighboring towns; and that afternoon and next day reporters began to arrive from everywhere to verify the sack and its history and write the whole thing up anew, and make dashing free-hand pictures of the sack, and of Richards's house, and the bank, and the Presbyterian church, and the Baptist church, and the public square, and the town-hall where the test would be applied and the money delivered; and damnable portraits of the Richardses, and Pinkerton the banker, and Cox, and the foreman, and Reverend Burgess, and the postmaster—and even of Jack Halliday, who was the loafing, good-natured, no-account, irreverent fisherman, hunter, boys' friend, stray-dogs' friend, typical "Sam Lawson" of the town. The little mean, smirking, oily Pinkerton showed the sack to all comers, and rubbed his sleek palms together pleasantly, and enlarged upon the town's fine old reputation for honesty and upon this wonderful indorsement of it, and hoped and believed that the example would now spread far and wide over the American world, and be epoch-making in the matter of moral regeneration. And so on, and so on.

By the end of a week things had quieted down again; the wild intoxication of pride and joy had sobered to a soft, sweet, silent delight—a sort of deep, nameless, unutterable content. All faces bore a look of peaceful, holy happiness.

Then a change came. It was a gradual change: so gradual that its beginnings were hardly noticed; maybe were not noticed at all, except by Jack Halliday, who always noticed everything; and always made fun of it, too, no matter what it was. He began to throw out chaffing remarks about people not looking quite so happy as they did a day or two ago; and next he claimed that the new aspect was deepening to positive sadness; next, that it was taking on a sick look; and finally he said that everybody was become so moody, thoughtful, and absent-minded that he could rob the meanest man in town of a cent out of the bottom of his breeches pocket and not disturb his revery.

At this stage—or at about this stage—a saying like this was dropped at bedtime—with a sigh, usually—by the head of each of the nineteen principal households: "Ah, what *could* have been the remark that Goodson made?"

And straightway—with a shudder—came this, from the man's wife: "Oh, *don't!* What horrible thing are you mulling in your mind? Put it away from you, for God's sake!"

But that question was wrung from those men again the next night—and got the same retort. But weaker.

And the third night the men uttered the question yet again—with anguish, and absently. This time—and the following night—the wives fidgeted feebly, and tried to say something. But didn't.

And the night after that they found their tongues and responded—longingly:

"Oh, if we *could* only guess!"

Halliday's comments grew daily more and more sparklingly disagreeable and disparaging. He went diligently about, laughing at the town, individually and in mass. But his laugh was the only one left in the village: it fell upon a hollow and mournful vacancy and emptiness. Not even a smile was findable anywhere. Halliday carried a cigar-box around on a tripod, playing that it was a camera, and halted all passers and aimed the thing and said, "Ready!—now look pleasant, please," but not even this capital joke could surprise the dreary faces into any softening.

So three weeks passed—one week was left. It was Saturday evening —after supper. Instead of the aforetime Saturday-evening flutter and bustle and shopping and larking, the streets were empty and desolate. Richards and his old wife sat apart in their little parlor—miserable and thinking. This was become their evening habit now: the lifelong habit which had preceded it, of reading, knitting, and contented chat, or receiving or paying neighborly calls, was dead and gone and forgotten, ages ago—two or three weeks ago; nobody talked now, nobody read, nobody visited—the whole village sat at home, sighing, worrying, silent. Trying to guess out that remark.

The postman left a letter. Richards glanced listlessly at the superscription and the postmark—unfamiliar, both—and tossed the letter on the table and resumed his might-have-beens and his hopeless dull miseries where he had left them off. Two or three hours later his wife got wearily up and was going away to bed without a good night—custom now—but she stopped near the letter and eyed it awhile with a dead interest, then broke it open, and began to skim it over. Richards, sitting there with his chair tilted back against the wall and his chin between his knees, heard something fall. It was his wife. He sprang to her side, but she cried out:

"Leave me alone, I am too happy. Read the letter—read it!"

He did. He devoured it, his brain reeling. The letter was from a distant state, and it said:

I am a stranger to you, but no matter: I have something to tell. I have just arrived home from Mexico, and learned about that episode. Of course you do not know who made that remark, but I know, and I am the only person living who does know. It was GOODSON. I knew him well, many years ago. I passed through your village that very night, and was his guest till the midnight train came along. I overheard him make that remark to the stranger in the dark—it was in Hale Alley. He and I talked of it the rest of the way home, and while smoking in his house. He mentioned many of your villagers in the course of his talk—most of them in a very uncomplimentary way, but two or three favorably; among these latter yourself. I say "favorably"—nothing stronger. I remember his saying he did not actually LIKE any person in the town—not one; but that you—I THINK he said you—am almost sure—had done him a very great service once, possibly without knowing the full value of it, and he wished he had a fortune, he would leave it to you when he died, and a curse apiece for the rest of the citizens. Now, then, if it was you that did him that service, you are his legitimate heir, and entitled to the sack of gold. I know that I can trust to your honor and honesty, for in a citizen of Hadleyburg these virtues are an unfailing inheritance, and so I am going to reveal to you the remark, well satisfied that if you are not the right man you will seek and find the right one and see that poor Goodson's debt of gratitude for the service referred to is paid. This is the remark: "YOU ARE FAR FROM BEING A BAD MAN: GO, AND REFORM."

HOWARD L. STEPHENSON

"Oh, Edward, the money is ours, and I am so grateful, *oh*, so grateful—kiss me, dear, it's forever since we kissed—and we needed it so—the money—and now you are free of Pinkerton and his bank, and nobody's slave any more; it seems to me I could fly for joy."

It was a happy half-hour that the couple spent there on the settee caressing each other; it was the old days come again—days that had begun with their courtship and lasted without a break till the stranger brought the deadly money. By and by the wife said:

"Oh, Edward, how lucky it was you did him that grand service, poor

Goodson! I never liked him, but I love him now. And it was fine and beautiful of you never to mention it or brag about it." Then, with a touch of reproach, "But you ought to have told *me,* Edward, you ought to have told your wife, you know."

"Well, I—er—well, Mary, you see—"

"Now stop hemming and hawing, and tell me about it, Edward. I always loved you, and now I'm proud of you. Everybody believes there was only one good generous soul in this village, and now it turns out that you—Edward, why don't you tell me?"

"Well—er—er— Why, Mary, I can't!"

"You *can't? Why* can't you?"

"You see, he—well, he—he made me promise I wouldn't."

The wife looked him over, and said, very slowly:

"Made—you—promise? Edward, what do you tell me that for?"

"Mary, do you think I would lie?"

She was troubled and silent for a moment, then she laid her hand within his and said:

"No . . . no. We have wandered far enough from our bearings—God spare us that! In all your life you have never uttered a lie. But now— now that the foundations of things seem to be crumbling from under us, we—we—" She lost her voice for a moment, then said, brokenly, "Lead us not into temptation. . . . I think you made the promise, Edward. Let it rest so. Let us keep away from that ground. Now—that is all gone by; let us be happy again; it is no time for clouds."

Edward found it something of an effort to comply, for his mind kept wandering—trying to remember what the service was that he had done Goodson.

The couple lay awake the most of the night, Mary happy and busy, Edward busy but not so happy. Mary was planning what she would do with the money. Edward was trying to recall that service. At first his conscience was sore on account of the lie he had told Mary—if it was a lie. After much reflection—suppose it *was* a lie? What then? Was it such a great matter? Aren't we always *acting* lies? Then why not *tell* them? Look at Mary—look what she had done. While he was hurrying off on his honest errand, what was she doing? Lamenting because the papers hadn't been destroyed and the money kept! Is theft better than lying?

That point lost its sting—the lie dropped into the background and left comfort behind it. The next point came to the front: *Had* he rendered that service? Well, here was Goodson's own evidence as reported in Stephenson's letter; there could be no better evidence than that—it was even *proof* that he had rendered it. Of course. So that point was settled. . . . No, not quite. He recalled with a wince that this unknown Mr. Stephenson was just a trifle unsure as to whether the performer of it was Richards or some other—and, oh dear, he had put Richards on his honor! He must himself decide whither that money must go—and Mr. Stephenson was not doubting that if he was the wrong man he would go honorably and find the right one. Oh, it was odious to put a man in such a situation—ah, why couldn't Stephenson have left out that doubt! What did he want to intrude that for?

Further reflection. How did it happen that *Richards's* name remained in Stephenson's mind as indicating the right man, and not some other man's name? That looked good. Yes, that looked very good. In fact, it went on looking better and better, straight along—until by and by it grew into positive *proof*. And then Richards put the matter at once out of his mind, for he had a private instinct that a proof once established is better left so.

He was feeling reasonably comfortable now, but there was still one other detail that kept pushing itself on his notice: of course he had done that service—that was settled; but what *was* that service? He must recall it—he would not go to sleep till he had recalled it; it would make his peace of mind perfect. And so he thought and thought. He thought of a dozen things—possible services, even probable services—but none of them seemed adequate, none of them seemed large enough, none of them seemed worth the money—worth the fortune Goodson had wished he could leave in his will. And besides, he couldn't remember having done them, anyway. Now, then—now, then—what *kind* of a service would it be that would make a man so inordinately grateful? Ah—the saving of his soul! That must be it. Yes, he could remember, now, how he once set himself the task of converting Goodson, and labored at it as much as—he was going to say three months; but upon closer examination it shrunk to a month, then to a week, then to a day, then to nothing. Yes, he remembered now, and with unwelcome vividness, that Goodson had told him to go to thunder and mind his own business—*he* wasn't hankering to follow Hadleyburg to heaven!

So that solution was a failure—he hadn't saved Goodson's soul. Richards was discouraged. Then after a little came another idea: had he saved Goodson's property? No, that wouldn't do—he hadn't any. His life? That is it! Of course. Why, he might have thought of it before. This time he was on the right track, sure. His imagination-mill was hard at work in a minute, now.

Thereafter during a stretch of two exhausting hours he was busy saving Goodson's life. He saved it in all kinds of difficult and perilous ways. In every case he got it saved satisfactorily up to a certain point; then, just as he was beginning to get well persuaded that it had really happened, a troublesome detail would turn up which made the whole thing impossible. As in the matter of drowning, for instance. In that case he had swum out and tugged Goodson ashore in an unconscious state with a great crowd looking on and applauding, but when he had got it all thought out and was just beginning to remember all about it, a whole swarm of disqualifying details arrived on the ground: the town would have known of the circumstance, Mary would have known of it, it would glare like a limelight in his own memory instead of being an inconspicuous service which he had possibly rendered "without knowing its full value." And at this point he remembered that he couldn't swim, anyway.

Ah—*there* was a point which he had been overlooking from the start: it had to be a service which he had rendered "possibly without knowing the full value of it." Why, really, that ought to be an easy hunt—much easier than those others. And sure enough, by and by he found it. Goodson, years and years ago, came near marrying a very sweet and pretty girl, named Nancy Hewitt, but in some way or other the match had been broken off; the girl died, Goodson remained a bachelor, and by and by became a soured one and a frank despiser of the human species. Soon after the girl's death the village found out, or thought it had found out, that she carried a spoonful of negro blood in her veins. Richards worked at these details a good while, and in the end he thought he remembered things concerning them which must have gotten mislaid in his memory through long neglect. He seemed to dimly remember that it was *he* that found out about the negro blood; that it was he that told the village; that the village told Goodson where they got it; that he thus saved Goodson from marrying the tainted girl; that he had done him this great service "without knowing the full value of it," in fact without knowing that he *was* doing it; but that Goodson knew the value of it, and what a narrow escape he had had, and so went to his grave grateful to his benefactor and wishing he had a fortune to leave him. It was all clear and simple now, and the more he went over it the more luminous and certain it grew; and at last, when he nestled to sleep satisfied and happy, he remembered the whole thing just as if it had been yesterday. In fact, he dimly remembered Goodson's *telling* him his gratitude once. Meantime Mary had spent six thousand dollars on a new house for herself and a pair of slippers for her pastor, and then had fallen peacefully to rest.

That same Saturday evening the postman had delivered a letter to each of the other principal citizens—nineteen letters in all. No two of the envelopes were alike, and no two of the superscriptions were in the same hand, but the letters inside were just like each other in every detail but one. They were exact copies of the letter received by Richards—handwriting and all—and were all signed by Stephenson, but in place of Richards's name each receiver's own name appeared.

All night long eighteen principal citizens did what their caste-brother Richards was doing at the same time—they put in their energies trying to remember what notable service it was that they had unconsciously done Barclay Goodson. In no case was it a holiday job; still they succeeded.

And while they were at this work, which was difficult, their wives put in the night spending the money, which was easy. During that one night the nineteen wives spent an average of seven thousand dollars each out of the forty thousand in the sack—a hundred and thirty-three thousand altogether.

Next day there was a surprise for Jack Halliday. He noticed that the faces of the nineteen chief citizens and their wives bore that expression of peaceful and holy happiness again. He could not understand it, neither was he able to invent any remarks about it that could damage it or disturb it. And so it was his turn to be dissatisfied with life. His private guesses at the reasons for the happiness failed in all instances, upon examination. When he met Mrs. Wilcox and noticed the placid ecstasy in her face, he said to himself, "Her cat has had kittens"—and went and asked the cook: it was not so; the cook had detected the happiness, but did not know the cause. When Halliday found the duplicate ecstasy in the face of "Shadbelly" Billson (village nickname), he was sure some neighbor of Billson's had broken his leg, but inquiry showed that this had not happened. The subdued ecstasy in Gregory Yates's face could mean but one thing—he was a mother-in-law short: it was another mistake. "And Pinkerton—Pinkerton—he has collected ten cents that he thought he was going to lose." And so on, and so on. In some cases the guesses had to remain in doubt, in the others they proved distinct errors. In the end Halliday said to himself, "Anyway it foots up that there's nineteen Hadleyburg families temporily in heaven: I don't know how it happened; I only know Providence is off duty to-day."

An architect and builder from the next state had lately ventured to set up a small business in this unpromising village, and his sign had now been hanging out a week. Not a customer yet; he was a discouraged

man, and sorry he had come. But his weather changed suddenly now.
First one and then another chief citizen's wife said to him privately:

"Come to my house Monday week—but say nothing about it for the
present. We think of building."

He got eleven invitations that day. That night he wrote his daughter
and broke off her match with her student. He said she could marry a
mile higher than that.

Pinkerton the banker and two or three other well-to-do men planned
country-seats—but waited. That kind don't count their chickens until
they are hatched.

The Wilsons devised a grand new thing—a fancy-dress ball. They
made no actual promises, but told all their acquaintanceship in confidence that they were thinking the matter over and thought they
should give it—"and if we do, you will be invited, of course." People
were surprised, and said, one to another, "Why, they are crazy, those
poor Wilsons, they can't afford it." Several among the nineteen said privately to their husbands, "It is a good idea: we will keep still till their
cheap thing is over, then *we* will give one that will make it sick."

The days drifted along, and the bill of future squanderings rose
higher and higher, wilder and wilder, more and more foolish and reckless. It began to look as if every member of the nineteen would not
only spend his whole forty thousand dollars before receiving-day, but
be actually in debt by the time he got the money. In some cases light-
headed people did not stop with planning to spend, they really spent
—on credit. They bought land, mortgages, farms, speculative stocks, fine
clothes, horses, and various other things, paid down the bonus, and
made themselves liable for the rest—at ten days. Presently the sober
second thought came, and Halliday noticed that a ghastly anxiety was
beginning to show up in a good many faces. Again he was puzzled,
and didn't know what to make of it. "The Wilcox kittens aren't dead,
for they weren't born; nobody's broken a leg; there's no shrinkage in
mother-in-laws; *nothing* has happened—it is an unsolvable mystery."

There was another puzzled man, too—the Rev. Mr. Burgess. For days,
wherever he went, people seemed to follow him or to be watching
out for him; and if he ever found himself in a retired spot, a member
of the nineteen would be sure to appear, thrust an envelope privately
into his hand, whisper "To be opened at the town-hall Friday evening,"
then vanish away like a guilty thing. He was expecting that there might
be one claimant for the sack—doubtful, however, Goodson being dead
—but it never occurred to him that all this crowd might be claimants.

When the great Friday came at last, he found that he had nineteen envelopes.

3

The town-hall had never looked finer. The platform at the end of it was backed by a showy draping of flags; at intervals along the walls were festoons of flags; the gallery fronts were clothed in flags; the supporting columns were swathed in flags; all this was to impress the stranger, for he would be there in considerable force, and in a large degree he would be connected with the press. The house was full. The 412 fixed seats were occupied; also the 68 extra chairs which had been packed into the aisles; the steps of the platform were occupied; some distinguished strangers were given seats on the platform; at the horseshoe of tables which fenced the front and sides of the platform sat a strong force of special correspondents who had come from everywhere. It was the best-dressed house the town had ever produced. There were some tolerably expensive toilets there, and in several cases the ladies who wore them had the look of being unfamiliar with that kind of clothes. At least the town thought they had that look, but the notion could have arisen from the town's knowledge of the fact that these ladies had never inhabited such clothes before.

The gold-sack stood on a little table at the front of the platform where all the house could see it. The bulk of the house gazed at it with a burning interest, a mouth-watering interest, a wistful and pathetic interest; a minority of nineteen couples gazed at it tenderly, lovingly, proprietarily, and the male half of this minority kept saying over to themselves the moving little impromptu speeches of thankfulness for the audience's applause and congratulations which they were presently going to get up and deliver. Every now and then one of these got a piece of paper out of his vest pocket and privately glanced at it to refresh his memory.

Of course there was a buzz of conversation going on—there always is; but at last when the Rev. Mr. Burgess rose and laid his hand on the sack he could hear his microbes gnaw, the place was so still. He related the curious history of the sack, then went on to speak in warm terms of Hadleyburg's old and well-earned reputation for spotless honesty, and of the town's just pride in this reputation. He said that this reputation was a treasure of priceless value; that under Providence its value had now become inestimably enhanced, for the recent episode had spread this fame far and wide, and thus had focused the eyes of the American world upon this village, and made its name for all time, as he hoped and believed, a synonym for commercial incorruptibility. [*Applause.*] "And who is to be the guardian of this noble treasure—the community as a whole? No! The responsibility is individual, not communal. From this day forth each and every one of you is in his own person its special guardian, and individually responsible that no harm shall come to it. Do you—does each of you—accept this great trust? [*Tumultuous assent.*] Then all is well. Transmit it to your children and to your children's children. To-day your purity is beyond reproach—see to it that it shall remain so. To-day there is not a person in your community who could be beguiled to touch a penny not his own—see to it that you abide in this grace. ["*We will! we will!*"] This is not the place to make comparisons between ourselves and other communities—some of them ungracious toward us; they have their ways, we have ours; let us be content. [*Applause.*] I am done. Under my hand, my friends, rests a stranger's eloquent recognition of what we are; through him the world will always henceforth know what we are. We do not know who he is, but in your name I utter your gratitude, and ask you to raise your voices in indorsement."

The house rose in a body and made the walls quake with the thunders of its thankfulness for the space of a long minute. Then it sat down, and Mr. Burgess took an envelope out of his pocket. The house held its breath while he slit the envelope open and took from it a slip of paper. He read its contents—slowly and impressively—the audience listening with tranced attention to this magic document, each of whose words stood for an ingot of gold:

"*The remark which I made to the distressed stranger was this: "You are very far from being a bad man: go, and reform.*"" Then he continued:

"We shall know in a moment now whether the remark here quoted corresponds with the one concealed in the sack; and if that shall prove to be so—and it undoubtedly will—this sack of gold belongs to a fellow-citizen who will henceforth stand before the nation as the symbol of the special virtue which has made our town famous throughout the land—Mr. Billson!"

The house had gotten itself all ready to burst into the proper tornado of applause; but instead of doing it, it seemed stricken with a paralysis; there was a deep hush for a moment or two, then a wave of whispered murmurs swept the place—of about this tenor: "*Billson!* oh, come, this is *too* thin! Twenty dollars to a stranger—or *anybody*—*Billson!* tell it to the marines!" And now at this point the house caught its breath all of a sudden in a new access of astonishment, for it discovered that whereas in one part of the hall Deacon Billson was standing up with his head meekly bowed, in another part of it Lawyer Wilson was doing the same. There was a wondering silence now for a while.

Everybody was puzzled, and nineteen couples were surprised and indignant.

Billson and Wilson turned and stared at each other. Billson asked, bitingly:

"Why do *you* rise, Mr. Wilson?"

"Because I have a right to. Perhaps you will be good enough to explain to the house why *you* rise?"

"With great pleasure. Because I wrote that paper."

"It is an impudent falsity! I wrote it myself."

It was Burgess's turn to be paralyzed. He stood looking vacantly at first one of the men and then the other, and did not seem to know what to do. The house was stupefied. Lawyer Wilson spoke up, now, and said,

"I ask the Chair to read the name signed to that paper."

That brought the Chair to itself, and it read out the name:

"'John Wharton *Billson*.'"

"There!" shouted Billson, "what have you got to say for yourself, now? And what kind of apology are you going to make to me and to this insulted house for the imposture which you have attempted to play here?"

"No apologies are due, sir; and as for the rest of it, I publicly charge you with pilfering my note from Mr. Burgess and substituting a copy of it signed with your own name. There is no other way by which you could have gotten hold of the test-remark; I alone, of living men, possessed the secret of its wording."

There was likely to be a scandalous state of things if this went on; everybody noticed with distress that the short-hand scribes were scribbling like mad; many people were crying "Chair, Chair! Order! order!" Burgess rapped with his gavel, and said:

"Let us not forget the proprieties due. There has evidently been a mistake somewhere, but surely that is all. If Mr. Wilson gave me an envelope—and I remember now that he did—I still have it."

He took one out of his pocket, opened it, glanced at it, looked surprised and worried, and stood silent a few moments. Then he waved his hand in a wandering and mechanical way, and made an effort or two to say something, then gave it up, despondently. Several voices cried out:

"Read it! read it! What is it?"

So he began in a dazed and sleep-walker fashion:

" '*The remark which I made to the unhappy stranger was this:* "*You are far from being a bad man.* [The house gazed at him, marveling.] *Go, and reform.*" ' [*Murmurs:* "Amazing! what can this mean?"] This one," said the Chair, "is signed Thurlow G. Wilson."

"There!" cried Wilson. "I reckon that settles it! I knew perfectly well my note was purloined."

"Purloined!" retorted Billson. "I'll let you know that neither you nor any man of your kidney must venture to—"

THE CHAIR "Order, gentlemen, order! Take your seats, both of you, please."

They obeyed, shaking their heads and grumbling angrily. The house was profoundly puzzled; it did not know what to do with this curious emergency. Presently Thompson got up. Thompson was the hatter. He would have liked to be a Nineteener; but such was not for him: his stock of hats was not considerable enough for the position. He said:

"Mr. Chairman, if I may be permitted to make a suggestion, can both of these gentlemen be right? I put it to you, sir, can both have happened to say the very same words to the stranger? It seems to me—"

The tanner got up and interrupted him. The tanner was a disgruntled man; he believed himself entitled to be a Nineteener, but he couldn't get recognition. It made him a little unpleasant in his ways and speech. Said he:

"Sho, *that's* not the point! *That* could happen—twice in a hundred years—but not the other thing. *Neither* of them gave the twenty dollars!"

[*A ripple of applause.*]

BILLSON "*I* did!"

WILSON "*I* did!"

Then each accused the other of pilfering.

THE CHAIR "Order! Sit down, if you please—both of you. Neither of the notes has been out of my possession at any moment."

A VOICE "Good—that settles *that!*"

THE TANNER "Mr. Chairman, one thing is now plain: one of these men has been eavesdropping under the other one's bed, and filching family secrets. If it is not unparliamentary to suggest it, I will remark that both are equal to it. [*The Chair.* "Order! order!"] I withdraw the remark, sir, and will confine myself to suggesting that *if* one of them has overheard the other reveal the test-remark to his wife, we shall catch him now."

A VOICE "How?"

THE TANNER "Easily. The two have not quoted the remark in exactly the same words. You would have noticed that, if there hadn't been a considerable stretch of time and an exciting quarrel inserted between the two readings."

A VOICE "Name the difference."

THE TANNER "The word *very* is in Billson's note, and not in the other."

MANY VOICES "That's so—he's right!"

THE TANNER "And so, if the Chair will examine the test-remark in the sack, we shall know which of these two frauds—[*The Chair.* "Order!"] —which of these two adventurers—[*The Chair.* "Order! order!"]—which of these two gentlemen—[*laughter and applause*]—is entitled to wear the belt as being the first dishonest blatherskite ever bred in this town —which he has dishonored, and which will be a sultry place for him from now out!" [*Vigorous applause.*]

MANY VOICES "Open it!—open the sack!"

Mr. Burgess made a slit in the sack, slid his hand in and brought out an envelope. In it were a couple of folded notes. He said:

"One of these is marked, 'Not to be examined until all written communications which have been addressed to the Chair—if any—shall have been read.' The other is marked '*The Test.*' Allow me. It is worded—to wit:

"'I do not require that the first half of the remark which was made to me by my benefactor shall be quoted with exactness, for it was not striking, and could be forgotten; but its closing fifteen words are quite striking, and I think easily rememberable; unless *these* shall be accurately reproduced, let the applicant be regarded as an impostor. My benefactor began by saying he seldom gave advice to any one, but that it always bore the hall-mark of high value when he did give it. Then he said this—and it has never faded from my memory: '*You are far from being a bad man—*'''

FIFTY VOICES "That settles it—the money's Wilson's! Wilson! Wilson! Speech! Speech!"

People jumped up and crowded around Wilson, wringing his hand and congratulating fervently—meantime the Chair was hammering with the gavel and shouting:

"Order, gentlemen! Order! Order! Let me finish reading, please."

When quiet was restored, the reading was resumed—as follows:

"'"*Go, and reform—or, mark my words—some day, for your sins, you will die and go to hell or Hadleyburg*—TRY AND MAKE IT THE FORMER.*"''

A ghastly silence followed. First an angry cloud began to settle darkly upon the faces of the citizenship; after a pause the cloud began to rise, and a tickled expression tried to take its place; tried so hard that it was only kept under with great and painful difficulty; the reporters, the Brixtonites, and other strangers bent their heads down and shielded their faces with their hands, and managed to hold in by main strength and heroic courtesy. At this most inopportune time burst upon the stillness the roar of a solitary voice—Jack Halliday's:

"*That's* got the hall-mark on it!"

Then the house let go, strangers and all. Even Mr. Burgess's gravity broke down presently, then the audience considered itself officially absolved from all restraint, and it made the most of its privilege. It was a good long laugh, and a tempestuously whole-hearted one, but it ceased at last—long enough for Mr. Burgess to try to resume, and for the people to get their eyes partially wiped; then it broke out again; and afterward yet again; then at last Burgess was able to get out these serious words:

"It is useless to try to disguise the fact—we find ourselves in the presence of a matter of grave import. It involves the honor of your town, it strikes at the town's good name. The difference of a single word between the test-remarks offered by Mr. Wilson and Mr. Billson was itself a serious thing, since it indicated that one or the other of these gentlemen had committed a theft—"

The two men were sitting limp, nerveless, crushed; but at these words both were electrified into movement, and started to get up—

"Sit down!" said the Chair, sharply, and they obeyed. "That, as I have said, was a serious thing. And it was—but for only one of them. But the matter has become graver; for the honor of *both* is now in formidable peril. Shall I go even further, and say in inextricable peril? *Both* left out the crucial fifteen words." He paused. During several moments he allowed the pervading stillness to gather and deepen its impressive effects, then added: "There would seem to be but one way whereby this could happen. I ask these gentlemen—Was there *collusion?—agreement?*"

A low murmur sifted through the house; its import was, "He's got them both."

Billson was not used to emergencies; he sat in a helpless collapse. But Wilson was a lawyer. He struggled to his feet, pale and worried, and said:

"I ask the indulgence of the house while I explain this most painful matter. I am sorry to say what I am about to say, since it must inflict irreparable injury upon Mr. Billson, whom I have always esteemed and respected until now, and in whose invulnerability to temptation I entirely believed—as did you all. But for the preservation of my own honor I must speak—and with frankness. I confess with shame—and I now beseech your pardon for it—that I said to the ruined stranger all of the words contained in the test-remark, including the disparaging fifteen. [*Sensation.*] When the late publication was made I recalled them, and I resolved to claim the sack of coin, for by every right I was entitled to it. Now I will ask you to consider this point, and weigh it well: that stranger's gratitude to me that night knew no bounds; he said himself that he could find no words for it that were adequate, and that if he should ever be able he would repay me a thousandfold. Now, then, I ask you this: Could I expect—could I believe—could I even remotely imagine—that, feeling as he did, he would do so ungrateful a thing as to add those quite unnecessary fifteen words to his test?—set a trap for me?—expose me as a slanderer of my own town before my own people assembled in a public hall? It was preposterous; it was impossible. His test would contain only the kindly opening clause of my remark. Of that I had no shadow of doubt. You would have thought as I did. You would not have expected a base betrayal from one whom you had befriended and against whom you had committed no offense. And so, with perfect confidence, perfect trust, I wrote on a piece of paper the opening words—ending with 'Go, and reform,'—and signed it. When I was about to put it in an envelope I was called into my back office, and without thinking I left the paper lying open on my desk." He stopped, turned his head slowly toward Billson, waited a moment, then added: "I ask you to note this: when I returned, a little later, Mr. Billson was retiring by my street door." [*Sensation.*]

In a moment Billson was on his feet and shouting:

"It's a lie! It's an infamous lie!"

THE CHAIR "Be seated, sir! Mr. Wilson has the floor."

Billson's friends pulled him into his seat and quieted him, and Wilson went on:

"Those are the simple facts. My note was now lying in a different place on the table from where I had left it. I noticed that, but attached no importance to it, thinking a draught had blown it there. That Mr. Billson would read a private paper was a thing which could not occur to me; he was an honorable man, and he would be above that. If you will allow me to say it, I think his extra word '*very*' stands explained; it is attributable to a defect of memory. I was the only man in the world who could furnish here any detail of the test-remark—by *honorable* means. I have finished."

There is nothing in the world like a persuasive speech to fuddle the mental apparatus and upset the convictions and debauch the emotions of an audience not practised in the tricks and delusions of oratory. Wilson sat down victorious. The house submerged him in tides of approving applause; friends swarmed to him and shook him by the hand and congratulated him, and Billson was shouted down and not allowed to say a word. The Chair hammered and hammered with its gavel, and kept shouting:

"But let us proceed, gentlemen, let us proceed!"

At last there was a measurable degree of quiet, and the hatter said: "But what is there to proceed with, sir, but to deliver the money?"

VOICES "That's it! That's it! Come forward, Wilson!"

THE HATTER "I move three cheers for Mr. Wilson, Symbol of the special virtue which—"

The cheers burst forth before he could finish; and in the midst of them—and in the midst of the clamor of the gavel also—some enthusiasts mounted Wilson on a big friend's shoulder and were going to fetch him in triumph to the platform. The Chair's voice now rose above the noise—

"Order! To your places! You forget that there is still a document to be read." When quiet had been restored he took up the document, and was going to read it, but laid it down again, saying, "I forgot; this is not to be read until all written communications received by me have first been read." He took an envelope out of his pocket, removed its inclosure, glanced at it—seemed astonished—held it out and gazed at it—stared at it.

Twenty or thirty voices cried out:

"What is it? Read it! read it!"

And he did—slowly, and wondering:

"*The remark which I made to the stranger*—[*Voices.* "Hello! how's this?"]—*was this: "You are far from being a bad man.* [*Voices.* "Great Scott!"] *Go, and reform,*" [*Voices.* "Oh, saw my leg off!"] Signed by Mr. Pinkerton, the banker."

The pandemonium of delight which turned itself loose now was of a sort to make the judicious weep. Those whose withers were unwrung laughed till the tears ran down; the reporters, in throes of laughter, set down disordered pot-hooks which would never in the world be decipherable; and a sleeping dog jumped up, scared out of its wits, and barked itself crazy at the turmoil. All manner of cries were scattered through the din: "We're getting rich—*two* Symbols of Incorruptibility! —without counting Billson!" "*Three!*—count Shadbelly in—we can't have too many!" "All right—Billson's elected!" "Alas, poor Wilson—victim of *two* thieves!"

A POWERFUL VOICE "Silence! The Chair's fished up something more out of its pocket."

VOICES "Hurrah! Is it something fresh? Read it! read! read!"

THE CHAIR [*reading*] "'The remark which I made,' etc.: "'You are far from being a bad man. Go,"' etc. Signed, 'Gregory Yates.'"

TORNADO OF VOICES "Four Symbols!" "'Rah for Yates!" "Fish again!"

The house was in a roaring humor now, and ready to get all the fun out of the occasion that might be in it. Several Nineteeners, looking pale and distressed, got up and began to work their way toward the aisles, but a score of shouts went up:

"The doors, the doors—close the doors; no Incorruptible shall leave this place! Sit down, everybody!"

The mandate was obeyed.

"Fish again! Read! read!"

The Chair fished again, and once more the familiar words began to fall from its lips—"'You are far from being a bad man.'"

"Name! name! What's his name?"

"'L. Ingoldsby Sargent.'"

"Five elected! Pile up the Symbols! Go on, go on!"

"'You are far from being a bad—'"

"Name! name!"

"'Nicholas Whitworth.'"

"Hooray! hooray! it's a symbolical day!"

Somebody wailed in, and began to sing this rhyme (leaving out "it's") to the lovely "Mikado" tune of "When a man's afraid, a beautiful maid—"; the audience joined in, with joy; then, just in time, somebody contributed another line—

And don't you this forget—

The house roared it out. A third line was at once furnished—

Corruptibles far from Hadleyburg are—

The house roared that one too. As the last note died, Jack Halliday's voice rose high and clear, freighted with a final line—

But the Symbols are here, you bet!

That was sung, with booming enthusiasm. Then the happy house started in at the beginning and sang the four lines through twice, with immense swing and dash, and finished up with a crashing three-times-three and a tiger for "Hadleyburg the Incorruptible and all Symbols of it which we shall find worthy to receive the hall-mark to-night."

Then the shoutings at the Chair began again, all over the place:

"Go on! go on! Read! read some more! Read all you've got!"

"That's it—go on! We are winning eternal celebrity!"

A dozen men got up now and began to protest. They said that this farce was the work of some abandoned joker, and was an insult to the whole community. Without a doubt these signatures were all forgeries—

"Sit down! sit down! Shut up! You are confessing. We'll find *your* names in the lot."

"Mr. Chairman, how many of those envelopes have you got?"

The Chair counted.

"Together with those that have been already examined, there are nineteen."

A storm of derisive applause broke out.

"Perhaps they all contain the secret. I move that you open them all and read every signature that is attached to a note of that sort—and read also the first eight words of the note."

"Second the motion!"

It was put and carried—uproariously. Then poor old Richards got up, and his wife rose and stood at his side. Her head was bent down, so that none might see that she was crying. Her husband gave her his arm, and so supporting her, he began to speak in a quavering voice:

"My friends, you have known us two—Mary and me—all our lives, and I think you have liked us and respected us—"

The Chair interrupted him:

"Allow me. It is quite true—that which you are saying, Mr. Richards: this town *does* know you two; it *does* like you; it *does* respect you; more—it honors you and *loves* you—"

Halliday's voice rang out:

"That's the hall-marked truth, too! If the Chair is right, let the house speak up and say it. Rise! Now, then—hip! hip! hip!—all together!"

The house rose in mass, faced toward the old couple eagerly, filled the air with a snow-storm of waving handkerchiefs, and delivered the cheers with all its affectionate heart.

The Chair then continued:

"What I was going to say is this: We know your good heart, Mr. Richards, but this is not a time for the exercise of charity toward offenders. [*Shouts of "Right! right!"*] I see your generous purpose in your face, but I cannot allow you to plead for these men—"

"But I was going to—"

"Please take your seat, Mr. Richards. We must examine the rest of these notes—simple fairness to the men who have already been exposed requires this. As soon as that has been done—I give you my word for this—you shall be heard."

MANY VOICES "Right!—the Chair is right—no interruption can be permitted at this stage! Go on!—the names! the names!—according to the terms of the motion!"

The old couple sat reluctantly down, and the husband whispered to the wife, "It is pitifully hard to have to wait; the shame will be greater than ever when they find we were only going to plead for *ourselves*."

Straightway the jollity broke loose again with the reading of the names.

"'You are far from being a bad man—' Signature, 'Robert J. Titmarsh.'

"'You are far from being a bad man—' Signature, 'Eliphalet Weeks.'

"'You are far from being a bad man—' Signature, 'Oscar B. Wilder.'"

At this point the house lit upon the idea of taking the eight words out of the Chairman's hands. He was not unthankful for that. Thenceforward he held up each note in its turn, and waited. The house droned out the eight words in a massed and measured and musical deep volume of sound (with a daringly close resemblance to a well-known church chant)—"'You are f-a-r from being a b-a-a-a-d man.'" Then the Chair said, "Signature, 'Archibald Wilcox.'" And so on, and so on, name after name, and everybody had an increasingly and gloriously good time except the wretched Nineteen. Now and then, when a particularly shining name was called, the house made the Chair wait while it chanted the whole of the test-remark from the beginning to the closing words, "And go to hell or Hadleyburg—try and make it the for-or-m-e-r!" and in these special cases they added a grand and agonized and imposing "A-a-a-a-men!"

The list dwindled, dwindled, dwindled, poor old Richards keeping tally of the count, wincing when a name resembling his own was pronounced, and waiting in miserable suspense for the time to come when it would be his humiliating privilege to rise with Mary and finish his plea, which he was intending to word thus: ". . . for until now we have never done any wrong thing, but have gone our humble way unreproached. We are very poor, we are old, and have no chick nor child to help us; we were sorely tempted, and we fell. It was my purpose when I got up before to make confession and beg that my name might not be read out in this public place, for it seemed to us that we could not bear it; but I was prevented. It was just; it was our place to suffer with the rest. It has been hard for us. It is the first time we have ever heard our name fall from any one's lips—sullied. Be merciful—for the sake of the better days; make our shame as light to bear as in your charity you can." At this point in his revery Mary nudged him, perceiving that his mind was absent. The house was chanting, "You are f-a-r," etc.

"Be ready," Mary whispered. "Your name comes now; he has read eighteen."

The chant ended.

"Next! next! next!" came volleying from all over the house.

Burgess put his hand into his pocket. The old couple, trembling, began to rise. Burgess fumbled a moment, then said,

"I find I have read them all."

Faint with joy and surprise, the couple sank into their seats, and Mary whispered:

"Oh, bless God, we are saved!—he has lost ours—I wouldn't give this for a hundred of those sacks!"

The house burst out with its "Mikado" travesty, and sang it three times with ever-increasing enthusiasm, rising to its feet when it reached for the third time the closing line—

> *But the Symbols are here, you bet!*

and finishing up with cheers and a tiger for "Hadleyburg purity and our eighteen immortal representatives of it."

Then Wingate, the saddler, got up and proposed cheers "for the cleanest man in town, the one solitary important citizen in it who didn't try to steal that money—Edward Richards."

They were given with great and moving heartiness; then somebody proposed that Richards be elected sole guardian and Symbol of the now Sacred Hadleyburg Tradition, with power and right to stand up and look the whole sarcastic world in the face.

Passed, by acclamation; then they sang the "Mikado" again, and ended it with:

> *And there's one Symbol left, you bet!*

There was a pause; then—

A VOICE "Now, then, who's to get the sack?"

THE TANNER (*with bitter sarcasm*) "That's easy. The money has to be divided among the eighteen Incorruptibles. They gave the suffering stranger twenty dollars apiece—and that remark—each in his turn—it took twenty-two minutes for the procession to move past. Staked the stranger—total contribution, $360. All they want is just the loan back—and interest—forty thousand dollars altogether."

MANY VOICES [*derisively*] "That's it! Divvy! divvy! Be kind to the poor—don't keep them waiting!"

THE CHAIR "Order! I now offer the stranger's remaining document. It says: 'If no claimant shall appear [*grand chorus of groans*] I desire that you open the sack and count out the money to the principal citizens of your town, they to take it in trust [*cries of "Oh! Oh! Oh!"*], and use it in such ways as to them shall seem best for the propagation and preservation of your community's noble reputation for incorruptible honesty [*more cries*]—a reputation to which their names and their efforts will add a new and far-reaching luster.' [*Enthusiastic outburst of sarcastic applause.*] That seems to be all. No—here is a postscript:

'P. S.—CITIZENS OF HADLEYBURG: *There* is *no* test-remark—*nobody made one.* [Great sensation.] *There wasn't any pauper stranger, nor any twenty-dollar contribution, nor any accompanying benediction and compliment—these are all inventions.* [General buzz and hum of astonishment and delight.] *Allow me to tell my story—it will take but a word or two. I passed through your town at a certain time, and received a deep offense which I had not earned. Any other man would have been content to kill one or two of you and call it square, but to me that would have been a trivial revenge, and inadequate; for the dead do not suffer. Besides, I could not kill you all—and, anyway, made as I am, even that would not have satisfied me. I wanted to damage every man in the place, and every woman—and not in their bodies or in their estate, but in their vanity—the place where feeble and foolish people are most vulnerable. So I disguised myself and came back and studied you. You were easy game. You had an old and lofty reputation for honesty, and naturally you were proud of it—it was your treasure of treasures, the very apple of your eye. As soon as I found out that you carefully and vigilantly kept yourselves and your children out of temptation, I knew how to proceed. Why, you simple creatures, the weakest of all weak things is a virtue which has not been tested in the fire. I laid a plan, and gathered a list of names. My project was to corrupt Hadleyburg the Incorruptible. My idea was to make liars and thieves of nearly half a hundred smirchless men and women who had never in their lives uttered a lie or stolen a penny. I was afraid of Goodson. He was neither born nor reared in Hadleyburg. I was afraid that if I started to operate my scheme by getting my letter laid before you, you would say to yourselves, "Goodson is the only man among us who would give away twenty dollars to a poor devil"—and then you might not bite at my bait. But Heaven took Goodson; then I knew I was safe, and I set my trap and baited it. It may be that I shall not catch all the men to whom I mailed the pretended test secret, but I shall catch the most of them, if I know Hadleyburg nature.* [Voices. "Right—he got every last one of them."] *I believe they will even steal ostensible* gamble-money, *rather than miss, poor, tempted, and mistrained fellows. I am hoping to eternally and everlastingly squelch your vanity and give Hadleyburg a new renown—one that will* stick—*and spread far. If I have succeeded, open the sack and summon the Committee on Propagation and Preservation of the Hadleyburg Reputation.'*

A CYCLONE OF VOICES "Open it! Open it! The Eighteen to the front! Committee on Propagation of the Tradition! Forward—the Incorruptibles!"

The Chair ripped the sack wide, and gathered up a handful of bright, broad, yellow coins, shook them together, then examined them—

"Friends, they are only gilded disks of lead!"

There was a crashing outbreak of delight over this news, and when the noise had subsided, the tanner called out:

"By right of apparent seniority in this business, Mr. Wilson is Chairman of the Committee on Propagation of the Tradition. I suggest that he step forward on behalf of his pals, and receive in trust the money."

A HUNDRED VOICES "Wilson! Wilson! Wilson! Speech! Speech!"

WILSON [*in a voice trembling with anger*] "You will allow me to say, and without apologies for my language, *damn* the money!"

A VOICE "Oh, and him a Baptist!"

A VOICE "Seventeen Symbols left! Step up, gentlemen, and assume your trust!"

There was a pause—no response.

THE SADDLER "Mr. Chairman, we've got *one* clean man left, anyway, out of the late aristocracy; and he needs money, and deserves it. I move that you appoint Jack Halliday to get up there and auction off that sack of gilt twenty-dollar pieces, and give the result to the right man—the man whom Hadleyburg delights to honor—Edward Richards."

This was received with great enthusiasm, the dog taking a hand again; the saddler started the bids at a dollar, the Brixton folk and Barnum's representative fought hard for it, the people cheered every jump that the bids made, the excitement climbed moment by moment higher and higher, the bidders got on their mettle and grew steadily more and more daring, more and more determined, the jumps went from a dollar up to five, then to ten, then to twenty, then fifty, then to a hundred, then—

At the beginning of the auction Richards whispered in distress to his wife: "O Mary, can we allow it? It—it—you see, it is an honor-reward, a testimonial to purity of character, and—and—can we allow it? Hadn't I better get up and—O Mary, what ought we to do?—what do you think we—[*Halliday's voice. "Fifteen I'm bid!—fifteen for the sack!—twenty! —ah, thanks!—thirty—thanks again! Thirty, thirty, thirty!—do I hear forty?—forty it is! Keep the ball rolling, gentlemen, keep it rolling!—fifty! thanks, noble Roman! going at fifty, fifty, fifty!—seventy!—ninety!— splendid!—a hundred!—pile it up, pile it up!—hundred and twenty— forty!—just in time!—hundred and fifty!—*TWO *hundred!—superb! Do I hear two h— thanks!—two hundred and fifty!—*"]

"It is another temptation, Edward—I'm all in a tremble—but, oh, we've escaped *one* temptation, and that ought to warn us to— ["*Six did I hear?—thanks!—six-fifty, six-f—* SEVEN *hundred!*"] And yet, Edward, when you think—nobody susp— ["*Eight hundred dollars!—hurrah!— make it nine!—Mr. Parsons, did I hear you say—thanks—nine!—this noble sack of virgin lead going at only nine hundred dollars, gilding and all —come! do I hear—a thousand!—gratefully yours!—did some one say eleven?—a sack which is going to be the most celebrated in the whole Uni—*"] O Edward" (beginning to sob), "we are *so* poor!—but—but— do as you think best—do as you think best."

Edward fell—that is, he sat still; sat with a conscience which was not satisfied, but which was overpowered by circumstances.

Meantime a stranger, who looked like an amateur detective gotten up as an impossible English earl, had been watching the evening's proceedings with manifest interest, and with a contented expression in his face; and he had been privately commenting to himself. He was now soliloquizing somewhat like this: "None of the Eighteen are bidding; that is not satisfactory; I must change that—the dramatic unities require it; they must buy the sack they tried to steal; they must pay a heavy price, too—some of them are rich. And another thing, when I make a mistake in Hadleyburg nature the man that puts that error upon me is entitled to a high honorarium, and some one must pay it. This poor old Richards has brought my judgment to shame; he is an honest man: —I don't understand it, but I acknowledge it. Yes, he saw my deuces *and* with a straight flush, and by rights the pot is his. And it shall be a jack-pot, too, if I can manage it. He disappointed me, but let that pass."

He was watching the bidding. At a thousand, the market broke; the prices tumbled swiftly. He waited—and still watched. One competitor dropped out; then another, and another. He put in a bid or two, now. When the bids had sunk to ten dollars, he added a five; some one raised him a three; he waited a moment, then flung in a fifty-dollar jump, and the sack was his—at $1,282. The house broke out in cheers —then stopped; for he was on his feet, and had lifted his hand. He began to speak.

"I desire to say a word, and ask a favor. I am a speculator in rarities, and I have dealings with persons interested in numismatics all over the world. I can make a profit on this purchase, just as it stands; but there is a way, if I can get your approval, whereby I can make every one of these leaden twenty-dollar pieces worth its face in gold, and perhaps more. Grant me that approval, and I will give part of my gains to your Mr. Richards, whose invulnerable probity you have so justly and so cordially recognized to-night; his share shall be ten thousand dollars, and I will hand him the money to-morrow. [*Great applause from the house.* But the "invulnerable probity" made the Richardses blush prettily; however, it went for modesty, and did no harm.] If you will pass my proposition by a good majority—I would like a two-thirds vote —I will regard that as the town's consent, and that is all I ask. Rarities are always helped by any device which will rouse curiosity and compel remark. Now if I may have your permission to stamp upon the faces of each of these ostensible coins the names of the eighteen gentlemen who—"

Nine-tenths of the audience were on their feet in a moment—dog and all—and the proposition was carried with a whirlwind of approving applause and laughter.

They sat down, and all the Symbols except "Dr." Clay Harkness got up, violently protesting against the proposed outrage, and threatening to—

"I beg you not to threaten me," said the stranger, calmly. "I know my legal rights, and am not accustomed to being frightened at bluster." [*Applause.*] He sat down. "Dr." Harkness saw an opportunity here. He was one of the two very rich men of the place, and Pinkerton was the other. Harkness was proprietor of a mint; that is to say, a popular patent medicine. He was running for the legislature on one ticket, and Pinkerton on the other. It was a close race and a hot one, and getting hotter every day. Both had strong appetites for money; each had bought a great tract of land, with a purpose; there was going to be a new railway, and each wanted to be in the legislature and help locate the route to his own advantage; a single vote might make the decision, and with it two or three fortunes. The stake was large, and Harkness was a daring speculator. He was sitting close to the stranger. He leaned over while one or another of the other Symbols was entertaining the house with protests and appeals, and asked, in a whisper.

"What is your price for the sack?"

"Forty thousand dollars."

"I'll give you twenty."

"No."

"Twenty-five"

"No."

"Say thirty."

"The price is forty thousand dollars; not a penny less."

"All right, I'll give it. I will come to the hotel at ten in the morning. I don't want it known: will see you privately."

"Very good." Then the stranger got up and said to the house:

"I find it late. The speeches of these gentlemen are not without merit, not without interest, not without grace; yet if I may be excused I will take my leave. I thank you for the great favor which you have shown me in granting my petition. I ask the Chair to keep the sack for me until to-morrow, and to hand these three five-hundred-dollar notes to Mr. Richards." They were passed up to the Chair. "At nine I will call for the sack, and at eleven will deliver the rest of the ten thousand to Mr. Richards in person, at his home. Good night."

Then he slipped out, and left the audience making a vast noise, which was composed of a mixture of cheers, the "Mikado" song, dog-disapproval, and the chant, "You are f-a-r from being a b-a-a-d man—a-a-a-a-men!"

4

At home the Richardses had to endure congratulations and compliments until midnight. Then they were left to themselves. They looked a little sad, and they sat silent and thinking. Finally Mary sighed and said,

"Do you think we are to blame, Edward—*much* to blame?" and her eyes wandered to the accusing triplet of big bank-notes lying on the table, where the congratulators had been gloating over them and reverently fingering them. Edward did not answer at once; then he brought out a sigh and said, hesitatingly:

"We—we couldn't help it, Mary. It—well, it was ordered. *All* things are."

Mary glanced up and looked at him steadily, but he didn't return the look. Presently she said:

"I thought congratulations and praises always tasted good. But—it seems to me, now—Edward?"

"Well?"

"Are you going to stay in the bank?"

"N-no."

"Resign?"

"In the morning—by note."

"It does seem best."

Richards bowed his head in his hands and muttered:

"Before, I was not afraid to let oceans of people's money pour through my hands, but—Mary, I am so tired, so tired—"

"We will go to bed."

At nine in the morning the stranger called for the sack and took it to the hotel in a cab. At ten Harkness had a talk with him privately. The stranger asked for and got five checks on a metropolitan bank—drawn to "Bearer"—four for $1,500 each, and one for $34,000. He put one of the former in his pocketbook, and the remainder, representing $38,500, he put in an envelope, and with these he added a note, which he wrote after Harkness was gone. At eleven he called at the Richards house and knocked. Mrs. Richards peeped through the shutters, then went and received the envelope, and the stranger disappeared without a word. She came back flushed and a little unsteady on her legs, and gasped out:

"I am sure I recognized him! Last night it seemed to me that maybe I had seen him somewhere before."

"He is the man that brought the sack here?"

"I am almost sure of it."

"Then he is the ostensible Stephenson, too, and sold every important citizen in this town with his bogus secret. Now if he has sent checks instead of money, we are sold, too, after we thought we had escaped. I was beginning to feel fairly comfortable once more, after my night's rest, but the look of that envelope makes me sick. It isn't fat enough; $8,500 in even the largest bank-notes makes more bulk than that."

"Edward, why do you object to checks?"

"Checks signed by Stephenson! I am resigned to take the $8,500 if it could come in bank-notes—for it does seem that it was so ordered, Mary—but I have never had much courage, and I have not the pluck to try to market a check signed with that disastrous name. It would be a trap. That man tried to catch me; we escaped somehow or other; and now he is trying a new way. If it is checks—"

"Oh, Edward, it is *too* bad!" and she held up the checks and began to cry.

"Put them in the fire! quick! we mustn't be tempted. It is a trick to make the world laugh at *us*, along with the rest, and— Give them to *me*, since you can't do it!" He snatched them and tried to hold his grip till he could get to the stove; but he was human, he was a cashier, and he stopped a moment to make sure of the signature. Then he came near to fainting.

"Fan me, Mary, fan me! They are the same as gold!"

"Oh, how lovely, Edward! Why?"

"Signed by Harkness. What can the mystery of that be, Mary?"

"Edward, do you think—"

"Look here—look at this! Fifteen—fifteen—fifteen—thirty-four. Thirty-eight thousand five hundred! Mary, the sack isn't worth twelve dollars, and Harkness—apparently—has paid about par for it."

"And does it all come to us, do you think—instead of the ten thousand?"

"Why, it looks like it. And the checks are made to 'Bearer,' too."

"Is that good, Edward? What is it for?"

"A hint to collect them at some distant bank, I reckon. Perhaps Harkness doesn't want the matter known. What is that—a note?"

"Yes. It was with the checks."

It was in the "Stephenson" handwriting, but there was no signature. It said:

"I am a disappointed man. Your honesty is beyond the reach of temptation. I had a different idea about it, but I wronged you in that, and I beg pardon, and do it sincerely. I honor you—and that is sincere too. This town is not worthy to kiss the hem of your garment. Dear sir, I made a square bet with myself that there were nineteen debauchable men in your self-righteous community. I have lost. Take the whole pot, you are entitled to it."

Richards drew a deep sigh, and said:

"It seems written with fire—it burns so. Mary—I am miserable again."

"I, too. Ah, dear, I wish—"

"To think, Mary—he *believes* in me."

"Oh, don't, Edward—I can't bear it."

"If those beautiful words were deserved, Mary—and God knows I believed I deserved them once—I think I could give the forty thousand dollars for them. And I would put that paper away, as representing more than gold and jewels, and keep it always. But now— We could not live in the shadow of its accusing presence, Mary."

He put it in the fire.

A messenger arrived and delivered an envelope.

Richards took from it a note and read it; it was from Burgess.

"You saved me, in a difficult time. I saved you last night. It was at cost of a lie, but I made the sacrifice freely, and out of a grateful heart. None in this village knows so well as I know how brave and good and noble you are. At bottom you cannot respect me, knowing as you do of that matter of which I am accused, and by the general voice condemned; but I beg that you will at least believe that I am a grateful man; it will help me to bear my burden."

[*Signed*]   BURGESS

"Saved, once more. And on such terms!" He put the note in the fire. "I—I wish I were dead, Mary, I wish I were out of it all."

"Oh, these are bitter, bitter days, Edward. The stabs, through their very generosity, are so deep—and they come so fast!"

Three days before the election each of two thousand voters suddenly found himself in possession of a prized memento—one of the renowned bogus double-eagles. Around one of its faces was stamped these words: "THE REMARK I MADE TO THE POOR STRANGER WAS—" Around the other face was stamped these: "GO, AND REFORM. [SIGNED] PINKERTON." Thus the entire remaining refuse of the renowned joke was emptied upon a single head, and with calamitous effect. It revived the recent vast laugh and concentrated it upon Pinkerton; and Harkness's election was a walkover.

Within twenty-four hours after the Richardses had received their checks their consciences were quieting down, discouraged; the old couple were learning to reconcile themselves to the sin which they had committed. But they were to learn, now, that a sin takes on new and real terrors when there seems a chance that it is going to be found out. This gives it a fresh and most substantial and important aspect. At church the morning sermon was of the usual pattern; it was the same old things said in the same old way; they had heard them a thousand times and found them innocuous, next to meaningless, and easy to sleep under; but now it was different: the sermon seemed to bristle with accusations; it seemed aimed straight and specially at people who were concealing deadly sins. After church they got away from the mob of

congratulators as soon as they could, and hurried homeward, chilled
to the bone at they did not know what—vague, shadowy, indefinite
fears. And by chance they caught a glimpse of Mr. Burgess as he turned
a corner. He paid no attention to their nod of recognition! He hadn't
seen it; but they did not know that. What could his conduct mean? It
might mean—it might mean—oh, a dozen dreadful things. Was it possible that he knew that Richards could have cleared him of guilt in that
bygone time, and had been silently waiting for a chance to even up
accounts? At home, in their distress they got to imagining that their
servant might have been in the next room listening when Richards revealed the secret to his wife that he knew of Burgess's innocence; next,
Richards began to imagine that he had heard the swish of a gown in
there at that time; next, he was sure he *had* heard it. They would call
Sarah in, on a pretext, and watch her face: if she had been betraying
them to Mr. Burgess, it would show in her manner. They asked her
some questions—questions which were so random and incoherent and
seemingly purposeless that the girl felt sure that the old people's minds
had been affected by their sudden good fortune; the sharp and watchful gaze which they bent upon her frightened her, and that completed
the business. She blushed, she became nervous and confused, and to
the old people these were plain signs of guilt—guilt of some fearful sort
or other—without doubt she was a spy and a traitor. When they were
alone again they began to piece many unrelated things together and
get horrible results out of the combination. When things had got about
to the worst, Richards was delivered of a sudden gasp, and his wife
asked:

"Oh, what is it?—what is it?"

"The note—Burgess's note! Its language was sarcastic, I see it now."
He quoted: "'At bottom you cannot respect me, *knowing*, as you do, of
that matter of which I am accused'—oh, it is perfectly plain, now, God
help me! He knows that I know! You see the ingenuity of the phrasing.
It was a trap—and like a fool, I walked into it. And Mary—?"

"Oh, it is dreadful—I know what you are going to say—he didn't return
your transcript of the pretended test-remark."

"No—kept it to destroy us with. Mary, he has exposed us to some
already. I know it—I know it well. I saw it in a dozen faces after
church. Ah, he wouldn't answer our nod of recognition—*he* knew what
he had been doing!"

In the night the doctor was called. The news went around in the
morning that the old couple were rather seriously ill—prostrated by the
exhausting excitement growing out of their great windfall, the congrat-

ulations, and the late hours, the doctor said. The town was sincerely distressed; for these old people were about all it had left to be proud of, now.

Two days later the news was worse. The old couple were delirious, and were doing strange things. By witness of the nurses, Richards had exhibited checks—for $8,500? No—for an amazing sum—$38,500! What could be the explanation of this gigantic piece of luck?

The following day the nurses had more news—and wonderful. They had concluded to hide the checks, lest harm come to them; but when they searched they were gone from under the patient's pillow—vanished away. The patient said:

"Let the pillow alone; what do you want?"

"We thought it best that the checks—"

"You will never see them again—they are destroyed. They came from Satan. I saw the hell-brand on them, and I knew they were sent to betray me to sin." Then he fell to gabbling strange and dreadful things which were not clearly understandable, and which the doctor admonished them to keep to themselves.

Richards was right; the checks were never seen again.

A nurse must have talked in her sleep, for within two days the forbidden gabblings were the property of the town; and they were of a surprising sort. They seemed to indicate that Richards had been a claimant for the sack himself, and that Burgess had concealed that fact and then maliciously betrayed it.

Burgess was taxed with this and stoutly denied it. And he said it was not fair to attach weight to the chatter of a sick old man who was out of his mind. Still, suspicion was in the air, and there was much talk.

After a day or two it was reported that Mrs. Richards's delirious deliveries were getting to be duplicates of her husband's. Suspicion flamed up into conviction, now, and the town's pride in the purity of its one undiscredited important citizen began to dim down and flicker toward extinction.

Six days passed, then came more news. The old couple were dying. Richards's mind cleared in his latest hour, and he sent for Burgess. Burgess said:

"Let the room be cleared. I think he wishes to say something in privacy."

"No!" said Richards: "I want witnesses. I want you all to hear my confession, so that I may die a man, and not a dog. I was clean—artificially—like the rest; and like the rest I fell when temptation came. I signed a lie, and claimed the miserable sack. Mr. Burgess remembered that I had done him a service, and in gratitude (and ignorance) he suppressed my claim and saved me. You know the thing that was charged against Burgess years ago. My testimony, and mine alone, could have cleared him, and I was a coward, and left him to suffer disgrace—"

"No—no—Mr. Richards, you—"

"My servant betrayed my secret to him—"

"No one has betrayed anything to me—"

—"and then he did a natural and justifiable thing, he repented of the saving kindness which he had done me, and he *exposed* me—as I deserved—"

"Never!—I make oath—"

"Out of my heart I forgive him."

Burgess's impassioned protestations fell upon deaf ears; the dying man passed away without knowing that once more he had done poor Burgess a wrong. The old wife died that night.

The last of the sacred Nineteen had fallen a prey to the fiendish sack; the town was stripped of the last rag of its ancient glory. Its mourning was not showy, but it was deep.

By act of the Legislature—upon prayer and petition—Hadleyburg was allowed to change its name to (never mind what—I will not give it away), and leave one word out of the motto that for many generations had graced the town's official seal.

It is an honest town once more, and the man will have to rise early that catches it napping again.

1899

The Death Disk[1]

1

This was in Oliver Cromwell's time. Colonel Mayfair was the youngest officer of his rank in the armies of the Commonwealth, he being but thirty years old. But young as he was, he was a veteran soldier, and tanned and war-worn, for he had begun his military life at seventeen; he had fought in many battles, and had won his high place in the service and in the admiration of men, step by step, by valor in the field. But he was in deep trouble now; a shadow had fallen upon his fortunes.

The winter evening was come, and outside were storm and darkness; within, a melancholy silence; for the Colonel and his young wife had talked their sorrow out, had read the evening chapter and prayed the evening prayer, and there was nothing more to do but sit hand in hand and gaze into the fire, and think—and wait. They would not have to wait long; they knew that, and the wife shuddered at the thought.

They had one child—Abby, seven years old, their idol. She would be coming presently for the good-night kiss, and the Colonel spoke now, and said:

"Dry away the tears and let us seem happy, for her sake. We must forget, for the time, that which is to happen."

"I will. I will shut them up in my heart, which is breaking."

"And we will accept what is appointed for us, and bear it in patience, as knowing that whatsoever He doeth is done in righteousness and meant in kindness—"

"Saying, His will be done. Yes, I can say it with all my mind and soul—I would I could say it with my heart. Oh, if I could! if this dear hand which I press and kiss for the last time—"

"'Sh! sweetheart, she is coming!"

A curly-headed little figure in nightclothes glided in at the door and ran to the father, and was gathered to his breast and fervently kissed once, twice, three times.

[1] The text for this story is a touching incident mentioned in Carlyle's *Letters and Speeches of Oliver Cromwell.* M. T.

"Why, papa, you mustn't kiss me like that: you rumple my hair."

"Oh, I am so sorry—so sorry: do you forgive me, dear?"

"Why, of course, papa. But *are* you sorry?—not pretending, but real, right down sorry?"

"Well, you can judge for yourself, Abby," and he covered his face with his hands and made believe to sob. The child was filled with remorse to see this tragic thing which she had caused, and she began to cry herself, and to tug at the hands, and say:

"Oh, don't, papa, please don't cry; Abby didn't mean it; Abby wouldn't ever do it again. Please, papa!" Tugging and straining to separate the fingers, she got a fleeting glimpse of an eye behind them, and cried out: "Why, you naughty papa, you are not crying at all! You are only fooling! And Abby is going to mamma, now: you don't treat Abby right."

She was for climbing down, but her father wound his arms about her and said: "No, stay with me, dear: papa *was* naughty, and confesses it, and is sorry—there, let him kiss the tears away—and he begs Abby's forgiveness, and will do anything Abby says he must do, for a punishment; they're all kissed away now, and not a curl rumpled—and whatever Abby commands—"

And so it was made up; and all in a moment the sunshine was back again and burning brightly in the child's face, and she was patting her father's cheeks and naming the penalty—"A story! a story!"

Hark!

The elders stopped breathing, and listened. Footsteps! faintly caught between the gusts of wind. They came nearer, nearer—louder, louder—then passed by and faded away. The elders drew deep breaths of relief, and the papa said: "A story, is it? A gay one?"

"No, papa: a dreadful one."

Papa wanted to shift to the gay kind, but the child stood by her rights—as per agreement, she was to have anything she commanded. He was a good Puritan soldier and had passed his word—he saw that he must make it good. She said:

"Papa, we mustn't always have gay ones. Nurse says people don't always have gay times. Is that true, papa? She *says* so."

The mamma sighed, and her thoughts drifted to her troubles again. The papa said, gently: "It is true, dear. Troubles have to come; it is a pity, but it is true."

"Oh, then tell a story about them, papa—a dreadful one, so that we'll shiver, and feel just as if it was *us*. Mamma, you snuggle up close, and hold one of Abby's hands, so that if it's too dreadful it'll be easier for us to bear it if we are all snuggled up together, you know. Now you can begin, papa."

"Well, once there were three Colonels—"

"Oh, goody! *I* know Colonels, just as easy! It's because you are one, and I know the clothes. Go on, papa."

"And in a battle they had committed a breach of discipline."

The large words struck the child's ear pleasantly, and she looked up, full of wonder and interest, and said:

"Is it something good to eat, papa?"

The parents almost smiled, and the father answered:

"No, quite another matter, dear. They exceeded their orders."

"Is *that* someth—"

"No; it's as uneatable as the other. They were ordered to feign an attack on a strong position in a losing fight, in order to draw the enemy about and give the Commonwealth's forces a chance to retreat; but in their enthusiasm they overstepped their orders, for they turned the feint into a fact, and carried the position by storm, and won the day and the battle. The Lord General was very angry at their disobedience, and praised them highly, and ordered them to London to be tried for their lives."

"Is it the great General Cromwell, papa?"

"Yes."

"Oh, I've seen *him*, papa! and when he goes by our house so grand on his big horse, with the soldiers, he looks so—so—well, I don't know just how, only he looks as if he isn't satisfied, and you can see the people are afraid of him; but *I'm* not afraid of him, because he didn't look like that at me."

"Oh, you dear prattler! Well, the Colonels came prisoners to London, and were put upon their honor, and allowed to go and see their families for the last—"

Hark!

They listened. Footsteps again; but again they passed by. The mamma leaned her head upon her husband's shoulder to hide her paleness.

"They arrived this morning."

The child's eyes opened wide.

"Why, papa! is it a *true* story?"

"Yes, dear."

"Oh, how good! Oh, it's ever so much better! Go on, papa. Why, mamma!—*dear* mamma, are you crying?"

"Never mind me, dear—I was thinking of the—of the—the poor families."

"But *don't* cry, mamma: it 'll all come out right—you'll see; stories always do. Go on, papa, to where they lived happy ever after; then she won't cry any more. You'll see, mamma. Go on, papa."

"First, they took them to the Tower before they let them go home."

"Oh, *I* know the Tower! We can see it from here. Go on, papa."

"I am going on as well as I can, in the circumstances. In the Tower the military court tried them for an hour, and found them guilty, and condemned them to be shot."

"*Killed*, papa?"

"Yes."

"Oh, how naughty! *Dear* mamma, you are crying again. Don't, mamma; it 'll soon come to the good place—you'll see. Hurry, papa, for mamma's sake; you don't go fast enough."

"I know I don't, but I suppose it is because I stop so much to reflect."

"But you mustn't *do* it, papa; you must go right on."

"Very well, then. The three Colonels—"

"Do you know them, papa?"

"Yes, dear."

"Oh, I wish I did! I love Colonels. Would they let me kiss them, do you think?" The Colonel's voice was a little unsteady when he answered:

"*One* of them would, my darling! There—kiss me for him."

"There, papa—and these two are for the others. I think they would let me kiss them, papa; for I would say, 'My papa is a Colonel, too, and brave, and he would do what you did; so it *can't* be wrong, no matter what those people say, and you needn't be the least bit ashamed'; then they would let me—wouldn't they, papa?"

"God knows they would, child!"

"Mamma!—oh, mamma, you mustn't. He's soon coming to the happy place; go on, papa."

"Then, some were sorry—they all were; that military court, I mean; and they went to the Lord General, and said they had done their duty —for it *was* their duty, you know—and now they begged that two of the Colonels might be spared, and only the other one shot. One would be sufficient for an example for the army, they thought. But the Lord General was very stern, and rebuked them forasmuch as, having done *their* duty and cleared their consciences, they would beguile him to do less, and so smirch his soldierly honor. But they answered that they were asking nothing of him that they would not do themselves if they stood in his great place and held in their hands the noble prerogative of mercy. That struck him, and he paused and stood thinking, some of the sternness passing out of his face. Presently he bid them wait, and he retired to his closet to seek counsel of God in prayer; and when he came again, he said: 'They shall cast lots. That shall decide it, and two of them shall live.' "

"And did they, papa, did they? And which one is to die?—ah, that poor man!"

"No. They refused."

"They wouldn't do it, papa?"

"No."

"Why?"

"They said that the one that got the fatal bean would be sentencing himself to death by his own voluntary act, and it would be but suicide, call it by what name one might. They said they were Christians, and the Bible forbade men to take their own lives. They sent back that word, and said they were ready—let the court's sentence be carried into effect."

"What does that mean, papa?"

"They—they will all be shot."

Hark!

The wind? No. Tramp—tramp—tramp—r-r-r-umble-dumdum, r-r-rumble-dumdum—

"Open—in the Lord General's name!"

"Oh, goody, papa, it's the soldiers!—I love the soldiers! Let *me* let them in, papa, let *me!*"

She jumped down, and scampered to the door and pulled it open, crying joyously: "Come in! come in! Here they are, papa! Grenadiers! *I* know the Grenadiers!"

The file marched in and straightened up in line at shoulder arms; its officer saluted, the doomed Colonel standing erect and returning the courtesy, the soldier wife standing at his side, white, and with features drawn with inward pain, but giving no other sign of her misery, the child gazing on the show with dancing eyes. . . .

One long embrace, of father, mother, and child; then the order, "To the Tower—forward!" Then the Colonel marched forth from the house with military step and bearing, the file following; then the door closed.

"Oh, mamma, didn't it come out beautiful! I *told* you it would; and they're going to the Tower, and he'll *see* them! He—"

"Oh, come to my arms, you poor innocent thing!" . . .

2

The next morning the stricken mother was not able to leave her bed; doctors and nurses were watching by her, and whispering together now and then; Abby could not be allowed in the room; she was told to run and play—mamma was very ill. The child, muffled in winter wraps, went out and played in the street awhile; then it struck her as strange, and also wrong, that her papa should be allowed to stay at the Tower in ignorance at such a time as this. This must be remedied; she would attend to it in person.

An hour later the military court were ushered into the presence of the Lord General. He stood grim and erect, with his knuckles resting upon the table, and indicated that he was ready to listen. The spokesman said: "We have urged them to reconsider; we have implored them: but they persist. They will not cast lots. They are willing to die, but not to defile their religion."

The Protector's face darkened, but he said nothing. He remained a time in thought, then he said: "They shall not all die; the lots shall be cast *for* them." Gratitude shone in the faces of the court. "Send for them. Place them in that room there. Stand them side by side with their faces to the wall and their wrists crossed behind them. Let me have notice when they are there."

When he was alone he sat down, and presently gave this order to an attendant: "Go, bring me the first little child that passes by."

The man was hardly out at the door before he was back again—leading Abby by the hand, her garments lightly powdered with snow. She went straight to the Head of the State, that formidable personage at the mention of whose name the principalities and powers of the earth trembled, and climbed up in his lap, and said:

"I know *you*, sir: you are the Lord General; I have seen you; I have seen you when you went by my house. Everybody was afraid; but *I* wasn't afraid, because you didn't look cross at *me*; you remember, don't you? I had on my red frock—the one with the blue things on it down the front. Don't you remember that?"

A smile softened the austere lines of the Protector's face, and he began to struggle diplomatically with his answer:

"Why, let me see—I—"

"I was standing right by the house—*my* house, you know."

"Well, you dear little thing, I ought to be ashamed, but you know—"

The child interrupted, reproachfully.

"Now you *don't* remember it. Why, I didn't forget *you*."

"Now I *am* ashamed: but I will never forget you again, dear; you have my word for it. You will forgive me now, won't you, and be good friends with me, always and forever?"

"Yes, indeed I will, though I don't know how you came to forget it; you must be very forgetful: but I am too, sometimes. I can forgive you without any trouble, for I think you *mean* to be good and do right, and I think you are just as kind—but you must snuggle me better, the way papa does—it's cold."

"You shall be snuggled to your heart's content, little new friend of mine, always to be *old* friend of mine hereafter, isn't it? You mind me of my little girl—not little any more, now—but she was dear, and sweet, and daintily made, like you. And she had your charm, little witch —your all-conquering sweet confidence in friend and stranger alike, that wins to willing slavery any upon whom its precious compliment falls. She used to lie in my arms, just as you are doing now; and charm the weariness and care out of my heart and give it peace, just as you are doing now; and we were comrades, and equals, and playfellows together. Ages ago it was, since that pleasant heaven faded away and vanished, and you have brought it back again;—take a burdened man's blessing for it, you tiny creature, who are carrying the weight of England while I rest!"

"Did you love her very, very, *very* much?"

"Ah, you shall judge by this: she commanded and I obeyed!"

"I think you are lovely! Will you kiss me?"

"Thankfully—and hold it a privilege, too. There—this one is for you; and there—this one is for her. You made it a request; and you could have made it a command, for you are representing her, and what you command I must obey."

The child clapped her hands with delight at the idea of this grand promotion—then her ear caught an approaching sound: the measured tramp of marching men.

"Soldiers!—soldiers, Lord General! Abby wants to see them!"

"You shall, dear; but wait a moment, I have a commission for you."

An officer entered and bowed low, saying, "They are come, your Highness," bowed again, and retired.

The Head of the Nation gave Abby three little disks of sealing-wax: two white, and one a ruddy red—for this one's mission was to deliver death to the Colonel who should get it.

"Oh, what a lovely red one! Are they for me?"

"No, dear; they are for others. Lift the corner of that curtain, there, which hides an open door; pass through, and you will see three men standing in a row, with their backs toward you and their hands behind their backs—so—each with one hand open, like a cup. Into each of the open hands drop one of those things, then come back to me."

Abby disappeared behind the curtain, and the Protector was alone. He said, reverently: "Of a surety that good thought came to me in my perplexity from Him who is an ever-present help to them that are in doubt and seek His aid. He knoweth where the choice should fall, and has sent His sinless messenger to do His will. Another would err, but He cannot err. Wonderful are His ways, and wise—blessed be His holy Name!"

The small fairy dropped the curtain behind her and stood for a moment conning with alert curiosity the appointments of the chamber of doom, and the rigid figures of the soldiery and the prisoners; then her face lighted merrily, and she said to herself: "Why, one of them is papa! I know his back. He shall have the prettiest one!" She tripped gaily forward and dropped the disks into the open hands, then peeped around under her father's arm and lifted her laughing face and cried out:

"Papa! papa! look what you've got. *I* gave it to you!"

He glanced at the fatal gift, then sunk to his knees and gathered his innocent little executioner to his breast in an agony of love and pity. Soldiers, officers, released prisoners, all stood paralyzed, for a moment, at the vastness of this tragedy, then the pitiful scene smote their hearts, their eyes filled, and they wept unashamed. There was deep and reverent silence during some minutes, then the officer of the guard moved reluctantly forward and touched his prisoner on the shoulder, saying, gently:

"It grieves me, sir, but my duty commands."

"Commands what?" said the child.

"I must take him away. I am so sorry."

"Take him away? Where?"

"To—to—God help me!—to another part of the fortress."

"Indeed you can't. My mamma is sick, and I am going to take him home." She released herself and climbed upon her father's back and put her arms around his neck. "Now Abby's ready, papa—come along."

"My poor child, I can't. I must go with them."

The child jumped to the ground and looked about her, wondering. Then she ran and stood before the officer and stamped her small foot indignantly and cried out:

"I told you my mamma is sick, and you might have listened. Let him go—you *must!*"

"Oh, poor child, would God I could, but indeed I must take him away. Attention, guard! . . . fall in! . . . shoulder arms!" . . .

Abby was gone—like a flash of light. In a moment she was back, dragging the Lord Protector by the hand. At this formidable apparition all present straightened up, the officers saluting and the soldiers presenting arms.

"Stop them, sir! My mamma is sick and wants my papa, and I *told* them so, but they never even listened to me, and are taking him away."

The Lord General stood as one dazed.

"*Your* papa, child? Is he your papa?"

"Why, of course—he was *always* it. Would I give the pretty red one to any other, when I love him so? No!"

A shocked expression rose in the Protector's face, and he said:

"Ah, God help me! through Satan's wiles I have done the cruelest thing that ever man did—and there is no help, no help! What can I do?"

Abby cried out, distressed and impatient: "Why you can make them let him go," and she began to sob. "Tell them to do it! You told me to command, and now the very first time I tell you to do a thing you don't do it!"

A tender light dawned in the rugged old face, and the Lord General laid his hand upon the small tyrant's head and said: "God be thanked for the saving accident of that unthinking promise; and you, inspired by Him, for reminding me of my forgotten pledge, O incomparable child! Officer, obey her command—she speaks by my mouth. The prisoner is pardoned; set him free!"

1901

Two Little Tales

FIRST STORY: THE MAN WITH A MESSAGE FOR THE DIRECTOR-GENERAL

Some days ago, in this second month of 1900, a friend made an afternoon call upon me here in London. We are of that age when men who are smoking away their times in chat do not talk quite so much about the pleasantnesses of life as about its exasperations. By and by this friend began to abuse the War Office. It appeared that he had a friend who had been inventing something which could be made very useful to the soldiers in South Africa. It was a light and very cheap and durable boot, which would remain dry in wet weather, and keep its shape and firmness. The inventor wanted to get the government's attention called to it, but he was an unknown man and knew the great officials would pay no heed to a message from him.

"This shows that he was an ass—like the rest of us," I said, interrupting. "Go on."

"But why have you said that? The man spoke the truth."

"The man spoke a lie. Go on."

"I will *prove* that he—"

"You can't prove anything of the kind. I am very old and very wise. You must not argue with me: it is irreverent and offensive. Go on."

"Very well. But you will presently see. I am not unknown, yet even *I* was not able to get the man's message to the Director-General of the Shoe-Leather Department."

"This is another lie. Pray go on."

"But I assure you on my honor that I failed."

"Oh, certainly. I knew *that*. You didn't need to tell me."

"Then where is the lie?"

"It is in your intimation that you were *not able* to get the Director-General's immediate attention to the man's message. It is a lie, because you *could* have gotten his immediate attention to it."

"I tell you I couldn't. In three months I haven't accomplished it."

"Certainly. Of course. I could know that without your telling me. You *could* have gotten his immediate attention if you had gone at it in a sane way; and so could the other man."

"I *did* go at it in a sane way."

"You didn't."

"How do *you* know? What do you know about the circumstances?"

"Nothing at all. But you didn't go at it in a sane way. That much I know to a certainty."

"How can you know it, when you don't know what method I used?"

"I know by the result. The result is perfect proof. You went at it in an insane way. I am very old and very w—"

"Oh, yes, I know. But will you let me tell you *how* I proceeded? I think that will settle whether it was insanity or not."

"No; that has already been settled. But go on, since you so desire to expose yourself. I am very o—"

"Certainly, certainly. I sat down and wrote a courteous letter to the Director-General of the Shoe-Leather Department, explai—"

"Do you know him personally?"

"No."

"You have scored one for my side. You began insanely. Go on."

"In the letter I made the great value and inexpensiveness of the invention clear, and offered to—"

"Call and see him? Of course you did. Score two against yourself. I am v—"

"He didn't answer for three days."

"Necessarily. Proceed."

"Sent me three gruff lines thanking me for my trouble, and proposing—"

"Nothing."

"That's it—proposing nothing. Then I wrote him more elaborately and—"

"Score three—"

—"and got no answer. At the end of a week I wrote and asked, with some touch of asperity, for an answer to that letter."

"Four. Go on."

"An answer came back saying the letter had not been received, and asking for a copy. I traced the letter through the post-office, and found that it *had* been received; but I sent a copy and said nothing. Two weeks passed without further notice of me. In the mean time I gradually got myself cooled down to a polite-letter temperature. Then I wrote and proposed an interview for next day, and said that if I did not hear from him in the mean time I should take his silence for assent."

"Score five."

"I arrived at twelve sharp, and was given a chair in the anteroom and told to wait. I waited until half past one; then I left, ashamed and angry. I waited another week, to cool down; then I wrote and made another appointment with him for next day noon."

"Score six."

"He answered, assenting. I arrived promptly, and kept a chair warm until half past two. I left then, and shook the dust of that place from my shoes for good and all. For rudeness, inefficiency, incapacity, indifference to the army's interests, the Director-General of the Shoe-Leather Department of the War Office is, in my o—"

"Peace! I am very old and very wise, and have seen many seemingly intelligent people who hadn't common sense enough to go at a simple and easy thing like this in a common-sense way. You are not a curiosity to me; I have personally known millions and billions like you. You have lost three months quite unnecessarily; the inventor has lost three months; the soldiers have lost three—nine months altogether. I will now read you a little tale which I wrote last night. Then you will call on the Director-General at noon to-morrow and transact your business."

"Splendid! Do you know him?"

"No; but listen to the tale."

SECOND STORY: HOW THE CHIMNEY-SWEEP GOT THE EAR OF THE EMPEROR

Summer was come, and all the strong were bowed by the burden of the awful heat, and many of the weak were prostrate and dying. For weeks the army had been wasting away with a plague of dysentery, that scourge of the soldier, and there was but little help. The doctors were in despair; such efficacy as their drugs and their science had once had—and it was not much at its best—was a thing of the past, and promised to remain so.

The Emperor commanded the physicians of greatest renown to appear before him for a consultation, for he was profoundly disturbed. He was very severe with them, and called them to account for letting his soldiers die; and asked them if they knew their trade, or didn't; and were they properly healers, or merely assassins? Then the principal assassin, who was also the oldest doctor in the land and the most venerable in appearance, answered and said:

"We have done what we could, your Majesty, and for a good reason it has been little. No medicine and no physician can cure that disease; only nature and a good constitution can do it. I am old, and I know. No doctor and no medicine can cure it—I repeat it and I emphasize it. Sometimes they seem to help nature a little—a very little—but as a rule, they merely do damage."

The Emperor was a profane and passionate man, and he deluged the doctors with rugged and unfamiliar names, and drove them from his presence.

Within a day he was attacked by that fell disease himself. The news flew from mouth to mouth, and carried consternation with it over all the land.

All the talk was about this awful disaster, and there was general depression, for few had hope. The Emperor himself was very melancholy, and sighed and said:

"The will of God be done. Send for the assassins again, and let us get over with it."

They came, and felt his pulse and looked at his tongue, and fetched the drug-store and emptied it into him, and sat down patiently to wait —for they were not paid by the job, but by the year.

2

Tommy was sixteen and a bright lad, but he was not in society. His rank was too humble for that, and his employment too base. In fact, it was the lowest of all employments, for he was second in command to his father, who emptied cesspools and drove a night-cart. Tommy's closest friend was Jimmy the chimney-sweep, a slim little fellow of fourteen, who was honest and industrious, and had a good heart, and supported a bedridden mother by his dangerous and unpleasant trade.

About a month after the Emperor fell ill, these two lads met one evening about nine. Tommy was on his way to his night-work, and of course was not in his Sundays, but in his dreadful work-clothes, and not smelling very well. Jimmy was on his way home from his day's labor, and was blacker than any other object imaginable, and he had his brushes on his shoulder and his soot-bag at his waist, and no feature of his sable face was distinguishable except his lively eyes.

They sat down on the curbstone to talk; and of course it was upon the one subject—the nation's calamity, the Emperor's disorder. Jimmy was full of a great project, and burning to unfold it. He said:

"Tommy, I can cure his Majesty. I know how to do it."

Tommy was surprised.

"What! You?"

"Yes, I."

"Why, you little fool, the best doctors can't."

"I don't care: I can do it. I can cure him in fifteen minutes."

"Oh, come off! What are you giving me?"

"The facts—that's all."

Jimmy's manner was so serious that it sobered Tommy, who said:

"I believe you are in earnest, Jimmy. Are you in earnest?"

"I give you my word."

"What is the plan? How'll you cure him?"

"Tell him to eat a slice of ripe watermelon."

It caught Tommy rather suddenly, and he was shouting with laughter

at the absurdity of the idea before he could put on a stopper. But he
sobered down when he saw that Jimmy was wounded. He patted
Jimmy's knee affectionately, not minding the soot, and said:

"I take the laugh all back. I didn't mean any harm, Jimmy, and I
won't do it again. You see, it seemed so funny, because wherever
there's a soldier-camp and dysentery, the doctors always put up a sign
saying anybody caught bringing watermelons there will be flogged with
the cat till he can't stand."

"I know it—the idiots!" said Jimmy, with both tears and anger in
his voice. "There's plenty of watermelons, and not one of all those soldiers ought to have died."

"But, Jimmy, what put the notion into your head?"

"It isn't a notion; it's a fact. Do you know that old gray-headed Zulu?
Well, this long time back he has been curing a lot of our friends, and
my mother has seen him do it, and so have I. It takes only one or two
slices of melon, and it don't make any difference whether the disease
is new or old; it cures it."

"It's very odd. But, Jimmy, if it is so, the Emperor ought to be told of
it."

"Of course; and my mother has told people, hoping they could get
the word to him; but they are poor working-folks and ignorant, and
don't know how to manage it."

"Of course they don't, the blunderheads," said Tommy, scornfully.
"*I'll* get it to him!"

"You? You night-cart polecat!" And it was Jimmy's turn to laugh. But
Tommy retorted sturdily:

"Oh, laugh if you like; but I'll *do* it!"

It had such an assured and confident sound that it made an impression, and Jimmy asked gravely:

"Do you know the Emperor?"

"Do *I* know him? Why, how you talk! Of course I don't."

"Then how'll you do it?"

"It's very simple and very easy. Guess. How would *you* do it, Jimmy?"

"Send him a letter. I never thought of it till this minute. But I'll bet
that's your way."

"I'll bet it ain't. Tell me, how would you send it?"

"Why, through the mail, of course."

Tommy overwhelmed him with scoffings, and said:

"Now, don't you suppose every crank in the empire is doing the same
thing? Do you mean to say you haven't thought of that?"

"Well—no," said Jimmy, abashed.

"You *might* have thought of it, if you weren't so young and inexperienced. Why, Jimmy, when even a common *general*, or a poet, or an actor, or anybody that's a little famous gets sick, all the cranks in the kingdom load up the mails with certain-sure quack cures for him. And so, what's bound to happen when it's the Emperor?"

"I suppose it's worse," said Jimmy, sheepishly.

"Well, I should think so! Look here, Jimmy: every single night we cart off as many as six loads of that kind of letters from the back yard of the palace, where they're thrown. Eighty thousand letters in one night! Do you reckon anybody reads them? Sho! not a single one. It's what would happen to your letter if you wrote it—which you won't, I reckon?"

"No," sighed Jimmy, crushed.

"But it's all right, Jimmy. Don't you fret: there's more than one way to skin a cat. *I'll* get the word to him."

"Oh, if you only *could*, Tommy, I should love you forever!"

"I'll do it, I tell you. Don't you worry; you depend on me."

"Indeed I will, Tommy, for you do know so much. You're not like other boys: they never know anything. How'll you manage, Tommy?"

Tommy was greatly pleased. He settled himself for reposeful talk, and said:

"Do you know that ragged poor thing that thinks he's a butcher because he goes around with a basket and sells cat's meat and rotten livers? Well, to begin with, I'll tell *him*."

Jimmy was deeply disappointed and chagrined, and said:

"Now, Tommy, it's a shame to talk so. You know my heart's in it, and it's not right."

Tommy gave him a love-pat, and said:

"Don't you be troubled, Jimmy. *I* know what I'm about. Pretty soon you'll see. That half-breed butcher will tell the old woman that sells chestnuts at the corner of the lane—she's his closest friend, and I'll ask him to; then, by request, she'll tell her rich aunt that keeps the little fruit-shop on the corner two blocks above; and that one will tell her particular friend, the man that keeps the game-shop; and he will tell his friend the sergeant of police; and the sergeant will tell his captain, and the captain will tell the magistrate, and the magistrate will tell his brother-in-law the county judge, and the county judge will tell the sheriff, and the sheriff will tell the Lord Mayor, and the Lord Mayor will tell the President of the Council, and the President of the Council will tell the—"

"By George, but it's a wonderful scheme, Tommy! How ever *did* you—"

"—Rear-Admiral, and the Rear will tell the Vice, and the Vice will tell the Admiral of the Blue, and the Blue will tell the Red, and the Red will tell the White, and the White will tell the First Lord of the Admiralty, and the First Lord will tell the Speaker of the House, and the Speaker—"

"Go it, Tommy; you're 'most there!"

"—will tell the Master of the Hounds, and the Master will tell the Head Groom of the Stables, and the Head Groom will tell the Chief Equerry, and the Chief Equerry will tell the First Lord in Waiting, and the First Lord will tell the Lord High Chamberlain, and the Lord High Chamberlain will tell the Master of the Household, and the Master of the Household will tell the little pet page that fans the flies off the Emperor, and the page will get down on his knees and whisper it to his Majesty—and the game's made!"

"I've *got* to get up and hurrah a couple of times, Tommy. It's the grandest idea that ever was. What ever put it into your head?"

"Sit down and listen, and I'll give you some wisdom—and don't you ever forget it as long as you live. Now, then, who is the closest friend you've got, and the one you couldn't and wouldn't ever refuse anything in the world to?"

"Why, it's you, Tommy. You know that."

"Suppose you wanted to ask a pretty large favor of the cat's-meat man. Well, you don't know him, and he would tell you to go to thunder, for he is that kind of a person; but he is my next best friend after you, and would run his legs off to do me a kindness—*any* kindness, he don't care what it is. Now, I'll ask you: which is the most common-sensible—for you to go and ask him to tell the chestnut-woman about your watermelon cure, or for you to get me to do it for you?"

"To get you to do it for me, of course. I wouldn't ever have thought of that, Tommy; it's splendid!"

"It's a *philosophy*, you see. Mighty good word—and large. It goes on this idea: everybody in the world, little and big, has one *special* friend, a friend that he's *glad* to do favors to—not sour about it, but *glad*—glad clear to the marrow. And so, I don't care where you start, you can get at anybody's ear that you want to—I don't care how low you are, nor how high he is. And it's so simple: you've only to find the *first* friend, that is all; that ends your part of the work. He finds the next friend himself, and that one finds the third, and so on, friend after friend, link after link, like a chain; and you can go up it or down it, as high as you like or as low as you like."

"It's just beautiful, Tommy."

"It's as simple and easy as a-b-c; but did you ever hear of anybody trying it? No; everybody is a fool. He goes to a stranger without any introduction, or writes him a letter, and of course he strikes a cold wave —and serves him gorgeously right. Now, the Emperor don't know me, but that's no matter—he'll eat his watermelon to-morrow. You'll see. Hihi—stop! It's the cat's-meat man. Good-by, Jimmy; I'll overtake him."

He did overtake him, and said:

"Say, will you do me a favor?"

"*Will* I? Well, I should *say!* I'm your man. Name it, and see me fly!"

"Go tell the chestnut-woman to put down everything and carry this message to her first-best friend, and tell the friend to pass it along." He worded the message, and said, "Now, then, rush!"

The next moment the chimney-sweep's word to the Emperor was on its way.

3

The next evening, toward midnight, the doctors sat whispering together in the imperial sick-room and they were in deep trouble, for the Emperor was in very bad case. They could not hide it from themselves that every time they emptied a fresh drug-store into him he got worse. It saddened them, for they were expecting that result. The poor emaciated Emperor lay motionless, with his eyes closed, and the page that was his darling was fanning the flies away and crying softly. Presently the boy heard the silken rustle of a portière, and turned and saw the Lord High Great Master of the Household peering in at the door and excitedly motioning to him to come. Lightly and swiftly the page tiptoed his way to his dear and worshiped friend the Master, who said:

"Only you can persuade him, my child, and oh, don't fail to do it! Take this, make him eat it, and he is saved."

"On my head be it. He shall eat it!"

It was a couple of great slices of ruddy, fresh watermelon.

The next morning the news flew everywhere that the Emperor was sound and well again, and had hanged the doctors. A wave of joy swept the land, and frantic preparations were made to illuminate.

After breakfast his Majesty sat meditating. His gratitude was unspeakable, and he was trying to devise a reward rich enough to properly testify it to his benefactor. He got it arranged in his mind, and called the page, and asked him if he had invented that cure. The boy said no— he got it from the Master of the Household.

He was sent away, and the Emperor went to devising again. The

Master was an earl; he would make him a duke, and give him a vast estate which belonged to a member of the Opposition. He had him called, and asked him if he was the inventor of the remedy. But the Master was an honest man, and said he got it of the Grand Chamberlain. He was sent away, and the Emperor thought some more. The Chamberlain was a viscount; he would make him an earl, and give him a large income. But the Chamberlain referred him to the First Lord in Waiting, and there was some more thinking; his Majesty thought out a smaller reward. But the First Lord in Waiting referred him back further, and he had to sit down and think out a further and becomingly and suitably smaller reward.

Then, to break the tediousness of the inquiry and hurry the business, he sent for the Grand High Chief Detective, and commanded him to trace the cure to the bottom, so that he could properly reward his benefactor.

At nine in the evening the High Chief Detective brought the word. He had traced the cure down to a lad named Jimmy, a chimney-sweep. The Emperor said, with deep feeling:

"Brave boy, he saved my life, and shall not regret it!"

And sent him a pair of his own boots; and the next best ones he had, too. They were too large for Jimmy, but they fitted the Zulu, so it was all right, and everything as it should be.

CONCLUSION TO THE FIRST STORY

"There—do you get the idea?"

"I am obliged to admit that I do. And it will be as you have said. I will transact the business to-morrow. I intimately know the Director-General's nearest friend. He will give me a note of introduction, with a word to say my matter is of real importance to the government. I will take it along, without an appointment, and send it in, with my card, and I sha'n't have to wait so much as half a minute."

That turned out true to the letter, and the government adopted the boots.

1901

The Belated Russian Passport

One fly makes a summer.—*Pudd'nhead Wilson's Calendar*

A great beer-saloon in the Friedrichstrasse, Berlin, toward mid-afternoon. At a hundred round tables gentlemen sat smoking and drinking; flitting here and there and everywhere were white-aproned waiters bearing foaming mugs to the thirsty. At a table near the main entrance were grouped half a dozen lively young fellows—American students—drinking good-by to a visiting Yale youth on his travels, who had been spending a few days in the German capital.

"But why do you cut your tour short in the middle, Parrish?" asked one of the students. "I wish I had your chance. What do you want to go home for?"

"Yes," said another, "what is the idea? You want to explain, you know, because it looks like insanity. Homesick?"

A girlish blush rose in Parrish's fresh young face, and after a little hesitation he confessed that that was his trouble.

"I was never away from home before," he said, "and every day I get more and more lonesome. I have not seen a friend for weeks, and it's been horrible. I meant to stick the trip through, for pride's sake, but seeing you boys has finished me. It's been heaven to me, and I can't take up that companionless dreariness again. If I had company—but I haven't, you know, so it's no use. They used to call me Miss Nancy when I was a small chap, and I reckon I'm that yet—girlish and timorous, and all that. I ought to have *been* a girl! I can't stand it; I'm going home."

The boys rallied him good-naturedly, and said he was making the mistake of his life; and one of them added that he ought at least to see St. Petersburg before turning back.

"Don't!" said Parrish, appealingly. "It was my dearest dream, and I'm throwing it away. Don't say a word more on that head, for I'm made of water, and can't stand out against anybody's persuasion. I *can't* go alone; I think I should die." He slapped his breast pocket, and added: "Here is my protection against a change of mind; I've bought ticket and sleeper for Paris, and I leave to-night. Drink, now—this is on me—bumpers—this is for home!"

The good-bys were said, and Alfred Parrish was left to his thoughts and his loneliness. But for a moment only. A sturdy middle-aged man with a brisk and businesslike bearing, and an air of decision and confidence suggestive of military training, came bustling from the next table, and seated himself at Parrish's side, and began to speak, with concentrated interest and earnestness. His eyes, his face, his person, his whole system, seemed to exude energy. He was full of steam—racing pressure—one could almost hear his gauge-cocks sing. He extended a frank hand, shook Parrish's cordially, and said, with a most convincing air of strenuous conviction:

"Ah, but you *mustn't;* really you mustn't; it would be the greatest mistake; you would always regret it. Be persuaded, I beg you; don't do it—don't!"

There was such a friendly note in it, and such a seeming of genuineness, that it brought a sort of uplift to the youth's despondent spirits, and a telltale moisture betrayed itself in his eyes, an unintentional confession that he was touched and grateful. The alert stranger noted that sign, was quite content with that response, and followed up his advantage without waiting for a spoken one:

"No, don't do it; it would be a mistake. I have heard everything that was said—you will pardon that—I was so close by that I couldn't help it. And it troubled me to think that you would cut your travels short when you really *want* to see St. Petersburg, and are right here almost in sight of it! Reconsider it—ah, you *must* reconsider it. It is such a short distance—it is very soon done and very soon over—and think what a memory it will be!"

Then he went on and made a picture of the Russian capital and its wonders, which made Alfred Parrish's mouth water and his roused spirits cry out with longing. Then—

"Of course you must see St. Petersburg—you *must!* Why, it will be a joy to you—a joy! I know, because I know the place as familiarly as I know my own birthplace in America. Ten years—I've known it ten years. Ask anybody there; they'll tell you; they all know me—Major Jackson. The very dogs know me. Do go; oh, you must go; you must, indeed."

Alfred Parrish was quivering with eagerness now. He would go. His face said it as plainly as his tongue could have done it. Then—the old shadow fell,—and he said, sorrowfully:

"Oh, no—no, it's no use; I can't. I should die of the loneliness."

The Major said, with astonishment: "The—loneliness! Why, I'm going *with* you!"

It was startlingly unexpected. And not quite pleasant. Things were moving too rapidly. Was this a trap? Was this stranger a sharper? Whence all this gratuitous interest in a wandering and unknown lad? Then he glanced at the Major's frank and winning and beaming face, and was ashamed; and wished he knew how to get out of this scrape without hurting the feelings of its contriver. But he was not handy in matters of diplomacy, and went at the difficulty with conscious awkwardness and small confidence. He said, with a quite overdone show of unselfishness:

"Oh no, no, you are too kind; I couldn't—I couldn't allow you to put yourself to such an inconvenience on my—"

"Inconvenience? None in the world, my boy; I was going to-night, anyway; I leave in the express at nine. Come! we'll go together. You sha'n't be lonely a single minute. Come along—say the word!"

So that excuse had failed. What to do now? Parrish was disheartened; it seemed to him that no subterfuge which his poor invention could contrive would ever rescue him from these toils. Still, he must make another effort, and he did; and before he had finished his new excuse he thought he recognized that it was unanswerable:

"Ah, but most unfortunately luck is against me, and it is impossible. Look at these"—and he took out his tickets and laid them on the table. "I am booked through to Paris, and I couldn't get these tickets and baggage coupons changed for St. Petersburg, of course, and would have to lose the money; and if I could afford to lose the money I should be rather short after I bought the new tickets—for there is all the cash I've got about me"—and he laid a five-hundred-mark bank-note on the table.

In a moment the Major had the tickets and coupons and was on his feet, and saying, with enthusiasm:

"Good! It's all right, and everything safe. They'll change the tickets and baggage pasters for *me;* they all know me—everybody knows me. Sit right where you are; I'll be back right away." Then he reached for the bank-note, and added, "I'll take this along, for there will be a little extra pay on the new tickets, maybe"—and the next moment he was flying out at the door.

2

Alfred Parrish was paralyzed. It was all so sudden. So sudden, so daring, so incredible, so impossible. His mouth was open, but his tongue wouldn't work; he tried to shout "Stop him," but his lungs were empty; he wanted to pursue, but his legs refused to do anything but tremble; then they gave way under him and let him down into his chair. His throat was dry, he was gasping and swallowing with dismay, his head was in a whirl. What must he do? He did not know. One thing seemed plain, however—he must pull himself together, and try to overtake that man. Of course the man could not get back the ticket-money, but would he throw the tickets away on that account? No; he would certainly go to the station and sell them to some one at half-price; and to-day, too, for they would be worthless to-morrow, by German custom. These reflections gave him hope and strength, and he rose and started. But he took only a couple of steps, then he felt a sudden sickness, and tottered back to his chair again, weak with a dread that his movement had been noticed—for the last round of beer was at his expense; it had not been paid for, and he hadn't a pfennig. He was a prisoner—Heaven only could know what might happen if he tried to leave the place. He was timid, scared, crushed; and he had not German enough to state his case and beg for help and indulgence.

Then his thoughts began to persecute him. How could he have been such a fool? What possessed him to listen to such a manifest adventurer? *And here comes the waiter!* He buried himself in the newspaper —trembling. The waiter passed by. It filled him with thankfulness. The hands of the clock seemed to stand still, yet he could not keep his eyes from them.

Ten minutes dragged by. The waiter again! Again he hid behind the paper. The waiter paused—apparently a week—then passed on.

Another ten minutes of misery—once more the waiter; this time he wiped off the table, and seemed to be a month at it; then paused two months, and went away.

Parrish felt that he could not endure another visit; he must take the chances: he must run the gantlet; he must escape. But the waiter stayed around about the neighborhood for five minutes—months and months seemingly, Parrish watching him with a despairing eye, and feeling the infirmities of age creeping upon him and his hair gradually turning gray.

At last the waiter wandered away—stopped at a table, collected a bill, wandered farther, collected another bill, wandered farther—Parrish's praying eye riveted on him all the time, his heart thumping, his breath coming and going in quick little gasps of anxiety mixed with hope.

The waiter stopped again to collect, and Parrish said to himself, it is

now or never! and started for the door. One step—two steps—three—
four—he was nearing the door—five—his legs shaking under him—was
that a swift step behind him?—the thought shriveled his heart—six steps
—seven, and he was out!—eight—nine—ten—eleven—twelve—there *is* a
pursuing step!—he turned the corner, and picked up his heels to fly—a
heavy hand fell on his shoulder, and the strength went out of his body.

It was the Major. He asked not a question, he showed no surprise. He
said, in his breezy and exhilarating fashion:

"Confound those people, they delayed me; that's why I was gone so
long. New man in the ticket-office, and he didn't know me, and
wouldn't make the exchange because it was irregular; so I had to hunt
up my old friend, the great mogul—the station-master, you know—hi,
there, cab! cab!—jump in, Parrish!—Russian consulate, cabby, and let
them fly!—so, as I say, that all cost time. But it's all right now, and
everything straight; your luggage reweighed, rechecked, fare-ticket and
sleeper changed, and I've got the documents for it in my pocket; also
the change—I'll keep it for you. Whoop along, cabby, whoop along; don't
let them go to sleep!"

Poor Parrish was trying his best to get in a word edgeways, as the cab
flew farther and farther from the bilked beer-hall, and now at last he
succeeded, and wanted to return at once and pay his little bill.

"Oh, never mind about that," said the Major, placidly; "that's all
right, they know me, everybody knows me—I'll square it next time I'm
in Berlin—push along, cabby, push along—no great lot of time to spare,
now."

They arrived at the Russian consulate, a moment after-hours, and
hurried in. No one there but a clerk. The Major laid his card on the desk,
and said, in the Russian tongue, "Now, then, if you'll visé this young
man's passport for Petersburg as quickly as—"

"But, dear sir, I'm not authorized, and the consul has just gone."

"Gone where?"

"Out in the country, where he lives."

"And he'll be back—"

"Not till morning."

"Thunder! Oh, well, look here, I'm Major Jackson—he knows me,
everybody knows me. You visé it yourself; tell him Major Jackson asked
you; it 'll be all right."

But it would be desperately and fatally irregular; the clerk could not
be persuaded; he almost fainted at the idea.

"Well, then, I'll tell you what you do," said the Major. "Here's stamps
and the fee—visé it in the morning, and start it along by mail."

The clerk said, dubiously, "He—well, he may perhaps do it, and so—"

"May? He *will!* He knows me—everybody knows me."

"Very well," said the clerk, "I will tell him what you say." He looked bewildered, and in a measure subjugated; and added, timidly: "But—but—you know you will beat it to the frontier twenty-four hours. There are no accommodations there for so long a wait."

"Who's going to *wait?* Not I, if the court knows herself."

The clerk was temporarily paralyzed, and said, "Surely, sir, you don't wish it sent to Petersburg!"

"And why not?"

"And the owner of it tarrying at the frontier, twenty-five miles away? It couldn't do him any good, in those circumstances."

"Tarry—the mischief! Who said he was going to do any tarrying?"

"Why, you know, of course, they'll stop him at the frontier if he has no passport."

"Indeed they won't! The Chief Inspector knows me—everybody does. I'll be responsible for the young man. You send it straight through to Petersburg—Hôtel de l'Europe, care Major Jackson: tell the consul not to worry, I'm taking all the risks myself."

The clerk hesitated, then chanced one more appeal:

"You must bear in mind, sir, that the risks are peculiarly serious, just now. The new edict is in force."

"What is it?"

"Ten years in Siberia for being in Russia without a passport."

"Mm—damnation!" He said it in English, for the Russian tongue is but a poor stand-by in spiritual emergencies. He mused a moment, then brisked up and resumed in Russian: "Oh, it's all right—label her St. Petersburg and let her sail! I'll fix it. They all know me there—all the authorities—everybody."

3

The Major turned out to be an adorable traveling-companion, and young Parrish was charmed with him. His talk was sunshine and rainbows, and lit up the whole region around, and kept it gay and happy and cheerful; and he was full of accommodating ways, and knew all about how to do things, and when to do them, and the best way. So the long journey was a fairy dream for that young lad who had been so lonely and forlorn and friendless so many homesick weeks. At last, when the two travelers were approaching the frontier, Parrish said something about passports; then started, as if recollecting something, and added:

"Why, come to think, I don't remember your bringing my passport away from the consulate. But you did, didn't you?"

"No; it's coming by mail," said the Major, comfortably.

"C—coming—by—mail!" gasped the lad; and all the dreadful things he had heard about the terrors and disasters of passportless visitors to Russia rose in his frightened mind and turned him white to the lips. "Oh, Major—oh, my goodness, what will become of me! How *could* you do such a thing?"

The Major laid a soothing hand upon the youth's shoulder and said:

"Now, don't you worry, my boy, don't you worry a bit. I'm taking care of you, and I'm not going to let any harm come to you. The Chief Inspector knows me, and I'll explain to him, and it 'll be all right—you'll see. Now don't you give yourself the least discomfort—I'll fix it all up, easy as nothing."

Alfred trembled, and felt a great sinking inside, but he did what he could to conceal his misery, and to respond with some show of heart to the Major's kindly pettings and reassurings.

At the frontier he got out and stood on the edge of the great crowd, and waited in deep anxiety while the Major plowed his way through the mass to "explain to the Chief Inspector." It seemed a cruelly long wait, but at last the Major reappeared. He said, cheerfully, "Damnation, it's a new inspector, and I don't know him!"

Alfred fell up against a pile of trunks, with a despairing, "Oh, dear, dear, I might have known it!" and was slumping limp and helpless to the ground, but the Major gathered him up and seated him on a box, and sat down by him, with a supporting arm around him, and whispered in his ear:

"Don't worry, laddie, don't—it's going to be all right; you just trust to me. The sub-inspector's as near-sighted as a shad. I watched him, and I know it's so. Now I'll tell you how to do. I'll go and get my passport chalked, then I'll stop right yonder inside the grille where you see those peasants with their packs. You be there, and I'll back up against the grille, and slip my passport to you through the bars, then you tag along after the crowd and hand it in, and trust to Providence and that shad. Mainly the shad. You'll pull through all right—now don't you be afraid."

"But, oh dear, dear, *your* description and *mine* don't tally any more than—"

"Oh, that's all right—difference between fifty-one and nineteen—just entirely imperceptible to that shad—don't you fret, it's going to come out as right as nails."

Ten minutes later Alfred was tottering toward the train, pale, and in a collapse, but he had played the shad successfully, and was as grateful as an untaxed dog that has evaded the police.

"I told you so," said the Major, in splendid spirits. "I knew it would come out all right if you trusted in Providence like a little trusting child and didn't try to improve on His ideas—it always does."

Between the frontier and Petersburg the Major laid himself out to restore his young comrade's life, and work up his circulation, and pull him out of his despondency, and make him feel again that life was a joy and worth living. And so, as a consequence, the young fellow entered the city in high feather and marched into the hotel in fine form, and registered his name. But instead of naming a room, the clerk glanced at him inquiringly, and waited. The Major came promptly to the rescue, and said, cordially:

"It's all right—you know me—set him down, I'm responsible." The clerk looked grave, and shook his head. The Major added: "It's all right, it'll be here in twenty-four hours—it's coming by mail. Here's mine, and his is coming, right along."

The clerk was full of politeness, full of deference, but he was firm. He said, in English:

"Indeed, I wish I could accommodate you, Major, and certainly I would if I could; but I have no choice, I must ask him to go; I cannot allow him to remain in the house a moment."

Parrish began to totter, and emitted a moan; the Major caught him and stayed him with an arm, and said to the clerk, appealingly:

"Come, you know me—everybody does—just let him stay here the one night, and I give you my word—"

The clerk shook his head, and said:

"But, Major, you are endangering me, you are endangering the house. I—I hate to do such a thing, but I—I *must* call the police."

"Hold on, don't do that. Come along, my boy, and don't you fret—it's going to come out all right. Hi, there, cabby! Jump in, Parrish. Palace of the General of the Secret Police—turn them loose, cabby! Let them go! Make them whiz! Now we're off, and don't you give yourself any uneasiness. Prince Bossloffsky knows me, knows me like a book; he'll soon fix things all right for us."

They tore through the gay streets and arrived at the palace, which was brilliantly lighted. But it was half past eight; the Prince was about going in to dinner, the sentinel said, and couldn't receive any one.

But he'll receive *me*," said the Major, robustly, and handed his card. "I'm Major Jackson. Send it in; it'll be all right."

The card was sent in, under protest, and the Major and his waif waited in a reception-room for some time. At length they were sent for, and conducted to a sumptuous private office and confronted with the Prince, who stood there gorgeously arrayed and frowning like a thunder-cloud. The Major stated his case, and begged for a twenty-four-hour stay of proceedings until the passport should be forthcoming.

"Oh, impossible!" said the Prince, in faultless English. "I marvel that you should have done so insane a thing as to bring the lad into the country without a passport, Major, I marvel at it; why, it's ten years in Siberia, and no help for it—catch him! support him!" for poor Parrish was making another trip to the floor. "Here—quick, give him this. There —take another draught; brandy's the thing, don't you find it so, lad? Now you feel better, poor fellow. Lie down on the sofa. How stupid it was of you, Major, to get him into such a horrible scrape." The Major eased the boy down with his strong arms, put a cushion under his head, and whispered in his ear:

"Look as damned sick as you can! Play it for all it's worth; he's touched, you see; got a tender heart under there somewhere; fetch a groan, and say, 'Oh, mamma, mamma'; it 'll knock him out, sure as guns."

Parrish was going to do these things anyway, from native impulse, so they came from him promptly, with great and moving sincerity, and the Major whispered: "Splendid! Do it again; Bernhardt couldn't beat it."

What with the Major's eloquence and the boy's misery, the point was gained at last; the Prince struck his colors, and said:

"Have it your way; though you deserve a sharp lesson and you ought to get it. I give you exactly twenty-four hours. If the passport is not here then, don't come near me; it's Siberia without hope of pardon."

While the Major and the lad poured out their thanks, the Prince rang in a couple of soldiers, and in their own language he ordered them to go with these two people, and not lose sight of the younger one a moment for the next twenty-four hours; and if, at the end of that term, the boy could not show a passport, impound him in the dungeons of St. Peter and St. Paul, and report.

The unfortunates arrived at the hotel with their guards, dined under their eyes, remained in Parrish's room until the Major went off to bed, after cheering up the said Parrish, then one of the soldiers locked himself and Parrish in, and the other one stretched himself across the door outside and soon went off to sleep.

So also did not Alfred Parrish. The moment he was alone with the solemn soldier and the voiceless silence his machine-made cheerfulness began to waste away, his medicated courage began to give off its supporting gases and shrink toward normal, and his poor little heart to shrivel like a raisin. Within thirty minutes he struck bottom; grief, misery, fright, despair, could go no lower. Bed? Bed was not for such as he; bed was not for the doomed, the lost! Sleep? He was not the Hebrew children, he could not sleep in the fire! He could only walk the floor. And not only could, but must. And did, by the hour. And mourned, and wept, and shuddered, and prayed.

Then all-sorrowfully he made his last dispositions, and prepared himself, as well as in him lay, to meet his fate. As a final act, he wrote a letter:

"MY DARLING MOTHER,—When these sad lines shall have reached you your poor Alfred will be no more. No; worse than that, far worse! Through my own fault and foolishness I have fallen into the hands of a sharper or a lunatic; I do not know which, but in either case I feel that I am lost. Sometimes I think he is a sharper, but most of the time I think he is only mad, for he has a kind, good heart, I know, and he certainly seems to try the hardest that ever a person tried to get me out of the fatal difficulties he has gotten me into.

"In a few hours I shall be one of a nameless horde plodding the snowy solitudes of Russia, under the lash, and bound for that land of mystery and misery and termless oblivion, Siberia! I shall not live to see it; my heart is broken and I shall die. Give my picture to *her*, and ask her to keep it in memory of me, and to so live that in the appointed time she may join me in that better world where there is no marriage nor giving in marriage, and where there are no more separations, and troubles never come. Give my yellow dog to Archy Hale, and the other one to Henry Taylor; my blazer I give to brother Will, and my fishing-things and Bible.

"There is no hope for me. I cannot escape; the soldier stands there with his gun and never takes his eyes off me, just blinks; there is no other movement, any more than if he was dead. I cannot bribe him, the maniac has my money. My letter of credit is in my trunk, and may never come—*will* never come, I know. Oh, what is to become of me! Pray for me, darling mother, pray for your poor Alfred. But it will do no good."

4

In the morning Alfred came out looking scraggy and worn when the Major summoned him to an early breakfast. They fed their guards, they lit cigars, the Major loosened his tongue and set it going, and under its magic influence Alfred gradually and gratefully became hopeful, measurably cheerful, and almost happy once more.

But he would not leave the house. Siberia hung over him black and threatening, his appetite for sights was all gone, he could not have borne the shame of inspecting streets and galleries and churches with a soldier at each elbow and all the world stopping and staring and commenting—no, he would stay within and wait for the Berlin mail and his fate. So, all day long the Major stood gallantly by him in his room, with one soldier standing stiff and motionless against the door with his musket at his shoulder, and the other one drowsing in a chair outside; and all day long the faithful veteran spun campaign yarns, described battles, reeled off explosive anecdotes, with unconquerable energy and sparkle and resolution, and kept the scared student alive and his pulses functioning. The long day wore to a close, and the pair, followed by their guards, went down to the great dining-room and took their seats.

"The suspense will be over before long, now," sighed poor Alfred.

Just then a pair of Englishmen passed by, and one of them said, "So we'll get no letters from Berlin to-night."

Parrish's breath began to fail him. The Englishmen seated themselves at a near-by table, and the other one said:

"No, it isn't as bad as that." Parrish's breathing improved. "There is later telegraphic news. The accident did detain the train formidably, but that is all. It will arrive here three hours late to-night."

Parrish did not get to the floor this time, for the Major jumped for him in time. He had been listening, and foresaw what would happen. He patted Parrish on the back, hoisted him out of his chair, and said, cheerfully:

"Come along, my boy, cheer up, there's absolutely nothing to worry about. I know a way out. Bother the passport; let it lag a week if it wants to, we can do without it."

Parrish was too sick to hear him; hope was gone, Siberia present; he moved off on legs of lead, upheld by the Major, who walked him to the American legation, heartening him on the way with assurances that on his recommendation the minister wouldn't hesitate a moment to grant him a new passport.

"I had that card up my sleeve all the time," he said. "The minister knows me—knows me familiarly—chummed together hours and hours under a pile of other wounded at Cold Harbor; been chummies ever since, in spirit, though we haven't met much in the body. Cheer up, laddie, everything's looking splendid! By gracious! I feel as cocky as a buck angel. Here we are, and our troubles are at an end! If we ever really had any."

There, alongside the door, was the trade-mark of the richest and freest and mightiest republic of all the ages: the pine disk, with the planked eagle spread upon it, his head and shoulders among the stars, and his claws full of out-of-date war material; and at that sight the tears came into Alfred's eyes, the pride of country rose in his heart, Hail Columbia boomed up in his breast, and all his fears and sorrows vanished away; for here he was safe, safe! not all the powers of the earth would venture to cross that threshold to lay a hand upon him!

For economy's sake the mightiest republic's legations in Europe consist of a room and a half on the ninth floor, when the tenth is occupied, and the legation furniture consists of a minister or an ambassador with a brakeman's salary, a secretary of legation who sells matches and mends crockery for a living, a hired girl for interpreter and general utility, pictures of the American liners, a chromo of the reigning President, a desk, three chairs, kerosene-lamp, a cat, a clock, and a cuspidor with the motto, "In God We Trust."

The party climbed up there, followed by the escort. A man sat at the desk writing official things on wrapping-paper with a nail. He rose and faced about; the cat climbed down and got under the desk; the hired girl squeezed herself up into the corner by the vodka-jug to make room; the soldiers squeezed themselves up against the wall alongside of her, with muskets at shoulder arms. Alfred was radiant with happiness and the sense of rescue.

The Major cordially shook hands with the official, rattled off his case in easy and fluent style, and asked for the desired passport.

The official seated his guests, then said: "Well, I am only the secretary of legation, you know, and I wouldn't like to grant a passport while the minister is on Russian soil. There is far too much responsibility."

"All right, send for him."

The secretary smiled, and said: "That's easier said than done. He's away up in the wilds, somewhere, on his vacation."

"Ger-reat Scott!" ejaculated the Major.

Alfred groaned; the color went out of his face, and he began to slowly collapse in his clothes. The secretary said, wonderingly:

"Why, what are you Great-Scotting about, Major? The Prince gave you twenty-four hours. Look at the clock; you're all right; you've half an hour left; the train is just due; the passport will arrive in time."

"Man, there's news! The train is three hours behind time! This boy's life and liberty are wasting away by minutes, and only thirty of them left! In half an hour he's the same as dead and damned to all eternity! By God, we *must* have the passport!"

"Oh, I am dying, I know it!" wailed the lad, and buried his face in his arms on the desk. A quick change came over the secretary, his placidity vanished away, excitement flamed up in his face and eyes, and he exclaimed:

"I see the whole ghastliness of the situation, but, Lord help us, what can I do? What can you suggest?"

"Why, hang it, give him the passport!"

"Impossible! Totally impossible! You know nothing about him; three days ago you had never heard of him; there's no way in the world to identify him. He is lost, lost—there's no possibility of saving him!"

The boy groaned again, and sobbed out, "Lord, Lord, it's the last of earth for Alfred Parrish!"

Another change came over the secretary.

In the midst of a passionate outburst of pity, vexation, and hopelessness, he stopped short, his manner calmed down, and he asked, in the indifferent voice which one uses in introducing the subject of the weather when there is nothing to talk about, "Is that your name?"

The youth sobbed out a yes.

"Where are you from?"

"Bridgeport."

The secretary shook his head—shook it again—and muttered to himself. After a moment:

"Born there?"

"No; New Haven."

"Ah-h." The secretary glanced at the Major, who was listening intently, with blank and unenlightened face, and indicated rather than said, "There is vodka there, in case the soldiers are thirsty." The Major sprang up, poured for them, and received their gratitude. The questioning went on.

"How long did you live in New Haven?"

"Till I was fourteen. Came back two years ago to enter Yale."

"When you lived there, what street did you live on?"

"Parker Street."

With a vague half-light of comprehension dawning in his eye, the Major glanced an inquiry at the secretary. The secretary nodded, the Major poured vodka again.

"What number?"

"It hadn't any."

The boy sat up and gave the secretary a pathetic look which said,

"Why do you want to torture me with these foolish things, when I am miserable enough without it?"

The secretary went on, unheeding: "What kind of a house was it?"

"Brick—two-story."

"Flush with the sidewalk?"

"No, small yard in front."

"Iron fence?"

"No, palings."

The Major poured vodka again—without instructions—poured brimmers this time; and his face had cleared and was alive now.

"What do you see when you enter the door?"

"A narrow hall; door at the end of it, and a door at your right."

"Anything else?"

"Hat-rack."

"Room at the right?"

"Parlor."

"Carpet?"

"Yes."

"Kind of carpet?"

"Old-fashioned Wilton."

"Figures?"

"Yes—hawking-party, horseback."

The Major cast an eye at the clock—only six minutes left! He faced about with the jug, and as he poured he glanced at the secretary, then at the clock—inquiringly. The secretary nodded; the Major covered the clock from view with his body a moment, and set the hands back half an hour; then he refreshed the men—double rations.

"Room beyond the hall and hat-rack?"

"Dining-room."

"Stove?"

"Grate."

"Did your people own the house?"

"Yes."

"Do they own it yet?"

"No; sold it when we moved to Bridgeport."

The secretary paused a little, then said, "Did you have a nickname among your playmates?"

The color slowly rose in the youth's pale cheeks, and he dropped his eyes. He seemed to struggle with himself a moment or two, then he said, plaintively, "They called me Miss Nancy."

The secretary mused awhile, then he dug up another question:

"Any ornaments in the dining-room?"

"Well, y—no."

"*None?* None at *all?*"

"No."

"The mischief! Isn't that a little odd? Think!"

The youth thought and thought; the secretary waited, slightly panting. At last the imperiled waif looked up sadly and shook his head.

"Think—*think!*" cried the Major, in anxious solicitude; and poured again.

"Come!" said the secretary, "not even a *picture?*"

"Oh, certainly! but you said ornament."

"Ah! What did your father think of it?"

The color rose again. The boy was silent.

"Speak," said the secretary.

"Speak," cried the Major, and his trembling hand poured more vodka outside the glasses than inside.

"I—I can't tell you what he said," murmured the boy.

"Quick! quick!" said the secretary; "out with it; there's no time to lose—home and liberty or Siberia and death depend upon the answer."

"Oh, have pity! he is a clergyman, and—"

"No matter; out with it, or—"

"He said it was the hell-firedest nightmare he ever struck!"

"Saved!" shouted the secretary, and seized his nail and a blank passport. "*I* identify you; I've lived in the house, and I painted the picture myself!"

"Oh, come to my arms, my poor rescued boy!" cried the Major. "We will always be grateful to God that He made this artist!—if He did."

1902

A Double-Barreled Detective Story

The first scene is in the country, in Virginia; the time, 1880. There has been a wedding, between a handsome young man of slender means and a rich young girl—a case of love at first sight and a precipitate marriage; a marriage bitterly opposed by the girl's widowed father.

Jacob Fuller, the bridegroom, is twenty-six years old, is of an old but unconsidered family which had by compulsion emigrated from Sedgemoor, and for King James's purse's profit, so everybody said—some maliciously the rest merely because they believed it. The bride is nineteen and beautiful. She is intense, high-strung, romantic, immeasurably proud of her Cavalier blood, and passionate in her love for her young husband. For its sake she braved her father's displeasure, endured his reproaches, listened with loyalty unshaken to his warning predictions, and went from his house without his blessing, proud and happy in the proofs she was thus giving of the quality of the affection which had made its home in her heart.

The morning after the marriage there was a sad surprise for her. Her husband put aside her proffered caresses, and said:

"Sit down. I have something to say to you. I loved you. That was before I asked your father to give you to me. His refusal is not my grievance—I could have endured that. But the things he said of me to you—that is a different matter. There—you needn't speak; I know quite well what they were; I got them from authentic sources. Among other things he said that my character was written in my face; that I was treacherous, a dissembler, a coward, and a brute without sense of pity or compassion: the 'Sedgemoor trade-mark,' he called it—and 'white-sleeve badge.' Any other man in my place would have gone to his house and shot him down like a dog. I wanted to do it, and was minded to do it, but a better thought came to me: to put him to shame; to break his heart; to kill him by inches. How to do it? Through my treatment of you, his idol! I would marry you; and then— Have patience. You will see."

From that moment onward, for three months, the young wife suffered all the humiliations, all the insults, all the miseries that the diligent and inventive mind of the husband could contrive, save physical injuries only. Her strong pride stood by her, and she kept the secret of her troubles. Now and then the husband said, "Why don't you go to your father and tell him?" Then he invented new tortures, applied them, and asked again. She always answered, "He shall never know by my mouth," and taunted him with his origin; said she was the lawful slave of a scion of slaves, and must obey, and would—up to that point, but no further; he could kill her if he liked, but he could not break her; it was not in the Sedgemoor breed to do it. At the end of the three months he said, with a dark significance in his manner, "I have tried all things but one"—and waited for her reply. "Try that," she said, and curled her lip in mockery.

That night he rose at midnight and put on his clothes, then said to her:

"Get up and dress!"

She obeyed—as always, without a word. He led her half a mile from the house, and proceeded to lash her to a tree by the side of the public road; and succeeded, she screaming and struggling. He gagged her then, struck her across the face with his cowhide, and set his blood-hounds on her. They tore the clothes off her, and she was naked. He called the dogs off, and said:

"You will be found—by the passing public. They will be dropping along about three hours from now, and will spread the news—do you hear? Good-by. You have seen the last of me."

He went away then. She moaned to herself:

"I shall bear a child—to *him!* God grant it may be a boy!"

The farmers released her by and by—and spread the news, which was natural. They raised the country with lynching intentions, but the bird had flown. The young wife shut herself up in her father's house; he shut himself up with her, and thenceforth would see no one. His pride was broken, and his heart; so he wasted away, day by day, and even his daughter rejoiced when death relieved him.

Then she sold the estate and disappeared.

2

In 1886 a young woman was living in a modest house near a secluded New England village, with no company but a little boy about five years old. She did her own work, she discouraged acquaintanceships, and had none. The butcher, the baker, and the others that served her could tell the villagers nothing about her further than that her name was Stillman, and that she called the child Archy. Whence she came they had not been able to find out, but they said she talked like a Southerner. The child had no playmates and no comrade, and no teacher but the mother. She taught him diligently and intelligently, and was satisfied with the results—even a little proud of them. One day Archy said:

"Mamma, am I different from other children?"

"Well, I suppose not. Why?"

"There was a child going along out there and asked me if the postman had been by and I said yes, and she said how long since I saw him and I said I hadn't seen him at all, and she said how did I know he'd been by, then, and I said because I smelt his track on the sidewalk, and she

said I was a dum fool and made a mouth at me. What did she do that
for?"

The young woman turned white, and said to herself, "It's a birth-
mark! The gift of the bloodhound is in him." She snatched the boy to
her breast and hugged him passionately, saying, "God has appointed
the way!" Her eyes were burning with a fierce light, and her breath
came short and quick with excitement. She said to herself: "The puzzle
is solved now; many a time it has been a mystery to me, the impossible
things the child has done in the dark, but it is all clear to me now."

She set him in his small chair, and said:

"Wait a little till I come, dear; then we will talk about the matter."

She went up to her room and took from her dressing-table several
small articles and put them out of sight: a nail-file on the floor under
the bed; a pair of nail-scissors under the bureau; a small ivory paper-
knife under the wardrobe. Then she returned, and said:

"There! I have left some things which I ought to have brought down."
She named them, and said, "Run up and bring them, dear."

The child hurried away on his errand and was soon back again with
the things.

"Did you have any difficulty, dear?"

"No, mamma; I only went where you went."

During his absence she had stepped to the bookcase, taken several
books from the bottom shelf, opened each, passed her hand over a page,
noting its number in her memory, then restored them to their places.
Now she said:

"I have been doing something while you have been gone, Archy. Do
you think you can find out what it was?"

The boy went to the bookcase and got out the books that had been
touched, and opened them at the pages which had been stroked.

The mother took him in her lap, and said:

"I will answer your question now, dear. I have found out that in one
way you are quite different from other people. You can see in the dark,
you can smell what other people cannot, you have the talents of a bloodhound. They are good and valuable things to have, but you must keep
the matter a secret. If people found it out, they would speak of you as
an odd child, a strange child, and children would be disagreeable to
you, and give you nicknames. In this world one must be like everybody
else if he doesn't want to provoke scorn or envy or jealousy. It is a great
and fine distinction which has been born to you, and I am glad; but you
will keep it a secret, for mamma's sake, won't you?"

The child promised, without understanding.

All the rest of the day the mother's brain was busy with excited thinkings; with plans, projects, schemes, each and all of them uncanny, grim, and dark. Yet they lit up her face; lit it with a fell light of their own; lit it with vague fires of hell. She was in a fever of unrest; she could not sit, stand, read, sew; there was no relief for her but in movement. She tested her boy's gift in twenty ways, and kept saying to herself all the time, with her mind in the past: "He broke my father's heart, and night and day all these years I have tried, and all in vain, to think out a way to break his. I have found it now—I have found it now."

When night fell, the demon of unrest still possessed her. She went on with her tests; with a candle she traversed the house from garret to cellar, hiding pins, needles, thimbles, spools, under pillows, under carpets, in cracks in the walls, under the coal in the bin; then sent the little fellow in the dark to find them; which he did, and was happy and proud when she praised him and smothered him with caresses.

From this time forward life took on a new complexion for her. She said, "The future is secure—I can wait, and enjoy the waiting." The most of her lost interests revived. She took up music again, and languages, drawing, painting, and the other long-discarded delights of her maidenhood. She was happy once more, and felt again the zest of life. As the years drifted by she watched the development of her boy, and was contented with it. Not altogether, but nearly that. The soft side of his heart was larger than the other side of it. It was his only defect, in her eyes. But she considered that his love for her and worship of her made up for it. He was a good hater—that was well; but it was a question if the materials of his hatreds were of as tough and enduring a quality as those of his friendships—and that was not so well.

The years drifted on. Archy was become a handsome, shapely, athletic youth, courteous, dignified, companionable, pleasant in his ways, and looking perhaps a trifle older than he was, which was sixteen. One evening his mother said she had something of grave importance to say to him, adding that he was old enough to hear it now, and old enough and possessed of character enough and stability enough to carry out a stern plan which she had been for years contriving and maturing. Then she told him her bitter story, in all its naked atrociousness. For a while the boy was paralyzed; then he said:

"I understand. We are Southerners; and by our custom and nature there is but one atonement. I will search him out and kill him."

"Kill him? No! Death is release, emancipation; death is a favor. Do I owe him favors? You must not hurt a hair of his head."

The boy was lost in thought awhile; then he said:

"You are all the world to me, and your desire is my law and my pleasure. Tell me what to do and I will do it."

The mother's eyes beamed with satisfaction, and she said:

"You will go and find him. I have known his hiding-place for eleven years; it cost me five years and more of inquiry, and much money, to locate it. He is a quartz-miner in Colorado, and well-to-do. He lives in Denver. His name is Jacob Fuller. There—it is the first time I have spoken it since that unforgettable night. Think! That name could have been yours if I had not saved you that shame and furnished you a cleaner one. You will drive him from that place; you will hunt him down and drive him again; and yet again, and again, and again, persistently, relentlessly, poisoning his life, filling it with mysterious terrors, loading it with weariness and misery, making him wish for death, and that he had a suicide's courage; you will make of him another Wandering Jew; he shall know no rest any more, no peace of mind, no placid sleep; you shall shadow him, cling to him, persecute him, till you break his heart, as he broke my father's and mine."

"I will obey, mother."

"I believe it, my child. The preparations are all made; everything is ready. Here is a letter of credit; spend freely, there is no lack of money. At times you may need disguises. I have provided them; also some other conveniences." She took from the drawer of the typewriter-table several squares of paper. They all bore these typewritten words:

$10,000 REWARD

It is believed that a certain man who is wanted in an Eastern state is sojourning here. In 1880, in the night, he tied his young wife to a tree by the public road, cut her across the face with a cowhide, and made his dogs tear her clothes from her, leaving her naked. He left her there, and fled the country. A blood-relative of hers has searched for him for seventeen years. Address . . . . , ... , Post-office. The above reward will be paid in cash to the person who will furnish the seeker, in a personal interview, the criminal's address.

"When you have found him and acquainted yourself with his scent, you will go in the night and placard one of these upon the building he occupies, and another one upon the post-office or in some other prominent place. It will be the talk of the region. At first you must give him several days in which to force a sale of his belongings at something approaching their value. We will ruin him by and by, but gradually; we must not impoverish him at once, for that could bring him to despair and injure his health, possibly kill him."

She took three or four more typewritten forms from the drawer—duplicates—and read one:

. . . . , ... , *18.* . . .

To Jacob Fuller:

You have . . . . . . days in which to settle your affairs. You will not be disturbed during that limit, which will expire at . . . . . . M., on the . . . . . . of . . . . You must then MOVE ON. If you are still in the place after the named hour, I will placard you on all the dead walls, detailing your crime once more, and adding the date, also the scene of it, with all names concerned, including your own. Have no fear of bodily injury—it will in no circumstances ever be inflicted upon you. You brought misery upon an old man, and ruined his life and broke his heart. What he suffered, you are to suffer.

"You will add no signature. He must receive this before he learns of the reward placard—before he rises in the morning—lest he lose his head and fly the place penniless."

"I shall not forget."

"You will need to use these forms only in the beginning—once may be enough. Afterward, when you are ready for him to vanish out of a place, see that he gets a copy of *this* form, which merely says:

MOVE ON. You have . . . . . . days.

"He will obey. That is sure."

3

Extracts from letters to the mother:

DENVER, *April 3, 1897*

I have now been living several days in the same hotel with Jacob Fuller. I have his scent; I could track him through ten divisions of infantry and find him. I have often been near him and heard him talk. He owns a good mine, and has a fair income from it; but he is not rich. He learned mining in a good way—by working at it for wages. He is a cheerful creature, and his forty-three years sit lightly upon him; he could pass for a younger man—say thirty-six or thirty-seven. He has never married again—passes himself off for a widower. He stands well, is liked, is popular, and has many friends. Even I feel a drawing toward him—the paternal blood in me making its claim. How blind and unreasoning and arbitrary are some of the laws of nature—the most of them, in fact! My task is become hard now—you realize it? you comprehend, and make allowances?—and the fire of it has cooled, more than I like to confess to myself. But I will carry it out. Even with the pleasure paled, the duty remains, and I will not spare him.

And for my help, a sharp resentment rises in me when I reflect that he who committed that odious crime is the only one who has not suffered by it. The lesson of it has manifestly reformed his character, and in the change he is happy. He, the guilty party, is absolved from all suffering; you, the innocent, are borne down with it. But be comforted —he shall harvest his share.

SILVER GULCH, *May 19*

I placarded Form No. 1 at midnight of April 3; an hour later I slipped Form No. 2 under his chamber door, notifying him to leave Denver at or before 11.50 the night of the 14th.

Some late bird of a reporter stole one of my placards, then hunted the town over and found the other one, and stole that. In this manner he accomplished what the profession call a "scoop"—that is, he got a valuable item, and saw to it that no other paper got it. And so his paper—the principal one in the town—had it in glaring type on the editorial page in the morning, followed by a Vesuvian opinion of our wretch a column long, which wound up by adding a thousand dollars to our reward on the paper's account! The journals out here know how to do the noble thing—when there's business in it.

At breakfast I occupied my usual seat—selected because it afforded a view of papa Fuller's face, and was near enough for me to hear the talk that went on at his table. Seventy-five or a hundred people were in the room, and all discussing that item, and saying they hoped the seeker would find that rascal and remove the pollution of his presence from the town—with a rail, or a bullet, or something.

When Fuller came in he had the Notice to Leave—folded up—in one hand, and the newspaper in the other; and it gave me more than half a pang to see him. His cheerfulness was all gone, and he looked old and pinched and ashy. And then—only think of the things he had to listen to! Mamma, he heard his own unsuspecting friends describe him with epithets and characterizations drawn from the very dictionaries and phrase-books of Satan's own authorized editions down below. And more than that, he had to agree with the verdicts and applaud

*them. His applause tasted bitter in his mouth, though; he could not
disguise that from me; and it was observable that his appetite was
gone; he only nibbled; he couldn't eat. Finally a man said:*

*"It is quite likely that that relative is in the room and hearing what
this town thinks of that unspeakable scoundrel. I hope so."*

*Ah, dear, it was pitiful the way Fuller winced, and glanced around
scared! He couldn't endure any more, and got up and left.*

*During several days he gave out that he had bought a mine in Mex-
ico, and wanted to sell out and go down there as soon as he could,
and give the property his personal attention. He played his cards well;
said he would take $40,000—a quarter in cash, the rest in safe notes; but
that as he greatly needed money on account of his new purchase, he
would diminish his terms for cash in full. He sold out for $30,000. And
then, what do you think he did? He asked for greenbacks, and took
them, saying the man in Mexico was a New-Englander, with a head
full of crotchets, and preferred greenbacks to gold or drafts. People
thought it queer, since a draft on New York could produce greenbacks
quite conveniently. There was talk of this odd thing, but only for a day;
that is as long as any topic lasts in Denver.*

*I was watching, all the time. As soon as the sale was completed and
the money paid—which was on the 11th—I began to stick to Fuller's
track without dropping it for a moment. That night—no, 12th, for it was
a little past midnight—I tracked him to his room, which was four doors
from mine in the same hall; then I went back and put on my muddy
day-laborer disguise, darkened my complexion, and sat down in my
room in the gloom, with a gripsack handy, with a change in it, and my
door ajar. For I suspected that the bird would take wing now. In half
an hour an old woman passed by, carrying a grip: I caught the familiar
whiff, and followed with my grip, for it was Fuller. He left the hotel
by a side entrance, and at the corner he turned up an unfrequented
street and walked three blocks in a light rain and a heavy darkness,
and got into a two-horse hack, which of course was waiting for him by
appointment. I took a seat (uninvited) on the trunk platform behind,
and we drove briskly off. We drove ten miles, and the hack stopped
at a way-station and was discharged. Fuller got out and took a seat on
a barrow under the awning, as far as he could get from the light; I
went inside, and watched the ticket-office. Fuller bought no ticket;
I bought none. Presently the train came along, and he boarded a car; I
entered the same car at the other end, and came down the aisle and
took the seat behind him. When he paid the conductor and named his*

objective point, I dropped back several seats, while the conductor was changing a bill, and when he came to me I paid to the same place—about a hundred miles westward.

From that time for a week on end he led me a dance. He traveled here and there and yonder—always on a general westward trend—but he was not a woman after the first day. He was a laborer, like myself, and wore bushy false whiskers. His outfit was perfect, and he could do the character without thinking about it, for he had served the trade for wages. His nearest friend could not have recognized him. At last he located himself here, the obscurest little mountain camp in Montana; he has a shanty, and goes out prospecting daily; is gone all day, and avoids society. I am living at a miner's boardinghouse, and it is an awful place: the bunks, the food, the dirt—everything.

We have been here four weeks, and in that time I have seen him but once; but every night I go over his track and post myself. As soon as he engaged a shanty here I went to a town fifty miles away and telegraphed that Denver hotel to keep my baggage till I should send for it. I need nothing here but a change of army shirts, and I brought that with me.

SILVER GULCH, *June 12*

The Denver episode has never found its way here, I think. I know the most of the men in camp, and they have never referred to it, at least in my hearing. Fuller doubtless feels quite safe in these conditions. He has located a claim, two miles away, in an out-of-the-way place in the mountains; it promises very well, and he is working it diligently. Ah, but the change in him! He never smiles, and he keeps quite to himself, consorting with no one—he who was so fond of company and so cheery only two months ago. I have seen him passing along several times recently—drooping, forlorn, the spring gone from his step, a pathetic figure. He calls himself David Wilson.

I can trust him to remain here until we disturb him. Since you insist, I will banish him again, but I do not see how he can be unhappier than he already is. I will go back to Denver and treat myself to a little season of comfort, and edible food, and endurable beds, and bodily decency; then I will fetch my things, and notify poor papa Wilson to move on.

DENVER, *June 19*

They miss him here. They all hope he is prospering in Mexico, and they do not say it just with their mouths, but out of their hearts. You know you can always tell. I am loitering here overlong, I confess it. But if you were in my place you would have charity for me. Yes, I know what you will say, and you are right: if I were in your place, and carried your scalding memories in my heart—

I will take the night train back to-morrow.

DENVER, *June* 20

God forgive us, mother, we are hunting the wrong man! I have not slept any all night. I am now waiting, at dawn, for the morning train —and how the minutes drag, how they drag!

This *Jacob Fuller* is a cousin of the guilty one. How stupid we have been not to reflect that the guilty one would never again wear his own name after that fiendish deed! The Denver Fuller is four years younger than the other one; he came here a young widower in '79, aged twenty-one—a year before you were married; and the documents to prove it are innumerable. Last night I talked with familiar friends of his who have known him from the day of his arrival. I said nothing, but a few days from now I will land him in this town again, with the loss upon his mine made good; and there will be a banquet, and a torch-light procession, and there will not be any expense on anybody but me. Do you call this "gush"? I am only a boy, as you well know; it is my privilege. By and by I shall not be a boy any more.

SILVER GULCH, *July* 3

Mother, he is gone! Gone, and left no trace. The scent was cold when I came. To-day I am out of bed for the first time since. I wish I were not a boy; then I could stand shocks better. They all think he went west. I start to-night, in a wagon—two or three hours of that, then I get a train. I don't know where I'm going, but I must go; to try to keep still would be torture.

Of course he has effaced himself with a new name and a disguise. This means that I may have to search the whole globe to find him. Indeed it is what I expect. Do you see, mother? It is I that am the Wandering Jew. The irony of it! We arranged that for another.

Think of the difficulties! And there would be none if I only could advertise for him. But if there is any way to do it that would not frighten him, I have not been able to think it out, and I have tried till my brains are addled. "If the gentleman who lately bought a mine in Mexico and sold one in Denver will send his address to" (to whom, mother!), "it will be explained to him that it was all a mistake; his forgiveness will be asked, and full reparation made for a loss which he *sustained in a certain matter." Do you see? He would think it a trap. Well, any one would. If I should say, "It is now known that he was not the man wanted, but another man—a man who once bore the same name, but discarded it for good reasons"—would that answer? But the Denver people would wake up then and say "Oho!" and they would remember about the suspicious greenbacks, and say, "Why did he run away if he wasn't the right man?—it is too thin." If I failed to find him he would be ruined there—there where there is no taint upon him now. You have a better head than mine. Help me.*

I have one clue, and only one. I know his handwriting. If he puts his new false name upon a hotel register and does not disguise it too much, it will be valuable to me if I ever run across it.

SAN FRANCISCO, *June 28, 1898*

You already know how well I have searched the states from Colorado to the Pacific, and how nearly I came to getting him once. Well, I have had another close miss. It was here, yesterday. I struck his trail, hot, on the street, and followed it on a run to a cheap hotel. That was a costly mistake; a dog would have gone the other way. But I am only part dog, and can get very humanly stupid when excited. He had been stopping in that house ten days; I almost know, now, that he stops long nowhere, the past six or eight months, but is restless and has to keep moving. I understand that feeling! and I know what it is to feel it. He still uses the name he had registered when I came so near catching him nine months ago—"James Walker"; doubtless the same he adopted when he fled from Silver Gulch. An unpretending man, and has small taste for fancy names. I recognized the hand easily, through its slight disguise. A square man, and not good at shams and pretenses.

They said he was just gone, on a journey; left no address; didn't say where he was going; looked frightened when asked to leave his address; had no baggage but a cheap valise; carried it off on foot—a "stingy old person, and not much loss to the house." "Old!" I suppose he is, now. I hardly heard; I was there but a moment. I rushed along his trail, and it led me to a wharf. Mother, the smoke of the steamer he had taken was just fading out on the horizon! I should have saved half an hour if I had gone in the right direction at first. I could have taken a fast tug, and should have stood a chance of catching that vessel. She is bound for Melbourne.

HOPE CAÑON, CALIFORNIA, *October 3, 1900*
You have a right to complain. "A letter a year" is a paucity; I freely

acknowledge it; but how can one write when there is nothing to write about but failures? No one can keep it up; it breaks the heart.

I told you—it seems ages ago, now—how I missed him at Melbourne, and then chased him all over Australasia for months on end.

Well, then, after that I followed him to India; almost saw him in Bombay; traced him all around—to Baroda, Rawal-Pindi, Lucknow, Lahore, Cawnpore, Allahabad, Calcutta, Madras—oh, everywhere; week after week, month after month, through the dust and swelter— always approximately on his track, sometimes close upon him, yet never catching him. And down to Ceylon, and then to— Never mind; by and by I will write it all out.

I chased him home to California, and down to Mexico, and back again to California. Since then I have been hunting him about the state from the first of last January down to a month ago. I feel almost sure he is not far from Hope Cañon; I traced him to a point thirty miles from here, but there I lost the trail; some one gave him a lift in a wagon, I suppose.

I am taking a rest, now—modified by searchings for the lost trail. I was tired to death, mother, and low-spirited, and sometimes coming uncomfortably near to losing hope; but the miners in this little camp are good fellows, and I am used to their sort this long time back; and their breezy ways freshen a person up and make him forget his troubles. I have been here a month. I am cabining with a young fellow named "Sammy" Hillyer, about twenty-five, the only son of his mother —like me—and loves her dearly, and writes to her every week—part of which is like me. He is a timid body, and in the matter of intellect— well, he cannot be depended upon to set a river on fire; but no matter, he is well liked; he is good and fine, and it is meat and bread and rest and luxury to sit and talk with him and have a comradeship again. I wish "James Walker" could have it. He had friends; he liked company. That brings up that picture of him, the time that I saw him last. The pathos of it! It comes before me often and often. At that very time, poor thing, I was girding up my conscience to make him move on again!

Hillyer's heart is better than mine, better than anybody's in the community, I suppose, for he is the one friend of the black sheep of the camp—Flint Buckner—and the only man Flint ever talks with or allows to talk with him. He says he knows Flint's history, and that it is trouble that has made him what he is, and so one ought to be as charitable toward him as one can. Now none but a pretty large heart could find space to accommodate a lodger like Flint Buckner, from all I hear about him outside. I think that this one detail will give you a better idea of

Sammy's character than any labored-out description I could furnish you of him. In one of our talks he said something about like this: "Flint is a kinsman of mine, and he pours out all his troubles to me—empties his breast from time to time, or I reckon it would burst. There couldn't be any unhappier man, Archy Stillman; his life had been made up of misery of mind—he isn't near as old as he looks. He has lost the feel of reposefulness and peace—oh, years and years ago! He doesn't know what good luck is—never has had any; often says he wishes he was in the other hell, he is so tired of this one."

4

No real gentleman will tell the naked truth in the presence of ladies.

It was a crisp and spicy morning in early October. The lilacs and laburnums, lit with the glory-fires of autumn, hung burning and flashing in the upper air, a fairy bridge provided by kind Nature for the wingless wild things that have their homes in the tree-tops and would visit together; the larch and the pomegranate flung their purple and yellow flames in brilliant broad splashes along the slanting sweep of the woodland; the sensuous fragrance of innumerable deciduous flowers rose upon the swooning atmosphere; far in the empty sky a solitary esophagus[1] slept upon motionless wing; everywhere brooded stillness, serenity, and the peace of God.

[1] From the Springfield *Republican*, April 12, 1902.

To the Editor of the Republican:

One of your citizens has asked me a question about the "esophagus," and I wish to answer him through you. This in the hope that the answer will get around, and save me some penmanship, for I have already replied to the same question more than several times, and am not getting as much holiday as I ought to have.

I published a short story lately, and it was in that that I put the esophagus. I will say privately that I expected it to bother some people —in fact, that was the intention—but the harvest has been larger than I was calculating upon. The esophagus has gathered in the guilty and the innocent alike, whereas I was only fishing for the innocent—the innocent and confiding. I knew a few of these would write and ask me; that would give me but little trouble; but I was not expecting that the wise and the learned would call upon me for succor. However, that has happened, and it is time for me to speak up and stop the inquiries if I can, for letter-writing is not restful to me, and I am not having so much fun out of this thing as I counted on. That you may understand the situation, I will insert a couple of sample inquiries. The first is from a public instructor in the Philippines:

SANTA CRUZ, *Ilocos, Sur, P. I.*
February 13, 1902

My dear Sir,—I have just been reading the first part of your latest story, entitled "A Double-barreled Detective Story," and am very much delighted with it. In Part IV, page 264, Harper's Magazine *for January, occurs this passage: "far in the empty sky a solitary 'esophagus' slept upon motionless wing; everywhere brooded stillness, serenity, and the peace of God." Now, there is one word I do not understand, namely, "esophagus." My only work of reference is the* Standard Dictionary, *but that fails to explain the meaning. If you can spare the time, I would be glad to have the meaning cleared up, as I consider the passage a very touching and beautiful one. It may seem foolish to you, but consider my lack of means away out in the northern part of Luzon.*

Yours very truly.

Do you notice? Nothing in the paragraph disturbed him but that one word. It shows that that paragraph was most ably constructed for the deception it was intended to put upon the reader. It was my intention that it should read plausibly, and it is now plain that it does; it was my intention that it should be emotional and touching, and you see, yourself, that it fetched this public instructor. Alas, if I had but left that one treacherous word out, I should have scored! scored everywhere; and the paragraph would have slidden through every reader's sensibilities like oil, and left not a suspicion behind.

The other sample inquiry is from a professor in a New England university. It contains one naughty word (which I cannot bear to suppress), but he is not in the theological department, so it is no harm:

Dear Mr. Clemens: "Far in the empty sky a solitary esophagus slept upon motionless wing."

It is not often I get a chance to read much periodical literature, but I have just gone through at this belated period, with much gratification and edification, your "Double-barreled Detective Story."

But what in hell is an esophagus? I keep one myself, but it never sleeps in the air or anywhere else. My profession is to deal with words, and esophagus interested me the moment I lighted upon it. But as a companion of my youth used to say, "I'll be eternally, co-eternally cussed" if I can make it out. Is it a joke, or I an ignoramus?

Between you and me, I was almost ashamed of having fooled that man, but for pride's sake I was not going to say so. I wrote and told him it was a joke—and that is what I am now saying to my Springfield inquirer. And I told him to carefully read the whole paragraph, and he would find not a vestige of sense in any detail of it. This also I commend to my Springfield inquirer.

I have confessed. I am sorry—partially. I will not do so any more—for the present. Don't ask me any more questions; let the esophagus have a rest—on his same old motionless wing.

MARK TWAIN

New York City, April 10, 1902

(*Editorial*)

☞ *The "Double-barreled Detective Story," which appeared in Harper's Magazine for January and February last, is the most elaborate of burlesques on detective fiction, with striking melodramatic passages in which it is difficult to detect the deception, so ably is it done. But the illusion ought not to endure even the first incident in the February number. As for the paragraph which has so admirably illustrated the skill of Mr. Clemens's ensemble and the carelessness of readers, here it is:*

"It was a crisp and spicy morning in early October. The lilacs and laburnums, lit with the glory-fires of autumn, hung burning and flashing in the upper air, a fairy bridge provided by kind nature for the wingless wild things that have their home in the tree-tops and would visit together; the larch and the pomegranate flung their purple and yellow flames in brilliant broad splashes along the slanting sweep of the woodland; the sensuous fragrance of innumerable deciduous flowers rose upon the swooning atmosphere; far in the empty sky a solitary esophagus slept upon motionless wings; everywhere brooded stillness, serenity, and the peace of God."

The success of Mark Twain's joke recalls to mind his story of the petrified man in the cavern, whom he described most punctiliously, first giving a picture of the scene, its impressive solitude, and all that; then going on to describe the majesty of the figure, casually mentioning that the thumb of his right hand rested against the side of his nose; then after further description observing that the fingers of the right hand were extended in a radiating fashion; and, recurring to the dignified attitude and position of the man, incidentally remarked that the thumb of the left hand was in contact with the little finger of the right —and so on. But was it so ingeniously written that Mark, relating the

*history years later in an article which appeared in that excellent maga-
zine of the past, the* Galaxy, *declared that no one ever found out the
joke, and, if we remember aright, that that astonishing old mockery was
actually looked for in the region where he, as a Nevada newspaper
editor, had located it. It is certain that Mark Twain's jumping frog has
a good many more "pints" than any other frog.*

October is the time—1900; Hope Cañon is the place, a silver-mining
camp away down in the Esmeralda region. It is a secluded spot, high
and remote; recent as to discovery; thought by its occupants to be rich
in metal—a year or two's prospecting will decide that matter one way
or the other. For inhabitants, the camp has about two hundred miners,
one white woman and child, several Chinese washermen, five squaws,
and a dozen vagrant buck Indians in rabbit-skin robes, battered plug
hats, and tin-can necklaces. There are no mills as yet; no church, no
newspaper. The camp has existed but two years; it has made no big
strike; the world is ignorant of its name and place.

On both sides of the cañon the mountains rise wall-like, three thousand feet, and the long spiral of straggling huts down in its narrow
bottom gets a kiss from the sun only once a day, when he sails over at
noon. The village is a couple of miles long; the cabins stand well apart
from each other. The tavern is the only "frame" house—the only house,
one might say. It occupies a central position, and is the evening resort
of the population. They drink there, and play seven-up and dominoes;
also billiards, for there is a table, crossed all over with torn places repaired with court-plaster; there are some cues, but no leathers; some
chipped balls which clatter when they run, and do not slow up gradually, but stop suddenly and sit down; there is a part of a cube of chalk,
with a projecting jag of flint in it; and the man who can score six on a
single break can set up the drinks at the bar's expense.

Flint Buckner's cabin was the last one of the village, going south;
his silver-claim was at the other end of the village, northward, and a
little beyond the last hut in that direction. He was a sour creature, unsociable, and had no companionships. People who had tried to get
acquainted with him had regretted it and dropped him. His history
was not known. Some believed that Sammy Hillyer knew it; others
said no. If asked, Hillyer said no, he was not acquainted with it. Flint
had a meek English youth of sixteen or seventeen with him, whom he
treated roughly, both in public and in private; and of course this lad
was applied to for information, but with no success. Fetlock Jones—
name of the youth—said that Flint picked him up on a prospecting

tramp, and as he had neither home nor friends in America, he had found it wise to stay and take Buckner's hard usage for the sake of the salary, which was bacon and beans. Further than this he could offer no testimony.

Fetlock had been in this slavery for a month now, and under his meek exterior he was slowly consuming to a cinder with the insults and humiliations which his master had put upon him. For the meek suffer bitterly from these hurts; more bitterly, perhaps, than do the manlier sort, who can burst out and get relief with words or blows when the limit of endurance has been reached. Good-hearted people wanted to help Fetlock out of his trouble, and tried to get him to leave Buckner; but the boy showed fright at the thought, and said he "dasn't." Pat Riley urged him, and said:

"You leave the damned hunks and come with me; don't you be afraid. I'll take care of *him*."

The boy thanked him with tears in his eyes, but shuddered and said he "dasn't risk it"; he said Flint would catch him alone, some time, in the night, and then— "Oh, it makes me sick, Mr. Riley, to think of it."

Others said, "Run away from him; we'll stake you; skip out for the coast some night." But all these suggestions failed; he said Flint would hunt him down and fetch him back, just for meanness.

The people could not understand this. The boy's miseries went steadily on, week after week. It is quite likely that the people would have understood if they had known how he was employing his spare time. He slept in an out-cabin near Flint's; and there, nights, he nursed his bruises and his humiliations, and studied and studied over a single problem—how he could murder Flint Buckner and not be found out. It was the only joy he had in life; these hours were the only ones in the twenty-four which he looked forward to with eagerness and spent in happiness.

He thought of poison. No—that would not serve; the inquest would reveal where it was procured and who had procured it. He thought of a shot in the back in a lonely place when Flint would be homeward bound at midnight—his unvarying hour for the trip. No—somebody might be near, and catch him. He thought of stabbing him in his sleep. No—he might strike an inefficient blow, and Flint would seize him. He examined a hundred different ways—none of them would answer; for in even the very obscurest and secretest of them there was always the fatal defect of a *risk*, a chance, a possibility that he might be found out. He would have none of that.

But he was patient, endlessly patient. There was no hurry, he said to himself. He would never leave Flint till he left him a corpse; there was no hurry—he would find the way. It was somewhere, and he would endure shame and pain and misery until he found it. Yes, somewhere there was a way which would leave not a trace, not even the faintest clue to the murderer—there was no hurry—he would find that way, and then—oh, then, it would just be good to be alive! Meantime he would diligently keep up his reputation for meekness; and also, as always theretofore, he would allow no one to hear him say a resentful or offensive thing about his oppressor.

Two days before the before-mentioned October morning Flint had bought some things, and he and Fetlock had brought them home to Flint's cabin: a fresh box of candles, which they put in the corner; a tin can of blasting-powder, which they placed upon the candle-box; a keg of blasting-powder, which they placed under Flint's bunk; a huge coil of fuse, which they hung on a peg. Fetlock reasoned that Flint's mining operations had outgrown the pick, and that blasting was about to begin now. He had seen blasting done, and he had a notion of the process, but he had never helped in it. His conjecture was right—blasting-time had come. In the morning the pair carried fuse, drills, and the powder-can to the shaft; it was now eight feet deep, and to get into it and out of it a short ladder was used. They descended, and by command Fetlock held the drill—without any instructions as to the right way to hold it—and Flint proceeded to strike. The sledge came down; the drill sprang out of Fetlock's hand, almost as a matter of course.

"You mangy son of a nigger, is that any way to hold a drill? Pick it up! Stand it up! There—hold fast. D—— you! *I'll* teach you!"

At the end of an hour the drilling was finished.

"Now, then, charge it."

The boy started to pour in the powder.

"Idiot!"

A heavy bat on the jaw laid the lad out.

"Get up! You can't lie sniveling there. Now, then, stick in the fuse *first*. *Now* put in the powder. Hold on, hold on! Are you going to fill the hole *all* up? Of all the sap-headed milksops I— Put in some dirt! Put in some gravel! Tamp it down! Hold on, hold on! Oh, great Scott! get out of the way!" He snatched the iron and tamped the charge himself, meantime cursing and blaspheming like a fiend. Then he fired the fuse, climbed out of the shaft, and ran fifty yards away, Fetlock following. They stood waiting a few minutes, then a great volume of smoke and rocks burst high into the air with a thunderous explosion; after a little there was a shower of descending stones; then all was serene again.

"I wish to God you'd been in it!" remarked the master.

They went down the shaft, cleaned it out, drilled another hole, and put in another charge.

"Look here! How much fuse are you proposing to waste? Don't you know how to time a fuse?"

"No, sir."

"You *don't!* Well, if you don't beat anything *I* ever saw!"

He climbed out of the shaft and spoke down:

"Well, idiot, are you going to be all day? Cut the fuse and light it!"

The trembling creature began:

"If you please, sir, I—"

"You talk back to *me?* Cut it and light it!"

The boy cut and lit.

"Ger-reat Scott! a one-minute fuse! I wish you were in—"

In his rage he snatched the ladder out of the shaft and ran. The boy was aghast.

"Oh, my God! Help! Help! Oh, save me!" he implored. "Oh, what can I do! What *can* I do!"

He backed against the wall as tightly as he could; the sputtering fuse frightened the voice out of him; his breath stood still; he stood gazing and impotent; in two seconds, three seconds, four he would be flying toward the sky torn to fragments. Then he had an inspiration. He sprang at the fuse; severed the inch of it that was left above ground, and was saved.

He sank down limp and half lifeless with fright, his strength gone; but he muttered with a deep joy:

"He has learnt me! I knew there was a way, if I would wait."

After a matter of five minutes Buckner stole to the shaft, looking worried and uneasy, and peered down into it. He took in the situation; he saw what had happened. He lowered the ladder, and the boy dragged himself weakly up it. He was very white. His appearance added something to Buckner's uncomfortable state, and he said, with a show of regret and sympathy which sat upon him awkwardly from lack of practice:

"It was an accident, you know. Don't say anything about it to anybody; I was excited, and didn't notice what I was doing. You're not looking well; you've worked enough for to-day; go down to my cabin and eat what you want, and rest. It's just an accident, you know, on account of my being excited."

"It scared me," said the lad, as he started away; "but I learnt something, so I don't mind it."

"Damned easy to please!" muttered Buckner, following him with his eye. "I wonder if he'll tell? Mightn't he? . . . I wish it *had* killed him."

The boy took no advantage of his holiday in the matter of resting; he employed it in work, eager and feverish and happy work. A thick growth of chaparral extended down the mountainside clear to Flint's cabin; the most of Fetlock's labor was done in the dark intricacies of that stubborn growth; the rest of it was done in his own shanty. At last all was complete, and he said:

"If he's got any suspicions that I'm going to tell on him, he won't keep them long, to-morrow. He will see that I am the same milksop as I always was—all day and the next. And the day after to-morrow night there 'll be an end of him; nobody will ever guess who finished him up nor how it was done. He dropped me the idea his own self, and that's odd."

5

The next day came and went.

It is now almost midnight, and in five minutes the new morning will begin. The scene is in the tavern billiard-room. Rough men in rough clothing, slouch-hats, breeches stuffed into boot-tops, some with vests, none with coats, are grouped about the boiler-iron stove, which has ruddy cheeks and is distributing a grateful warmth; the billiard-balls are clacking; there is no other sound—that is, within; the wind is fitfully moaning without. The men look bored; also expectant. A hulking broad-shouldered miner, of middle age, with grizzled whiskers, and an unfriendly eye set in an unsociable face, rises, slips a coil of fuse upon his arm, gathers up some other personal properties, and departs without word or greeting to anybody. It is Flint Buckner. As the door closes behind him a buzz of talk breaks out.

"The regularest man that ever was," said Jake Parker, the blacksmith: "you can tell when it's twelve just by him leaving, without looking at your Waterbury."

"And it's the only virtue he's got, as fur as I know," said Peter Hawes, miner.

"He's just a blight on this society," said Wells-Fargo's man, Ferguson. "If I was running this shop I'd make him say something, *some* time or other, or vamos the ranch." This with a suggestive glance at the bar-keeper, who did not choose to see it, since the man under discussion was a good customer, and went home pretty well set up, every night, with refreshments furnished from the bar.

"Say," said Ham Sandwich, miner, "does any of you boys ever recollect of him asking you to take a drink?"

"*Him?* Flint *Buckner?* Oh, Laura!"

This sarcastic rejoinder came in a spontaneous general outburst in one form of words or another from the crowd. After a brief silence, Pat Riley, miner, said:

"He's the 15-puzzle, that cuss. And his boy's another one. *I* can't make them out."

"Nor anybody else," said Ham Sandwich; "and if they are 15-puzzles, how are you going to rank up that other one? When it comes to A 1 right-down solid mysteriousness, he lays over both of them. *Easy*—don't he?"

"You bet!"

Everybody said it. Every man but one. He was the new-comer—Peterson. He ordered the drinks all round, and asked who No. 3 might be. All answered at once, "Archy Stillman!"

"Is he a mystery?" asked Peterson.

"Is *he* a mystery? Is Archy *Stillman* a mystery?" said Wells-Fargo's man, Ferguson. "Why, the fourth dimension's foolishness to *him.*"

For Ferguson was learned.

Peterson wanted to hear all about him; everybody wanted to tell him; everybody began. But Billy Stevens, the barkeeper, called the house to order, and said one at a time was best. He distributed the drinks, and appointed Ferguson to lead. Ferguson said:

"Well, he's a boy. And that is just about all we know about him. You can pump him till you are tired; it ain't any use; you won't get anything. At least about his intentions, or line of business, or where he's from, and such things as that. And as for getting at the nature and get-up of his main big chief mystery, why, he'll just change the subject, that's all. You can *guess* till you're black in the face—it's your privilege—but suppose you do, where do you arrive at? Nowhere, as near as I can make out."

"What *is* his big chief one?"

"Sight, maybe. Hearing, maybe. Instinct, maybe. Magic, maybe. Take your choice—grownups, twenty-five; children and servants, half price. Now I'll tell you what he can do. You can start here, and just disappear; you can go and hide wherever you want to, I don't care where it is, nor how far—and he'll go straight and put his finger on you."

"You don't mean it!"

"I just do, though. Weather's nothing to him—elemental conditions is nothing to him—he don't even take notice of them."

"Oh, come! Dark? Rain? Snow? Hey?"

"It's all the same to *him*. He don't give a damn."

"Oh, *say*—including *fog*, per'aps?"

"*Fog!* he's got an eye 't can plunk through it like a bullet."

"Now, boys, honor bright, what's he giving me?"

"It's a fact!" they all shouted. "Go on, Wells-Fargo."

"Well, sir, you can leave him here, chatting with the boys, and you can slip out and go to any cabin in this camp and open a book—yes, sir, a dozen of them—and take the page in your memory, and he'll start out and go straight to that cabin and open every one of them books at the right page, and call it off, and never make a mistake."

"He must be the devil!"

"More than one has thought it. Now I'll tell you a perfectly wonderful thing that he done. The other night he—"

There was a sudden great murmur of sounds outside, the door flew open, and an excited crowd burst in, with the camp's one white woman in the lead and crying:

"My child! my child! she's lost and gone! For the love of God help me to find Archy Stillman; we've hunted everywhere!"

Said the barkeeper:

"Sit down, sit down, Mrs. Hogan, and don't worry. He asked for a bed three hours ago, tuckered out tramping the trails the way he's always doing, and went up-stairs. Ham Sandwich, run up and roust him out; he's in No. 14."

The youth was soon down-stairs and ready. He asked Mrs. Hogan for particulars.

"Bless you, dear, there ain't any; I wish there was. I put her to sleep at seven in the evening, and when I went in there an hour ago to go to bed myself, she was gone. I rushed for your cabin, dear, and you wasn't there, and I've hunted for you ever since, at every cabin down the gulch, and now I've come up again, and I'm that distracted and scared and heartbroke; but, thanks to God, I've found you at last, dear heart, and you'll find my child. Come on! come quick!"

"Move right along; I'm with you, madam. Go to your cabin first."

The whole company streamed out to join the hunt. All the southern half of the village was up, a hundred men strong, and waiting outside, a vague dark mass sprinkled with twinkling lanterns. The mass fell into columns by threes and fours to accommodate itself to the narrow road, and strode briskly along southward in the wake of the leaders. In a few minutes the Hogan cabin was reached.

"There's the bunk," said Mrs. Hogan; "there's where she was; it's where I laid her at seven o'clock; but where she is now, God only knows."

"Hand me a lantern," said Archy. He set it on the hard earth floor and knelt by it, pretending to examine the ground closely. "Here's her track," he said, touching the ground here and there and yonder with his finger. "Do you see?"

Several of the company dropped upon their knees and did their best to see. One or two thought they discerned something like a track; the others shook their heads and confessed that the smooth hard surface had no marks upon it which their eyes were sharp enough to discover. One said, "Maybe a child's foot could make a mark on it, but *I* don't see how."

Young Stillman stepped outside, held the light to the ground, turned leftward, and moved three steps, closely examining; then said, "I've got the direction—come along; take the lantern, somebody."

He strode off swiftly southward, the files following, swaying and bending in and out with the deep curves of the gorge. Thus a mile, and the mouth of the gorge was reached; before them stretched the sagebrush plain, dim, vast, and vague. Stillman called a halt, saying, "We mustn't start wrong, now; we must take the direction again."

He took a lantern and examined the ground for a matter of twenty yards; then said, "Come on; it's all right," and gave up the lantern. In and out among the sage-bushes he marched, a quarter of a mile, bearing gradually to the right; then took a new direction and made another great semicircle; then changed again and moved due west nearly half a mile—and stopped.

"She gave it up, here, poor little chap. Hold the lantern. You can see where she sat."

But this was in a slick alkali flat which was surfaced like steel, and no person in the party was quite hardy enough to claim an eyesight that could detect the track of a cushion on a veneer like that. The bereaved mother fell upon her knees and kissed the spot, lamenting.

"But where is she, then?" some one said. "She didn't stay here. We can see *that* much, anyway."

Stillman moved about in a circle around the place, with the lantern, pretending to hunt for tracks.

"Well!" he said presently, in an annoyed tone, "I don't understand it." He examined again. "No use. She was here—that's certain; she never *walked* away from here—and that's certain. It's a puzzle; I can't make it out."

The mother lost heart then.

"Oh, my God! oh, blessed Virgin! some flying beast has got her. I'll never see her again!"

"Ah, *don't* give up," said Archy. "We'll find her—don't give up."

"God bless you for the words, Archy Stillman!" and she seized his hand and kissed it fervently.

Peterson, the new-comer, whispered satirically in Ferguson's ear:

"Wonderful performance to find this place, wasn't it? Hardly worth while to come so far, though; any other supposititious place would have answered just as well—hey?"

Ferguson was not pleased with the innuendo. He said, with some warmth:

"Do you mean to insinuate that the child hasn't been here? I tell you the child *has* been here! Now if you want to get yourself into as tidy a little fuss as—"

"All right!" sang out Stillman. "Come, everybody, and look at this! It was right under our noses all the time, and we didn't see it."

There was a general plunge for the ground at the place where the child was alleged to have rested, and many eyes tried hard and hopefully to see the thing that Archy's finger was resting upon. There was a pause, then a several-barreled sigh of disappointment. Pat Riley and Ham Sandwich said, in the one breath:

"What is it, Archy? There's nothing here."

"Nothing? Do you call *that* nothing?" and he swiftly traced upon the ground a form with his finger. "There—don't you recognize it now? It's Injun Billy's track. He's got the child."

"God be praised!" from the mother.

"Take away the lantern. I've got the direction. Follow!"

He started on a run, racing in and out among the sage-bushes a matter of three hundred yards, and disappeared over a sand-wave; the others struggled after him, caught him up, and found him waiting. Ten steps away was a little wickiup, a dim and formless shelter of rags and old horse-blankets, a dull light showing through its chinks.

"You lead, Mrs. Hogan," said the lad. "It's your privilege to be first."

All followed the sprint she made for the wickiup, and saw, with her, the picture its interior afforded. Injun Billy was sitting on the ground; the child was asleep beside him. The mother hugged it with a wild embrace, which included Archy Stillman, the grateful tears running down her face, and in a choked and broken voice she poured out a golden stream of that wealth of worshiping endearments which has its home in full richness nowhere but in the Irish heart.

"I find her bymeby it is ten o'clock," Billy explained. "She 'sleep out yonder, ve'y tired—face wet, been cryin', 'spose; fetch her home, feed her, she heap much hungry—go 'sleep 'gin."

In her limitless gratitude the happy mother waived rank and hugged him too, calling him "the angel of God in disguise." And he probably was in disguise if he was that kind of an official. He was dressed for the character.

At half past one in the morning the procession burst into the village singing, "When Johnny Comes Marching Home," waving its lanterns, and swallowing the drinks that were brought out all along its course. It concentrated at the tavern, and made a night of what was left of the morning.

6

The next afternoon the village was electrified with an immense sensation. A grave and dignified foreigner of distinguished bearing and appearance had arrived at the tavern, and entered this formidable name upon the register:

SHERLOCK HOLMES

The news buzzed from cabin to cabin, from claim to claim; tools were dropped, and the town swarmed toward the center of interest. A man passing out at the northern end of the village shouted it to Pat Riley, whose claim was the next one to Flint Buckner's. At that time Fetlock Jones seemed to turn sick. He muttered to himself:

"Uncle *Sherlock!* The mean luck of it!—that *he* should come just when . . ." He dropped into a reverie, and presently said to himself: "But what's the use of being afraid of *him?* Anybody that knows him the way I do knows he can't detect a crime except where he plans it all out beforehand and arranges the clues and hires some fellow to commit it according to instructions. . . . Now there ain't going to *be* any clues this time—so, what show has he got? None at all. No, sir; everything's ready. If I was to risk putting it off— . . . No, I won't run any risk like that. Flint Buckner goes out of this world to-night, for sure." Then another trouble presented itself. "Uncle Sherlock 'll be wanting to talk home matters with me this evening, and how am I going to get rid of him? for I've *got* to be at my cabin a minute or two about eight o'clock." This was an awkward matter, and cost him much thought. But he found a way to beat the difficulty. "We'll go for a walk, and I'll leave him in the road a minute, so that he won't see what it is I do: the best way to throw a detective off the track, anyway, is to have him along when you are preparing the thing. Yes, that's the safest —I'll take him with me."

Meantime the road in front of the tavern was blocked with villagers waiting and hoping for a glimpse of the great man. But he kept his room, and did not appear. None but Ferguson, Jake Parker the blacksmith, and Ham Sandwich had any luck. These enthusiastic admirers of the great scientific detective hired the tavern's detained-baggage lockup, which looked into the detective's room across a little alleyway ten or twelve feet wide, ambushed themselves in it, and cut some peep-holes in the window-blind. Mr. Holmes's blinds were down; but by and by he raised them. It gave the spies a hair-lifting but pleasurable thrill to find themselves face to face with the Extraordinary Man who had filled the world with the fame of his more than human ingenuities. There he sat—not a myth, not a shadow, but real, alive, compact of substance, and almost within touching distance with the hand.

"Look at that head!" said Ferguson, in an awed voice. "By gracious! *that's* a head!"

"You bet!" said the blacksmith, with deep reverence. "Look at his nose! look at his eyes! Intellect? Just a battery of it!"

"And that paleness," said Ham Sandwich. "Comes from thought— that's what it comes from. Hell! duffers like us don't know what real thought *is*."

"No more we don't," said Ferguson. "What we take for thinking is just blubber-and-slush."

"Right you are, Wells-Fargo. And look at that frown—that's *deep* thinking—away down, down, forty fathom into the bowels of things. He's on the track of something."

"Well, he is, and don't you forget it. Say—look at that awful gravity —look at that pallid solemness—there ain't any corpse can lay over it."

"No, sir, not for dollars! And it's his'n by hereditary rights, too; he's been dead four times a'ready, and there's history for it. Three times natural, once by accident. I've heard say he smells damp and cold, like a grave. And he—"

"'Sh! Watch him! There—he's got his thumb on the bump on the near corner of his forehead, and his forefinger on the off one. His think-works is just a-*grinding* now, you bet your other shirt."

"That's so. And now he's gazing up toward heaven and stroking his mustache slow, and—"

"Now he has rose up standing, and is putting his clues together on his left fingers with his right finger. See? he touches the forefinger—now middle finger—now ring-finger—"

"Stuck!"

"Look at him scowl! He can't seem to make out *that* clue. So he—"

"See him smile!—like a tiger—and tally off the other fingers like nothing! He's got it, boys; he's got it sure!"

"Well, I should *say!* I'd hate to be in that man's place that he's after."

Mr. Holmes drew a table to the window, sat down with his back to the spies, and proceeded to write. The spies withdrew their eyes from the peep-holes, lit their pipes, and settled themselves for a comfortable smoke and talk. Ferguson said, with conviction:

"Boys, it's no use talking, he's a wonder! He's got the signs of it all over him."

"You hain't ever said a truer word than that, Wells-Fargo," said Jake Parker. "Say, wouldn't it 'a' been nuts if he'd a-been here last night?"

"Oh, by George, but wouldn't it!" said Ferguson. "Then we'd have seen *scientific* work. Intellect—just pure intellect—away up on the upper levels, dontchuknow. Archy is all right, and it don't become anybody to belittle *him*, I can tell you. But his gift is only just eyesight, sharp as an owl's, as near as I can make it out just a grand natural animal talent, no more, no less, and prime as far as it goes, but no intellect in it, and for awfulness and marvelousness no more to be compared to what this man does than—than— Why, let me tell you what *he'd* have done. He'd have stepped over to Hogan's and glanced—just *glanced*, that's all—at the premises, and that's enough. See everything? Yes, sir, to the last little *de*tail; and he'd know more about that place than the Hogans would know in seven years. Next, he would sit down on the bunk, just as ca'm, and say to Mrs. Hogan— *Say*, Ham, consider that you are Mrs. Hogan. I'll ask the questions; you answer them."

"All right; go on."

"'Madam, if you please—attention—do not let your mind wander. Now, then—sex of the child?'

"'Female, your Honor.'

"'Um—female. Very good, very good. Age?'

"'Turned six, your Honor.'

"'Um—young, weak—two miles. Weariness will overtake it then. It will sink down and sleep. We shall find it two miles away, or less. Teeth?'

"'Five, your Honor, and one a-coming.'

"'Very good, very good, *very* good, indeed.' You see, boys, *he* knows a clue when he sees it, when it wouldn't mean a dern thing to anybody else. 'Stockings, madam? Shoes?'

"'Yes, your Honor—both.'

"'Yarn, perhaps? Morocco?'

"'Yarn, your Honor. And kip.'

"'Um—kip. This complicates the matter. However, let it go—we shall manage. Religion?'

"'Catholic, your Honor.'

"'Very good. Snip me a bit from the bed blanket, please. Ah, thanks. Part wool—foreign make. Very well. A snip from some garment of the child's, please. Thanks. Cotton. Shows wear. An excellent clue, excellent. Pass me a pallet of the floor dirt, if you'll be so kind. Thanks, many thanks. Ah, admirable, admirable! *Now* we know where we are, I think.' You see, boys, he's got all the clues he wants now; he don't need anything more. Now, then, what does this Extraordinary Man do? He lays those snips and that dirt out on the table and leans over them on his elbows, and puts them together side by side and studies them— mumbles to himself, 'Female'; changes them around—mumbles, 'Six years old'; changes them this way and that—again mumbles: 'Five teeth —one a-coming—Catholic—yarn—cotton—kip—damn that kip.' Then he straightens up and gazes toward heaven, and plows his hands through his hair—plows and plows, muttering, 'Damn that kip!' Then he stands up and frowns, and begins to tally off his clues on his fingers—and gets stuck at the ring-finger. But only just a minute—then his face glares all up in a smile like a house afire, and he straightens up stately and majestic, and says to the crowd, 'Take a lantern, a couple of you, and go down to Injun Billy's and fetch the child—the rest of you go 'long home to bed; good-night, madam; good-night, gents.' And he bows like the Matterhorn, and pulls out for the tavern. That's *his* style, and the *Only* —scientific, intellectual—all over in fifteen minutes—no poking around all over the sage-brush range an hour and a half in a mass-meeting crowd for *him,* boys—you hear *me!*"

"By Jackson, it's grand!" said Ham Sandwich. "Wells-Fargo, you've got him down to a dot. He ain't painted up any exacter to the life in the books. By George, I can juse *see* him—can't you, boys?"

"You bet you! It's just a photograft, that's what it is."

Ferguson was profoundly pleased with his success, and grateful. He sat silently enjoying his happiness a little while, then he murmured, with a deep awe in his voice,

"I wonder if God made him?"

There was no response for a moment; then Ham Sandwich said, reverently:

"Not all at one time, I reckon."

7

At eight o'clock that evening two persons were groping their way past Flint Buckner's cabin in the frosty gloom. They were Sherlock Holmes and his nephew.

"Stop here in the road a moment, uncle," said Fetlock, "while I run to my cabin; I won't be gone a minute."

He asked for something—the uncle furnished it—then he disappeared in the darkness, but soon returned, and the talking-walk was resumed. By nine o'clock they had wandered back to the tavern. They worked their way through the billiard-room, where a crowd had gathered in the hope of getting a glimpse of the Extraordinary Man. A royal cheer was raised. Mr. Holmes acknowledged the compliment with a series of courtly bows, and as he was passing out his nephew said to the assemblage:

"Uncle Sherlock's got some work to do, gentlemen, that 'll keep him till twelve or one; but he'll be down again then, or earlier if he can, and hopes some of you'll be left to take a drink with him."

"By George, he's just a duke, boys! Three cheers for Sherlock Holmes, the greatest man that ever lived!" shouted Ferguson. "Hip, hip, hip—"

"Hurrah! hurrah! hurrah! Tiger!"

The uproar shook the building, so hearty was the feeling the boys put into their welcome. Up-stairs the uncle reproached the nephew gently, saying:

"What did you get me into that engagement for?"

"I reckon you don't want to be unpopular, do you, uncle? Well, then, don't you put on any exclusiveness in a mining-camp, that's all. The boys admire you; but if you was to leave without taking a drink with them, they'd set you down for a snob. And besides, you said you had home talk enough in stock to keep us up and at it half the night."

The boy was right, and wise—the uncle acknowledged it. The boy was wise in another detail which he did not mention—except to himself: "Uncle and the others will come handy—in the way of nailing an *alibi* where it can't be budged."

He and his uncle talked diligently about three hours. Then, about midnight, Fetlock stepped down-stairs and took a position in the dark a dozen steps from the tavern, and waited. Five minutes later Flint Buckner came rocking out of the billiard-room and almost brushed him as he passed.

"I've *got* him!" muttered the boy. He continued to himself, looking after the shadowy form: "Good-by—good-by for good, Flint Buckner; you called my mother a—well, never mind what: it's all right, now; you're taking your last walk, friend."

He went musing back into the tavern. "From now till one is an hour. We'll spend it with the boys: it's good for the *alibi*."

He brought Sherlock Holmes to the billiard-room, which was jammed with eager and admiring miners; the guest called the drinks, and the fun began. Everybody was happy; everybody was complimentary; the ice was soon broken, songs, anecdotes, and more drinks followed, and the pregnant minutes flew. At six minutes to one, when the jollity was at its highest—

Boom!

There was silence instantly. The deep sound came rolling and rumbling from peak to peak up the gorge, then died down, and ceased. The spell broke, then, and the men made a rush for the door, saying:

"Something's blown up!"

Outside, a voice in the darkness said, "It's away down the gorge; I saw the flash."

The crowd poured down the cañon—Holmes, Fetlock, Archy Stillman, everybody. They made the mile in a few minutes. By the light of a lantern they found the smooth and solid dirt floor of Flint Buckner's cabin; of the cabin itself not a vestige remained, not a rag nor a splinter. Nor any sign of Flint. Search-parties sought here and there and yonder, and presently a cry went up.

"Here he is!"

It was true. Fifty yards down the gulch they had found him—that is, they had found a crushed and lifeless mass which represented him. Fetlock Jones hurried thither with the others and looked.

The inquest was a fifteen-minute affair. Ham Sandwich, foreman of the jury, handed up the verdict, which was phrased with a certain unstudied literary grace, and closed with this finding, to wit: that "deceased came to his death by his own act or some other person or persons unknown to this jury not leaving any family or similar effects behind but his cabin which was blown away and God have mercy on his soul amen."

Then the impatient jury rejoined the main crowd, for the storm-center of interest was there—Sherlock Holmes. The miners stood silent and reverent in a half-circle, inclosing a large vacant space which included the front exposure of the site of the late premises. In this considerable space the Extraordinary Man was moving about, attended by his nephew with a lantern. With a tape he took measurements of the cabin site; of the distance from the wall of chaparral to the road; of the height of the chaparral bushes; also various other measurements. He gathered a rag here, a splinter there, and a pinch of earth yonder, inspected them profoundly, and preserved them. He took the "lay" of the place with a pocket-compass, allowing two seconds for magnetic variation. He took the time (Pacific) by his watch, correcting it for local time. He paced off the distance from the cabin site to the corpse, and corrected that for tidal differentiation. He took the altitude with a pocket-aneroid, and the temperature with a pocket-thermometer. Finally he said, with a stately bow:

"It is finished. Shall we return, gentlemen?"

He took up the line of march for the tavern, and the crowd fell into his wake, earnestly discussing and admiring the Extraordinary Man, and interlarding guesses as to the origin of the tragedy and who the author of it might be.

"My, but it's grand luck having him here—hey, boys?" said Ferguson.

"It's the biggest thing of the century," said Ham Sandwich. "It 'll go all over the world; you mark my words."

"*You* bet!" said Jake Parker, the blacksmith. "It 'll boom this camp. Ain't it so, Wells-Fargo?"

"Well, as you want my opinion—if it's any sign of how *I* think about it, I can tell you this: yesterday I was holding the Straight Flush claim at two dollars a foot; I'd like to see the man that can get it at sixteen to-day."

"Right you are, Wells-Fargo! It's the grandest luck a new camp ever struck. Say, did you see him collar them little rags and dirt and things? What an eye! He just can't overlook a clue—'taint *in* him."

"That's so. And they wouldn't mean a thing to anybody else; but to him, why, they're just a book—large print at that."

"Sure's you're born! Them odds and ends have got their little old secret, and they think there ain't anybody can pull it; but, land! when he sets his grip there they've got to squeal, and don't you forget it."

"Boys, I ain't sorry, now, that he wasn't here to roust out the child; this is a bigger thing, by a long sight. Yes, sir, and more tangled up and scientific and intellectual."

"I reckon we're all of us glad it's turned out this way. Glad? 'George! it ain't any name for it. Dontchuknow, Archy could 've *learnt* something if he'd had the nous to stand by and take notice of how that man works the system. But no; he went poking up into the chaparral and just missed the whole thing."

"It's true as gospel; I seen it myself. Well, Archy's young. He'll know better one of these days."

"Say, boys, who do you reckon done it?"

That was a difficult question, and brought out a world of unsatisfying conjecture. Various men were mentioned as possibilities, but one by one they were discarded as not being eligible. No one but young Hillyer had been intimate with Flint Buckner; no one had really had a quarrel with him; he had affronted every man who had tried to make up to him, although not quite offensively enough to require bloodshed. There was one name that was upon every tongue from the start, but it was the last to get utterance—Fetlock Jones's. It was Pat Riley that mentioned it.

"Oh, well," the boys said, "of course we've all thought of him, because he had a million rights to kill Flint Buckner, and it was just his plain duty to do it. But all the same there's two things we can't get around: for one thing, he hasn't got the sand; and for another, he wasn't anywhere near the place when it happened."

"I know it," said Pat. "He was there in the billiard-room with us when it happened."

"Yes, and was there all the time for an hour *before* it happened."

"It's so. And lucky for him, too. He'd have been suspected in a minute if it hadn't been for that."

8

The tavern dining-room had been cleared of all its furniture save one six-foot pine table and a chair. This table was against one end of the room; the chair was on it; Sherlock Holmes, stately, imposing, impressive, sat in the chair. The public stood. The room was full. The tobacco-smoke was dense, the stillness profound.

The Extraordinary Man raised his hand to command additional silence; held it in the air a few moments; then, in brief, crisp terms he put forward question after question, and noted the answers with "Um-ums," nods of the head, and so on. By this process he learned all about Flint Buckner, his character, conduct, and habits, that the people were able to tell him. It thus transpired that the Extraordinary Man's nephew was the only person in the camp who had a killing-grudge against Flint Buckner. Mr. Holmes smiled compassionately upon the witness, and asked, languidly:

"Do any of you gentlemen chance to know where the lad Fetlock Jones was at the time of the explosion?"

A thunderous response followed:

"In the billiard-room of this house!"

"Ah. And had he just come in?"

"Been there all of an hour!"

"Ah. It is about—about—well, about how far might it be to the scene of the explosion?"

"All of a mile!"

"Ah. It isn't *much* of an alibi, 'tis true, but—"

A storm-burst of laughter, mingled with shouts of "By jiminy, but he's chain-lightning!" and "Ain't you sorry you spoke, Sandy?" shut off the rest of the sentence, and the crushed witness drooped his blushing face in pathetic shame. The inquisitor resumed:

"The lad Jones's somewhat *distant* connection with the case" (*laughter*) "having been disposed of, let us now call the *eye*-witnesses of the tragedy, and listen to what they have to say."

He got out his fragmentary clues and arranged them on a sheet of cardboard on his knee. The house held its breath and watched.

"We have the longitude and the latitude, corrected for magnetic variation, and this gives us the exact location of the tragedy. We have the altitude, the temperature, and the degree of humidity prevailing—inestimably valuable, since they enable us to estimate with precision the degree of influence which they would exercise upon the mood and disposition of the assassin at that time of the night."

(*Buzz of admiration; muttered remark, "By George, but he's deep!"*) He fingered his clues. "And now let us ask these mute witnesses to speak to us.

"Here we have an empty linen shot-bag. What is its message? This: that robbery was the motive, not revenge. What is its further message? This: that the assassin was of inferior intelligence—shall we say light-witted, or perhaps approaching that? How do we know this? Because a person of sound intelligence would not have proposed to rob the man Buckner, who never had much money with him. But the assassin might have been a stranger? Let the bag speak again. I take from it this article. It is a bit of silver-bearing quartz. It is peculiar. Examine it, please—you—and you—and you. Now pass it back, please. There is but one lode on this coast which produces just that character and color of quartz; and that is a lode which crops out for nearly two miles on a stretch, and in my opinion is destined, at no distant day, to confer upon its locality a globe-girdling celebrity, and upon its two hundred owners riches beyond the dreams of avarice. Name that lode, please."

"The Consolidated Christian Science and Mary Ann!" was the prompt response.

A wild crash of hurrahs followed, and every man reached for his neighbor's hand and wrung it, with tears in his eyes; and Wells-Fargo Ferguson shouted, "The Straight Flush is on the lode, and up she goes to a hundred and fifty a foot—you hear *me!*"

When quiet fell, Mr. Holmes resumed:

"We perceive, then, that three facts are established, to wit: the assassin was approximately light-witted; he was not a stranger; his motive was robbery, not revenge. Let us proceed. I hold in my hand a small fragment of fuse, with the recent smell of fire upon it. What is its testimony? Taken with the corroborative evidence of the quartz, it reveals to us that the assassin was a miner. What does it tell us further? This, gentlemen: that the assassination was consummated by means of an explosive. What else does it say? This: that the explosive was located against the side of the cabin nearest the road—the front side—for within six feet of that spot I found it.

"I hold in my fingers a burnt Swedish match—the kind one rubs on a safety-box. I found it in the road, six hundred and twenty-two feet from the abolished cabin. What does it say? This: that the train was fired from that point. What further does it tell us? This: that the assassin was left-handed. How do I know this? I should not be able to explain to you, gentlemen, how I know it, the signs being so subtle that only long experience and deep study can enable one to detect them. But the signs are here, and they are reinforced by a fact which you must have often noticed in the great detective narratives—that *all* assassins are left-handed."

"By Jackson, *that's* so!" said Ham Sandwich, bringing his great hand down with a resounding slap upon his thigh; "blamed if I ever thought of it before."

"Nor I!" "Nor I!" cried several. "Oh, there can't anything escape *him* —look at his eye!"

"Gentlemen, distant as the murderer was from his doomed victim, he did not wholly escape injury. This fragment of wood which I now exhibit to you struck him. It drew blood. Wherever he is, he bears the telltale mark. I picked it up where he stood when he fired the fatal train." He looked out over the house from his high perch, and his countenance began to darken; he slowly raised his hand, and pointed:

"There stands the assassin!"

For a moment the house was paralyzed with amazement; then twenty voices burst out with:

"Sammy Hillyer? Oh, *hell,* no! *Him?* It's pure foolishness!"

"Take care, gentlemen—be not hasty. Observe—he has the blood-mark on his brow."

Hillyer turned white with fright. He was near to crying. He turned this way and that, appealing to every face for help and sympathy; and held out his supplicating hands toward Holmes and began to plead:

"*Don't,* oh, don't! I never did it; I give my word I never did it. The way I got this hurt on my forehead was—"

"Arrest him, constable!" cried Holmes. "I will swear out the warrant."

The constable moved reluctantly forward—hesitated—stopped.

Hillyer broke out with another appeal. "Oh, Archy, don't let them do it; it would kill mother! *You* know how I got the hurt. Tell them, and save me, Archy; save me!"

Stillman worked his way to the front, and said:

"Yes, I'll save you. Don't be afraid." Then he said to the house, "Never mind how he got the hurt; it hasn't anything to do with this case, and isn't of any consequence."

"God bless you, Archy, for a true friend!"

"Hurrah for Archy! Go in, boy, and play 'em a knock-down flush to their two pair 'n' a jack!" shouted the house, pride in their home talent and a patriotic sentiment of loyalty to it rising suddenly in the public heart and changing the whole attitude of the situation.

Young Stillman waited for the noise to cease; then he said:

"I will ask Tom Jeffries to stand by that door yonder, and Constable Harris to stand by the other one here, and not let anybody leave the room."

"Said and done. Go on, old man!"

"The criminal is present, I believe. I will show him to you before long, in case I am right in my guess. Now I will tell you all about the tragedy, from start to finish. The motive *wasn't* robbery; it was revenge. The murderer *wasn't* light-witted. He *didn't* stand six hundred and twenty-two feet away. He *didn't* get hit with a piece of wood. He *didn't* place the explosive against the cabin. He *didn't* bring a shot-bag with him, and he *wasn't* left-handed. With the exception of these errors, the distinguished guest's statement of the case is substantially correct."

A comfortable laugh rippled over the house; friend nodded to friend, as much as to say, "That's the word, with the bark *on* it. Good lad, good boy. *He* ain't lowering his flag any!"

The guest's serenity was not disturbed. Stillman resumed:

"I also have some witnesses; and I will presently tell you where you can find some more." He held up a piece of coarse wire; the crowd

craned their necks to see. "It has a smooth coating of melted tallow on it. And here is a candle which is burned half-way down. The remaining half of it has marks cut upon it an inch apart. Soon I will tell you where I found these things. I will now put aside reasonings, guesses, the impressive hitchings of odds and ends of clues together, and the other showy theatricals of the detective trade, and tell you in a plain, straightforward way just how this dismal thing happened."

He paused a moment, for effect—to allow silence and suspense to intensify and concentrate the house's interest; then he went on:

"The assassin studied out his plan with a good deal of pains. It was a good plan, very ingenious, and showed an intelligent mind, not a feeble one. It was a plan which was well calculated to ward off all suspicion from its inventor. In the first place, he marked a candle into spaces an inch apart, and lit it and timed it. He found it took three hours to burn four inches of it. I tried it myself for half an hour, awhile ago, up-stairs here, while the inquiry into Flint Buckner's character and ways was being conducted in this room, and I arrived in that way at the rate of a candle's consumption when sheltered from the wind. Having proved his trial candle's rate, he blew it out—I have already shown it to you—and put his inch-marks on a fresh one.

"He put the fresh one into a tin candlestick. Then at the five-hour mark he bored a hole through the candle with a red-hot wire. I have already shown you the wire, with a smooth coat of tallow on it—tallow that had been melted and had cooled.

"With labor—very hard labor, I should say—he struggled up through the stiff chaparral that clothes the steep hillside back of Flint Buckner's place, tugging an empty flour-barrel with him. He placed it in that absolutely secure hiding-place, and in the bottom of it he set the candlestick. Then he measured off about thirty-five feet of fuse—the barrel's distance from the back of the cabin. He bored a hole in the side of the barrel—here is the large gimlet he did it with. He went on and finished his work; and when it was done, one end of the fuse was in Buckner's cabin, and the other end, with a notch chipped in it to expose the powder, was in the hole in the candle—timed to blow the place up at one o'clock this morning, provided the candle was lit about eight o'clock yesterday evening—which I am betting it was—and provided there was an explosive in the cabin and connected with that end of the fuse—which I am also betting there was, though I can't prove it. Boys, the barrel is there in the chaparral, the candle's remains are in it in the tin stick; the burnt-out fuse is in the gimlet-hole, the other end is down the hill where the late cabin stood. I saw them all an hour or two ago, when the Professor here was measuring off unimplicated vacancies and collecting relics that hadn't anything to do with the case."

He paused. The house drew a long, deep breath, shook its strained cords and muscles free and burst into cheers. "Dang him!" said Ham Sandwich, "that's why he was snooping around in the chaparral, instead of picking up points out of the P'fessor's game. Looky here—*he* ain't no fool, boys."

"No, sir! Why, great Scott—"

But Stillman was resuming:

"While we were out yonder an hour or two ago, the owner of the gimlet and the trial candle took them from a place where he had concealed them—it was not a good place—and carried them to what he probably thought was a better one, two hundred yards up in the pine woods, and hid them there, covering them over with pine needles. It was there that I found them. The gimlet exactly fits the hole in the barrel. And now—"

The Extraordinary Man interrupted him. He said, sarcastically:

"We have had a very pretty fairy tale, gentlemen—very pretty indeed. Now I would like to ask this young man a question or two."

Some of the boys winced, and Ferguson said:

"I'm afraid Archy's going to catch it now."

The others lost their smiles and sobered down. Mr. Holmes said:

"Let us proceed to examine into this fairy tale in a consecutive and orderly way—by geometrical progression, so to speak—linking detail to detail in a steadily advancing and remorselessly consistent and unassailable march upon this tinsel toy fortress of error, the dream fabric of a callow imagination. To begin with, young sir, I desire to ask you but three questions at present—*at present*. Did I understand you to say it was your opinion that the supposititious candle was lighted at about eight o'clock yesterday evening?"

"Yes, sir—about eight."

"Could you say exactly eight?"

"Well, no, I couldn't be that exact."

"Um. If a person had been passing along there just about that time, he would have been almost sure to encounter that assassin, do you think?"

"Yes, I should think so."

"Thank you, that is all. For the present. I say, all *for the present*."

"Dern him! he's laying for Archy," said Ferguson.

"It's so," said Ham Sandwich. "I don't like the look of it."

Stillman said, glancing at the guest, "I was along there myself at half-past eight—no, about nine."

"In-deed? This is interesting—this is very interesting. Perhaps you encountered the assassin?"

"No, I encountered no one."

"Ah. Then—if you will excuse the remark—I do not quite see the relevancy of the information."

"It has none. At present. I say it has none—at present."

He paused. Presently he resumed: "I did not encounter the assassin, but I am on his track, I am sure, for I believe he is in this room. I will ask you all to pass one by one in front of me—here, where there is a good light—so that I can see your feet."

A buzz of excitement swept the place, and the march began, the guest looking on with an iron attempt at gravity which was not an unqualified success. Stillman stooped, shaded his eyes with his hand, and gazed down intently at each pair of feet as it passed. Fifty men tramped monotonously by—with no result. Sixty. Seventy. The thing was beginning to look absurd. The guest remarked, with suave irony:

"Assassins appear to be scarce this evening."

The house saw the humor if it, and refreshed itself with a cordial laugh. Ten or twelve more candidates tramped by—no, *danced* by, with airy and ridiculous capers which convulsed the spectators—then suddenly Stillman put out his hand and said:

"This is the assassin!"

"Fetlock Jones, by the great Sanhedrim!" roared the crowd; and at once let fly a pyrotechnic explosion and dazzle and confusion of stirring remarks inspired by the situation.

At the height of the turmoil the guest stretched out his hand, commanding peace. The authority of a great name and a great personality laid its mysterious compulsion upon the house, and it obeyed. Out of the panting calm which succeeded, the guest spoke, saying, with dignity and feeling:

"*This* is serious. It strikes at an innocent life. Innocent beyond suspicion! Innocent beyond peradventure! Hear me *prove* it; observe how simple a fact can brush out of existence this witless lie. Listen. My friends, that lad was never out of my sight yesterday evening at *any* time!"

It made a deep impression. Men turned their eyes upon Stillman with grave inquiry in them. His face brightened, and he said:

"I *knew* there was another one!" He stepped briskly to the table and glanced at the guest's feet, then up at his face, and said: "You were *with* him! You were not fifty steps from him when he lit the candle that by and by fired the powder!" (*Sensation.*) "And what is more, you furnished the matches yourself!"

Plainly the guest seemed hit; it looked so to the public. He opened his mouth to speak; the words did not come freely.

"This—er—this is insanity—this—"

Stillman pressed his evident advantage home. He held up a charred match.

"Here is one of them. I found it in the barrel—and there's *another* one there."

The guest found his voice at once.

"*Yes*—and put them there yourself!"

It was recognized a good shot. Stillman retorted.

"It is *wax*—a breed unknown to this camp. I am ready to be searched for the box. Are you?"

The guest was staggered this time—the dullest eye could see it. He fumbled with his hands; once or twice his lips moved, but the words did not come. The house waited and watched, in tense suspense, the stillness adding effect to the situation. Presently Stillman said, gently:

"We are waiting for your decision."

There was silence again during several moments; then the guest answered, in a low voice:

"I refuse to be searched."

There was no noisy demonstration, but all about the house one voice after another muttered:

"That settles it! He's Archy's meat."

What to do now? Nobody seemed to know. It was an embarrassing situation for the moment—merely, of course, because matters had taken such a sudden and unexpected turn that these unpractised minds were not prepared for it, and had come to a standstill, like a stopped clock, under the shock. But after a little the machinery began to work again, tentatively, and by twos and threes the men put their heads together and privately buzzed over this and that and the other proposition. One of these propositions met with much favor; it was, to confer upon the assassin a vote of thanks for removing Flint Buckner, and let him go. But the cooler heads opposed it, pointing out that addled brains in the Eastern states would pronounce it a scandal, and make no end of foolish noise about it. Finally the cool heads got the upper hand, and obtained general consent to a proposition of their own; their leader then called the house to order and stated it—to this effect: that Fetlock Jones be jailed and put upon trial.

The motion was carried. Apparently there was nothing further to do now, and the people were glad, for, privately, they were impatient to get out and rush to the scene of the tragedy, and see whether that barrel and the other things were really there or not.

But no—the break-up got a check. The surprises were not over yet. For a while Fetlock Jones had been silently sobbing, unnoticed in the absorbing excitements which had been following one another so persistently for some time; but when his arrest and trial were decreed, he broke out despairingly, and said:

"No! it's no use. I don't want any jail, I don't want any trial; I've had all the hard luck I want, and all the miseries. Hang me now, and let me out! It would all come out, anyway—there couldn't anything save me. He has told it all, just as if he'd been with me and seen it—I don't know how he found out; and you'll find the barrel and things, and then I wouldn't have any chance any more. I killed him; and *you'd* have done it too, if he'd treated you like a dog, and you only a boy, and weak and poor, and not a friend to help you."

"And served him damned well right!" broke in Ham Sandwich. "Looky here, boys—"

From the constable: "Order! Order, gentlemen!"

A voice: "Did your uncle know what you was up to?"

"No, he didn't."

"Did he give you the matches, sure enough?"

"Yes, he did; but he didn't know what I wanted them for."

"When you was out on such a business as that, how did you venture to risk having him along—and him a *detective?* How's that?"

The boy hesitated, fumbled with his buttons in an embarrassed way, then said, shyly:

"I know about detectives, on account of having them in the family; and if you don't want them to find out about a thing, it's best to have them around when you do it."

The cyclone of laughter which greeted this naïve discharge of wisdom did not modify the poor little waif's embarrassment in any large degree.

9

From a letter to Mrs. Stillman, dated merely "Tuesday."

Fetlock Jones was put under lock and key in an unoccupied log cabin, and left there to await his trial. Constable Harris provided him with a couple of days' rations, instructed him to keep a good guard over himself, and promised to look in on him as soon as further supplies should be due.

Next morning a score of us went with Hillyer, out of friendship, and helped him bury his late relative, the unlamented Buckner, and I acted as first assistant pall-bearer, Hillyer acting as chief. Just as we had finished our labors a ragged and melancholy stranger, carrying an old hand-bag, limped by with his head down, and I caught the scent I had chased around the globe! It was the odor of Paradise to my perishing hope!

In a moment I was at his side and had laid a gentle hand upon his shoulder. He slumped to the ground as if a stroke of lightning had withered him in his tracks; and as the boys came running he struggled to his knees and put up his pleading hands to me, and out of his chattering jaws he begged me to persecute him no more, and said:

"You have hunted me around the world, Sherlock Holmes, yet God is my witness I have never done any man harm!"

A glance at his wild eyes showed us that he was insane. That was my work, mother! The tidings of your death can some day repeat the misery I felt in that moment, but nothing else can ever do it. The boys lifted him up, and gathered about him, and were full of pity of him, and said the gentlest and touchingest things to him, and said cheer up and don't be troubled, he was among friends now, and they would take care of him, and protect him, and hang any man that laid a hand on him. They are just like so many mothers, the rough mining-camp boys are, when you wake up the south side of their hearts; yes, and just like so many reckless and unreasoning children when you wake up the opposite of that muscle. They did everything they could think of to comfort him, but nothing succeeded until Wells-Fargo Ferguson, who is a clever strategist, said:

"If it's only Sherlock Holmes that's troubling you, you needn't worry any more."

"Why?" asked the forlorn lunatic, eagerly.

"Because he's dead again."

"Dead! Dead! Oh, don't trifle with a poor wreck like me. *Is* he dead? On honor, now—is he telling me true, boys?"

"True as you're standing there!" said Ham Sandwich, and they all backed up the statement in a body.

"They hung him in San Bernardino last week," added Ferguson, clinching the matter, "whilst he was searching around after you. Mistook him for another man. They're sorry, but they can't help it now."

"They're a-building him a monument," said Ham Sandwich, with the air of a person who had contributed to it, and knew.

"James Walker" drew a deep sigh—evidently a sigh of relief—and said nothing; but his eyes lost something of their wildness, his countenance cleared visibly, and its drawn look relaxed a little. We all went to our cabin, and the boys cooked him the best dinner the camp could furnish the materials for, and while they were about it Hillyer and I outfitted him from hat to shoe-leather with new clothes of ours, and made a comely and presentable old gentleman of him. "Old" is the right word, and a pity, too: old by the droop of him, and the frost upon his hair, and the marks which sorrow and distress have left upon his face; though he is only in his prime in the matter of years. While he ate, we smoked and chatted; and when he was finishing he found his voice at last, and of his own accord broke out with his personal history. I cannot furnish his exact words, but I will come as near it as I can.

THE "WRONG MAN'S" STORY

It happened like this: I was in Denver. I had been there many years; sometimes I remember how many, sometimes I don't—but it isn't any matter. All of a sudden I got a notice to leave, or I would be exposed for a horrible crime committed long before—years and years before—in the East.

I knew about that crime, but I was not the criminal; it was a cousin of mine of the same name. What should I better do? My head was all disordered by fear, and I didn't know. I was allowed very little time—only one day, I think it was. I would be ruined if I was published, and the people would lynch me, and not believe what I said. It is always the way with lynchings: when they find out it is a mistake they are sorry, but it is too late—the same as it was with Mr. Holmes, you see. So I said I would sell out and get money to live on, and run away until it blew over and I could come back with my proofs. Then I escaped in the night and went a long way off in the mountains somewhere, and lived disguised and had a false name.

I got more and more troubled and worried, and my troubles made me see spirits and hear voices, and I could not think straight and clear on any subject, but got confused and involved and had to give it up, because my head hurt so. It got to be worse and worse; more spirits and more voices. They were about me all the time; at first only in the night, then in the day too. They were always whispering around my bed and plotting against me, and it broke my sleep and kept me fagged out, because I got no good rest.

And then came the worst. One night the whispers said, "We'll never manage, because we can't *see* him, and so can't point him out to the people."

They sighed; then one said: "We must bring Sherlock Holmes. He can be here in twelve days."

They all agreed, and whispered and jibbered with joy. But my heart broke; for I had read about that man, and knew what it would be to have him upon my track, with his superhuman penetration and tireless energies.

The spirits went away to fetch him, and I got up at once in the middle of the night and fled away, carrying nothing but the hand-bag that had my money in it—thirty thousand dollars; two-thirds of it are in the bag there yet. It was forty days before that man caught up on my track. I just escaped. From habit he had written his real name on a tavern register, but had scratched it out and written "Dagget Barclay" in the place of it. But fear gives you a watchful eye and keen, and I read the true name through the scratches, and fled like a deer.

He has hunted me all over this world for three years and a half— the Pacific states, Australasia, India—everywhere you can think of; then back to Mexico and up to California again, giving me hardly any rest; but that name on the registers always saved me, and what is left of me is alive yet. And I am *so* tired! A cruel time he has given me, yet I give you my honor I have never harmed him nor any man.

That was the end of the story, and it stirred those boys to bloodheat, be sure of it. As for me—each word burnt a hole in me where it struck.

We voted that the old man should bunk with us, and be my guest and Hillyer's. I shall keep my own counsel, naturally; but as soon as he is well rested and nourished, I shall take him to Denver and rehabilitate his fortunes.

The boys gave the old fellow the bone-smashing good-fellowship handshake of the mines, and then scattered away to spread the news.

At dawn next morning Wells-Fargo Ferguson and Ham Sandwich called us softly out, and said, privately:

"That news about the way that old stranger has been treated has spread all around, and the camps are up. They are piling in from everywhere, and are going to lynch the P'fessor. Constable Harris is in a dead funk, and has telephoned the sheriff. Come along!"

We started on a run. The others were privileged to feel as they chose, but in my heart's privacy I hoped the sheriff would arrive in time; for

I had small desire that Sherlock Holmes should hang for my deeds, as you can easily believe. I had heard a good deal about the sheriff, but for reassurance's sake I asked:

"Can he stop a mob?"

"Can *he* stop a mob! Can Jack *Fairfax* stop a mob! Well, I should smile! Ex-desperado—nineteen scalps on his string. Can *he!* Oh, I *say!*"

As we tore up the gulch, distant cries and shouts and yells rose faintly on the still air, and grew steadily in strength as we raced along. Roar after roar burst out, stronger and stronger, nearer and nearer; and at last, when we closed up upon the multitude massed in the open area in front of the tavern, the crash of sound was deafening. Some brutal roughs from Daly's gorge had Holmes in their grip, and he was the calmest man there; a contemptuous smile played about his lips, and if any fear of death was in his British heart, his iron personality was master of it and no sign of it was allowed to appear.

"Come to a vote, men!" This from one of the Daly gang, Shadbelly Higgins. "Quick! is it hang, or shoot?"

"Neither!" shouted one of his comrades. "He'd be alive again in a week; burning's the only permanency for *him.*"

The gangs from all the outlying camps burst out in a thundercrash of approval, and went struggling and surging toward the prisoner, and closed around him, shouting, "Fire! fire's the ticket!" They dragged him to the horse-post, backed him against it, chained him to it, and piled wood and pine cones around him waist-deep. Still the strong face did not blench, and still the scornful smile played about the thin lips.

"A match! fetch a match!"

Shadbelly struck it, shaded it with his hand, stooped, and held it under a pine cone. A deep silence fell upon the mob. The cone caught, a tiny flame flickered about it a moment or two. I seemed to catch the sound of distant hoofs—it grew more distinct—still more and more distinct, more and more definite, but the absorbed crowd did not appear to notice it. The match went out. The man struck another, stooped, and again the flame rose; this time it took hold and began to spread— here and there men turned away their faces. The executioner stood with the charred match in his fingers, watching his work. The hoof-beats turned a projecting crag, and now they came thundering down upon us. Almost the next moment there was a shout:

"The sheriff!"

And straightway he came tearing into the midst, stood his horse almost on his hind feet, and said:

"Fall back, you gutter-snipes!"

He was obeyed. By all but their leader. He stood his ground, and his hand went to his revolver. The sheriff covered him promptly, and said:

"Drop your hand, you parlor desperado. Kick the fire away. Now unchain the stranger."

The parlor desperado obeyed. Then the sheriff made a speech; sitting his horse at martial ease, and not warming his words with any touch of fire, but delivering them in a measured and deliberate way, and in a tone which harmonized with their character and made them impressively disrespectful.

"You're a nice lot—now ain't you? Just about eligible to travel with this bilk here—Shadbelly Higgins—this loud-mouthed sneak that shoots people in the back and calls himself a desperado. If there's anything I do particularly despise, it's a lynching mob; I've never seen one that had a man in it. It has to tally up a hundred against one before it can pump up pluck enough to tackle a sick tailor. It's made up of cowards, and so is the community that breeds it; and ninety-nine times out of a hundred the sheriff's another one." He paused—apparently to turn that last idea over in his mind and taste the juice of it—then he went on: "The sheriff that lets a mob take a prisoner away from him is the lowest-down coward there is. By the statistics there was a hundred and eighty-two of them drawing sneak pay in America last year. By the way it's going, pretty soon there 'll be a new disease in the doctor-books—*sheriff complaint*." That idea pleased him—any one could see it. "People will say, 'Sheriff sick again?' 'Yes; got the same old thing.' And next there 'll be a new title. People won't say, 'He's running for sheriff of Rapaho County,' for instance; they'll say, 'He's running for Coward of Rapaho.' Lord, the idea of a grown-up person being afraid of a lynch mob!"

He turned an eye on the captive, and said, "Stranger, who are you, and what have you been doing?"

"My name is Sherlock Holmes, and I have not been doing anything."

It was wonderful, the impression which the sound of that name made on the sheriff, notwithstanding he must have come posted. He spoke up with feeling, and said it was a blot on the country that a man whose marvelous exploits had filled the world with their fame and their ingenuity, and whose histories of them had won every reader's heart by the brilliancy and charm of their literary setting, should be visited under the Stars and Stripes by an outrage like this. He apologized in the name of the whole nation, and made Holmes a most handsome bow, and told Constable Harris to see him to his quarters, and hold himself personally responsible if he was molested again. Then he turned to the mob and said:

"Hunt your holes, you scum!" which they did; then he said: "Follow me, Shadbelly; I'll take care of your case myself. No—keep your pop-gun; whenever I see the day that I'll be afraid to have you behind me with that thing, it 'll be time for me to join last year's hundred and eighty-two"; and he rode off in a walk, Shadbelly following.

When we were on our way back to our cabin, toward breakfast-time, we ran upon the news that Fetlock Jones had escaped from his lock-up in the night and is gone! Nobody is sorry. Let his uncle track him out if he likes; it is in his line; the camp is not interested.

10

Ten days later.

"James Walker" is all right in body now, and his mind shows improvement too. I start with him for Denver to-morrow morning.

Next night. Brief note, mailed at a way-station.

As we were starting, this morning, Hillyer whispered to me: "Keep this news from Walker until you think it safe and not likely to disturb his mind and check his improvement: the ancient crime he spoke of was really committed—and by his cousin, as he said. *We buried the real criminal* the other day—the unhappiest man that has lived in a century —Flint Buckner. His real name was Jacob Fuller!" There, mother, by help of me, an unwitting mourner, your husband and my father is in his grave. Let him rest.

1902

The Five Boons of Life

1

In the morning of life came the good fairy with her basket, and said: "Here are gifts. Take one, leave the others. And be wary, choose wisely; oh, choose wisely! for only one of them is valuable."

The gifts were five: Fame, Love, Riches, Pleasure, Death. The youth said, eagerly:

"There is no need to consider"; and he chose Pleasure.

He went out into the world and sought out the pleasures that youth delights in. But each in its turn was short-lived and disappointing, vain and empty; and each, departing, mocked him. In the end he said: "These years I have wasted. If I could but choose again, I would choose wisely."

2

The fairy appeared, and said:

"Four of the gifts remain. Choose once more; and oh, remember—time is flying, and only one of them is precious."

The man considered long, then chose Love; and did not mark the tears that rose in the fairy's eyes.

After many, many years the man sat by a coffin, in an empty home. And he communed with himself, saying: "One by one they have gone away and left me; and now she lies here, the dearest and the last. Desolation after desolation has swept over me; for each hour of happiness the treacherous trader, Love, has sold me I have paid a thousand hours of grief. Out of my heart of hearts I curse him."

3

"Choose again." It was the fairy speaking. "The years have taught you wisdom—surely it must be so. Three gifts remain. Only one of them has any worth—remember it, and choose warily."

The man reflected long, then chose Fame; and the fairy, sighing, went her way.

Years went by and she came again, and stood behind the man where he sat solitary in the fading day, thinking. And she knew his thought:

"My name filled the world, and its praises were on every tongue, and it seemed well with me for a little while. How little a while it was! Then came envy; then detraction; then calumny; then hate; then persecution. Then derision, which is the beginning of the end. And last of all came pity, which is the funeral of fame. Oh, the bitterness and misery of renown! target for mud in its prime, for contempt and compassion in its decay."

4

"Choose yet again." It was the fairy's voice. "Two gifts remain. And do not despair. In the beginning there was but one that was precious, and it is still here."

"Wealth—which is power! How blind I was!" said the man. "Now, at last, life will be worth the living. I will spend, squander, dazzle. These mockers and despisers will crawl in the dirt before me, and I will feed my hungry heart with their envy. I will have all luxuries, all joys, all enchantments of the spirit, all contentments of the body that man holds dear. I will buy, buy, buy! deference, respect, esteem, worship—every pinchbeck grace of life the market of a trivial world can furnish forth. I have lost much time, and chosen badly heretofore, but let that pass; I was ignorant then, and could but take for best what seemed so."

Three short years went by, and a day came when the man sat shivering in a mean garret; and he was gaunt and wan and hollow-eyed, and clothed in rags; and he was gnawing a dry crust and mumbling:

"Curse all the world's gifts, for mockeries and gilded lies! And miscalled, every one. They are not gifts, but merely lendings. Pleasure, Love, Fame, Riches: they are but temporary disguises for lasting realities—Pain, Grief, Shame, Poverty. The fairy said true; in all her store there was but one gift which was precious, only one that was not valueless. How poor and cheap and mean I know those others now to be, compared with that inestimable one, that dear and sweet and kindly one, that steeps in dreamless and enduring sleep the pains that persecute the body, and the shames and griefs that eat the mind and heart. Bring it! I am weary, I would rest."

5

The fairy came, bringing again four of the gifts, but Death was wanting. She said:

"I gave it to a mother's pet, a little child. It was ignorant, but trusted me, asking me to choose for it. You did not ask me to choose."

"Oh, miserable me! What is there left for me?"

"What not even you have deserved: the wanton insult of Old Age."

1902

Was It Heaven? Or Hell?

1

"You told a *lie?*"

"You confess it—you actually confess it—you told a lie!"

2

The family consisted of four persons: Margaret Lester, widow, aged thirty-six; Helen Lester, her daughter, aged sixteen; Mrs. Lester's maiden aunts, Hannah and Hester Gray, twins, aged sixty-seven. Waking and sleeping, the three women spent their days and nights in adoring the young girl; in watching the movements of her sweet spirit in the mirror of her face; in refreshing their souls with the vision of her bloom and beauty; in listening to the music of her voice; in gratefully recognizing how rich and fair for them was the world with this presence in it; in shuddering to think how desolate it would be with this light gone out of it.

By nature—and inside—the aged aunts were utterly dear and lovable and good, but in the matter of morals and conduct their training had been so uncompromisingly strict that it had made them exteriorly austere, not to say stern. Their influence was effective in the house; so effective that the mother and the daughter conformed to its moral and religious requirements cheerfully, contentedly, happily, unquestionably. To do this was become second nature to them. And so in this peaceful heaven there were no clashings, no irritations, no fault-findings, no heart-burnings.

In it a lie had no place. In it a lie was unthinkable. In it speech was restricted to absolute truth, iron-bound truth, implacable and uncom-

promising truth, let the resulting consequences be what they might.
At last, one day, under stress of circumstances, the darling of the house
sullied her lips with a lie—and confessed it, with tears and self-upbraid-
ings. There are not any words that can paint the consternation of the
aunts. It was as if the sky had crumpled up and collapsed and the
earth had tumbled to ruin with a crash. They sat side by side, white
and stern, gazing speechless upon the culprit, who was on her knees
before them with her face buried first in one lap and then the other,
moaning and sobbing, and appealing for sympathy and forgiveness and
getting no response, humbly kissing the hand of the one, then of the
other, only to see it withdrawn as suffering defilement by those soiled
lips.

Twice, at intervals, Aunt Hester said, in frozen amazement:

"You told a *lie*?"

Twice, at intervals, Aunt Hannah followed with the muttered and
amazed ejaculation:

"You confess it—you actually confess it—you told a lie!"

It was all they could say. The situation was new, unheard of, incredible; they could not understand it, they did not know how to take
hold of it, it approximately paralyzed speech.

At length it was decided that the erring child must be taken to her
mother, who was ill, and who ought to know what had happened.
Helen begged, besought, implored that she might be spared this further
disgrace, and that her mother might be spared the grief and pain of it;
but this could not be: duty required this sacrifice, duty takes precedence of all things, nothing can absolve one from a duty, with a duty no
compromise is possible.

Helen still begged, and said the sin was her own, her mother had
had no hand in it—why must she be made to suffer for it?

But the aunts were obdurate in their righteousness, and said the law
that visited the sins of the parent upon the child was by all right and
reason reversible; and therefore it was but just that the innocent mother
of a sinning child should suffer her rightful share of the grief and pain
and shame which were the allotted wages of the sin.

The three moved toward the sick-room.

At this time the doctor was approaching the house. He was still a
good distance away, however. He was a good doctor and a good man,
and he had a good heart, but one had to know him a year to get over
hating him, two years to learn to endure him, three to learn to like him,
and four or five to learn to love him. It was a slow and trying education,

but it paid. He was of great stature; he had a leonine head, a leonine face, a rough voice, and an eye which was sometimes a pirate's and sometimes a woman's, according to the mood. He knew nothing about etiquette, and cared nothing about it; in speech, manner, carriage, and conduct he was the reverse of conventional. He was frank, to the limit; he had opinions on all subjects; they were always on tap and ready for delivery, and he cared not a farthing whether his listener liked them or didn't. Whom he loved he loved, and manifested it; whom he didn't love he hated, and published it from the housetops. In his young days he had been a sailor, and the salt-airs of all the seas blew from him yet. He was a sturdy and loyal Christian, and believed he was the best one in the land, and the only one whose Christianity was perfectly sound, healthy, full-charged with common sense, and had no decayed places in it. People who had an ax to grind, or people who for any reason wanted to get on the soft side of him, called him The Christian—a phrase whose delicate flattery was music to his ears, and whose capital T was such an enchanting and vivid object to him that he could *see* it when it fell out of a person's mouth even in the dark. Many who were fond of him stood on their consciences with both feet and brazenly called him by that large title habitually, because it was a pleasure to them to do anything that would please him; and with eager and cordial malice his extensive and diligently cultivated crop of enemies gilded it, beflowered it, expanded it to "The *Only* Christian." Of these two titles, the latter had the wider currency; the enemy, being greatly in the majority, attended to that. Whatever the doctor believed, he believed with all his heart, and would fight for it whenever he got the chance; and if the intervals between chances grew to be irksomely wide, he would invent ways of shortening them himself. He was severely conscientious, according to his rather independent lights, and whatever he took to be a duty he performed, no matter whether the judgment of the professional moralists agreed with his own or not. At sea, in his young days, he had used profanity freely, but as soon as he was converted he made a rule, which he rigidly stuck to ever afterward, never to use it except on the rarest occasions, and then only when duty commanded. He had been a hard drinker at sea, but after his conversion he became a firm and outspoken teetotaler, in order to be an example to the young, and from that time forth he seldom drank; never, indeed, except when it seemed to him to be a duty—a condition which sometimes occurred a couple of times a year, but never as many as five times.

Necessarily, such a man is impressionable, impulsive, emotional. This one was, and had no gift at hiding his feelings; or if he had it he took no trouble to exercise it. He carried his soul's prevailing weather in his face, and when he entered a room the parasols or the umbrellas went up—figuratively speaking—according to the indications. When the soft light was in his eye it meant approval, and delivered a benediction; when he came with a frown he lowered the temperature ten degrees. He was a well-beloved man in the house of his friends, but sometimes a dreaded one.

He had a deep affection for the Lester household, and its several members returned this feeling with interest. They mourned over his kind of Christianity, and he frankly scoffed at theirs; but both parties went on loving each other just the same.

He was approaching the house—out of the distance; the aunts and the culprit were moving toward the sick-chamber.

3

The three last named stood by the bed; the aunts austere, the transgressor softly sobbing. The mother turned her head on the pillow; her tired eyes flamed up instantly with sympathy and passionate mother-love when they fell upon her child, and she opened the refuge and shelter of her arms.

"Wait!" said Aunt Hannah, and put out her hand and stayed the girl from leaping into them.

"Helen," said the other aunt, impressively, "tell your mother all. Purge your soul; leave nothing unconfessed."

Standing stricken and forlorn before her judges, the young girl mourned her sorrowful tale through to the end, then in a passion of appeal cried out:

"Oh, mother, can't you forgive me? won't you forgive me?—I am so desolate!"

"Forgive you, my darling? Oh, come to my arms!—there, lay your head upon my breast, and be at peace. If you had told a thousand lies—"

There was a sound—a warning—the clearing of a throat. The aunts glanced up, and withered in their clothes—there stood the doctor, his face a thunder-cloud. Mother and child knew nothing of his presence; they lay locked together, heart to heart, steeped in immeasurable content, dead to all things else. The physician stood many moments glaring and glooming upon the scene before him; studying it, analyzing it, searching out its genesis; then he put up his hand and beckoned to the aunts. They came trembling to him, and stood humbly before him and waited. He bent down and whispered:

"Didn't I tell you this patient must be protected from all excitement? What the hell have you been doing? Clear out of the place!"

They obeyed. Half an hour later he appeared in the parlor, serene, cheery, clothed in sunshine, conducting Helen, with his arm about her waist, petting her, and saying gentle and playful things to her; and she also was her sunny and happy self again.

"Now, then," he said, "good-by, dear. Go to your room, and keep away from your mother, and behave yourself. But wait—put out your tongue. There, that will do—you're as sound as a nut!" He patted her cheek and added, "Run along now; I want to talk to these aunts."

She went from the presence. His face clouded over again at once; and as he sat down he said:

"You two have been doing a lot of damage—and maybe some good. Some good, yes—such as it is. That woman's disease is typhoid! You've brought it to a show-up, I think, with your insanities, and that's a service—such as it is. I hadn't been able to determine what it was before."

With one impulse the old ladies sprang to their feet, quaking with terror.

"Sit down! What are you proposing to do?"

"Do? We must fly to her. We—"

"You'll do nothing of the kind; you've done enough harm for one day. Do you want to squander all your capital of crimes and follies on a single deal? Sit down, I tell you. I have arranged for her to sleep; she needs it; if you disturb her without my orders, I'll brain you—if you've got the materials for it."

They sat down, distressed and indignant, but obedient, under compulsion. He proceeded:

"Now, then, I want this case explained. *They* wanted to explain it to me—as if there hadn't been emotion and excitement enough already. You knew my orders; how did you dare to go in there and get up that riot?"

Hester looked appealingly at Hannah; Hannah returned a beseeching look at Hester—neither wanted to dance to this unsympathetic orchestra. The doctor came to their help. He said:

"Begin, Hester."

Fingering at the fringes of her shawl, and with lowered eyes, Hester said, timidly:

"We should not have disobeyed for any ordinary cause, but this was vital. This was a duty. With a duty one has no choice; one must put all lighter considerations aside and perform it. We were obliged to arraign her before her mother. She had told a lie."

The doctor glowered upon the woman a moment, and seemed to be trying to work up in his mind an understanding of a wholly incomprehensible proposition; then he stormed out:

"She told a lie! *Did* she? God bless my soul! I tell a million a day! And so does every doctor. And so does everybody—including you—for that matter. And *that* was the important thing that authorized you to venture to disobey my orders and imperil that woman's life! Look here, Hester Gray, this is pure lunacy; that girl *couldn't* tell a lie that was intended to injure a person. The thing is impossible—absolutely impossible. You know it yourselves—both of you; you know it perfectly well."

Hannah came to her sister's rescue:

"Hester didn't mean that it was that kind of a lie, and it wasn't. But it was a lie."

"Well, upon my word, I never heard such nonsense! Haven't you got sense enough to discriminate between lies? Don't you know the difference between a lie that helps and a lie that hurts?"

"*All* lies are sinful," said Hannah, setting her lips together like a vise; "all lies are forbidden."

The Only Christian fidgeted impatiently in his chair. He wanted to attack this proposition, but he did not quite know how or where to begin. Finally he made a venture:

"Hester, wouldn't you tell a lie to shield a person from an undeserved injury or shame?"

"No."

"Not even a friend?"

"No."

"Not even your dearest friend?"

"No. I would not."

The doctor struggled in silence awhile with this situation; then he asked:

"Not even to save him from bitter pain and misery and grief?"

"No. Not even to save his life."

Another pause. Then:

"Nor his soul?"

There was a hush—a silence which endured a measurable interval—then Hester answered, in a low voice, but with decision:

"Nor his soul."

No one spoke for a while; then the doctor said:

"Is it with you the same, Hannah?"

"Yes," she answered.

"I ask you both—why?"

"Because to tell such a lie, or any lie, is a sin, and could cost us the loss of our own souls—*would*, indeed, if we died without time to repent."

"Strange . . . strange . . . it is past belief." Then he asked, roughly: "Is such a soul as that *worth* saving?" He rose up, mumbling and grumbling, and started for the door, stumping vigorously along. At the threshold he turned and rasped out an admonition: "Reform! Drop this mean and sordid and selfish devotion to the saving of your shabby little souls, and hunt up something to do that's got some dignity to it! *Risk* your souls! risk them in good causes; then if you lose them, why should you care? Reform!"

The good old gentlewomen sat paralyzed, pulverized, outraged, insulted, and brooded in bitterness and indignation over these blasphemies. They were hurt to the heart, poor old ladies, and said they could never forgive these injuries.

"Reform!"

They kept repeating that word resentfully. "Reform—and learn to tell lies!"

Time slipped along, and in due course a change came over their spirits. They had completed the human being's first duty—which is to think about himself until he has exhausted the subject, then he is in a condition to take up minor interests and think of other people. This changes the complexion of his spirits—generally wholesomely. The minds of the two old ladies reverted to their beloved niece and the fearful disease which had smitten her; instantly they forgot the hurts their self-love had received, and a passionate desire rose in their hearts to go to the help of the sufferer and comfort her with their love, and minister to her, and labor for her the best they could with their weak hands, and joyfully and affectionately wear out their poor old bodies in her dear service if only they might have the privilege.

"And we shall have it!" said Hester, with the tears running down her face. "There are no nurses comparable to us, for there are no others that will stand their watch by that bed till they drop and die, and God knows we would do that."

"Amen," said Hannah, smiling approval and indorsement through the mist of moisture that blurred her glasses. "The doctor knows us, and knows we will not disobey again; and he will call no others. He will not dare!"

"Dare?" said Hester, with temper, and dashing the water from her eyes; "he will dare anything—that Christian devil! But it will do no good for him to try it this time—but, laws! Hannah! after all's said and done, he is gifted and wise and good, and he would not think of such a thing. . . . It is surely time for one of us to go to that room. What is keeping him? Why doesn't he come and say so?"

They caught the sound of his approaching step. He entered, sat down, and began to talk.

"Margaret is a sick woman," he said. "She is still sleeping, but she will wake presently; then one of you must go to her. She will be worse before she is better. Pretty soon a night-and-day watch must be set. How much of it can you two undertake?"

"All of it!" burst from both ladies at once.

The doctor's eyes flashed, and he said, with energy:

"You *do* ring true, you brave old relics! And you *shall* do all of the nursing you can, for there's none to match you in that divine office in this town; but you can't do all of it, and it would be a crime to let you." It was grand praise, golden praise, coming from such a source, and it took nearly all the resentment out of the aged twins' hearts. "Your Tilly and my old Nancy shall do the rest—good nurses both, white souls with black skins, watchful, loving, tender—just perfect nurses!—and competent liars from the cradle. . . . Look you! keep a little watch on Helen; she is sick, and is going to be sicker."

The ladies looked a little surprised, and not credulous; and Hester said:

"How is that? It isn't an hour since you said she was as sound as a nut."

The doctor answered, tranquilly:

"It was a lie."

The ladies turned upon him indignantly, and Hannah said:

"How can you make an odious confession like that, in so indifferent a tone, when you know how we feel about all forms of—"

"Hush! You are as ignorant as cats, both of you, and you don't know what you are talking about. You are like all the rest of the moral moles; you lie from morning till night, but because you don't do it with your mouths, but only with your lying eyes, your lying inflections, your deceptively misplaced emphases, and your misleading gestures, you turn up your complacent noses and parade before God and the world as saintly and unsmirched Truth-Speakers, in whose cold-storage souls a lie would freeze to death if it got there! Why will you humbug yourselves with that foolish notion that no lie is a lie except a spoken one? What is the difference between lying with your eyes and lying with your mouth? There is none; and if you would reflect a moment you would see that it is so. There isn't a human being that doesn't tell a gross of lies every day of his life; and you—why, between you, you tell thirty thousand; yet you flare up here in a lurid hypocritical horror because I tell that child a benevolent and sinless lie to protect her from her imagination, which would get to work and warm up her blood to a fever in an hour, if I were disloyal enough to my duty to let it. Which I should probably do if I were interested in saving my soul by such disreputable means.

"Come, let us reason together. Let us examine details. When you two were in the sick-room raising that riot, what would you have done if you had known I was coming?"

"Well, what?"

"You would have slipped out and carried Helen with you—wouldn't you?"

The ladies were silent.

"What would be your object and intention?"

"Well, what?"

"To keep me from finding out your guilt; to beguile me to infer that Margaret's excitement proceeded from some cause not known to you. In a word, to tell me a lie—a silent lie. Moreover, a possibly harmful one."

The twins colored, but did not speak.

"You not only tell myriads of silent lies, but you tell lies with your mouths—you two."

"*That* is not so!"

"It is so. But only harmless ones. You never dream of uttering a harmful one. Do you know that that is a concession—and a confession?"

"How do you mean?"

"It is an unconscious concession that harmless lies are not criminal; it is a confession that you constantly *make* that discrimination. For instance, you declined old Mrs. Foster's invitation last week to meet those odious Higbies at supper—in a polite note in which you expressed regret and said you were very sorry you could not go. It was a lie. It was as unmitigated a lie as was ever uttered. Deny it, Hester—with another lie."

Hester replied with a toss of her head.

"That will not do. Answer. Was it a lie, or wasn't it?"

The color stole into the cheeks of both women, and with a struggle and an effort they got out their confession:

"It was a lie."

"Good—the reform is beginning; there is hope for you yet; you will not tell a lie to save your dearest friend's soul, but you will spew out one without a scruple to save yourself the discomfort of telling an unpleasant truth."

He rose. Hester, speaking for both, said, coldly:

"We have lied; we perceive it; it will occur no more. To lie is a sin. We shall never tell another one of any kind whatsoever, even lies of courtesy or benevolence, to save any one a pang or a sorrow decreed for him by God."

"Ah, how soon you will fall! In fact, you have fallen already; for what you have just uttered is a lie. Good-by. Reform! One of you go to the sick-room now."

4

Twelve days later.

Mother and child were lingering in the grip of the hideous disease. Of hope for either there was little. The aged sisters looked white and worn, but they would not give up their posts. Their hearts were breaking, poor old things, but their grit was steadfast and indestructible. All the twelve days the mother had pined for the child, and the child for the mother, but both knew that the prayer of these longings could not be granted. When the mother was told—on the first day—that her disease was typhoid, she was frightened, and asked if there was danger that Helen could have contracted it the day before, when she was in the sick-chamber on that confession visit. Hester told her the doctor had poo-pooed the idea. It troubled Hester to say it, although it was true, for she had not believed the doctor; but when she saw the mother's joy in the news, the pain in her conscience lost something of its force— a result which made her ashamed of the constructive deception which she had practised, though not ashamed enough to make her distinctly and definitely wish she had refrained from it. From that moment the sick woman understood that her daughter must remain away, and she said she would reconcile herself to the separation the best she could, for she would rather suffer death than have her child's health imperiled. That afternoon Helen had to take to her bed, ill. She grew worse during the night. In the morning her mother asked after her:

"Is she well?"

Hester turned cold; she opened her lips, but the words refused to come. The mother lay languidly looking, musing, waiting; suddenly she turned white and gasped out:

"Oh, my God! what is it? is she sick?"

Then the poor aunt's tortured heart rose in rebellion, and words came:

"No—be comforted; she is well."

The sick woman put all her happy heart in her gratitude:

"Thank God for those dear words! Kiss me. How I worship you for saying them!"

Hester told this incident to Hannah, who received it with a rebuking look, and said, coldly:

"Sister, it was a lie."

Hester's lips trembled piteously; she choked down a sob, and said:

"Oh, Hannah, it was a sin, but I could not help it. I could not endure the fright and the misery that were in her face."

"No matter. It was a lie. God will hold you to account for it."

"Oh, I know it, I know it," cried Hester, wringing her hands, "but even if it were now, I could not help it. I know I should do it again."

"Then take my place with Helen in the morning. I will make the report myself."

Hester clung to her sister, begging and imploring.

"Don't, Hannah, oh, don't—you will kill her."

"I will at least speak the truth."

In the morning she had a cruel report to bear to the mother, and she braced herself for the trial. When she returned from her mission, Hester was waiting, pale and trembling, in the hall. She whispered:

"Oh, how did she take it—that poor, desolate mother?"

Hannah's eyes were swimming in tears. She said:

"God forgive me, I told her the child was well!"

Hester gathered her to her heart, with a grateful "God bless you, Hannah!" and poured out her thankfulness in an inundation of worshiping praises.

After that, the two knew the limit of their strength, and accepted their fate. They surrendered humbly, and abandoned themselves to the hard requirements of the situation. Daily they told the morning lie, and confessed their sin in prayer; not asking forgiveness, as not being worthy of it, but only wishing to make record that they realized their wickedness and were not desiring to hide it or excuse it.

Daily, as the fair young idol of the house sank lower and lower, the sorrowful old aunts painted her glowing bloom and her fresh young beauty to the wan mother, and winced under the stabs her ecstasies of joy and gratitude gave them.

In the first days, while the child had strength to hold a pencil, she wrote fond little love-notes to her mother, in which she concealed her illness; and these the mother read and reread through happy eyes wet

with thankful tears, and kissed them over and over again, and treasured them as precious things under her pillow.

Then came a day when the strength was gone from the hand, and the mind wandered, and the tongue babbled pathetic incoherences. This was a sore dilemma for the poor aunts. There were no love-notes for the mother. They did not know what to do. Hester began a carefully studied and plausible explanation, but lost the track of it and grew confused; suspicion began to show in the mother's face, then alarm. Hester saw it, recognized the imminence of the danger, and descended to the emergency, pulling herself resolutely together and plucking victory from the open jaws of defeat. In a placid and convincing voice she said:

"I thought it might distress you to know it, but Helen spent the night at the Sloanes'. There was a little party there, and, although she did not want to go, and you so sick, we persuaded her, she being young and needing the innocent pastimes of youth, and we believing you would approve. Be sure she will write the moment she comes."

"How good you are, and how dear and thoughtful for us both! Approve? Why, I thank you with all my heart. My poor little exile! Tell her I want her to have every pleasure she can—I would not rob her of one. Only let her keep her health, that is all I ask. Don't let that suffer; I could not bear it. How thankful I am that she escaped this infection —and what a narrow risk she ran, Aunt Hester! Think of that lovely face all dulled and burned with fever. I can't bear the thought of it. Keep her health. Keep her bloom! I can see her now, the dainty creature—with the big, blue, earnest eyes; and sweet, oh, so sweet and gentle and winning! Is she as beautiful as ever, dear Aunt Hester?"

"Oh, more beautiful and bright and charming than ever she was before, if such a thing can be"—and Hester turned away and fumbled with the medicine-bottles, to hide her shame and grief.

5

After a little, both aunts were laboring upon a difficult and baffling work in Helen's chamber. Patiently and earnestly, with their stiff old fingers, they were trying to forge the required note. They made failure after failure, but they improved little by little all the time. The pity of it all, the pathetic humor of it, there was none to see; they themselves were unconscious of it. Often their tears fell upon the notes and spoiled them; sometimes a single misformed word made a note risky which could have been ventured but for that; but at last Hannah pro-

duced one whose script was a good enough imitation of Helen's to pass
any but a suspicious eye, and bountifully enriched it with the petting
phrases and loving nicknames that had been familiar on the child's lips
from her nursery days. She carried it to the mother, who took it with
avidity, and kissed it, and fondled it, reading its precious words over
and over again, and dwelling with deep contentment upon its closing
paragraph:

"Mousie darling, if I could only see you, and kiss your eyes, and feel
your arms about me! I am so glad my practising does not disturb you.
Get well soon. Everybody is good to me, but I am so lonesome without
you, dear mamma."

"The poor child, I know just how she feels. She cannot be quite
happy without me; and I—oh, I live in the light of her eyes! Tell her
she must practise all she pleases; and, Aunt Hannah—tell her I can't
hear the piano this far, nor her dear voice when she sings: God knows
I wish I could. No one knows how sweet that voice is to me; and to
think—some day it will be silent! What are you crying for?"

"Only because—because—it was just a memory. When I came away
she was singing, 'Loch Lomond.' The pathos of it! It always moves me
so when she sings that."

"And me, too. How heartbreakingly beautiful it is when some youth-
ful sorrow is brooding in her breast and she sings it for the mystic healing it brings. . . . Aunt Hannah?"

"Dear Margaret?"

"I am very ill. Sometimes it comes over me that I shall never hear
that dear voice again."

"Oh, don't—don't, Margaret! I can't bear it!"

Margaret was moved and distressed, and said, gently:

"There—there—let me put my arms around you. Don't cry. There—
put your cheek to mine. Be comforted. I wish to live. I will live if I can.
Ah, what could she do without me! . . . Does she often speak of me?
—but I know she does."

"Oh, all the time—all the time!"

"My sweet child! She wrote the note the moment she came home?"

"Yes—the first moment. She would not wait to take off her things."

"I knew it. It is her dear, impulsive, affectionate way. I knew it without asking, but I wanted to hear you say it. The petted wife knows she
is loved, but she makes her husband tell her so every day, just for the
joy of hearing it. . . . She used the pen this time. That is better; the
pencil-marks could rub out, and I should grieve for that. Did you suggest that she use the pen?"

"Y—no—she—it was her own idea."

The mother looked her pleasure, and said:

"I was hoping you would say that. There was never such a dear and thoughtful child! . . . Aunt Hannah?"

"Dear Margaret?"

"Go and tell her I think of her all the time, and worship her. Why —you are crying again. Don't be so worried about me, dear; I think there is nothing to fear, yet."

The grieving messenger carried her message, and piously delivered it to unheeding ears. The girl babbled on unaware; looking up at her with wondering and startled eyes flaming with fever, eyes in which was no light of recognition:

"Are you—no, you are not my mother. I want her—oh, I want her! She was here a minute ago—I did not see her go. Will she come? will she come quickly? will she come now? . . . There are so many houses . . . and they oppress me so . . . and everything whirls and turns and whirls . . . oh, my head, my head!"—and so she wandered on and on, in her pain, flitting from one torturing fancy to another, and tossing her arms about in a weary and ceaseless persecution of unrest.

Poor old Hannah wetted the parched lips and softly stroked the hot brow, murmuring endearing and pitying words, and thanking the Father of all that the mother was happy and did not know.

6

Daily the child sank lower and steadily lower towards the grave, and daily the sorrowing old watchers carried gilded tidings of her radiant health and loveliness to the happy mother, whose pilgrimage was also now nearing its end. And daily they forged loving and cheery notes in the child's hand, and stood by with remorseful consciences and bleeding hearts, and wept to see the grateful mother devour them and adore them and treasure them away as things beyond price, because of their sweet source, and sacred because her child's hand had touched them.

At last came that kindly friend who brings healing and peace to all. The lights were burning low. In the solemn hush which precedes the dawn vague figures flitted soundless along the dim hall and gathered silent and awed in Helen's chamber, and grouped themselves about her bed, for a warning had gone forth, and they knew. The dying girl lay with closed lids, and unconscious, the drapery upon her breast faintly rising and falling as her wasting life ebbed away. At intervals a sigh or a muffled sob broke upon the stillness. The same haunting thought was in all minds there: the pity of this death, the going out into the great darkness, and the mother not here to help and hearten and bless.

Helen stirred; her hands began to grope wistfully about as if they sought something—she had been blind some hours. The end was come; all knew it. With a great sob Hester gathered her to her breast, crying, "Oh, my child, my darling!" A rapturous light broke in the dying girl's face, for it was mercifully vouchsafed her to mistake those sheltering arms for another's; and she went to her rest murmuring, "Oh, mamma, I am so happy—I so longed for you—now I can die."

Two hours later Hester made her report. The mother asked:
"How is it with the child?"
"She is well."

7

A sheaf of white crape and black was hung upon the door of the house, and there it swayed and rustled in the wind and whispered its tidings. At noon the preparation of the dead was finished, and in the coffin lay the fair young form, beautiful, and in the sweet face a great peace. Two mourners sat by it, grieving and worshiping—Hannah and the black woman Tilly. Hester came, and she was trembling, for a great trouble was upon her spirit. She said:
"She asks for a note."

Hannah's face blanched. She had not thought of this; it had seemed that that pathetic service was ended. But she realized now that that could not be. For a little while the two women stood looking into each other's face, with vacant eyes; then Hannah said:
"There is no way out of it—she must have it; she will suspect, else."
"And she would find out."
"Yes. It would break her heart." She looked at the dead face, and her eyes filled. "I will write it," she said.

Hester carried it. The closing line said:
"Darling Mousie, dear sweet mother, we shall soon be together again. Is not that good news? And it is true; they all say it is true."

The mother mourned, saying:
"Poor child, how will she bear it when she knows? I shall never see her again in life. It is hard, so hard. She does not suspect? You guard her from that?"
"She thinks you will soon be well."

"How good you are, and careful, dear Aunt Hester! None goes near her who could carry the infection?"

"It would be a crime."

"But you *see* her?"

"With a distance between—yes."

"That is so good. Others one could not trust; but you two guardian angels—steel is not so true as you. Others would be unfaithful; and many would deceive, and lie."

Hester's eyes fell, and her poor old lips trembled.

"Let me kiss you for her, Aunt Hester; and when I am gone, and the danger is past, place the kiss upon her dear lips some day, and say her mother sent it, and all her mother's broken heart is in it."

Within the hour, Hester, raining tears upon the dead face, performed her pathetic mission.

8

Another day dawned, and grew, and spread its sunshine in the earth. Aunt Hannah brought comforting news to the failing mother, and a happy note, which said again, "We have but a little time to wait, darling mother, then we shall be together."

The deep note of a bell came moaning down the wind.

"Aunt Hannah, it is tolling. Some poor soul is at rest. As I shall be soon. You will not let her forget me?"

"Oh, God knows she never will!"

"Do not you hear strange noises, Aunt Hannah? It sounds like the shuffling of many feet."

"We hoped you would not hear it, dear. It is a little company gathering, for—for Helen's sake, poor little prisoner. There will be music—and she loves it so. We thought you would not mind."

"Mind? Oh no, no—oh, give her everything her dear heart can desire. How good you two are to her, and how good to me! God bless you both always!"

After a listening pause:

"How lovely! It is her organ. Is she playing it herself, do you think?" Faint and rich and inspiring the chords floated to her ears on the still air. "Yes, it is her touch, dear heart, I recognize it. They are singing. Why—it is a hymn! and the sacredest of all, the most touching, the most consoling. . . . It seems to open the gates of paradise to me. . . . If I could die now. . . ."

Faint and far the words rose out of the stillness:

Nearer, my God, to Thee,
Nearer to Thee,
E'en though it be a cross
That raiseth me.

With the closing of the hymn another soul passed to its rest, and they that had been one in life were not sundered in death. The sisters, mourning and rejoicing, said:

"How blessed it was that she never knew!"

9

At midnight they sat together, grieving, and the angel of the Lord appeared in the midst transfigured with a radiance not of earth: and speaking, said:

"For liars a place is appointed. There they burn in the fires of hell from everlasting unto everlasting. Repent!"

The bereaved fell upon their knees before him and clasped their hands and bowed their gray heads, adoring. But their tongues clove to the roof of their mouths, and they were dumb.

"Speak! that I may bear the message to the chancery of heaven and bring again the decree from which there is no appeal."

Then they bowed their heads yet lower, and one said:

"Our sin is great, and we suffer shame; but only perfect and final repentance can make us whole; and we are poor creatures who have learned our human weakness, and we know that if we were in those hard straits again our hearts would fail again, and we should sin as before. The strong could prevail, and so be saved, but we are lost."

They lifted their heads in supplication. The angel was gone. While they marveled and wept he came again; and bending low, he whispered the decree.

10

Was it Heaven? Or Hell?

1902

A Dog's Tale

My father was a St. Bernard, my mother was a collie, but I am a Presbyterian. This is what my mother told me; I do not know these nice distinctions myself. To me they are only fine large words meaning nothing. My mother had a fondness for such; she liked to say them, and see other dogs look surprised and envious, as wondering how she got so much education. But, indeed, it was not real education; it was only show: she got the words by listening in the dining-room and draw-ing-room when there was company, and by going with the children to Sunday-school and listening there; and whenever she heard a large word she said it over to herself many times, and so was able to keep it until there was a dogmatic gathering in the neighborhood, then she would get it off, and surprise and distress them all, from pocket-pup to mastiff, which rewarded her for all her trouble. If there was a stran-ger he was nearly sure to be suspicious, and when he got his breath again he would ask her what it meant. And she always told him. He was never expecting this, but thought he would catch her; so when she told him, he was the one that looked ashamed, whereas he had thought it was going to be she. The others were always waiting for this, and glad of it and proud of her, for they knew what was going to happen, be-cause they had had experience. When she told the meaning of a big word they were all so taken up with admiration that it never occurred to any dog to doubt if it was the right one; and that was natural, be-cause, for one thing, she answered up so promptly that it seemed like a dictionary speaking, and for another thing, where could they find out whether it was right or not? for she was the only cultivated dog there was. By and by, when I was older, she brought home the word Unin-tellectual, one time, and worked it pretty hard all the week at different gatherings, making much unhappiness and despondency; and it was at this time that I noticed that during that week she was asked for the meaning at eight different assemblages, and flashed out a fresh defini-tion every time, which showed me that she had more presence of mind than culture, though I said nothing, of course. She had one word which she always kept on hand, and ready, like a life-preserver, a kind of emergency word to strap on when she was likely to get washed over-board in a sudden way—that was the word Synonymous. When she hap-pened to fetch out a long word which had had its day weeks before and its prepared meanings gone to her dump-pile, if there was a stran-ger there of course it knocked him groggy for a couple of minutes, then he would come to, and by that time she would be away down the wind on another tack, and not expecting anything; so when he'd hail and ask her to cash in, I (the only dog on the inside of her game) could see her canvas flicker a moment—but only just a moment—then it would belly out taut and full, and she would say, as calm as a sum-mer's day, "It's synonymous with supererogation," or some godless long reptile of a word like that, and go placidly about and skim away on the next tack, perfectly comfortable, you know, and leave that stranger looking profane and embarrassed, and the initiated slatting the floor with their tails in unison and their faces transfigured with a holy joy.

And it was the same with phrases. She would drag home a whole phrase, if it had a grand sound, and play it six nights and two matinées, and explain it a new way every time—which she had to, for all she cared for was the phrase; she wasn't interested in what it meant, and knew those dogs hadn't wit enough to catch her, anyway. Yes, she was a daisy! She got so she wasn't afraid of anything, she had such confidence in the ignorance of those creatures. She even brought anecdotes that she had heard the family and the dinner-guests laugh and shout over; and as a rule she got the nub of one chestnut hitched onto another chestnut, where, of course, it didn't fit and hadn't any point; and when she delivered the nub she fell over and rolled on the floor and laughed and barked in the most insane way, while I could see that she was wondering to herself why it didn't seem as funny as it did when she first heard it. But no harm was done; the others rolled and barked too, privately ashamed of themselves for not seeing the point, and never suspecting that the fault was not with them and there wasn't any to see.

You can see by these things that she was of a rather vain and frivolous character; still, she had virtues, and enough to make up, I think. She had a kind heart and gentle ways, and never harbored resentments for injuries done her, but put them easily out of her mind and forgot them; and she taught her children her kindly way, and from her we learned also to be brave and prompt in time of danger, and not to run away, but face the peril that threatened friend or stranger, and help him the best we could without stopping to think what the cost might be to us. And she taught us not by words only, but by example, and that is the best way and the surest and the most lasting. Why, the brave things she did, the splendid things! she was just a soldier; and so modest about it—well, you couldn't help admiring her, and you couldn't help imitating her; not even a King Charles spaniel could remain entirely despicable in her society. So, as you see, there was more to her than her education.

2

When I was well grown, at last, I was sold and taken away, and I never saw her again. She was broken-hearted, and so was I, and we cried; but she comforted me as well as she could, and said we were sent into this world for a wise and good purpose, and must do our duties without repining, take our life as we might find it, live it for the best good of others, and never mind about the results; they were not our affair. She said men who did like this would have a noble and beautiful reward by and by in another world, and although we animals would not go there, to do well and right without reward would give to our brief lives a worthiness and dignity which in itself would be a reward. She had gathered these things from time to time when she had gone to the Sunday-school with the children, and had laid them up in her memory more carefully than she had done with those other words and phrases; and she had studied them deeply, for her good and ours. One may see by this that she had a wise and thoughtful head, for all there was so much lightness and vanity in it.

So we said our farewells, and looked our last upon each other through our tears; and the last thing she said—keeping it for the last to make me remember it the better, I think—was, "In memory of me, when there is a time of danger to another do not think of yourself, think of your mother, and do as she would do."

Do you think I could forget that? No.

3

It was such a charming home!—my new one; a fine great house, with pictures, and delicate decorations, and rich furniture, and no gloom anywhere, but all the wilderness of dainty colors lit up with flooding sunshine; and the spacious grounds around it, and the great garden— oh, greensward, and noble trees, and flowers, no end! And I was the same as a member of the family; and they loved me, and petted me, and did not give me a new name, but called me by my old one that was dear to me because my mother had given it me—Aileen Mavourneen.

She got it out of a song; and the Grays knew that song, and said it was a beautiful name.

Mrs. Gray was thirty, and so sweet and so lovely, you cannot imagine it; and Sadie was ten, and just like her mother, just a darling slender little copy of her, with auburn tails down her back, and short frocks; and the baby was a year old, and plump and dimpled, and fond of me, and never could get enough of hauling on my tail, and hugging me, and laughing out its innocent happiness; and Mr. Gray was thirty-eight, and tall and slender and handsome, a little bald in front, alert, quick in his movements, businesslike, prompt, decided, unsentimental, and with that kind of trim-chiseled face that just seems to glint and sparkle with frosty intellectuality! He was a renowned scientist. I do not know what the word means, but my mother would know how to use it and get effects. She would know how to depress a rat-terrier with it and make a lap-dog look sorry he came. But that is not the best one; the best one was Laboratory. My mother could organize a Trust on that one that would skin the tax-collars off the whole herd. The laboratory was not a book, or a picture, or a place to wash your hands in, as the college president's dog said—no, that is the lavatory; the laboratory is quite different, and is filled with jars, and bottles, and electrics, and wires, and strange machines; and every week other scientists came there and sat in the place, and used the machines, and discussed, and made what they called experiments and discoveries; and often I came, too, and stood around and listened, and tried to learn, for the sake of my mother, and in loving memory of her, although it was a pain to me, as realizing what she was losing out of her life and I gaining nothing at all; for try as I might, I was never able to make anything out of it at all.

Other times I lay on the floor in the mistress's work-room and slept, she gently using me for a foot-stool, knowing it pleased me, for it was a caress; other times I spent an hour in the nursery, and got well tousled and made happy; other times I watched by the crib there, when the baby was asleep and the nurse out for a few minutes on the baby's affairs; other times I romped and raced through the grounds and the garden with Sadie till we were tired out, then slumbered on the grass in the shade of a tree while she read her book; other times I went visiting among the neighbor dogs—for there were some most pleasant ones not far away, and one very handsome and courteous and graceful one, a curly-haired Irish setter by the name of Robin Adair, who was a Presbyterian like me, and belonged to the Scotch minister.

The servants in our house were all kind to me and were fond of me, and so, as you see, mine was a pleasant life. There could not be a happier dog than I was, nor a gratefuler one. I will say this for myself, for it is only the truth: I tried in all ways to do well and right, and honor my mother's memory and her teachings, and earn the happiness that had come to me, as best I could.

By and by came my little puppy, and then my cup was full, my happiness was perfect. It was the dearest little waddling thing, and so smooth and soft and velvety, and had such cunning little awkward paws, and such affectionate eyes, and such a sweet and innocent face; and it made me so proud to see how the children and their mother adored it, and fondled it, and exclaimed over every little wonderful thing it did. It did seem to me that life was just too lovely to—

Then came the winter. One day I was standing a watch in the nursery. That is to say, I was asleep on the bed. The baby was asleep in the crib, which was alongside the bed, on the side next the fireplace. It was the kind of crib that has a lofty tent over it made of a gauzy stuff that you can see through. The nurse was out, and we two sleepers were alone. A spark from the wood-fire was shot out, and it lit on the slope of the tent. I suppose a quiet interval followed, then a scream from the baby woke me, and there was that tent flaming up toward the ceiling! Before I could think, I sprang to the floor in my fright, and in a second was half-way to the door; but in the next half-second my mother's farewell was sounding in my ears, and I was back on the bed again. I reached my head through the flames and dragged the baby out by the waist-band, and tugged it along, and we fell to the floor together in a cloud of smoke; I snatched a new hold, and dragged the screaming little creature along and out at the door and around the bend of the hall, and was still tugging away, all excited and happy and proud, when the master's voice shouted:

"Begone, you cursed beast!" and I jumped to save myself; but he was wonderfully quick, and chased me up, striking furiously at me with his cane, I dodging this way and that, in terror, and at last a strong blow fell upon my left foreleg, which made me shriek and fall, for the moment, helpless; the cane went up for another blow, but never descended, for the nurse's voice rang wildly out, "The nursery's on fire!" and the master rushed away in that direction, and my other bones were saved.

The pain was cruel, but, no matter, I must not lose any time; he might come back at any moment; so I limped on three legs to the other end of the hall, where there was a dark little stairway leading up into a garret where old boxes and such things were kept, as I had heard say, and where people seldom went. I managed to climb up there, then I searched my way through the dark among the piles of things, and hid in the secretest place I could find. It was foolish to be afraid there, yet still I was; so afraid that I held in and hardly even whimpered, though it would have been such a comfort to whimper, because that eases the pain, you know. But I could lick my leg, and that did me some good.

For half an hour there was a commotion downstairs, and shoutings, and rushing footsteps, and then there was quiet again. Quiet for some minutes, and that was grateful to my spirit, for then my fears began to go down; and fears are worse than pains—oh, much worse. Then came a sound that froze me. They were calling me—calling me by name—hunting for me!

It was muffled by distance, but that could not take the terror out of it, and it was the most dreadful sound to me that I had ever heard. It went all about, everywhere, down there: along the halls, through all the rooms, in both stories, and in the basement and the cellar; then outside, and farther and farther away—then back, and all about the house again, and I thought it would never, never stop. But at last it did, hours and hours after the vague twilight of the garret had long ago been blotted out by black darkness.

Then in that blessed stillness my terrors fell little by little away, and I was at peace and slept. It was a good rest I had, but I woke before the twilight had come again. I was feeling fairly comfortable, and I could think out a plan now. I made a very good one; which was, to creep down, all the way down the back stairs, and hide behind the cellar door, and slip out and escape when the iceman came at dawn, while he was inside filling the refrigerator; then I would hide all day, and start on my journey when night came; my journey to—well, anywhere where they would not know me and betray me to the master. I was feeling almost cheerful now; then suddenly I thought: Why, what would life be without my puppy!

That was despair. There was no plan for me; I saw that; I must stay where I was; stay, and wait, and take what might come—it was not my affair; that was what life is—my mother had said it. Then—well, then the calling began again! All my sorrows came back. I said to myself, the master will never forgive. I did not know what I had done to make him so bitter and so unforgiving, yet I judged it was something a dog could not understand, but which was clear to a man and dreadful.

They called and called—days and nights, it seemed to me. So long that the hunger and thirst near drove me mad, and I recognized that I was getting very weak. When you are this way you sleep a great deal, and I did. Once I woke in an awful fright—it seemed to me that the calling was right there in the garret! And so it was: it was Sadie's voice, and she was crying; my name was falling from her lips all broken, poor thing, and I could not believe my ears for the joy of it when I heard her say:

"Come back to us—oh, come back to us, and forgive—it is all so sad without our—"

I broke in with *such* a grateful little yelp, and the next moment Sadie was plunging and stumbling through the darkness and the lumber and shouting for the family to hear, "She's found, she's found!"

The days that followed—well, they were wonderful. The mother and Sadie and the servants—why, they just seemed to worship me. They couldn't seem to make me a bed that was fine enough; and as for food, they couldn't be satisfied with anything but game and delicacies that were out of season; and every day the friends and neighbors flocked in to hear about my heroism—that was the name they called it by, and it means agriculture. I remember my mother pulling it on a kennel once, and explaining it that way, but didn't say what agriculture was, except that it was synonymous with intramural incandescence; and a dozen times a day Mrs. Gray and Sadie would tell the tale to newcomers, and say I risked my life to save the baby's, and both of us had burns to prove it, and then the company would pass me around and pet me and exclaim about me, and you could see the pride in the eyes of Sadie and her mother; and when the people wanted to know what made me limp, they looked ashamed and changed the subject, and sometimes when people hunted them this way and that way with questions about it, it looked to me as if they were going to cry.

And this was not all the glory; no, the master's friends came, a whole twenty of the most distinguished people, and had me in the laboratory, and discussed me as if I was a kind of discovery; and some of them said it was wonderful in a dumb beast, the finest exhibition of instinct they could call to mind; but the master said, with vehemence, "It's far above instinct; it's *reason*, and many a man, privileged to be saved and go with you and me to a better world by right of its possession, has less of it than this poor silly quadruped that's foreordained to perish"; and then he laughed, and said: "Why, look at me—I'm a sarcasm! bless you, with all my grand intelligence, the only thing I inferred was that the dog had gone mad and was destroying the child, whereas but for the beast's intelligence—it's *reason*, I tell you!—the child would have perished!"

They disputed and disputed, and *I* was the very center and subject of it all, and I wished my mother could know that this grand honor had come to me; it would have made her proud.

Then they discussed optics, as they called it, and whether a certain injury to the brain would produce blindness or not, but they could not agree about it, and said they must test it by experiment by and by; and next they discussed plants, and that interested me, because in the summer Sadie and I had planted seeds—I helped her dig the holes, you know—and after days and days a little shrub or a flower came up there, and it was a wonder how that could happen; but it did, and I wished I could talk—I would have told those people about it and shown them how much I knew, and been all alive with the subject; but I didn't care for the optics; it was dull, and when they came back to it again it bored me, and I went to sleep.

Pretty soon it was spring, and sunny and pleasant and lovely, and the sweet mother and the children patted me and the puppy good-by, and went away on a journey and a visit to their kin, and the master wasn't any company for us, but we played together and had good times, and the servants were kind and friendly, so we got along quite happily and counted the days and waited for the family.

And one day those men came again, and said, now for the test, and they took the puppy to the laboratory, and I limped three-leggedly along, too, feeling proud, for any attention shown the puppy was a pleasure to me, of course. They discussed and experimented, and then suddenly the puppy shrieked, and they set him on the floor, and he went staggering around, with his head all bloody, and the master clapped his hands and shouted:

"There, I've won—confess it! He's as blind as a bat!"

And they all said:

"It's so—you've proved your theory, and suffering humanity owes you a great debt from henceforth," and they crowded around him, and wrung his hand cordially and thankfully, and praised him.

But I hardly saw or heard these things, for I ran at once to my little darling, and snuggled close to it where it lay, and licked the blood, and it put its head against mine, whimpering softly, and I knew in my heart it was a comfort to it in its pain and trouble to feel its mother's touch, though it could not see me. Then it dropped down, presently, and its little velvet nose rested upon the floor, and it was still, and did not move any more.

Soon the master stopped discussing a moment, and rang in the footman, and said, "Bury it in the far corner of the garden," and then went on with the discussion, and I trotted after the footman, very happy and grateful, for I knew the puppy was out of its pain now, because it was asleep. We went far down the garden to the farthest end, where the children and the nurse and the puppy and I used to play in the summer in the shade of a great elm, and there the footman dug a hole, and I saw he was going to plant the puppy, and I was glad, because it would grow and come up a fine handsome dog, like Robin Adair, and be a beautiful surprise for the family when they came home; so I tried to help him dig, but my lame leg was no good, being stiff, you know, and you have to have two, or it is no use. When the footman had finished and covered little Robin up, he patted my head, and there were tears in his eyes, and he said: "Poor little doggie, you SAVED *his* child."

I have watched two whole weeks, and he doesn't come up! This last week a fright has been stealing upon me. I think there is something terrible about this. I do not know what it is, but the fear makes me sick, and I cannot eat, though the servants bring me the best of food; and they pet me so, and even come in the night, and cry, and say, "Poor doggie—do give it up and come home; *don't* break our hearts!" and all this terrifies me the more, and makes me sure something has happened. And I am so weak; since yesterday I cannot stand on my feet any more. And within this hour the servants, looking toward the sun where it was sinking out of sight and the night chill coming on, said things I could not understand, but they carried something cold to my heart.

"Those poor creatures! They do not suspect. They will come home in the morning, and eagerly ask for the little doggie that did the brave deed, and who of us will be strong enough to say the truth to them: 'The humble little friend is gone where go the beasts that perish.'"

1903

The $30,000 Bequest

Lakeside was a pleasant little town of five or six thousand inhabitants, and a rather pretty one, too, as towns go in the Far West. It had church accommodations for thirty-five thousand, which is the way of the Far West and the South, where everybody is religious, and where each of the Protestant sects is represented and has a plant of its own.

Rank was unknown in Lakeside—unconfessed, anyway; everybody knew everybody and his dog, and a sociable friendliness was the prevailing atmosphere.

Saladin Foster was book-keeper in the principal store, and the only high-salaried man of his profession in Lakeside. He was thirty-five years old, now; he had served that store for fourteen years; he had begun in his marriage-week at four hundred dollars a year, and had climbed steadily up, a hundred dollars a year, for four years; from that time forth his wage had remained eight hundred—a handsome figure indeed, and everybody conceded that he was worth it.

His wife, Electra, was a capable helpmeet, although—like himself—a dreamer of dreams and a private dabbler in romance. The first thing she did, after her marriage—child as she was, aged only nineteen—was to buy an acre of ground on the edge of the town, and pay down the cash for it—twenty-five dollars, all her fortune. Saladin had less, by fifteen. She instituted a vegetable garden there, got it farmed on shares by the nearest neighbor, and made it pay her a hundred per cent. a year. Out of Saladin's first year's wage she put thirty dollars in the savings-bank, sixty out of his second, a hundred out of his third, a hundred and fifty out of his fourth. His wage went to eight hundred a year, then, and meantime two children had arrived and increased the expenses, but she banked two hundred a year from the salary, nevertheless, thenceforth. When she had been married seven years she built and furnished a pretty and comfortable two-thousand-dollar house in the midst of her garden-acre, paid half of the money down and moved her family in. Seven years later she was out of debt and had several hundred dollars out earning its living.

Earning it by the rise in landed estate; for she had long ago bought another acre or two and sold the most of it at a profit to pleasant people who were willing to build, and would be good neighbors and furnish a general comradeship for herself and her growing family. She had an independent income from safe investments of about a hundred dollars a year; her children were growing in years and grace; and she was a pleased and happy woman. Happy in her husband, happy in her children, and the husband and the children were happy in her. It is at this point that this history begins.

The youngest girl, Clytemnestra—called Clytie for short—was eleven; her sister, Gwendolen—called Gwen for short—was thirteen; nice girls, and comely. The names betray the latent romance-tinge in the parental blood, the parents' names indicate that the tinge was an inheritance. It was an affectionate family, hence all four of its members had pet names. Saladin's was a curious and unsexing one—Sally; and so was Electra's—Aleck. All day long Sally was a good and diligent book-keeper and salesman; all day long Aleck was a good and faithful mother and housewife, and thoughtful and calculating business woman; but in the cozy living-room at night they put the plodding world away, and lived in another and a fairer, reading romances to each other, dreaming dreams, comrading with kings and princes and stately lords and ladies in the flash and stir and splendor of noble palaces and grim and ancient castles.

2

Now came great news! Stunning news—joyous news, in fact. It came from a neighboring state, where the family's only surviving relative lived. It was Sally's relative—a sort of vague and indefinite uncle or second or third cousin by the name of Tilbury Foster, seventy and a bachelor, reputed well off and correspondingly sour and crusty. Sally had tried to make up to him once, by letter, in a bygone time, and had not made that mistake again. Tilbury now wrote to Sally, saying he should shortly die, and should leave him thirty thousand dollars, cash; not for love, but because money had given him most of his troubles and exasperations, and he wished to place it where there was good hope that it would continue its malignant work. The bequest would be found in his will, and would be paid over. *Provided,* that Sally should be able to prove to the executors that he had *taken no notice of the gift by spoken word or by letter, had made no inquiries concerning the moribund's progress toward the everlasting tropics, and had not attended the funeral.*

As soon as Aleck had partially recovered from the tremendous emotions created by the letter, she sent to the relative's habitat and subscribed for the local paper.

Man and wife entered into a solemn compact, now, to never mention the great news to any one while the relative lived, lest some ignorant person carry the fact to the death-bed and distort it and make it appear that they were disobediently thankful for the bequest, and just the same as confessing it and publishing it, right in the face of the prohibition.

For the rest of the day Sally made havoc and confusion with his books, and Aleck could not keep her mind on her affairs, nor even take up a flower-pot or book or a stick of wood without forgetting what she had intended to do with it. For both were dreaming.

"Thir-ty thousand dollars!"

All day long the music of those inspiring words sang through those people's heads.

From her marriage-day forth, Aleck's grip had been upon the purse, and Sally had seldom known what it was to be privileged to squander a dime on non-necessities.

"Thir-ty thousand dollars!" the song went on and on. A vast sum, an unthinkable sum!

All day long Aleck was absorbed in planning how to invest it, Sally in planning how to spend it.

There was no romance-reading that night. The children took themselves away early, for the parents were silent, distraught, and strangely unentertaining. The good-night kisses might as well have been impressed upon vacancy, for all the response they got; the parents were not aware of the kisses, and the children had been gone an hour before their absence was noticed. Two pencils had been busy during that hour—note-making; in the way of plans. It was Sally who broke the stillness at last. He said, with exultation:

"Ah, it 'll be grand, Aleck! Out of the first thousand we'll have a horse and a buggy for summer, and a cutter and a skin lap-robe for winter."

Aleck responded with decision and composure—

"Out of the *capital?* Nothing of the kind. Not if it was a million!"

Sally was deeply disappointed; the glow went out of his face.

"Oh, Aleck!" he said, reproachfully. "We've always worked so hard and been so scrimped; and now that we are rich, it does seem—"

He did not finish, for he saw her eye soften; his supplication had touched her. She said, with gentle persuasiveness:

"We must not spend the capital, dear, it would not be wise. Out of the income from it—"

"That will answer, that will answer, Aleck! How dear and good you are! There will be a noble income, and if we can spend that—"

"Not *all* of it, dear, not all of it, but you can spend a part of it. That is, a reasonable part. But the whole of the capital—every penny of it—must be put right to work, and kept at it. You see the reasonableness of that, don't you?"

"Why, ye-s. Yes, of course. But we'll have to wait so long. Six months before the first interest falls due."

"Yes—maybe longer."

"Longer, Aleck? Why? Don't they pay half-yearly?"

"*That* kind of an investment—yes; but I sha'n't invest in that way."

"What way, then?"

"For big returns."

"Big. That's good. Go on, Aleck. What is it?"

"Coal. The new mines. Cannel. I mean to put in ten thousand. Ground floor. When we organize, we'll get three shares for one."

"By George, but it sounds good, Aleck! Then the shares will be worth —how much? And when?"

"About a year. They'll pay ten per cent. half-yearly, and be worth thirty thousand. I know all about it; the advertisement is in the Cincinnati paper here."

"Land, thirty thousand for ten—in a year! Let's jam in the whole capital and pull out ninety! I'll write and subscribe right now—to-morrow it may be too late."

He was flying to the writing-desk, but Aleck stopped him and put him back in his chair. She said:

"Don't lose your head so. We mustn't subscribe till we've got the money; don't you know that?"

Sally's excitement went down a degree or two, but he was not wholly appeased.

"Why, Aleck, we'll *have* it, you know—and so soon, too. He's probably out of his troubles before this; it's a hundred to nothing he's selecting his brimstone-shovel this very minute. Now, I think—"

Aleck shuddered, and said:

"How *can* you, Sally! Don't talk in that way, it is perfectly scandalous."

"Oh well, make it a halo, if you like, *I* don't care for his outfit, I was only just talking. Can't you let a person talk?"

"But why should you *want* to talk in that dreadful way? How would you like to have people talk so about *you*, and you not cold yet?"

"Not likely to be, for *one* while, I reckon, if my last act was giving away money for the sake of doing somebody a harm with it. But never mind about Tilbury, Aleck, let's talk about something worldly. It does seem to me that that mine is the place for the whole thirty. What's the objection?"

"All the eggs in one basket—that's the objection."

"All right, if you say so. What about the other twenty? What do you mean to do with that?"

"There is no hurry; I am going to look around before I do anything with it."

"All right, if your mind's made up," sighed Sally. He was deep in thought awhile, then he said:

"There'll be twenty thousand profit coming from the ten a year from now. We can spend that, can't we, Aleck?"

Aleck shook her head.

"No, dear," she said, "it won't sell high till we've had the first semi-annual dividend. You can spend part of that."

"Shucks, only *that*—and a whole year to wait! Confound it, I—"

"Oh, do be patient! It might even be declared in three months—it's quite within the possibilities."

"Oh, jolly! oh, thanks!" and Sally jumped up and kissed his wife in gratitude. "It 'll be three thousand—three whole thousand! how much of it can we spend, Aleck? Make it liberal—do, dear, that's a good fellow."

Aleck was pleased; so pleased that she yielded to the pressure and conceded a sum which her judgment told her was a foolish extravagance—a thousand dollars. Sally kissed her half a dozen times and even in that way could not express all his joy and thankfulness. This new access of gratitude and affection carried Aleck quite beyond the bounds of prudence, and before she could restrain herself she had made her darling another grant—a couple of thousand out of the fifty or sixty which she meant to clear within a year out of the twenty which still remained of the bequest. The happy tears sprang to Sally's eyes, and he said:

"Oh, I want to hug you!" And he did it. Then he got his notes and sat down and began to check off, for first purchase, the luxuries which he should earliest wish to secure. "Horse—buggy—cutter—lap-robe—patent-leathers—dog—plug-hat—church-pew—stem-winder—new teeth—*say*, Aleck!"

"Well?"

"Ciphering away, aren't you? That's right. Have you got the twenty thousand invested yet?"

"No, there's no hurry about that; I must look around first, and think."

"But you are ciphering; what's it about?"

"Why, I have to find work for the thirty thousand that comes out of the coal, haven't I?"

"Scott, what a head! I never thought of that. How are you getting along? Where have you arrived?"

"Not very far—two years or three. I've turned it over twice; once in oil and once in wheat."

"Why, Aleck, it's splendid! How does it aggregate?"

"I think—well, to be on the safe side, about a hundred and eighty thousand clear, though it will probably be more."

"My! isn't it wonderful? By gracious! luck has come our way at last, after all the hard sledding. Aleck!"

"Well?"

"I'm going to cash in a whole three hundred on the missionaries—what real right have we to care for expenses!"

"You couldn't do a nobler thing, dear; and it's just like your generous nature, you unselfish boy."

The praise made Sally poignantly happy, but he was fair and just enough to say it was rightfully due to Aleck rather than to himself, since but for her he should never have had the money.

Then they went up to bed, and in their delirium of bliss they forgot and left the candle burning in the parlor. They did not remember until they were undressed; then Sally was for letting it burn; he said they could afford it, if it was a thousand. But Aleck went down and put it out.

A good job, too; for on her way back she hit on a scheme that would turn the hundred and eighty thousand into half a million before it had had time to get cold.

3

The little newspaper which Aleck had subscribed for was a Thursday sheet; it would make the trip of five hundred miles from Tilbury's village and arrive on Saturday. Tilbury's letter had started on Friday, more than a day too late for the benefactor to die and get into that week's issue, but in plenty of time to make connection for the next output. Thus the Fosters had to wait almost a complete week to find out whether anything of a satisfactory nature had happened to him or not. It was a long, long week, and the strain was a heavy one. The pair could hardly have borne it if their minds had not had the relief of wholesome diversion. We have seen that they had that. The woman was piling up fortunes right along, the man was spending them—spending all his wife would give him a chance at, at any rate.

At last the Saturday came, and the *Weekly Sagamore* arrived. Mrs. Eversly Bennett was present. She was the Presbyterian parson's wife, and was working the Fosters for a charity. Talk now died a sudden death—on the Foster side. Mrs. Bennett presently discovered that her hosts were not hearing a word she was saying; so she got up, wondering and indignant, and went away. The moment she was out of the house, Aleck eagerly tore the wrapper from the paper, and her eyes and Sally's swept the columns for the death-notices. Disappointment! Tilbury was not anywhere mentioned. Aleck was a Christian from the cradle, and duty and the force of habit required her to go through the motions. She pulled herself together and said, with a pious two-per-cent. trade joyousness:

"Let us be humbly thankful that he has been spared; and—"

"Damn his treacherous hide, I wish—"

"Sally! For shame!"

"I don't care!" retorted the angry man. "It's the way *you* feel, and if you weren't so immorally pious you'd be honest and say so."

Aleck said, with wounded dignity:

"I do not see how you can say such unkind and unjust things. There is no such thing as immoral piety."

Sally felt a pang, but tried to conceal it under a shuffling attempt to save his case by changing the form of it—as if changing the form while retaining the juice could deceive the expert he was trying to placate. He said:

"I didn't mean so bad as that, Aleck; I didn't really mean immoral piety, I only meant—meant—well, conventional piety, you know; er—shop piety; the—the—why, *you* know what I mean. Aleck—the—well, where you put up the plated article and play it for solid, you know, without intending anything improper, but just out of trade habit, ancient policy, petrified custom, loyalty to—to—hang it, I can't find the right words, but *you* know what I mean, Aleck, and that there isn't any harm in it. I'll try again. You see, it's this way. If a person—"

"You have said quite enough," said Aleck, coldly; "let the subject be dropped."

"*I'm* willing," fervently responded Sally, wiping the sweat from his forehead and looking the thankfulness he had no words for. Then, musingly, he apologized to himself. "I certainly held threes—I *know* it —but I drew and didn't fill. That's where I'm so often weak in the game. If I had stood pat—but I didn't. I never do. I don't know enough."

Confessedly defeated, he was properly tame now and subdued. Aleck forgave him with her eyes.

The grand interest, the supreme interest, came instantly to the front again; nothing could keep it in the background many minutes on a stretch. The couple took up the puzzle of the absence of Tilbury's death-notice. They discussed it every which way, more or less hopefully, but they had to finish where they began, and concede that the only really sane explanation of the absence of the notice must be—and without doubt was—that Tilbury was not dead. There was something sad about it, something even a little unfair, maybe, but there it was, and had to be put up with. They were agreed as to that. To Sally it seemed a strangely inscrutable dispensation; more inscrutable than usual, he thought; one of the most unnecessarily inscrutable he could call to mind, in fact— and said so, with some feeling; but if he was hoping to draw Aleck he failed; she reserved her opinion, if she had one; she had not the habit of taking injudicious risks in any market, worldly or other.

The pair must wait for next week's paper—Tilbury had evidently postponed. That was their thought and their decision. So they put the subject away, and went about their affairs again with as good heart as they could.

Now, if they had but known it, they had been wronging Tilbury all the time. Tilbury had kept faith, kept it to the letter; he was dead, he had died to schedule. He was dead more than four days now and used to it; entirely dead, perfectly dead, as dead as any other new person in the cemetery; dead in abundant time to get into that week's *Saga-more*, too, and only shut out by an accident; an accident which could not happen to a metropolitan journal, but which happens easily to a poor little village rag like the *Sagamore*. On this occasion, just as the editorial page was being locked up, a gratis quart of strawberry water-ice arrived from Hostetter's Ladies' and Gents' Ice-Cream Parlors, and the stickful of rather chilly regret over Tilbury's translation got crowded out to make room for the editor's frantic gratitude.

On its way to the standing-galley Tilbury's notice got pied. Otherwise it would have gone into some future edition, for *Weekly Sagamores* do not waste "live" matter, and in their galleys "live" matter is immortal, unless a pi accident intervenes. But a thing that gets pied is dead, and for such there is no resurrection; its chance of seeing print is gone, for-ever and ever. And so, let Tilbury like it or not, let him rave in his grave to his fill, no matter—no mention of his death would ever see the light in the *Weekly Sagamore*.

4

Five weeks drifted tediously along. The *Sagamore* arrived regularly on the Saturdays, but never once contained a mention of Tilbury Foster. Sally's patience broke down at this point, and he said, resentfully:

"Damn his livers, he's immortal!"

Aleck gave him a very severe rebuke, and added, with icy solemnity:

"How would you feel if you were suddenly cut off just after such an awful remark had escaped out of you?"

Without sufficient reflection Sally responded:

"I'd feel I was lucky I hadn't got caught with it *in* me."

Pride had forced him to say something, and as he could not think of any rational thing to say he flung that out. Then he stole a base—as he called it—that is, slipped from the presence, to keep from getting brayed in his wife's discussion-mortar.

Six months came and went. The *Sagamore* was still silent about Tilbury. Meantime, Sally had several times thrown out a feeler—that is, a hint that he would like to know. Aleck had ignored the hints. Sally now resolved to brace up and risk a frontal attack. So he squarely proposed to disguise himself and go to Tilbury's village and surreptitiously find out as to the prospects. Aleck put her foot on the dangerous project with energy and decision. She said:

"What can you be thinking of? You do keep my hands full! You have to be watched all the time, like a little child, to keep you from walking into the fire. You'll stay right where you are!"

"Why, Aleck, I could do it and not be found out—I'm certain of it."

"Sally Foster, don't you know you would have to inquire around?"

"Of course, but what of it? Nobody would suspect who I was."

"Oh, listen to the man! Some day you've got to prove to the executors that you never inquired. What then?"

He had forgotten that detail. He didn't reply; there wasn't anything to say. Aleck added:

"Now then, drop that notion out of your mind, and don't ever meddle with it again. Tilbury set that trap for you. Don't you know it's a trap? He is on the watch, and fully expecting you to blunder into it. Well, he is going to be disappointed—at least while I am on deck. Sally!"

"Well?"

"As long as you live, if it's a hundred years, don't you ever make an inquiry. Promise!"

"All right," with a sigh and reluctantly.

Then Aleck softened and said:

"Don't be impatient. We are prospering; we can wait; there is no hurry. Our small dead-certain income increases all the time; and as to futures, I have not made a mistake yet—they are piling up by the thousands and the tens of thousands. There is not another family in the state with such prospects as ours. Already we are beginning to roll in eventual wealth. You know that, don't you?"

"Yes, Aleck, it's certainly so."

"Then be grateful for what God is doing for us, and stop worrying.

You do not believe we could have achieved these prodigious results without His special help and guidance, do you?"

Hesitatingly, "N-no, I suppose not." Then, with feeling and admiration, "And yet, when it comes to judiciousness in watering a stock or putting up a hand to skin Wall Street I don't give in that *you* need any outside amateur help, if I do wish I—"

"Oh, *do* shut up! I know you do not mean any harm or any irreverence, poor boy, but you can't seem to open your mouth without letting out things to make a person shudder. You keep me in constant dread. For you and for all of us. Once I had no fear of the thunder, but now when I hear it I—"

Her voice broke, and she began to cry, and could not finish. The sight of this smote Sally to the heart, and he took her in his arms and petted her and comforted her and promised better conduct, and upbraided himself and remorsefully pleaded for forgiveness. And he was in earnest, and sorry for what he had done and ready for any sacrifice that could make up for it.

And so, in privacy, he thought long and deeply over the matter, resolving to do what should seem best. It was easy to *promise* reform; indeed he had already promised it. But would that do any real good, any permanent good? No, it would be but temporary—he knew his weakness, and confessed it to himself with sorrow—he could not keep the promise. Something surer and better must be devised; and he devised it. At cost of precious money which he had long been saving up, shilling by shilling, he put a lightning-rod on the house.

At a subsequent time he relapsed.

What miracles habit can do! and how quickly and how easily habits are acquired—both trifling habits and habits which profoundly change us. If by accident we wake at two in the morning a couple of nights in succession, we have need to be uneasy, for another repetition can turn the accident into a habit; and a month's dallying with whisky—but we all know these commonplace facts.

The castle-building habit, the day-dreaming habit—how it grows! what a luxury it becomes; how we fly to its enchantments at every idle moment, how we revel in them, steep our souls in them, intoxicate ourselves with their beguiling fantasies—oh yes, and how soon and how easily our dream life and our material life become so intermingled and so fused together that we can't quite tell which is which, any more.

By and by Aleck subscribed for a Chicago daily and for the *Wall Street Pointer*. With an eye single to finance she studied these as diligently all the week as she studied her Bible Sundays. Sally was lost in admiration, to note with what swift and sure strides her genius and judgment developed and expanded in the forecasting and handling of the securities of both the material and spiritual markets. He was proud of her nerve and daring in exploiting worldly stocks, and just as proud of her conservative caution in working her spiritual deals. He noted that she never lost her head in either case; that with a splendid courage she often went short on worldly futures, but heedfully drew the line there—she was always long on the others. Her policy was quite sane and simple, as she explained it to him: what she put into earthly futures was for speculation, what she put into spiritual futures was for investment; she was willing to go into the one on a margin, and take chances, but in the case of the other, "margin her no margins"—she wanted to cash in a hundred cents per dollar's worth, and have the stock transferred on the books.

It took but a very few months to educate Aleck's imagination and Sally's. Each day's training added something to the spread and effectiveness of the two machines. As a consequence, Aleck made imaginary money much faster than at first she had dreamed of making it, and Sally's competency in spending the overflow of it kept pace with the strain put upon it, right along. In the beginning, Aleck had given the coal speculation a twelvemonth in which to materialize, and had been loath to grant that this term might possibly be shortened by nine months. But that was the feeble work, the nursery work, of a financial fancy that had had no teaching, no experience, no practice. These aids soon came, then that nine months vanished, and the imaginary ten-thousand-dollar investment came marching home with three hundred per cent. profit on its back!

It was a great day for the pair of Fosters. They were speechless for joy. Also speechless for another reason: after much watching of the market, Aleck had lately, with fear and trembling, made her first flyer on a "margin," using the remaining twenty thousand of the bequest in this risk. In her mind's eye she had seen it climb, point by point—always with a chance that the market would break—until at last her anxieties were too great for further endurance—she being new to the margin business and unhardened, as yet—and she gave her imaginary broker an imaginary order by imaginary telegraph to sell. She said forty thousand dollars' profit was enough. The sale was made on the very day that the coal venture had returned with its rich freight. As I have said, the couple were speechless. They sat dazed and blissful that night, trying to realize the immense fact, the overwhelming fact, that they were actually worth a hundred thousand dollars in clean, imaginary cash. Yet so it was.

It was the last time that ever Aleck was afraid of a margin; at least afraid enough to let it break her sleep and pale her cheek to the extent that this first experience in that line had done.

Indeed it was a memorable night. Gradually the realization that they were rich sank securely home into the souls of the pair, then they began to place the money. If we could have looked out through the eyes of these dreamers, we should have seen their tidy little wooden house disappear, and a two-story brick with a cast-iron fence in front of it take its place; we should have seen a three-globed gas-chandelier grow down from the parlor ceiling; we should have seen the homely rag carpet turn to noble Brussels, a dollar and a half a yard; we should have seen the plebeian fireplace vanish away and a recherché, big base-burner with isinglass windows take position and spread awe around. And we should have seen other things, too; among them the buggy, the lap-robe, the stove-pipe hat, and so on.

From that time forth, although the daughters and the neighbors saw only the same old wooden house there, it was a two-story brick to Aleck and Sally; and not a night went by that Aleck did not worry about the imaginary gas-bills, and get for all comfort Sally's reckless retort: "What of it? We can afford it."

Before the couple went to bed, that first night that they were rich, they had decided that they must celebrate. They must give a party—that was the idea. But how to explain it—to the daughters and the neighbors? They could not expose the fact that they were rich. Sally was willing, even anxious, to do it; but Aleck kept her head and would not allow it. She said that although the money was as good as in, it would be as well to wait until it was actually in. On that policy she took her stand, and would not budge. The great secret must be kept, she said—kept from the daughters and everybody else.

The pair were puzzled. They must celebrate, they were determined to celebrate, but since the secret must be kept, what could they celebrate? No birthdays were due for three months. Tilbury wasn't available, evidently he was going to live forever; what the nation *could* they celebrate? That was Sally's way of putting it; and he was getting impatient, too, and harassed. But at last he hit it—just by sheer inspiration, as it seemed to him—and all their troubles were gone in a moment; they would celebrate the Discovery of America. A splendid idea!

Aleck was almost too proud of Sally for words—she said *she* never would have thought of it. But Sally, although he was bursting with delight in the compliment and with wonder at himself, tried not to let on, and said it wasn't really anything, anybody could have done it. Whereat Aleck, with a prideful toss of her happy head, said:

"Oh, certainly! Anybody could—oh, anybody! Hosannah Dilkins, for instance! Or maybe Adelbert Peanut—oh, *dear*—yes! Well, I'd like to see them try it, that's all. Dear-me-suz, if they could think of the discovery of a forty-acre island it's more than *I* believe they could; and as for a whole continent, why, Sally Foster, you know perfectly well it would strain the livers and lights out of them and *then* they couldn't!"

The dear woman, she knew he had talent; and if affection made her over-estimate the size of it a little, surely it was a sweet and gentle crime, and forgiveable for its source's sake.

5

The celebration went off well. The friends were all present, both the young and the old. Among the young were Flossie and Gracie Peanut and their brother Adelbert, who was a rising young journeyman tinner, also Hosannah Dilkins, Jr., journeyman plasterer, just out of his apprenticeship. For many months Adelbert and Hosannah had been showing interest in Gwendolen and Clytemnestra Foster, and the parents of the girls had noticed this with private satisfaction. But they suddenly realized now that that feeling had passed. They recognized that the changed financial conditions had raised up a social bar between their daughters and the young mechanics. The daughters could now look higher—and must. Yes, must. They need marry nothing below the grade of lawyer or merchant; poppa and momma would take care of this; there must be no mésalliances.

However, these thinkings and projects of theirs were private, and did not show on the surface, and therefore threw no shadow upon the celebration. What showed upon the surface was a serene and lofty contentment and a dignity of carriage and gravity of deportment which compelled the admiration and likewise the wonder of the company. All noticed it, all commented upon it, but none was able to divine the secret of it. It was a marvel and a mystery. There several persons remarked, without suspecting what clever shots they were making:

"It's as if they'd come into property."

That was just it, indeed.

Most mothers would have taken hold of the matrimonial matter in the old regulation way; they would have given the girls a talking to, of a solemn sort and untactful—a lecture calculated to defeat its own purpose, by producing tears and secret rebellion; and the said mothers would have further damaged the business by requesting the young mechanics to discontinue their attentions. But this mother was different. She was practical. She said nothing to any of the young people concerned, nor to any one else except Sally. He listened to her and understood; understood and admired. He said:

"I get the idea. Instead of finding fault with the samples on view, thus hurting feelings and obstructing trade without occasion, you merely offer a higher class of goods for the money, and leave nature to take her course. It's wisdom, Aleck, solid wisdom, and sound as a nut. Who's your fish? Have you nominated him yet?"

No, she hadn't. They must look the market over—which they did. To start with, they considered and discussed Bradish, rising young lawyer, and Fulton, rising young dentist. Sally must invite them to dinner. But not right away; there was no hurry, Aleck said. Keep an eye on the pair, and wait; nothing would be lost by going slowly in so important a matter.

It turned out that this was wisdom, too; for inside of three weeks Aleck made a wonderful strike which swelled her imaginary hundred thousand to four hundred thousand of the same quality. She and Sally were in the clouds that evening. For the first time they introduced champagne at dinner. Not real champagne, but plenty real enough for the amount of imagination expended on it. It was Sally that did it, and Aleck weakly submitted. At bottom both were troubled and ashamed, for he was a high-up Son of Temperance, and at funerals wore an apron which no dog could look upon and retain his reason and his opinion; and she was a W. C. T. U., with all that that implies of boiler-iron virtue and unendurable holiness. But there it was; the pride of riches was beginning its disintegrating work. They had lived to prove, once more, a sad truth which had been proven many times before in the world: that whereas principle is a great and noble protection against showy and degrading vanities and vices, poverty is worth six of it. More than four hundred thousand dollars to the good! They took up the matrimonial matter again. Neither the dentist nor the lawyer was mentioned; there was no occasion, they were out of the running. Disqualified. They discussed the son of the pork-packer and the son of the village banker. But finally, as in the previous case, they concluded to wait and think, and go cautiously and sure.

Luck came their way again. Aleck, ever watchful, saw a great and risky chance, and took a daring flyer. A time of trembling, of doubt, of awful uneasiness followed, for non-success meant absolute ruin and nothing short of it. Then came the result, and Aleck, faint with joy, could hardly control her voice when she said:

"The suspense is over, Sally—and we are worth a cold million!"

Sally wept for gratitude, and said:

"Oh, Electra, jewel of women, darling of my heart, we are free at last, we roll in wealth, we need never scrimp again. It's a case for Veuve Cliquot!" and he got out a pint of spruce-beer and made sacrifice, he saying "Damn the expense," and she rebuking him gently with reproachful but humid and happy eyes.

They shelved the pork-packer's son and the banker's son, and sat down to consider the Governor's son and the son of the Congressman.

6

It were a weariness to follow in detail the leaps and bounds the Foster fictitious finances took from this time forth. It was marvelous, it was dizzying, it was dazzling. Everything Aleck touched turned to fairy gold, and heaped itself glittering toward the firmament. Millions upon millions poured in, and still the mighty stream flowed thundering along, still its vast volume increased. Five millions—ten millions—twenty—thirty—was there never to be an end?

Two years swept by in a splendid delirium, the intoxicated Fosters scarcely noticing the flight of time. They were now worth three hundred million dollars; they were in every board of directors of every prodigious combine in the country; and still, as time drifted along, the millions went on piling up, five at a time, ten at a time, as fast as they could tally them off, almost. The three hundred doubled itself—then doubled again—and yet again—and yet once more.

Twenty-four hundred millions!

The business was getting a little confused. It was necessary to take an account of stock, and straighten it out. The Fosters knew it, they felt it, they realized that it was imperative; but they also knew that to do it properly and perfectly the task must be carried to a finish without a break when once it was begun. A ten-hours' job; and where could *they* find ten leisure hours in a bunch? Sally was selling pins and sugar and calico all day and every day; Aleck was cooking and washing dishes and sweeping and making beds all day and every day, with none to help, for the daughters were being saved up for high society. The Fosters knew there was one way to get the ten hours, and only one. Both were ashamed to name it; each waited for the other to do it. Finally Sally said:

"Somebody's got to give in. It's up to me. Consider that I've named it—never mind pronouncing it out aloud."

Aleck colored, but was grateful. Without further remark, they fell. Fell, and—broke the Sabbath. For that was their only free ten-hour stretch. It was but another step in the downward path. Others would follow. Vast wealth has temptations which fatally and surely undermine the moral structure of persons not habituated to its possession.

They pulled down the shades and broke the Sabbath. With hard and patient labor they overhauled their holdings and listed them. And a long-drawn procession of formidable names it was! Starting with the Railway Systems, Steamer Lines, Standard Oil, Ocean Cables, Diluted Telegraph, and all the rest, and winding up with Klondike, De Beers, Tammany Graft, and Shady Privileges in the Post-office Department.

Twenty-four hundred millions, and all safely planted in Good Things, gilt-edged and interest-bearing. Income, $120,000,000 a year. Aleck fetched a long purr of soft delight, and said:

"Is it enough?"

"It is, Aleck."

"What shall we do?"

"Stand pat."

"Retire from business?"

"That's it."

"I am agreed. The good work is finished; we will take a long rest and enjoy the money."

"Good! Aleck!"

"Yes, dear?"

"How much of the income can we spend?"

"The whole of it."

It seemed to her husband that a ton of chains fell from his limbs. He did not say a word; he was happy beyond the power of speech.

After that, they broke the Sabbaths right along, as fast as they turned up. It is the first wrong steps that count. Every Sunday they put in the whole day, after morning service, on inventions—inventions of ways to spend the money. They got to continuing this delicious dissipation until past midnight; and at every séance Aleck lavished millions upon great charities and religious enterprises, and Sally lavished like sums upon matters to which (at first) he gave definite names. Only at first. Later the names gradually lost sharpness of outline, and eventually faded into "sundries," thus becoming entirely—but safely—undescriptive. For Sally was crumbling. The placing of these millions added seriously and most uncomfortably to the family expenses—in tallow candles. For a while Aleck was worried. Then, after a little, she ceased to worry, for the occasion of it was gone. She was pained, she was grieved, she was ashamed; but she said nothing, and so became an accessory. Sally was taking candles; he was robbing the store. It is ever thus. Vast wealth, to the person unaccustomed to it, is a bane; it eats into the flesh and bone of his morals. When the Fosters were poor, they could have been trusted with untold candles. But now they—but let us not dwell upon it. From candles to apples is but a step: Sally got to taking apples; then soap; then maple-sugar; then canned goods; then crockery. How easy it is to go from bad to worse, when once we have started upon a downward course!

Meantime, other effects had been milestoning the course of the Fosters' splendid financial march. The fictitious brick dwelling had given place to an imaginary granite one with a checker-board mansard roof; in time this one disappeared and gave place to a still grander home— and so on and so on. Mansion after mansion, made of air, rose, higher, broader, finer, and each in its turn vanished away; until now in these latter great days, our dreamers were in fancy housed, in a distant region, in a sumptuous vast palace which looked out from a leafy summit upon a noble prospect of vale and river and receding hills steeped in tinted mists—and all private, all the property of the dreamers; a palace swarming with liveried servants, and populous with guests of fame and power, hailing from all the world's capitals, foreign and domestic.

This palace was far, far away toward the rising sun, immeasurably remote, astronomically remote, in Newport, Rhode Island, Holy Land of High Society, ineffable Domain of the American Aristocracy. As a rule they spent a part of every Sabbath—after morning service—in this sumptuous home, the rest of it they spent in Europe, or in dawdling around in their private yacht. Six days of sordid and plodding fact life at home on the ragged edge of Lakeside and straitened means, the seventh in Fairyland—such had become their program and their habit.

In their sternly restricted fact life they remained as of old—plodding, diligent, careful, practical, economical. They stuck loyally to the little Presbyterian Church, and labored faithfully in its interests and stood by its high and tough doctrines with all their mental and spiritual energies. But in their dream life they obeyed the invitations of their fancies, whatever they might be, and howsoever the fancies might change. Aleck's fancies were not very capricious, and not frequent, but Sally's scattered a good deal. Aleck, in her dream life, went over to the Episcopal camp, on account of its large official titles; next she became High-church on account of the candles and shows; and next she naturally changed to Rome, where there were cardinals and more candles. But these excursions were a nothing to Sally's. His dream life was a glowing and continuous and persistent excitement, and he kept every part of it fresh and sparkling by frequent changes, the religious part along with the rest. He worked his religions hard, and changed them with his shirt.

The liberal spendings of the Fosters upon their fancies began early in their prosperities, and grew in prodigality step by step with their advancing fortunes. In time they became truly enormous. Aleck built a university or two per Sunday; also a hospital or two; also a Rowton hotel or so; also a batch of churches; now and then a cathedral; and once, with untimely and ill-chosen playfulness, Sally said, "It was a cold day when she didn't ship a cargo of missionaries to persuade unreflecting Chinamen to trade off twenty-four carat Confucianism for counterfeit Christianity."

This rude and unfeeling language hurt Aleck to the heart, and she went from the presence crying. That spectacle went to his own heart, and in his pain and shame he would have given worlds to have those unkind words back. She had uttered no syllable of reproach—and that cut him. Not one suggestion that he look at his own record—and she could have made, oh, so many, and such blistering ones! Her generous silence brought a swift revenge, for it turned his thoughts upon himself, it summoned before him a spectral procession, a moving vision of his life as he had been leading it these past few years of limitless prosperity, and as he sat there reviewing it his cheeks burned and his soul was steeped in humiliation. Look at her life—how fair it was, and tending ever upward; and look at his own—how frivolous, how charged with mean vanities, how selfish, how empty, how ignoble! And its trend—never upward, but downward, ever downward!

He instituted comparisons between her record and his own. He had found fault with her—so he mused—he! And what could he say for himself? When she built her first church what was he doing? Gathering other blasé multimillionaires into a Poker Club; defiling his own palace with it; losing hundreds of thousands to it at every sitting, and sillily vain of the admiring notoriety it made for him. When she was building her first university, what was he doing? Polluting himself with a gay and dissipated secret life in the company of other fast bloods, multimillionaires in money and paupers in character. When she was building her first foundling asylum, what was he doing? Alas! When she was projecting her noble Society for the Purifying of the Sex, what was he doing? Ah, what, indeed! When she and the W. C. T. U. and the Woman with the Hatchet, moving with resistless march, were sweeping the fatal bottle from the land, what was he doing? Getting drunk three times a day. When she, builder of a hundred cathedrals, was being gratefully welcomed and blest in papal Rome and decorated with the Golden Rose which she had so honorably earned, what was he doing? Breaking the bank at Monte Carlo.

He stopped. He could go no farther; he could not bear the rest. He rose up, with a great resolution upon his lips: this secret life should be revealed, and confessed; no longer would he live it clandestinely; he would go and tell her All.

And that is what he did. He told her All; and wept upon her bosom; wept, and moaned, and begged for her forgiveness. It was a profound shock, and she staggered under the blow, but he was her own, the core of her heart, the blessing of her eyes, her all in all, she could deny him nothing, and she forgave him. She felt that he could never again be quite to her what he had been before; she knew that he could only repent, and not reform; yet all morally defaced and decayed as he was, was he not her own, her very own, the idol of her deathless worship? She said she was his serf, his slave, and she opened her yearning heart and took him in.

7

One Sunday afternoon some time after this they were sailing the summer seas in their dream yacht, and reclining in lazy luxury under the awning of the after-deck. There was silence, for each was busy with his own thoughts. These seasons of silence had insensibly been growing more and more frequent of late; the old nearness and cordiality were waning. Sally's terrible revelation had done its work; Aleck had tried hard to drive the memory of it out of her mind, but it would not go, and the shame and bitterness of it were poisoning her gracious dream life. She could see now (on Sundays) that her husband was becoming a bloated and repulsive Thing. She could not close her eyes to this, and in these days she no longer looked at him, Sundays, when she could help it.

But she—was she herself without blemish? Alas, she knew she was not. She was keeping a secret from him, she was acting dishonorably toward him, and many a pang it was costing her. *She was breaking the compact, and concealing it from him.* Under strong temptation she had gone into business again; she had risked their whole fortune in a purchase of all the railway systems and coal and steel companies in the country on a margin, and she was now trembling, every Sabbath hour, lest through some chance word of hers he find it out. In her misery and remorse for this treachery she could not keep her heart from going out to him in pity; she was filled with compunctions to see him lying there, drunk and content, and never suspecting. Never suspecting—trusting her with a perfect and pathetic trust, and she holding over him by a thread a possible calamity of so devastating a—

"Say—Aleck?"

The interrupting words brought her suddenly to herself. She was grateful to have that persecuting subject from her thoughts, and she answered, with much of the old-time tenderness in her tone:

"Yes, dear."

"Do you know, Aleck, I think we are making a mistake—that is, you are. I mean about the marriage business." He sat up, fat and froggy and benevolent, like a bronze Buddha, and grew earnest. "Consider —it's more than five years. You've continued the same policy from the start: with every rise, always holding on for five points higher. Always when I think we are going to have some weddings, you see a bigger thing ahead, and I undergo another disappointment. I think you are too hard to please. Some day we'll get left. First, we turned down the dentist and the lawyer. That was all right—it was sound. Next, we turned down the banker's son and the pork-butcher's heir—right again, and sound. Next, we turned down the Congressman's son and the Governor's—right as a trivet, I confess it. Next the Senator's son and the son of the Vice-President of the United States—perfectly right, there's no permanency about those little distinctions. Then you went for the aristocracy; and I thought we had struck oil at last—yes. We would make a plunge at the Four Hundred, and pull in some ancient lineage, venerable, holy, ineffable, mellow with the antiquity of a hundred and fifty years, disinfected of the ancestral odors of salt-cod and pelts all of a century ago, and unsmirched by a day's work since; and then! why, then the marriages, of course. But no, along comes a pair of real aristocrats from Europe, and straightway you throw over the half-breeds. It was awfully discouraging, Aleck! Since then, what a procession! You turned down the baronets for a pair of barons; you turned down the barons for a pair of viscounts; the viscounts for a pair of earls; the earls for a pair of marquises; the marquises for a brace of dukes. Now, Aleck, cash in!—you've played the limit. You've got a job lot of four dukes under the hammer; of four nationalities; all sound in wind and limb and pedigree, all bankrupt and in debt up to the ears. They come high, but we can afford it. Come, Aleck, don't delay any longer, don't keep up the suspense: take the whole lay-out, and leave the girls to choose!"

Aleck had been smiling blandly and contentedly all through this arraignment of her marriage policy; a pleasant light, as of triumph with perhaps a nice surprise peeping out through it, rose in her eyes, and she said, as calmly as she could:

"Sally, what would you say to—*royalty?*"

Prodigious! Poor man, it knocked him silly, and he fell over the garboard strake and barked his shin on the cat-heads. He was dizzy for a moment, then he gathered himself up and limped over and sat down by his wife and beamed his old-time admiration and affection upon her in floods, out of his bleary eyes.

"By George!" he said, fervently, "Aleck, you *are* great—the greatest woman in the whole earth! I can't ever learn the whole size of you. I can't ever learn the immeasurable deeps of you. Here I've been considering myself qualified to criticize your game. *I!* Why, if I had stopped to think, I'd have known you had a lone hand up your sleeve. Now, dear heart, I'm all red-hot impatience—tell me about it!"

The flattered and happy woman put her lips to his ear and whispered a princely name. It made him catch his breath, it lit his face with exultation.

"Land!" he said, "it's a stunning catch! He's got a gambling-hell, and a graveyard, and a bishop, and a cathedral—all his very own. And all gilt-edged five-hundred-per-cent. stock, every detail of it; the tidiest little property in Europe. And that graveyard—it's the selectest in the world: none but suicides admitted; *yes*, sir, and the free-list suspended, too, *all* the time. There isn't much land in the principality, but there's enough: eight hundred acres in the graveyard and forty-two outside. It's a *sovereignty*—that's the main thing; *land's* nothing. There's plenty land, Sahara's drugged with it."

Aleck glowed; she was profoundly happy. She said:

"Think of it, Sally—it is a family that has never married outside the Royal and Imperial Houses of Europe: our grandchildren will sit upon thrones!"

"True as you live, Aleck—and bear scepters, too; and handle them as naturally and nonchalantly as I handle a yardstick. It's a grand catch, Aleck. He's corralled, is he? Can't get away? You didn't take him on a margin?"

"No. Trust me for that. He's not a liability, he's an asset. So is the other one."

"Who is it, Aleck?"

"His Royal Highness Sigismund-Siegfried-Lauenfeld-Dinkelspiel-

Schwartzenberg Blutwurst, Hereditary Grand Duke of Katzenyammer."

"No! You can't mean it!"

"It's as true as I'm sitting here, I give you my word," she answered.

His cup was full, and he hugged her to his heart with rapture, saying:

"How wonderful it all seems, and how beautiful! It's one of the oldest and noblest of the three hundred and sixty-four ancient German principalities, and one of the few that was allowed to retain its royal estate when Bismarck got done trimming them. I know that farm, I've been there. It's got a rope-walk and a candle-factory and an army. Standing army. Infantry and cavalry. Three soldiers and a horse. Aleck, it's been a long wait, and full of heartbreak and hope deferred, but God knows I am happy now. Happy, and grateful to you, my own, who have done it all. When is it to be?"

"Next Sunday."

"Good. And we'll want to do these weddings up in the very regalest style that's going. It's properly due to the royal quality of the parties of the first part. Now as I understand it, there is only one kind of marriage that is sacred to royalty, exclusive to royalty: it's the morganatic."

"What do they call it that for, Sally?"

"I don't know; but anyway it's royal, and royal only."

"Then we will insist upon it. More—I will compel it. It is morganatic marriage or none."

"That settles it!" said Sally, rubbing his hands with delight. "And it will be the very first in America. Aleck, it will make Newport sick."

Then they fell silent, and drifted away upon their dream wings to the far regions of the earth to invite all the crowned heads and their families and provide gratis transportation for them.

8

During three days the couple walked upon air, with their heads in the clouds. They were but vaguely conscious of their surroundings; they saw all things dimly, as through a veil; they were steeped in dreams, often they did not hear when they were spoken to; they often did not understand when they heard; they answered confusedly or at random; Sally sold molasses by weight, sugar by the yard, and furnished soap when asked for candles, and Aleck put the cat in the wash and fed milk to the soiled linen. Everybody was stunned and amazed, and went about muttering, "What *can* be the matter with the Fosters?"

Three days. Then came events! Things had taken a happy turn, and

for forty-eight hours Aleck's imaginary corner had been booming. Up
—up—still up! Cost point was passed. Still up—and up—and up! Five
points above cost—then ten—fifteen—twenty! Twenty points cold profit
on the vast venture, now, and Aleck's imaginary brokers were shouting frantically by imaginary long-distance, "Sell! sell! for Heaven's sake
sell!"

She broke the splendid news to Sally, and he, too, said, "Sell! sell—
oh, don't make a blunder, now, you own the earth!—sell, sell!" But she
set her iron will and lashed it amidships, and said she would hold on
for five points more if she died for it.

It was a fatal resolve. The very next day came the historic crash, the
record crash, the devastating crash, when the bottom fell out of Wall
Street, and the whole body of gilt-edged stocks dropped ninety-five
points in five hours, and the multimillionaire was seen begging his
bread in the Bowery. Aleck sternly held her grip and "put up" as long
as she could, but at last there came a call which she was powerless to
meet, and her imaginary brokers sold her out. Then, and not till then,
the man in her was vanished, and the woman in her resumed sway. She
put her arms about her husband's neck and wept, saying:

"I am to blame, do not forgive me, I cannot bear it. We are paupers!
Paupers, and I am so miserable. The weddings will never come off; all
that is past; we could not even buy the dentist, now."

A bitter reproach was on Sally's tongue: "I *begged* you to sell, but
you—" He did not say it; he had not the heart to add a hurt to that
broken and repentant spirit. A nobler thought came to him and he said:

"Bear up, my Aleck, all is not lost! You really never invested a penny
of my uncle's bequest, but only its unmaterialized future; what we have
lost was only the increment harvested from that future by your incomparable financial judgment and sagacity. Cheer up, banish these griefs;
we still have the thirty thousand untouched; and with the experience
which you have acquired, think what you will be able to do with it in
a couple of years! The marriages are not off, they are only postponed."

These were blessed words. Aleck saw how true they were, and their
influence was electric; her tears ceased to flow, and her great spirit
rose to its full stature again. With flashing eye and grateful heart, and
with hand uplifted in pledge and prophecy, she said:

"Now and here I proclaim—"

But she was interrupted by a visitor. It was the editor and proprietor
of the *Sagamore*. He had happened into Lakeside to pay a duty-call
upon an obscure grandmother of his who was nearing the end of her
pilgrimage, and with the idea of combining business with grief he had

looked up the Fosters, who had been so absorbed in other things for the past four years that they had neglected to pay up their subscription. Six dollars due. No visitor could have been more welcome. He would know all about Uncle Tilbury and what his chances might be getting to be, cemeterywards. They could, of course, ask no questions, for that would squelch the bequest, but they could nibble around on the edge of the subject and hope for results. The scheme did not work. The obtuse editor did not know he was being nibbled at; but at last, chance accomplished what art had failed in. In illustration of something under discussion which required the help of metaphor, the editor said:

"Land, it's as tough as Tilbury Foster!—as *we* say."

It was sudden, and it made the Fosters jump. The editor noticed it, and said, apologetically:

"No harm intended, I assure you. It's just a saying; just a joke, you know—nothing in it. Relation of yours?"

Sally crowded his burning eagerness down, and answered with all the indifference he could assume:

"I—well, not that I know of, but we've heard of him." The editor was thankful, and resumed his composure. Sally added: "Is he—is he—well?"

"Is he *well*? Why, bless you he's in Sheol these five years!"

The Fosters were trembling with grief, though it felt like joy. Sally said, non-committally—and tentatively:

"Ah, well, such is life, and none can escape—not even the rich are spared."

The editor laughed.

"If you are including Tilbury," said he, "it don't apply. *He* hadn't a cent; the town had to bury him."

The Fosters sat petrified for two minutes; petrified and cold. Then, white-faced and weak-voiced, Sally asked:

"Is it true? Do you *know* it to be true?"

"Well, I should say! I was one of the executors. He hadn't anything to leave but a wheelbarrow, and he left that to me. It hadn't any wheel, and wasn't any good. Still, it was something, and so, to square up, I scribbled off a sort of a little obituarial send-off for him, but it got crowded out."

The Fosters were not listening—their cup was full, it could contain no more. They sat with bowed heads, dead to all things but the ache at their hearts.

An hour later. Still they sat there, bowed, motionless, silent, the visitor long ago gone, they unaware.

Then they stirred, and lifted their heads wearily, and gazed at each other wistfully, dreamily, dazed; then presently began to twaddle to each other in a wandering and childish way. At intervals they lapsed into silences, leaving a sentence unfinished, seemingly either unaware of it or losing their way. Sometimes, when they woke out of these silences they had a dim and transient consciousness that something had happened to their minds; then with a dumb and yearning solicitude they would softly caress each other's hands in mutual compassion and support, as if they would say: "I am near you, I will not forsake you, we will bear it together; somewhere there is release and forgetfulness, somewhere there is a grave and peace; be patient, it will not be long."

They lived yet two years, in mental night, always brooding, steeped in vague regrets and melancholy dreams, never speaking; then release came to both on the same day.

Toward the end the darkness lifted from Sally's ruined mind for a moment, and he said:

"Vast wealth, acquired by sudden and unwholesome means, is a snare. It did us no good, transient were its feverish pleasures; yet for its sake we threw away our sweet and simple and happy life—let others take warning by us."

He lay silent awhile, with closed eyes; then as the chill of death crept upward toward his heart, and consciousness was fading from his brain, he muttered:

"Money had brought him misery, and he took his revenge upon us, who had done him no harm. He had his desire: with base and cunning calculation he left us but thirty thousand, knowing we would try to increase it, and ruin our life and break our hearts. Without added expense he could have left us far above desire of increase, far above the temptation to speculate, and a kinder soul would have done it; but in him was no generous spirit, no pity, no—"

1904

A Horse's Tale

PART I

1 SOLDIER BOY—PRIVATELY TO HIMSELF

I am Buffalo Bill's horse. I have spent my life under his saddle—with him in it, too, and he is good for two hundred pounds, without his clothes; and there is no telling how much he does weigh when he is out on the war-path and has his batteries belted on. He is over six feet, is young, hasn't an ounce of waste flesh, is straight, graceful, springy in his motions, quick as a cat, and has a handsome face, and black hair dangling down on his shoulders, and is beautiful to look at; and nobody is braver than he is, and nobody is stronger, except myself. Yes, a person that doubts that he is fine to see should see him in his beaded buckskins, on my back and his rifle peeping above his shoulder, chasing a hostile trail, with me going like the wind and his hair streaming out behind from the shelter of his broad slouch. Yes, he is a sight to look at then—and I'm part of it myself.

I am his favorite horse, out of dozens. Big as he is, I have carried him eighty-one miles between nightfall and sunrise on the scout; and I am good for fifty, day in and day out, and all the time. I am not large, but I am built on a business basis. I have carried him thousands and thousands of miles on scout duty for the army, and there's not a gorge, nor a pass, nor a valley, nor a fort, nor a trading post, nor a buffalo-range in the whole sweep of the Rocky Mountains and the Great Plains that we don't know as well as we know the bugle-calls. He is Chief of Scouts to the Army of the Frontier, and it makes us very important. In such a position as I hold in the military service one needs to be of good family and possess an education much above the common to be worthy of the place. I am the best-educated horse outside of the hippodrome, everybody says, and the best-mannered. It may be so, it is not for me to say; modesty is the best policy, I think. Buffalo Bill taught me the most of what I know, my mother taught me much, and I taught myself the rest. Lay a row of moccasins before me—Pawnee,

Sioux, Shoshone, Cheyenne, Blackfoot, and as many other tribes as you please—and I can name the tribe every moccasin belongs to by the make of it. Name it in horse-talk, and could do it in American if I had speech.

I know some of the Indian signs—the signs they make with their hands, and by signal-fires at night and columns of smoke by day. Buffalo Bill taught me how to drag wounded soldiers out of the line of fire with my teeth; and I've done it, too; at least I've dragged *him* out of the battle when he was wounded. And not just once, but twice. Yes, I know a lot of things. I remember forms, and gaits, and faces; and you can't disguise a person that's done me a kindness so that I won't know him thereafter wherever I find him. I know the art of searching for a trail, and I know the stale track from the fresh. I can keep a trail all by myself, with Buffalo Bill asleep in the saddle; ask him—he will tell you so. Many a time, when he has ridden all night, he has said to me at dawn, "Take the watch, Boy; if the trail freshens, call me." Then he goes to sleep. He knows he can trust me, because I have a reputation. A scout horse that has a reputation does not play with it.

My mother was all American—no alkali-spider about *her*, I can tell you; she was of the best blood of Kentucky, the bluest Blue-grass aristocracy, very proud and acrimonious—or maybe it is ceremonious. I don't know which it is. But it is no matter; size is the main thing about a word, and that one's up to standard. She spent her military life as colonel of the Tenth Dragoons, and saw a deal of rough service—distinguished service it was, too. I mean, she *carried* the Colonel; but it's all the same. Where would he be without his horse? He wouldn't arrive. It takes two to make a colonel of dragoons. She was a fine dragoon horse, but never got above that. She was strong enough for the scout service, and had the endurance, too, but she couldn't quite come up to the speed required; a scout horse has to have steel in his muscle and lightning in his blood.

My father was a bronco. Nothing as to lineage—that is, nothing as to recent lineage—but plenty good enough when you go a good way back. When Professor Marsh was out here hunting bones for the chapel of Yale University he found skeletons of horses no bigger than a fox, bedded in the rocks, and he said they were ancestors of my father. My mother heard him say it; and he said those skeletons were two million years old, which astonished her and made her Kentucky pretensions look small and pretty antiphonal, not to say oblique. Let me see. . . . I used to know the meaning of those words, but . . . well, it was years ago, and 'tisn't as vivid now as it was when they were fresh.

That sort of words doesn't keep, in the kind of climate we have out here. Professor Marsh said those skeletons were fossils. So that makes me part blue grass and part fossil; if there is any older or better stock, you will have to look for it among the Four Hundred, I reckon. I am satisfied with it. And am a happy horse, too, though born out of wedlock.

And now we are back at Fort Paxton once more, after a forty-day scout, away up as far as the Big Horn. Everything quiet. Crows and Blackfeet squabbling—as usual—but no outbreaks, and settlers feeling fairly easy.

The Seventh Cavalry still in garrison, here; also the Ninth Dragoons, two artillery companies, and some infantry. All glad to see me, including General Alison, commandant. The officers' ladies and children well, and called upon me—with sugar. Colonel Drake, Seventh Cavalry, said some pleasant things; Mrs. Drake was very complimentary; also Captain and Mrs. Marsh, Company B, Seventh Cavalry; also the Chaplain, who is always kind and pleasant to me, because I kicked the lungs out of a trader once. It was Tommy Drake and Fanny Marsh that furnished the sugar—nice children, the nicest at the post, I think.

That poor orphan child is on her way from France—everybody is full of the subject. Her father was General Alison's brother; married a beautiful young Spanish lady ten years ago, and has never been in America since. They lived in Spain a year or two, then went to France. Both died some months ago. This little girl that is coming is the only child. General Alison is glad to have her. He has never seen her. He is a very nice old bachelor, but is an old bachelor just the same and isn't more than about a year this side of retirement by age limit; and so what does he know about taking care of a little maid nine years old? If I could have her it would be another matter, for I know all about children, and they adore me. Buffalo Bill will tell you so himself.

I have some of this news from overhearing the garrison-gossip, the rest of it I got from Potter, the General's dog. Potter is the great Dane. He is privileged, all over the post, like Shekels, the Seventh Cavalry's dog, and visits everybody's quarters and picks up everything that is going, in the way of news. Potter has no imagination, and no great deal of culture, perhaps, but he has a historical mind and a good memory, and so he is the person I depend upon mainly to post me up when I get back from a scout. That is, if Shekels is out on depredation and I can't get hold of him.

2   LETTER FROM ROUEN—TO GENERAL ALISON

My dear Brother-in-law,—Please let me write again in Spanish, I cannot trust my English, and I am aware, from what your brother used to say, that army officers educated at the Military Academy of the United States are taught our tongue. It is as I told you in my other letter: both my poor sister and her husband, when they found they could not recover, expressed the wish that you should have their little Catherine—as knowing that you would presently be retired from the army—rather than that she should remain with me, who am broken in health, or go to your mother in California, whose health is also frail.

You do not know the child, therefore I must tell you something about her. You will not be ashamed of her looks, for she is a copy in little of her beautiful mother—and it is that Andalusian beauty which is not surpassable, even in your country. She has her mother's charm and grace and good heart and sense of justice, and she has her father's vivacity and cheerfulness and pluck and spirit of enterprise, with the affectionate disposition and sincerity of both parents.

My sister pined for her Spanish home all these years of exile; she was always talking of Spain to the child, and tending and nourishing the love of Spain in the little thing's heart as a precious flower; and she died happy in the knowledge that the fruitage of her patriotic labors was as rich as even she could desire.

Cathy is a sufficiently good little scholar, for her nine years; her mother taught her Spanish herself, and kept it always fresh upon her ear and her tongue by hardly ever speaking with her in any other tongue; her father was her English teacher, and talked with her in that language almost exclusively; French has been her everyday speech for more than seven years among her playmates here; she has a good working use of governess—German and Italian. It is true that there is always a faint foreign fragrance about her speech, no matter what language she is talking, but it is only just noticeable, nothing more, and is rather a charm than a mar, I think. In the ordinary child-studies Cathy is neither before nor behind the average child of nine, I should say. But I can say this for her: in love for her friends and in high-mindedness and good-heartedness she has not many equals, and in my opinion no superiors. And I beg of you, let her have her way with the dumb animals—they are her worship. It is an inheritance from her mother. She knows but little of cruelties and oppressions—keep them from her sight if you can. She would flare up at them and make trouble, in her small but quite decided and resolute way; for she has a character of her own, and lacks neither promptness nor initiative. Sometimes her judgment is at fault, but I think her intentions are always right. Once when she was a little creature of three or four years she suddenly brought her tiny foot down upon the floor in an apparent outbreak of indignation, then fetched it a backward wipe, and stooped down to examine the result. Her mother said:

"Why, what is it, child? What has stirred you so?"

"Mamma, the big ant was trying to kill the little one."

"And so you protected the little one."

"Yes, mamma, because he had no friend, and I wouldn't let the big one kill him."

"But you have killed them both."

Cathy was distressed, and her lip trembled. She picked up the remains and laid them upon her palm, and said:

"Poor little anty, I'm so sorry; and I didn't mean to kill you, but there wasn't any other way to save you, it was such a hurry."

She is a dear and sweet little lady, and when she goes it will give me a sore heart. But she will be happy with you, and if your heart is old and tired, give it into her keeping; she will make it young again, she will refresh it, she will make it sing. Be good to her, for all our sakes!

My exile will soon be over now. As soon as I am a little stronger I shall see my Spain again; and that will make *me* young again!

MERCEDES

3   GENERAL ALISON TO HIS MOTHER

I am glad to know that you are all well, in San Bernardino.

. . . That grandchild of yours has been here—well, I do not quite know how many days it is; nobody can keep account of days or anything else where she is! Mother, she did what the Indians were never able to do. She took the Fort—took it the first day! Took me, too; took the colonels, the captains, the women, the children, and the dumb brutes; took Buffalo Bill, and all his scouts; took the garrison—to the last man; and in forty-eight hours the Indian encampment was hers, illustrious old Thunder-Bird and all. Do I seem to have lost my solemnity, my gravity, my poise, my dignity? You would lose your own, in my circumstances. Mother, you never saw such a winning little devil. She is all energy, and spirit, and sunshine, and interest in everybody and everything, and pours out her prodigal love upon every creature that will take it, high or low, Christian or pagan, feathered or furred;

and none has declined it to date, and none ever will, I think. But she has a temper, and sometimes it catches fire and flames up, and is likely to burn whatever is near it; but it is soon over, the passion goes as quickly as it comes. Of course she has an Indian name already; Indians always rechristen a stranger early. Thunder-Bird attended to her case. He gave her the Indian equivalent for firebug, or firefly. He said:

"'Times, ver' quiet, ver' soft, like summer night, but when she mad she blaze."

Isn't it good? Can't you see the flare? She's beautiful, mother, beautiful as a picture; and there is a touch of you in her face, and of her father—poor George! and in her unresting activities, and her fearless ways, and her sunbursts and cloudbursts, she is always bringing George back to me. These impulsive natures are dramatic. George was dramatic, so is this Lightning-Bug, so is Buffalo Bill. When Cathy first arrived—it was in the forenoon—Buffalo Bill was away, carrying orders to Major Fuller, at Five Forks, up in the Clayton Hills. At mid-afternoon I was at my desk, trying to work, and this sprite had been making it impossible for half an hour. At last I said:

"Oh, you bewitching little scamp, *can't* you be quiet just a minute or two, and let your poor old uncle attend to a part of his duties?"

"I'll try, uncle; I will, indeed," she said.

"Well, then, that's a good child—kiss me. Now, then, sit up in that chair, and set your eye on that clock. There—that's right. If you stir—if you so much as wink—for four whole minutes, I'll bite you!"

It was very sweet and humble and obedient she looked, sitting there, still as a mouse; I could hardly keep from setting her free and telling her to make as much racket as she wanted to. During as much as two minutes there was a most unnatural and heavenly quiet and repose, then Buffalo Bill came thundering up to the door in all his scout finery, flung himself out of the saddle, said to his horse, "Wait for me, Boy," and stepped in, and stopped dead in his tracks—gazing at the child. She forgot orders, and was on the floor in a moment, saying:

"Oh, you are so beautiful! Do you like me?"

"No, I don't, I love you!" and he gathered her up with a hug, and then set her on his shoulder—apparently nine feet from the floor.

She was at home. She played with his long hair, and admired his big hands and his clothes and his carbine, and asked question after question, as fast as he could answer, until I excused them both for half an hour, in order to have a chance to finish my work. Then I heard Cathy exclaiming over Soldier Boy; and he was worthy of her raptures, for he is a wonder of a horse, and has a reputation which is as shining as his own silken hide.

4 CATHY TO HER AUNT MERCEDES

Oh, it is wonderful here, aunty dear, just paradise! Oh, if you could only see it! everything so wild and lovely; such grand plains, stretching such miles and miles and miles, all the most delicious velvety sand and sage-brush, and rabbits as big as a dog, and such tall and noble jackassful ears that that is what they name them by; and such vast mountains, and so rugged and craggy and lofty, with cloud-shawls wrapped around their shoulders, and looking so solemn and awful and satisfied; and the charming Indians, oh, how you would dote on them, aunty dear, and they would on you, too, and they would let you hold their babies, the way they do me, and they *are* the fattest, and brownest, and sweetest little things, and never cry, and wouldn't if they had pins sticking in them, which they haven't, because they are poor and can't afford it; and the horses and mules and cattle and dogs—hundreds and hundreds and hundreds, and not an animal that you can't do what you please with, except uncle Thomas, but *I* don't mind him, he's lovely; and oh, if you could hear the bugles: *too—too—too-too—too —too,* and so on—per-fectly beautiful! Do you recognize that one? It's the first toots of the *reveille;* it goes, dear me, *so* early in the morning! —then I and every other soldier on the whole place are up and out in a minute, except uncle Thomas, who is most unaccountably lazy, I don't know why, but I have talked to him about it, and I reckon it will be better, now. He hasn't any faults much, and is charming and sweet, like Buffalo Bill, and Thunder-Bird, and Mammy Dorcas, and Soldier Boy, and Shekels, and Potter, and Sour-Mash, and—well, they're *all* that, just angels, as you may say.

The very first day I came, I don't know how long ago it was, Buffalo Bill took me on Soldier Boy to Thunder-Bird's camp, not the big one which is out on the plain, which is White Cloud's, he took me to *that* one next day, but this one is four or five miles up in the hills and crags, where there is a great shut-in meadow, full of Indian lodges and dogs and squaws and everything that is interesting, and a brook of the clearest water running through it, with white pebbles on the bottom and trees all along the banks cool and shady and good to wade in, and as the sun goes down it is dimmish in there, but away up against the sky you see the big peaks towering up and shining bright and vivid in the sun, and sometimes an eagle sailing by them, not flapping a wing, the same as if he was asleep; and young Indians and girls romping and laughing and carrying on, around the spring and the pool, and not much clothes on except the girls, and dogs fighting, and the squaws busy at work, and the bucks busy resting, and the old men sitting in a bunch smoking, and passing the pipe not to the left but to the right, which means there's been a row in the camp and they are settling it if they can, and children playing *just* the same as any other children, and little boys shooting at a mark with bows, and I cuffed one of them because he hit a dog with a club that wasn't doing anything, and he resented it but before long he wished he hadn't: but this sentence is getting too long and I will start another. Thunder-Bird put on his Sunday-best war outfit to let me see him, and he was splendid to look at, with his face painted red and bright and intense like a fire-coal and a valance of eagle feathers from the top of his head all down his back, and he had his tomahawk, too, and his pipe, which has a stem which is longer than my arm, and I never had such a good time in an Indian camp in my life, and I learned a lot of words of the language, and next day BB took me to the camp out on the Plains, four miles, and I had another good time and got acquainted with some more Indians and dogs; and the big chief, by the name of White Cloud, gave me a pretty little bow and arrows and I gave him my red sash-ribbon, and in four days I could shoot very well with it and beat any white boy of my size at the post; and I have been to those camps plenty of times since; and I have learned to ride, too, BB taught me, and every day he practises me and praises me, and every time I do better than ever he lets me have a scamper on Soldier Boy, and *that's* the last agony of pleasure! for he is the charmingest horse, and so beautiful and shiny and black, and hasn't another color on him anywhere, except a white star in his forehead, not just an imitation star, but a real one, with four points, shaped exactly like a star that's handmade, and if you should cover him all up but his star you would know him anywhere, even in Jerusalem or Australia, by that. And I got acquainted with a good many of the Seventh Cavalry, and the dragoons, and officers, and families, and horses, in the first few days, and some more in the next few and the next few and the next few, and now I know more soldiers and horses than you can think, no matter how hard you try. I am keeping up my studies every now and then, but there isn't much time for it. I love you so! and I send you a hug and a kiss.   CATHY

P.S.—I belong to the Seventh Cavalry and Ninth Dragoons; I am an officer, too, and do not have to work on account of not getting any wages.

5   GENERAL ALISON TO MERCEDES

She has been with us a good nice long time, now. You are troubled
about your sprite because this is such a wild frontier, hundreds of miles
from civilization, and peopled only by wandering tribes of savages?
You fear for her safety? Give yourself no uneasiness about her. Dear
me, she's in a nursery! and she's got more than eighteen hundred
nurses. It would distress the garrison to suspect that you think they
can't take care of her. They think they can. They would tell you so
themselves. You see, the Seventh Cavalry has never had a child of its
very own before, and neither has the Ninth Dragoons; and so they are
like all new mothers, they think there is no other child like theirs, no
other child so wonderful, none that is so worthy to be faithfully and
tenderly looked after and protected. These bronzed veterans of mine
are very good mothers, I think, and wiser than some other mothers;
for they let her take lots of risks, and it is a good education for her;
and the more risks she takes and comes successfully out of, the prouder
they are of her. They adopted her, with grave and formal military ceremonies of their own invention—solemnities is the truer word; solemnities that were so profoundly solemn and earnest, that the spectacle
would have been comical if it hadn't been so touching. It was a good
show, and as stately and complex as guard-mount and the trooping of
the colors; and it had its own special music, composed for the occasion
by the bandmaster of the Seventh; and the child was as serious as the
most serious war-worn soldier of them all; and finally when they
throned her upon the shoulder of the oldest veteran, and pronounced
her "well and truly adopted," and the bands struck up and all saluted
and she saluted in return, it was better and more moving than any kindred thing I have seen on the stage, because stage things are make-
believe, but this was real and the players' hearts were in it.

It happened several weeks ago, and was followed by some additional
solemnities. The men created a couple of new ranks, thitherto unknown to the army regulations, and conferred them upon Cathy, with
ceremonies suitable to a duke. So now she is Corporal-General of the
Seventh Cavalry, and Flag-Lieutenant of the Ninth Dragoons, with the
privilege (decreed by the men) of writing U.S.A. after her name! Also,
they presented her a pair of shoulder-straps—both dark blue, the one
with F. L. on it, the other with C. G. Also, a sword. She wears them.
Finally, they granted her the *salute*. I am witness that that ceremony
is faithfully observed by both parties—and most gravely and decorously,

too. I have never seen a soldier smile yet, while delivering it, nor Cathy in returning it.

Ostensibly I was not present at these proceedings, and am ignorant of them; but I was where I could see. I was afraid of one thing—the jealousy of the other children of the post; but there is nothing of that, I am glad to say. On the contrary, they are proud of their comrade and her honors. It is a surprising thing, but it is true. The children are devoted to Cathy, for she has turned their dull frontier life into a sort of continuous festival; also they know her for a stanch and steady friend, a friend who can always be depended upon, and does not change with the weather.

She has become a rather extraordinary rider, under the tutorship of a more than extraordinary teacher—BB, which is her pet name for Buffalo Bill. She pronounces it *beeby*. He has not only taught her seventeen ways of breaking her neck, but twenty-two ways of avoiding it. He has infused into her the best and surest protection of a horseman —*confidence*. He did it gradually, systematically, little by little, a step at a time, and each step made sure before the next was essayed. And so he inched her along up through terrors that had been discounted by training before she reached them, and therefore were not recognizable as terrors when she got to them. Well, she is a daring little rider, now, and is perfect in what she knows of horsemanship. By and by she will know the art like a West Point cadet, and will exercise it as fearlessly. She doesn't know anything about sidesaddles. Does that distress you? And she is a fine performer, without any saddle at all. Does that discomfort you? Do not let it; she is not in any danger, I give you my word.

You said that if my heart was old and tired she would refresh it, and you said truly. I do not know how I got along without her, before. I was a forlorn old tree, but now that this blossoming vine has wound itself about me and become the life of my life, it is very different. As a furnisher of business for me and for Mammy Dorcas she is exhaustlessly competent, but I like my share of it and of course Dorcas likes hers, for Dorcas "raised" George, and Cathy is George over again in so many ways that she brings back Dorcas's youth and the joys of that long-vanished time. My father tried to set Dorcas free twenty years ago, when we still lived in Virginia, but without success; she considered herself a member of the family, and wouldn't go. And so, a member of the family she remained, and has held that position unchallenged ever since, and holds it now; for when my mother sent her here from San Bernardino when we learned that Cathy was coming, she only changed from one division of the family to the other. She has the warm heart of her race, and its lavish affections, and when Cathy arrived the pair were mother and child in five minutes, and that is what they are to date and will continue. Dorcas really thinks she raised George, and that is one of her prides, but perhaps it was a mutual raising, for their ages were the same—thirteen years short of mine. But they were playmates, at any rate; as regards that, there is no room for dispute.

Cathy thinks Dorcas is the best Catholic in America except herself. She could not pay any one a higher compliment than that, and Dorcas could not receive one that would please her better. Dorcas is satisfied that there has never been a more wonderful child than Cathy. She has conceived the curious idea that Cathy is *twins,* and that one of them is a boy-twin and failed to get segregated—got submerged, is the idea. To argue with her that this is nonsense is a waste of breath—her mind is made up, and arguments do not affect it. She says:

"Look at her; she loves dolls, and girl-plays, and everything a girl loves, and she's gentle and sweet, and ain't cruel to dumb brutes—now that's the girl-twin, but she loves boy-plays, and drums and fifes and soldiering, and rough-riding, and ain't afraid of anybody or anything— and that's the boy-twin; 'deed you needn't tell *me* she's only *one* child; no, sir, she's twins, and one of them got shet up out of sight. Out of sight, but that don't make any difference, that boy is in there, and you can see him look out of her eyes when her temper is up."

Then Dorcas went on, in her simple and earnest way, to furnish illustrations.

"Look at that raven, Marse Tom. Would anybody befriend a raven but that child? Of course they wouldn't; it ain't natural. Well, the Injun boy had the raven tied up, and was all the time plaguing it and starving it, and she pitied the po' thing, and tried to buy it from the boy, and the tears was in her eyes. That was the girl-twin, you see. She offered him her thimble, and he flung it down; she offered him all the doughnuts she had, which was two, and he flung them down; she offered him half a paper of pins, worth forty ravens, and he made a mouth at her and jabbed one of them in the raven's back. That was the limit, you know. It called for the other twin. Her eyes blazed up, and she jumped for him like a wild-cat, and when she was done with him she was rags and he wasn't anything but an allegory. That was most undoubtedly the other twin, you see, coming to the front. No, sir; don't tell *me* he ain't in there. I've seen him with my own eyes—and plenty of times, at that."

"Allegory? What is an allegory?"

"I don't know, Marse Tom, it's one of her words; she loves the big ones, you know, and I pick them up from her; they sound good and I can't help it."

"What happened after she had converted the boy into an allegory?"

"Why, she untied the raven and confiscated him by force and fetched him home, and left the doughnuts and things on the ground. Petted him, of course, like she does with every creature. In two days she had him so stuck after her that she—well, *you* know how he follows her everywhere, and sets on her shoulder often when she rides her break-neck rampages—all of which is the girl-twin to the front, you see—and he does what he pleases, and is up to all kinds of devilment, and is a perfect nuisance in the kitchen. Well, they all stand it, but they wouldn't if it was another person's bird."

Here she began to chuckle comfortably, and presently she said:

"Well, you know, she's a nuisance herself, Miss Cathy is, she *is* so busy, and into everything, like that bird. It's all just as innocent, you know, and she don't mean any harm, and is so good and dear; and it ain't her fault, it's her nature; her interest is always a-working and always red-hot, and she *can't* keep quiet. Well, yesterday it was 'Please, Miss Cathy, don't do that'; and, 'Please, Miss Cathy, let that alone'; and, 'Please, Miss Cathy, don't make so much noise'; and so on and so on, till I reckon I had found fault fourteen times in fifteen minutes; then she looked up at me with her big brown eyes that can plead so, and said in that odd little foreign way that goes to your heart:

"'Please, mammy, make me a compliment.'"

"And of course you did it, you old fool?"

"Marse Tom, I just grabbed her up to my breast and says, 'Oh, you po' dear little motherless thing, you ain't got a fault in the world, and you can do anything you want to, and tear the house down, and yo' old black mammy won't say a word!'"

"Why, of course, of course—*I* knew you'd spoil the child."

She brushed away her tears, and said with dignity:

"Spoil the child? spoil *that* child, Marse Tom? There can't *anybody* spoil her. She's the king bee of this post, and everybody pets her and is her slave, and yet, as you know, your own self, she ain't the least little bit spoiled." Then she eased her mind with this retort: "Marse Tom, she makes you do anything she wants to, and you can't deny it; so if she could be spoilt, she'd been spoilt long ago, because you are the very *worst!* Look at that pile of cats in your chair, and you sitting on a candle-box, just as patient; it's because they're her cats."

If Dorcas were a soldier, I could punish her for such large frankness as that. I changed the subject, and made her resume her illustrations. She had scored against me fairly, and I wasn't going to cheapen her victory by disputing it. She proceeded to offer this incident in evidence on her twin theory:

"Two weeks ago when she got her finger mashed open, she turned pretty pale with the pain, but she never said a word. I took her in my lap, and the surgeon sponged off the blood and took a needle and thread and began to sew it up; it had to have a lot of stitches, and each one made her scrunch a little, but she never let go a sound. At last the surgeon was so full of admiration that he said, 'Well, you *are* a brave little thing!' and she said, just as ca'm and simple as if she was talking about the weather, 'There isn't anybody braver but the Cid!' You see? it was the boy-twin that the surgeon was a-dealing with."

"Who is the Cid?"

"I don't know, sir—at least only what she says. She's always talking about him, and says he was the bravest hero Spain ever had, or any other country. They have it up and down, the children do, she standing up for the Cid, and they working George Washington for all he is worth."

"Do they quarrel?"

"No; it's only disputing, and bragging, the way children do. They want her to be an American, but she can't be anything but a Spaniard, she says. You see, her mother was always longing for home, po' thing! and thinking about it, and so the child is just as much a Spaniard as if she'd always lived there. She thinks she remembers how Spain looked, but I reckon she don't, because she was only a baby when they moved to France. She is very proud to be a Spaniard."

Does that please you, Mercedes? Very well, be content; your niece is loyal to her allegiance: her mother laid deep the foundations of her love for Spain, and she will go back to you as good a Spaniard as you are yourself. She had made me promise to take her to you for a long visit when the War Office retires me.

I attend to her studies myself; has she told you that? Yes, I am her school-master, and she makes pretty good progress, I think, everything considered. Everything considered—being translated—means holidays. But the fact is, she was not born for study, and it comes hard. Hard for me, too; it hurts me like a physical pain to see that free spirit of the air and the sunshine laboring and grieving over a book; and sometimes when I find her gazing far away towards the plains and the blue mountains with the longing in her eyes, I have to throw open the prison

doors; I can't help it. A quaint little scholar she is, and makes plenty
of blunders. Once I put the question:

"What does the Czar govern?"

She rested her elbow on her knee and her chin on her hand and
took that problem under deep consideration. Presently she looked up
and answered, with a rising inflection implying a shade of uncertainty,

"The dative case?"

Here are a couple of her expositions which were delivered with tranquil confidence:

"*Chaplain,* diminutive of chap. *Lass* is masculine, *lassie* is feminine."

She is not a genius, you see, but just a normal child; they all make
mistakes of that sort. There is a glad light in her eye which is pretty
to see when she finds herself able to answer a question promptly and
accurately, without any hesitation; as, for instance, this morning:

"Cathy dear, what is a cube?"

"Why, a native of Cuba."

She still drops a foreign word into her talk now and then, and there
is still a subtle foreign flavor or fragrance about even her exactest English—and long may this abide! for it has for me a charm that is very
pleasant. Sometimes her English is daintily prim and bookish and cap-
tivating. She has a child's sweet tooth, but for her health's sake I try to
keep its inspirations under check. She is obedient—as is proper for a
titled and recognized military personage, which she is—but the chain
presses sometimes. For instance, we were out for a walk, and passed
by some bushes that were freighted with wild gooseberries. Her face
brightened and she put her hands together and delivered herself of
this speech, most feelingly:

"Oh, if I was permitted a vice it would be the *gourmandise!*"

Could I resist that? No. I gave her a gooseberry.

You ask about her languages. They take care of themselves; they will
not get rusty here; our regiments are not made up of natives alone—
far from it. And she is picking up Indian tongues diligently.

6 SOLDIER BOY AND THE MEXICAN PLUG

"When did you come?"

"Arrived at sundown."

"Where from?"

"Salt Lake."

"Are you in the service?"

"No. Trade."

"Pirate trade, I reckon."

"What do you know about it?"

"I saw you when you came. I recognized your master. He is a bad sort. Trap-robber, horse-thief, squaw-man, renegado—Hank Butters—I know him very well. Stole you, didn't he?"

"Well, it amounted to that."

"I thought so. Where is his pard?"

"He stopped at White Cloud's camp."

"He is another of the same stripe, is Blake Haskins." (*Aside.*) They are laying for Buffalo Bill again, I guess. (*Aloud.*) "What is your name?"

"Which one?"

"Have you got more than one?"

"I get a new one every time I'm stolen. I used to have an honest name, but that was early; I've forgotten it. Since then I've had thirteen *aliases*."

"Aliases? What is alias?"

"A false name."

"Alias. It's a fine large word, and is in my line; it has quite a learned and cerebrospinal incandescent sound. Are you educated?"

"Well, no, I can't claim it. I can take down bars, I can distinguish oats from shoe-pegs, I can blaspheme a saddle-boil with the college-bred, and I know a few other things—not many; I have had no chance, I have always had to work; besides, I am of low birth and no family. You speak my dialect like a native, but you are not a Mexican Plug, you are a gentleman, I can see that; and educated, of course."

"Yes, I am of old family, and not illiterate. I am a fossil."

"A which?"

"Fossil. The first horses were fossils. They date back two million years."

"Gr-eat sand and sage-brush! do you mean it?"

"Yes, it is true. The bones of my ancestors are held in reverence and worship, even by men. They do not leave them exposed to the weather when they find them, but carry them three thousand miles and enshrine them in their temples of learning, and worship them."

"It is wonderful! I knew you must be a person of distinction, by your fine presence and courtly address, and by the fact that you are not subjected to the indignity of hobbles, like myself and the rest. Would you tell me your name?"

"You have probably heard of it—Soldier Boy."

"What!—the renowned, the illustrious?"

"Even so."

"It takes my breath! Little did I dream that ever I should stand face to face with the possessor of that great name. Buffalo Bill's horse! Known from the Canadian border to the deserts of Arizona, and from the eastern marches of the Great Plains to the foot-hills of the Sierra! Truly this is a memorable day. You still serve the celebrated Chief of Scouts?"

"I am still his property, but he has lent me, for a time, to the most noble, the most gracious, the most excellent, her Excellency Catherine, Corporal-General Seventh Cavalry and Flag-Lieutenant Ninth Dragoons, U.S.A.,—on whom be peace!"

"Amen. Did you say *her* Excellency?"

"The same. A Spanish lady, sweet blossom of a ducal house. And truly a wonder; knowing everything, capable of everything; speaking all the languages, master of all sciences, a mind without horizons, a heart of gold, the glory of her race! On whom be peace!"

"Amen. It is marvelous!"

"Verily. I knew many things, she has taught me others. I am educated. I will tell you about her."

"I listen—I am enchanted."

"I will tell a plain tale, calmly, without excitement, without eloquence. When she had been here four or five weeks she was already erudite in military things, and they made her an officer—a double officer. She rode the drill every day, like any soldier; and she could take the bugle and direct the evolutions herself. Then, on a day, there was a grand race, for prizes—none to enter but the children. Seventeen children entered, and she was the youngest. Three girls, fourteen boys —good riders all. It was a steeplechase, with four hurdles, all pretty high. The first prize was a most cunning half-grown silver bugle, and mighty pretty, with red silk cord and tassels. Buffalo Bill was very anxious; for he had taught her to ride, and he did most dearly want her to win that race, for the glory of it. So he wanted her to ride me, but she wouldn't; and she reproached him, and said it was unfair and unright, and taking advantage; for what horse in this post or any other could stand a chance against me? and she was very severe with him, and said, 'You ought to be ashamed—you are proposing to me conduct unbecoming an officer and a gentleman.' So he just tossed her up in the air about thirty feet and caught her as she came down, and said he *was* ashamed; and put up his handkerchief and pretended to cry, which nearly broke her heart, and she petted him, and begged him to forgive her, and said she would do anything in the world he could ask but that; but he said he ought to go hang himself, and he *must,* if he could get a rope; it was nothing but right he should, for he never, never could forgive himself; and then *she* began to cry, and they both sobbed, the way you could hear him a mile, and she clinging around his neck and pleading, till at last he was comforted a little, and gave his solemn promise he wouldn't hang himself till after the race; and wouldn't do it at all if she won it, which made her happy, and she said she would win it or die in the saddle; so then everything was pleasant again and both of them content. He can't help playing jokes on her, he is so fond of her and she is so innocent and unsuspecting; and when she finds it out she cuffs him and is in a fury, but presently forgives him because it's *him;* and maybe the very next day she's caught with another joke; you see she can't learn any better, because she hasn't any deceit in her, and that kind aren't ever expecting it in another person.

"It was a grand race. The whole post was there, and there was such another whooping and shouting when the seventeen kids came flying down the turf and sailing over the hurdles—oh, beautiful to see! Half-way down, it was kind of neck and neck, and anybody's race and no-body's. Then, what should happen but a cow steps out and puts her head down to munch grass, with her broadside to the battalion, and they a-coming like the wind; they split apart to flank her, but *she?*— why, she drove the spurs home and soared over that cow like a bird! and on she went, and cleared the last hurdle solitary and alone, the army letting loose the grand yell, and she skipped from the horse the same as if he had been standing still, and made her bow, and every-body crowded around to congratulate, and they gave her the bugle, and she put it to her lips and blew 'boots and saddles' to see how it would go, and BB was as proud as you can't think! And he said, 'Take Soldier Boy, and don't pass him back till I ask for him!' and I can tell you he wouldn't have said that to any other person on this planet. That was two months and more ago, and nobody has been on my back since but the Corporal-General Seventh Cavalry and Flag-Lieutenant of the Ninth Dragoons, U.S.A.,—on whom be peace!"

"Amen. I listen—tell me more."

"She set to work and organized the Sixteen, and called it the First Battalion Rocky Mountain Rangers, U.S.A., and she wanted to be bu-gler, but they elected her Lieutenant-General *and* Bugler. So she ranks her uncle the commandant, who is only a Brigadier. And doesn't she train those little people! Ask the Indians, ask the traders, ask the sol-diers; they'll tell you. She has been at it from the first day. Every morning they go clattering down into the plain, and there she sits on my back with her bugle at her mouth and sounds the orders and puts them through the evolutions for an hour or more; and it is too beautiful for anything to see those ponies dissolve from one formation into another, and waltz about, and break, and scatter, and form again, always moving, always graceful, now trotting, now galloping, and so on, sometimes near by, sometimes in the distance, all just like a state ball, you know, and sometimes she can't hold herself any longer, but sounds the 'charge,' and turns me loose! and you can take my word for it, if the battalion hasn't *too* much of a start we catch up and go over the breastworks with the front line.

"Yes, they are soldiers, those little people; and healthy, too, not ailing any more, the way they used to be sometimes. It's because of her drill. She's got a fort, now—Fort Fanny Marsh. Major-General Tommy Drake planned it out, and the Seventh and Dragoons built it. Tommy is the Colonel's son, and is fifteen and the oldest in the Battalion; Fanny Marsh is Brigadier-General, and is next oldest—over thirteen. She is daughter of Captain Marsh, Company B, Seventh Cavalry. Lieutenant-General Alison is the youngest by considerable; I think she is about nine and a half or three-quarters. Her military rig, as Lieutenant-General, isn't for business, it's for dress parade, because the ladies made it. They say they got it out of the Middle Ages—out of a book—and it is all red and blue and white silks and satins and velvets; tights, trunks, sword, doublet with slashed sleeves, short cape, cap with just one feather in it; I've heard them name these things; they got them out of the book; she's dressed like a page, of old times, they say. It's the daintiest outfit that ever was—you will say so, when you see it. She's lovely in it—oh, just a dream! In some ways she is just her age, but in others she's as old as her uncle, I think. She is very learned. She teaches her uncle his book. I have seen her sitting by with the book and reciting to him what is in it, so that he can learn to do it himself.

"Every Saturday she hires little Injuns to garrison her fort; then she lays siege to it, and makes military approaches by make-believe trenches in make-believe night, and finally at make-believe dawn she draws her sword and sounds the assault and takes it by storm. It is for practice. And she has invented a bugle-call all by herself, out of her own head, and it's a stirring one, and the prettiest in the service. It's to call *me* —it's never used for anything else. She taught it to me, and told me what it says: 'It is I, Soldier—come!' and when those thrilling notes come floating down the distance I hear them without fail, even if I am two miles away; and then—oh, then you should see my heels get down to business!

"And she has taught me how to say good-morning and good-night to her, which is by lifting my right hoof for her to shake; and also how to say good-by; I do that with my left foot—but only for practice, because there hasn't been any but make-believe good-bying yet, and I hope there won't ever be. It would make me cry if I ever had to put up my left foot in earnest. She has taught me how to salute, and I can do it as well as a soldier. I bow my head low, and lay my right hoof against my cheek. She taught me that because I got into disgrace once, through ignorance. I am privileged, because I am known to be honorable and trustworthy, and because I have a distinguished record in the service; so they don't hobble me nor tie me to stakes or shut me tight in stables, but let me wander around to suit myself. Well, trooping the colors is a very solemn ceremony, and everybody must stand uncovered when the flag goes by, the commandant and all; and once I was there, and ignorantly walked across right in front of the band, which was an awful disgrace. Ah, the Lieutenant-General was so ashamed, and so distressed that I should have done such a thing before all the world, that she couldn't keep the tears back; and then she taught me the salute, so that if I ever did any other unmilitary act through ignorance I could do my salute and she believed everybody would think it was apology enough and would not press the matter. It is very nice and distinguished; no other horse can do it; often the men salute me, and I return it. I am privileged to be present when the Rocky Mountain Rangers troop the colors and I stand solemn, like the children, and I salute when the flag goes by. Of course when she goes to her fort her sentries sing out 'Turn out the guard!' and then . . . do you catch that refreshing early-morning whiff from the mountain-pines and the wild flowers? The night is far spent; we'll hear the bugles before long. Dorcas, the black woman, is very good and nice; she takes care of the Lieutenant-General, and is Brigadier-General Alison's mother, which makes her mother-in-law to the Lieutenant-General. That is what Shekels says. At least it is what I think he says, though I never can understand him quite clearly. He—"

"Who is Shekels?"

"The Seventh Cavalry dog. I mean, if he *is* a dog. His father was a coyote and his mother was a wild-cat. It doesn't really make a dog out of him, does it?"

"Not a real dog, I should think. Only a kind of a general dog, at most, I reckon. Though this is a matter of ichthyology, I suppose; and if it is, it is out of my depth, and so my opinion is not valuable, and I don't claim much consideration for it."

"It isn't ichthyology; it is dogmatics, which is still more difficult and tangled up. Dogmatics always are."

"Dogmatics is quite beyond me, quite; so I am not competing. But on general principles it is my opinion that a colt out of a coyote and a wild-cat is no square dog, but doubtful. That is my hand, and I stand pat."

"Well, it is as far as I can go myself, and be fair and conscientious. I have always regarded him as a doubtful dog, and so has Potter. Potter is the great Dane. Potter says he is no dog, and not even poultry—though I do not go quite so far as that."

"And I wouldn't, myself. Poultry is one of those things which no person can get to the bottom of, there is so much of it and such variety. It is just wings, and wings, and wings, till you are weary: turkeys, and geese, and bats, and butterflies, and angels, and grasshoppers, and flying-fish, and—well, there is really no end to the tribe; it gives me the heaves just to think of it. But this one hasn't any wings, has he?"

"No."

"Well, then, in my belief he is more likely to be dog than poultry. I have not heard of poultry that hadn't wings. Wings is the *sign* of poultry; it is what you tell poultry by. Look at the mosquito."

"What do you reckon he is, then? He must be something."

"Why, he could be a reptile; anything that hasn't wings is a reptile."

"Who told you that?"

"Nobody told me, but I overheard it."

"Where did you overhear it?"

"Years ago. I was with the Philadelphia Institute expedition in the Bad Lands under Professor Cope, hunting mastodon bones, and I overheard him say, his own self, that any plantigrade circumflex vertebrate bacterium that hadn't wings and was uncertain was a reptile. Well, then, has this dog any wings? No. Is he a plantigrade circumflex vertebrate bacterium? Maybe so, maybe not; but without ever having seen him, and judging only by his illegal and spectacular parentage, I will bet the odds of a bale of hay to a bran mash that he looks it. Finally, is he uncertain? That is the point—is he uncertain? I will leave it to you if you have ever heard of a more uncertainer dog than what this one is?"

"No, I never have."

"Well, then, he's a reptile. That's settled."

"Why, look here, whatsyourname—"

"Last alias, 'Mongrel.'"

"A good one, too. I was going to say, you are better educated than you have been pretending to be. I like cultured society, and I shall cultivate your acquaintance. Now as to Shekels, whenever you want to know about any private thing that is going on at this post or in White Cloud's camp or Thunder-Bird's, he can tell you; and if you make friends with him he'll be glad to, for he is a born gossip, and picks up all the tittle-tattle. Being the whole Seventh Cavalry's reptile, he doesn't belong to anybody in particular, and hasn't any military duties; so he comes and goes as he pleases, and is popular with all the house cats and other authentic sources of private information. He understands all the languages, and talks them all, too. With an accent like gritting your teeth, it is true, and with a grammar that is no improvement on blasphemy—still, with practice you get at the meat of what he says, and it serves. . . . Hark! That's the reveille. . . .

THE REVEILLE*

"Faint and far, but isn't it clear, isn't it sweet? There's no music like the bugle to stir the blood, in the still solemnity of the morning twilight, with the dim plain stretching away to nothing and the spectral mountains slumbering against the sky. You'll hear another note in a minute— faint and far and clear, like the other one, and sweeter still, you'll notice. Wait . . . listen. There it goes! It says, '*It is I, Soldier—come!*' . . .

SOLDIER BOY'S BUGLE CALL

. . . Now then, watch me leave a blue streak behind!"

*At West Point the bugle is supposed to be saying:
"I can't get 'em up,
I can't get 'em up,
I can't get 'em up in the morning!"

7   SOLDIER BOY AND SHEKELS

"Did you do as I told you? Did you look up the Mexican Plug?"

"Yes, I made his acquaintance before night and got his friendship."

"I liked him. Did you?"

"Not at first. He took me for a reptile, and it troubled me, because I didn't know whether it was a compliment or not. I couldn't ask him, because it would look ignorant. So I didn't say anything, and soon I liked him very well indeed. Was it a compliment, do you think?"

"Yes, that is what it was. They are very rare, the reptiles; very few left, now-a-days."

"Is that so? What is a reptile?"

"It is a plantigrade circumflex vertebrate bacterium that hasn't any wings and is uncertain."

"Well, it—it sounds fine, it surely does."

"And it *is* fine. You may be thankful you are one."

"I am. It seems wonderfully grand and elegant for a person that is so humble as I am; but I am thankful, I am indeed, and will try to live up to it. It is hard to remember. Will you say it again, please, and say it slow?"

"Plantigrade circumflex vertebrate bacterium that hasn't any wings and is uncertain."

"It *is* beautiful, anybody must grant it; beautiful, and of a noble sound. I hope it will not make me proud and stuck-up—I should not like to be that. It is much more distinguished and honorable to be a reptile than a dog, don't you think, Soldier?"

"Why, there's no comparison. It is awfully aristocratic. Often a duke is called a reptile; it is set down so, in history."

"Isn't that grand! Potter wouldn't ever associate with me, but I reckon he'll be glad to when he finds out what I am."

"You can depend upon it."

"I will thank Mongrel for this. He is a very good sort, for a Mexican Plug. Don't you think he is?"

"It is my opinion of him; and as for his birth, he cannot help that. We cannot all be reptiles, we cannot all be fossils; we have to take what comes and be thankful it is no worse. It is the true philosophy."

"For those others?"

"Stick to the subject, please. Did it turn out that my suspicions were right?"

"Yes, perfectly right. Mongrel has heard them planning. They are after BB's life, for running them out of Medicine Bow and taking their stolen horses away from them."

"Well, they'll get him yet, for sure."

"Not if he keeps a sharp lookout."

"*He* keep a sharp lookout! He never does; he despises them, and all their kind. His life is always being threatened, and so it has come to be monotonous."

"Does he know they are here?"

"Oh yes, he knows it. He is always the earliest to know who comes and who goes. But he cares nothing for them and their threats; he only laughs when people warn him. They'll shoot him from behind a tree the first he knows. Did Mongrel tell you their plans?"

"Yes. They have found out that he starts for Fort Clayton day after to-morrow, with one of his scouts; so they will leave to-morrow, letting on to go south, but they will fetch around north all in good time."

"Shekels, I don't like the look of it."

8 THE SCOUT-START. BB AND LIEUTENANT-GENERAL ALISON

BB (*saluting.*): "Good! handsomely done! The Seventh couldn't beat it! You do certainly handle your Rangers like an expert, General. And where are you bound?"

"Four miles on the trail to Fort Clayton."

"Glad am I, dear! What's the idea of it?"

"Guard of honor for you and Thorndike."

"Bless—your—*heart!* I'd rather have it from you than from the Commander-in-Chief of the armies of the United States, you incomparable little soldier!—and I don't need to take any oath to that, for you believe it."

"I *thought* you'd like it, BB."

"*Like* it? Well, I should say so! Now then—all ready—sound the advance, and away we go!"

9 SOLDIER BOY AND SHEKELS AGAIN

Well, this is the way it happened. We did the escort duty; then we came back and struck for the plain and put the Rangers through a rousing drill—oh, for hours! Then we sent them home under Brigadier-General Fanny Marsh; then the Lieutenant-General and I went off on a gallop over the plains for about three hours, and were lazying along home in the middle of the afternoon, when we met Jimmy Slade, the drummer-boy, and he saluted and asked the Lieutenant-General if she had heard the news, and she said no, and he said:

"'Buffalo Bill has been ambushed and badly shot this side of Clayton, and Thorndike the scout, too; Bill couldn't travel, but Thorndike could, and he brought the news, and Sergeant Wilkes and six men of Company B are gone, two hours ago, hotfoot, to get Bill. And they say—'

"'*Go!*' she shouted to me—and I went."

"Fast?"

"Don't ask foolish questions. It was an awful pace. For four hours nothing happened, and not a word said, except that now and then she said, 'Keep it up, Boy, keep it up, sweetheart; we'll save him!' I kept it up. Well, when the dark shut down, in the rugged hills, that poor little chap had been tearing around in the saddle all day, and I noticed by the slack knee-pressure that she was tired and tottery, and I got dreadfully afraid; but every time I tried to slow down and let her go to sleep, so I could stop, she hurried me up again; and so, sure enough, at last over she went!

"Ah, that was a fix to be in! for she lay there and didn't stir, and what was I to do? I couldn't leave her to fetch help, on account of the wolves. There was nothing to do but stand by. It was dreadful. I was afraid she was killed, poor little thing! But she wasn't. She came to, by and by, and said, 'Kiss me, Soldier,' and those were blessed words. I kissed her—often; I am used to that, and we like it. But she didn't get up, and I was worried. She fondled my nose with her hand, and talked to me, and called me endearing names—which is her way—but she caressed with the same hand all the time. The other arm was broken, you see, but I didn't know it, and she didn't mention it. She didn't want to distress me, you know.

"Soon the big gray wolves came, and hung around, and you could hear them snarl, and snap at each other, but you couldn't see anything of them except their eyes, which shone in the dark like sparks and stars. The Lieutenant-General said, 'If I had the Rocky Mountain Rangers here, we would make those creatures climb a tree.' Then she made believe that the Rangers were in hearing, and put up her bugle and blew the 'assembly'; and then, 'boots and saddles'; then the 'trot'; 'gallop'; '*charge!*' Then she blew the 'retreat,' and said, 'That's for you, you rebels; the Rangers don't ever retreat!'

"The music frightened them away, but they were hungry, and kept coming back. And of course they got bolder and bolder, which is their way. It went on for an hour, then the tired child went to sleep, and it was pitiful to hear her moan and nestle, and I couldn't do anything for her. All the time I was laying for the wolves. They are in my line; I have had experience. At last the boldest one ventured within my lines, and I landed him among his friends with some of his skull still on him, and they did the rest. In the next hour I got a couple more, and they went the way of the first one, down the throats of the detachment. That satisfied the survivors, and they went away and left us in peace.

"We hadn't any more adventures, though I kept awake all night and was ready. From midnight on the child got very restless, and out of her head, and moaned, and said, 'Water, water—thirsty'; and now and then, 'Kiss me, Soldier'; and sometimes she was in her fort and giving orders to her garrison; and once she was in Spain, and thought her mother was with her. People say a horse can't cry; but they don't know, because we cry inside.

"It was an hour after sunup that I heard the boys coming, and recognized the hoof-beats of Pomp and Cæsar and Jerry, old mates of mine; and a welcomer sound there couldn't ever be.

"Buffalo Bill was in a horse-litter, with his leg broken by a bullet, and Mongrel and Blake Haskins's horse were doing the work. Buffalo Bill and Thorndike had killed both of those toughs.

"When they got to us, and Buffalo Bill saw the child lying there so white, he said, 'My God!' and the sound of his voice brought her to herself, and she gave a little cry of pleasure and struggled to get up, but couldn't, and the soldiers gathered her up like the tenderest women, and their eyes were wet and they were not ashamed, when they saw her arm dangling; and so were Buffalo Bill's, and when they laid her in his arms he said, 'My darling, how does this come?' and she said, 'We came to save you, but I was tired, and couldn't keep awake, and fell off and hurt myself, and couldn't get on again.' 'You came to save me, you dear little rat? It was too lovely of you!' 'Yes, and Soldier stood by me, which you know he would, and protected me from the wolves; and if he got a chance he kicked the life out of some of them—for you know he would, BB.' The sergeant said, 'He laid out three of them, sir, and here's the bones to show for it.' 'He's a grand horse,' said BB; 'he's the grandest horse that ever was! and has saved your life, Lieutenant-General Alison, and shall protect it the rest of his life—he's yours for a kiss!' He got it, along with a passion of delight, and he said, 'You are feeling better now, little Spaniard—do you think you could blow the advance?' She put up the bugle to do it, but he said wait a minute first. Then he and the sergeant set her arm and put it in splints, she wincing but not whimpering; then we took up the march for home, and that's the end of the tale; and I'm her horse. Isn't she a brick, Shekels?"

"Brick? She's more than a brick, more than a thousand bricks—she's a reptile!"

"It's a compliment out of your heart, Shekels. God bless you for it!"

10   GENERAL ALISON AND DORCAS

"Too much company for her, Marse Tom. Betwixt you, and Shekels, and the Colonel's wife, and the Cid—"

"The Cid? Oh, I remember—the raven."

"—and Mrs. Captain Marsh and Famine and Pestilence the baby *coyotes,* and Sour-Mash and her pups, and Sardanapalus and her kittens— hang these names she gives the creatures, they warp my jaw—and Potter: you—all sitting around *in* the house, and Soldier Boy at the window the entire time, it's a wonder to me she comes along as well as she does. She—"

"You want her all to yourself, you stingy old thing!"

"Marse Tom, you know better. It's too much company. And then the idea of her receiving reports all the time from her officers, and acting upon them, and giving orders, the same as if she was well! It ain't good for her, and the surgeon don't like it, and tried to persuade her not to and couldn't; and when he *ordered* her, she was that outraged and indignant, and was very severe on him, and accused him of insubordination, and said it didn't become him to give orders to an officer of her rank. Well, he saw he had excited her more and done more harm than all the rest put together, so he was vexed at himself and wished he had kept still. Doctors *don't* know much, and that's a fact. She's too much interested in things—she ought to rest more. She's all the time sending messages to BB, and to soldiers and Injuns and whatnot, and to the animals."

"To the animals?"

"Yes, sir."

"Who carries them?"

"Sometimes Potter, but mostly it's Shekels."

"Now come! who can find fault with such pretty make-believe as that?"

"But it ain't make-believe, Marse Tom. She does send them."

"Yes, I don't doubt that part of it."

"Do you doubt they get them, sir?"

"Certainly. Don't you?"

"No, sir. Animals talk to one another. I know it perfectly well, Marse Tom, and I ain't saying it by guess."

"What a curious superstition!"

"It ain't a superstition, Marse Tom. Look at that Shekels—look at him, *now*. Is he listening, or ain't he? *Now* you see! he's turned his head away. It's because he was caught—caught in the act. I'll ask you— could a Christian look any more ashamed than what he looks now?— *lay down!* You see? he was going to sneak out. Don't tell *me*, Marse Tom! If animals don't talk, I miss *my* guess. And Shekels is the worst. He goes and tells the animals everything that happens in the officers' quarters; and if he's short of facts, he invents them. He hasn't any more principle than a blue jay; and as for morals, he's empty. Look at him now; look at him grovel. He knows what I am saying, and he knows it's the truth. You see, yourself, that he can feel shame; it's the only virtue he's got. It's wonderful how they find out everything that's going on—the animals. They—"

"Do you really believe they do, Dorcas?"

"I don't only just believe it, Marse Tom, I know it. Day before yesterday they knew something was going to happen. They were that excited, and whispering around together; why, anybody could see that they— But my! I must get back to her, and I haven't got to my errand yet."

"What is it, Dorcas?"

"Well, it's two or three things. One is, the doctor don't salute when he comes . . . Now, Marse Tom, it ain't anything to laugh at, and so—"

"Well, then, forgive me; I didn't mean to laugh—I got caught unprepared."

"You see, she don't want to hurt the doctor's feelings, so she don't say anything to him about it; but she is always polite, herself, and it hurts that kind for people to be rude to them."

"I'll have that doctor hanged."

"Marse Tom, she don't *want* him hanged. She—"

"Well, then, I'll have him boiled in oil."

"But she don't *want* him boiled. I—"

"Oh, very well, very well, I only want to please her; I'll have him skinned."

"Why, *she* don't want him skinned; it would break her heart. Now—"

"Woman, this is perfectly unreasonable. What in the nation *does* she want?"

"Marse Tom, if you would only be a little patient, and not fly off the handle at the least little thing. Why, she only wants you to speak to him."

"Speak to him! Well, upon my word! All this unseemly rage and row about such a—a— Dorcas, I never saw you carry on like this before. You have alarmed the sentry; he thinks I am being assassinated; he thinks there's a mutiny, a revolt, an insurrection; he—"

"Marse Tom, you are just putting on; you know it perfectly well; I don't know what makes you act like that—but you always did, even when you was little, and you can't get over it, I reckon. Are you over it now, Marse Tom?"

"Oh, well, yes; but it would try anybody to be doing the best he could, offering every kindness he could think of, only to have it rejected with contumely and . . . Oh, well, let it go; it's no matter—I'll talk to the doctor. Is that satisfactory, or are you going to break out again?"

"Yes, sir, it is; and it's only right to talk to him, too, because it's just as she says; she's trying to keep up discipline in the Rangers, and this insubordination of his is a bad example for them—now ain't it so, Marse Tom?"

"Well, there *is* reason in it, I can't deny it; so I will speak to him, though at bottom I think hanging would be more lasting. What is the rest of your errand, Dorcas?"

"Of course her room is Ranger headquarters now, Marse Tom, while she's sick. Well, soldiers of the cavalry and the dragoons that are off duty come and get her sentries to let them relieve them and serve in their place. It's only out of affection, sir, and because they know military honors please her, and please the children too, for her sake; and they don't bring their muskets; and so—"

"I've noticed them there, but didn't twig the idea. They are standing guard, are they?"

"Yes, sir, and she is afraid you will reprove them and hurt their feelings, if you see them there; so she begs, if—if you don't mind coming in the back way—"

"Bear me up, Dorcas; don't let me faint."

"There—sit up and behave, Marse Tom. You are not going to faint; you are only pretending—you used to act just so when you was little; it does seem a long time for you to get grown up."

"Dorcas, the way the child is progressing, I shall be out of my job before long—she'll have the whole post in her hands. I must make a stand, I must not go down without a struggle. These encroachments. . . . Dorcas, what do you think she will think of next?"

"Marse Tom, she don't mean any harm."

"Are you sure of it?"

"Yes, Marse Tom."

"You feel sure she has no ulterior designs?"

"I don't know what that is, Marse Tom, but I know she hasn't."

"Very well, then, for the present I am satisfied. What else have you come about?"

"I reckon I better tell you the whole thing first, Marse Tom, then tell you what she wants. There's been an *émeute,* as she calls it. It was before she got back with BB. The officer of the day reported it to her this morning. It happened at her fort. There was a fuss betwixt Major-General Tommy Drake and Lieutenant-Colonel Agnes Frisbie, and he snatched her doll away, which is made of white kid stuffed with sawdust, and tore every rag of its clothes off, right before them all, and is under arrest, and the charge is conduct un—"

"Yes, I know—conduct unbecoming an officer and a gentleman—a plain case, too, it seems to me. This is a serious matter. Well, what is her pleasure?"

"Well, Marse Tom, she has summoned a court-martial, but the doctor don't think she is well enough to preside over it, and she says there ain't anybody competent but her, because there's a major-general concerned; and so she—she—well, she says, would you preside over it for her? . . . Marse Tom, *sit* up! You ain't any more going to faint than Shekels is."

"Look here, Dorcas, go along back, and be tactful. Be persuasive; don't fret her; tell her it's all right, the matter is in my hands, but it isn't good form to hurry so grave a matter as this. Explain to her that we have to go by precedent, and that I believe this one to be new. In fact, you can say I know that nothing just like it has happened in our army, therefore I must be guided by European precedents, and must go cautiously and examine them carefully. Tell her not to be impatient, it will take me several days, but it will all come out right, and I will come over and report progress as I go along. Do you get the idea, Dorcas?"

"I don't know as I do, sir."

"Well, it's this. You see, it won't ever do for me, a brigadier in the regular army, to preside over that infant court-martial—there isn't any precedent for it, don't you see. Very well. I will go on examining authorities and reporting progress until she is well enough to get me out of this scrape by presiding herself. Do you get it now?"

"Oh, yes, sir, I get it, and it's good, I'll go and fix it with her. *Lay down!* and stay where you are."

"Why, what harm is he doing?"

"Oh, it ain't any harm, but it just vexes me to see him act so."

"What was he doing?"

"Can't you see, and him in such a sweat? He was starting out to spread it all over the post. *Now* I reckon you won't deny, any more, that they go and tell everything they hear, now that you've seen it with yo' own eyes."

"Well, I don't like to acknowledge it, Dorcas, but I don't see how I can consistently stick to my doubts in the face of such overwhelming proof as this dog is furnishing."

"There, now, you've got in yo' right mind at last! I wonder you can be so stubborn, Marse Tom. But you always was, even when you was little. I'm going now."

"Look here; tell her that in view of the delay, it is my judgment that she ought to enlarge the accused on his parole."

"Yes, sir, I'll tell her. Marse Tom?"

"Well?"

"She can't get to Soldier Boy, and he stands there all the time, down in the mouth and lonesome; and she says will you shake hands with him and comfort him? Everybody does."

"It's a curious kind of lonesomeness; but, all right, I will."

11   SEVERAL MONTHS LATER. ANTONIO AND THORNDIKE

"Thorndike, isn't that Plug you're riding an asset of the scrap you and Buffalo Bill had with the late Blake Haskins and his pal a few months back?"

"Yes, this is Mongrel—and not a half-bad horse, either."

"I've noticed he keeps up his lick first-rate. Say—isn't it a gaudy morning?"

"Right you are!"

"Thorndike, it's Andalusian! and when that's said, all's said."

"Andalusian *and* Oregonian, Antonio! Put it that way, and you have my vote. Being a native up there, I know. You being Andalusian-born—"

"Can speak with authority for that patch of paradise? Well, I can. Like the Don! like Sancho! This is the correct Andalusian dawn now— crisp, fresh, dewy, fragrant, pungent—"

" 'What though the spicy breezes
  Blow soft o'er Ceylon's isle—'

—*git* up, you old cow! stumbling like that when we've just been praising you! out on a scout and can't live up to the honor any better than
that? Antonio, how long have you been out here in the Plains and the
Rockies?"

"More than thirteen years."

"It's a long time. Don't you ever get homesick?"

"Not till now."

"Why *now?*—after such a long cure."

"These preparations of the retiring commandant's have started it up."

"Of course. It's natural."

"It keeps me thinking about Spain. I know the region where the
Seventh's child's aunt lives; I know all the lovely country for miles
around; I'll bet I've seen her aunt's villa many a time; I'll bet I've been
in it in those pleasant old times when I was a Spanish gentleman."

"They say the child is wild to see Spain."

"It's so; I know it from what I hear."

"Haven't you talked with her about it?"

"No. I've avoided it. I should soon be as wild as she is. That would
not be comfortable."

"I wish I was going, Antonio. There's two things I'd give a lot to see.
One's a railroad."

"She'll see one when she strikes Missouri."

"The other's a bull-fight."

"I've seen lots of them; I wish I could see another."

"I don't know anything about it, except in a mixed-up, foggy way,
Antonio, but I know enough to know it's grand sport."

"The grandest in the world! There's no other sport that begins with
it. I'll tell you what I've seen, then you can judge. It was my first, and
it's as vivid to me now as it was when I saw it. It was a Sunday afternoon, and beautiful weather, and my uncle, the priest, took me as a
reward for being a good boy and because of my own accord and without
anybody asking me I had bankrupted my savings-box and given the
money to a mission that was civilizing the Chinese and sweetening their
lives and softening their hearts with the gentle teachings of our religion,
and I wish you could have seen what we saw that day, Thorndike.

"The amphitheater was packed, from the bull-ring to the highest row
—twelve thousand people in one circling mass, one slanting, solid mass
—royalties, nobles, clergy, ladies, gentlemen, state officials, generals, ad-
mirals, soldiers, sailors, lawyers, thieves, merchants, brokers, cooks,
housemaids, scullery-maids, doubtful women, dudes, gamblers, beggars,
loafers, tramps, American ladies, gentlemen, preachers, English ladies,

gentlemen, preachers, German ditto, French ditto, and so on and so on, all the world represented: Spaniards to admire and praise, foreigners to enjoy and go home and find fault—there they were, one solid, sloping, circling sweep of rippling and flashing color under the downpour of the summer sun—just a garden, a gaudy, gorgeous flower-garden! Children munching oranges, six thousand fans fluttering and glimmering, everybody happy, everybody chatting gayly with their intimates, lovely girl-faces smiling recognition and salutation to other lovely girl-faces, gray old ladies and gentlemen dealing in the like exchanges with each other—ah, such a picture of cheery contentment and glad anticipation! not a mean spirit, nor a sordid soul, nor a sad heart there—ah, Thorndike, I wish I could see it again.

"Suddenly, the martial note of a bugle cleaves the hum and murmur —clear the ring!

"They clear it. The great gate is flung open, and the procession marches in, splendidly costumed and glittering: the marshals of the day, then the picadores on horseback, then the matadores on foot, each surrounded by his quadrille of *chulos*. They march to the box of the city fathers, and formally salute. The key is thrown, the bull-gate is unlocked. Another bugle blast—the gate flies open, the bull plunges in, furious, trembling, blinking in the blinding light, and stands there, a magnificent creature, center of those multitudinous and admiring eyes, brave, ready for battle, his attitude a challenge. He sees his enemy: horsemen sitting motionless, with long spears in rest, upon blindfolded broken-down nags, lean and starved, fit only for sport and sacrifice, then the carrion-heap.

"The bull makes a rush, with murder in his eye, but a picador meets him with a spear-thrust in the shoulder. He flinches with the pain, and the picador skips out of danger. A burst of applause for the picador, hisses for the bull. Some shout "Cow!" at the bull, and call him offensive names. But he is not listening to them, he is there for business; he is not minding the cloak-bearers that come fluttering around to confuse him; he chases this way, he chases that way, and hither and yon, scattering the nimble banderillos in every direction like a spray, and receiving their maddening darts in his neck as they dodge and fly—oh, but it's a lively spectacle, and brings down the house! Ah, you should hear the thundering roar that goes up when the game is at its wildest and brilliant things are done!

"Oh, that first bull, that day, was great! From the moment the spirit of war rose to flood-tide in him and he got down to his work, he began to do wonders. He tore his way through his persecutors, flinging one of them clear over the parapet; he bowled a horse and his rider down, and plunged straight for the next, got home with his horns, wounding both horse and man; on again, here and there and this way and that; and one after another he tore the bowels out of two horses so that they gushed to the ground, and ripped a third one so badly that although they rushed him to cover and shoved his bowels back and stuffed the rents with tow and rode him against the bull again, he couldn't make the trip; he tried to gallop, under the spur, but soon reeled and tottered and fell, all in a heap. For a while, that bull-ring was the most thrilling and glorious and inspiring sight that ever was seen. The bull absolutely cleared it, and stood there alone! monarch of the place. The people went mad for pride in him, and joy and delight, and you couldn't hear yourself think, for the roar and boom and crash of applause."

"Antonio, it carries me clear out of myself just to hear you tell it; it must have been perfectly splendid. If I live, I'll see a bull-fight yet before I die. Did they kill him?"

"Oh yes; that is what the bull is for. They tired him out, and got him at last. He kept rushing the matador, who always slipped smartly and gracefully aside in time, waiting for a sure chance; and at last it came; the bull made a deadly plunge for him—was avoided neatly, and as he sped by, the long sword glided silently into him, between left shoulder and spine—in and in, to the hilt. He crumpled down, dying."

"Ah, Antonio, it *is* the noblest sport that ever was. I would give a year of my life to see it. Is the bull always killed?"

"Yes. Sometimes a bull is timid, finding himself in so strange a place, and he stands trembling, or tries to retreat. Then everybody despises him for his cowardice and wants him punished and made ridiculous; so they hough him from behind, and it is the funniest thing in the world to see him hobbling around on his severed legs; the whole vast house goes into hurricanes of laughter over it; I have laughed till the tears ran down my cheeks to see it. When he has furnished all the sport he can, he is not any longer useful, and is killed."

"Well, it is perfectly grand, Antonio, perfectly beautiful. Burning a nigger don't begin."

12   MONGREL AND THE OTHER HORSE

"Sage-Brush, you have been listening?"

"Yes."

"Isn't it strange?"

"Well, no, Mongrel, I don't know that it is."

"Why don't you?"

"I've seen a good many human beings in my time. They are created as they are; they cannot help it. They are only brutal because that is their make; brutes would be brutal if it was *their* make."

"To me, Sage-Brush, man is most strange and unaccountable. Why should he treat dumb animals that way when they are not doing any harm?"

"Man is not always like that, Mongrel; he is kind enough when he is not excited by religion."

"Is the bull-fight a religious service?"

"I think so. I have heard so. It is held on Sunday."

(*A reflective pause, lasting some moments.*) Then:

"When we die, Sage-Brush, do we go to heaven and dwell with man?"

"My father thought not. He believed we do not have to go there unless we deserve it."

PART II   IN SPAIN

13   GENERAL ALISON TO HIS MOTHER

It was a prodigious trip, but delightful, of course, through the Rockies and the Black Hills and the mighty sweep of the Great Plains to civilization and the Missouri border—where the railroading began and the delightfulness ended. But no one is the worse for the journey; certainly not Cathy, nor Dorcas, nor Soldier Boy; and as for me, I am not complaining.

Spain is all that Cathy had pictured it—and more, she says. She is in a fury of delight, the maddest little animal that ever was, and all for joy. She thinks she remembers Spain, but that is not very likely, I suppose. The two—Mercedes and Cathy—devour each other. It is a rapture of love, and beautiful to see. It is Spanish; that describes it. Will this be a short visit?

No. It will be permanent. Cathy has elected to abide with Spain and her aunt. Dorcas says she (Dorcas) foresaw that this would happen; and also says that she wanted it to happen, and says the child's own country is the right place for her, and that she ought not to have been sent to me, I ought to have gone to her. I thought it insane to take Soldier Boy to Spain, but it was well that I yielded to Cathy's pleadings; if he had been left behind, half of her heart would have remained with him, and she would not have been contented. As it is, everything has fallen out for the best, and we are all satisfied and comfortable. It may be that Dorcas and I will see America again some day; but also it is a case of maybe not.

We left the post in the early morning. It was an affecting time. The women cried over Cathy, so did even those stern warriors the Rocky Mountain Rangers; Shekels was there, and the Cid, and Sardanapalus, and Potter, and Mongrel, and Sour-Mash, Famine, and Pestilence, and Cathy kissed them all and wept; details of the several arms of the garrison were present to represent the rest, and say good-by and God bless you for all the soldiery; and there was a special squad from the Seventh, with the oldest veteran at its head, to speed the Seventh's Child with grand honors and impressive ceremonies; and the veteran had a touching speech by heart, and put up his hand in salute and tried to say it, but his lips trembled and his voice broke, but Cathy bent down from the saddle and kissed him on the mouth and turned his defeat to victory, and a cheer went up.

The next act closed the ceremonies, and was a moving surprise. It may be that you have discovered, before this, that the rigors of military law and custom melt insensibly away and disappear when a soldier or a regiment or the garrison wants to do something that will please Cathy. The bands conceived the idea of stirring her soldierly heart with a farewell which would remain in her memory always, beautiful and un-fading, and bring back the past and its love for her whenever she should think of it; so they got their project placed before General Burnaby, my successor, who is Cathy's newest slave, and in spite of poverty of precedents they got his permission. The bands knew the child's favorite military airs. By this hint you know what is coming, but Cathy didn't. She was asked to sound the "reveille," which she did.

With the last note the bands burst out with a crash: and woke the

mountains with the "Star-Spangled Banner" in a way to make a body's
heart swell and thump and his hair rise! It was enough to break a
person all up, to see Cathy's radiant face shining out through her gladness and tears. By request she blew the "assembly," now. . . .

THE ASSEMBLY

. . . Then the bands thundered in, with "Rally round the flag, boys,
rally once again!" Next, she blew another call ("to the Standard") . . .

TO THE STANDARD

. . . and the bands responded with "When we were marching
through Georgia." Straightway she sounded "boots and saddles," that
thrilling and most expediting call. . . .

BOOTS AND SADDLES

. . . and the bands could hardly hold in for the final note; then they
turned their whole strength loose on "Tramp, tramp, tramp, the boys
are marching," and everybody's excitement rose to blood-heat.

Now an impressive pause—then the bugle sang "TAPS"—translatable,
this time, into "Good-by, and God keep us all!" for taps is the soldier's
nightly release from duty, and farewell: plaintive, sweet, pathetic, for

the morning is never sure, for him; always it is possible that he is hearing it for the last time. . . .

TAPS

. . . Then the bands turned their instruments towards Cathy and burst in with that rollicking frenzy of a tune, "Oh, we'll all get blind drunk when Johnny comes marching home—yes, we'll all get blind drunk when Johnny comes marching home!" and followed it instantly with "Dixie," that antidote for melancholy, merriest and gladdest of all military music on any side of the ocean—and that was the end. And so—farewell!

I wish you could have been there to see it all, hear it all, and feel it: and get yourself blown away with the hurricane huzza that swept the place as a finish.

When we rode away, our main body had already been on the road an hour or two—I speak of our camp equipage; but we didn't move off alone: when Cathy blew the "advance" the Rangers cantered out in column of fours, and gave us escort, and were joined by White Cloud and Thunder-Bird in all their gaudy bravery, and by Buffalo Bill and four subordinate scouts. Three miles away, in the Plains, the Lieutenant-General halted, sat her horse like a military statue, the bugle at her lips, and put the Rangers through the evolutions for half an hour; and finally, when she blew the "charge," she led it herself. "Not for the last time," she said, and got a cheer, and we said good-by all around, and faced eastward and rode away.

Postscript. A Day Later. Soldier Boy was stolen last night. Cathy is almost beside herself, and we cannot comfort her. Mercedes and I are not much alarmed about the horse, although this part of Spain is in something of a turmoil, politically, at present, and there is a good deal of lawlessness. In ordinary times the thief and the horse would soon be captured. We shall have them before long, I think.

14   SOLDIER BOY—TO HIMSELF

It is five months. Or is it six? My troubles have clouded my memory. I think I have been all over this land, from end to end, and now I am back again since day before yesterday, to that city which we passed through, that last day of our long journey, and which is near her country home. I am a tottering ruin and my eyes are dim, but I recognized it. If she could see me she would know me and sound my call. I wish I could hear it once more; it would revive me, it would bring back her face and the mountains and the free life, and I would come—if I were dying I would come! She would not know *me*, looking as I do, but she would know me by my star. But she will never see me, for they do not let me out of this shabby stable—a foul and miserable place, with most two wrecks like myself for company.

How many times have I changed hands? I think it is twelve times— I cannot remember; and each time it was down a step lower, and each time I got a harder master. They have been cruel, every one; they have worked me night and day in degraded employments, and beaten me; they have fed me ill and some days not at all. And so I am but bones, now, with a rough and frowsy skin humped and cornered upon my shrunken body—that skin which was once so glossy, that skin which she loved to stroke with her hand. I was the pride of the mountains and the Great Plains; now I am a scarecrow and despised. These piteous wrecks that are my comrades here say we have reached the bottom of the scale, the final humiliation; they say that when a horse is no longer worth the weeds and discarded rubbish they feed to him, they sell him to the bull-ring for a glass of brandy, to make sport for the people and perish for their pleasure.

To die—that does not disturb me; we of the service never care for death. But if I could see her once more! if I could hear her bugle sing again and say, "It is I, Soldier—come!"

15 GENERAL ALISON TO MRS. DRAKE, THE COLONEL'S WIFE

To return, now, to where I was, and tell you the rest. We shall never know how she came to be there; there is no way to account for it. She was always watching for black and shiny and spirited horses—watching, hoping, despairing, hoping again; always giving chase and sounding her call, upon the meagerest chance of a response, and breaking her heart over the disappointment; always inquiring, always interested in sales-stables and horse accumulations in general. How she got there must remain a mystery.

At the point which I had reached in a preceding paragraph of this account, the situation was as follows: two horses lay dying; the bull had scattered his persecutors for the moment, and stood raging, panting, pawing the dust in clouds over his back, when the man that had been wounded returned to the ring on a remount, a poor blindfolded

wreck that yet had something ironically military about his bearing—
and the next moment the bull had ripped him open and his bowels
were dragging upon the ground and the bull was charging his swarm
of pests again. Then came pealing through the air a bugle-call that
froze my blood—*"It is I, Soldier—come!"* I turned; Cathy was flying
down through the massed people; she cleared the parapet at a bound,
and sped towards that riderless horse, who staggered forward towards
the remembered sound; but his strength failed, and he fell at her feet,
she lavishing kisses upon him and sobbing, the house rising with one
impulse, and white with horror! Before help could reach her the bull
was back again—

She was never conscious again in life. We bore her home, all mangled and drenched in blood, and knelt by her and listened to her broken
and wandering words, and prayed for her passing spirit, and there was
no comfort—nor ever will be, I think. But she was happy, for she was
far away under another sky, and comrading again with her Rangers,
and her animal friends, and the soldiers. Their names fell softly and
caressingly from her lips, one by one, with pauses between. She was
not in pain, but lay with closed eyes, vacantly murmuring, as one who
dreams. Sometimes she smiled, saying nothing; sometimes she smiled
when she uttered a name—such as Shekels, or BB, or Potter. Sometimes
she was at her fort, issuing commands; sometimes she was careering
over the plains at the head of her men; sometimes she was training her
horse; once she said, reprovingly, "You are giving me the wrong foot;
give me the left—don't you know it is good-by?"

After this, she lay silent some time; the end was near. By and by
she murmured, "Tired . . . sleepy . . . take Cathy, mamma." Then,
"Kiss me, Soldier." For a little time she lay so still that we were doubtful if she breathed. Then she put out her hand and began to feel grop-
ingly about; then said, "I cannot find it; blow 'taps.'"* It was the end.

TAPS

°"Lights Out"

1906

Hunting the Deceitful Turkey

When I was a boy my uncle and his big boys hunted with the rifle, the youngest boy Fred and I with a shotgun—a small single-barrelled shotgun which was properly suited to our size and strength; it was not much heavier than a broom. We carried it turn about, half an hour at a time. I was not able to hit anything with it, but I liked to try. Fred and I hunted feathered small game, the others hunted deer, squirrels, wild turkeys, and such things. My uncle and the big boys were good shots. They killed hawks and wild geese and such like on the wing; and they didn't wound or kill squirrels, they *stunned* them. When the dogs treed a squirrel, the squirrel would scamper aloft and run out on a limb and flatten himself along it, hoping to make himself invisible in that way—and not quite succeeding. You could see his wee little ears sticking up. You couldn't see his nose, but you knew where it was. Then the hunter, despising a "rest" for his rifle, stood up and took offhand aim at the limb and sent a bullet into it immediately under the squirrel's nose, and down tumbled the animal, unwounded but unconscious; the dogs gave him a shake and he was dead. Sometimes when the distance was great and the wind not accurately allowed for, the bullet would hit the squirrel's head; the dogs could do as they pleased with that one —the hunter's pride was hurt, and he wouldn't allow it to go into the gamebag.

In the first faint gray of the dawn the stately wild turkeys would be stalking around in great flocks, and ready to be sociable and answer invitations to come and converse with other excursionists of their kind. The hunter concealed himself and imitated the turkey-call by sucking the air through the legbone of a turkey which had previously answered a call like that and lived only just long enough to regret it. There is nothing that furnishes a perfect turkey-call except that bone. Another of Nature's treacheries, you see. She is full of them; half the time she doesn't know which she likes best—to betray her child or protect it. In the case of the turkey she is badly mixed: she gives it a bone to be used in getting it into trouble, and she also furnishes it with a trick for getting itself out of the trouble again. When a mamma-turkey answers an invitation and finds she has made a mistake in accepting it, she does as the mamma-partridge does—remembers a previous engagement and goes limping and scrambling away, pretending to be very lame; and at the same time she is saying to her not-visible children, "Lie low, keep still, don't expose yourselves; I shall be back as soon as I have beguiled this shabby swindler out of the country."

When a person is ignorant and confiding, this immoral device can have tiresome results. I followed an ostensibly lame turkey over a considerable part of the United States one morning, because I believed in her and could not think she would deceive a mere boy, and one who was trusting her and considering her honest. I had the single-barrelled shotgun, but my idea was to catch her alive. I often got within rushing distance of her, and then made my rush; but always, just as I made my final plunge and put my hand down where her back had been, it wasn't there; it was only two or three inches from there and I brushed the tail-feathers as I landed on my stomach—a very close call, but still not quite close enough; that is, not close enough for success, but just close enough to convince me that I could do it next time. She always waited for me, a little piece away, and let on to be resting and greatly fatigued; which was a lie, but I believed it, for I still thought her honest long after I ought to have begun to doubt her, suspecting that this was no way for a high-minded bird to be acting. I followed, and followed, and followed, making my periodical rushes, and getting up and brushing the dust off, and resuming the voyage with patient confidence; indeed, with a confidence which grew, for I could see by the change of climate and vegetation that we were getting up into the high latitudes, and as she always looked a little tireder and a little more discouraged after each rush, I judged that I was safe to win, in the end, the competition being purely a matter of staying power and the advantage lying with me from the start because she was lame.

Along in the afternoon I began to feel fatigued myself. Neither of us had had any rest since we first started on the excursion, which was upwards of ten hours before, though latterly we had paused awhile after rushes, I letting on to be thinking about something else; but neither of us sincere, and both of us waiting for the other to call game but in no real hurry about it, for indeed those little evanescent snatches of rest were very grateful to the feelings of us both; it would naturally be so, skirmishing along like that ever since dawn and not a bite in the meantime; at least for me, though sometimes as she lay on her side fanning herself with a wing and praying for strength to get out of this difficulty a grasshopper happened along whose time had come, and that was well for her, and fortunate, but I had nothing—nothing the whole day.

More than once, after I was very tired, I gave up taking her alive, and was going to shoot her, but I never did it, although it was my right, for I did not believe I could hit her; and besides, she always stopped and posed, when I raised the gun, and this made me suspicious that she knew about me and my marksmanship, and so I did not care to expose myself to remarks.

I did not get her, at all. When she got tired of the game at last, she rose from almost under my hand and flew aloft with the rush and whir of a shell and lit on the highest limb of a great tree and sat down and crossed her legs and smiled down at me, and seemed gratified to see me so astonished.

I was ashamed, and also lost; and it was while wandering the woods hunting for myself that I found a deserted log cabin and had one of the best meals there that in my life-days I have eaten. The weed-grown garden was full of ripe tomatoes, and I ate them ravenously, though I had never liked them before. Not more than two or three times since have I tasted anything that was so delicious as those tomatoes. I surfeited myself with them, and did not taste another one until I was in middle life. I can eat them now, but I do not like the look of them. I suppose we have all experienced a surfeit at one time or another. Once, in stress of circumstances, I ate part of a barrel of sardines, there being nothing else at hand, but since then I have always been able to get along without sardines.

1906

Extract from Captain Stormfield's Visit to Heaven

1

Well, when I had been dead about thirty years, I begun to get a little anxious. Mind you, I had been whizzing through space all that time, like a comet. *Like* a comet! Why, Peters, I laid over the lot of them! Of course there warn't any of them going my way, as a steady thing, you know, because they travel in a long circle like the loop of a lasso, whereas I was pointed as straight as a dart for the Hereafter; but I happened on one every now and then that was going my way for an hour or so, and then we had a bit of a brush together. But it was generally pretty one-sided, because I sailed by them the same as if they were standing still. An ordinary comet don't make more than about 200,000 miles a minute. Of course when I came across one of that sort —like Encke's and Halley's comets, for instance—it warn't anything but just a flash and a vanish, you see. You couldn't rightly call it a race. It was as if the comet was a gravel-train and I was a telegraph despatch. But after I got outside of our astronomical system, I used to flush a comet occasionally that was something *like*. *We* haven't got any such comets—ours don't begin. One night I was swinging along at a good round gait, everything taut and trim, and the wind in my favor—I judged I was going about a million miles a minute—it might have been more, it couldn't have been less—when I flushed a most uncommonly big one about three points off my starboard bow. By his stern lights I judged he was bearing about northeast-and-by-north-half-east. Well, it was so near my course that I wouldn't throw away the chance; so I fell off a point, steadied my helm, and went for him. You should have heard me whiz, and seen the electric fur fly! In about a minute and a half I was fringed out with an electrical nimbus that flamed around for miles and miles and lit up all space like broad day. The comet was burning blue in the distance, like a sickly torch, when I first sighted him, but he begun to grow bigger and bigger as I crept up on him. I slipped up on him so fast that when I had gone about 150,000,000 miles I was close enough to be swallowed up in the phosphorescent glory of his wake, and I couldn't see anything for the glare. Thinks I, it won't do to run into him, so I shunted to one side and tore along. By and by I closed up abreast of his tail. Do you know what it was like? It was like a gnat closing up on the continent of America. I forged along. By and by I had sailed along his coast for a little upwards of a hundred and fifty million miles, and then I could see by the shape of him that I hadn't even got up to his waistband yet. Why, Peters, *we* don't know anything about comets, down here. If you want to see comets that *are* comets, you've got to go outside of our solar system—where there's room for them, you understand. My friend, I've seen comets out there that couldn't even lay down inside the *orbits* of our noblest comets without their tails hanging over.

Well, I boomed along another hundred and fifty million miles, and got up abreast his shoulder, as you may say. I was feeling pretty fine, I tell you; but just then I noticed the officer of the deck come to the side and hoist his glass in my direction. Straight off I heard him sing out—

"Below there, ahoy! Shake her up, shake her up! Heave on a hundred million billion tons of brimstone!"

"Ay—ay, sir!"

"Pipe the starboard watch! All hands on deck!"

"Ay—ay, sir!"

"Send two hundred thousand million men aloft to shake out royals and sky-scrapers!"

"Ay—ay, sir!"

"Hand the stuns'ls! Hang out every rag you've got! Clothe her from stem to rudder-post!"

"Ay—ay, sir!"

In about a second I begun to see I'd woke up a pretty ugly customer, Peters. In less than ten seconds that comet was just a blazing cloud of red-hot canvas. It was piled up into the heavens clean out of sight—the old thing seemed to swell out and occupy all space; the sulphur smoke from the furnaces—oh, well, nobody can describe the way it rolled and tumbled up into the skies, and nobody can half describe the way it smelt. Neither can anybody begin to describe the way that monstrous craft begun to crash along. And such another powwow—thousands of bo's'n's whistles screaming at once, and a crew like the populations of a hundred thousand worlds like ours all swearing at once. Well, I never heard the like of it before.

We roared and thundered along side by side, both doing our level best, because I'd never struck a comet before that could lay over me, and so I was bound to beat this one or break something. I judged I had some reputation in space, and I calculated to keep it. I noticed I wasn't gaining as fast, now, as I was before, but still I was gaining. There was a power of excitement on board the comet. Upwards of a hundred billion passengers swarmed up from below and rushed to the side and begun to bet on the race. Of course this careened her and damaged her speed. My, but wasn't the mate mad! He jumped at that crowd, with his trumpet in his hand, and sung out—

"Amidships! amidships, you——!¹ or I'll brain the last idiot of you!"

Well, sir, I gained and gained, little by little, till at last I went skimming sweetly by the magnificent old conflagration's nose. By this time

¹ The Captain could not remember what this word was. He said it was in a foreign tongue.

the captain of the comet had been rousted out, and he stood there in the red glare for'ard, by the mate, in his shirtsleeves and slippers, his hair all rats' nests and one suspender hanging, and how sick those two men did look! I just simply couldn't help putting my thumb to my nose as I glided away and singing out:

"Ta-ta! ta-ta! Any word to send to your family?"

Peters, it was a mistake. Yes, sir, I've often regretted that—it was a mistake. You see, the captain had given up the race, but that remark was too tedious for him—he couldn't stand it. He turned to the mate, and says he—

"Have we got brimstone enough of our own to make the trip?"

"Yes, sir."

"Sure?"

"Yes, sir—more than enough."

"How much have we got in cargo for Satan?"

"Eighteen hundred thousand billion quintillions of kazarks."

"Very well, then, let his boarders freeze till the next comet comes. Lighten ship! Lively, now, lively, men! Heave the whole cargo overboard!"

Peters, look me in the eye, and be calm. I found out, over there, that a kazark is exactly the bulk of a *hundred and sixty-nine worlds like ours!* They hove all that load overboard. When it fell it wiped out a considerable raft of stars just as clean as if they'd been candles and somebody blowed them out. As for the race, that was at an end. The minute she was lightened the comet swung along by me the same as if I was anchored. The captain stood on the stern, by the after-davits, and put his thumb to his nose and sung out—

"Ta-ta! ta-ta! Maybe *you've* got some message to send your friends in the Everlasting Tropics!"

Then he hove up his other suspender and started for'ard, and inside of three-quarters of an hour his craft was only a pale torch again in the distance. Yes, it was a mistake, Peters—that remark of mine. I don't reckon I'll ever get over being sorry about it. I'd 'a' beat the bully of the firmament if I'd kept my mouth shut.

But I've wandered a little off the track of my tale; I'll get back on my course again. Now you see what kind of speed I was making. So, as I said, when I had been tearing along this way about thirty years I begun to get uneasy. Oh, it was pleasant enough, with a good deal to find out, but then it was kind of lonesome, you know. Besides, I wanted to get somewhere. I hadn't shipped with the idea of cruising forever. First off, I liked the delay, because I judged I was going to fetch up in pretty warm quarters when I got through; but towards the last I begun to feel that I'd rather go to—well, most any place, so as to finish up the uncertainty.

Well, one night—it was always night, except when I was rushing by some star that was occupying the whole universe with its fire and its glare—light enough then, of course, but I necessarily left it behind in a minute or two and plunged into a solid week of darkness again. The stars ain't so close together as they look to be. Where was I? Oh yes; one night I was sailing along, when I discovered a tremendous long row of blinking lights away on the horizon ahead. As I approached, they begun to tower and swell and look like mighty furnaces. Says I to myself—

"By George, I've arrived at last—and at the wrong place, just as I expected!"

Then I fainted. I don't know how long I was insensible, but it must have been a good while, for, when I came to, the darkness was all gone and there was the loveliest sunshine and the balmiest, fragrantest air in its place. And there was such a marvelous world spread out before me—such a glowing, beautiful, bewitching country. The things I took for furnaces were gates, miles high, made all of flashing jewels, and they pierced a wall of solid gold that you couldn't see the top of, nor yet the end of, in either direction. I was pointed straight for one of these gates, and a-coming like a house afire. Now I noticed that the skies were black with millions of people, pointed for those gates. What a roar they made, rushing through the air! The ground was as thick as ants with people, too—billions of them, I judge.

I lit. I drifted up to a gate with a swarm of people, and when it was my turn the head clerk says, in a businesslike way—

"Well, quick! Where are you from?"

"San Francisco," says I.

"San Fran—*what?*" says he.

"San Francisco."

He scratched his head and looked puzzled, then he says—

"Is it a planet?"

By George, Peters, think of it! *"Planet?"* says I; "it's a city. And moreover, it's one of the biggest and finest and—"

"There, there!" says he, "no time here for conversation. We don't deal in cities here. Where are you from in a *general* way?"

"Oh," I says, "I beg your pardon. Put me down for California."

I had him *again*, Peters! He puzzled a second, then he says, sharp and irritable—

"I don't know any such planet— is it a constellation?"

"Oh, my goodness!" says I. "Constellation, says you? No—it's a State."

"Man, we don't deal in States here. *Will* you tell me where you are from *in general—at large*, don't you understand?"

"Oh, now I get your idea," I says. "I'm from America,—the United States of America."

Peters, do you know I had him *again?* If I hadn't I'm a clam! His face was as blank as a target after a militia shooting-match. He turned to an under clerk and says—

"Where is America? *What* is America?"

The under clerk answered up prompt and says—

"There ain't any such orb."

"*Orb?*" says I. "Why, what are you talking about, young man? It ain't an orb; it's a country; it's a continent. Columbus discovered it; I reckon likely you've heard of *him*, anyway. America—why, sir, America—"

"Silence!" says the head clerk. "Once for all, where—are—you—*from?*"

"Well," says I, "I don't know anything more to say—unless I lump things, and just say I'm from the world."

"Ah," says he, brightening up, "now that's something like! *What* world?"

Peters, he had *me*, that time. I looked at him, puzzled, he looked at me, worried. Then he burst out—

"Come, come, what world?"

Says I, "Why, *the* world, of course."

"*The* world!" he says. "H'm! there's billions of them! . . . Next!"

That meant for me to stand aside. I done so, and a sky-blue man with seven heads and only one leg hopped into my place. I took a walk. It just occurred to me, then, that all the myriads I had seen swarming to that gate, up to this time, were just like that creature. I tried to run across somebody I was acquainted with, but they were out of acquaintances of mine just then. So I thought the thing all over and finally sidled back there pretty meek and feeling rather stumped, as you may say.

"Well?" said the head clerk.

"Well, sir," I says, pretty humble, "I don't seem to make out which world it is I'm from. But you may know it from this—it's the one the Saviour saved."

He bent his head at the Name. Then he says, gently—

"The worlds He has saved are like to the gates of heaven in number

—none can count them. What astronomical system is your world in?—perhaps that may assist."

"It's the one that has the sun in it—and the moon—and Mars"—he shook his head at each name—hadn't ever heard of them, you see—"and Neptune—and Uranus—and Jupiter—"

"Hold on!" says he—"hold on a minute! Jupiter . . . Jupiter . . . Seems to me we had a man from there eight or nine hundred years ago—but people from that system very seldom enter by this gate." All of a sudden he begun to look me so straight in the eye that I thought he was going to bore through me. Then he says, very deliberate, "Did you come *straight here* from your system?"

"Yes, sir," I says—but I blushed the least little bit in the world when I said it.

He looked at me very stern, and says—

"That is not true; and this is not the place for prevarication. You wandered from your course. How did that happen?"

Says I, blushing again—

"I'm sorry, and I take back what I said, and confess. I raced a little with a comet one day—only just the least little bit—only the tiniest lit—"

"So—so," says he—and without any sugar in his voice to speak of. I went on, and says—

"But I only fell off just a bare point, and I went right back on my course again the minute the race was over."

"No matter—that divergence has made all this trouble. It has brought you to a gate that is billions of leagues from the right one. If you had gone to your own gate they would have known all about your world at once and there would have been no delay. But we will try to accommodate you." He turned to an under clerk and says—

"What system is Jupiter in?"

"I don't remember, sir, but I think there is such a planet in one of the little new systems away out in one of the thinly worlded corners of the universe. I will see."

He got a balloon and sailed up and up and up, in front of a map that was as big as Rhode Island. He went on up till he was out of sight, and by and by he came down and got something to eat and went up again. To cut a long story short, he kept on doing this for a day or two, and finally he came down and said he thought he had found that solar system, but it might be fly-specks. So he got a microscope and went back. It turned out better than he feared. He had rousted out our system, sure enough. He got me to describe our planet and its distance from the sun, and then he says to his chief—

"Oh, I know the one he means, now, sir. It is on the map. It is called the Wart."

"Says I to myself, "Young man, it wouldn't be wholesome for you to go down *there* and call it the Wart."

Well, they let me in, then, and told me I was safe forever and wouldn't have any more trouble.

Then they turned from me and went on with their work, the same as if they considered my case all complete and shipshape. I was a good deal surprised at this, but I was diffident about speaking up and reminding them. I did so hate to do it, you know; it seemed a pity to bother them, they had so much on their hands. Twice I thought I would give up and let the thing go; so twice I started to leave, but immediately I thought what a figure I should cut stepping out amongst the redeemed in such a rig, and that made me hang back and come to anchor again. People got to eying me—clerks, you know—wondering why I didn't get under way. I couldn't stand this long—it was too uncomfortable. So at last I plucked up courage and tipped the head clerk a signal. He says—

"What! you here yet? What's wanting?"

Says I, in a low voice and very confidential, making a trumpet with my hands at his ear—

"I beg pardon, and you mustn't mind my reminding you, and seeming to meddle, but hain't you forgot something?"

He studied a second, and says—

"Forgot something? . . . No, not that I know of."

"Think," says I.

He thought. Then he says—

"No, I can't seem to have forgot anything. What is it?"

"Look at me," says I, "look me all over."

He done it.

"Well?" says he.

"Well," says I, "you don't notice anything? If I branched out amongst the elect looking like this, wouldn't I attract considerable attention?—wouldn't I be a little conspicuous?"

"Well," he says, "I don't see anything the matter. What do you lack?"

"Lack! Why, I lack my harp, and my wreath, and my halo, and my hymn-book, and my palm branch—I lack everything that a body naturally requires up here, my friend."

Puzzled? Peters, he was the worst puzzled man you ever saw. Finally he says—

"Well, you seem to be a curiosity every way a body takes you. I never heard of these things before."

I looked at the man awhile in solid astonishment; then I says—

"Now, I hope you don't take it as an offence, for I don't mean any, but really, for a man that has been in the Kingdom as long as I reckon you have, you do seem to know powerful little about its customs."

"Its customs!" says he. "Heaven is a large place, good friend. Large empires have many and diverse customs. Even small dominions have, as you doubtless know by what you have seen of the matter on a small scale in the Wart. How can you imagine I could ever learn the varied customs of the countless kingdoms of heaven? It makes my head ache to think of it. I know the customs that prevail in those portions inhabited by peoples that are appointed to enter by my own gate—and hark ye, that is quite enough knowledge for one individual to try to pack into his head in the thirty-seven millions of years I have devoted night and day to that study. But the idea of learning the customs of the whole appalling expanse of heaven—O man, how insanely you talk! Now I don't doubt that this odd costume you talk about is the fashion in that district of heaven you belong to, but you won't be conspicuous in this section without it."

I felt all right, if that was the case, so I bade him good-day and left. All day I walked towards the far end of a prodigious hall of the office, hoping to come out into heaven any moment, but it was a mistake. That hall was built on the general heavenly plan—it naturally couldn't be small. At last I got so tired I couldn't go any farther; so I sat down to rest, and begun to tackle the queerest sort of strangers and ask for information, but I didn't get any; they couldn't understand my language, and I could not understand theirs. I got dreadfully lonesome. I was so downhearted and homesick I wished a hundred times I never had died. I turned back, of course. About noon next day, I got back at last and was on hand at the booking-office once more. Says I to the head clerk—

"I begin to see that a man's got to be in his own heaven to be happy."

"Perfectly correct," says he. "Did you imagine the same heaven would suit all sorts of men?"

"Well, I had that idea—but I see the foolishness of it. Which way am I to go to get to my district?"

He called the under clerk that had examined the map, and he gave me general directions. I thanked him and started; but he says—

"Wait a minute; it is millions of leagues from here. Go outside and stand on that red wishing-carpet; shut your eyes, hold your breath, and wish yourself there."

"I'm much obliged," says I; "why didn't you dart me through when I first arrived?"

"We have a good deal to think of here; it was your place to think of it and ask for it. Good-by; we probably sha'n't see you in this region for a thousand centuries or so."

"In that case, *o revoor*," says I.

I hopped onto the carpet and held my breath and shut my eyes and wished I was in the booking-office of my own section. The very next instant a voice I knew sung out in a business kind of a way—

"A harp and a hymn-book, pair of wings and a halo, size 13, for Cap'n Eli Stormfield, of San Francisco!—make him out a clean bill of health, and let him in."

I opened my eyes. Sure enough, it was a Pi Ute Injun I used to know in Tulare County; mighty good fellow—I remembered being at his funeral, which consisted of him being burnt and the other Injuns gauming their faces with his ashes and howling like wild-cats. He was powerful glad to see me, and you may make up your mind I was just as glad to see him, and felt that I was in the right kind of a heaven at last.

Just as far as your eye could reach, there was swarms of clerks, running and bustling around, tricking out thousands of Yanks and Mexicans and English and Arabs, and all sorts of people in their new outfits; and when they gave me my kit and I put on my halo and I took a look in the glass, I could have jumped over a house for joy, I was so happy. "Now *this* is something like!" says I. "Now," says I, "I'm all right—show me a cloud."

Inside of fifteen minutes I was a mile on my way towards the cloud-banks and about a million people along with me. Most of us tried to fly, but some got crippled and nobody made a success of it. So we concluded to walk, for the present, till we had had some wing practice.

We begun to meet swarms of folks who were coming back. Some had harps and nothing else; some had hymn-books and nothing else; some had nothing at all; all of them looked meek and uncomfortable; one young fellow hadn't anything left but his halo, and he was carrying that in his hand; all of a sudden he offered it to me and says—

"Will you hold it for me a minute?"

Then he disappeared in the crowd. I went on. A woman asked me to hold her palm branch, and then *she* disappeared. A girl got me to hold her harp for her, and by George, *she* disappeared; and so on and so on, till I was about loaded down to the guards. Then comes a smiling old gentleman and asked me to hold *his* things. I swabbed off the perspiration and says, pretty tart—

"I'll have to get you to excuse me, my friend,—*I* ain't no hat-rack."

About this time I begun to run across piles of those traps, lying in the road. I just quietly dumped my extra cargo along with them. I looked around, and, Peters, that whole nation that was following me were loaded down the same as I'd been. The return crowd had got them to hold their things a minute, you see. They all dumped their loads, too, and we went on.

When I found myself perched on a cloud, with a million other people, I never felt so good in my life. Says I, "Now this is according to the promises; I've been having my doubts, but now I *am* in heaven, sure enough." I gave my palm branch a wave or two, for luck, and then I tautened up my harp-strings and struck in. Well, Peters, you can't imagine anything like the row we made. It was grand to listen to, and made a body thrill all over, but there was considerable many tunes going on at once, and that was a drawback to the harmony, you understand; and then there was a lot of Injun tribes, and they kept up such another war-whooping that they kind of took the tuck out of the music. By and by I quit performing, and judged I'd take a rest. There was quite a nice mild old gentleman sitting next me, and I noticed he didn't take a hand; I encouraged him, but he said he was naturally bashful, and was afraid to try before so many people. By and by the old gentleman said he never could seem to enjoy music somehow. The fact was, I was beginning to feel the same way; but I didn't say anything. Him and I had a considerable long silence, then, but of course it warn't noticeable in that place. After about sixteen or seventeen hours, during which I played and sung a little, now and then—always the same tune, because I didn't know any other—I laid down my harp and begun to fan myself with my palm branch. Then we both got to sighing pretty regular. Finally, says he—

"Don't you know any tune but the one you've been pegging at all day?"

"Not another blessed one," says I.

"Don't you reckon you could learn another one?" says he.

"Never," says I; "I've tried to, but I couldn't manage it."

"It's a long time to hang to the one—eternity, you know."

"Don't break my heart," says I; "I'm getting low-spirited enough already."

After another long silence, says he—

"Are you glad to be here?"

Says I, "Old man, I'll be frank with you. This *ain't* just as near my idea of bliss as I thought it was going to be, when I used to go to church."

Says he, "What do you say to knocking off and calling it half a day?"

"That's me," says I. "I never wanted to get off watch so bad in my life."

So we started. Millions were coming to the cloud-bank all the time, happy and hosannahing; millions were leaving it all the time, looking mighty quiet, I tell you. We laid for the new-comers, and pretty soon I'd got them to hold all my things a minute, and then I was a free man again and most outrageously happy. Just then I ran across old Sam Bartlett, who had been dead a long time, and stopped to have a talk with him. Says I—

"Now tell me—is this to go on forever? Ain't there anything else for a change?"

Says he—

"I'll set you right on that point very quick. People take the figurative language of the Bible and the allegories for literal, and the first thing they ask for when they get here is a halo and a harp, and so on. Nothing that's harmless and reasonable is refused a body here, if he asks it in the right spirit. So they are outfitted with these things without a word. They go and sing and play just about one day, and that's the last you'll ever see them in the choir. They don't need anybody to tell them that that sort of thing wouldn't make a heaven—at least not a heaven that a sane man could stand a week and remain sane. That cloud-bank is placed where the noise can't disturb the old inhabitants, and so there ain't any harm in letting everybody get up there and cure himself as soon as he comes.

"Now you just remember this—heaven is as blissful and lovely as it can be; but it's just the busiest place you ever heard of. There ain't any idle people here after the first day. Singing hymns and waving palm branches through all eternity is pretty when you hear about it in the pulpit, but it's as poor a way to put in valuable time as a body could contrive. It would just make a heaven of warbling ignoramuses, don't you see? Eternal Rest sounds comforting in the pulpit, too. Well, you try it once, and see how heavy time will hang on your hands. Why, Stormfield, a man like you, that had been active and stirring all his life, would go mad in six months in a heaven where he hadn't anything to do. Heaven is the very last place to come to *rest* in,—and don't you be afraid to bet on that!"

Says I—

"Sam, I'm as glad to hear it as I thought I'd be sorry. I'm glad I come, now."

Says he—

"Cap'n, ain't you pretty physically tired?"

Says I—

"Sam, it ain't any name for it! I'm dog-tired."

"Just so—just so. You've earned a good sleep, and you'll get it. You've earned a good appetite, and you'll enjoy your dinner. It's the same here as it is on earth—you've got to earn a thing, square and honest, before you enjoy it. You can't enjoy first and earn afterwards. But there's this difference, here: you can choose your own occupation, and all the powers of heaven will be put forth to help you make a success of it, if you do your level best. The shoemaker on earth that had the soul of a poet in him won't have to make shoes here."

"Now that's all reasonable and right," says I. "Plenty of work, and the kind you hanker after; no more pain, no more suffering—"

"Oh, hold on; there's plenty of pain here—but it don't kill. There's plenty of suffering here, but it don't last. You see, happiness ain't a *thing in itself*—it's only a *contrast* with something that ain't pleasant. That's all it is. There ain't a thing you can mention that is happiness in its own self—it's only so by contrast with the other thing. And so, as soon as the novelty is over and the force of the contrast dulled, it ain't happiness any longer, and you have to get something fresh. Well, there's plenty of pain and suffering in heaven—consequently there's plenty of contrasts, and just no end of happiness."

Says I, "It's the sensiblest heaven I've heard of yet, Sam, though it's about as different from the one I was brought up on as a live princess is different from her own wax figger."

Along in the first months I knocked around about the Kingdom, making friends and looking at the country, and finally settled down in a pretty likely region, to have a rest before taking another start. I went on making acquaintances and gathering up information. I had a good deal of talk with an old bald-headed angel by the name of Sandy Mc-Williams. He was from somewhere in New Jersey. I went about with him, considerable. We used to lay around, warm afternoons, in the shade of a rock, on some meadow-ground that was pretty high and out of the marshy slush of his cranberry-farm, and there we used to talk about all kinds of things, and smoke pipes. One day, says I—

"About how old might you be, Sandy?"

"Seventy-two."

"I judged so. How long you been in heaven?"

"Twenty-seven years, come Christmas."

"How old was you when you come up?"

"Why, seventy-two, of course."

"You can't mean it!"

"Why can't I mean it?"

"Because, if you was seventy-two then, you are naturally ninety-nine now."

"No, but I ain't. I stay the same age I was when I come."

"Well," says I, "come to think, there's something just here that I want to ask about. Down below, I always had an idea that in heaven we would all be young, and bright, and spry."

"Well, you *can* be young if you want to. You've only got to wish."

"Well, then, why didn't you wish?"

"I did. They all do. You'll try it, some day, like enough; but you'll get tired of the change pretty soon."

"Why?"

"Well, I'll tell you. Now you've always been a sailor; did you ever try some other business?"

"Yes, I tried keeping grocery, once, up in the mines; but I couldn't stand it; it was too dull—no stir, no storm, no life about it; it was like being part dead and part alive, both at the same time. I wanted to be one thing or t'other. I shut up shop pretty quick and went to sea."

"That's it. Grocery people like it, but you couldn't. You see you wasn't used to it. Well, I wasn't used to being young, and I couldn't seem to take any interest in it. I was strong, and handsome, and had curly hair,—yes, and wings, too!—gay wings like a butterfly. I went to picnics and dances and parties with the fellows, and tried to carry on and talk nonsense with the girls, but it wasn't any use; I couldn't take to it—fact is, it was an awful bore. What I wanted was early to bed and early to rise, and something to *do*; and when my work was done, I wanted to sit quiet, and smoke and think—not tear around with a parcel of giddy young kids. You can't think what I suffered whilst I was young."

"How long was you young?"

"Only two weeks. That was plenty for me. Laws, I was so lonesome! You see, I was full of the knowledge and experience of seventy-two years; the deepest subject those young folks could strike was only *a-b-c* to me. And to hear them argue—oh, my! it would have been funny, if it hadn't been so pitiful. Well, I was so hungry for the ways and the sober talk I was used to, that I tried to ring in with the old people, but they wouldn't have it. They considered me a conceited young upstart, and gave me the cold shoulder. Two weeks was a-plenty for me.

I was glad to get back my bald head again, and my pipe, and my old drowsy reflections in the shade of a rock or a tree."

"Well," says I, "do you mean to say you're going to stand still at seventy-two, forever?"

"I don't know, and I ain't particular. But I ain't going to drop back to twenty-five any more—I know that, mighty well. I know a sight more than I did twenty-seven years ago, and I enjoy learning, all the time, but I don't seem to get any older. That is, bodily—my mind gets older, and stronger, and better seasoned, and more satisfactory."

Says I, "If a man comes here at ninety, don't he ever set himself back?"

"Of course he does. He sets himself back to fourteen; tries it a couple of hours, and feels like a fool; sets himself forward to twenty; it ain't much improvement; tries thirty, fifty, eighty, and finally ninety—finds he is more at home and comfortable at the same old figure he is used to than any other way. Or, if his mind begun to fail him on earth at eighty, that's where he finally sticks up here. He sticks at the place where his mind was last at its best, for there's where his enjoyment is best, and his ways most set and established."

"Does a chap of twenty-five stay always twenty-five, and look it?"

"If he is a fool, yes. But if he is bright, and ambitious and industrious, the knowledge he gains and the experience he has, change his ways and thoughts and likings, and make him find his best pleasure in the company of people above that age; so he allows his body to take on that look of as many added years as he needs to make him comfortable and proper in that sort of society; he lets his body go on taking the look of age, according as he progresses, and by and by he will be bald and wrinkled outside, and wise and deep within."

"Babies the same?"

"Babies the same. Laws, what asses we used to be, on earth, about these things! We said we'd be always young in heaven. We didn't say *how* young—we didn't think of that, perhaps—that is, we didn't all think alike, anyway. When I was a boy of seven, I suppose I thought we'd all be twelve, in heaven; when I was twelve, I suppose I thought we'd all be eighteen or twenty in heaven; when I was forty, I begun to go back; I remember I hoped we'd all be about *thirty* years old in heaven. Neither a man nor a boy ever thinks the age he *has* is exactly the best one—he puts the *right* age a few years older or a few years younger than he is. Then he makes the ideal age the general age of the heavenly people. And he expects everybody to *stick* at that age—stand stock-still—and expects them to enjoy it!— Now just think of the idea

of standing still in heaven! Think of a heaven made up entirely of hoop-rolling, marble-playing cubs of seven years!—or of awkward, diffident, sentimental immaturities of nineteen!—or of vigorous people of thirty, healthy-minded, brimming with ambition, but chained hand and foot to that one age and its limitations like so many helpless galley-slaves! Think of the dull sameness of a society made up of people all of one age and one set of looks, habits, tastes and feelings. Think how superior to it earth would be, with its variety of types and faces and ages, and the enlivening attrition of the myriad interests that come into pleasant collision in such a variegated society."

"Look here," says I, "do you know what you're doing?"

"Well, what am I doing?"

"You are making heaven pretty comfortable in one way, but you are playing the mischief with it in another."

"How d'you mean?"

"Well," I says, "take a young mother that's lost her child, and—"

"'Sh!" he says. "Look!"

It was a woman. Middle-aged, and had grizzled hair. She was walking slow, and her head was bent down, and her wings hanging limp and droopy; and she looked ever so tired, and was crying, poor thing! She passed along by, with her head down, that way, and the tears running down her face, and didn't see us. Then Sandy said, low and gentle, and full of pity:

"*She's* hunting for her child! No, *found* it, I reckon. Lord, how she's changed! But I recognized her in a minute, though it's twenty-seven years since I saw her. A young mother she was, about twenty-two or four, or along there; and blooming and lovely and sweet—oh, just a flower! And all her heart and all her soul was wrapped up in her child, her little girl, two years old. And it died, and she went wild with grief, just wild! Well, the only comfort she had was that she'd see her child again, in heaven—'never more to part,' she said, and kept on saying it over and over, 'never more to part.' And the words made her happy; yes, they did; they made her joyful; and when I was dying, twenty-seven years ago, she told me to find her child the first thing, and say she was coming—'soon, soon, *very* soon, she hoped and believed!'"

"Why, it's pitiful, Sandy."

He didn't say anything for a while, but sat looking at the ground, thinking. Then he says, kind of mournful:

"And now she's come!"

"Well? Go on."

"Stormfield, maybe she hasn't found the child, but I think she has.

Looks so to me. I've seen cases before. You see, she's kept that child in her head just the same as it was when she jounced it in her arms a little chubby thing. But here it didn't elect to *stay* a child. No, it elected to grow up, which it did. And in these twenty-seven years it has learned all the deep scientific learning there is to learn, and is studying and studying and learning and learning more and more, all the time, and don't give a damn for anything *but* learning; just learning, and discussing gigantic problems with people like herself."

"Well?"

"Stormfield, don't you see? Her mother knows *cranberries*, and how to tend them, and pick them, and put them up, and market them; and not another blamed thing! Her and her daughter can't be any more company for each other *now* than mud turtle and bird o' paradise. Poor thing, she was looking for a baby to jounce; *I* think she's struck a disapp'intment."

"Sandy, what will they do—stay unhappy forever in heaven?"

"No, they'll come together and get adjusted by and by. But not this year, and not next. By and by."

2

I had been having considerable trouble with my wings. The day after I helped the choir I made a dash or two with them, but was not lucky. First off, I flew thirty yards, and then fouled an Irishman and brought him down—brought us both down, in fact. Next, I had a collision with a Bishop—and bowled him down, of course. We had some sharp words, and I felt pretty cheap, to come banging into a grave old person like that, with a million strangers looking on and smiling to themselves.

I saw I hadn't got the hang of the steering, and so couldn't rightly tell where I was going to bring up when I started. I went afoot the rest of the day, and let my wings hang. Early next morning I went to a private place to have some practice. I got up on a pretty high rock, and got a good start, and went swooping down, aiming for a bush a little over three hundred yards off; but I couldn't seem to calculate for the wind, which was about two points abaft my beam. I could see I was going considerable to looard of the bush, so I worked my starboard wing slow and went ahead strong on the port one, but it wouldn't answer; I could see I was going to broach to, so I slowed down on both, and lit. I went back to the rock and took another chance at it. I aimed two or three points to starboard of the bush—yes, more than that— enough so as to make it nearly a head-wind. I done well enough, but made pretty poor time. I could see, plain enough, that on a head-wind, wings was a mistake. I could see that a body could sail pretty close to the wind, but he couldn't go in the wind's eye. I could see that if I wanted to go a-visiting any distance from home, and the wind was ahead, I might have to wait days, maybe, for a change; and I could see, too, that these things could not be any use at all in a gale; if you tried to run before the wind, you would make a mess of it, for there isn't any way to shorten sail—like reefing, you know—you have to take it *all* in—shut your feathers down flat to your sides. That would *land* you, of course. You could lay to, with your head to the wind—that is the best you could do, and right hard work you'd find it, too. If you tried any other game, you would founder, sure.

I judge it was about a couple of weeks or so after this that I dropped old Sandy McWilliams a note one day—it was a Tuesday—and asked him to come over and take his manna and quails with me next day; and the first thing he did when he stepped in was to twinkle his eye in a sly way, and say,—

"Well, Cap, what you done with your wings?"

I saw in a minute that there was some sarcasm done up in that rag somewheres, but I never let on. I only says,—

"Gone to the wash."

"Yes," he says, in a dry sort of way, "they mostly go to the wash—about this time—I've often noticed it. Fresh angels are powerful neat. When do you look for 'em back?"

"Day after to-morrow," says I.

He winked at me, and smiled.

Says I,—

"Sandy, out with it. Come—no secrets among friends. I notice you don't ever wear wings—and plenty others don't. I've been making an ass of myself—is that it?"

"That is about the size of it. But it is no harm. We all do it at first. It's perfectly natural. You see, on earth we jumped to such foolish conclusions as to things up here. In the pictures we always saw the angels with wings on—and that was all right; but we jumped to the conclusion that that was their way of getting around—and that was all wrong. The wings ain't anything but a uniform, that's all. When they are in the field—so to speak,—they always wear them; you never see an angel going with a message anywhere without his wings, any more than you would see a military officer presiding at a court-martial without his uniform, or a postman delivering letters, or a policeman walking his beat, in plain clothes. But they ain't to *fly* with! The wings are for show, not for use. Old experienced angels are like officers of the regular army—they dress plain, when they are off duty. New angels are like the militia—never shed the uniform—always fluttering and floundering around in their wings, butting people down, flapping here, and there, and everywhere, always imagining they are attracting the admiring eye—well, they just think they are the very most important people in heaven. And when you see one of them come sailing around with one wing tipped up and t'other down, you make up your mind he is saying to himself: 'I wish Mary Ann in Arkansaw could see me now. I reckon she'd wish she hadn't shook me.' No, they're just for show, that's all—only just for show."

"I judge you've got it about right, Sandy," says I.

"Why, look at it yourself," says he. "*You* ain't built for wings—no man is. You know what a grist of years it took you to come here from the earth—and yet you were booming along faster than any cannon-ball could go. Suppose you had to fly that distance with your wings—wouldn't eternity have been over before you got here? Certainly. Well, angels have to go to the earth every day—millions of them—to appear in visions to dying children and good people, you know—it's the heft of their business. They appear with their wings, of course, because they are on official service, and because the dying persons wouldn't know they were angels if they hadn't wings—but do you reckon they fly with them? It stands to reason they don't. The wings would wear out before they got half-way; even the pinfeathers would be gone; the wing frames would be as bare as kite sticks before the paper is pasted on. The distances in heaven are billions of times greater; angels have to go all over heaven every day; could they do it with their wings alone? No, indeed; they wear the wings for style, but they travel any distance in an instant by *wishing*. The wishing-carpet of the Arabian Nights was a sensible idea—but our earthly idea of angels flying these awful distances with their clumsy wings was foolish.

"Our young saints, of both sexes, wear wings all the time—blazing red ones, and blue and green, and gold, and variegated, and rainbowed, and ring-streaked-and-striped ones—and nobody finds fault. It is suitable to their time of life. The things are beautiful, and they set the young people off. They are the most striking and lovely part of their outfit—a halo don't *begin*."

"Well," says I, "I've tucked mine away in the cupboard, and I allow to let them lay there till there's mud."

"Yes—or a reception."

"What's that?"

"Well, you can see one to-night if you want to. There's a barkeeper from Jersey City going to be received."

"Go on—tell me about it."

"This barkeeper got converted at a Moody and Sankey meeting, in New York, and started home on the ferryboat, and there was a collision and he got drowned. He is of a class that thinks all heaven goes wild with joy when a particularly hard lot like him is saved; they think all heaven turns out hosannahing to welcome them; they think there isn't anything talked about in the realms of the blest but their case, for that day. This barkeeper thinks there hasn't been such another stir here in years, as his coming is going to raise.— And I've always noticed this peculiarity about a dead barkeeper—he not only expects all hands to turn out when he arrives, but he expects to be received with a torchlight procession."

"I reckon he is disappointed, then."

"No, he isn't. No man is allowed to be disappointed here. Whatever he wants, when he comes—that is, any reasonable and unsacrilegious thing—he can have. There's always a few millions or billions of young folks around who don't want any better entertainment than to fill up their lungs and swarm out with their torches and have a high time over a barkeeper. It tickles the barkeeper till he can't rest, it makes a charming lark for the young folks, it don't do anybody any harm, it don't cost a rap, and it keeps up the place's reputation for making all comers happy and content."

"Very good. I'll be on hand and see them land the barkeeper."

"It is manners to go in full dress. You want to wear your wings, you know, and your other things."

"Which ones?"

"Halo, and harp, and palm branch, and all that."

"Well," says I, "I reckon I ought to be ashamed of myself, but the fact is I left them laying around that day I resigned from the choir. I haven't got a rag to wear but this robe and the wings."

"That's all right. You'll find they've been raked up and saved for you. Send for them."

"I'll do it, Sandy. But what was it you was saying about unsacrilegious things, which people expect to get, and will be disappointed about?"

"Oh, there are a lot of such things that people expect and don't get. For instance, there's a Brooklyn preacher by the name of Talmage, who is laying up a considerable disappointment for himself. He says, every now and then in his sermons, that the first thing he does when he gets to heaven, will be to fling his arms around Abraham, Isaac and Jacob, and kiss them and weep on them. There's millions of people down there on earth that are promising themselves the same thing. As many as sixty thousand people arrive here every single day, that want to run straight to Abraham, Isaac and Jacob, and hug them and weep on them. Now mind you, sixty thousand a day is a pretty heavy contract for those old people. If they were a mind to allow it, they wouldn't ever have anything to do, year in and year out, but stand up and be hugged and wept on thirty-two hours in the twenty-four. They would be tired out and as wet as muskrats all the time. What would heaven be, to *them?* It would be a mighty good place to get out of—you know that, yourself. Those are kind and gentle old Jews, but they ain't any fonder of kissing the emotional high-lights of Brooklyn than you be. You mark my words, Mr. T.'s endearments are going to be declined, with thanks. There are limits to the privileges of the elect, even in heaven. Why, if Adam was to show himself to every new comer that wants to call and gaze at him and strike him for his autograph, he would never have time to do anything else but just that. Talmage has said he is going to give Adam some of his attentions, as well as A., I. and J. But he will have to change his mind about that."

"Do you think Talmage will really come here?"

"Why, certainly, he will; but don't you be alarmed; he will run with his own kind, and there's plenty of them. That is the main charm of heaven—there's all kinds here—which wouldn't be the case if you let the preachers tell it. Anybody can find the sort he prefers, here, and he just lets the others alone, and they let him alone. When the Deity builds a heaven, it is built right, and on a liberal plan."

Sandy sent home for his things, and I sent for mine, and about nine in the evening we begun to dress. Sandy says,—

"This is going to be a grand time for you, Stormy. Like as not some of the patriarchs will turn out."

"No, but will they?"

"Like as not. Of course they are pretty exclusive. They hardly ever show themselves to the common public. I believe they never turn out except for an eleventh-hour convert. They wouldn't do it then, only earthly tradition makes a grand show pretty necessary on that kind of an occasion."

"Do they all turn out, Sandy?"

"Who?—all the patriarchs? Oh, no—hardly ever more than a couple. You will be here fifty thousand years—maybe more—before you get a glimpse of all the patriarchs and prophets. Since I have been here, Job has been to the front once, and once Ham and Jeremiah both at the same time. But the finest thing that has happened in my day was a year or so ago; that was Charles Peace's reception—him they called 'the Bannercross Murderer'—an Englishman. There were four patriarchs and two prophets on the Grand Stand that time—there hasn't been anything like it since Captain Kidd came; Abel was there—the first time in twelve hundred years. A report got around that Adam was coming; well, of course, Abel was enough to bring a crowd, all by himself, but there is nobody that can draw like Adam. It was a false report, but it got around, anyway, as I say, and it will be a long day before I see the like of it again. The reception was in the English department, of course, which is eight hundred and eleven million miles from the New Jersey line. I went, along with a good many of my neighbors, and it was a sight to see, I can tell you. Flocks came from all the departments. I saw Esquimaux there, and Tartars, Negroes, Chinamen—people from everywhere. You see a mixture like that in the Grand Choir, the first day you land here, but you hardly ever see it again. There were billions of people; when they were singing or hosannahing, the noise was wonderful; and even when their tongues were still the drumming of the wings was nearly enough to burst your head, for all the sky was as thick as if it was snowing angels. Although Adam was not there, it was a great time anyway, because we had three archangels on the Grand Stand—it is a seldom thing that even one comes out."

"What did they look like, Sandy?"

"Well, they had shining faces, and shining robes, and wonderful rainbow wings, and they stood eighteen feet high, and wore swords, and held their heads up in a noble way, and looked like soldiers."

"Did they have halos?"

"No—anyway, not the hoop kind. The archangels and the upper-class patriarchs wear a finer thing than that. It is a round, solid, splendid glory of gold, that is blinding to look at. You have often seen a patriarch in a picture, on earth, with that thing on—you remember it?—he looks as if he had his head in a brass platter. That don't give you the right idea of it at all—it is much more shining and beautiful."

"Did you talk with those archangels and patriarchs, Sandy?"

"Who—I? Why, what can you be thinking about, Stormy? I ain't worthy to speak to such as they."

"Is Talmage?"

"Of course not. You have got the same mixed-up idea about these things that everybody has down there. I had it once, but I got over it. Down there they talk of the heavenly King—and that is right—but then they go right on speaking as if this was a republic and everybody was on a dead level with everybody else, and privileged to fling his arms around anybody he comes across, and be hail-fellow-well-met with all the elect, from the highest down. How tangled up and absurd that is! How are you going to have a republic under a king? How are you going to have a republic at all, where the head of the government is absolute, holds his place forever, and has no parliament, no council to meddle or make in his affairs, nobody voted for, nobody elected, nobody in the whole universe with a voice in the government, nobody asked to take a hand in its matters, and nobody *allowed* to do it? Fine republic, ain't it?"

"Well, yes—it *is* a little different from the idea I had—but I thought I might go around and get acquainted with the grandees, anyway— not exactly splice the main-brace with them, you know, but shake hands and pass the time of day."

"Could Tom, Dick and Harry call on the Cabinet of Russia and do that?—on Prince Gortschakoff, for instance?"

"I reckon not, Sandy."

"Well, this is Russia—only more so. There's not the shadow of a re- public about it anywhere. There are ranks, here. There are viceroys, princes, governors, sub-governors, sub-sub-governors, and a hundred orders of nobility, grading along down from grand-ducal archangels, stage by stage, till the general level is struck, where there ain't any titles. Do you know what a prince of the blood is, on earth?"

"No."

"Well, a prince of the blood don't belong to the royal family exactly, and he don't belong to the mere nobility of the kingdom; he is lower than the one, and higher than t'other. That's about the position of the patriarchs and prophets here. There's some mighty high nobility here —people that you and I ain't worthy to polish sandals for—and *they* ain't worthy to polish sandals for the patriarchs and prophets. That gives you a kind of an idea of their rank, don't it? You begin to see how high up they are, don't you? Just to get a two-minute glimpse of one of them is a thing for a body to remember and tell about for a thousand years. Why, Captain, just think of this: if Abraham was to set his foot down here by this door, there would be a railing set up around that foot-track right away, and a shelter put over it, and people would flock here from all over heaven, for hundreds and hundreds of years, to look at it. Abraham is one of the parties that Mr. Talmage, of Brook- lyn, is going to embrace, and kiss, and weep on, when he comes. He wants to lay in a good stock of tears, you know, or five to one he will go dry before he gets a chance to do it."

"Sandy," says I, "I had an idea that I was going to be equal with everybody here, too, but I will let that drop. It don't matter, and I am plenty happy enough anyway."

"Captain, you are happier than you would be, the other way. These old patriarchs and prophets have got ages the start of you; they know more in two minutes than you know in a year. Did you ever try to have a sociable improving-time discussing winds, and currents and variations of compass with an undertaker?"

"I get your idea, Sandy. He couldn't interest me. He would be an ignoramus in such things—he would bore me, and I would bore him."

"You have got it. You would bore the patriarchs when you talked, and when they talked they would shoot over your head. By and by you would say, 'Good morning, your Eminence, I will call again'—but you wouldn't. Did you ever ask the slush-boy to come up in the cabin and take dinner with you?"

"I get your drift again, Sandy. I wouldn't be used to such grand people as the patriarchs and prophets, and I would be sheepish and tongue-tied in their company, and mighty glad to get out of it. Sandy, which is the highest rank, patriarch or prophet?"

"Oh, the prophets hold over the patriarchs. The newest prophet, even, is of a sight more consequence than the oldest patriarch. Yes, sir, Adam himself has to walk behind Shakespeare."

"Was Shakespeare a prophet?"

"Of course he was; and so was Homer, and heaps more. But Shakespeare and the rest have to walk behind a common tailor from Tennessee, by the name of Billings; and behind a horse-doctor named Sakka, from Afghanistan. Jeremiah, and Billings and Buddha walk together, side by side, right behind a crowd from planets not in our astronomy; next come a dozen or two from Jupiter and other worlds; next come Daniel, and Sakka and Confucius; next a lot from systems outside of ours; next come Ezekiel, and Mahomet, Zoroaster, and a knife-grinder from ancient Egypt; then there is a long string, and after them, away down toward the bottom, come Shakespeare and Homer, and a shoemaker named Marais, from the back settlements of France."

"Have they really rung in Mahomet and all those other heathens?"

"Yes—they all had their message, and they all get their reward. The man who don't get his reward on earth, needn't bother—he will get it here, sure."

"But why did they throw off on Shakespeare, that way, and put him away down there below those shoemakers and horse-doctors and knife-grinders—a lot of people nobody ever heard of?"

"That is the heavenly justice of it—they warn't rewarded according to their deserts, on earth, but here they get their rightful rank. That tailor Billings, from Tennessee, wrote poetry that Homer and Shakespeare couldn't begin to come up to; but nobody would print it, nobody read it but his neighbors, an ignorant lot, and they laughed at it. Whenever the village had a drunken frolic and a dance, they would drag him in and crown him with cabbage leaves, and pretend to bow down to him; and one night when he was sick and nearly starved to death, they had him out and crowned him, and then they rode him on a rail about the village, and everybody followed along, beating tin pans and yelling. Well, he died before morning. He wasn't ever expecting to go to heaven, much less that there was going to be any fuss made over him, so I reckon he was a good deal surprised when the reception broke on him."

"Was you there, Sandy?"

"Bless you, no!"

"Why? Didn't you know it was going to come off?"

"Well, I judge I did. It was the talk of these realms—not for a day, like this barkeeper business, but for twenty years before the man died."

"Why the mischief didn't you go, then?"

"Now how you talk! The like of me go meddling around at the reception of a prophet? A mudsill like me trying to push in and help receive an awful grandee like Edward J. Billings? Why, I should have been laughed at for a billion miles around. I shouldn't ever heard the last of it."

"Well, who did go, then?"

"Mighty few people that you and I will ever get a chance to see, Captain. Not a solitary commoner ever has the luck to see a reception of a prophet, I can tell you. All the nobility, and all the patriarchs and prophets—every last one of them—and all the archangels, and all the princes and governors and viceroys, were there,—and no small fry—not a single one. And mind you, I'm not talking about only the grandees from our world, but the princes and patriarchs and so on from all the worlds that shine in our sky, and from billions more that belong in systems upon systems away outside of the one our sun is in. There were some prophets and patriarchs there that ours ain't a circumstance to, for rank and illustriousness and all that. Some were from Jupiter and other worlds in our own system, but the most celebrated were three poets, Saa, Bo and Soof, from great planets in three different and very remote systems. These three names are common and familiar in every nook and corner of heaven, clear from one end of it to the other—fully

EXTRACT FROM CAPTAIN STORMFIELD'S VISIT TO HEAVEN 589

as well known as the eighty Supreme Archangels, in fact—whereas our
Moses, and Adam, and the rest, have not been heard of outside of our
world's little corner of heaven, except by a few very learned men scattered here and there—and they always spell their names wrong, and
get the performances of one mixed up with the doings of another, and
they almost always locate them simply *in our solar system*, and think
that is enough without going into little details such as naming the particular world they are from. It is like a learned Hindoo showing off how
much he knows by saying Longfellow lived in the United States—as if
he lived all over the United States, and as if the country was so small
you couldn't throw a brick there without hitting him. Between you and
me, it does gravel me, the cool way people from those monster worlds
outside our system snub our little world, and even our system. Of course
we think a good deal of Jupiter, because our world is only a potato to
it, for size; but then there are worlds in other systems that Jupiter isn't
even a mustard-seed to—like the planet Goobra, for instance, which you
couldn't squeeze inside the orbit of Halley's comet without straining
the rivets. Tourists from Goobra (I mean parties that lived and died
there—natives) come here, now and then, and inquire about our world,
and when they find out it is so little that a streak of lightning can flash
clear around it in the eighth of a second, they have to lean up against
something to laugh. Then they screw a glass into their eye and go to
examining *us*, as if we were a curious kind of foreign bug, or something
of that sort. One of them asked me how long our day was; and when I
told him it was twelve hours long, as a general thing, he asked me if
people where I was from considered it worth while to get up and wash
for such a day as that. That is the way with those Goobra people—they
can't seem to let a chance go by to throw it in your face that their day
is three hundred and twenty-two of our years long. This young snob
was just of age—he was six or seven thousand of his days old—say two
million of our years—and he had all the puppy airs that belong to that
time of life—that turning-point when a person has got over being a boy
and yet ain't quite a man exactly. If it had been anywhere else but in
heaven, I would have given him a piece of my mind. Well, anyway,
Billings had the grandest reception that has been seen in thousands of
centuries, and I think it will have a good effect. His name will be carried pretty far, and it will make our system talked about, and maybe
our world, too, and raise us in the respect of the general public of
heaven. Why, look here—Shakespeare walked backwards before that
tailor from Tennessee, and scattered flowers for him to walk on, and
Homer stood behind his chair and waited on him at the banquet. Of

course that didn't go for much *there,* amongst all those big foreigners
from other systems, as they hadn't heard of Shakespeare or Homer
either, but it would amount to considerable down there on our little
earth if they could know about it. I wish there was something *in* that
miserable spiritualism, so we could send them word. That Tennessee
village would set up a monument to Billings, then, and his autograph
would outsell Satan's. Well, they had grand times at that reception—a
small-fry noble from Hoboken told me all about it—Sir Richard Duffer,
Baronet."

"What, Sandy, a nobleman from Hoboken? How is that?"

"Easy enough. Duffer kept a sausage-shop and never saved a cent
in his life because he used to give all his spare meat to the poor, in a
quiet way. Not tramps,—no, the other sort—the sort that will starve before they will beg—honest square people out of work. Dick used to
watch hungry-looking men and women and children, and track them
home, and find out all about them from the neighbors, and then feed
them and find them work. As nobody ever *saw* him give anything to
anybody, he had the reputation of being mean; he died with it, too,
and everybody said it was a good riddance; but the minute he landed
here, they made him a baronet, and the very first words Dick the
sausage-maker of Hoboken heard when he stepped upon the heavenly
shore were, 'Welcome, Sir Richard Duffer!' It surprised him some, because he thought he had reasons to believe he was pointed for a warmer
climate than this one."

All of a sudden the whole region fairly rocked under the crash of
eleven hundred and one thunder blasts, all let off at once, and Sandy
says,—

"There, that's for the barkeep."

I jumped up and says,—

"Then let's be moving along, Sandy; we don't want to miss any of
this thing, you know."

"Keep your seat," he says; "he is only just telegraphed, that is all."

"How?"

"That blast only means that he has been sighted from the signal-
station. He is off Sandy Hook. The committees will go down to meet
him, now, and escort him in. There will be ceremonies and delays;
they won't be coming up the Bay for a considerable time, yet. It is
several billion miles away, anyway."

"*I* could have been a barkeeper and a hard lot just as well as not," says I, remembering the lonesome way I arrived, and how there wasn't any committee nor anything.

"I notice some regret in your voice," says Sandy, "and it is natural enough; but let bygones be bygones; you went according to your lights, and it is too late now to mend the thing."

"No, let it slide, Sandy, I don't mind. But you've got a Sandy Hook *here*, too, have you?"

"We've got everything here, just as it is below. All the States and Territories of the Union, and all the kingdoms of the earth and the islands of the sea are laid out here just as they are on the globe—all the same shape they are down there, and all graded to the relative size, only each State and realm and island is a good many billion times bigger here than it is below. There goes another blast."

"What is that one for?"

"That is only another fort answering the first one. They each fire eleven hundred and one thunder blasts at a single dash—it is the usual salute for an eleventh-hour guest; a hundred for each hour and an extra one for the guest's sex; if it was a woman we would know it by their leaving off the extra gun."

"How do we know there's eleven hundred and one, Sandy, when they all go off at once?—and yet we certainly do know."

"Our intellects are a good deal sharpened up, here, in some ways, and that is one of them. Numbers and sizes and distances are so great, here, that we have to be made so we can *feel* them—our old ways of counting and measuring and ciphering wouldn't ever give us an idea of them, but would only confuse us and oppress us and make our heads ache."

After some more talk about this, I says: "Sandy, I notice that I hardly ever see a white angel; where I run across one white angel, I strike as many as a hundred million copper-colored ones—people that can't speak English. How is that?"

"Well, you will find it the same in any State or Territory of the American corner of heaven you choose to go to. I have shot along, a whole week on a stretch, and gone millions and millions of miles, through perfect swarms of angels, without ever seeing a single white one, or hearing a word I could understand. You see, America was occupied a billion years and more, by Injuns and Aztecs, and that sort of folks, before a white man ever set his foot in it. During the first three hundred years after Columbus's discovery, there wasn't ever more than one good lecture audience of white people, all put together, in America—I mean the whole thing, British Possessions and all; in the beginning of our century there were only 6,000,000 or 7,000,000—say seven; 12,000,000 or 14,000,000 in 1825; say 23,000,000 in 1850; 40,000,000 in 1875. Our death-rate has always been 20 in 1000 per annum. Well, 140,000 died the first year of the century; 280,000 the twenty-fifth year; 500,000 the fiftieth year; about a million the seventy-fifth year. Now I am going to be liberal about this thing, and consider that fifty million whites have died in America from the beginning up to to-day—make it sixty, if you want to; make it a hundred million—it's no difference about a few millions one way or t'other. Well, now, you can see, yourself, that when you come to spread a little dab of people like that over these hundreds of billions of miles of American territory here in heaven, it is like scattering a ten-cent box of homœopathic pills over the Great Sahara and expecting to find them again. You can't expect us to amount to anything in heaven, and we *don't*—now that is the simple fact, and we have got to do the best we can with it. The learned men from other planets and other systems come here and hang around à while, when they are touring around the Kingdom, and then go back to their own section of heaven and write a book of travels, and they give America about five lines in it. And what do they say about us? They say this wilderness is populated with a scattering few hundred thousand billions of red angels, with now and then a curiously complected *diseased* one. You see, they think we whites and the occasional nigger are Injuns that have been bleached out or blackened by some leprous disease or other—for some peculiarly rascally *sin*, mind you. It is a mighty sour pill for us all, my friend—even the modestest of us, let alone the other kind, that think they are going to be received like a long-lost government bond, and hug Abraham into the bargain. I haven't asked you any of the particulars, Captain, but I judge it goes without saying—if my experience is worth anything—that there wasn't much of a hooraw made over you when you arrived—now was there?"

"Don't mention it, Sandy," says I, coloring up a little; "I wouldn't have had the family see it for any amount you are a mind to name. Change the subject, Sandy, change the subject."

"Well, do you think of settling in the California department of bliss?"

"I don't know. I wasn't calculating on doing anything really definite in that direction till the family come. I thought I would just look around, meantime, in a quiet way, and make up my mind. Besides, I know a good many dead people, and I was calculating to hunt them up and swap a little gossip with them about friends, and old times, and one thing or another, and ask them how they like it here, as far as they have got. I reckon my wife will want to camp in the California range, though, because most all her departed will be there, and she likes to be with folks she knows."

"Don't you let her. You see what the Jersey district of heaven is, for whites; well, the California district is a thousand times worse. It swarms with a mean kind of leather-headed mud-colored angels—and your nearest white neighbors is likely to be a million miles away. *What a man mostly misses, in heaven, is company*—company of his own sort and color and language. I have come near settling in the European part of heaven once or twice on that account."

"Well, why didn't you, Sandy?"

"Oh, various reasons. For one thing, although you *see* plenty of whites there, you can't understand any of them hardly, and so you go about as hungry for talk as you do here. I like to look at a Russian or a German or an Italian—I even like to look at a Frenchman if I ever have the luck to catch him engaged in anything that ain't indelicate—but *looking* don't cure the hunger—what you want is talk."

"Well, there's England, Sandy—the English district of heaven."

"Yes, but it is not so very much better than this end of the heavenly domain. As long as you run across Englishmen born this side of three hundred years ago, you are all right; but the minute you get back of Elizabeth's time the language begins to fog up, and the further back you go the foggier it gets. I had some talk with one Langland and a man by the name of Chaucer—old-time poets—but it was no use, I couldn't quite understand them and they couldn't quite understand me. I have had letters from them since, but it is such broken English I can't make it out. Back of those men's time the English are just simply foreigners, nothing more, nothing less; they talk Danish, German, Norman French, and sometimes a mixture of all three; back of *them*, they talk Latin, and ancient British, Irish, and Gaelic; and then back of these come billions and billions of pure savages that talk a gibberish that Satan himself couldn't understand. The fact is, where you strike one man in the English settlements that you can understand, you wade through awful swarms that talk something you can't make head nor tail of. You see, every country on earth has been overlaid so often, in the course of a billion years, with different kinds of people and different sorts of languages, that this sort of mongrel business was bound to be the result in heaven."

"Sandy," says I, "did you see a good many of the great people history tells about?"

"Yes—plenty. I saw kings and all sorts of distinguished people."

"Do the kings rank just as they did below?"

"No; a body can't bring his rank up here with him. Divine right is a good-enough earthly romance, but it don't go, here. Kings drop down to the general level as soon as they reach the realms of grace. I knew Charles the Second very well—one of the most popular comedians in the English section—draws first rate. There are better, of course—people that were never heard of on earth—but Charles is making a very good reputation indeed, and is considered a rising man. Richard the Lion-hearted is in the prize-ring, and coming into considerable favor. Henry the Eighth is a tragedian, and the scenes where he kills people are done to the very life. Henry the Sixth keeps a religious-book stand."

"Did you ever see Napoleon, Sandy?"

"Often—sometimes in the Corsican range, sometimes in the French. He always hunts up a conspicuous place, and goes frowning around with his arms folded and his field-glass under his arm, looking as grand, gloomy and peculiar as his reputation calls for, and very much bothered because he don't stand as high, here, for a soldier, as he expected to."

"Why, who stands higher?"

"Oh, a *lot* of people *we* never heard of before—the shoemaker and horse-doctor and knife-grinder kind, you know—clodhoppers from goodness knows where, that never handled a sword or fired a shot in their lives—but the soldiership was in them, though they never had a chance to show it. But here they take their right place, and Cæsar and Napoleon and Alexander have to take a back seat. The greatest military genius our world ever produced was a bricklayer from somewhere back of Boston—died during the Revolution—by the name of Absalom Jones. Wherever he goes, crowds flock to see him. You see, everybody knows that if he had had a chance he would have shown the world some generalship that would have made all generalship before look like child's play and 'prentice work. But he never got a chance; he tried heaps of times to enlist as a private, but he had lost both thumbs and a couple of front teeth, and the recruiting sergeant wouldn't pass him. However, as I say, everybody knows, now, what he *would* have been, and so they flock by the million to get a glimpse of him whenever they hear he is going to be anywhere. Cæsar, and Hannibal, and Alexander, and Napoleon are all on his staff, and ever so many more great generals; but the public hardly care to look at *them* when *he* is around. Boom! There goes another salute. The barkeeper's off quarantine now."

Sandy and I put on our things. Then we made a wish, and in a second we were at the reception-place. We stood on the edge of the ocean of space, and looked out over the dimness, but couldn't make out anything. Close by us was the Grand Stand—tier on tier of dim thrones rising up toward the zenith. From each side of it spread away the tiers of seats for the general public. They spread away for leagues and leagues —you couldn't see the ends. They were empty and still, and hadn't a cheerful look, but looked dreary, like a theater before anybody comes —gas turned down. Sandy says,—

"We'll sit down here and wait. We'll see the head of the procession come in sight away off yonder pretty soon, now."

Says I,—

"It's pretty lonesome, Sandy; I reckon there's a hitch somewheres. Nobody but just you and me—it ain't much of a display for the barkeeper."

"Don't you fret, it's all right. There'll be one more gun-fire—then you'll see."

In a little while we noticed a sort of a lightish flush, away off on the horizon.

"Head of the torchlight procession," says Sandy.

It spread, and got lighter and brighter; soon it had a strong glare like a locomotive headlight; it kept on getting brighter and brighter till it was like the sun peeping above the horizon-line at sea—the big red rays shot high up into the sky.

"Keep your eyes on the Grand Stand and the miles of seats—sharp!" says Sandy, "and listen for the gun-fire."

Just then it burst out, "Boom-boom-boom!" like a million thunderstorms in one, and made the whole heavens rock. Then there was a sudden and awful glare of light all about us, and in that very instant every one of the millions of seats was occupied, and as far as you could see, in both directions, was just a solid pack of people, and the place was all splendidly lit up! It was enough to take a body's breath away. Sandy says,—

"That is the way we do it here. No time fooled away; nobody straggling in after the curtain's up. Wishing is quicker work than traveling. A quarter of a second ago these folks were millions of miles from here. When they heard the last signal, all they had to do was to wish, and here they are."

The prodigious choir struck up,—

> *We long to hear thy voice,*
> *To see thee face to face.*

It was noble music, but the uneducated chipped in and spoilt it, just as the congregations used to do on earth.

The head of the procession begun to pass, now, and it was a wonder-ful sight. It swept along, thick and solid, five hundred thousand angels abreast, and every angel carrying a torch and singing—the whirring thunder of the wings made a body's head ache. You could follow the line of the procession back, and slanting upward into the sky, far away in a glittering snaky rope, till it was only a faint streak in the distance. The rush went on and on, for a long time, and at last, sure enough, along comes the barkeeper, and then everybody rose, and a cheer went up that made the heavens shake, I tell you! He was all smiles, and had his halo tilted over one ear in a cocky way, and was the most satisfied-looking saint I ever saw. While he marched up the steps of the Grand Stand, the choir struck up,—

> *The whole wide heaven groans,*
> *And waits to hear that voice.*

There were four gorgeous tents standing side by side in the place of honor, on a broad railed platform in the center of the Grand Stand, with a shining guard of honor round about them. The tents had been shut up all this time. As the barkeeper climbed along up, bowing and smiling to everybody, and at last got to the platform, these tents were jerked up aloft all of a sudden, and we saw four noble thrones of gold, all caked with jewels, and in the two middle ones sat old white-whisk-ered men, and in the two others a couple of the most glorious and gaudy giants, with platter halos and beautiful armor. All the millions went down on their knees, and stared, and looked glad, and burst out into a joyful kind of murmurs. They said,—

"Two archangels!—that is splendid. Who can the others be?"

The archangels gave the barkeeper a stiff little military bow; the two old men rose; one of them said, "Moses and Esau welcome thee!" and then all the four vanished, and the thrones were empty.

The barkeeper looked a little disappointed, for he was calculating to hug those old people, I judge; but it was the gladdest and proudest multitude you ever saw—because they had seen Moses and Esau. Everybody was saying, "Did you see them?—I did—Esau's side face was to me, but I saw Moses full in the face, just as plain as I see you this min-ute!"

The procession took up the barkeeper and moved on with him again, and the crowd broke up and scattered. As we went along home, Sandy said it was a great success, and the barkeeper would have a right to be proud of it forever. And he said *we* were in luck, too; said we might attend receptions for forty thousand years to come, and not have a chance to see a brace of such grand moguls as Moses and Esau. We found afterwards that we had come near seeing another patriarch, and likewise a genuine prophet besides, but at the last moment they sent regrets. Sandy said there would be a monument put up there, where Moses and Esau had stood, with the date and circumstances, and all about the whole business, and travelers would come for thousands of years and gawk at it, and climb over it, and scribble their names on it.

1907

A Fable

Once upon a time an artist who had painted a small and very beautiful picture placed it so that he could see it in the mirror. He said, "This doubles the distance and softens it, and it is twice as lovely as it was before."

The animals out in the woods heard of this through the housecat, who was greatly admired by them because he was so learned, and so refined and civilized, and so polite and high-bred, and could tell them so much which they didn't know before, and were not certain about afterward. They were much excited about this new piece of gossip, and they asked questions, so as to get at a full understanding of it. They asked what a picture was, and the cat explained.

"It is a flat thing," he said; "wonderfully flat, marvelously flat, enchantingly flat and elegant. And, oh, so beautiful!"

That excited them almost to a frenzy, and they said they would give the world to see it. Then the bear asked:

"What is it that makes it so beautiful?"

"It is the looks of it," said the cat.

This filled them with admiration and uncertainty, and they were more excited than ever. Then the cow asked:

"What is a mirror?"

"It is a hole in the wall," said the cat. "You look in it, and there you see the picture, and it is so dainty and charming and ethereal and inspiring in its unimaginable beauty that your head turns round and round, and you almost swoon with ecstasy."

The ass had not said anything as yet; he now began to throw doubts. He said there had never been anything as beautiful as this before, and probably wasn't now. He said that when it took a whole basketful of sesquipedalian adjectives to whoop up a thing of beauty, it was time for suspicion.

It was easy to see that these doubts were having an effect upon the animals, so the cat went off offended. The subject was dropped for a couple of days, but in the meantime curiosity was taking a fresh start, and there was a revival of interest perceptible. Then the animals assailed the ass for spoiling what could possibly have been a pleasure to them, on a mere suspicion that the picture was not beautiful, without any evidence that such was the case. The ass was not troubled; he was calm, and said there was one way to find out who was in the right, himself or the cat: he would go and look in that hole, and come back and tell what he found there. The animals felt relieved and grateful, and asked him to go at once—which he did.

But he did not know where he ought to stand; and so, through error, he stood between the picture and the mirror. The result was that the picture had no chance, and didn't show up. He returned home and said:

"The cat lied. There was nothing in that hole but an ass. There wasn't a sign of a flat thing visible. It was a handsome ass, and friendly, but just an ass, and nothing more."

The elephant asked:

"Did you see it good and clear? Were you close to it?"

"I saw it good and clear, O Hathi, King of Beasts. I was so close that I touched noses with it."

"This is very strange," said the elephant; "the cat was always truthful before—as far as we could make out. Let another witness try. Go, Baloo, look in the hole, and come and report."

So the bear went. When he came back, he said:

"Both the cat and the ass have lied; there was nothing in the hole but a bear."

Great was the surprise and puzzlement of the animals. Each was now anxious to make the test himself and get at the straight truth. The elephant sent them one at a time.

First, the cow. She found nothing in the hole but a cow.

The tiger found nothing in it but a tiger.

The lion found nothing in it but a lion.

The leopard found nothing in it but a leopard.

The camel found a camel, and nothing more.

Then Hathi was wroth, and said he would have the truth, if he had to go and fetch it himself. When he returned, he abused his whole subjectry for liars, and was in an unappeasable fury with the moral and mental blindness of the cat. He said that anybody but a near-sighted fool could see that there was nothing in the hole but an elephant.

MORAL, BY THE CAT

You can find in a text whatever you bring, if you will stand between it and the mirror of your imagination. You may not see your ears, but they will be there.

1909

The Mysterious Stranger

It was in 1590—winter. Austria was far away from the world, and asleep; it was still the Middle Ages in Austria, and promised to remain so forever. Some even set it away back centuries upon centuries and said that by the mental and spiritual clock it was still the Age of Belief in Austria. But they meant it as a compliment, not a slur, and it was so taken, and we were all proud of it. I remember it well, although I was only a boy; and I remember, too, the pleasure it gave me.

Yes, Austria was far from the world, and asleep, and our village was in the middle of that sleep, being in the middle of Austria. It drowsed in peace in the deep privacy of a hilly and woodsy solitude where news from the world hardly ever came to disturb its dreams, and was infinitely content. At its front flowed the tranquil river, its surface painted with cloud-forms and the reflections of drifting arks and stone-boats; behind it rose the woody steeps to the base of the lofty precipice; from the top of the precipice frowned a vast castle, its long stretch of towers and bastions mailed in vines; beyond the river, a league to the left, was a tumbled expanse of forest-clothed hills cloven by winding gorges where the sun never penetrated; and to the right a precipice overlooked the river, and between it and the hills just spoken of lay a far-reaching plain dotted with little homesteads nested among orchards and shade trees.

The whole region for leagues around was the hereditary property of a prince, whose servants kept the castle always in perfect condition for occupancy, but neither he nor his family came there oftener than once in five years. When they came it was as if the lord of the world had arrived, and had brought all the glories of its kingdoms along; and when they went they left a calm behind which was like the deep sleep which follows an orgy.

Eseldorf was a paradise for us boys. We were not overmuch pestered with schooling. Mainly we were trained to be good Christians; to revere the Virgin, the Church, and the saints above everything. Beyond these matters we were not required to know much; and, in fact, not allowed to. Knowledge was not good for the common people, and could make them discontented with the lot which God had appointed for them, and God would not endure discontentment with His plans. We had two priests. One of them, Father Adolf, was a very zealous and strenuous priest, much considered.

There may have been better priests, in some ways, than Father Adolf, but there was never one in our commune who was held in more solemn and awful respect. This was because he had absolutely no fear of the Devil. He was the only Christian I have ever known of whom that could be truly said. People stood in deep dread of him on that account; for they thought that there must be something supernatural about him, else he could not be so bold and so confident. All men speak in bitter disapproval of the Devil, but they do it reverently, not flippantly; but Father Adolf's way was very different; he called him by every name he could lay his tongue to, and it made everyone shudder that heard him; and often he would even speak of him scornfully and scoffingly; then the people crossed themselves and went quickly out of his presence, fearing that something fearful might happen.

Father Adolf had actually met Satan face to face more than once, and defied him. This was known to be so. Father Adolf said it himself. He never made any secret of it, but spoke it right out. And that he was speaking true there was proof in at least one instance, for on that occasion he quarreled with the enemy, and intrepidly threw his bottle at him; and there, upon the wall of his study, was the ruddy splotch where it struck and broke.

But it was Father Peter, the other priest, that we all loved best and were sorriest for. Some people charged him with talking around in conversation that God was all goodness and would find a way to save all his poor human children. It was a horrible thing to say, but there was never any absolute proof that Father Peter said it; and it was out of character for him to say it, too, for he was always good and gentle and truthful. He wasn't charged with saying it in the pulpit, where all the congregation could hear and testify, but only outside, in talk; and it is easy for enemies to manufacture *that*. Father Peter had an enemy and a very powerful one, the astrologer who lived in a tumbled old tower up the valley, and put in his nights studying the stars. Every one knew he could foretell wars and famines, though that was not so hard, for there was always a war and generally a famine somewhere. But he could also read any man's life through the stars in a big book he had, and find lost property, and every one in the village except Father Peter stood in awe of him. Even Father Adolf, who had defied the Devil, had a wholesome respect for the astrologer when he came through our village wearing his tall, pointed hat and his long, flowing robe with stars on it, carrying his big book, and a staff which was known to have magic power. The bishop himself sometimes listened to the astrologer, it was said, for, besides studying the stars and prophesying, the astrologer made a great show of piety, which would impress the bishop, of course.

But Father Peter took no stock in the astrologer. He denounced him openly as a charlatan—a fraud with no valuable knowledge of any kind, or powers beyond those of an ordinary and rather inferior human being, which naturally made the astrologer hate Father Peter and wish to ruin him. It was the astrologer, as we all believed, who originated the story about Father Peter's shocking remark and carried it to the bishop. It was said that Father Peter had made the remark to his niece, Marget, though Marget denied it and implored the bishop to believe her and spare her old uncle from poverty and disgrace. But the bishop wouldn't listen. He suspended Father Peter indefinitely, though he wouldn't go so far as to excommunicate him on the evidence of only one witness; and now Father Peter had been out a couple of years, and our other priest, Father Adolf, had his flock.

Those had been hard years for the old priest and Marget. They had been favorites, but of course that changed when they came under the shadow of the bishop's frown. Many of their friends fell away entirely, and the rest became cool and distant. Marget was a lovely girl of eighteen when the trouble came, and she had the best head in the village, and the most in it. She taught the harp, and earned all her clothes and pocket money by her own industry. But her scholars fell off one by one now; she was forgotten when there were dances and parties among the youth of the village; the young fellows stopped coming to the house, all except Wilhelm Meidling—and he could have been spared; she and her uncle were sad and forlorn in their neglect and disgrace, and the sunshine was gone out of their lives. Matters went worse and worse, all through the two years. Clothes were wearing out, bread was harder and harder to get. And now, at last, the very end was come. Solomon Isaacs had lent all the money he was willing to put on the house, and gave notice that to-morrow he would foreclose.

2

Three of us boys were always together, and had been so from the cradle, being fond of one another from the beginning, and this affection deepened as the years went on—Nikolaus Bauman, son of the principal judge of the local court; Seppi Wohlmeyer, son of the keeper of the principal inn, the "Golden Stag," which had a nice garden, with shade trees reaching down to the riverside, and pleasure boats for hire; and I was the third—Theodor Fischer, son of the church organist, who was also leader of the village musicians, teacher of the violin, composer, tax-collector of the commune, sexton, and in other ways a useful citizen, and respected by all. We knew the hills and the woods as well as the birds knew them; for we were always roaming them when we had leisure—at least, when we were not swimming or boating or fishing, or playing on the ice or sliding down hill.

And we had the run of the castle park, and very few had that. It was because we were pets of the oldest servingman in the castle—Felix Brandt; and often we went there, nights, to hear him talk about old times and strange things, and to smoke with him (he taught us that) and to drink coffee; for he had served in the wars, and was at the siege of Vienna; and there, when the Turks were defeated and driven away, among the captured things were bags of coffee, and the Turkish prisoners explained the character of it and how to make a pleasant drink out of it, and now he always kept coffee by him, to drink himself and also to astonish the ignorant with. When it stormed he kept us all night; and while it thundered and lightened outside he told us about ghosts and horrors of every kind, and of battles and murders and mutilations, and such things, and made it pleasant and cozy inside; and he told these things from his own experience largely. He had seen many ghosts in his time, and witches and enchanters, and once he was lost in a fierce storm at midnight in the mountains, and by the glare of the lightning had seen the Wild Huntsman rage on the blast with his specter dogs chasing after him through the driving cloud-rack. Also he had seen an incubus once, and several times he had seen the great bat that sucks the blood from the necks of people while they are asleep, fanning them softly with its wings and so keeping them drowsy till they die.

He encouraged us not to fear supernatural things, such as ghosts, and said they did no harm, but only wandered about because they were lonely and distressed and wanted kindly notice and compassion; and in time we learned not to be afraid, and even went down with him in the night to the haunted chamber in the dungeons of the castle. The ghost appeared only once, and it went by very dim to the sight and floated noiseless through the air, and then disappeared; and we scarcely trembled, he had taught us so well. He said it came up sometimes in the night and woke him by passing its clammy hand over his face, but it did him no hurt; it only wanted sympathy and notice. But the strangest thing was that he had seen angels—actual angels out of heaven—and had talked with them. They had no wings, and wore clothes, and talked and looked and acted just like any natural person, and you would never know them for angels except for the wonderful things they did which a mortal could not do, and the way they suddenly disappeared while you were talking with them, which was also a thing which no mortal could do. And he said they were pleasant and cheerful, not gloomy and melancholy, like ghosts.

It was after that kind of a talk one May night that we got up next morning and had a good breakfast with him and then went down and crossed the bridge and went away up into the hills on the left to a woody hill-top which was a favorite place of ours, and there we stretched out on the grass in the shade to rest and smoke and talk over these strange things, for they were in our minds yet, and impressing us. But we couldn't smoke, because we had been heedless and left our flint and steel behind.

Soon there came a youth strolling toward us through the trees, and he sat down and began to talk in a friendly way, just as if he knew us. But we did not answer him, for he was a stranger and we were not used to strangers and were shy of them. He had new and good clothes on, and was handsome and had a winning face and a pleasant voice, and was easy and graceful and unembarrassed, not slouchy and awkward and diffident, like other boys. We wanted to be friendly with him, but didn't know how to begin. Then I thought of the pipe, and wondered if it would be taken as kindly meant if I offered it to him. But I remembered that we had no fire, so I was sorry and disappointed. But he looked up bright and pleased, and said:

"Fire? Oh, that is easy; I will furnish it."

I was so astonished I couldn't speak; for I had not said anything. He took the pipe and blew his breath on it, and the tobacco glowed red, and spirals of blue smoke rose up. We jumped up and were going to run, for that was natural; and we did run a few steps, although he was yearningly pleading for us to stay, and giving us his word that he would not do us any harm, but only wanted to be friends with us and have company. So we stopped and stood, and wanted to go back, being full of curiosity and wonder, but afraid to venture. He went on coaxing, in his soft, persuasive way; and when we saw that the pipe did not blow up and nothing happened, our confidence returned by little and little, and presently our curiosity got to be stronger than our fear, and we ventured back—but slowly, and ready to fly at any alarm.

He was bent on putting us at ease, and he had the right art; one could not remain doubtful and timorous where a person was so earnest and simple and gentle, and talked so alluringly as he did; no, he won us over, and it was not long before we were content and comfortable and chatty, and glad we had found this new friend. When the feeling of constraint was all gone we asked him how he had learned to do that strange thing, and he said he hadn't learned it at all; it came natural to him—like other things—other curious things.

"What ones?"

"Oh, a number; I don't know how many."

"Will you let us see you do them?"

"Do—please!" the others said.

"You won't run away again?"

"No—indeed we won't. Please do. Won't you?"

"Yes, with pleasure; but you mustn't forget your promise, you know."

We said we wouldn't, and he went to a puddle and came back with water in a cup which he had made out of a leaf, and blew upon it and threw it out, and it was a lump of ice the shape of the cup. We were astonished and charmed, but not afraid any more; we were very glad to be there, and asked him to go on and do some more things. And he did. He said he would give us any kind of fruit we liked, whether it was in season or not. We all spoke at once;

"Orange!"

"Apple!"

"Grapes!"

"They are in your pockets," he said, and it was true. And they were of the best, too, and we ate them and wished we had more, though none of us said so.

"You will find them where those came from," he said, "and everything else your appetites call for; and you need not name the thing you wish; as long as I am with you, you have only to wish and find."

And he said true. There was never anything so wonderful and so interesting. Bread, cakes, sweets, nuts—whatever one wanted, it was there. He ate nothing himself, but sat and chatted, and did one curious thing after another to amuse us. He made a tiny toy squirrel out of clay, and it ran up a tree and sat on a limb overhead and barked down at us. Then he made a dog that was not much larger than a mouse, and it treed the squirrel and danced about the tree, excited and barking, and was as alive as any dog could be. It frightened the squirrel from tree to tree and followed it up until both were out of sight in the forest. He made birds out of clay and set them free, and they flew away, singing.

At last I made bold to ask him to tell us who he was.

"An angel," he said, quite simply, and set another bird free and clapped his hands and made it fly away.

A kind of awe fell upon us when we heard him say that, and we were afraid again; but he said we need not be troubled, there was no occasion for us to be afraid of an angel, and he liked us, anyway. He went on chatting as simply and unaffectedly as ever; and while he talked he made a crowd of little men and women the size of your finger, and they went diligently to work and cleared and leveled off a space a couple of yards square in the grass and began to build a cunning little castle in it, the women mixing the mortar and carrying it up the scaffoldings in pails on their heads, just as our work-women have always done, and the men laying the courses of masonry—five hundred of these toy people swarming briskly about and working diligently and wiping the sweat off their faces as natural as life. In the absorbing interest of watching those five hundred little people make the castle grow step by step and course by course, and take shape and symmetry, that feeling and awe soon passed away and we were quite comfortable and at home again. We asked if we might make some people, and he said yes, and told Seppi to make some cannon for the walls, and told Nikolaus to make some halberdiers, with breastplates and greaves and helmets, and I was to make some cavalry, with horses, and in allotting these tasks he called us by our names, but did not say how he knew them. Then Seppi asked him what his own name was, and he said, tranquilly, "Satan," and held out a chip and caught a little woman on it who was falling from the scaffolding and put her back where she belonged, and said, "She is an idiot to step backward like that and not notice what she is about."

It caught us suddenly, that name did, and our work dropped out of our hands and broke to pieces—a cannon, a halberdier, and a horse. Satan laughed, and asked what was the matter. I said, "Nothing, only it seemed a strange name for an angel." He asked why.

"Because it's—it's—well, it's his name, you know."

"Yes—he is my uncle."

He said it placidly, but it took our breath for a moment and made our hearts beat. He did not seem to notice that, but mended our halberdiers and things with a touch, handing them to us finished, and said, "Don't you remember?—he was an angel himself, once."

"Yes—it's true," said Seppi; "I didn't think of that."

"Before the Fall he was blameless."

"Yes," said Nikolaus, "he was without sin."

"It is a good family—ours," said Satan; "there is not a better. He is the only member of it that has ever sinned."

I should not be able to make any one understand how exciting it all was. You know that kind of quiver that trembles around through you when you are seeing something so strange and enchanting and wonderful that it is just a fearful joy to be alive and look at it; and you know how you gaze, and your lips turn dry and your breath comes short, but you wouldn't be anywhere but there, not for the world. I was bursting to ask one question—I had it on my tongue's end and could hardly hold it back—but I was ashamed to ask it; it might be a rudeness. Satan set an ox down that he had been making, and smiled up at me and said:

"It wouldn't be a rudeness, and I should forgive it if it was. Have I seen him? Millions of times. From the time that I was a little child a thousand years old I was his second favorite among the nursery angels of our blood and lineage—to use a human phrase—yes, from that time until the Fall, eight thousand years, measured as you count time."

"Eight—thousand!"

"Yes." He turned to Seppi, and went on as if answering something that was in Seppi's mind: "Why, naturally I look like a boy, for that is what I am. With us what you call time is a spacious thing; it takes a long stretch of it to grow an angel to full age." There was a question in my mind, and he turned to me and answered it, "I am sixteen thousand years old—counting as you count." Then he turned to Nikolaus and said: "No, the Fall did not affect me nor the rest of the relationship. It was only he that I was named for who ate of the fruit of the tree and then beguiled the man and the woman with it. We others are still ignorant of sin; we are not able to commit it; we are without blemish, and shall abide in that estate always. We—" Two of the little workmen were quarreling, and in buzzing little bumblebee voices they were cursing and swearing at each other; now came blows and blood; then they locked themselves together in a life-and-death struggle. Satan reached out his hand and crushed the life out of them with his fingers, threw them away, wiped the red from his fingers on his handkerchief, and went on talking where he had left off: "We cannot do wrong; neither have we any disposition to do it, for we do not know what it is."

It seemed a strange speech, in the circumstances, but we barely noticed that, we were so shocked and grieved at the wanton murder he had committed—for murder it was, that was its true name, and it was without palliation or excuse, for the men had not wronged him in any way. It made us miserable, for we loved him, and had thought him so noble and so beautiful and gracious, and had honestly believed he was an angel; and to have him do this cruel thing—ah, it lowered him so, and we had had such pride in him. He went right on talking, just as if nothing had happened, telling about his travels, and the interesting things he had seen in the big worlds of our solar systems and of other solar systems far away in the remotenesses of space, and about the customs of the immortals that inhabit them, somehow fascinating us, enchanting us, charming us in spite of the pitiful scene that was now under our eyes, for the wives of the little dead men had found the crushed and shapeless bodies and were crying over them, and sobbing and lamenting, and a priest was kneeling there with his hands crossed upon his breast, praying; and crowds and crowds of pitying friends were massed about them, reverently uncovered, with their bare heads bowed, and many with the tears running down—a scene which Satan paid no attention to until the small noise of the weeping and praying began to annoy him, then he reached out and took the heavy board seat out of our swing and brought it down and mashed all those people into the earth just as if they had been flies, and went on talking just the same.

An angel, and kill a priest! An angel who did not know how to do wrong, and yet destroys in cold blood hundreds of helpless poor men and women who had never done him any harm! It made us sick to see that awful deed, and to think that none of those poor creatures was prepared except the priest, for none of them had ever heard a mass or seen a church. And we were witnesses; we had seen these murders done and it was our duty to tell, and let the law take its course.

But he went on talking right along, and worked his enchantments upon us again with that fatal music of his voice. He made us forget everything; we could only listen to him, and love him, and be his slaves, to do with us as he would. He made us drunk with the joy of

being with him, and of looking into the heaven of his eyes, and of feeling the ecstasy that thrilled along our veins from the touch of his hand.

3

The Stranger had seen everything, he had been everywhere, he knew
everything, and he forgot nothing. What another must study, he
learned at a glance; there were no difficulties for him. And he made
things live before you when he told about them. He saw the world
made; he saw Adam created; he saw Samson surge against the pillars
and bring the temple down in ruins about him; he saw Cæsar's death;
he told of the daily life in heaven; he had seen the damned writhing
in the red waves of hell; and he made us see all these things, and it was
as if we were on the spot and looking at them with our own eyes. And
we felt them, too, but there was no sign that they were anything to
him beyond mere entertainments. Those visions of hell, those poor
babes and women and girls and lads and men shrieking and supplicating in anguish—why, we could hardly bear it, but he was as bland about
it as if it had been so many imitation rats in an artificial fire.

And always when he was talking about men and women here on the
earth and their doings—even their grandest and sublimest—we were
secretly ashamed, for his manner showed that to him they and their
doings were of paltry poor consequence; often you would think he was
talking about flies, if you didn't know. Once he even said, in so many
words, that our people down here were quite interesting to him, notwithstanding they were so dull and ignorant and trivial and conceited,
and so diseased and rickety, and such a shabby, poor, worthless lot all
around. He said it in a quite matter-of-course way and without bitterness, just as a person might talk about bricks or manure or any other
thing that was of no consequence and hadn't feelings. I could see he
meant no offense, but in my thoughts I set it down as not very good
manners.

"Manners!" he said. "Why, it is merely the truth, and truth is good
manners; manners are a fiction. The castle is done. Do you like it?"

Any one would have been obliged to like it. It was lovely to look at,
it was so shapely and fine, and so cunningly perfect in all its particulars,
even to the little flags waving from the turrets. Satan said we must put
the artillery in place now, and station the halberdiers and display the
cavalry. Our men and horses were a spectacle to see, they were so little
like what they were intended for; for, of course, we had no art in making such things. Satan said they were the worst he had seen; and when

he touched them and made them alive, it was just ridiculous the way they acted, on account of their legs not being of uniform lengths. They reeled and sprawled around as if they were drunk, and endangered everybody's lives around them, and finally fell over and lay helpless and kicking. It made us all laugh, though it was a shameful thing to see. The guns were charged with dirt, to fire a salute, but they were so crooked and so badly made that they all burst when they went off, and killed some of the gunners and crippled the others. Satan said we would have a storm now, and an earthquake, if we liked, but we must stand off a piece, out of danger. We wanted to call the people away, too, but he said never mind them; they were of no consequence, and we could make more, some time or other, if we needed them.

A small storm-cloud began to settle down black over the castle, and the miniature lightning and thunder began to play, and the ground to quiver, and the wind to pipe and wheeze, and the rain to fall, and all the people flocked into the castle for shelter. The cloud settled down blacker and blacker, and one could see the castle only dimly through it; the lightning blazed out flash upon flash and pierced the castle and set it on fire, and the flames shone out red and fierce through the cloud, and the people came flying out, shrieking, but Satan brushed them back, paying no attention to our begging and crying and imploring; and in the midst of the howling of the wind and volleying of the thunder the magazine blew up, the earthquake rent the ground wide, and the castle's wreck and ruin tumbled into the chasm, which swallowed it from sight, and closed upon it, with all that innocent life, not one of the five hundred poor creatures escaping. Our hearts were broken; we could not keep from crying.

"Don't cry," Satan said; "they were of no value."

"But they are gone to hell!"

"Oh, it is no matter; we can make plenty more."

It was of no use to try to move him; evidently he was wholly without feeling, and could not understand. He was full of bubbling spirits, and as gay as if this were a wedding instead of a fiendish massacre. And he was bent on making us feel as he did, and of course his magic accomplished his desire. It was no trouble to him; he did whatever he pleased with us. In a little while we were dancing on that grave, and he was playing to us on a strange, sweet instrument which he took out of his pocket; and the music—but there is no music like that, unless perhaps in heaven, and that was where he brought it from, he said. It made one mad, for pleasure; and we could not take our eyes from him, and the looks that went out of our eyes came from our hearts, and their dumb speech was worship. He brought the dance from heaven, too, and the bliss of paradise was in it.

Presently he said he must go away on an errand. But we could not bear the thought of it, and clung to him, and pleaded with him to stay; and that pleased him, and he said so, and said he would not go yet, but would wait a little while and we would sit down and talk a few minutes longer; and he told us Satan was only his real name, and he was to be known by it to us alone, but he had chosen another one to be called by in the presence of others; just a common one, such as people have— Philip Traum.

It sounded so odd and mean for such a being! But it was his decision, and we said nothing; his decision was sufficient.

We had seen wonders this day; and my thoughts began to run on the pleasure it would be to tell them when I got home, but he noticed those thoughts, and said:

"No, all these matters are a secret among us four. I do not mind your trying to tell them, if you like, but I will protect your tongues, and nothing of the secret will escape from them."

It was a disappointment, but it couldn't be helped, and it cost us a sigh or two. We talked pleasantly along, and he was always reading our thoughts and responding to them, and it seemed to me that this was the most wonderful of all the things he did, but he interrupted my musings and said:

"No, it would be wonderful for you, but it is not wonderful for me. I am not limited like you. I am not subject to human conditions. I can measure and understand your human weaknesses, for I have studied them; but I have none of them. My flesh is not real, although it would seem firm to your touch; my clothes are not real; I am a spirit. Father Peter is coming." We looked around, but did not see any one. "He is not in sight yet, but you will see him presently."

"Do you know him, Satan?"

"No."

"Won't you talk with him when he comes? He is not ignorant and dull, like us, and he would so like to talk with you. Will you?"

"Another time, yes, but not now. I must go on my errand after a little. There he is now; you can see him. Sit still, and don't say anything."

We looked up and saw Father Peter approaching through the chestnuts. We three were sitting together in the grass, and Satan sat in front of us in the path. Father Peter came slowly along with his head down, thinking, and stopped within a couple of yards of us and took off his hat and got out his silk handkerchief, and stood there mopping his face and looking as if he were going to speak to us, but he didn't. Presently he muttered, "I can't think what brought me here; it seems as if I were in my study a minute ago—but I suppose I have been dreaming along for an hour and have come all this stretch without noticing; for I am not myself in these troubled days." Then he went mumbling along to himself and walked straight through Satan, just as if nothing were there. It made us catch our breath to see it. We had the impulse to cry out, the way you nearly always do when a startling thing happens, but something mysteriously restrained us and we remained quiet, only breathing fast. Then the trees hid Father Peter after a little, and Satan said:

"It is as I told you—I am only a spirit."

"Yes, one perceives it now," said Nikolaus, "but we are not spirits. It is plain he did not see you, but were we invisible, too? He looked at us, but he didn't seem to see us."

"No, none of us was visible to him, for I wished it so."

It seemed almost too good to be true, that we were actually seeing these romantic and wonderful things, and that it was not a dream. And there he sat, looking just like anybody—so natural and simple and charming, and chatting along again the same as ever, and—well, words cannot make you understand what we felt. It was an ecstasy; and an ecstasy is a thing that will not go into words; it feels like music, and one cannot tell about music so that another person can get the feeling of it. He was back in the old ages once more now, and making them live before us. He had seen so much, so much! It was just a wonder to look at him and try to think how it must seem to have such experience behind one.

But it made you seem sorrowfully trivial, and the creature of a day, and such a short and paltry day, too. And he didn't say anything to raise up your drooping pride—no, not a word. He always spoke of men in the same old indifferent way—just as one speaks of bricks and ma-nure-piles and such things; you could see that they were of no conse-quence to him, one way or the other. He didn't mean to hurt us, you could see that; just as we don't mean to insult a brick when we dis-parage it; a brick's emotions are nothing to us; it never occurs to us to think whether it has any or not.

Once when he was bunching the most illustrious kings and con-querors and poets and prophets and pirates and beggars together—just a brick-pile—I was shamed into putting in a word for man, and asked him why he made so much difference between men and himself. He had to struggle with that a moment; he didn't seem to understand how I could ask such a strange question. Then he said:

"The difference between man and me? The difference between a mortal and an immortal? between a cloud and a spirit?" He picked up a wood-louse that was creeping along a piece of bark: "What is the difference between Cæsar and this?"

I said, "One cannot compare things which by their nature and by the interval between them are not comparable."

"You have answered your own question," he said. "I will expand it. Man is made of dirt—I saw him made. I am not made of dirt. Man is a museum of diseases, a home of impurities; he comes to-day and is gone to-morrow; he begins as dirt and departs as stench; I am of the aristocracy of the Imperishables. And man has the *Moral Sense*. You understand? He has the *Moral Sense*. That would seem to be difference enough between us, all by itself."

He stopped there, as if that settled the matter. I was sorry, for at that time I had but a dim idea of what the Moral Sense was. I merely knew that we were proud of having it, and when he talked like that about it, it wounded me, and I felt as a girl feels who thinks her dearest finery is being admired and then overhears strangers making fun of it. For a while we were all silent, and I, for one, was depressed. Then Satan began to chat again, and soon he was sparkling along in such a cheerful and vivacious vein that my spirits rose once more. He told some very cunning things that put us in a gale of laughter; and when he was telling about the time that Samson tied the torches to the foxes' tails and set them loose in the Philistines' corn, and Samson sitting on the fence slapping his thighs and laughing, with the tears running down his cheeks, and lost his balance and fell off the fence, the memory of that picture got him to laughing, too, and we did have a most lovely and jolly time. By and by he said:

"I am going on my errand now."

"Don't!" we all said. "Don't go; stay with us. You won't come back."

"Yes, I will; I give you my word."

"When? To-night? Say when."

"It won't be long. You will see."

"We like you."

"And I you. And as a proof of it I will show you something fine to see. Usually when I go I merely vanish; but now I will dissolve myself and let you see me do it."

He stood up, and it was quickly finished. He thinned away and thinned away until he was a soap-bubble, except that he kept his shape. You could see the bushes through him as clearly as you see things through a soap-bubble, and all over him played and flashed the delicate iridescent colors of the bubble, and along with them was that thing shaped like a window-sash which you always see on the globe of the bubble. You have seen a bubble strike the carpet and lightly bound along two or three times before it bursts. He did that. He sprang— touched the grass—bounded—floated along—touched again—and so on, and presently exploded—puff! and in his place was vacancy.

It was a strange and beautiful thing to see. We did not say anything, but sat wondering and dreaming and blinking; and finally Seppi roused up and said, mournfully sighing:

"I suppose none of it has happened."

Nikolaus sighed and said about the same.

I was miserable to hear them say it, for it was the same cold fear that was in my own mind. Then we saw poor old Father Peter wandering along back, with his head bent down, searching the ground. When he was pretty close to us he looked up and saw us, and said, "How long have you been here, boys?"

"A little while, Father."

"Then it is since I came by, and maybe you can help me. Did you come up by the path?"

"Yes, Father."

"That is good. I came the same way. I have lost my wallet. There wasn't much in it, but a very little is much to me, for it was all I had. I suppose you haven't seen anything of it?"

"No, Father, but we will help you hunt."

"It is what I was going to ask you. Why, here it is!"

We hadn't noticed it; yet there it lay, right where Satan stood when he began to melt—if he did melt and it wasn't a delusion. Father Peter picked it up and looked very much surprised.

"It is mine," he said, "but not the contents. This is fat; mine was flat; mine was light; this is heavy." He opened it; it was stuffed as full as it could hold with gold coins. He let us gaze our fill; and of course we did gaze, for we had never seen so much money at one time before. All our mouths came open to say "Satan did it!" but nothing came out. There it was, you see—we couldn't tell what Satan didn't want told; he had said so himself.

"Boys, did you do this?"

It made us laugh. And it made him laugh, too, as soon as he thought what a foolish question it was.

"Who has been here?"

Our mouths came open to answer, but stood so for a moment, because we couldn't say "Nobody," for it wouldn't be true, and the right word didn't seem to come; then I thought of the right one, and said it:

"Not a human being."

"That is so," said the others, and let their mouths go shut.

"It is not so," said Father Peter, and looked at us very severely. "I came by here a while ago, and there was no one here, but that is nothing; some one has been here since. I don't mean to say that the person didn't pass here before you came, and I don't mean to say you saw him, but some one did pass, that I know. On your honor—you saw no one?"

"Not a human being."

"That is sufficient; I know you are telling me the truth."

He began to count the money on the path, we on our knees eagerly helping to stack it in little piles.

"It's eleven hundred ducats odd!" he said. "Oh dear! if it were only mine—and I need it so!" and his voice broke and his lips quivered.

"It is yours, sir!" we all cried out at once, "every heller!"

"No—it isn't mine. Only four ducats are mine; the rest . . . !" He fell to dreaming, poor old soul, and caressing some of the coins in his hands, and forgot where he was, sitting there on his heels with his old gray head bare; it was pitiful to see. "No," he said, waking up, "it isn't mine. I can't account for it. I think some enemy . . . it must be a trap."

Nikolaus said: "Father Peter, with the exception of the astrologer you haven't a real enemy in the village—nor Marget, either. And not even a half-enemy that's rich enough to chance eleven hundred ducats to do you a mean turn. I'll ask you if that's so or not?"

He couldn't get around that argument, and it cheered him up. "But it isn't mine, you see—it isn't mine, in any case."

He said it in a wistful way, like a person that wouldn't be sorry, but glad, if anybody would contradict him.

"It is yours, Father Peter, and we are witness to it. Aren't we, boys?"

"Yes, we are—and we'll stand by it, too."

"Bless your hearts, you do almost persuade me; you do, indeed. If I had only a hundred-odd ducats of it! The house is mortgaged for it, and we've no home for our heads if we don't pay to-morrow. And that four ducats is all we've got in the—"

"It's yours, every bit of it, and you've got to take it—we are bail that it's all right. Aren't we, Theodor? Aren't we, Seppi?"

We two said yes, and Nikolaus stuffed the money back into the shabby old wallet and made the owner take it. So he said he would use two hundred of it, for his house was good enough security for that, and would put the rest at interest till the rightful owner came for it; and on our side we must sign a paper showing how he got the money —a paper to show to the villagers as proof that he had not got out of his troubles dishonestly.

4

It made immense talk next day, when Father Peter paid Solomon Isaacs in gold and left the rest of the money with him at interest. Also, there was a pleasant change; many people called at the house to congratulate him, and a number of cool old friends became kind and friendly again; and, to top all, Marget was invited to a party.

And there was no mystery; Father Peter told the whole circumstance just as it happened, and said he could not account for it, only it was the plain hand of Providence, so far as he could see.

One or two shook their heads and said privately it looked more like the hand of Satan; and really that seemed a surprisingly good guess for ignorant people like that. Some came slyly buzzing around and tried to coax us boys to come out and "tell the truth;" and promised they wouldn't ever tell, but only wanted to know for their own satisfaction, because the whole thing was so curious. They even wanted to buy the secret, and pay money for it; and if we could have invented something that would answer—but we couldn't; we hadn't the ingenuity, so we had to let the chance go by, and it was a pity.

We carried that secret around without any trouble, but the other one, the big one, the splendid one, burned the very vitals of us, it was so hot to get out and we so hot to let it out and astonish people with it. But we had to keep it in; in fact, it kept itself in. Satan said it would, and it did. We went off every day and got to ourselves in the woods so that we could talk about Satan, and really that was the only subject we thought of or cared anything about; and day and night we watched for him and hoped he would come, and we got more and more impatient all the time. We hadn't any interest in the other boys any more, and wouldn't take part in their games and enterprises. They seemed so tame, after Satan; and their doings so trifling and commonplace after his adventures in antiquity and the constellations, and his miracles and meltings and explosions, and all that.

During the first day we were in a state of anxiety on account of one thing, and we kept going to Father Peter's house on one pretext or another to keep track of it. That was the gold coin; we were afraid it would crumble and turn to dust, like fairy money. If it did— But it didn't. At the end of the day no complaint had been made about it, so after that we were satisfied that it was real gold, and dropped the anxiety out of our minds.

There was a question which we wanted to ask Father Peter, and finally we went there the second evening, a little diffidently, after drawing straws, and I asked it as casually as I could, though it did not sound as casual as I wanted, because I didn't know how:

"What is the Moral Sense, sir?"

He looked down, surprised, over his great spectacles, and said, "Why, it is the faculty which enables us to distinguish good from evil."

It threw some light, but not a glare, and I was a little disappointed, also to some degree embarrassed. He was waiting for me to go on, so, in default of anything else to say, I asked, "Is it valuable?"

"Valuable? Heavens! lad, it is the one thing that lifts man above the beasts that perish and makes him heir to immortality!"

This did not remind me of anything further to say, so I got out, with the other boys, and we went away with that indefinite sense you have often had of being filled but not fatted. They wanted me to explain, but I was tired.

We passed out through the parlor, and there was Marget at the spinnet teaching Marie Lueger. So one of the deserting pupils was back; and an influential one, too; the others would follow. Marget jumped up and ran and thanked us again, with tears in her eyes—this was the third time—for saving her and her uncle from being turned into the street, and we told her again we hadn't done it; but that was her way, she never could be grateful enough for anything a person did for her; so we let her have her say. And as we passed through the garden, there was Wilhelm Meidling sitting there waiting, for it was getting toward the edge of the evening, and he would be asking Marget to take a walk along the river with him when she was done with the lesson. He was a young lawyer, and succeeding fairly well and working his way along, little by little. He was very fond of Marget, and she of him. He had not deserted along with the others, but had stood his ground all through. His faithfulness was not lost on Marget and her uncle. He hadn't so very much talent, but he was handsome and good, and these are a kind of talents themselves and help along. He asked us how the lesson was getting along, and we told him it was about done. And maybe it was so; we didn't know anything about it, but we judged it would please him, and it did, and didn't cost us anything.

5

On the fourth day comes the astrologer from his crumbling old tower up the valley, where he had heard the news, I reckon. He had a private talk with us, and we told him what we could, for we were mightily in dread of him. He sat there studying and studying awhile to himself; then he asked:

"How many ducats did you say?"

"Eleven hundred and seven, sir."

Then he said, as if he were talking to himself: "It is ver-y singular. Yes . . . very strange. A curious coincidence." Then he began to ask questions, and went over the whole ground from the beginning, we answering. By and by he said: "Eleven hundred and six ducats. It is a large sum."

"Seven," said Seppi, correcting him.

"Oh, seven, was it? Of course a ducat more or less isn't of consequence, but you said eleven hundred and six before."

It would not have been safe for us to say he was mistaken, but we knew he was. Nikolaus said, "We ask pardon for the mistake, but we meant to say seven."

"Oh, it is no matter, lad; it was merely that I noticed the discrepancy. It is several days, and you cannot be expected to remember precisely. One is apt to be inexact when there is no particular circumstance to impress the count upon the memory."

"But there was one, sir," said Seppi, eagerly.

"What was it, my son?" asked the astrologer, indifferently.

"First, we all counted the piles of coin, each in turn, and all made it the same—eleven hundred and six. But I had slipped one out, for fun, when the count began, and now I slipped it back and said, 'I think there is a mistake—there are eleven hundred and seven; let us count again.' We did, and of course I was right. They were astonished; then I told how it came about."

The astrologer asked us if this was so, and we said it was.

"That settles it," he said. "I know the thief now. Lads, the money was stolen."

Then he went away, leaving us very much troubled, and wondering what he could mean. In about an hour we found out; for by that time it was all over the village that Father Peter had been arrested for stealing a great sum of money from the astrologer. Everybody's tongue was loose and going. Many said it was not in Father Peter's character and must be a mistake; but the others shook their heads and said misery and want could drive a suffering man to almost anything. About one detail there were no differences; all agreed that Father Peter's account of how the money came into his hands was just about unbelievable— it had such an impossible look. They said it might have come into the astrologer's hands in some such way, but into Father Peter's, never! Our characters began to suffer now. We were Father Peter's only witnesses; how much did he probably pay us to back up his fantastic tale? People talked that kind of talk to us pretty freely and frankly, and were full of scoffings when we begged them to believe really we had told only the truth. Our parents were harder on us than any one else. Our fathers said we were disgracing our families, and they commanded us to purge ourselves of our lie, and there was no limit to their anger when we continued to say we had spoken true. Our mothers cried over us and begged us to give back our bribe and get back our honest names and save our families from shame, and come out and honorably confess. And at last we were so worried and harassed that we tried to tell the whole thing, Satan and all—but no, it wouldn't come out. We were hoping and longing all the time that Satan would come and help us out of our trouble, but there was no sign of him.

Within an hour after the astrologer's talk with us, Father Peter was in prison and the money sealed up and in the hands of the officers of the law. The money was in a bag, and Solomon Isaacs said he had not touched it since he had counted it; his oath was taken that it was the same money, and that the amount was eleven hundred and seven ducats. Father Peter claimed trial by the ecclesiastical court, but our other priest, Father Adolf, said an ecclesiastical court hadn't jurisdiction over a suspended priest. The bishop upheld him. That settled it; the case would go to trial in the civil court. The court would not sit for some time to come. Wilhelm Meidling would be Father Peter's lawyer and do the best he could, of course, but he told us privately that a weak case on his side and all the power and prejudice on the other made the outlook bad.

So Marget's new happiness died a quick death. No friends came to condole with her, and none were expected; an unsigned note withdrew her invitation to the party. There would be no scholars to take lessons. How could she support herself? She could remain in the house, for the mortgage was paid off, though the government and not poor Solomon Isaacs had the mortgage-money in its grip for the present. Old Ursula, who was cook, chambermaid, housekeeper, laundress, and everything else for Father Peter, and had been Marget's nurse in earlier years, said God would provide. But she said that from habit, for she was a good Christian. She meant to help in the providing, to make sure, if she could find a way.

We boys wanted to go and see Marget and show friendliness for her, but our parents were afraid of offending the community and wouldn't let us. The astrologer was going around inflaming everybody against Father Peter, and saying he was an abandoned thief and had stolen eleven hundred and seven gold ducats from him. He said he knew he was a thief from that fact, for it was exactly the sum he had lost and which Father Peter pretended he had "found."

In the afternoon of the fourth day after the catastrophe old Ursula appeared at our house and asked for some washing to do, and begged my mother to keep this secret, to save Marget's pride, who would stop this project if she found it out, yet Marget had not enough to eat and was growing weak. Ursula was growing weak herself, and showed it; and she ate of the food that was offered her like a starving person, but could not be persuaded to carry any home, for Marget would not eat charity food. She took some clothes down to the stream to wash them, but we saw from the window that handling the bat was too much for her strength; so she was called back and a trifle of money offered her, which she was afraid to take lest Marget should suspect; then she took it, saying she would explain that she found it in the road. To keep it from being a lie and damning her soul, she got me to drop it while she watched; then she went along by there and found it, and exclaimed with surprise and joy, and picked it up and went her way. Like the rest of the village, she could tell every-day lies fast enough and without taking any precautions against fire and brimstone on their account; but this was a new kind of lie, and it had a dangerous look because she hadn't had any practice in it. After a week's practice it wouldn't have given her any trouble. It is the way we are made.

I was in trouble, for how would Marget live? Ursula could not find a coin in the road every day—perhaps not even a second one. And I was ashamed, too, for not having been near Marget, and she so in need of friends; but that was my parents' fault, not mine, and I couldn't help it.

I was walking along the path, feeling very downhearted, when a most cheery and tingling freshening-up sensation went rippling through me, and I was too glad for any words, for I knew by that sign that Satan was by. I had noticed it before. Next moment he was alongside of me and I was telling him all my trouble and what had been happening to Marget and her uncle. While we were talking we turned a curve and saw old Ursula resting in the shade of a tree, and she had a lean stray kitten in her lap and was petting it. I asked her where she got it, and she said it came out of the woods and followed her; and she said it probably hadn't any mother or any friends and she was going to take it home and take care of it. Satan said:

"I understand you are very poor. Why do you want to add another mouth to feed? Why don't you give it to some rich person?"

Ursula bridled at this and said: "Perhaps you would like to have it. You must be rich, with your fine clothes and quality airs." Then she sniffed and said: "Give it to the rich—the idea! The rich don't care for anybody but themselves; it's only the poor that have feeling for the poor, and help them. The poor and God. God will provide for this kitten."

"What makes you think so?"

Ursula's eyes snapped with anger. "Because I know it!" she said. "Not a sparrow falls to the ground without His seeing it."

"But it falls, just the same. What good is seeing it fall?"

Old Ursula's jaws worked, but she could not get any word out for the moment, she was so horrified. When she got her tongue she stormed out, "Go about your business, you puppy, or I will take a stick to you!"

I could not speak, I was so scared. I knew that with his notions about the human race Satan would consider it a matter of no consequence to strike her dead, there being "plenty more;" but my tongue stood still, I could give her no warning. But nothing happened; Satan remained tranquil—tranquil and indifferent. I suppose he could not be insulted by Ursula any more than the king could be insulted by a tumble-bug. The old woman jumped to her feet when she made her remark, and did it as briskly as a young girl. It had been many years since she had done the like of that. That was Satan's influence; he was a fresh breeze to the weak and the sick, wherever he came. His presence affected even the lean kitten, and it skipped to the ground and began to chase a leaf. This surprised Ursula, and she stood looking at the creature and nodding her head wonderingly, her anger quite forgotten.

"What's come over it?" she said. "Awhile ago it could hardly walk."

"You have not seen a kitten of that breed before," said Satan.

Ursula was not proposing to be friendly with the mocking stranger, and she gave him an ungentle look and retorted: "Who asked you to come here and pester me, I'd like to know? And what do you know about what I've seen and what I haven't seen?"

"You haven't seen a kitten with the hair-spines on its tongue pointing to the front, have you?"

"No—nor you, either."

"Well, examine this one and see."

Ursula was become pretty spry, but the kitten was spryer, and she could not catch it, and had to give it up. Then Satan said:

"Give it a name, and maybe it will come."

Ursula tried several names, but the kitten was not interested.

"Call it Agnes. Try that."

The creature answered to the name and came. Ursula examined its tongue. "Upon my word, it's true!" she said. "I have not seen this kind of a cat before. Is it yours?"

"No."

"Then how did you know its name so pat?"

"Because all cats of that breed are named Agnes; they will not answer to any other."

Ursula was impressed. "It is the most wonderful thing!" Then a shadow of trouble came into her face, for her superstitions were aroused, and she reluctantly put the creature down, saying: "I suppose I must let it go; I am not afraid—no, not exactly that, though the priest—well, I've heard people—indeed, many people . . . And, besides, it is quite well now and can take care of itself." She sighed, and turned to go, murmuring: "It is such a pretty one, too, and would be such company —and the house is so sad and lonesome these troubled days . . . Miss Marget so mournful and just a shadow, and the old master shut up in jail."

"It seems a pity not to keep it," said Satan.

Ursula turned quickly—just as if she were hoping some one would encourage her.

"Why?" she asked, wistfully.

"Because this breed brings luck."

"Does it? Is it true? Young man, do you know it to be true? How does it bring luck?"

"Well, it brings money, anyway."

Ursula looked disappointed. "Money? A cat bring money? The idea! You could never sell it here; people do not buy cats here; one can't even give them away." She turned to go.

"I don't mean sell it. I mean have an income from it. This kind is called the Lucky Cat. Its owner finds four silver groschen in his pocket every morning."

I saw the indignation rising in the old woman's face. She was insulted. This boy was making fun of her. That was her thought. She thrust her hands into her pockets and straightened up to give him a piece of her mind. Her temper was all up, and hot. Her mouth came open and let out three words of a bitter sentence, . . . then it fell silent, and the anger in her face turned to surprise or wonder or fear, or something, and she slowly brought out her hands from her pockets and opened them and held them so. In one was my piece of money, in the other lay four silver groschen. She gazed a little while, perhaps to see if the groschen would vanish away; then she said, fervently:

"It's true—it's true—and I'm ashamed and beg forgiveness, O dear master and benefactor!" And she ran to Satan and kissed his hand, over and over again, according to the Austrian custom.

In her heart she probably believed it was a witch-cat and an agent of the Devil; but no matter, it was all the more certain to be able to keep its contract and furnish a daily good living for the family, for in matters of finance even the piousest of our peasants would have more confidence in an arrangement with the Devil than with an archangel. Ursula started homeward, with Agnes in her arms, and I said I wished I had her privilege of seeing Marget.

Then I caught my breath, for we were there. There in the parlor, and Marget standing looking at us, astonished. She was feeble and pale, but I knew that those conditions would not last in Satan's atmosphere, and it turned out so. I introduced Satan—that is, Philip Traum —and we sat down and talked. There was no constraint. We were simple folk, in our village, and when a stranger was a pleasant person we were soon friends. Marget wondered how we got in without her hearing us. Traum said the door was open, and we walked in and waited until she should turn around and greet us. This was not true; no door was open; we entered through the walls or the roof or down the chimney, or somehow; but no matter, what Satan wished a person to believe, the person was sure to believe, and so Marget was quite satisfied with that explanation. And then the main part of her mind was on Traum, anyway; she couldn't keep her eyes off him, he was so beautiful. That gratified me, and made me proud. I hoped he would show off some, but he didn't. He seemed only interested in being friendly and telling lies. He said he was an orphan. That made Marget pity him. The water came into her eyes. He said he had never known his mamma; she passed away while he was a young thing; and said his papa was in shattered health, and had no property to speak of—in fact, none of any earthly value—but he had an uncle in business down in the tropics, and he was very well off and had a monopoly, and it was from this uncle that he drew his support. The very mention of a kind uncle was enough to remind Marget of her own, and her eyes filled again. She said she hoped their two uncles would meet, some day. It made me shudder. Philip said he hoped so, too; and that made me shudder again.

"Maybe they will," said Marget. "Does your uncle travel much?"

"Oh yes, he goes all about; he has business everywhere."

And so they went on chatting, and poor Marget forgot her sorrow for one little while, anyway. It was probably the only really bright and cheery hour she had known lately. I saw she liked Philip, and I knew she would. And when he told her he was studying for the ministry I could see that she liked him better than ever. And then, when he promised to get her admitted to the jail so that she could see her uncle, that was the capstone. He said he would give the guards a little present, and she must always go in the evening after dark, and say nothing, "but just show this paper and pass in, and show it again when you come out"—and he scribbled some queer marks on the paper and gave it to her, and she was ever so thankful, and right away was in a fever for the sun to go down; for in that old, cruel time prisoners were not allowed to see their friends, and sometimes they spent years in the jails without ever seeing a friendly face. I judged that the marks on the paper were an enchantment, and that the guards would not know what they were doing, nor have any memory of it afterward; and that was indeed the way of it. Ursula put her head in at the door now and said:

"Supper's ready, miss." Then she saw us and looked frightened, and motioned me to come to her, which I did, and she asked if we had told about the cat. I said no, and she was relieved, and said please don't; for if Miss Marget knew, she would think it was an unholy cat and would send for a priest and have its gifts all purified out of it, and then there wouldn't be any more dividends. So I said we wouldn't tell, and she was satisfied. Then I was beginning to say good-by to Marget, but Satan interrupted and said, ever so politely—well, I don't remember just the words, but anyway he as good as invited himself to supper, and me, too. Of course Marget was miserably embarrassed, for she had no reason to suppose there would be half enough for a sick bird. Ursula heard him, and she came straight into the room, not a bit pleased. At first she was astonished to see Marget looking so fresh and rosy, and said so; then she spoke up in her native tongue, which was Bohemian, and said—as I learned afterward—"Send him away, Miss Marget; there's not victuals enough."

Before Marget could speak, Satan had the word, and was talking back to Ursula in her own language—which was a surprise to her, and for her mistress, too. He said, "Didn't I see you down the road awhile ago?"

"Yes, sir."

"Ah, that pleases me; I see you remember me." He stepped to her and whispered: "I told you it is a Lucky Cat. Don't be troubled; it will provide."

That sponged the slate of Ursula's feelings clean of its anxieties, and a deep, financial joy shone in her eyes. The cat's value was augmenting. It was getting full time for Marget to take some sort of notice of Satan's invitation, and she did it in the best way, the honest way that was natural to her. She said she had little to offer, but that we were welcome if we would share it with her.

We had supper in the kitchen, and Ursula waited at table. A small fish was in the frying-pan, crisp and brown and tempting, and one could see that Marget was not expecting such respectable food as this. Ursula brought it, and Marget divided it between Satan and me, declining to take any of it herself; and was beginning to say she did not care for fish to-day, but she did not finish the remark. It was because she noticed that another fish had appeared in the pan. She looked surprised, but did not say anything. She probably meant to inquire of Ursula about this later. There were other surprises: flesh and game and wines and fruits—things which had been strangers in that house lately; but Marget made no exclamations, and now even looked unsurprised, which was Satan's influence, of course. Satan talked right along, and was entertaining, and made the time pass pleasantly and cheerfully; and although he told a good many lies, it was no harm in him, for he was only an angel and did not know any better. They do not know right from wrong; I knew this, because I remembered what he had said about it. He got on the good side of Ursula. He praised her to Marget, confidentially, but speaking just loud enough for Ursula to hear. He said she was a fine woman, and he hoped some day to bring her and his uncle together. Very soon Ursula was mincing and simpering around in a ridiculous girly way, and smoothing out her gown and prinking at herself like a foolish old hen, and all the time pretending she was not hearing what Satan was saying. I was ashamed, for it showed us to be what Satan considered us, a silly race and trivial. Satan said his uncle entertained a great deal, and to have a clever woman presiding over the festivities would double the attractions of the place.

"But your uncle is a gentleman, isn't he?" asked Marget.

"Yes," said Satan indifferently; "some even call him a Prince, out of compliment, but he is not bigoted; to him personal merit is everything, rank nothing."

My hand was hanging down by my chair; Agnes came along and licked it; by this act a secret was revealed. I started to say, "It is all a mistake; this is just a common, ordinary cat; the hair-needles on her tongue point inward, not outward." But the words did not come, because they couldn't. Satan smiled upon me, and I understood.

When it was dark Marget took food and wine and fruit, in a basket, and hurried away to the jail, and Satan and I walked toward my home. I was thinking to myself that I should like to see what the inside of the jail was like; Satan overheard the thought, and the next moment we were in the jail. We were in the torture-chamber, Satan said. The rack was there, and the other instruments, and there was a smoky lantern or two hanging on the walls and helping to make the place look dim and dreadful. There were people there—and executioners—but as they took no notice of us, it meant that we were invisible. A young man lay bound, and Satan said he was suspected of being a heretic, and the executioners were about to inquire into it. They asked the man to confess to the charge, and he said he could not, for it was not true. Then they drove splinter after splinter under his nails, and he shrieked with the pain. Satan was not disturbed, but I could not endure it, and had to be whisked out of there. I was faint and sick, but the fresh air revived me, and we walked toward my home. I said it was a brutal thing.

"No, it was a human thing. You should not insult the brutes by such a misuse of that word; they have not deserved it," and he went on talking like that. "It is like your paltry race—always lying, always claiming virtues which it hasn't got, always denying them to the higher animals, which alone possess them. No brute ever does a cruel thing—that is the monopoly of those with the Moral Sense. When a brute inflicts pain he does it innocently; it is not wrong; for him there is no such thing as wrong. And he does not inflict pain for the pleasure of inflicting it—only man does that. Inspired by that mongrel Moral Sense of his! A sense whose function is to distinguish between right and wrong, with liberty to choose which of them he will do. Now what advantage can he get out of that? He is always choosing, and in nine cases out of ten he prefers the wrong. There shouldn't be any wrong; and without the Moral Sense there couldn't be any. And yet he is such an unreasoning creature that he is not able to perceive that the Moral Sense degrades him to the bottom layer of animated beings and is a shameful possession. Are you feeling better? Let me show you something."

6

In a moment we were in a French village. We walked through a great factory of some sort, where men and women and little children were toiling in heat and dirt and a fog of dust; and they were clothed in rags, and drooped at their work, for they were worn and half starved, and weak and drowsy. Satan said:

"It is some more Moral Sense. The proprietors are rich, and very holy; but the wage they pay to these poor brothers and sisters of theirs is only enough to keep them from dropping dead with hunger. The work-hours are fourteen per day, winter and summer—from six in the morning till eight at night—little children and all. And they walk to and from the pigsties which they inhabit—four miles each way, through mud and slush, rain, snow, sleet, and storm, daily, year in and year out. They get four hours of sleep. They kennel together, three families in a room, in unimaginable filth and stench; and disease comes, and they die off like flies. Have they committed a crime, these mangy things? No. What have they done, that they are punished so? Nothing at all, except getting themselves born into your foolish race. You have seen how they treat a misdoer there in the jail; now you see how they treat the innocent and the worthy. Is your race logical? Are these ill-smelling innocents better off than that heretic? Indeed, no; his punishment is trivial compared with theirs. They broke him on the wheel and smashed him to rags and pulp after we left, and he is dead now, and free of your precious race; but these poor slaves here—why, they have been dying for years, and some of them will not escape from life for years to come. It is the Moral Sense which teaches the factory proprietors the difference between right and wrong—you perceive the result. They think themselves better than dogs. Ah, you are such an illogical, unreasoning race! And paltry—oh, unspeakably!"

Then he dropped all seriousness and just overstrained himself making fun of us, and deriding our pride in our warlike deeds, our great heroes, our imperishable fames, our mighty kings, our ancient aristocracies, our venerable history—and laughed and laughed till it was enough to make a person sick to hear him; and finally he sobered a little and said, "But, after all, it is not all ridiculous; there is a sort of pathos about it when one remembers how few are your days, how childish your pomps, and what shadows you are!"

Presently all things vanished suddenly from my sight, and I knew what it meant. The next moment we were walking along in our village;

and down toward the river I saw the twinkling lights of the Golden
Stag. Then in the dark I heard a joyful cry:

"He's come again!"

It was Seppi Wohlmeyer. He had felt his blood leap and his spirits
rise in a way that could mean only one thing, and he knew Satan was
near, although it was too dark to see him. He came to us, and we
walked along together, and Seppi poured out his gladness like water.
It was as if he were a lover and had found his sweetheart who had
been lost. Seppi was a smart and animated boy, and had enthusiasm
and expression, and was a contrast to Nikolaus and me. He was full
of the last new mystery, now—the disappearance of Hans Oppert, the
village loafer. People were beginning to be curious about it, he said.
He did not say anxious—curious was the right word, and strong enough.
No one had seen Hans for a couple of days.

"Not since he did that brutal thing, you know," he said.

"What brutal thing?" It was Satan that asked.

"Well, he is always clubbing his dog, which is a good dog, and his
only friend, and is faithful, and loves him, and does no one any harm;
and two days ago he was at it again, just for nothing—just for pleasure
—and the dog was howling and begging, and Theodor and I begged,
too, but he threatened us, and struck the dog again with all his might
and knocked one of his eyes out, and he said to us, 'There, I hope you
are satisfied now; that's what you have got for him by your damned
meddling'—and he laughed, the heartless brute." Seppi's voice trembled with pity and anger. I guessed what Satan would say, and he said
it.

"There is that misused word again—that shabby slander. Brutes do
not act like that, but only men."

"Well, it was inhuman, anyway."

"No, it wasn't, Seppi; it was human—quite distinctly human. It is not
pleasant to hear you libel the higher animals by attributing to them
dispositions which they are free from, and which are found nowhere
but in the human heart. None of the higher animals is tainted with the
disease called the Moral Sense. Purify your language, Seppi; drop those
lying phrases out of it."

He spoke pretty sternly—for him—and I was sorry I hadn't warned
Seppi to be more particular about the word he used. I knew how he
was feeling. He would not want to offend Satan; he would rather offend all his kin. There was an uncomfortable silence, but relief soon
came, for that poor dog came along now, with his eye hanging down,
and went straight to Satan, and began to moan and mutter brokenly,

and Satan began to answer in the same way, and it was plain that they were talking together in the dog language. We all sat down in the grass, in the moonlight, for the clouds were breaking away now, and Satan took the dog's head in his lap and put the eye back in its place, and the dog was comfortable, and he wagged his tail and licked Satan's hand, and looked thankful and said the same; I knew he was saying it, though I did not understand the words. Then the two talked together a bit, and Satan said:

"He says his master was drunk."

"Yes, he was," said we.

"And an hour later he fell over the precipice there beyond the Cliff Pasture."

"We know the place; it is three miles from here."

"And the dog has been often to the village, begging people to go there, but he was only driven away and not listened to."

We remembered it, but hadn't understood what he wanted.

"He only wanted help for the man who had misused him, and he thought only of that, and has had no food nor sought any. He has watched by his master two nights. What do you think of your race? Is heaven reserved for it, and this dog ruled out, as your teachers tell you? Can your race add anything to this dog's stock of morals and magnanimities?" He spoke to the creature, who jumped up, eager and happy, and apparently ready for orders and impatient to execute them. "Get some men; go with the dog—he will show you that carrion; and take a priest along to arrange about insurance, for death is near."

With the last word he vanished, to our sorrow and disappointment. We got the men and Father Adolf, and we saw the man die. Nobody cared but the dog; he mourned and grieved, and licked the dead face, and could not be comforted. We buried him where he was, and without a coffin, for he had no money, and no friend but the dog. If we had been an hour earlier the priest would have been in time to send that poor creature to heaven, but now he was gone down into the awful fires, to burn forever. It seemed such a pity that in a world where so many people have difficulty to put in their time, one little hour could not have been spared for this poor creature who needed it so much, and to whom it would have made the difference between eternal joy and eternal pain. It gave an appalling idea of the value of an hour, and I thought I could never waste one again without remorse and terror. Seppi was depressed and grieved, and said it must be so much better to be a dog and not run such awful risks. We took this one home with us and kept him for our own. Seppi had a very good thought as we were walking along, and it cheered us up and made us feel much better. He said the dog had forgiven the man that had wronged him so, and maybe God would accept that absolution.

There was a very dull week, now, for Satan did not come, nothing much was going on, and we boys could not venture to go and see Marget, because the nights were moonlit and our parents might find us out if we tried. But we came across Ursula a couple of times taking a walk in the meadows beyond the river to air the cat, and we learned from her that things were going well. She had natty new clothes on and bore a prosperous look. The four groschen a day were arriving without a break, but were not being spent for food and wine and such things—the cat attended to all that.

Marget was enduring her forsakenness and isolation fairly well, all things considered, and was cheerful, by help of Wilhelm Meidling. She spent an hour or two every night in the jail with her uncle, and had fattened him up with the cat's contributions. But she was curious to know more about Philip Traum, and hoped I would bring him again. Ursula was curious about him herself, and asked a good many questions about his uncle. It made the boys laugh, for I had told them the nonsense Satan had been stuffing her with. She got no satisfaction out of us, our tongues being tied.

Ursula gave us a small item of information: money being plenty now, she had taken on a servant to help about the house and run errands. She tried to tell it in a commonplace, matter-of-course way, but she was so set up by it and so vain of it that her pride in it leaked out pretty plainly. It was beautiful to see her veiled delight in this grandeur, poor old thing, but when we heard the name of the servant we wondered if she had been altogether wise; for although we were young, and often thoughtless, we had fairly good perception on some matters. This boy was Gottfried Narr, a dull, good creature, with no harm in him and nothing against him personally; still, he was under a cloud, and properly so, for it had not been six months since a social blight had mildewed the family—his grandmother had been burned as a witch. When that kind of a malady is in the blood it does not always come out with just one burning. Just now was not a good time for Ursula and Marget to be having dealings with a member of such a family, for the witch-terror had risen higher during the past year than it had ever reached in the memory of the oldest villagers. The mere mention of a witch was almost enough to frighten us out of our wits. This was natural enough, because of late years there were more kinds of witches than there used to be; in old times it had been only old women, but of late years they

were of all ages—even children of eight and nine; it was getting so that
anybody might turn out to be a familiar of the Devil—age and sex
hadn't anything to do with it. In our little region we had tried to extir-
pate the witches, but the more of them we burned the more of the
breed rose up in their places.

Once, in a school for girls only ten miles away, the teachers found
that the back of one of the girls was all red and inflamed, and they
were greatly frightened, believing it to be the Devil's marks. The girl
was scared, and begged them not to denounce her, and said it was only
fleas; but of course it would not do to let the matter rest there. All the
girls were examined, and eleven out of the fifty were badly marked,
the rest less so. A commission was appointed, but the eleven only cried
for their mothers and would not confess. Then they were shut up, each
by herself, in the dark, and put on black bread and water for ten days
and nights; and by that time they were haggard and wild, and their
eyes were dry and they did not cry any more, but only sat and mum-
bled, and would not take the food. Then one of them confessed, and
said they had often ridden through the air on broomsticks to the
witches' Sabbath, and in a bleak place high up in the mountains had
danced and drunk and caroused with several hundred other witches
and the Evil One, and all had conducted themselves in a scandalous
way and had reviled the priests and blasphemed God. That is what
she said—not in narrative form, for she was not able to remember any
of the details without having them called to her mind one after the
other; but the commission did that, for they knew just what questions
to ask, they being all written down for the use of witch-commissioners
two centuries before. They asked, "Did you do so and so?" and she always said yes, and looked weary and tired, and took no interest in it.
And so when the other ten heard that this one confessed, they confessed, too, and answered yes to the questions. Then they were burned
at the stake all together, which was just and right; and everybody went
from all the countryside to see it. I went, too; but when I saw that one
of them was a bonny, sweet girl I used to play with, and looked so
pitiful there chained to the stake, and her mother crying over her and
devouring her with kisses and clinging around her neck, and saying,
"Oh, my God! oh, my God!" it was too dreadful, and I went away.

It was bitter cold weather when Gottfried's grandmother was burned.
It was charged that she had cured bad headaches by kneading the
person's head and neck with her fingers—as she said—but really by the
Devil's help, as everybody knew. They were going to examine her, but
she stopped them, and confessed straight off that her power was from

the Devil. So they appointed to burn her next morning, early, in our market-square. The officer who was to prepare the fire was there first, and prepared it. She was there next—brought by the constables, who left her and went to fetch another witch. Her family did not come with her. They might be reviled, maybe stoned, if the people were excited. I came, and gave her an apple. She was squatting at the fire, warming herself and waiting; and her old lips and hands were blue with the cold. A stranger came next. He was a traveler, passing through; and he spoke to her gently, and, seeing nobody but me there to hear, said he was sorry for her. And he asked if what she confessed was true, and she said no. He looked surprised and still more sorry then, and asked her:

"Then why did you confess?"

"I am old and very poor," she said, "and I work for my living. There was no way but to confess. If I hadn't they might have set me free. That would ruin me, for no one would forget that I had been suspected of being a witch, and so I would get no more work, and wherever I went they would set the dogs on me. In a little while I would starve. The fire is best; it is soon over. You have been good to me, you two, and I thank you."

She snuggled closer to the fire, and put out her hands to warm them, the snow-flakes descending soft and still on her old gray head and making it white and whiter. The crowd was gathering now, and an egg came flying and struck her in the eye, and broke and ran down her face. There was a laugh at that.

I told Satan all about the eleven girls and the old woman, once, but it did not affect him. He only said it was the human race, and what the human race did was of no consequence. And he said he had seen it made; and it was not made of clay; it was made of mud—part of it was, anyway. I knew what he meant by that—the Moral Sense. He saw the thought in my head, and it tickled him and made him laugh. Then he called a bullock out of a pasture and petted it and talked with it, and said:

"There—he wouldn't drive children mad with hunger and fright and loneliness, and then burn them for confessing to things invented for them which had never happened. And neither would he break the hearts of innocent, poor old women and make them afraid to trust themselves among their own race; and he would not insult them in their death-agony. For he is not besmirched with the Moral Sense, but is as the angels are, and knows no wrong, and never does it."

Lovely as he was, Satan could be cruelly offensive when he chose; and he always chose when the human race was brought to his attention. He always turned up his nose at it, and never had a kind word for it.

Well, as I was saying, we boys doubted if it was a good time for Ursula to be hiring a member of the Narr family. We were right. When the people found it out they were naturally indignant. And, moreover, since Marget and Ursula hadn't enough to eat themselves, where was the money coming from to feed another mouth? That is what they wanted to know; and in order to find out they stopped avoiding Gottfried and began to seek his society and have sociable conversations with him. He was pleased—not thinking any harm and not seeing the trap—and so he talked innocently along, and was no discreeter than a cow.

"Money!" he said; "they've got plenty of it. They pay me two groschen a week, besides my keep. And they live on the fat of the land, I can tell you; the prince himself can't beat their table."

This astonishing statement was conveyed by the astrologer to Father Adolf on a Sunday morning when he was returning from mass. He was deeply moved, and said:

"This must be looked into."

He said there must be witchcraft at the bottom of it, and told the villagers to resume relations with Marget and Ursula in a private and unostentatious way, and keep both eyes open. They were told to keep their own counsel, and not rouse the suspicions of the household. The villagers were at first a bit reluctant to enter such a dreadful place, but the priest said they would be under his protection while there, and no harm could come to them, particularly if they carried a trifle of holy water along and kept their beads and crosses handy. This satisfied them and made them willing to go; envy and malice made the baser sort even eager to go.

And so poor Marget began to have company again, and was as pleased as a cat. She was like 'most anybody else—just human, and happy in her prosperities and not averse from showing them off a little; and she was humanly grateful to have the warm shoulder turned to her and be smiled upon by her friends and the village again; for of all the hard things to bear, to be cut by your neighbors and left in contemptuous solitude is maybe the hardest.

The bars were down, and we could all go there now, and we did— our parents and all—day after day. The cat began to strain herself. She provided the top of everything for those companies, and in abundance —among them many a dish and many a wine which they had not tasted before and which they had not even heard of except at second-hand from the prince's servants. And the tableware was much above ordinary, too.

Marget was troubled at times, and pursued Ursula with questions to an uncomfortable degree; but Ursula stood her ground and stuck to it that it was Providence, and said no word about the cat. Marget knew that nothing was impossible to Providence, but she could not help having doubts that this effort was from there, though she was afraid to say so, lest disaster come of it. Witchcraft occurred to her, but she put the thought aside, for this was before Gottfried joined the household, and she knew Ursula was pious and a bitter hater of witches. By the time Gottfried arrived Providence was established, unshakably intrenched, and getting all the gratitude. The cat made no murmur, but went on composedly improving in style and prodigality by experience.

In any community, big or little, there is always a fair proportion of people who are not malicious or unkind by nature, and who never do unkind things except when they are overmastered by fear, or when their self-interest is greatly in danger, or some such matter as that. Eseldorf had its proportion of such people, and ordinarily their good and gentle influence was felt, but these were not ordinary times—on account of the witch-dread—and so we did not seem to have any gentle and compassionate hearts left, to speak of. Every person was frightened at the unaccountable state of things at Marget's house, not doubting that witchcraft was at the bottom of it, and fright frenzied their reason. Naturally there were some who pitied Marget and Ursula for the danger that was gathering about them, but naturally they did not say so; it would not have been safe. So the others had it all their own way, and there was none to advise the ignorant girl and the foolish woman and warn them to modify their doings. We boys wanted to warn them, but we backed down when it came to the pinch, being afraid. We found that we were not manly enough nor brave enough to do a generous action when there was a chance that it could get us into trouble. Neither of us confessed this poor spirit to the others, but did as other people would have done—dropped the subject and talked about something else. And I knew we all felt mean, eating and drinking Marget's fine things along with those companies of spies, and petting her and complimenting her with the rest, and seeing with self-reproach how foolishly happy she was, and never saying a word to put her on her guard. And, indeed, she was happy, and as proud as a princess, and so grateful to have friends again. And all the time these people were watching with all their eyes and reporting all they saw to Father Adolf.

But he couldn't make head or tail of the situation. There must be an enchanter somewhere on the premises, but who was it? Marget was not seen to do any jugglery, nor was Ursula, nor yet Gottfried; and still the wines and dainties never ran short, and a guest could not call for a thing and not get it. To produce these effects was usual enough with witches and enchanters—that part of it was not new; but to do it without any incantations, or even any rumblings or earthquakes or lightnings or apparitions—that was new, novel, wholly irregular. There was nothing in the books like this. Enchanted things were always unreal. Gold turned to dirt in an unenchanted atmosphere, food withered away and vanished. But this test failed in the present case. The spies brought samples: Father Adolf prayed over them, exorcised them, but it did no good; they remained sound and real, they yielded to natural decay only, and took the usual time to do it.

Father Adolf was not merely puzzled, he was also exasperated; for these evidences very nearly convinced him—privately—that there was no witchcraft in the matter. It did not wholly convince him, for this could be a new kind of witchcraft. There was a way to find out as to this: if this prodigal abundance of provender was not brought in from the outside, but produced on the premises, there was witchcraft, sure.

7

Marget announced a party, and invited forty people; the date for it was seven days away. This was a fine opportunity. Marget's house stood by itself, and it could be easily watched. All the week it was watched night and day. Marget's household went out and in as usual, but they carried nothing in their hands, and neither they nor others brought anything to the house. This was ascertained. Evidently rations for forty people were not being fetched. If they were furnished any sustenance it would have to be made on the premises. It was true that Marget went out with a basket every evening, but the spies ascertained that she always brought it back empty.

The guests arrived at noon and filled the place. Father Adolf followed; also, after a little, the astrologer, without invitation. The spies had informed him that neither at the back nor the front had any parcels been brought in. He entered, and found the eating and drinking going on finely, and everything progressing in a lively and festive way. He glanced around and perceived that many of the cooked delicacies and all of the native and foreign fruits were of a perishable character, and he also recognized that these were fresh and perfect. No apparitions, no incantations, no thunder. That settled it. This was witchcraft.

And not only that, but of a new kind—a kind never dreamed of before. It was a prodigious power, an illustrious power; he resolved to discover its secret. The announcement of it would resound throughout the world, penetrate to the remotest lands, paralyze all the nations with amazement—and carry his name with it, and make him renowned forever. It was a wonderful piece of luck, a splendid piece of luck; the glory of it made him dizzy.

All the house made room for him; Marget politely seated him; Ursula ordered Gottfried to bring a special table for him. Then she decked it and furnished it, and asked for his orders.

"Bring me what you will," he said.

The two servants brought supplies from the pantry, together with white wine and red—a bottle of each. The astrologer, who very likely had never seen such delicacies before, poured out a beaker of red wine, drank it off, poured another, then began to eat with a grand appetite.

I was not expecting Satan, for it was more than a week since I had seen or heard of him, but now he came in—I knew it by the feel, though people were in the way and I could not see him. I heard him apologizing for intruding; and he was going away, but Marget urged him to stay, and he thanked her and stayed. She brought him along, introducing him to the girls, and to Meidling, and to some of the elders; and there was quite a rustle of whispers: "It's the young stranger we hear so much about and can't get sight of, he is away so much." "Dear, dear, but he is beautiful—what is his name?" "Philip Traum." "Ah, it fits him!" (You see, "Traum" is German for "Dream.") "What does he do?" "Studying for the ministry, they say." "His face is his fortune—he'll be a cardinal some day." "Where is his home?" "Away down somewhere in the tropics, they say—has a rich uncle down there." And so on. He made his way at once; everybody was anxious to know him and talk with him. Everybody noticed how cool and fresh it was, all of a sudden, and wondered at it, for they could see that the sun was beating down the same as before, outside, and the sky was clear of clouds, but no one guessed the reason, of course.

The astrologer had drunk his second beaker; he poured out a third. He set the bottle down, and by accident overturned it. He seized it before much was spilled, and held it up to the light, saying, "What a pity—it is royal wine." Then his face lighted with joy or triumph, or something, and he said, "Quick! Bring a bowl."

It was brought—a four-quart one. He took up that two-pint bottle and began to pour; went on pouring, the red liquor gurgling and gushing into the white bowl and rising higher and higher up its sides, everybody staring and holding their breath—and presently the bowl was full to the brim.

"Look at the bottle," he said, holding it up; "it is full yet!" I glanced at Satan, and in that moment he vanished. Then Father Adolf rose up, flushed and excited, crossed himself, and began to thunder in his great voice, "This house is bewitched and accursed!" People began to cry and shriek and crowd toward the door. "I summon this detected household to—"

His words were cut off short. His face became red, then purple, but he could not utter another sound. Then I saw Satan, a transparent film, melt into the astrologer's body; then the astrologer put up his hand, and apparently in his own voice said, "Wait—remain where you are." All stopped where they stood. "Bring a funnel!" Ursula brought it, trembling and scared, and he stuck it in the bottle and took up the great bowl and began to pour the wine back, the people gazing and dazed with astonishment, for they knew the bottle was already full before he began. He emptied the whole of the bowl into the bottle, then smiled out over the room, chuckled, and said, indifferently: "It is nothing—anybody can do it! With my powers I can even do much more."

A frightened cry burst out everywhere. "Oh, my God, he is possessed!" and there was a tumultuous rush for the door which swiftly emptied the house of all who did not belong in it except us boys and Meidling. We boys knew the secret, and would have told it if we could, but we couldn't. We were very thankful to Satan for furnishing that good help at the needful time.

Marget was pale, and crying; Meidling looked kind of petrified; Ursula the same; but Gottfried was the worst—he couldn't stand, he was so weak and scared. For he was of a witch family, you know, and it would be bad for him to be suspected. Agnes came loafing in, looking pious and unaware, and wanted to rub up against Ursula and be petted, but Ursula was afraid of her and shrank away from her, but pretending she was not meaning any incivility, for she knew very well it wouldn't answer to have strained relations with that kind of a cat. But we boys took Agnes and petted her, for Satan would not have befriended her if he had not had a good opinion of her, and that was indorsement enough for us. He seemed to trust anything that hadn't the Moral Sense.

Outside, the guests, panic-stricken, scattered in every direction and fled in a pitiable state of terror; and such a tumult as they made with their running and sobbing and shrieking and shouting that soon all the village came flocking from their houses to see what had happened, and they thronged the street and shouldered and jostled one another in excitement and fright; and then Father Adolf appeared, and they fell apart in two walls like the cloven Red Sea, and presently down this lane the astrologer came striding and mumbling, and where he passed the lanes surged back in packed masses, and fell silent with awe, and their eyes stared and their breasts heaved, and several women fainted; and when he was gone by the crowd swarmed together and followed him at a distance, talking excitedly and asking questions and finding out the facts. Finding out the facts and passing them on to others, with improvements—improvements which soon enlarged the bowl of wine to a barrel, and made the one bottle hold it all and yet remain empty to the last.

When the astrologer reached the market-square he went straight to a juggler, fantastically dressed, who was keeping three brass balls in the air, and took them from him and faced around upon the approaching crowd and said: "This poor clown is ignorant of his art. Come forward and see an expert perform."

So saying, he tossed the balls up one after another and set them whirling in a slender bright oval in the air, and added another, then another and another, and soon—no one seeing whence he got them— adding, adding, adding, the oval lengthening all the time, his hands moving so swiftly that they were just a web or a blur and not distinguishable as hands; and such as counted said there were now a hundred balls in the air. The spinning great oval reached up twenty feet in the air and was a shining and glinting and wonderful sight. Then he folded his arms and told the balls to go on spinning without his help— and they did it. After a couple of minutes he said, "There, that will do," and the oval broke and came crashing down, and the balls scattered abroad and rolled every whither. And wherever one of them came the people fell back in dread, and no one would touch it. It made him laugh, and he scoffed at the people and called them cowards and old women. Then he turned and saw the tight-rope, and said foolish people were daily wasting their money to see a clumsy and ignorant varlet degrade that beautiful art; now they should see the work of a master. With that he made a spring into the air and lit firm on his feet on the rope. Then he hopped the whole length of it back and forth on one foot, with his hands clasped over his eyes; and next he began to throw somersaults, both backward and forward, and threw twenty-seven.

The people murmured, for the astrologer was old, and always before had been halting of movement and at times even lame, but he was nimble enough now and went on with his antics in the liveliest manner.

Finally he sprang lightly down and walked away, and passed up the road and around the corner and disappeared. Then that great, pale, silent, solid crowd drew a deep breath and looked into one another's faces as if they said: "Was it real? Did you see it, or was it only I—and I was dreaming?" Then they broke into a low murmur of talking, and fell apart in couples, and moved toward their homes, still talking in that awed way, with faces close together and laying a hand on an arm and making other such gestures as people make when they have been deeply impressed by something.

We boys followed behind our fathers, and listened, catching all we could of what they said; and when they sat down in our house and continued their talk they still had us for company. They were in a sad mood, for it was certain, they said, that disaster for the village must follow this awful visitation of witches and devils. Then my father remembered that Father Adolf had been struck dumb at the moment of his denunciation.

"They have not ventured to lay their hands upon an anointed servant of God before," he said; "and how they could have dared it this time I cannot make out, for he wore his crucifix. Isn't it so?"

"Yes," said the others, "we saw it."

"It is serious, friends, it is very serious. Always before, we had a protection. It has failed."

The others shook, as with a sort of chill, and muttered those words over—"It has failed." "God has forsaken us."

"It is true," said Seppi Wohlmeyer's father; "there is nowhere to look for help."

"The people will realize this," said Nikolaus's father, the judge, "and despair will take away their courage and their energies. We have indeed fallen upon evil times."

He sighed, and Wohlmeyer said, in a troubled voice: "The report of it all will go about the country, and our village will be shunned as being under the displeasure of God. The Golden Stag will know hard times."

"True, neighbor," said my father; "all of us will suffer—all in repute, many in estate. And, good God!—"

"What is it?"

"That can come—to finish us!"

"Name it—um Gottes Willen!"

"The Interdict!"

It smote like a thunderclap, and they were like to swoon with the terror of it. Then the dread of this calamity roused their energies, and they stopped brooding and began to consider ways to avert it. They discussed this, that, and the other way, and talked till the afternoon was far spent, then confessed that at present they could arrive at no decision. So they parted sorrowfully, with oppressed hearts which were filled with bodings.

While they were saying their parting words I slipped out and set my course for Marget's house to see what was happening there. I met many people, but none of them greeted me. It ought to have been surprising, but it was not, for they were so distraught with fear and dread that they were not in their right minds, I think; they were white and haggard, and walked like persons in a dream, their eyes open but seeing nothing, their lips moving but uttering nothing, and worriedly clasping and unclasping their hands without knowing it.

At Marget's it was like a funeral. She and Wilhelm sat together on the sofa, but said nothing, and not even holding hands. Both were steeped in gloom, and Marget's eyes were red from the crying she had been doing. She said:

"I have been begging him to go, and come no more, and so save himself alive. I cannot bear to be his murderer. This house is bewitched, and no inmate will escape the fire. But he will not go, and he will be lost with the rest."

Wilhelm said he would not go; if there was danger for her, his place was by her, and there he would remain. Then she began to cry again, and it was all so mournful that I wished I had stayed away. There was a knock, now, and Satan came in, fresh and cheery and beautiful, and brought that winy atmosphere of his and changed the whole thing. He never said a word about what had been happening, nor about the awful fears which were freezing the blood in the hearts of the community, but began to talk and rattle on about all manner of gay and pleasant things: and next about music—an artful stroke which cleared away the remnant of Marget's depression and brought her spirits and her interests broad awake. She had not heard any one talk so well and so knowingly on that subject before, and she was so uplifted by it and so charmed that what she was feeling lit up her face and came out in her words; and Wilhelm noticed it and did not look as pleased as he ought to have done. And next Satan branched off into poetry, and recited some, and did it well, and Marget was charmed again; and again Wilhelm was not as pleased as he ought to have been, and this time Marget noticed it and was remorseful.

I fell asleep to pleasant music that night—the patter of rain upon the panes and the dull growling of distant thunder. Away in the night

Satan came and roused me and said: "Come with me. Where shall we go?"

"Anywhere—so it is with you."

Then there was a fierce glare of sunlight, and he said, "This is China."

That was a grand surprise, and made me sort of drunk with vanity and gladness to think I had come so far—so much, much farther than anybody else in our village, including Bartel Sperling, who had such a great opinion of his travels. We buzzed around over that empire for more than half an hour, and saw the whole of it. It was wonderful, the spectacles we saw; and some were beautiful, others too horrible to think. For instance— However, I may go into that by and by, and also why Satan chose China for this excursion instead of another place; it would interrupt my tale to do it now. Finally we stopped flitting and lit.

We sat upon a mountain commanding a vast landscape of mountain-range and gorge and valley and plain and river, with cities and villages slumbering in the sunlight, and a glimpse of blue sea on the farther verge. It was a tranquil and dreamy picture, beautiful to the eye and restful to the spirit. If we could only make a change like that whenever we wanted to, the world would be easier to live in than it is, for change of scene shifts the mind's burdens to the other shoulder and banishes old, shop-worn wearinesses from mind and body both.

We talked together, and I had the idea of trying to reform Satan and persuade him to lead a better life. I told him about all those things he had been doing, and begged him to be more considerate and stop making people unhappy. I said I knew he did not mean any harm, but that he ought to stop and consider the possible consequences of a thing before launching it in that impulsive and random way of his; then he would not make so much trouble. He was not hurt by this plain speech; he only looked amused and surprised, and said:

"What? I do random things? Indeed, I never do. I stop and consider possible consequences? Where is the need? I know what the conse-quences are going to be—always."

"Oh, Satan, then how could you do these things?"

"Well, I will tell you, and you must understand if you can. You belong to a singular race. Every man is a suffering-machine and a hap-piness-machine combined. The two functions work together harmoni-ously, with a fine and delicate precision, on the give-and-take principle. For every happiness turned out in the one department the other stands ready to modify it with a sorrow or a pain—maybe a dozen. In most cases the man's life is about equally divided between happiness and unhappiness. When this is not the case the unhappiness predominates —always; never the other. Sometimes a man's make and disposition are such that his misery-machine is able to do nearly all the business. Such a man goes through life almost ignorant of what happiness is. Everything he touches, everything he does, brings a misfortune upon him. You have seen such people? To that kind of a person life is not an advantage, is it? It is only a disaster. Sometimes for an hour's happiness a man's machinery makes him pay years of misery. Don't you know that? It happens every now and then. I will give you a case or two presently. Now the people of your village are nothing to me—you know that, don't you?"

I did not like to speak out too flatly, so I said I had suspected it.

"Well, it is true that they are nothing to me. It is not possible that they should be. The difference between them and me is abysmal, immeasurable. They have no intellect."

"No intellect?"

"Nothing that resembles it. At a future time I will examine what man calls his mind and give you the details of that chaos, then you will see and understand. Men have nothing in common with me—there is no point of contact; they have foolish little feelings and foolish little vanities and impertinences and ambitions; their foolish little life is but a laugh, a sigh, and extinction; and they have no sense. Only the Moral Sense. I will show you what I mean. Here is a red spider, not so big as a pin's head. Can you imagine an elephant being interested in him— caring whether he is happy or isn't, or whether he is wealthy or poor, or whether his sweetheart returns his love or not, or whether his mother is sick or well, or whether he is looked up to in society or not, or whether his enemies will smite him or his friends desert him, or whether his hopes will suffer blight or his political ambitions fail, or whether he shall die in the bosom of his family or neglected and despised in a foreign land? These things can never be important to the elephant; they are nothing to him; he cannot shrink his sympathies to the microscopic size of them. Man is to me as the red spider is to the elephant. The elephant has nothing against the spider—he cannot get down to that remote level; I have nothing against man. The elephant is indifferent; I am indifferent. The elephant would not take the trouble to do the spider an ill turn; if he took the notion he might do him a good turn, if it came in his way and cost nothing. I have done men good service, but no ill turns.

"The elephant lives a century, the red spider a day; in power, intellect, and dignity the one creature is separated from the other by a distance which is simply astronomical. Yet in these, as in all qualities, man is immeasurably further below me than is the wee spider below the elephant.

"Man's mind clumsily and tediously and laboriously patches little trivialities together and gets a result—such as it is. My mind creates! Do you get the force of that? Creates anything it desires—and in a moment. Creates without material. Creates fluids, solids, colors—anything, everything—out of the airy nothing which is called Thought. A man imagines a silk thread, imagines a machine to make it, imagines a picture, then by weeks of labor embroiders it on canvas with the thread. I think the whole thing, and in a moment it is before you—created.

"I think a poem, music, the record of a game of chess—anything—and it is there. This is the immortal mind—nothing is beyond its reach. Nothing can obstruct my vision; the rocks are transparent to me, and darkness is daylight. I do not need to open a book; I take the whole of its contents into my mind at a single glance, through the cover; and in a million years I could not forget a single word of it, or its place in the volume. Nothing goes on in the skull of man, bird, fish, insect, or other creature which can be hidden from me. I pierce the learned man's brain with a single glance, and the treasures which cost him threescore years to accumulate are mine; he can forget, and he does forget, but I retain.

"Now, then, I perceive by your thoughts that you are understanding me fairly well. Let us proceed. Circumstances might so fall out that the elephant could like the spider—supposing he can see it—but he could not love it. His love is for his own kind—for his equals. An angel's love is sublime, adorable, divine, beyond the imagination of man—infinitely beyond it! But it is limited to his own august order. If it fell upon one of your race for only an instant, it would consume its object to ashes. No, we cannot love men, but we can be harmlessly indifferent to them; we can also like them, sometimes. I like you and the boys, I like Father Peter, and for your sakes I am doing all these things for the villagers."

He saw that I was thinking a sarcasm, and he explained his position.

"I have wrought well for the villagers, though it does not look like it on the surface. Your race never know good fortune from ill. They are always mistaking the one for the other. It is because they cannot see into the future. What I am doing for the villagers will bear good fruit some day; in some cases to themselves; in others, to unborn generations of men. No one will ever know that I was the cause, but it will be none the less true, for all that. Among you boys you have a game: you stand a row of bricks on end a few inches apart; you push a brick, it knocks its neighbor over, the neighbor knocks over the next brick—and so on till all the row is prostrate. That is human life. A child's first act knocks over the initial brick, and the rest will follow inexorably. If you could see into the future, as I can, you would see everything that was going to happen to that creature; for nothing can change the order of its life after the first event has determined it. That is, nothing will change it, because each act unfailingly begets an act, that act begets another, and so on to the end, and the seer can look forward down the line and see just when each act is to have birth, from cradle to grave."

"Does God order the career?"

"Foreordain it? No. The man's circumstances and environment order it. His first act determines the second and all that follow after. But suppose, for argument's sake, that the man should skip one of these acts; an apparently trifling one, for instance; suppose that it had been appointed that on a certain day, at a certain hour and minute and second and fraction of a second he should go to the well, and he didn't go. That man's career would change utterly, from that moment; thence to the grave it would be wholly different from the career which his first act as a child had arranged for him. Indeed, it might be that if he had gone to the well he would have ended his career on a throne, and that omitting to do it would set him upon a career that would lead to beggary and a pauper's grave. For instance: if at any time—say in boyhood—Columbus had skipped the triflingest little link in the chain of acts projected and made inevitable by his first childish act, it would have changed his whole subsequent life, and he would have become a priest and died obscure in an Italian village, and America would not have been discovered for two centuries afterward. I know this. To skip any one of the billion acts in Columbus's chain would have wholly changed his life. I have examined his billion of possible careers, and in only one of them occurs the discovery of America. You people do not suspect that all of your acts are of one size and importance, but it is true; to snatch at an appointed fly is as big with fate for you as in any other appointed act—"

"As the conquering of a continent, for instance?"

"Yes. Now, then, no man ever does drop a link—the thing has never happened! Even when he is trying to make up his mind as to whether he will do a thing or not, that itself is a link, an act, and has its proper place in his chain; and when he finally decides an act, that also was the thing which he was absolutely certain to do. You see, now, that a man will never drop a link in his chain. He cannot. If he made up his mind to try, that project would itself be an unavoidable link—a thought bound to occur to him at that precise moment, and made certain by the first act of his babyhood."

It seemed so dismal!

"He is a prisoner for life," I said sorrowfully, "and cannot get free."

"No, of himself he cannot get away from the consequences of his first childish act. But I can free him."

I looked up wistfully.

"I have changed the careers of a number of your villagers."

I tried to thank him, but found it difficult, and let it drop.

"I shall make some other changes. You know that little Lisa Brandt?"

"Oh yes, everybody does. My mother says she is so sweet and so lovely that she is not like any other child. She says she will be the pride of the village when she grows up; and its idol, too, just as she is now."

"I shall change her future."

"Make it better?" I asked.

"Yes. And I will change the future of Nikolaus."

I was glad, this time, and said, "I don't need to ask about his case; you will be sure to do generously by him."

"It is my intention."

Straight off I was building that great future of Nicky's in my imagination, and had already made a renowned general of him and hofmeister at the court, when I noticed that Satan was waiting for me to get ready to listen again. I was ashamed of having exposed my cheap imaginings to him, and was expecting some sarcasms, but it did not happen. He proceeded with his subject:

"Nicky's appointed life is sixty-two years."

"That's grand!" I said.

"Lisa's, thirty-six. But, as I told you, I shall change their lives and those ages. Two minutes and a quarter from now Nikolaus will wake out of his sleep and find the rain blowing in. It was appointed that he should turn over and go to sleep again. But I have appointed that he shall get up and close the window first. That trifle will change his career entirely. He will rise in the morning two minutes later than the chain of his life had appointed him to rise. By consequence, thenceforth nothing will ever happen to him in accordance with the details of the old chain." He took out his watch and sat looking at it a few moments, then said: "Nikolaus has risen to close the window. His life is changed, his new career has begun. There will be consequences."

It made me feel creepy; it was uncanny.

"But for this change certain things would happen twelve days from now. For instance, Nikolaus would save Lisa from drowning. He would arrive on the scene at exactly the right moment—four minutes past ten, the long-ago appointed instant of time—and the water would be shoal, the achievement easy and certain. But he will arrive some seconds too late, now; Lisa will have struggled into deeper water. He will do his best, but both will drown."

"Oh, Satan! oh, dear Satan!" I cried, with the tears rising in my eyes, "save them! Don't let it happen. I can't bear to lose Nikolaus, he is my loving playmate and friend; and think of Lisa's poor mother!"

I clung to him and begged and pleaded, but he was not moved. He made me sit down again, and told me I must hear him out.

"I have changed Nikolaus's life, and this has changed Lisa's. If I had not done this, Nikolaus would save Lisa, then he would catch cold from his drenching; one of your race's fantastic and desolating scarlet fevers would follow, with pathetic aftereffects; for forty-six years he would lie in his bed a paralytic log, deaf, dumb, blind, and praying night and day for the blessed relief of death. Shall I change his life back?"

"Oh no! Oh, not for the world! In charity and pity leave it as it is."

"It is best so. I could not have changed any other link in his life and done him so good a service. He had a billion possible careers, but not one of them was worth living; they were charged full with miseries and disasters. But for my intervention he would do his brave deed twelve days from now—a deed begun and ended in six minutes—and get for all reward those forty-six years of sorrow and suffering I told you of. It is one of the cases I was thinking of awhile ago when I said that sometimes an act which brings the actor an hour's happiness and self-satisfaction is paid for—or punished—by years of suffering."

I wondered what poor little Lisa's early death would save her from. He answered the thought:

"From ten years of pain and slow recovery from an accident, and then from nineteen years' pollution, shame, depravity, crime, ending with death at the hands of the executioner. Twelve days hence she will die; her mother would save her life if she could. Am I not kinder than her mother?"

"Yes—oh, indeed yes; and wiser."

"Father Peter's case is coming on presently. He will be acquitted, through unassailable proofs of his innocence."

"Why, Satan, how can that be? Do you really think it?"

"Indeed, I know it. His good name will be restored, and the rest of his life will be happy."

"I can believe it. To restore his good name will have that effect."

"His happiness will not proceed from that cause. I shall change his life that day, for his good. He will never know his good name has been restored."

In my mind—and modestly—I asked for particulars, but Satan paid no attention to my thought. Next, my mind wandered to the astrologer, and I wondered where he might be.

"In the moon," said Satan, with a fleeting sound which I believed was a chuckle. "I've got him on the cold side of it, too. He doesn't know where he is, and is not having a pleasant time; still, it is good enough for him, a good place for his star studies. I shall need him presently; then I shall bring him back and possess him again. He has a long and cruel and odious life before him, but I will change that, for I have no feeling against him and am quite willing to do him a kindness. I think I shall get him burned."

He had such strange notions of kindness! But angels are made so, and do not know any better. Their ways are not like our ways; and, besides, human beings are nothing to them; they think they are only freaks. It seems to me odd that he should put the astrologer so far away; he could have dumped him in Germany just as well, where he would be handy.

"Far away?" said Satan. "To me no place is far away; distance does not exist for me. The sun is less than a hundred million miles from here, and the light that is falling upon us has taken eight minutes to come; but I can make that flight, or any other, in a fraction of time so minute that it cannot be measured by a watch. I have but to think the journey, and it is accomplished."

I held out my hand and said, "The light lies upon it; think it into a glass of wine, Satan."

He did it. I drank the wine.

"Break the glass," he said.

I broke it.

"There—you see it is real. The villagers thought the brass balls were magic stuff and as perishable as smoke. They were afraid to touch them. You are a curious lot—your race. But come along; I have business. I will put you to bed." Said and done. Then he was gone; but his voice came back to me through the rain and darkness saying, "Yes, tell Seppi, but no other."

It was the answer to my thought.

8

Sleep would not come. It was not because I was proud of my travels and excited about having been around the big world to China, and feeling contemptuous of Bartel Sperling, "the traveler," as he called himself, and looked down upon us others because he had been to Vienna once and was the only Eseldorf boy who had made such a journey and seen the world's wonders. At another time that would have kept me awake, but it did not affect me now. No, my mind was filled with Nikolaus, my thoughts ran upon him only, and the good days we had seen together at romps and frolics in the woods and the fields and the river in the long summer days, and skating and sliding in the winter when our parents thought we were in school. And now he was going out of this young life, and the summers and winters would come and go, and we others would rove and play as before, but his place would be vacant; we should see him no more. To-morrow he would not suspect, but would be as he had always been, and it would shock me to hear him laugh, and see him do lightsome and frivolous things, for to me he would be a corpse, with waxen hands and dull eyes, and I should see the shroud around his face; and next day he would not suspect, nor the next, and all the time his handful of days would be wasting swiftly away and that awful thing coming nearer and nearer, his fate closing steadily around him and no one knowing it but Seppi and me. Twelve days—only twelve days. It was awful to think of. I noticed that in my thoughts I was not calling him by his familiar names, Nick and Nicky, but was speaking of him by his full name, and reverently, as one speaks of the dead. Also, as incident after incident of our comradeship came thronging into my mind out of the past, I noticed that they were mainly cases where I had wronged him or hurt him, and they rebuked me and reproached me, and my heart was wrung with remorse, just as it is when we remember our unkindnesses to friends who have passed beyond the veil, and we wish we could have them back again, if only for a moment, so that we could go on our knees to them and say, "Have pity, and forgive."

Once when we were nine years old he went a long errand of nearly two miles for the fruiterer, who gave him a splendid big apple for reward, and he was flying home with it, almost beside himself with astonishment and delight, and I met him, and he let me look at the apple, not thinking of treachery, and I ran off with it, eating it as I ran, he following me and begging; and when he overtook me I offered him the core, which was all that was left; and I laughed. Then he turned away, crying, and said he had meant to give it to his little sister. That smote me, for she was slowly getting well of a sickness, and it would have been a proud moment for him, to see her joy and surprise and have her caresses. But I was ashamed to say I was ashamed, and only said something rude and mean, to pretend I did not care, and he made no reply in words, but there was a wounded look in his face as he turned away toward his home which rose before me many times in after years, in the night, and reproached me and made me ashamed again. It had grown dim in my mind, by and by, then it disappeared; but it was back now, and not dim.

Once at school, when we were eleven, I upset my ink and spoiled four copy-books, and was in danger of severe punishment; but I put it upon him, and he got the whipping.

And only last year I had cheated him in a trade, giving him a large fish-hook which was partly broken through for three small sound ones. The first fish he caught broke the hook, but he did not know I was blamable, and he refused to take back one of the small hooks which my conscience forced me to offer him, but said, "A trade is a trade; the hook was bad, but that was not your fault."

No, I could not sleep. These little, shabby wrongs upbraided me and tortured me, and with a pain much sharper than one feels when the wrongs have been done to the living. Nikolaus was living, but no matter; he was to me as one already dead. The wind was still moaning about the eaves, the rain still pattering upon the panes.

In the morning I sought out Seppi and told him. It was down by the river. His lips moved, but he did not say anything, he only looked dazed and stunned, and his face turned very white. He stood like that a few moments, the tears welling into his eyes, then he turned away and I locked my arm in his and we walked along thinking, but not speaking. We crossed the bridge and wandered through the meadows and up among the hills and the woods, and at last the talk came and flowed freely, and it was all about Nikolaus and was a recalling of the life we had lived with him. And every now and then Seppi said, as if to himself:

"Twelve days!—less than twelve days."

We said we must be with him all the time; we must have all of him we could; the days were precious now. Yet we did not go to seek him. It would be like meeting the dead, and we were afraid. We did not say it, but that was what we were feeling. And so it gave us a shock when we turned a curve and came upon Nikolaus face to face. He shouted, gaily:

"Hi-hi! What is the matter? Have you seen a ghost?"

We couldn't speak, but there was no occasion; he was willing to talk for us all, for he had just seen Satan and was in high spirits about it. Satan had told him about our trip to China, and he had begged Satan to take him a journey, and Satan had promised. It was to be a far journey, and wonderful and beautiful; and Nikolaus had begged him to take us, too, but he said no, he would take us some day, maybe, but not now. Satan would come for him on the 13th, and Nikolaus was already counting the hours, he was so impatient.

That was the fatal day. We were already counting the hours, too.

We wandered many a mile, always following paths which had been our favorites from the days when we were little, and always we talked about the old times. All the blitheness was with Nikolaus; we others could not shake off our depression. Our tone toward Nikolaus was so strangely gentle and tender and yearning that he noticed it, and was pleased; and we were constantly doing him deferential little offices of courtesy, and saying, "Wait, let me do that for you," and that pleased him, too. I gave him seven fish-hooks—all I had—and made him take them; and Seppi gave him his new knife and a humming-top painted red and yellow—atonements for swindles practised upon him formerly, as I learned later, and probably no longer remembered by Nikolaus now. These things touched him, and he could not have believed that we loved him so; and his pride in it and gratefulness for it cut us to the heart, we were so undeserving of them. When we parted at last, he was radiant, and said he had never had such a happy day.

As we walked along homeward, Seppi said, "We always prized him, but never so much as now, when we are going to lose him."

Next day and every day we spent all of our spare time with Nikolaus; and also added to it time which we (and he) stole from work and other duties, and this cost the three of us some sharp scoldings, and some threats of punishment. Every morning two of us woke with a start and a shudder, saying, as the days flew along, "Only ten days left;" "only nine days left;" "only eight;" "only seven." Always it was narrowing. Always Nikolaus was gay and happy, and always puzzled because we were not. He wore his invention to the bone trying to invent ways to cheer us up, but it was only a hollow success; he could see that our jollity had no heart in it, and that the laughs we broke into came up against some obstruction or other and suffered damage and decayed into a sigh. He tried to find out what the matter was, so that he could help us out of our trouble or make it lighter by sharing it with us; so we had to tell many lies to deceive him and appease him.

But the most distressing thing of all was that he was always making plans, and often they went beyond the 13th! Whenever that happened it made us groan in spirit. All his mind was fixed upon finding some way to conquer our depression and cheer us up; and at last, when he had but three days to live, he fell upon the right idea and was jubilant over it—a boys-and-girls' frolic and dance in the woods, up there where we first met Satan, and this was to occur on the 14th. It was ghastly, for that was his funeral day. We couldn't venture to protest; it would only have brought a "Why?" which we could not answer. He wanted us to help him invite his guests, and we did it—one can refuse nothing to a dying friend. But it was dreadful, for really we were inviting them to his funeral.

It was an awful eleven days; and yet, with a lifetime stretching back between to-day and then, they are still a grateful memory to me, and beautiful. In effect they were days of companionship with one's sacred dead, and I have known no comradeship that was so close or so precious. We clung to the hours and the minutes, counting them as they wasted away, and parting with them with that pain and bereavement which a miser feels who sees his hoard filched from him coin by coin by robbers and is helpless to prevent it.

When the evening of the last day came we stayed out too long; Seppi and I were in fault for that; we could not bear to part with Nikolaus; so it was very late when we left him at his door. We lingered near awhile, listening; and that happened which we were fearing. His father gave him the promised punishment, and we heard his shrieks. But we listened only a moment, then hurried away, remorseful for this thing which we had caused. And sorry for the father, too; our thought being, "If he only knew—if he only knew!"

In the morning Nikolaus did not meet us at the appointed place, so we went to his home to see what the matter was. His mother said:

"His father is out of all patience with these goings-on, and will not have any more of it. Half the time when Nick is needed he is not to be found; then it turns out that he has been gadding around with you two. His father gave him a flogging last night. It always grieved me before, and many's the time I have begged him off and saved him, but this time he appealed to me in vain, for I was out of patience myself."

"I wish you had saved him just this one time," I said, my voice trembling a little; "it would ease a pain in your heart to remember it some day."

She was ironing at the time, and her back was partly toward me. She turned about with a startled or wondering look in her face and said, "What do you mean by that?"

I was not prepared, and didn't know anything to say; so it was awkward, for she kept looking at me; but Seppi was alert and spoke up:

"Why, of course it would be pleasant to remember, for the very reason we were out so late was that Nikolaus got to telling how good you are to him, and how he never got whipped when you were by to save him; and he was so full of it, and we were so full of the interest of it, that none of us noticed how late it was getting."

"Did he say that? Did he?" and she put her apron to her eyes.

"You can ask Theodor—he will tell you the same."

"It is a dear, good lad, my Nick," she said. "I am sorry I let him get whipped; I will never do it again. To think—all the time I was sitting here last night, fretting and angry at him, he was loving me and praising me! Dear, dear, if we could only know! Then we shouldn't ever go wrong; but we are only poor, dumb beasts groping around and making mistakes. I sha'n't ever think of last night without a pang."

She was like all the rest; it seemed as if nobody could open a mouth, in these wretched days, without saying something that made us shiver. They were "groping around," and did not know what true, sorrowfully true things they were saying by accident.

Seppi asked if Nikolaus might go out with us.

"I am sorry," she answered, "but he can't. To punish him further, his father doesn't allow him to go out of the house to-day."

We had a great hope! I saw it in Seppi's eyes. We thought, "If he cannot leave the house, he cannot be drowned." Seppi asked, to make sure:

"Must he stay in all day, or only the morning?"

"All day. It's such a pity, too; it's a beautiful day, and he is so unused to being shut up. But he is busy planning his party, and maybe that is company for him. I do hope he isn't too lonesome."

Seppi saw that in her eye which emboldened him to ask if we might go up and help him pass his time.

"And welcome!" she said, right heartily. "Now I call that real friendship, when you might be abroad in the fields and the woods, having a happy time. You are good boys, I'll allow that, though you don't always find satisfactory ways of improving it. Take these cakes—for yourselves—and give him this one, from his mother."

The first thing we noticed when we entered Nikolaus's room was the time—a quarter to 10. Could that be correct? Only such a few minutes to live! I felt a contraction at my heart. Nikolaus jumped up and gave us a glad welcome. He was in good spirits over his plannings for his party and had not been lonesome.

"Sit down," he said, "and look at what I've been doing. And I've finished a kite that you will say is a beauty. It's drying, in the kitchen; I'll fetch it."

He had been spending his penny savings in fanciful trifles of various kinds, to go as prizes in the games, and they were marshaled with fine and showy effect upon the table. He said:

"Examine them at your leisure while I get mother to touch up the kite with her iron if it isn't dry enough yet."

Then he tripped out and went clattering down-stairs, whistling.

We did not look at the things; we couldn't take any interest in anything but the clock. We sat staring at it in silence, listening to the ticking, and every time the minute-hand jumped we nodded recognition —one minute fewer to cover in the race for life or for death. Finally Seppi drew a deep breath and said:

"Two minutes to ten. Seven minutes more and he will pass the death-point. Theodor, he is going to be saved! He's going to—"

"Hush! I'm on needles. Watch the clock and keep still."

Five minutes more. We were panting with the strain and the excitement. Another three minutes, and there was a footstep on the stair.

"Saved!" And we jumped up and faced the door.

The old mother entered, bringing the kite. "Isn't it a beauty?" she said. "And, dear me, how he has slaved over it—ever since daylight, I think, and only finished it awhile before you came." She stood it against the wall, and stepped back to take a view of it. "He drew the pictures his own self, and I think they are very good. The church isn't so very good, I'll have to admit, but look at the bridge—any one can recognize the bridge in a minute. He asked me to bring it up. . . . Dear me! it's seven minutes past ten, and I—"

"But where is he?"

"He? Oh, he'll be here soon; he's gone out a minute."

"Gone out?"

"Yes. Just as he came down-stairs little Lisa's mother came in and said the child had wandered off somewhere, and as she was a little uneasy I told Nikolaus to never mind about his father's orders—go and look her up. . . . Why, how white you two do look! I do believe you are sick. Sit down; I'll fetch something. That cake has disagreed with you. It is a little heavy, but I thought—"

She disappeared without finishing her sentence, and we hurried at once to the back window and looked toward the river. There was a great crowd at the other end of the bridge, and people were flying toward that point from every direction.

"Oh, it is all over—poor Nikolaus! Why, oh, why did she let him get out of the house!"

"Come away," said Seppi, half sobbing, "come quick—we can't bear to meet her; in five minutes she will know."

But we were not to escape. She came upon us at the foot of the stairs, with her cordials in her hands, and made us come in and sit down and take the medicine. Then she watched the effect, and it did not satisfy her; so she made us wait longer, and kept upbraiding herself for giving us the unwholesome cake.

Presently the thing happened which we were dreading. There was a sound of tramping and scraping outside, and a crowd came solemnly in, with heads uncovered, and laid the two drowned bodies on the bed.

"Oh, my God!" that poor mother cried out, and fell on her knees, and put her arms about her dead boy and began to cover the wet face with kisses. "Oh, it was I that sent him, and I have been his death. If I had obeyed, and kept him in the house, this would not have happened. And I am rightly punished; I was cruel to him last night, and him begging me, his own mother, to be his friend."

And so she went on and on, and all the women cried, and pitied her, and tried to comfort her, but she could not forgive herself and could not be comforted, and kept on saying if she had not sent him out he would be alive and well now, and she was the cause of his death.

It shows how foolish people are when they blame themselves for anything they have done. Satan knows, and he said nothing happens that your first act hasn't arranged to happen and made inevitable; and so, of your own motion you can't ever alter the scheme or do a thing that will break a link. Next we heard screams, and Frau Brandt came wildly plowing and plunging through the crowd with her dress in disorder and hair flying loose, and flung herself upon her dead child with moans and kisses and pleadings and endearments; and by and by she rose up almost exhausted with her outpourings of passionate emotion, and clenched her fist and lifted it toward the sky, and her tear-drenched face grew hard and resentful, and she said:

"For nearly two weeks I have had dreams and presentiments and warnings that death was going to strike what was most precious to me, and day and night and night and day I have groveled in the dirt before Him praying Him to have pity on my innocent child and save it from harm—and here is His answer!"

Why, He had saved it from harm—but she did not know.

She wiped the tears from her eyes and cheeks, and stood awhile gazing down at the child and caressing its face and its hair with her hands; then she spoke again in that bitter tone: "But in His hard heart is no compassion. I will never pray again."

She gathered her dead child to her bosom and strode away, the crowd falling back to let her pass, and smitten dumb by the awful words they had heard. Ah, that poor woman! It is as Satan said, we do not know good fortune from bad, and are always mistaking the one for the other. Many a time since I have heard people pray to God to spare the life of sick persons, but I have never done it.

Both funerals took place at the same time in our little church next day. Everybody was there, including the party guests. Satan was there, too; which was proper, for it was on account of his efforts that the funerals had happened. Nikolaus had departed this life without absolution, and a collection was taken up for masses, to get him out of purgatory. Only two-thirds of the required money was gathered, and the parents were going to try to borrow the rest, but Satan furnished it. He told us privately that there was no purgatory, but he had contributed in order that Nikolaus's parents and their friends might be saved from worry and distress. We thought it very good of him, but he said money did not cost him anything.

At the graveyard the body of little Lisa was seized for debt by a carpenter to whom the mother owed fifty groschen for work done the year before. She had never been able to pay this, and was not able now. The carpenter took the corpse home and kept it four days in his cellar, the mother weeping and imploring about his house all the time; then he buried it in his brother's cattle-yard, without religious ceremonies. It drove the mother wild with grief and shame, and she forsook her work and went daily about the town, cursing the carpenter and blaspheming the laws of the emperor and the church, and it was pitiful to see. Seppi asked Satan to interfere, but he said the carpenter and the rest were members of the human race and were acting quite neatly for that species of animal. He would interfere if he found a horse acting in such a way, and we must inform him when we came across that kind of horse doing that kind of a human thing, so that he could stop it. We believed this was sarcasm, for of course there wasn't any such horse.

But after a few days we found that we could not abide that poor woman's distress, so we begged Satan to examine her several possible careers, and see if he could not change her, to her profit, to a new one.

He said the longest of her careers as they now stood gave her forty-two years to live, and her shortest one twenty-nine, and that both were charged with grief and hunger and cold and pain. The only improvement he could make would be to enable her to skip a certain three minutes from now; and he asked us if he should do it. This was such a short time to decide in that we went to pieces with nervous excitement, and before we could pull ourselves together and ask for particulars he said the time would be up in a few more seconds; so then we gasped out, "Do it!"

"It is done," he said; "she was going around a corner; I have turned her back; it has changed her career."

"Then what will happen, Satan?"

"It is happening now. She is having words with Fischer, the weaver. In his anger Fischer will straightway do what he would not have done but for this accident. He was present when she stood over her child's body and uttered those blasphemies."

"What will he do?"

"He is doing it now—betraying her. In three days she will go to the stake."

We could not speak; we were frozen with horror, for if we had not meddled with her career she would have been spared this awful fate. Satan noticed these thoughts, and said:

"What you are thinking is strictly human-like—that is to say, foolish. The woman is advantaged. Die when she might, she would go to heaven. By this prompt death she gets twenty-nine years more of heaven than she is entitled to, and escapes twenty-nine years of misery here."

A moment before we were bitterly making up our minds that we would ask no more favors of Satan for friends of ours, for he did not seem to know any way to do a person a kindness but by killing him; but the whole aspect of the case was changed now, and we were glad of what we had done and full of happiness in the thought of it.

After a little I began to feel troubled about Fischer, and asked, timidly, "Does this episode change Fischer's life-scheme, Satan?"

"Change it? Why, certainly. And radically. If he had not met Frau Brandt awhile ago he would die next year, thirty-four years of age. Now he will live to be ninety, and have a pretty prosperous and comfortable life of it, as human lives go."

We felt a great joy and pride in what we had done for Fischer, and were expecting Satan to sympathize with this feeling; but he showed no sign and this made us uneasy. We waited for him to speak, but he didn't; so, to assuage our solicitude we had to ask him if there was any defect in Fischer's good luck. Satan considered the question a moment, then said, with some hesitation:

"Well, the fact is, it is a delicate point. Under his several former possible life-careers he was going to heaven."

We were aghast. "Oh, Satan! and under this one—"

"There, don't be so distressed. You were sincerely trying to do him a kindness; let that comfort you."

"Oh, dear, dear, that cannot comfort us. You ought to have told us what we were doing, then we wouldn't have acted so."

But it made no impression on him. He had never felt a pain or a sorrow, and did not know what they were, in any really informing way. He had no knowledge of them except theoretically—that is to say, intellectually. And of course that is no good. One can never get any but a loose and ignorant notion of such things except by experience. We tried our best to make him comprehend the awful thing that had been done and how we were compromised by it, but he couldn't seem to get hold of it. He said he did not think it important where Fischer went to; in heaven he would not be missed, there were "plenty there." We tried to make him see that he was missing the point entirely; that Fischer, and not other people, was the proper one to decide about the importance of it; but it all went for nothing; he said he did not care for Fischer—there were plenty more Fischers.

The next minute Fischer went by on the other side of the way, and it made us sick and faint to see him, remembering the doom that was upon him, and we the cause of it. And how unconscious he was that anything had happened to him! You could see by his elastic step and his alert manner that he was well satisfied with himself for doing that hard turn for poor Frau Brandt. He kept glancing back over his shoulder expectantly. And, sure enough, pretty soon Frau Brandt followed after, in charge of the officers and wearing jingling chains. A mob was in her wake, jeering and shouting, "Blasphemer and heretic!" and some among them were neighbors and friends of her happier days. Some were trying to strike her, and the officers were not taking as much trouble as they might to keep them from it.

"Oh, stop them, Satan!" It was out before we remembered that he could not interrupt them for a moment without changing their whole after-lives. He puffed a little puff toward them with his lips and they began to reel and stagger and grab at the empty air; then they broke apart and fled in every direction, shrieking, as if in intolerable pain.

He had crushed a rib of each of them with that little puff. We could not help asking if their life-chart was changed.

"Yes, entirely. Some have gained years, some have lost them. Some few will profit in various ways by the change, but only that few."

We did not ask if we had brought poor Fischer's luck to any of them. We did not wish to know. We fully believed in Satan's desire to do us kindnesses, but we were losing confidence in his judgment. It was at this time that our growing anxiety to have him look over our life-charts and suggest improvements began to fade out and give place to other interests.

For a day or two the whole village was a chattering turmoil over Frau Brandt's case and over the mysterious calamity that had over-taken the mob, and at her trial the place was crowded. She was easily convicted of her blasphemies, for she uttered those terrible words again and said she would not take them back. When warned that she was imperiling her life, she said they could take it in welcome, she did not want it, she would rather live with the professional devils in perdition than with these imitators in the village. They accused her of breaking all those ribs by witchcraft, and asked her if she was not a witch? She answered scornfully:

"No. If I had that power would any of you holy hypocrites be alive five minutes? No; I would strike you all dead. Pronounce your sentence and let me go; I am tired of your society."

So they found her guilty, and she was excommunicated and cut off from the joys of heaven and doomed to the fires of hell; then she was clothed in a coarse robe and delivered to the secular arm, and con-ducted to the market-place, the bell solemnly tolling the while. We saw her chained to the stake, and saw the first film of blue smoke rise on the still air. Then her hard face softened, and she looked upon the packed crowd in front of her and said, with gentleness:

"We played together once, in long-agone days when we were inno-cent little creatures. For the sake of that, I forgive you."

We went away then, and did not see the fires consume her, but we heard the shrieks, although we put our fingers in our ears. When they ceased we knew she was in heaven, notwithstanding the excommuni-cation; and we were glad of her death and not sorry that we had brought it about.

One day, a little while after this, Satan appeared again. We were always watching out for him, for life was never very stagnant when he was by. He came upon us at that place in the woods where we had

first met him. Being boys, we wanted to be entertained; we asked him
to do a show for us.

"Very well," he said; "would you like to see a history of the progress
of the human race?—its development of that product which it calls civilization?"

We said we should.

So, with a thought, he turned the place into the Garden of Eden, and
we saw Abel praying by his altar; then Cain came walking toward him
with his club, and did not seem to see us, and would have stepped
on my foot if I had not drawn it in. He spoke to his brother in a language which we did not understand; then he grew violent and threatening, and we knew what was going to happen, and turned away our
heads for the moment; but we heard the crash of the blows and heard
the shrieks and the groans; then there was silence, and we saw Abel
lying in his blood and gasping out his life, and Cain standing over him
and looking down at him, vengeful and unrepentant.

Then the vision vanished, and was followed by a long series of unknown wars, murders, and massacres. Next we had the Flood, and the
Ark tossing around in the stormy waters, with lofty mountains in the
distance showing veiled and dim through the rain. Satan said:

"The progress of your race was not satisfactory. It is to have another
chance now."

The scene changed, and we saw Noah overcome with wine.

Next, we had Sodom and Gomorrah, and "the attempt to discover
two or three respectable persons there," as Satan described it. Next,
Lot and his daughters in the cave.

Next came the Hebraic wars, and we saw the victors massacre the
survivors and their cattle, and save the young girls alive and distribute
them around.

Next we had Jael; and saw her slip into the tent and drive the nail
into the temple of her sleeping guest; and we were so close that when
the blood gushed out it trickled in a little, red stream to our feet, and
we could have stained our hands in it if we had wanted to.

Next we had Egyptian wars, Greek wars, Roman wars, hideous
drenchings of the earth with blood; and we saw the treacheries of the
Romans toward the Carthaginians, and the sickening spectacle of the
massacre of those brave people. Also we saw Cæsar invade Britain—
"not that those barbarians had done him any harm, but because he
wanted their land, and desired to confer the blessings of civilization
upon their widows and orphans," as Satan explained.

Next, Christianity was born. Then ages of Europe passed in review

before us, and we saw Christianity and Civilization march hand in
hand through those ages, "leaving famine and death and desolation in
their wake, and other signs of the progress of the human race," as Satan
observed.

And always we had wars, and more wars, and still other wars—all
over Europe, all over the world. "Sometimes in the private interest of
royal families," Satan said, "sometimes to crush a weak nation; but
never a war started by the aggressor for any clean purpose—there is no
such war in the history of the race."

"Now," said Satan, "you have seen your progress down to the present, and you must confess that it is wonderful—in its way. We must
now exhibit the future."

He showed us slaughters more terrible in their destruction of life,
more devastating in their engines of war, than any we had seen.

"You perceive," he said, "that you have made continual progress.
Cain did his murder with a club; the Hebrews did their murders with
javelins and swords; the Greeks and Romans added protective armor
and the fine arts of military organization and generalship; the Christian
has added guns and gunpowder; a few centuries from now he will have
so greatly improved the deadly effectiveness of his weapons of slaughter that all men will confess that without Christian civilization war
must have remained a poor and trifling thing to the end of time."

Then he began to laugh in the most unfeeling way, and make fun
of the human race, although he knew that what he had been saying
shamed us and wounded us. No one but an angel could have acted so;
but suffering is nothing to them; they do not know what it is, except
by hearsay.

More than once Seppi and I had tried in a humble and diffident
way to convert him, and as he had remained silent we had taken his
silence as a sort of encouragement; necessarily, then, this talk of his
was a disappointment to us, for it showed that we had made no deep
impression upon him. The thought made us sad, and we knew then
how the missionary must feel when he has been cherishing a glad hope
and has seen it blighted. We kept our grief to ourselves, knowing that
this was not the time to continue our work.

Satan laughed his unkind laugh to a finish; then he said: "It is a
remarkable progress. In five or six thousand years five or six high civilizations have risen, flourished, commanded the wonder of the world,
then faded out and disappeared; and not one of them except the latest
ever invented any sweeping and adequate way to kill people. They all
did their best—to kill being the chiefest ambition of the human race

and the earliest incident in its history—but only the Christian civilization has scored a triumph to be proud of. Two or three centuries from now it will be recognized that all the competent killers are Christians; then the pagan world will go to school to the Christian—not to acquire his religion, but his guns. The Turk and the Chinaman will buy those to kill missionaries and converts with."

By this time his theater was at work again, and before our eyes nation after nation drifted by, during two or three centuries, a mighty procession, an endless procession, raging, struggling, wallowing through seas of blood, smothered in battle-smoke through which the flags glinted and the red jets from the cannon darted; and always we heard the thunder of the guns and the cries of the dying.

"And what does it amount to?" said Satan, with his evil chuckle. "Nothing at all. You gain nothing; you always come out where you went in. For a million years the race has gone on monotonously propagating itself and monotonously reperforming this dull nonsense—to what end? No wisdom can guess! Who gets a profit out of it? Nobody but a parcel of usurping little monarchs and nobilities who despise you; would feel defiled if you touched them; would shut the door in your face if you proposed to call; whom you slave for, fight for, die for, and are not ashamed of it, but proud; whose existence is a perpetual insult to you and you are afraid to resent it; who are mendicants supported by your alms, yet assume toward you the airs of benefactor toward beggar; who address you in the language of master to slave, and are answered in the language of slave to master; who are worshiped by you with your mouth, while in your heart—if you have one—you despise yourselves for it. The first man was a hypocrite and a coward, qualities which have not yet failed in his line; it is the foundation upon which all civilizations have been built. Drink to their perpetuation! Drink to their augmentation! Drink to—" Then he saw by our faces how much we were hurt, and he cut his sentence short and stopped chuckling, and his manner changed. He said, gently: "No, we will drink one another's health, and let civilization go. The wine which has flown to our hands out of space by desire is earthly, and good enough for that other toast; but throw away the glasses; we will drink this one in wine which has not visited this world before."

We obeyed, and reached up and received the new cups as they descended. They were shapely and beautiful goblets, but they were not made of any material that we were acquainted with. They seemed to be in motion, they seemed to be alive; and certainly the colors in them were in motion. They were very brilliant and sparkling, and of every

tint, and they were never still, but flowed to and fro in rich tides which
met and broke and flashed out dainty explosions of enchanting color.
I think it was most like opals washing about in waves and flashing out
their splendid fires. But there is nothing to compare the wine with.
We drank it, and felt a strange and witching ecstasy as of heaven go
stealing through us, and Seppi's eyes filled and he said worshipingly:

"We shall be there some day, and then—"

He glanced furtively at Satan, and I think he hoped Satan would
say, "Yes, you will be there some day," but Satan seemed to be thinking
about something else, and said nothing. This made me feel ghastly, for
I knew he had heard; nothing, spoken or unspoken, ever escaped him.
Poor Seppi looked distressed, and did not finish his remark. The goblets
rose and clove their way into the sky, a triplet of radiant sundogs, and
disappeared. Why didn't they stay? It seemed a bad sign, and depressed me. Should I ever see mine again? Would Seppi ever see his?

9

It was wonderful, the mastery Satan had over time and distance. For
him they did not exist. He called them human inventions, and said
they were artificialities. We often went to the most distant parts of the
globe with him, and stayed weeks and months, and yet were gone only
a fraction of a second, as a rule. You could prove it by the clock. One
day when our people were in such awful distress because the witch
commission were afraid to proceed against the astrologer and Father
Peter's household, or against any, indeed, but the poor and the friendless, they lost patience and took to witch-hunting on their own score,
and began to chase a born lady who was known to have the habit of
curing people by devilish arts, such as bathing them, washing them,
and nourishing them instead of bleeding them and purging them
through the ministrations of a barber-surgeon in the proper way. She
came flying down, with the howling and cursing mob after her, and
tried to take refuge in houses, but the doors were shut in her face. They
chased her more than half an hour, we following to see it, and at last
she was exhausted and fell, and they caught her. They dragged her to
a tree and threw a rope over the limb, and began to make a noose in
it, some holding her, meantime, and she crying and begging, and her
young daughter looking on and weeping, but afraid to say or do anything.

They hanged the lady, and I threw a stone at her, although in my
heart I was sorry for her; but all were throwing stones and each was

watching his neighbor, and if I had not done as the others did it would have been noticed and spoken of. Satan burst out laughing.

All that were near by turned upon him, astonished and not pleased. It was an ill time to laugh, for his free and scoffing ways and his supernatural music had brought him under suspicion all over the town and turned many privately against him. The big blacksmith called attention to him now, raising his voice so that all should hear, and said:

"What are you laughing at? Answer! Moreover, please explain to the company why you threw no stone."

"Are you sure I did not throw a stone?"

"Yes. You needn't try to get out of it; I had my eye on you."

"And I—I noticed you!" shouted two others.

"Three witnesses," said Satan: "Mueller, the blacksmith; Klein, the butcher's man; Pfeiffer, the weaver's journeyman. Three very ordinary liars. Are there any more?"

"Never mind whether there are others or not, and never mind about what you consider us—three's enough to settle your matter for you. You'll prove that you threw a stone, or it shall go hard with you."

"That's so!" shouted the crowd, and surged up as closely as they could to the center of interest.

"And first you will answer that other question," cried the blacksmith, pleased with himself for being mouthpiece to the public and hero of the occasion. "What are you laughing at?"

Satan smiled and answered, pleasantly: "To see three cowards stoning a dying lady when they were so near death themselves."

You could see the superstitious crowd shrink and catch their breath, under the sudden shock. The blacksmith, with a show of bravado, said:

"Pooh! What do you know about it?"

"I? Everything. By profession I am a fortuneteller, and I read the hands of you three—and some others—when you lifted them to stone the woman. One of you will die to-morrow week; another of you will die to-night; the third has but five minutes to live—and yonder is the clock!"

It made a sensation. The faces of the crowd blanched, and turned mechanically toward the clock. The butcher and the weaver seemed smitten with an illness, but the blacksmith braced up and said, with spirit:

"It is not long to wait for prediction number one. If it fails, young master, you will not live a whole minute after, I promise you that."

No one said anything; all watched the clock in a deep stillness which was impressive. When four and a half minutes were gone the blacksmith gave a sudden gasp and clapped his hands upon his heart, saying, "Give me breath! Give me room!" and began to sink down. The crowd surged back, no one offering to support him, and he fell lumbering to the ground and was dead. The people stared at him, then at Satan, then at one another; and their lips moved, but no words came. Then Satan said:

"Three saw that I threw no stone. Perhaps there are others; let them speak."

It struck a kind of panic into them, and, although no one answered him, many began to violently accuse one another, saying, "You said he didn't throw," and getting for reply, "It is a lie, and I will make you eat it!" And so in a moment they were in a raging and noisy turmoil, and beating and banging one another; and in the midst was the only indifferent one—the dead lady hanging from her rope, her troubles forgotten, her spirit at peace.

So we walked away, and I was not at ease, but was saying to myself, "He told them he was laughing at them, but it was a lie—he was laughing at me."

That made him laugh again, and he said, "Yes, I was laughing at you, because, in fear of what others might report about you, you stoned the woman when your heart revolted at the act—but I was laughing at the others, too."

"Why?"

"Because their case was yours."

"How is that?"

"Well, there were sixty-eight people there, and sixty-two of them had no more desire to throw a stone than you had."

"Satan!"

"Oh, it's true. I know your race. It is made up of sheep. It is governed by minorities, seldom or never by majorities. It suppresses its feelings and its beliefs and follows the handful that makes the most noise. Sometimes the noisy handful is right, sometimes wrong; but no matter, the crowd follows it. The vast majority of the race, whether savage or civilized, are secretly kind-hearted and shrink from inflicting pain, but in the presence of the aggressive and pitiless minority they don't dare to assert themselves. Think of it! One kind-hearted creature spies upon another, and sees to it that he loyally helps in iniquities which revolt both of them. Speaking as an expert, I know that ninety-nine out of a hundred of your race were strongly against the killing of witches when that foolishness was first agitated by a handful of pious lunatics in the long ago. And I know that even to-day, after ages of transmitted prejudice and silly teaching, only one person in twenty puts any real heart into the harrying of a witch. And yet apparently everybody hates witches and wants them killed. Some day a handful will rise up on the other side and make the most noise—perhaps even a single daring man with a big voice and a determined front will do it—and in a week all the sheep will wheel and follow him, and witch-hunting will come to a sudden end.

"Monarchies, aristocracies, and religions are all based upon that large defect in your race—the individual's distrust of his neighbor, and his desire, for safety's or comfort's sake, to stand well in his neighbor's eye. These institutions will always remain, and always flourish, and always oppress you, affront you, and degrade you, because you will always be and remain slaves of minorities. There was never a country where the majority of the people were in their secret hearts loyal to any of these institutions."

I did not like to hear our race called sheep, and said I did not think they were.

"Still, it is true, lamb," said Satan. "Look at you in war—what mutton you are, and how ridiculous!"

"In war? How?"

"There has never been a just one, never an honorable one—on the part of the instigator of the war. I can see a million years ahead, and this rule will never change in so many as half a dozen instances. The loud little handful—as usual—will shout for the war. The pulpit will—warily and cautiously—object—at first; the great, big, dull bulk of the nation will rub its sleepy eyes and try to make out why there should be a war, and will say, earnestly and indignantly, "It is unjust and dishonorable, and there is no necessity for it." Then the handful will shout louder. A few fair men on the other side will argue and reason against the war with speech and pen, and at first will have a hearing and be applauded; but it will not last long; those others will outshout them, and presently the anti-war audiences will thin out and lose popularity. Before long you will see this curious thing: the speakers stoned from the platform, and free speech strangled by hordes of furious men who in their secret hearts are still at one with those stoned speakers—as earlier —but do not dare to say so. And now the whole nation—pulpit and all —will take up the war-cry, and shout itself hoarse, and mob any honest man who ventures to open his mouth; and presently such mouths will cease to open. Next the statesmen will invent cheap lies, putting the blame upon the nation that is attacked, and every man will be glad of those conscience-soothing falsities, and will diligently study them, and refuse to examine any refutations of them; and thus he will by and by convince himself that the war is just, and will thank God for the better sleep he enjoys after this process of grotesque self-deception."

10

Days and days went by now, and no Satan. It was dull without him. But the astrologer, who had returned from his excursion to the moon, went about the village, braving public opinion, and getting a stone in the middle of his back now and then when some witch-hater got a safe chance to throw it and dodge out of sight. Meantime two influences had been working well for Marget. That Satan, who was quite indifferent to her, had stopped going to her house after a visit or two had hurt her pride, and she had set herself the task of banishing him from her heart. Reports of Wilhelm Meidling's dissipation brought to her from time to time by old Ursula had touched her with remorse, jealousy of Satan being the cause of it; and so now, these two matters working upon her together, she was getting a good profit out of the combination—her interest in Satan was steadily cooling, her interest in Wilhelm as steadily warming. All that was needed to complete her conversion was that Wilhelm should brace up and do something that should cause favorable talk and incline the public toward him again.

The opportunity came now. Marget sent and asked him to defend her uncle in the approaching trial, and he was greatly pleased, and stopped drinking and began his preparations with diligence. With more diligence than hope, in fact, for it was not a promising case. He had many interviews in his office with Seppi and me, and threshed out our testimony pretty thoroughly, thinking to find some valuable grains among the chaff, but the harvest was poor, of course.

If Satan would only come! That was my constant thought. He could invent some way to win the case; for he had said it would be won, so he necessarily knew how it could be done. But the days dragged on, and still he did not come. Of course I did not doubt that it would win, and that Father Peter would be happy for the rest of his life, since Satan had said so; yet I knew I should be much more comfortable if he would come and tell us how to manage it. It was getting high time for Father Peter to have a saving change toward happiness, for by general report he was worn out with his imprisonment and the ignominy that was burdening him, and was like to die of his miseries unless he got relief soon.

At last the trial came on, and the people gathered from all around to witness it; among them many strangers from considerable distances. Yes, everybody was there except the accused. He was too feeble in body for the strain. But Marget was present, and keeping up her hope and her spirit the best she could. The money was present, too. It was emptied on the table, and was handled and caressed and examined by such as were privileged.

The astrologer was put in the witness-box. He had on his best hat and robe for the occasion.

QUESTION You claim that this money is yours?

ANSWER I do.

Q. How did you come by it?

A. I found the bag in the road when I was returning from a journey.

Q. When?

A. More than two years ago.

Q. What did you do with it?

A. I brought it home and hid it in a secret place in my observatory, intending to find the owner if I could.

Q. You endeavored to find him?

A. I made diligent inquiry during several months, but nothing came of it.

Q. And then?

A. I thought it not worth while to look further, and was minded to use the money in finishing the wing of the foundling-asylum connected with the priory and nunnery. So I took it out of its hiding-place and counted it to see if any of it was missing. And then—

Q. Why do you stop? Proceed.

A. I am sorry to have to say this, but just as I had finished and was restoring the bag to its place, I looked up and there stood Father Peter behind me.

Several murmured, "That looks bad," but others answered, "Ah, but he is such a liar!"

Q. That made you uneasy?

A. No; I thought nothing of it at the time, for Father Peter often came to me unannounced to ask for a little help in his need.

Marget blushed crimson at hearing her uncle falsely and impudently charged with begging, especially from one he had always denounced as a fraud, and was going to speak, but remembered herself in time and held her peace.

Q. Proceed.

A. In the end I was afraid to contribute the money to the foundling-asylum, but elected to wait yet another year and continue my inquiries.

When I heard of Father Peter's find I was glad, and no suspicion entered my mind; when I came home a day or two later and discovered that my own money was gone I still did not suspect until three circumstances connected with Father Peter's good fortune struck me as being singular coincidences.

Q. Pray name them.

A. Father Peter had found his money in a path—I had found mine in a road. Father Peter's find consisted exclusively of gold ducats—mine also. Father Peter found eleven hundred and seven ducats—I exactly the same.

This closed his evidence, and certainly it made a strong impression on the house; one could see that.

Wilhelm Meidling asked him some questions, then called us boys, and we told our tale. It made the people laugh, and we were ashamed. We were feeling pretty badly, anyhow, because Wilhelm was hopeless, and showed it. He was doing as well as he could, poor young fellow, but nothing was in his favor, and such sympathy as there was was now plainly not with his client. It might be difficult for court and people to believe the astrologer's story, considering his character, but it was almost impossible to believe Father Peter's. We were already feeling badly enough, but when the astrologer's lawyer said he believed he would not ask us any questions—for our story was a little delicate and it would be cruel for him to put any strain upon it—everybody tittered, and it was almost more than we could bear. Then he made a sarcastic little speech, and got so much fun out of our tale, and it seemed so ridiculous and childish and every way impossible and foolish, that it made everybody laugh till the tears came; and at last Marget could not keep up her courage any longer, but broke down and cried, and I was so sorry for her.

Now I noticed something that braced me up. It was Satan standing alongside of Wilhelm! And there was such a contrast!—Satan looked so confident, had such a spirit in his eyes and face, and Wilhelm looked so depressed and despondent. We two were comfortable now, and judged that he would testify and persuade the bench and the people that black was white and white black, or any other color he wanted it. We glanced around to see what the strangers in the house thought of him, for he was beautiful, you know—stunning, in fact—but no one was noticing him; so we knew by that that he was invisible.

The lawyer was saying his last words; and while he was saying them Satan began to melt into Wilhelm. He melted into him and disappeared; and then there was a change, when his spirit began to look out of Wilhelm's eyes.

That lawyer finished quite seriously, and with dignity. He pointed to the money, and said:

"The love of it is the root of all evil. There it lies, the ancient tempter, newly red with the shame of its latest victory—the dishonor of a priest of God and his two poor juvenile helpers in crime. If it could but speak, let us hope that it would be constrained to confess that of all its conquests this was the basest and the most pathetic."

He sat down. Wilhelm rose and said:

"From the testimony of the accuser I gather that he found this money in a road more than two years ago. Correct me, sir, if I misunderstood you."

The astrologer said his understanding of it was correct.

"And the money so found was never out of his hands thenceforth up to a certain definite date—the last day of last year. Correct me, sir, if I am wrong."

The astrologer nodded his head. Wilhelm turned to the bench and said:

"If I prove that this money here was not that money, then it is not his?"

"Certainly not; but this is irregular. If you had such a witness it was your duty to give proper notice of it and have him here to—" He broke off and began to consult with the other judges. Meantime that other lawyer got up excited and began to protest against allowing new witnesses to be brought into the case at this late stage.

The judges decided that his contention was just and must be allowed.

"But this is not a new witness," said Wilhelm. "It has already been partly examined. I speak of the coin."

"The coin? What can the coin say?"

"It can say it is not the coin that the astrologer once possessed. It can say it was not in existence last December. By its date it can say this."

And it was so! There was the greatest excitement in the court while that lawyer and the judges were reaching for coins and examining them and exclaiming. And everybody was full of admiration of Wilhelm's brightness in happening to think of that neat idea. At last order was called and the court said:

"All of the coins but four are of the date of the present year. The court tenders its sincere sympathy to the accused, and its deep regret that he, an innocent man, through an unfortunate mistake, has suffered the undeserved humiliation of imprisonment and trial. The case is dismissed."

So the money could speak, after all, though that lawyer thought it couldn't. The court rose, and almost everybody came forward to shake hands with Marget and congratulate her, and then to shake with Wilhelm and praise him; and Satan had stepped out of Wilhelm and was standing around looking on full of interest, and people walking through him every which way, not knowing he was there. And Wilhelm could not explain why he only thought of the date on the coins at the last moment, instead of earlier; he said it just occurred to him, all of a sudden, like an inspiration, and he brought it right out without any hesitation, for, although he didn't examine the coins, he seemed, somehow, to know it was true. That was honest of him, and like him; another would have pretended he had thought of it earlier, and was keeping it back for a surprise.

He had dulled down a little now; not much, but still you could notice that he hadn't that luminous look in his eyes that he had while Satan was in him. He nearly got it back, though, for a moment when Marget came and praised him and thanked him and couldn't keep him from seeing how proud she was of him. The astrologer went off dissatisfied and cursing, and Solomon Isaacs gathered up the money and carried it away. It was Father Peter's for good and all, now.

Satan was gone. I judged that he had spirited himself away to the jail to tell the prisoner the news; and in this I was right. Marget and the rest of us hurried thither at our best speed, in a great state of rejoicing.

Well, what Satan had done was this: he had appeared before that poor prisoner, exclaiming, "The trial is over, and you stand forever disgraced as a thief—by verdict of the court!"

The shock unseated the old man's reason. When we arrived, ten minutes later, he was parading pompously up and down and delivering commands to this and that and the other constable or jailer, and calling them Grand Chamberlain, and Prince This and Prince That, and Admiral of the Fleet, Field Marshal in Command, and all such fustian, and was as happy as a bird. He thought he was Emperor!

Marget flung herself on his breast and cried, and indeed everybody was moved almost to heartbreak. He recognized Marget, but could not understand why she should cry. He patted her on the shoulder and said:

"Don't do it, dear; remember, there are witnesses, and it is not becoming in the Crown Princess. Tell me your trouble—it shall be mended; there is nothing the Emperor cannot do." Then he looked around and saw old Ursula with her apron to her eyes. He was puzzled at that, and said, "And what is the matter with you?"

Through her sobs she got out words explaining that she was distressed to see him—"so." He reflected over that a moment, then muttered, as if to himself: "A singular old thing, the Dowager Duchess—means well, but is always snuffling and never able to tell what it is about. It is because she doesn't know." His eyes fell on Wilhelm. "Prince of India," he said, "I divine that it is you that the Crown Princess is concerned about. Her tears shall be dried; I will no longer stand between you; she shall share your throne; and between you you shall inherit mine. There, little lady, have I done well? You can smile now—isn't it so?"

He petted Marget and kissed her, and was so contented with himself and with everybody that he could not do enough for us all, but began to give away kingdoms and such things right and left, and the least that any of us got was a principality. And so at last, being persuaded to go home, he marched in imposing state; and when the crowds along the way saw how it gratified him to be hurrahed at, they humored him to the top of his desire, and he responded with condescending bows and gracious smiles, and often stretched out a hand and said, "Bless you, my people!"

As pitiful a sight as ever I saw. And Marget, and old Ursula crying all the way.

On my road home I came upon Satan, and reproached him with deceiving me with that lie. He was not embarrassed, but said, quite simply and composedly:

"Ah, you mistake; it was the truth. I said he would be happy the rest of his days, and he will, for he will always think he is the Emperor, and his pride in it and his joy in it will endure to the end. He is now, and will remain, the one utterly happy person in this empire."

"But the method of it, Satan, the method! Couldn't you have done it without depriving him of his reason?"

It was difficult to irritate Satan, but that accomplished it.

"What an ass you are!" he said. "Are you so unobservant as not to have found out that sanity and happiness are an impossible combination? No sane man can be happy, for to him life is real, and he sees what a fearful thing it is. Only the mad can be happy, and not many of those. The few that imagine themselves kings or gods are happy, the rest are no happier than the sane. Of course, no man is entirely in his right mind at any time, but I have been referring to the extreme cases. I have taken from this man that trumpery thing which the race regards as a Mind; I have replaced his tin life with a silver-gilt fiction; you see the result—and you criticize! I said I would make him permanently happy, and I have done it. I have made him happy by the only means possible to his race—and you are not satisfied!" He heaved a discouraged sigh, and said, "It seems to me that this race is hard to please."

There it was, you see. He didn't seem to know any way to do a person a favor except by killing him or making a lunatic out of him. I apologized, as well as I could; but privately I did not think much of his processes—at that time.

Satan was accustomed to say that our race lived a life of continuous and uninterrupted self-deception. It duped itself from cradle to grave with shams and delusions which it mistook for realities, and this made its entire life a sham. Of the score of fine qualities which it imagined it had and was vain of, it really possessed hardly one. It regarded itself as gold, and was only brass. One day when he was in this vein he mentioned a detail—the sense of humor. I cheered up then, and took issue. I said we possessed it.

"There spoke the race!" he said; "always ready to claim what it hasn't got, and mistake its ounce of brass filings for a ton of gold-dust. You have a mongrel perception of humor, nothing more; a multitude of you possess that. This multitude see the comic side of a thousand low-grade and trivial things—broad incongruities, mainly; grotesqueries, absurdities, evokers of the horse-laugh. The ten thousand high-grade comicalities which exist in the world are sealed from their dull vision. Will a day come when the race will detect the funniness of these juvenilities and laugh at them—and by laughing at them destroy them? For your race, in its poverty, has unquestionably one really effective weapon—laughter. Power, money, persuasion, supplication, persecution—these can lift at a colossal humbug—push it a little—weaken it a little, century by century; but only laughter can blow it to rags and atoms at a blast. Against the assault of laughter nothing can stand. You are always fussing and fighting with your other weapons. Do you ever use that one? No; you leave it lying rusting. As a race, do you ever use it at all? No; you lack sense and the courage."

We were traveling at the time and stopped at a little city in India and looked on while a juggler did his tricks before a group of natives. They were wonderful, but I knew Satan could beat that game, and I begged him to show off a little, and he said he would. He changed himself into a native in turban and breech-cloth, and very considerately conferred on me a temporary knowledge of the language.

The juggler exhibited a seed, covered it with earth in a small flower-pot, then put a rag over the pot; after a minute the rag began to rise; in ten minutes it had risen a foot; then the rag was removed and a little tree was exposed, with leaves upon it and ripe fruit. We ate the fruit, and it was good. But Satan said:

"Why do you cover the pot? Can't you grow the tree in the sunlight?"

"No," said the juggler; "no one can do that."

"You are only an apprentice; you don't know your trade. Give me the seed. I will show you." He took the seed and said, "What shall I raise from it?"

"It is a cherry seed; of course you will raise a cherry."

"Oh no; that is a trifle; any novice can do that. Shall I raise an orange-tree from it?"

"Oh yes!" and the juggler laughed.

"And shall I make it bear other fruits as well as oranges?"

"If God wills!" and they all laughed.

Satan put the seed in the ground, put a handful of dust on it, and said, "Rise!"

A tiny stem shot up and began to grow, and grew so fast that in five minutes it was a great tree, and we were sitting in the shade of it. There was a murmur of wonder, then all looked up and saw a strange and pretty sight, for the branches were heavy with fruits of many kinds and colors—oranges, grapes, bananas, peaches, cherries, apricots, and so on. Baskets were brought, and the unlading of the tree began; and the people crowded around Satan and kissed his hand, and praised him, calling him the prince of jugglers. The news went about the town, and everybody came running to see the wonder—and they remembered to bring baskets, too. But the tree was equal to the occasion; it put out new fruits as fast as any were removed; baskets were filled by the score and by the hundred, but always the supply remained undiminished. At last a foreigner in white linen and sun-helmet arrived, and ex-claimed, angrily:

"Away from here! Clear out, you dogs; the tree is on my lands and is my property."

The natives put down their baskets and made humble obeisance. Sa-tan made humble obeisance, too, with his fingers to his forehead, in the native way, and said:

"Please let them have their pleasure for an hour, sir—only that, and no longer. Afterward you may forbid them; and you will still have more fruit than you and the state together can consume in a year."

This made the foreigner very angry, and he cried out, "Who are you, you vagabond, to tell your betters what they may do and what they mayn't!" and he struck Satan with his cane and followed this error with a kick.

The fruits rotted on the branches, and the leaves withered and fell. The foreigner gazed at the bare limbs with the look of one who is surprised, and not gratified. Satan said:

"Take good care of the tree, for its health and yours are bound together. It will never bear again, but if you tend it well it will live long. Water its roots once in each hour every night—and do it yourself; it must not be done by proxy, and to do it in daylight will not answer. If you fail only once in any night, the tree will die, and you likewise. Do not go home to your own country any more—you would not reach there; make no business or pleasure engagements which require you to go outside your gate at night—you cannot afford the risk; do not rent or sell this place—it would be injudicious."

The foreigner was proud and wouldn't beg, but I thought he looked as if he would like to. While he stood gazing at Satan we vanished away and landed in Ceylon.

I was sorry for that man; sorry Satan hadn't been his customary self and killed him or made him a lunatic. It would have been a mercy. Satan overheard the thought, and said:

"I would have done it but for his wife, who has not offended me. She is coming to him presently from their native land, Portugal. She is well, but has not long to live, and has been yearning to see him and persuade him to go back with her next year. She will die without knowing he can't leave that place."

"He won't tell her?"

"He? He will not trust that secret with any one; he will reflect that it could be revealed in sleep, in the hearing of some Portuguese guest's servant some time or other."

"Did none of those natives understand what you said to him?"

"None of them understood, but he will always be afraid that some of them did. That fear will be torture to him, for he has been a harsh master to them. In his dreams he will imagine them chopping his tree down. That will make his days uncomfortable—I have already arranged for his nights."

It grieved me, though not sharply, to see him take such a malicious satisfaction in his plans for this foreigner.

"Does he believe what you told him, Satan?"

"He thought he didn't, but our vanishing helped. The tree, where there had been no tree before—that helped. The insane and uncanny variety of fruits—the sudden withering—all these things are helps. Let him think as he may, reason as he may, one thing is certain, he will water the tree. But between this and night he will begin his changed career with a very natural precaution—for him."

"What is that?"

"He will fetch a priest to cast out the tree's devil. You are such a humorous race—and don't suspect it."

"Will he tell the priest?"

"No. He will say a juggler from Bombay created it, and that he wants the juggler's devil driven out of it, so that it will thrive and be fruitful again. The priest's incantations will fail; then the Portuguese will give up that scheme and get his watering-pot ready."

"But the priest will burn the tree. I know it; he will not allow it to remain."

"Yes, and anywhere in Europe he would burn the man, too. But in India the people are civilized, and these things will not happen. The man will drive the priest away and take care of the tree."

I reflected a little, then said, "Satan, you have given him a hard life, I think."

"Comparatively. It must not be mistaken for a holiday."

We flitted from place to place around the world as we had done before, Satan showing me a hundred wonders, most of them reflecting in some way the weakness and triviality of our race. He did this now every few days—not out of malice—I am sure of that—it only seemed to amuse and interest him, just as a naturalist might be amused and interested by a collection of ants.

11

For as much as a year Satan continued these visits, but at last he came less often, and then for a long time he did not come at all. This always made me lonely and melancholy. I felt that he was losing interest in our tiny world and might at any time abandon his visits entirely. When one day he finally came to me I was overjoyed, but only for a little while. He had come to say good-by, he told me, and for the last time. He had investigations and undertakings in other corners of the universe, he said, that would keep him busy for a longer period than I could wait for his return.

"And you are going away, and will not come back any more?"

"Yes," he said. "We have comraded long together, and it has been pleasant—pleasant for both; but I must go now, and we shall not see each other any more."

"In this life, Satan, but in another? We shall meet in another, surely?"

Then, all tranquilly and soberly, he made the strange answer, "*There is no other.*"

A subtle influence blew upon my spirit from his, bringing with it a vague, dim, but blessed and hopeful feeling that the incredible words might be true—even *must* be true.

"Have you never suspected this, Theodor?"

"No. How could I? But if it can only be true—"

"It is true."

A gust of thankfulness rose in my breast, but a doubt checked it before it could issue in words, and I said, "But—but—we have seen that future life—seen it in its actuality, and so—"

"It was a vision—it had no existence."

I could hardly breathe for the great hope that was struggling in me. "A vision?—a vi—"

"*Life itself is only a vision, a dream.*"

It was electrical. By God! I had had that very thought a thousand times in my musings!

"*Nothing* exists; all is a dream. God—man—the world—the sun, the moon, the wilderness of stars—a dream, all a dream; they have no existence. *Nothing exists save empty space—and you!*"

"I!"

"And you are not you—you have no body, no blood, no bones, you are but a *thought*. I myself have no existence; I am but a dream—your dream, creature of your imagination. In a moment you will have realized this, then you will banish me from your visions and I shall dissolve into the nothingness out of which you made me. . . .

"I am perishing already—I am failing—I am passing away. In a little while you will be alone in shoreless space, to wander its limitless solitudes without friend or comrade forever—for you will remain a *thought*, the only existent thought, and by your nature inextinguishable, indestructible. But I, your poor servant, have revealed you to yourself and set you free. Dream other dreams, and better!

"Strange! that you should not have suspected years ago—centuries, ages, eons, ago!—for you have existed, companionless, through all the eternities. Strange, indeed, that you should not have suspected that your universe and its contents were only dreams, visions, fiction!

Strange, because they are so frankly and hysterically insane—like all dreams: a God who could make good children as easily as bad, yet preferred to make bad ones; who could have made every one of them happy, yet never made a single happy one; who made them prize their bitter life, yet stingily cut it short; who gave his angels eternal happiness unearned, yet required his other children to earn it; who gave his angels painless lives, yet cursed his other children with biting miseries and maladies of mind and body; who mouths justice and invented hell —mouths mercy and invented hell—mouths Golden Rules, and forgiveness multiplied by seventy times seven, and invented hell; who mouths morals to other people and has none himself; who frowns upon crimes, yet commits them all; who created man without invitation, then tries to shuffle the responsibility for man's acts upon man, instead of honorably placing it where it belongs, upon himself; and finally, with altogether divine obtuseness, invites this poor, abused slave to worship him! . . .

"You perceive, *now*, that these things are all impossible except in a dream. You perceive that they are pure and puerile insanities, the silly creations of an imagination that is not conscious of its freaks—in a word, that they are a dream, and you the maker of it. The dream-marks are all present; you should have recognized them earlier.

"It is true, that which I have revealed to you; there is no God, no universe, no human race, no earthly life, no heaven, no hell. It is all a dream—a grotesque and foolish dream. Nothing exists but you. And you are but a *thought*—a vagrant thought, a useless thought, a homeless thought, wandering forlorn among the empty eternities!"

He vanished, and left me appalled; for I knew, and realized, that all he had said was true.

1916